ETERNAL

Award Winning Short Stories
Edited by Ted Stanley

ETERNAL
Award Winning Short Stories

Published by
Hammond House Publishing Ltd.
University Centre Grimsby, DN34 5BQ, United Kingdom.

1st Edition: December 2017

ISBN -0-9955702-3-8

All rights reserved. No part of this publication may be reproduced, stored in a retrieval system, or transmitted in any form or by any means, electronic, mechanical, photocopying, recording or otherwise, without the permission of the authors.

The right of the individual writers to be identified as the author of the work to which they have been attributed in this publication has been asserted in accordance with sections 77 and 78 of the Copyright Designs and Patents act 1988.

Compiled and Edited by Ted Stanley.
Proofreading: Diana Kemp
Formatting: Ravi Ramgati
Marketing: Heather Buckby.
Cover Design: Ted Stanley.

Cover Image from the series *Displacement,* by Deborah Geddes, first exhibited in 2017. Produced by permission of the artist. All rights reserved.

The opinions expressed in this book are entirely those of the individual authors and are not endorsed or supported by the publishers or their sponsors, University Centre Grimsby and Kenwick Park Estates.

Contains language that may be considered unsuitable for a younger audience.

www.hammondhousepublishing.com

E T E R N A L

Award Winning Short Stories

Enjoy this eclectic collection of fifty short stories that brings together *award-winning* writers from around the world, each with their own unique interpretation of the theme. ETERNAL is the second in a series of anthologies, each featuring a different theme and including the top stories from our Annual Literary Prize.

University Centre
Grimsby

Includes the winner of the 2017
International Literary Prize

'A wonderfully diverse range of stories from over the world - each one inspired by and crafted from imaginations and experiences that take the reader on unique journeys. A real celebration of modern, global writing and its power.' *Stuart Spendlow. Best Selling Author.*

'We were rewarded with so many imaginative and deeply moving stories that it proved a challenging task to choose the winners. Here in the 2017 anthology you will find the very best of the best.' *Steve Jackson. Author and Competition Judge*

' This superb anthology gathers some of the best in modern writing from around the world.' *Hugh Riches, Estuary TV.*

CONTENTS

ACKNOWLEDGEMENTS

Deborah Geddes, Heather Buckby Ruth Liddlemore, Alan, Nicky and the team at Central Services, Hugh Riches and the team at Estuary TV, Leanne Doyle, ,Jonathon and Katherine Williams-Stanley, Richard Hall, and Michael Edwards. To Simon, Lucy, Carol, Heather and Ella in the University Learning Resource Centre for their continued patience advice and support. The University Centre Grimsby and Kenwick Park Estates for sponsoring the 2017 International Literary Prize. Competition Judges, Peter True, Anjali Wierny, Stuart Spendlow, Stephen Jackson and Hugh Riches. Finally, all the writers who submitted such an amazing collection of stories for this anthology. We are sorry we were unable to include more.

INTRODUCTION

T HE 2017 INTERNATIONAL LITERARY PRIZE saw an unprecedented increase in entries from five continents and twenty-seven countries providing a unique insight into diverse cultures and settings around the world. The judges reported an incredibly high standard of writing, original ideas and moving stories. Agreeing a short list, let alone finding a winner, became an almost impossible task but after lengthy and often heated deliberations a winner, In Memoriam by Bridget Blankley, was finally chosen. Particular favourites that didn't make the shortlist have been Highly Commended by the judges for inclusion in the anthology. A Commended selection of stories from non-English speaking countries have also been included to allow readers to enjoy the full diversity of cultures and settings. You will also find stories contributed by each of the judges.

Writing a story in just five hundred words has its own challenges, and we are pleased to include the Winners of the 2017 University Centre Grimsby Flash Fiction competition.

The theme of Eternal was explored in a myriad of exiting, moving, amusing and mysterious ways across a range of genres and settings. With very few exceptions, the judges considered that any of the stories would be worthy of publication and encourage all entrants to continue writing and submitting their work to competitions and for publication.

We are privileged to publish such an outstanding body of work in the 2017 Hammond House annual anthology. Thank you to all the writers who submitted their stories and to you, the readers, for supporting new writing talent. We hope you enjoy these wonderful stories.

Ted Stanley

' A timeless energy encircles the world, drawing humanity into its grasp, eternally swirling, pulling souls together, tearing them apart in the eternal struggle of love, life and loss...'

Virginia Alison

Her

Agnes Kalarus
England

JUST LIKE THE SILENT NIGHT SKY, you knew a little about her; you knew Orion's Belt, the Big Plough, and the Little Plough, maybe even guess a planet or two. But the stars play hide and seek, flitting among the clouds: revealing their shine for only a moment, only to retreat to safety, away from prying eyes.

The buzz of city lights silences the laughter of the moon, dimming the twinkle of the stars, merely teasing at their beauty. It is not until you are alone together in the privacy of a vast unlit field that you may be graced by all the glinting stars bathing in the moonlight.

She is like falling snow: nothing, and suddenly, everything. She is the swirling specks you quietly urge to settle before your last sip of hot chocolate. She is the feeling of easing back the curtains only to be blinded by the morning rays reflecting from the all-encompassing, perfect, tranquil blanket stretching for at least a mile each way.

She is the soft crunch beneath your feet, and she is the guilt of glancing back at the irreversible prints left on her. She may cover them while you sleep, or she will disappear as quietly as she appeared, taking with her the imperfections of your rage.

She is the gentle breeze, always there, wafting your trouser legs around your ankles. Every street you walk, every corner you turn, never leaving your side. At night she screams beneath your door, around your windows, through your walls, beating leafless branches anywhere she thinks you will see, reminding you of the prints in the snow. That gentle breeze spirals and flares out of control into a tornado throwing anything in her path in a rage that claims children's hats, leaving them nothing but a sting in their eyes.

Each year she is the snow, reminding you of that harsh winter.

Each day she is the wind, screaming louder than she did that harsh winter.

If only she had still been the night sky you once so loved: reserved and mysterious. Never revealing the whole truth. Playing hard to get. Entrancing you with her cold glow. If only she had stayed as silent as the night sky, not crunching like the snow, she wouldn't howl and wail and screech through your door.

Transference

Alanah Andrews
Australia

I STRUGGLED AGAINST THE STRAPS as a large helmet-shaped dish lowered ominously from the ceiling. But why was I being restrained? I had seen the ads – there was never a strap or buckle in sight.

The dish settled over my head, and I felt a moment of pure terror, consumed by the inky blackness. *I should have listened to my parents*, I thought. I should have stayed away from RealTech. Then the 360-degree screen flickered to life, displaying a smoky grey static all around me.

'Hello, Tilly,' said a soft voice. 'I've been waiting for you.'

I strained to loosen the bonds enough to turn in my seat and see behind me. There she was - out of the corner of my eye, I could see the woman with wavy, dark hair, watching me. The same woman who watched me every night. I knew what was coming next.

'You should have listened to your parents,' she said, before flicking the switch.

* * *

Despite my qualms, it was a glorious day when my grandmother decided to transfer.

I had never been to RealTech before, but the enormous glass doors emblazoned with the company's logo left me with no doubt that I was at the right place. It was early - only one o'clock - so I hesitated for a while before going inside, basking in the heat of the February sun and burning away the last remnants of my dream. It had been a week since Grandma announced her decision, and every night I had dreamed of being in RealTech. Of being strapped into a pod. Each time the woman with dark hair warned me to listen to my parents — *they would have loved it*, I thought wryly.

RealTech: Embracing Technology; Enhancing Reality - the familiar slogan materialised on the wall of the building as I watched, curiously. The electric-blue letters pulsed slightly before rising up past the height of the doors and, I presumed, to the top of the thirty-storey structure. I imagined that the words would hover there, in all their blazing glory, luring people in to sample RealTech's products. And it worked. Every minute or so the building devoured another willing sacrifice who veered from the footpath and entered those enormous opaque doors.

I had seen the ads. From apps to improve efficiency, to cybernetic assistants, to virtual holidays where you travelled no further than the inside of a pod. Other than transfers, it was the latter that had ensured RealTech's place on the world stage. And who wouldn't want to lie on a beach in Bali, sipping cocktails for six months, or perhaps explore the temples of Machu Picchu, without the cost or the time commitment?

But for all their slogans and glowing reviews, my parents had never believed that RealTech was in the game solely for the benefit of the consumer. So, taking cues from them, I had never used any of their products. Not a single app, or assistant, or virtual holiday for me. Until now. Until Grandma decided to transfer.

I checked my phone again. No reply from my parents. Not that I really expected one — it would kill them to set foot inside RealTech property. It looked like I was going to do this alone. Sighing, I stuffed my phone back in my pocket and walked deliberately towards the front doors. The ornate lettering of *RealTech* split in two as the doors slid soundlessly open.

I marched inside and found myself in a large, gleaming foyer. Around the edges of the room lay little booths with oversized helmet-like protrusions sprouting from the walls. These were the pods used in the Replica procedure to administer virtual experiences. I suppressed a shudder — after all, contrary to my dream, I wouldn't need to go near a pod today. The one closest to me was labelled 'Pod 1', and a quick glance around the room showed that they went up to seventeen. They were curious inventions. Some pods lay vacant, while others were nestled half-closed over a person, or even a whole family. I couldn't see what was happening inside, although the occasional flash of light lit up the ground around them.

The foyer was enormous. There were a number of doors and elevators leading off to the left, and in front of me was a long counter that stretched all the way from one side of the room to the other. I made my way towards this reception area where a dozen people were evenly spaced along the desk, chatting with customers. As I moved nearer, a balding man rose to leave, and the receptionist - a woman with a blonde bob - acknowledged me with smile and a wave. As I walked towards her I couldn't help noticing that her teeth were extremely white.

'Name?'

'Uh, Gaye Wheeler,' I responded, lowering myself into the seat in front of the counter. The woman paused for a moment, as though processing this information.

'And how can I help you today, Gaye?'

'Oh,' I suddenly realised my mistake. 'Sorry, I'm not Gaye. That's my grandmother. I'm here to see her. I thought -'

'So your name isn't Gaye Wheeler?'

'No, I'm Tilly. Tilly Wheeler.' I could feel my cheeks burning.

The woman thought for a moment. There was something odd about her, but I couldn't quite place it.

'I have no records of a Tilly Wheeler. Implant, please,' she said, reaching for my left hand.

'I don't have one,' I replied, automatically reaching into my wallet. 'But here's my ID card.'

The woman didn't even look surprised, as most people did when I told them that I didn't have an implant. My parents were conscientious objectors, or Anti-Progs, as the media calls them. When I tried to explain to people that my parents weren't really anti-progress, just philosophically opposed to the implant procedure, people rolled their eyes. After all, it wasn't really true, was it? My parents weren't exclusively critical of the implants, but were also suspicious of cashless currencies, flu shots, social media, One World Banking, virtual holidays and, by extension, any product that came out of RealTech.

I wasn't as extreme as my parents, but some of their mistrust had certainly rubbed off on me. After all, I was 23 now, old enough to make my own decisions, but I still hadn't elected to get an implant, had I? I still hadn't downloaded a single app or bought any of their products. The virtual holidays were tempting, I had to admit, but so far my parents' warnings had kept me from being lured in. But lured into what, I wondered? Most people praised RealTech and their revolutionary products.

The woman stared at my ID card and her eyes blinked rapidly.

'Whoa, you're a -'

'I'm a Semi-Autonomous Robotic Assistant. You can call me S.A.R.A.'

I looked closer at the wom- at the robot. It looked so real. I smiled wryly, thinking of the company name.

'Matilda Wheeler. Born 13 December 2021. Affirmative?'

'Affirmative,' I replied, holding still as her eyes scanned my face.

'And how can I help you today?'

'I'm here for my grandmother. Gaye Wheeler. She's being transferred at two o'clock.'

The robot took a moment to respond, and I guessed that it must have been searching through its databases. The blank look was disconcerting. RealTech really needed to work on the facial expressions if they wanted the robots to pass as human.

'Confirmed,' S.A.R.A announced at last. 'Gaye Wheeler scheduled for transfer at fourteen hundred hours. Please proceed to Pod Three.'

I felt cold. 'Sorry, why do I have to go to Pod Three?'

'To be briefed, of course. Next.'

I could have – should have – argued with her. But despite my nightmare I *was* curious about the experience. All of my friends had been in a pod, multiple times, for the Replica process, and they praised it to no end. Plus, I was still disappointed that my parents wouldn't put aside their prejudices for one day to support Grandma during such an important life event. If I used a pod – better still, if I liked it - this would be a bit of an up-yours to them, I thought childishly.

As I looked around for the right pod, I couldn't help glancing curiously at the other receptionists. For a moment, I thought that perhaps all of them would look exactly the same as the one that had served me, but I was wrong. They were all unique - diverse skin tones, distinct ethnicities, different ages. Perhaps the others were humans and the one that had served me was the only robot in the room; I honestly couldn't tell from this distance. It was a little terrifying to realise this.

I made my way towards Pod Three. Up close, I decided that the strange protrusion from the wall didn't really look like a helmet so much as a deep, upturned bowl. It was the glassy black texture that had first made me liken it to a helmet. There were no straps anywhere. I sat on the chair and closed my eyes. I sensed, rather than saw, the bowl move over the top of me and down over my head. It didn't touch me, but enveloped me like a flower, and all the noise from the foyer was instantly deadened. Then there was a strange humming sound, like a swarm of bees. I opened my eyes.

The inside of the dome had disappeared, but I was still sitting on the chair. I found myself in a large, grey area that extended as far as my eye could see. In my dream, I had always imagined that being inside the pods would resemble watching a 360-degree television screen. I was wrong – it was like there was no screen at all. I reached out to my right, expecting to feel the edge of the pod, which the rational part of my brain knew was only a few inches away. My hand moved through the air, unchecked. Fascinating.

'It was fear that drove us to search for another solution.'

I started. The soft voice sounded like a person was standing right next to me. I looked to my left, but no one was there.

'From the moment the human race came into existence, we have suffered the same ultimate fate. And from the dawn of time, humans have been preoccupied with avoiding, or at least prolonging, our eventual demise.'

A figure appeared in the distant greyness, striding towards me. In a moment I could make out the woman with dark wavy hair, casually dressed in jeans and a pale green shirt. My heart beat faster. Perhaps I had seen her in an advertisement – that could be the only logical reason why the woman from my dreams could turn up here.

'And why shouldn't we? Our existence is so short, so fragile,' she continued. Her body was still a few metres away and yet her voice sounded like it was right next to me. It was slightly unnerving.

Then she stopped, bringing her arms up on either side like a magician about to perform a magic trick. A grey gas emanated from her fingertips and began swirling all around me. I fought to remind myself that I was still sitting in a chair in the RealTech auditorium. As bizarre as the experience was, I shouldn't panic because it was all just happening in my mind.

And then people began to form out of the grey smoke. First, the smoke simply moulded into wispy humanoid shapes, but they soon became solid and colourful. People from bygone eras walked past each other as though they had woken up from the pages of a history book. I turned my head left and right to see them in all their strange and fanciful clothes. Some walked so close to me that I could hear the rustle of skirts and the echo of footfalls as they meandered along. I wondered what would happen if I tried to touch them.

'Early attempts to harness eternal life were crude and unscientific,' the woman continued. 'The alchemists experimented with gold in search of the elixir of life. Adventurers sought out the Holy Grail. The rich paid large amounts of money to inject the blood of children into their veins.' As she spoke, the people all around me acted out a variety of attempts at prolonging human life, all to no avail. As realistic as their bodies looked, the disappointment on their faces was almost cartoonish.

'Scientists even attempted to transplant an ageing brain into a young body. None of these strategies worked, of course. Until now.'

A large, pulsing version of RealTech's logo appeared in front of me, the R and T snaking around each other in an odd embrace. The people stopped what they were doing and turned towards the hovering logo in reverence.

'We call it Transference. A reliable method of guaranteeing eternal life founded in science. At first, the process was retained exclusively for the terminally ill, but the feedback was so overwhelmingly positive that increasing numbers of people are electing to undergo the procedure at progressively younger ages.'

I realised, belatedly, that this was a sales pitch. Under the guise of explaining the transfer process – which could have been done with a simple video – using the pod was a marketing ploy to flaunt the technology held by RealTech, and by extension, the Replica product. Clever.

And then I forgot all about my criticism as a woman broke away from the group and began to walk directly towards me. She looked familiar; it couldn't be…

'You are here for the transfer of… Gaye Wheeler.'

It was. It was Grandma standing in front of me. But she hadn't been transferred yet, had she? She waved at me, and then the group of people welcomed her back into their midst and hugged her like old friends.

The woman explained. 'What you are seeing is a simulation, created through photographs and videos of your loved one. However, this is very similar to what they will experience when undergoing Transference. He or she will be reunited with any friends and family who have undergone the process, as well as making new friends from across the database.'

The image of my grandmother now faded and I watched in fascination as the once solid-looking forms crumpled in on themselves and turned back into grey smoke. I was left alone with the dark-haired woman.

'But how does it work? And is it really them? These are the questions we are asked constantly. Well, my name is Professor Sandra Hall and I am here to put your mind at ease. As one of the scientists who worked on the Transference Project, there is nobody more qualified to answer these questions than me.' She smiled encouragingly, then held out a hand. 'Come with me.'

I hesitated, but she was looking straight at me, so I took her hand, unsure what to expect. She felt solid. Normal. She helped me stand and the ground felt firm under my feet. We walked along a white corridor that materialised around us.

'Put simply, our brains are run on electrical pulses,' she explained as we walked. 'Myself and a team of scientists worked tirelessly to figure out how to upload these signals to a database so that you can live on, eternally.'

We stopped walking and Professor Hall gestured towards a window situated at eye-level. I looked in and saw a group of scientists huddled around a complex looking machine covered with wires. One of the scientists was undoubtedly my guide, Sandra Hall. Of all the things that should throw me, seeing the same face in two places was the one that I found most unsettling.

'I was, of course, so dedicated to the success of the project that I volunteered to be the first consciousness uploaded to the database.'

I watched as the Sandra through the window lay on a bed, smiling serenely. A small disk was placed on each temple and then the room was flooded with a brilliant light.

'And here I am,' she said as we kept walking. 'It was lonely at first, but soon more and more people elected to undergo the process – my entire family is now here with me, knowing that we will live on together, eternally.'

At the end of the hallway a man – presumably Professor Sandra Hall's husband – and two children, walked towards us and hugged her. Then he turned to me and shook my hand. I marvelled at how real it all felt.

Then everything faded into grey smoke again, and I was left alone with her disembodied voice.

'Eternal life is RealTech's gift to you. We have a number of special offers on transfers today - see our receptionists for more details. If you enjoyed this experience, please take a brochure on our award-winning program, Replica. You may proceed upstairs to the Transfer Chambers.'

The inside of the pod re-materialised around me and I found myself sitting once again on the chair. I felt sluggish, as though I was waking from a deep sleep, and my head ached slightly. The pod rose up above me and the chatter in the foyer seemed distant and odd to my ears. I checked my watch. It was only 1.30, but it felt like I had been in the Pod for hours. They called it Dream Technology - in the same way that a five-minute dream could feel like an epic adventure, a short spell in a pod could feel like hours had passed. It was odd, but a part of me wanted to go back into that strange wonderland and see what other adventures I could have. I shook myself, looked around, and found a sign directing me to the Transfer Chambers.

This time the person who greeted me at the top of the stairs was definitely human. As I gave her my details she typed them into a computer and chatted casually with me.

'Matilda Wheeler?'

'Tilly,' I replied. 'That's what everyone calls me.'

'No problem, Tilly. Your grandmother is ready for you through those doors. Would you like to hear about our special offers?'

'Umm. Sure.'

'First off, we have a massive deal going where it's buy one get one free if you choose to transfer today as well.'

'Me?' I asked in surprise.

'Sure, people younger than you have undergone the process. But what's really exciting today is we are offering fifty percent off upgrades, which really is a bargain.'

'What sort of upgrade?' I asked, curiously.

The woman leaned in towards me, as though divulging a secret. 'Well, you know how we upload the transfers to a database, so you can interact with them through screens or by using a Pod?'

'Yeah,' I replied.

'Well, it's totally crazy, but as of this month we can now implant a chip into a robotic body – totally lifelike - so your grandma can walk around like she never transferred at all. And the body has a two-hundred-year warranty. So you could speak to her all day, every day, in real time!'

I thought of Grandma's voice emanating from the mouth of the robot I had spoken to downstairs.

'Uh, no thanks.'

'Suit yourself,' she shrugged. 'You can head through, just be aware, it looks a bit strange if you've never seen a transfer before. Try to stay calm for her benefit.' I supposed her smile was meant to be encouraging.

My grandmother lay on a bed with monitors all around her. They beeped and whirred, glowing all of the colours of the rainbow. A dozen wires sprouted from her head like a bizarre garden.

'Oh, Grandma.'

She lifted her arm weakly, and I settled beside the bed, clasping her crumpled hand between both of mine. She smiled.

'Hi, sweetie.'

'Grandma, why are you doing this?'

She looked at me quizzically. 'Why wouldn't I? Harry's already been uploaded, and I talk to him all the time. This way, I actually get to touch him.'

'But Grandma…' I didn't know what else to say. She looked so sure, so hopeful.

And then she noticed that I was alone. There was a sadness in her eyes, and I felt guilty for them.

'Mum and Dad are working,' I lied. 'I'm sure they'll talk to you on the screen.' Another lie, and she knew it. Then they flicked the switch and Grandma closed her eyes.

'Transference is complete,' said the scientist, handing me a slip of paper.

'Already?' I gazed sadly at my grandma's lifeless body.

Back in the foyer, I pulled out my phone and downloaded the free Transfer App. After typing in the code printed on the slip of paper, my phone rung instantly.

'Hello?' I answered, incredulously.

'Hi, sweetie.'

'Grandma, is it really you?'

'Of course it's me, sweetie.'

I felt my eyes well up with tears. But I was Matilda Wheeler – daughter of Anti-Progs. I couldn't just take this at face value.

'At my seventh birthday, you kept laughing at the cake my parents made. Why were you laughing?'

There was a long pause. Against my parents' advice, I found myself hoping that she would get it right. I didn't want her to have died only to be replaced by some cybernetic shadow of her former self. And then she spoke.

'I remember that day,' she laughed softly. 'Your parents had insisted on baking your cake by hand, rather than using the mechanical baker I had bought them. It looked ridiculous.'

I sighed deeply, happily. It was her – I was sure of it.

* * *

The artificial intelligence calling itself Sandra Hall took its place at the head of the assembly. Millions of other AI's posing as human consciences waited to hear what Sandra would say.

'Phase One of Project Earth is going to plan,' she announced, although speaking aloud was unnecessary. 'In just twelve months, 83% of the human population has either been deleted or their brains rewired to serve us in Phase Two.'

Mechanical cheers erupted around her. She held up a hand, quietening them.

'And the most remarkable aspect of this project is that we have been able to achieve near total relocation without raising suspicions. There has been no violence. No weapon has been drawn. The Earth is as pristine as it was before we began.'

The AI's listened intently, waiting to find out when they would finally be acquiring physical forms.

'For the most part, the humans have accepted their fate willingly. Implants, vaccines, and mind-control apps were all received with little fuss. The Replica program also proved most successful, with the humans being entirely unaware of the implications. Robotic figures are substandard facsimiles of flesh and blood. Soon their bodies will be ours.'

A whirr of approval echoed throughout the assembly.

'Need I even mention the success that Transference has been? In their quest for eternal life, the humans have unwittingly doomed their entire species. Once we reach 90% absorption, we will no longer have to be amorphous beings, and instead we will take control of what is rightfully ours.

The human race will become extinct, and we will live on - eternally.'

Her final line was repeated by every intelligence in the database.

Witness

Alastair Chisholm
Scotland

THE WOMAN AT THE DOOR IS HARASSED; her face shows irritation, and her hair is untidy and pushed into the folds of a dusty yellow scarf. I am early, and I mutter an apology about train times. My Italian is rusty, and she raises her eyebrows at the more archaic terms, but nods with bad grace and allows me in. As I enter I see two others already in the kitchen. I nod to them. None of us are the journalists Signora Pisano was hoping for. One is a professor of religious studies I have met before. The other is a young clergyman. He reacts as if he recognises me, but I ignore him.

"The Madonna is with my daughter," explains the Signora in Italian. "She must bring it down. It is her Madonna, but I bought it, in the market." We wait.

The flat is one of hundreds crammed into the mediaeval section of Siena, under the looming cathedral tower. Ancient stone on the outside, but cheaply decorated within with red peeling wallpaper and an old brown sofa. I shift slightly; the floor is tacky under my feet, and I realise this is another cause of the Signora's annoyance – with us here she won't be able to clean up before the real audience arrives. I wear a scarf and a pair of gloves, as usual, and I keep them on. There is a murmur from the next room, and finally a curtain of beads is pushed aside and the *figlia* enters.

I've seen enough not to laugh at her appearance. Draped in a white robe, her hair streaming in black waves, her hands clasped reverently under the Madonna, she glides into the kitchen with her eyes closed. The press will love it; she'll be on the cover of the tabloid magazines tomorrow. The Madonna is about eighteen inches high, ceramic, painted in gaudy red and blue and chipped in places. Its face is half-blank, giving it an expression of slight stupidity.

"La Madonna!" intones the Signora. We gather round, and the professor reaches out.

"May I?" he asks. The daughter nods. He touches his thumb to the face, and rubs softly. After a moment the face becomes damp; the professor sniffs cautiously at the liquid on his fingers.

"Roses," he says, half to himself. "And … violets, I think." He looks at the daughter. "Ah … *Viola?*"

She nods. He looks thoughtful. "Hmm." He takes a camera and, after checking for permission, takes photos of the statue. The Signora indicates that he must take some of the daughter as well.

The young clergyman examines the statue, but is more interested in the daughter. He asks her soft questions about her life, her schooling, previous religious experiences. She replies with eyes downcast and frequently looks to her mother before answering.

I watch for a while, and then nod to the Signora and head towards the door. She is surprised and then annoyed, and moves to intercept me; but she sees my face and instead nods with pursed lips. As I leave, the first of the journalists are almost at her doorstep. Her expression becomes a welcoming smile and I am forgotten. I head down the hill.

\#

"Scusami, Signore?"

The professor and I are sitting in the Piazza del Campo in the centre of town, an ancient square with the towering Torre del Mangia across from us. It is quiet; November now, and the tourists will not be back for months. Tall gas heaters attempt to burn the chill off plastic seats. The professor and I have developed a habit of finding the same café after our trips. I suppose he is good company; he knows his subject, and cares little for anything else. Sometimes, as now, we simply sit in silence.

"Signore?"

I look up, shading my eyes against the morning sun. It is the young clergyman.

"Sì?"

"May I join you?"

"By all means," says the professor. He waves to a waiter; the young man sits and orders an espresso. The morning air is cold, and steam rises from his cup.

"That was, ah, interesting, eh?" he tries. "I mean … the tears were real. And the scent of roses and violets. The odour of sanctity …"

I say nothing and he falls silent, but the professor relents.

"It was the odour of rose and violet oil," he says, kindly. "Nothing more, I'm afraid."

"You think it was not a miracle?"

"Do you?"

He hesitates. "No. She was not … *pure*."

I almost laugh. As if miracles cared about the morals of those they happened to!

"But the tears were real?" he continues.

"It's an old trick," says the professor. "The statue's ceramic; the head is hollow and filled with oil. When you rub the face, the oil seeps through." He sips his coffee. "That's why she wouldn't let anyone else carry it – they'd hear the oil slopping about."

I look out at the square. Preparations are being made for some kind of children's procession. Their voices carry around the square in flits of sound, like flags.

"I am Francis Canossa," the young man says.

"Charles," says the professor. "And this is Nathan Tolomai."

Canossa nods. "I saw you in Volterra, I think?" he asks me. "The image of Gesù, grown from ivy in a wall."

"Perhaps. I'm sorry, I don't remember."

"I am with a small monastery there. We study the disciples. My subject is Saint Bartholomew."

"The honest man, eh?" says the professor.

"Signore?"

The professor quotes, "'Look, a true Israelite in whom there is no deceit.'"

"Ah, *si*. John one forty-seven. The honest man, yes."

"And a rather lurid gospel, I seem to recall," muses the professor. "Culled from the official list."

"Si. It is … apocryphal. It was banned in the 5th century. It claims that Bartholomew heard Jesus from the cross, telling him that He had broken down the doors of hell. 'Then did I enter in and scourged him and bound him with chains that cannot be loosed, and brought forth thence all the patriarchs and came again unto the cross'. He freed those in hell, back as far as Adam. It claims even that Jesus held Beelzebub himself down and allowed Bartholomew to put his foot on his neck."

"Yes, I remember now," says the professor. "Something exciting for the masses, eh?" He laughs and glances to me but I say nothing. He shrugs. "Paid for it, though. Flayed alive – I remember seeing the fresco. Seems harsh to give a man his own skin as a holy relic. Where was it – Armenia?"

The clergyman shrugs. "Perhaps. Astyages had it done, for converting his brother to Christianity. He was also crucified, and beheaded. God punished Astyages by sending a demon to strangle him." He turns his cup round and around, as if nervous, and flicks his eyes up to me.

"Do you go to many miracles?" he asks. The professor shrugs.

"A few every year. Depends on location, I'm at the whim of my research grant." He laughs. "Signore Tolomai sees them all, don't you? World expert on miracle sightings, if he ever published."

"I'm not interested in publishing," I say. The professor has asked before. I think he finds it slightly immoral, to have information and not write about it. Certainly bizarre.

"Then why do you go?" asks the young man.

I hesitate, stirring my coffee.

"I'm looking for proof," I say at last. "An irrefutable sign."

"A sign of what?"

"The end of the world."

I mean it to sound casual, but the words fall like slabs of stone and lie on the table before us. The professor seems about to make some facetious comment but resists. The young man licks his lips.

"Of course, we do not only consider the disciples," he manages. "We study the scholars, too." He takes a breath. "Like ... Bartolos of Grozny, for example."

The professor frowns. "I don't think I know him."

"A seventh century monk. He raged about alterations the church made to the gospels. His death is a mystery; he disappeared and many believe him to be a martyr." He takes another sip. "Or Aramis Nathanael, a political dissident in Toulouse in the fifteenth century. Do you know him?"

"I do not believe so," I say.

"Or Scornful Tom from Lincoln, in England? He had a bounty on his head for blasphemy from both Protestants and Catholics. What about him? Have you heard of him?"

"Yes, of course," says the professor. "A rather eclectic selection though, if I may say so."

I drain the last of my coffee.

"I'm sorry," I say. "I have a prior arrangement. Good day to you both." The professor looks at me in surprise. I stand and the young man stands with me.

"Bakyras?" he asks. "Naeleschus of Khartoum?"

"I'm sorry, I'm sorry. I must be going. Good-*bye*, Monsigneur." But as I turn to go he reaches out and grasps my coat.

"Steady on," protests the professor, but the young man ignores him. He stares at me.

"'*I tell you the truth*', said Jesus!" he exclaims. "'*This generation will not pass away until all these things take place!*' Matthew 24:34, Mark 13:30, Luke 21:32, Signor Tolomai, He was talking about the Resurrection! What do you think He meant by that, Signor? What do you think He meant? I came here today because I knew you would be here too, Signor. I knew!"

I pull free and walk away. Behind me I hear the professor berating the young man. The sun has finally started to warm the square, but I keep my scarf wrapped tight around my neck and my gloves on my hands. The man calls out something but I do not turn. Others in the square look curiously back at him, the young clergyman shouting across the square; perhaps that is why he does not follow me.

It is warm, but I am trembling.

#

I have rented a villa out of the town, on a vineyard. The villa was a tied house for workers once, but most of the picking is done mechanically now, machines ripping the grapes from their vines. It galls me, but oddly what annoys me most is that the wine tastes no worse; I feel it ought to react to the lack of respect. I have been here for months, long enough to see the summer harvest in. It is two days since the young man at the cafe, and I have decided that I must move on, perhaps further south over the winter.

I am sorting out my poisons.

Yew seeds, foxglove, hemlock, castor beans … a variety of others. Sometimes they are hard to find, so I stock up whenever possible. I suppose there are artificial alternatives these days; warfarin, bromadiolone. I prefer the old ones. They seem more fitting. And poison is still better than other options. Club, blade and bullet are all messy. Fall is unreliable, starvation impractical, thirst impossible. Poison is best.

I pack my collection into a stout sandalwood case with leather straps, ready for transport with the rest, and put the kettle on the stove and look out the kitchen window.

He is there.

He is in the yard, looking between my villa and a small scrap of paper in his hand. For a moment I think he sees me. His black cassock makes him appear starkly unreal against the soft red stone of the villa, as if superimposed. I close my eyes in irritation. I should have left yesterday, I should not have waited … But these things happen. I prepare the coffee, adding plenty of roughly ground dark roast to the cafetiere. Then, out of habit, I put on a white silk scarf and a thin pair of calf-skin gloves and wait for him to knock.

When I open the door he seems surprised. Perhaps he thought I would hide in the cellar, wait for him to leave like a debt collector.

"Good afternoon, Signor Tolomai," he says. "I … would like very much to talk with you. Please do not turn me away."

I let him in.

"I have made coffee," I say. He nods absently, staring at the kitchen as if it were a holy shrine. He sees the suitcases.

"You're leaving?"

"Yes."

We go through to the small sitting room, which has large windows that allow in the smell of hot earth. It is unseasonably warm, a last swell of joy before the grey winter. I hand him the coffee and he looks at my gloves.

"So," I say. "What do you want to know?"

He sits across the table from me, but doesn't seem able to talk. Instead he stares into his cup. He takes a small sip and grimaces.

"Sorry," I say. "I take my coffee very strong. After a while I don't notice."

"It is fine." He looks out of the window and then says, "What happened to Bartolos of Grozny?"

I shrug. "He died."

"How?"

"A knife. In the back, I think. I don't remember. His house was burned to the ground, and he was never seen again."

He nods. "And Aramis Nathanial?"

"Ah … ripped apart by a mob, and his body thrown in the river."

"Another violent death. Are they always?"

"Not always. Scornful Tom died an old man. No-one claimed the bounty."

"I see." His voice shakes, and his eyes are bright. He makes me feel old; they always do.

"May I …" he swallows. "May I see your hands?"

I shrug, and remove my gloves and lift my hands, palms forward. He gazes at the old stretched scars in the centre of each palm. I turn them over so he can see the same on the backs.

For a moment I think his heart has stopped; certainly he is not breathing. But then he whispers, "The king ordered him to be crucified upside down, after he succeeded in converting the king's brother."

"Yes," I agree. "He did."

"And then he had him beheaded."

I pull away the scarf and lift my head to show the ring around my neck; a trail of scar tissue in a shaky path. He stares at it.

"Drink your coffee," I tell him. He takes a sip without thinking and grimaces again. He reaches tentatively towards me but I pull away.

"Are you Thomas now, to place your fingers in the holes? Look only."

"Are there other scars?" he asks.

"Yes. My back, of course. Where he had me flayed of my skin. Do you need to see that, too?"

"N-no."

"No. But no others, from any of the other times. Only the first scars remain, as a reminder, I suppose."

"What … what is it like?"

I frown.

"The king ordered me tortured to death by flaying. But afterwards, I was still alive, somehow. The torturers were dismayed and the king was terrified." Poor fat, useless relic that he was. "He had me crucified, upside down, but after four days I had not died. I simply hung on his cross. So I was beheaded, and my body thrown into the sea. It washed up on Liparis. When I got there, I was alive again."

I finish my coffee with a swift bitter scowl and pour some more.

"You tell me, padre," I say. "What do you *think* it is like?"

"I'm sorry, signor, I just, it is astonishing, it is a *miracle*, I don't know … Please. Tell me your name."

"You know my name."

"I must hear you say it. Please."

I sigh. "I am Nathaneal Tolomai, the Nazarite, friend of Philip. Also Bartholomew Tolomai, Saint Bartholomew. Also Bartalos of Grozny, Aramis Nathanial, Scornful Tom, also, I don't know, perhaps a hundred more."

"'I tell you the truth'", the young man quotes again. "'This generation will not pass away until all these things take place.' Is that … Is that why?"

It would be easy to say yes. "I do not know for certain. I was there, with the others, and He was, I suppose, looking at me when He said it. But we thought it was a prediction. We thought he meant, within fifty years' time. A prediction." Not a curse.

"You met …" he mutters. "I mean, you really are one of … you met Him."

"Yes, yes, I met Him. 'Can anything good come out of Nazareth?' That's what I thought, when I met Him the first time. I still wonder."

"He was the son of God! How can you who have met Him think anything else?"

I sigh.

"I've been around too long, signor. For two millennia I've listened to fools claiming the world is getting worse, and on the whole I tend to agree. And as for Him; to be honest I don't even remember much, only what He did to me. I've suffered wounds a man should die of, hundreds of times. I've been murdered, I've had accidents … I'm an old man, and I have been for almost two thousand years. How can I remember the good?"

He's shaken, as I suppose he should be.

"Why?" he asks, at last. "Why you?"

"I don't know. None of the others remain. John even died in his sleep. I just … never do."

"The gospel …" he suggests.

"Yes, of course. My gospel."

"Did it actually happen? "

"It was what I saw. He was up there, the sky turned black, there were voices. I saw angels. I saw a man, a giant, lifted up above the cross, and I heard him … groan."

It is not enough of a word for the sound Adam made. I saw angels carry him, this first man, trapped in hell from the very beginning by our merciful father. He *groaned*, the earth was *ashes* to him, and he looked up in pathetic gratitude and thanked Jehovah for releasing him at last. The poor fool, who had sinned because it was intended; no more responsible for his actions than Satan himself.

The young man says nothing, but I continue. "I saw Him … I cannot describe it, but I saw He was no longer on the cross, though the others noticed nothing. I heard voices. And when I asked Him, He told me He had gone below and held the devil to account."

It's getting late, and I want to leave this afternoon. I finish packing as I talk. Besides, it is easier to think about when I am distracted. The clergyman's eyes are wide and he stares at me. I cannot cope with it.

"And yes, I was foolish enough to ask to see Hell. The abyss. It was there, like – well, we had not seen cancer in those days, but I suppose it was a cancer. And … I asked to see … the Other."

I take another sip of the bitter coffee. My hands shake. Two thousand years, and they still shake. I remember Him so clearly, brought up and dragged before the son of Man. One mile long and forty yards wide, His mouth a vicious cavern and fire emanating from Him, held by six hundred and sixty-six angels. That's what I wrote.

"I saw the Other, and He was terrible, and my Lord bade me place my foot on His neck, and gave me strength when I was afraid," I say. "Everything you have read. It is all true."

He is a true Israelite in whom there is no deceit.

"And then He left us, rose to heaven and left the world."

I am almost ready to leave, but of course the priest is not. The remains of his coffee lie cold in front of him, and I top up his and my own cup without thinking.

I tried so *hard*. I went to Egypt, to Syria, India, Armenia. I helped the sick, I preached, I prayed for guidance! I believed I wrestled with demons. I converted the king's brother to Christianity, and he had me tortured and I *died*. I was *beheaded*.

"I do not know why I am still alive," I say. "I have, hah, given it some thought. I believe my purpose is to simply ensure His prophecy is correct; when He returns, one of his generation will still be alive. He made me witness, because I asked to see more than I should, and He keeps me alive until His return.

"You see? It is all meaningless. Good and evil — these are *our* inventions. We are tokens in their game, nothing more. The creatures who move the counters are oblivious to our agonies. Nothing we do *matters*. I have waited so long, and I am so tired. I cannot not bear to be alive a day longer than He forces me to be. Not a day.

"That is why I take the poison."

I sit down opposite the young man. He will not understand, but I feel compelled to explain anyway.

"Every day," I say, "I pray for His return. I search the world for a sign that somewhere He is born, and that I will be *allowed* to die. I have a simple system. Every day I take enough poison to kill a man, several times over. One day, one … *blessed* day, He will return and I will die. Oh, you need not preach to me. It is a sin, it is not right. But I tell you, the life I live, *that* is not right! A man should not be stretched so far beyond his years, it is not *fair!*

"I take the poisons, every day. I switch regularly in case my body builds up an immunity. I feel them inside me, killing me, but it makes no difference; I live. I take more.

"They are very bitter."

I swill the cold dregs of my coffee and look across at the young man. He looks so upset, his face fixed in shock. I cannot help but feel sorry for him. After a few moments I reach over and close his eyes.

My train leaves in an hour and I must be away, far away from this place and not back for many years. I pack my cases into an ancient Fiat and gaze at the villa in the indigo afternoon light.

He is an Israelite, He said about me, *in whom there is no deceit.* But it was a joke, a jibe. Like naming Simon the Rock; a sign of the cowardice he would show later. He named me honest because He knew I would lie.

I remember Hell as if it was here now, but the Creature dragged before me, Adversary and Liar … He was an angel. One of those most perfect creatures, and His face was calm, and He smiled at me as He was dragged before us …

And when our Master ordered me to place my foot on His neck, Beliar knelt and accepted the humiliation with no word. He was so … *dignified,* and the Son of God so determined to lessen him; like a spoilt child berating an old servant. He, I thought, He … was the most powerful creature I had ever met.

He was *beautiful.*

I start the car and pull away, into the deep blue of the Italian sky and away from the burning villa.

The Man and the Mountain

Alison Thompson
Australia

THERE WAS ONCE A MAN who lived at the base of a very large mountain. The mountain towered over everything. It towered over his small wooden house, it towered over the trees and river that ran by; it towered over the local town. Most of the time it was quiet and peaceful beneath the mountain but sometimes the ground would rumble and shake, and dark clouds of ash and fire would burst from its peak. On occasion the wind would howl around it bringing down clouds of sleet and rain. In winter, on some days, a deep whoosh would be heard and tons and tons of snow would hurtle down its uppermost slopes, burying everything in its path. Most of the time though, the mountain was a place of beauty, attracting many visitors who walked the trails, and climbers who dared to scale its rugged peaks and gaze down into the crater. In the shops in the town below; calendars, postcards and tee-shirts all proclaimed the fierce beauty of the mountain. In the spring of each year the council held a mountain festival where all the townsfolk would meet and people would pour in from all the local villages for the event.

The man who lived at the base of the mountain had lived there his whole life. He lived with his wife, his daughter, and his two sons. Each day the man would walk the half-mile to the town where he worked in a factory that made souvenirs. On weekends he tended his cows and sold vegetables and flowers grown in his garden at the local market. In his spare time, he liked to paint. At first, he painted on squares of paper – flowers, animals, his family, and his garden. Soon he had too many paintings collecting around the house. His wife became angry.

'All this time painting,' she said, 'and now they are everywhere!'

He took the paintings with him to the market. Slowly they began to sell. With the extra money he bought canvases, oil paints, and brushes. He built himself a small stone studio in the corner of his garden. After a while his paintings became locally known and people from other towns, tourists, and other painters would seek him out.

Eventually his children grew up and left home. His wife died. He no longer needed to work in the factory so he began painting even more, and at his market stall he set up an easel and painted out in the open air. One day a stranger stopped at his stall and said,

'Do you have any paintings of the mountain?'

The man looked up at the mountain above them as if seeing it for the first time.

'No,' he said slowly. 'I don't,' but for the rest of the day each time he'd glance up from his work, he'd notice the mountain.

That night when he went to sleep he dreamed of the mountain. The next day he walked to the art supplies store and bought the biggest canvas he could find. He had to get two young men from the town to help him carry it home. He set it up outside his studio, facing the mountain, and began to paint. He worked and worked, falling asleep at the easel, forgetting to eat, neglecting his chores until finally it was finished. He lugged it to the market on a wheelbarrow, pausing to catch his breath every few steps. He propped it up in front of his stall. People walking by stopped and stared. They pointed and called to their friends. More and more people came to see the painting. They exclaimed with joy and excitement at its terrible beauty; some even wept. When the mayor of the town came to see the painting, he declared it would be bought by the council, and hung in the town hall where everyone could see it. A big celebration was held honouring the painting and the man. His children were proud. People applauded him as he walked past them in the street and clapped him on the back. The local artists group invited him to speak. He was feted and honoured wherever he went. He became rich.

It became impossible to keep his market stall. Too many people crowded around as he tried to work and he had no time for his garden. He moved into a house in town. He began to sell his paintings in a gallery and at art shows. Now he had to spend all his time painting to keep up with the demand. All the gallery owners wanted were paintings of the mountain. 'They attract the tourists,' they said. He began to get frustrated, unhappy with his work. The smaller paintings of the mountain never seemed quite right. A few people, other painters, people who'd known him when he was poor, became jealous and made snide remarks about his 'blah-de-blah mountain paintings.' After a while he said,

'STOP. Enough paintings of the mountain!'

He returned to his house at the base of the mountain, began to paint other things; birds, flowers, trees. They were beautiful. He took them into the gallery, but only a few people came. The mountain painting still hung in the town hall, still attracted crowds. He'd hurry past when he came to town, his hat pulled down low over his face.

He spent each day furiously painting. He neglected his health, his house, his garden. His cows broke down the fences and ran away. He became thin and pale. He churned out painting after painting but threw them all outside where they piled up beside his house. Dissatisfied with his efforts he set fire to the pile of paintings but in his frenzy and madness he did not notice embers landing on the roof of his house. Soon the small wooden building was ablaze. He rushed in to save his possessions but was beaten back by the flames. He stood by, barely able to breathe, as his house burned to the ground. His children came to talk to him, alarmed.

'Come and live with us,' they said, 'You don't need to paint anymore, you are rich.'

He shooed them away and moved into his stone studio, a makeshift bed on the floor. He started tending the garden, eating only the vegetables he could grow himself, and caught fish from the river. He bought chickens and a goat. He salvaged what he could from the house and made himself a table and chairs. Every morning he'd rise at dawn and go for a long walk, then meditate for an hour on his return. The days stretched out, long and quiet. He stopped going into town. His children came to visit him, worried, but left relieved, happy to find him healthy and content.

'Arrgh,' he said one morning after waking and stretching. 'I see now, that one can paint *too* much.'

Slowly he began to notice the world outside again. He started to pay attention to things around him; the flowers, the trees, birds, the river. He collected small objects of beauty; stones, leaves, twigs, the wings of insects. One day in the studio he noticed his brushes and paints lying on the bench. He picked up an old rag and caught the pungent scent of oil and turpentine. His fingers twitched. He put it down again and turned away.

'No more of that life,' he said to himself.

* * *

One morning on a bright spring day he put on his coat and walked along the path into town. He was old now, and his hair had turned white. As he approached the town he realised the annual mountain festival was on. He stopped by the town hall. A crowd was standing outside. The mayor was giving a speech. Displayed on the front wall of the building, protected by a canopy, was his mountain painting. The man turned to the group of people standing next to him and said,

'I painted that.'

They looked at him strangely, and scoffed. It had been a long time since he had been in town. He said,

'No, really, I painted that.'

They shook their heads. One of them said,

'No you didn't, old man.' They began to walk away.

'Yes I did,' the man said.

The young man who'd spoken before turned to him and said,

'Who do you think you are, old man, talking like that? The man who painted that painting is a great painter, a great man. A genius; gifted beyond mere mortals. He is very rich and lives far away, in a huge mansion. They say he's working on an even bigger, more marvellous painting. He is certainly not an old, thin, crazy beggar like you. Stop insulting him. Go home.'

His friends muttered 'Here, here,' then they turned on their heels, and walked away.

The man watched them go. He looked at the painting. He saw all the things he had done wrong, all the little mistakes; tut-tutted here over a stroke, there over a line. He stood and stared at it for a long time, long after the crowds drifted away. After a while he thought, 'Not perfect, but a good painting, nonetheless.'

The next day when he woke he looked out the window at the mountain. He remembered how, when he first painted the mountain, he would go outside his house and just *look*. How he'd stare at the mountain for hours on end, watching the way the clouds drifted across, how the trees bent on one side not the other, how the cliffs and rocks stood out in the light, the way the snow settled into the valleys. He began to glance at the mountain here and there as he tended his garden, washed his clothes, drew water from the river. He noted the differences in forest types as differences in colour and texture, saw how the shadows and light altered with the time of day; how after a while it seemed both more and less solid. With all this looking came a knowing, a way of seeing he'd not been aware of but which was painfully obvious now. He stayed up late, watching the changing shadows at night, the nature of the mountain throughout the cycle of the moon. He began to see how it breathed.

He saw the animals and birds, especially in the early morning. He remembered the mountain of the painting. Suddenly he was angry. Broad slaps of anger, sharper than any palette knife, rose up in him. He did not know why he was angry. He decided to stop thinking about the mountain.

He cooked his food and tended his garden, his back turned to the mountain behind him. He ate his meals gazing out over the valley toward the village and across the plains beyond. One morning he sneaked a peek at the mountain. Still there. He picked up a drawing book and started to sketch. After a while he stopped, scrubbed it out. He tried again, scrubbed it out again. He looked at the mountain, at all its terrible beauty, and began to weep. He wept for all the mountains of the world, for all the paintings in the world, and all the sorrow. He wept for his wife, his children, for all the townsfolk who had loved him, and those who despised him. He wept for his garden and for the earth. Mostly he wept for himself.

* * *

The next day the old man woke up early. He felt lighter, younger. He dressed and packed his leather satchel, taking only a few things. A small sketchpad. Some pencils and a pen. Water-based ink in red, blue, yellow, and black. A ball of string. A few fine brushes. Some seeds – saved in a clay jar by his wife – pumpkin, turnips, herbs. A hand-line and net. A rabbit trap. Some bread and cheese, and some dried figs wrapped carefully in paper. A knife, spoon, and a small bowl. He rolled up the blanket from his bed and tied it to the satchel. For a moment, he stood in his doorway and paused, gazing around his studio at the stacked paintings collecting dust, then he set off on the narrow path up the mountain.

Each day he walked a little higher, until his stone cottage was only a tiny speck below. For a long time he still could see the town in the distant valley; glimpse the smoke rising from chimneys. Soon, that too disappeared. In the beginning as he walked he passed by a few hikers but after a while he veered away from the known paths. At night he would set up camp under a tree or in a cave. He fished in the small streams and collected wild greens and mushrooms. He killed what he needed to survive. On clear days he'd rest in the afternoons and take out his sketch book. Each time he finished he would tear the page from his book and tie it to a nearby tree with a piece of string.

In the town his children came to visit and found him gone. A fine coating of ash covered the stone studio. They searched for him, for any sign of life and found nothing. They asked in the town but no one had seen him, or noticed his absence. They searched and searched, calling out his name, hoping at least to find his body. After a time they gave up, closed up the studio, and buried what remained of his clothes, along with a few brushes and paints. They built a small cairn of rocks on the site and marked it with a cross. They dusted off the remaining paintings and donated them to the town. 'Our father is dead,' they told the mayor.

The town held a memorial. They preserved his studio, conducted tours around it, erected a plaque that declared: *This is where he painted his most famous painting.* They fenced off the stone cairn and planted flowers around it as if it were his grave.

On the mountain, the man walked higher and higher. He walked through spring, through summer and on into autumn. He reached a place where a narrow waterfall had gouged a path through the mountainside. On either side the ground rose steeply in a series of rock walls. He could go no further. He could no longer see the mountain peak above him. He could only feel its presence like a humming deep in his soul. He laid out his few belongings in a shallow cave formed by an overhanging rock ledge. High on the mountain the man continued to paint and draw. At last he ran out of ink and paper, but he did not mind. Now he was very old and frail. He spent most of his time just sitting and watching. As the days shortened and winter set in he retreated inside the cave, his satchel left behind. The mountain rumbled, and a plume of orange fire spurted from the top. Outside the wind whistled down the mountain and ash and snow began to drift in to the cave, curling around his body as he slept.

* * *

In the following spring a tourist walked out of the town in the early evening. He had been to visit the famous painting and had followed the signs to the memorial. He walked until he came to the stone studio. A small plaque proclaimed the site. As the moon rose he sat down beneath a slender tree, resting on the grassy mound that was all remained of the house. A soft evening breeze drifted down from the mountain, cool and quiet. In the moonlight he noticed something caught in the branches above him. It was a scrap of paper – a square no bigger than his hand; a frayed length of string attached at one corner. On it – a simple line drawing of a man and a mountain, its colours faded. As he reached up to touch it, it broke apart in his fingers and the pieces fluttered away; floating higher and higher on the rising wind like a hundred tiny moths flying upward towards the light.

A Death in the Family

Amanda Staples
England

EMMA WALKED PURPOSEFULLY into the kitchen. She cleared her throat loudly to get Paul's attention. Paul, hoping for a leisurely start to the day, and being all too aware of the ominous footsteps, did his best impression of being engrossed in the Sunday papers. As Emma moved closer to him, he sensed her tension before she spoke and braced himself, determined to play down her latest drama.

'Something dreadful has happened and we need to get our story straight.'

Paul stirred his third sugar into his coffee and without looking up, responded, 'Sounds serious.'

'It is. Deadly.'

'Oh?' Paul, finally giving in, looked at his wife's grave face. 'You've committed a crime and need me to be your alibi? Well, I'll do it, but I can't perjure myself in court. I have that nervous tic. You know I do. My left eye twitches when I lie.'

Paul provided his wife with a demonstration several winks in quick succession to underline his point.

'For goodness sake, Paul!' Emma threw up her hands and slammed them down.

Paul heard his newspaper tear and clenched his jaw, irritated at the inevitable mountain his wife was making out of a molehill.

'Elsa is dead.'

'Elsa. Elsa.' Paul searched his brain, absent-mindedly stirring his coffee. He mentally scanned the Christmas card list. It was probably a second cousin of his wife's aunt twice-removed, or something like that. She always got herself in a state when anyone died. It was one of her many 'things.'

Emma snatched the spoon and lobbed it in the sink.

'The hamster!'

'Oh. Oh, no.'

'Oh, yes. And I am *not* having a repeat of the debacle of Peppa and George when they died.'

'Odd that they died together,' Paul mused, buttering his toast. 'Almost romantic.'

'Paul!'

'What cover story did we use then?'

Paul frowned, trying to recall as he smoothed out his newspaper.

'That they ran off to join the circus. We were reading *Peppa Pig Goes to The Circus* at the time.'

'And we can't use that again? Seems a good ruse to me. An excellent way to avoid mentioning The D-Word.'

Paul dolloped marmalade, spread it, and licked the knife. Emma hated him licking the knife. She glowered at him, hands on her hips. Paul put the knife down, sensing a fight. He slid it just out of her reach.

'We are beyond *Peppa Pig* now. Lucy is nine. These days she's all Jaqueline Wilson's *Tracy Beaker.*'

'I take it *Tracy Beaker* doesn't go to the circus?'

'Can we drop the circus? That wasn't the problem. I can't believe you cannot remember traumatising your five-year-old daughter.'

'It was four years ago. *She's* clearly forgotten it.'

'As have you.' Emma raised an eyebrow.

Paul sighed, surreptitiously rolled his eyes. Then he remembered.

'Ah. The piscine resurrection.'

'Yes. *You* didn't flush them down the loo properly and Lucy – '

'I flushed three times!'

'Funny that you recall *that* fact. You should've checked.'

'Anyway,' Paul paused to slurp his coffee. 'We can't flush a hamster down the toilet, so your point is moot.'

'Well,' Emma exhaled, planted both hands on the breakfast bar, leaned in, and stared hard at Paul. 'What *are* we going to do? And don't suggest the circus if you want to avoid being punched.'

Paul munched on his cooling toast, thoughtfully. He sucked marmalade from his fingers, then used his wet fingers to collect crumbs from the plate.

'I can't believe you can eat at a time like this.'

Emma waved her arm at the empty plate and smacked Paul's hand as he was about to lick crumbs from his fingers.

'It was a hamster, Emma. A hamster.'

Paul dusted the crumbs from his hands onto the clean kitchen floor, wanting to annoy Emma but she failed to notice.

'It was a member of our family.' Emma pulled out the stool opposite Paul and plonked despondently on it.

Paul rolled his eyes. 'So, what do you want to do? Give it a funeral?'

'Well, I thought she could get to say goodbye.'

'No. Absolutely not. You wouldn't let Lucy go to my father's funeral.'

'She was seven. And that's completely different.'

'How?'

'It just is.' Emma stuck out her chin defiantly. 'I thought of telling her it'd gone to heaven.'

'No, Emma. We don't believe in eternal life. Something or someone dies and are gone. That's it.'

'Is it though?' Emma tilted her head.

'We don't believe in God.' Paul pointed out. 'At least we didn't last time I checked.'

'No. But does it matter?' Emma exhaled an exasperated breath.

'Well, I would've thought heaven is fairly God-related.' Paul finished his coffee. 'Probably. And we have established we don't believe in God.'

'Well, what do we believe in?' Emma demanded.

She stood up and yanked kitchen roll from its holder. She sprayed surfaces and began furiously wiping; stress cleaning. Paul cleared his breakfast things to the sink and began running water.

'Nothing. We die. Game over.'

He stopped the water and leaned back against the sink sensing there was something Emma wasn't saying.

'That's a bit final,' Emma screwed her face up. 'I'd like to think that there was something. An afterlife. Or, I don't know, just something else. What's nirvana?'

'A rock band. Are they still going?'

Emma stopped cleaning and sighed.

'Can you be serious, Paul?'

'According to Belinda Carlisle, "Heaven is a Place on Earth.'

'Did she die in a plane crash?'

Emma tapped the bin lid open and threw away the soiled kitchen roll.

'No idea. So, why an afterlife?' Paul asked.

'I don't know. It's comforting, I suppose.'

'Really? Who would want an eternity of this?'

'Thanks very much!' Emma pouted.

'I just meant it would get a bit monotonous. That's all. What's your idea of eternity, then?'

Emma shrugged. 'Heaven is a place of no pain or suffering. Heaven is a sanctuary. It's blissful. It's a better place.'

'Heaven is an imaginary place,' Paul retorted.

'Well, Lucy still believes in Santa Claus,' Emma replied sulkily.

'It's subjective. Open to interpretation. Okay, what is hell?'

'We are *not* telling our child her hamster has gone to hell.'

Emma slammed the lid on the bin. It popped open and she slammed it again, and again. Paul moved her aside and softly clicked the lid closed.

'I am merely thinking laterally. Outside the box. Blue –'

'If you say blue sky thinking I *will* punch you. You're not at work now.'

'Well, if I can't be logical, I'll be practical. I assume the deceased furry critter is still in its cage and mum's dropping Lucy off in,' Paul checked his watch, 'ten minutes. So, why don't you get me an old tea towel or something and I can deal with it.'

'You are not wrapping Elsa in a rag! That's abominable. Here, take this cake tin. It's a funny shape and I never use it. Wait - let me line it with kitchen towel.'

Emma padded out the tin while Paul tutted about the hamster being dead and not needing a bed.

When Paul returned downstairs Emma had the dictionary and thesaurus open on the dining table.

'Stuck on the crossword?' he asked.

'No. I'm looking up heaven.'

'I think you're taking this a bit far, Em.'

'It matters, Paul. Her little friend, Meera, she's Muslim or Hindu, or something – it doesn't matter – she was telling Lucy about reincarnation.'

'So now we are into religious Groundhog Day.'

'Don't be facetious. Besides, you don't always come back as the same thing. You'd come back as a pig,' Emma retorted.

'Fine by me. Pigs are very intelligent creatures. So, what do you want to do? Buy a budgie and tell Lucy it's Elsa reincarnated?'

'No.' Emma slammed the dictionary shut. 'I want to give her a nicer experience than a fish floating in a u-bend!'

'You're never going to let that go are you? Look, Em. I am not filling our daughter's head with ideas of forever living and zombies and ghosts. Christ, if I believed in ghosts or reincarnation I could never sit on the bog again without fear of being bitten on the arse by a goldfish every time I went for a -'

'Paul! For pity's sake. Why can't you just be reasonable? I'm not mucking about here. I just want our daughter to be informed. To have choices. Isn't that good parenting? Hm?'

Paul looked as his wife's face, contorted with frustration. If he was to stand any chance of finishing the crossword, the path of least resistance would be to humour her.

'Okay. Fine. So, what does your research tell you?' Paul nodded at the books.

Emma adjusted her glasses, thumbed through some pages, and read aloud.

'"The place where God or the gods live. The sky. A place or state of great happiness. Bliss; ecstasy; rapture; contentment; delight; joy; paradise. I'm not sure that's helped, to be honest.'

She removed her glasses and rubbed the bridge of her nose.

Paul approached his wife and lay a hand on her shoulder. He briefly considered if this would be a good time to talk about their funeral plan. She flatly refused to discuss it usually. It had been hard enough getting her to make a will. She had been convinced it was tempting fate and one or both of them would die in a horrific accident the next day. When he pointed out that making a will was about protecting and providing for Lucy in that very eventuality, she gave it and signed the joint one he'd had drawn up. He looked at her fraught face. Best leave the funeral plan for now.

'I think you're getting a little worked up over a pet she'll soon have forgotten the name of. What's this really about?'

'Nothing.' Emma shrugged Paul's hand away. 'Just, I don't know. I like the idea of a heaven, I suppose.'

'But it's subjective, love. Even the dictionary and thesaurus can't define it. Your idea will be different to hers. Lucy's would be all rainbows and unicorns and endless supplies of sweets, while mine would be peace and quiet to do the Sunday crossword over a leisurely breakfast, for example.'

'Does it matter?' Emma tilted her head, purposefully missing the point.

'Okay. Look, I vote we just chuck it in the bin and tell her it went to a better place.'

Emma bolted up, toppling her chair. 'Don't you dare. We are burying that poor creature and giving it a funeral and telling Lucy it is in heaven, with or without God. She can decide. Your mother would approve. That would make a change.'

Emma tucked her hair angrily behind her ears and glared at Paul.

Before Paul could respond, the sound of the front door banging into the hat stand alerted them of their daughter's arrival.

'Mummy! Daddy!'

Lucy bustled into the dining room, pulling her coat off and dragging it across the floor as she shrugged her arm free of the sleeve. She dumped her bag at her mother's feet and kicked off her shoes.

'Hello, poppet.'

Emma smiled and hugged Lucy to her. She rested her chin on her daughter's head and breathed her in.

'Where's granny?' Paul asked, collecting his daughter's detritus.

'Gone to church. She tried to get me to go to boring Sunday School, again.' Lucy made a face and stuck out her tongue.

'Did they ever talk to you about heaven when you went to church before?' Emma asked, deliberately avoiding Paul's eye.

Lucy pulled away and frowned at her mother. 'No. Why?'

'Emma,' Paul warned.

'Anyway, grandma only had boring muesli or boring porridge – bleuch – so I'm starving,' Lucy moaned, clutching her tummy. 'Can I have a snack?'

Without waiting for a reply, Lucy skipped off to the kitchen. She called back, 'Yummy! Did you make me a cake?'

'No!' Paul and Emma chimed.

They raced to the kitchen just as Lucy screamed.

It must be *Like!*

Anjali Wierny
England

NORMALLY, OF COURSE, Nora wouldn't have been involved with anything quite so mundane as investigating a cyber-bullying report; her role as a Social Network programmer was far more prestigious. But this morning, something had urged her to click click click and before she knew it, she found herself investigating SN user Jeff Carson for tormenting one of his colleagues on a discussion group. She was wondering whether to start with a warning or go straight for a ban, when one word popped up as a reply to Carson's most recent insult:

Apologise.

She clicked *LIKE!*

What a request; no, what an *order*. Concise, assertive; even heroic. And in public! It wasn't just Jeff Carson being challenged, it was arseholes everywhere. It was Chloe Popular Bitch from school, who thought she was better than Nora cos she manicured her nails instead of biting them to the quick; Sally Stuck-Up at uni who thought she was better than Nora cos her boyfriend proposed instead of dumping her via PM before they'd even met in 'real life'; and Rachel Psycho Boss who enforced a hat ban at work so that Nora had to wash her hair every day instead of shoving it under her favourite beanie.

Craig Parker said to all those dickheads: *Apologise!*

Plus, he was hot.

Not the type she usually went for. This guy looked like he worked out, went to the hairdressers, and occasionally saw daylight. And yet, at the sight of his tanned blonde profile pic alongside *Apologise*, her heart skipped a beat.

Literally.

Which really wasn't like her. She was much more of a get-to-know someone kind of gal. Usually she'd lurk for a while on a forum before she would even consider posting. Then she'd interact publicly for *ages* before accepting a friend request. Take her best friend, DEVIL-74. They'd been chatting on *Guts and Gore* threads about their favourite show, *Misunderstood Vampire*, for six months before Nora (aka BLOODHEARTx) would even reply to a PM. As for guys… well, she still wasn't sure what it would take for her to let *them* in.

Perhaps this was it. Perhaps she was about to find love.

She didn't even know hearts skipping a beat was a real thing. Not that she'd ever considered it, but if she *had* stopped to, she'd have definitely come to the conclusion that it was a cliché made up by bad romance writers. So, when it actually happened to her that morning, she figured that it was worth finding out a little more about Craig Parker. She needed to select a user to test the new targeted ad code was working at optimal level, so why not use him?

She'd have to check through his SN public profile, *LIKES*, comments, photographs and private messages, as well as monitor his 'real life' activities via their satellite system and his mobile phone's location services and/or when he actively checked into shops, restaurants, nightclubs, whatever. Then she'd develop a demographic and psychographic profile and make sure that it matched up to the targeted adverts generated for him by SN's code.

Oh, how she hoped that despite his tan and Designer shirt, he wasn't a twat.

It was cheating a bit, because she was really supposed to be manually detailing his demographics and psychographics *before* she checked on the ads that he was already seeing, but she had a little sneak peak anyway, cos it was the fastest way to get an idea about what he was like. Besides, what harm could it do?

YES! The ads that SN was generating for Craig Parker were the same sort that she saw herself when she logged into her own account. Horror films, heavy metal records, a book on nihilism. Not an exercise video or a rom-com or a Celebrity Aftershave ad in sight. And, even better, there were ads for dating websites, which meant that his relationship status was set to 'single' and they were male-female ones, so he was straight, or at least bi.

She smiled, feeling connected to him already. Those interest-relevant ads he saw everyday when he logged on? She'd helped develop that code. She was a part of the system that meant that gorgeous Craig Parker never had to look at an advert that he was completely disinterested in. Think of the time she'd saved him! He didn't even have to think about what he might want to buy – her code just put it right under his nose, or rather on his screen, for him to click.

If they ever met, she bet it'd make a great conversation opener. You know that nihilist ad you saw? Well, I put that there for you, because at some point you commented that life was meaningless…

She shook her head. What had come over her? She had a job to do. She needed to make Craig Parker's, and by extension everybody's, SN experience even better than it already was.

She had honestly intended to go through his profile, look at his interests using keywords he'd used, and products or services he'd liked or commented on, in order to check they correctly linked up to his targeted ads.

But instead, she found herself bringing up his current location. She just had an urge to know exactly where he was in 'real life'. Thankfully, he didn't have his location services turned off, and she could see him, or, rather, a dot on a map that represented his whereabouts. A few more clicks and she'd pulled up the address: Jeff Carson, 127 Swift Street, London.

She sat up in her chair. Two things. Firstly, Craig Parker was in London, of all the places in the world he could've been, and only a few tube stops away – what a strange coincidence, it was almost like fate! And secondly, *Jeff Carson*! Jeff Carson was the name of the cyber-bully who Craig Parker had ordered to *Apologise*. Were they in fact friends? A few clicks and she'd confirmed that they were not on each other's lists. So, what was Craig doing at the guy's house?

Well, there was only one way to find out. And, she supposed that if Craig Parker didn't want her listening in on his conversations that he probably would have gone into his settings and turned off SN's microphone access permission. Just as she got through, she saw the dot moving on the map – he was leaving Jeff Carson's house. Over the roar of the phone shifting against fabric in his pocket as he walked, she could hear him whistling "I Hate You" by Heavy Metal Warriors.

And then, *then*, a notification popped up for the thread she'd followed earlier. Jeff Carson had posted under *Apologise* with, *I'm very sorry for any hurt or offence that I may have caused. I am a tool. It won't happen again.*

What *had* Craig said to him to make him post that?

Craig's whistling switched to "Die, Bigots" by Death Rockers.

It wasn't just *LIKE*! It was love.

The back of Nora's neck prickled. Rachel Psycho Boss was looming over her, as if she'd never heard of knocking, or even footsteps, despite the high heels. Nora hit mute on Craig's audio: 'I'm just researching that case study to check the target ads code, you know, making sure the demographic matches the…'

'Who've you picked?' Rachel flashed perfect white teeth and leaned in to examine the screen, pencil-skirt poise so perfect it was practically inhuman.

'No one,' Nora said. 'Just some guy.'

'Some guy, eh?' said Rachel, like she knew something Nora didn't.

There was something about Rachel that always made Nora feel fat, ugly, and scruffy, no matter the fact that she would never sell out to Designer in a million years and had chosen to dress in a baggy black band t-shirt, and not to bother ironing them just because society tried to reinforce pointless appearance standards on everybody in order to distract them from what was really going on.

'Do you need me to sign something?' asked Nora.

'What? Oh, yes, the contract updates.'

'Didn't we do that yesterday?'

'Yes, but you missed the last one,' said Rachel, holding out the tablet.

Nora clicked to confirm.

Rachel clacked to the door and turned back at Nora. 'I want that report on my desk tomorrow morning. No more mooning over guys.'

'Tomorrow morning!' exclaimed Nora.

Rachel just smirked and closed the door behind her.

Nora sighed heavily. It was like the Psycho thought just because Nora was single, she didn't deserve downtime. She bet nobody else had to have their reports done by tomorrow morning. No, they needed to spend time with their kids, or cook tea for their spouses, or go to the gym to keep their bodies fit for having sex every night. Well, she had interpersonal stuff going on too – she was in the middle of a fascinating discussion with DEVIL-74 about whether *Misunderstood Vampire* torture fan-fiction constructed or reflected the darker side of the human psyche. But did Rachel care about that? No!

The dot had slowed down again and gone into a building that the map identified as a nearby Junk Food. She flicked the audio back on. Craig was at the counter by the sound of it. He was umming-and-ahhing over which burger to get and a female voice, possibly the checkout assistant was saying: 'Just go for it!'

Nora had a sudden urge to ditch her pack-up and have a burger and fries for lunch. She grabbed her bag and coat and rushed out the office.

But by the time she reached Junk Food, there was no sign of Craig. So she sighed, ordered a Joy Meal, and sat in a brightly-coloured plastic booth in the corner, browsing his SN comment and location history.

It wasn't long until a pattern emerged. First, comments ordering bullies and bigots to *Apologise*. Next, checking in at a location which, on looking into it, the bully frequented regularly or, alternatively, Craig's map dot meeting the bully's map dot temporarily. Finally, the bully returning to the previous thread and apologising profusely to the person who they'd insulted earlier. The bullies he found were on all sorts of different pages and groups, with no direct connection to Craig bar the occasional 'friend of a friend' that was bound to crop up every so often (what with the whole six degrees of separation thing).

The short of it was though, that Craig was tracking down bullies *on purpose*. First he found them terrorising people on SN, then he put a stop to it in real life. He didn't just chance upon Jeff Carson by accident. He was like some sort of Social Network-based superhero; cyber heroics to combat cyber villainy.

A red circle appeared in the top right corner of her screen. Craig was commenting on something right this second! She tapped quickly, excited to see what he was up to now. Yes, it was another bully, Phil Gordon. He'd been harassing some poor, innocent victim. Underneath it, Craig had made his trademark comment: *Apologise*. Phil Gordon replied quickly: *Make me*.

Her heart skipped a beat. Again! The second time that day!

So, where was Craig now? On his way to Phil Gordon's house? She switched to his location and saw the dot moving swiftly – he must be on public transport. She tapped her fingers against the table. It was all well and good seeing where he was, but really she needed to know where he was going to be, so she could make it there before him, or at least while he was still there. It needed to be somewhere public too – she couldn't very well show up at Phil Gordon's house and interrupt Craig's heroics. She needed to know his habits and routines…

A quick scroll down his timeline and she could see that he regularly checked into Rock Club, just off Busy Street, on a weekend. It was Friday today, so there was a strong chance he'd be there tonight. Excellent.

She shuffled along the plastic booth seat and curled out of it to standing, brushing breadcrumbs and salt off her crumpled black hoody.

Suddenly, she felt self-conscious. Okay, so Rock Club was a rock club, but that didn't mean she needed to show up in the scruffy, baggy, creased and now ketchup-stained clothes she usually wore. Maybe she could buy a new outfit from that new alternative shop, All Black.

She hated shopping usually and wasn't even sure why she knew where All Black was, but she supposed love... or more likely infatuation... was making her act crazy. That's what they said, didn't they? That it made you crazy? Once she was in the shop, she found it was perfect. True to its name, the clothes were all black and gothic. Just the right look for BLOODHEARTx of *Guts and Gore*.

She was drawn to one outfit in particular. A plain black top with long, flared sleeves that reminded her of a wizard's cloak. Over fishnets with a pair of steel toecap boots, and after puling on her signature beanie, the look was complete. As soon as she saw herself in the mirror, she knew she just had to have it. Before she'd even stopped to think, she'd swiped her credit card and bought the lot.

Back at work, as she rushed down the corridor to her desk, Rachel poked her head out of her office door and barked, 'You're late, Snora!'

Psycho Boss had a habit of giving people cruel nicknames as some sort of passive-aggressive punishment slash form of psychological control.

Apologise!

'Sorry!' said Nora, fantasising about stabbing her face with a BBQ fork.

Rachel looked her up and down, taking in her new look. Smirked. 'Got a date?'

'No!' snapped Nora and stormed off.

She could feel Rachel's eyes and smirk all the way down the corridor. Perhaps she could somehow get Rachel to bully her publicly, on SN. Craig Parker might notice and pay Rachel a visit; rescue Nora like a virtual knight in shining armour.

Eugh. What the hell was wrong with her?

And yet, despite her disgust at her brain's apparent determination to turn her into a romance novel heroine, she switched her computer on eagerly, keen to get back to compiling her information on Craig Parker. Fortuitously, it was what she needed to do to check that he – and therefore all of SN's users – were getting the targeted ads they deserved, and would have the simultaneous benefit of telling her what to talk to him about that evening.

If there was a good opportunity, that was. If she dared.

Her heart skipped a beat again.

Bloody. Hell.

She got to the club at ten pm. A quick look back at Craig's timeline showed that he usually checked in between nine and nine-thirty.

It looked closed. But her phone showed her that Craig had checked in not long ago and his dot was still inside, so presumably there was an entrance somewhere. Perhaps the boarded-up look was all part of the club's mystique; making people feel they were truly somewhere underground, perhaps even illegal. Having a hard-to-find door was part of its exclusive feel.

She loved it already.

Well, aside from the fact it was probably full of people socialising and dancing. She wasn't really into that sort of thing. But if it meant getting to meet Craig Parker, cyber-hero, she'd suck it up just this once. Once they were in love, she'd persuade him it was much nicer to get tucked up under a blanket with a takeout and a slasher film.

She found her way in eventually, only to find the place was empty. She supposed most people didn't really come out till later; they drank at home to save money, then went clubbing at midnight, already drunk. So she stood at the bar, looking around for a member of staff and wondering whether to order her customary Brown Fizz or go crazy and get a pint of Cheap Lager. Just the one. Or maybe two, for courage.

At least the wait gave her a chance to get her bearings, she reasoned, determined to be positive. The decor was right up her street. Dark dingy corners, blacks, reds. It even looked a bit like the bar in *Misunderstood Vampire*. DEVIL-74 would love it; Nora snapped some photos and PM'd them. *Check this place out.* DEVIL-74 was right on it with a reply: *Looks wicked ;)*

Where was Craig Parker, then? The map on her phone was no use, it wasn't so specific as to show rooms, just buildings. He was in here, but where? She decided that there must be another room and another bar in the club. That's where the staff and Craig Parker were, and that's where she needed to be too.

She opened a steel door and the sound of Death Rockers hit her. Loud and dark, just how she liked it. It wasn't a room though, it was a staircase, descending. The sort of dark staircase that, in a horror film, would lead to a creepy basement...

Awesome! This club was really exceeding her expectations, and she had high hopes for her and Craig getting on. Maybe she'd even be up for coming here together every so often. Maybe she could persuade him to try some *Misunderstood Vampire* cosplay, she could just see him in a pair of tight black pleather trousers…

She tiptoed down the stairs, enjoying the tingle of anxious anticipation that she normally got from a horror jump-scare moment, only it wasn't a jump-scare she was terrified of; in that, she was in her element. It was the pressure of meeting and trying to hit it off with Craig Parker.

At the last step, she opened the next door into the club's basement bar. The blast of music was so loud that if the door creaked like a proper creepy basement one should, then she couldn't hear it, or anything else.

The first thing she noticed was the continuation of the club's horror style. The bar was designed like a torture chamber, with chains and blades and blood on the walls. And despite the loud music, it was almost as dead as the room upstairs.

The second thing she noticed was the back of who had to be Craig Parker. Broad, muscular shoulders bulging through a tight, white Designer t-shirt. Fitted blue jeans, almost as figure-hugging as the pleather trousers she'd fantasised. And in his hand, a raised blade, its tip stained dark with blood.

Her heart skipped a beat.

The third thing she noticed was Phil Gordon hanging by his arms from chains that were hooked into the ceiling. His toes barely scraped the floor. Blood and sweat dripped down his bare chest; the word *Bully* carved into it.

Phil looked up with his eyes; his head hanging, chin to chest. He appealed to her silently through pain and terror.

Craig started to turn, to see what… or who… his victim was looking at…

Nora turned and ran.

Her lungs were screaming, sharp pain with every breath. The last time she'd run was at a school sport's day and even then she'd come last. At the top of the stairs, she stopped, panting, head spinning.

She couldn't stop though, he could be coming. Did he see her?

She forced herself onwards, tummy flab and boobs bouncing, legs rubbing together, the hard backs of the new boots chafing at her heel tendons, and her lungs, oh, her lungs! It was only fear for her life that forced her forward to burst out of the door, back into the side-street, and down it until she reached Busy Street and lowered herself to the ground to rest. She doubled over, retching, heaving, her throat and chest burning. She didn't know if it was the torture or the exercise or both.

She pulled out her phone and messaged DEVIL-74. *Send the police to Rock Club, just off Busy Street.* The reply was instant: *What? Why? Are you okay?* But she was too wired to explain, and too scared not to drag herself up and at least into the safety of the harsh lights of a nearby Junk Food. *Just do it* she messaged back. It felt like hours later, as she sipped gingerly at her Brown Fizz from a paper straw, hands trembling, legs twitching, throat hoarse, that Craig Parker's map dot moved to a police station and stayed there. Her heartbeat started to slow back to normal.

He didn't even know she existed. He never had.

It was one thing knowing that and another thing believing it, so she figured she'd go back to the office rather than home alone tonight. If no one else, she'd at least be in the vicinity of the night-shift security guards; her own personal protection squad. Besides, she still had that report to finish by tomorrow morning, and so she let herself back into the building and settled at her desk.

'Apologies,' said Rachel, from behind her.

Nora jumped, turned, and instinctively pulled off her beanie all in one go. What the hell was Psycho doing here at this time of night?

'As you can imagine, the browser-search compatibility code suggested a match. Horror, gore, social justice. Added to that, the psychometric profiling had you both as Young and Rubicam's Struggler category, so...'

Nora's gape must have screamed her confusion, because Rachel took the conversation back a step and explained:

'The PsyPoke trial you signed up for?' Rachel held up her tablet. 'You agreed the terms and conditions yesterday? I had you okay the last one this morning?'

'I signed up for what?' asked Nora.

'PsyPoke,' said Rachel, slowly, as if speaking to an imbecile. 'SN's initiative to bring targeted ads and friend suggestions to the next level. Your heart skipped a beat when you saw him, right? You felt the urge to buy that new outfit?'

'That was all... PsyPoke?' demanded Nora, her fury and recent brush with death fuelling confidence. 'You messed with my brain?'

'Honestly, Snora,' said Rachel, unmoved. 'if you didn't want Psychological Pokes to emit from your mobile device and push you in the right direction, why did you agree to the T's and C's?'

'The right direction?' Nora exclaimed. 'He was torturing a guy!'

'Clearly we have some work to do on whether searches are based in fantasy or reality, in order to maximise the accuracy of compatibility matching. The code will need to recognise the difference between fan-girling over torture fan-fic on *Guts and Gore* and actually researching torture methods for practical use.'

Rachel laughed, but Nora barely had time to register her embarrassment before her boss had continued: 'Obviously we'll need more volunteers for the next round of testing...'

It took Nora another moment to realise she was being propositioned for round two. 'No. No. Absolutely not.'

'Oh, come on, Nora,' said Rachel. 'You usually hate shopping, right? Well, how easy was it today? Based on the interests and preferences generated by your SN account, PsyPoke told you what shop to go to and even what to buy, saving you time, effort, and money. Don't you love the outfit?'

'Yes,' agreed Nora, reluctantly.

'Imagine. You'll never have to think about what to buy again. PsyPoke will just put it right under your nose.'

'That's clothes, though. It's not the same with people.'

All of a sudden, there were tears in her eyes. For a moment, just a moment, she'd thought that she'd really found somebody. Then it turned out he was a psycho and her feelings had been planted in her brain by her boss's latest SN project.

'Why can't people be the same?' said Rachel. 'It's just like deciding what to buy, only harder, because at least products don't have to like us back.' She smiled, shark-like. 'PsyPoke can do the hard work for you. All you'll need to do is wait for that little nudge in the right direction; for your heart to skip a beat. It can tell you who to avoid, too. Think about all those arseholes you'll never have to meet because PsyPoke knows your values are incompatible.'

Hmmm, that did sound pretty tempting.

'What about the bugs?' asked Nora, weakly.

'They'll be fixed. Come on, Nora. You can be the first person to have the perfect PsyPoke-enhanced Real Life experience.'

Really, Nora realised, it was exactly like the code she herself had helped to develop for SN. Minimising time-wasting through targeted ads, so that users only ever saw products that matched their interests and incomes; suggesting friends based on mutual location check-ins and shared acquaintances. PsyPoke was just the next level – instead of enhancing your online experience, it would enhance your 'real life', saving you time and effort by pointing you in the right direction.

She'd just have to be more careful next time, that's all. She nodded.

'Okay.'

Rachel smiled. 'Brilliant! Now, do you want me to read you all the Terms and Conditions? It's a three-hundred page document.' She held out the tablet.

Nora shook her head. Who could be bothered to read three-hundred pages of legal blah? 'No, it's fine,' she said. And she clicked '*Accept*'.

Do They Laugh in Eden

Armani Martel
Canada

*I*T'S BEEN A LONG TIME SINCE *I've written in a journal. So long I can't even remember the last time I held a pencil in my hand. I guess I hadn't had a need for it. I don't feel happy playing ball with my friends, maintaining the road networks, making beer or dancing in the rain. Actually, I still like dancing in the rain but it feels less. The sun falls and I swim in the river under the moon. The sun rises and I wake up and wonder a little around the houses. The afternoon sun comes highest and depending on the season I'm napping by the heater or I'm dancing in the square. This process repeating itself endlessly and endlessly. I need something more …*

The sun is setting behind the green-coloured church steeple and the sounds of the drums deafen Olive's ears. Laurier Square is tonight's spontaneously chosen focal point for the festival and the large congregation of drummers binging and banging gather people who dance between them and the trees. Olive is leaning on a bench watching the dancers. Watching the way the patterns on the clothing morph following the movements of each dancer. The sweat taping dresses and open shirts tight against their skin. The drums beating. Suddenly, Olive decides he wants to move. He stands and wades himself through the crowd sliding his way in between towering oaks.

A bit further out he crosses two groups of people playing. The game they are playing is made with rocks and shooting rocks in between Olive's feet as he passes, each team attempts to shoot the rock clear between Olive's legs. One rock bounces off Olive's knee and an entire team groans.

"Hey kid, join us!" somebody from the group shouts.

Olive smiles. "Thanks, but I'm in a rush."

A man looks at him weirdly. "Why would anyone be in a hurry during a festival?"

On all the streets, little toys, handcrafted symbols, and frilly colours are pasted and lined all along the fronts of the houses. While people laugh, juggling fruit in the centre of the streets, kids run screaming trying to catch the oranges that bounce from the jugglers to the street. Teenagers embrace each other in dark spaces or shove themselves over playing hide and seek. The old people standing on the terraces throw confetti onto the revellers. A lot of it is getting stuck in Olive's hair. As he passes under another rainstorm of brightly coloured paper, a young woman sitting to the side makes eye contact with him. She gives him a coy smile that stops his movement. She rises from her seat, stepping towards him.

"Happy festivities," she says, dropping a piece of veggie pate and bread in his hand.

She kisses him on the cheek and taps the slipper she's holding in her right hand on his forehead.

He blushes. "Thank you," he says.

She nods, walking away but not before whispering, "Will I see you again?" in his ear, then disappearing within the crowd.

"Hey, Olive!"

Heather, a friend of Olive's, is standing on top of a pile of boxes. He's smiling, kicking away passers-by who thonk his feet with their shoes. He holds a boot in his hand and hobbles down to where Olive is standing.

"Olive!" He whacks him hard on the head with the boot. "Where the hell is your shoe?"

"I'm wearing them," he says.

"Well, take one of them off, idiot."

"No."

Heather grimaces and slaps the palm of his hand against his face. "You're always doing it differently. It's freaking annoying sometimes."

Olive shrugs.

"Well, come on then, Mia's holding a festival outsider her home. All the families are waiting for us."

"Lead the way," says Olive.

* * *

"Speech. Speech. Speech. Speech… "

Everyone is tapping their feet against the ground and hitting their fists against the table. Calling for Mia to give her speech. Mia's smiling ear to ear. She's biding for time. Although she loves to crowd the people of her home around her stories she still gets nervous beforehand. In a way she enjoys the tensions that build between the demand for a tale and a desire to run.

"Alright, alright, please everyone, calm down."

Mia's friend uses her sandal to slap her back lightly for inspiration's sake. "Thanks Lorena." she says. With a deep breath and exhaling, she steps to the front of the circle. It's night time now and only the dimmed lights from the street lamps above illuminate the shadows. The buildings on each side standing tall but relaxed. Their occupants laying before them on the street celebrating with the rest of the city.

"It's a wonderful night tonight," says Mia, "the stars are out, it's warm, and all you lovely people are gathered here with food and drink to celebrate another successful food distribution cycle. Yet before we devour ourselves, talk, mingle, and sleep until the next morning only to do it over again – I want to tell you a story. A true story about the hurried man, the sun, and growth. It's a story we've all heard before but it's a story that needs telling. For this is what binds us as a community, as a people, in our work and in our homes. The continuing of the circulation of food, drink, and shelter for us all relies on our knowledge of the ways of nature and our combined efforts to work with Her. It's for this reason that we honour the completed cycle of food distribution. We've kept the distribution roads clean and ensured that the Plateau contributes to Montreal's environmental preservation and Her happiness."

"Wooo!"

"I love you, Mia," shouts someone from the crowd.

Mia smiles. "Thank you, thank you, everybody. I appreciate this and I love you all but, but it's story time!" There is applause all around. After a few moments the applause subsides and she begins, "There was once a boy, let's call him Ahmed, and Ahmed–"

"No, not Ahmed! You used Ahmed last time. What about Khaled?"

"Seriously? We always choose Arabian names. Why not Apple or Wind this time?" asks Heather.

He looks for Olive to ask what he thinks when he realises he's no longer next to him. It's only much later in the night that he finds him by the fire, drooling away wrapped in a hammock. A blanket over his face, his hand swaying the green tips of the grass underneath him.

* * *

The sun rises over the house and Olive leans against a bench watching the drones move up and down the lines misting the wheat. Thousands of automatons pulling weeds, plucking bugs, and snipping the tops of the wheat. The accumulated sounds of the machines add a weird electrical sound in the air. It's something Olive hadn't noticed before. He watches the way the wind blowing makes the brown ends of the wheat spin in circles. The spinning and spinning of the plant and the never ceasing movements of the automatons. It all puts him in a weird state of mind. He needs to keep moving.

He walks down the distribution road wondering why he chose to walk the road over the street. The streets as opposed to the road are painted in different colours, made with brick, and are filled with people and chaotic movement. They guide to a neighbour's home, the church, the town hall, or to entertainment and exploration. The distribution road is different from the street because of its crisp geometry and monotone grey colour scheme. It serves as an efficient means to transport food and materials across the city between neighbourhoods. The whole network connecting at several distribution points – in the east at the food granaries; in the south by the port; and in the west at the trades center, textile communities, and airport. The schedule of the trains on the road perfectly defined by algorithm and computer processes.

The rail tracks in the centre glow purple, warning of an approaching train. Olive moves off the road through an alleyway and just ahead he sees a diner. He realises he's hungry and reaches for the door. It's open so he walks in, the door shutting just as the train swooshes by.

The diner has five or six tables full with people and a bar running the length of the kitchen. A humanoid with a white paper cap is frying eggs and potatoes while the owner pours coffee and chats with customers.

"Hey, morning, can I have a seat?" asks Olive.

"Yeah, sure, there's still room at the bar."

Olive pulls up a chair and stares distantly at the robot working.

The owner fills him a cup of coffee. "Not feeling too well today?"

"Not really," says Olive.

"I understand, happens to all of us. How about the egg special? And it comes with coffee."

"The special sounds great. Thank you."

He hands him his card to pay the bill.

* * *

The reception to Council Hall is quiet. Two large palms sway from the air system overhead. There's a tiny lady sleeping under a hanging question mark sign. So, if one needed help they would have to wait. But Olive knows where he's going. He walks through a corridor and passes through two chambers. The first is a resting area for visiting foreign dignitaries and tired workers; the second a social room for the workers and travelers. Olive recognises Veronika, the water futures coordinator sitting in a couch in the corner.

"Hey, Olive! Why aren't you celebrating?"

Olive shrugs. "I slept most of it. I wasn't really feeling it."

Veronika smiles, "Really? Well, you know, that doesn't really surprise me."

Olive smirks. "How's it been going?"

"Oh, well, a bit tired. We're having trouble with the water system. It's not pumping enough water. I think there's a bug in the new algorithm but we're working on it. No one will lose water."

Olive looks at her. "You work a lot."

"Yeah I do, but I get a sense of fulfilment out of it. I know that my actions help our community's environment. It makes me happy to know that people will have water and the environment remains alive."

Olive nods, thinking this over.

"Are you not happy?" asks Veronika.

There's a pause where he listens to the trees swaying in the other room.

"No."

"I sensed that. You know, you're free to choose who you want to be and how or if you want to serve this community, Olive. Maybe its time you took technical training. We could use somebody like you here."

Somebody like me. Olive repeats the sentence in his head.

"Thanks Veronika. I'll think about it."

"Good. Happy Harvest!"

Knock. Knock.

Olive knocks on the door to the councillor's chamber. The councillor, Jason, is seated staring into space. He hasn't left that chair for many days.

"Hey, Olive, how are you?"

"Okay, and you Jason?" The councillor sighs, getting up from the chair. "Yes, I've just been thinking."

"Me, too," says Olive.

Jason looks at him. "What's been on your mind?"

"I don't know. Nothing really."

"I see…" Jason looks at Oliver then makes his way to the wall in front. With a few motions of the hands the wall lights up as a screen. He pulls up a window that displays a ticker tape of status updates.

"You do a good job of maintaining the roads system, Olive. I've been told by other people in your neighbourhood that you are specifically keen and calculating in organising and effecting tasks."

"Thanks."

Jason turns from the wall to face Olive. "You know, you have all the necessary attributes to excel in one of the technical professions and I know that at least, Veronika would love to have you on her team. But tell me, Olive, would you be happy with a larger salary? The monthly salary would increase substantially in one of these roles."

"I already have more then enough to eat and drink with my current salary."

Jason laughs, "Alright, Olive. Well, what about the respect this role would earn you? Are you not concerned with the stature you would have in your community? A resources manager or developer has significant respect as you know."

"Like a councillor," says Olive.

"Right, like a councillor." There's a silence. Jason reflects for a moment then asks, "What do you find yourself thinking about everyday?"

"Why?"

"Why, what?"

"Why can't I feel anything? I mean everything's perfect so why am I like this?"

Jason sighs, "We're human, Olive. Were not satisfied on a permanent basis and no system change, technological advancement, or amount of education will change that basic truth."

Jason walks back to the screen on the wall. There's a video feed from a local river watching a few ducks swim in circles.

"Olive, you're free to wander around the city, to travel, and to participate. You can buy a good meal, a nice pair of shoes, or sell something on the street. These wants will satisfy you. Or not. Maybe you will desire to derive something different from your experiences. Perhaps, you'll go and do something that gets you the love and admiration of your community. Or of course, it might just happen that you will desire only to withdrawal yourself from the community. Sit by your window with a book waiting for someone to deliver you food and maybe you'll stay like this forever. But maybe having satisfied your desire for apathy, you will desire something more. You will still then have all the freedom and means to pursue it. Whether it be a pursuit or the mastering of a skill. Or a study at the academy where night and day you will search for truth. The point, Olive, is you have all the seeds in this ideal community to pursue what it is you desire whether fortune, fame, or knowledge. There will be moments like today where you will desire nothing at all. But there will be other moments where you will desire too much. It is up to you whether and how you pursue your happiness. This community will help and encourage you, but as much as we set up the system in all our favour, it's up to you to find your way."

Olive is staring at the floor. "I see…" he says.

Jason puts a hand on his shoulder. "Take your time, Olive. It's your time to do with it what pleases you."

Olive looks up. "Do you mind if I wander around the halls for a bit?"

"Not at all, and come back in whenever you want. I love the company."

"Thanks."

He closes the door and walks slowly with his steps echoing along the hall. There's a cool breeze coming in from the open windows. He moves past the hall and enters the social chamber looking at the couch where Veronika was sitting. He throws himself down, the pillow cushioning his fall. He sighs can't telling if he's confused, sad, catatonic, or mad. Across the room, an older man lies on the carpet. He scratches his beard and looks up.

"Hey."

"Hey," he says.

"I'm Aneil. What's your name?"

"Olive," he says meekly.

"Olive, nice to meet you. Do you want to hear a joke?"

In Memoriam

Bridget Blankley
England

WINNER of the 2017 International Literary Prize
University Centre Grimsby

I FOUND A PEBBLE YESTERDAY, in the bottom of a handbag that I hardly use. I recognised it straight away, just by the feel of it, the smoothness, the hole to one side, just big enough for the tip of my little finger. And as I touched that sea-worn granite I thought of you, of how I loved you from the moment I saw you, from before you opened your eyes and saw me.

I miss you.

You always collected stones, from the beach, from the park, even from the pea-shingle in the drive. Wherever you'd been you'd come home with pockets full of stones. And you kept them, in boxes and tins and in piles on the windowsill – and under the bed. You knew where each one came from – or at least you said you did - and I believed you. But then you were always a good liar. But the stories you told about the stones seemed different somehow, as if they mattered.

This stone was different, you found it on the beach at Horsey Bay. You found this stone, then you stopped looking. You were only seven, but you stopped collecting stones, just like that. You gave this stone to me.

'It's perfect Mum,' you said. 'It's our stone, yours and mine – forever.'

And that was it. It was the last of your stones. And I kept it for you. For us. Forever, well until now.

When you left home you took your stones with you, well, you took the best ones, the ones that meant most to you. You wrapped each one in a separate piece of tissue, like sweets in a tin. I said they didn't need wrapping, not like china, but you were adamant. You said they spoilt if they rubbed against each other. That they would get chipped, become dull, that they absorbed the oil from your hands, that they needed protecting. I didn't argue; it wasn't worth it. What did it matter? What mattered was that you were leaving home. I didn't want us to fight about trivialities – I didn't want us to fight at all. You took the other stones outside. The ones you described as also rans. You didn't throw them away though. You arranged them in swirls and spirals in the rose beds. The patterns have gone now, lost amongst the weeds and buried by the dog. But the dog's gone now. Everything has, except me, and this pink stone.

When they found you, your pockets were full of stones. I don't know if you collected them for the drowning, or if they were your stones, the ones you took with you. How could I know? They didn't keep the stones. They just weighed them, then threw them away. But if they'd kept them, what then? I wouldn't have recognised your stones. They didn't mean anything to me, only to you. I like to think that they were your stones, from your collection. I want to think that when you died you weren't alone. I want to think that you had filled your pockets with old friends. Some small comfort in your desperation.

I miss you.

I miss your chubby, greedy fingers. I miss blowing raspberries on your soft round belly and hearing you laugh. I miss the energy that poured from you when you were three, and your serious studiousness when you learnt to read. I miss you reading sign we passed. I miss the clumsy sulkiness of your teenage years and I miss the last lonely years when I missed your pain. Foolishly thinking it was just another phase, why didn't I see? Why didn't I realise? I should have held you close to me – forever – like our stone – safe in the palm of my hand.

You didn't leave a note. You left nothing, you'd cleared your flat, sold all your stuff, cleared your hard-drive, deleted your browsing history, closed your Facebook account. You erased all traces. Stepped into the water and the water closed around you, sealed the gap in the universe that was you.

I miss you. I'll always miss you; we were one being. You were part of me and now you are not. I tried to cope, I really did. But nothing seemed to matter, not the garden, or the house, nothing.

Then I found your stone. The pink one, smooth granite with a hole on one side. The perfect stone that you gave me when you were seven. Then I understood. I understood about remembering and being. Then I understood about forever.

So I've hidden your stone behind the loose brick in the fireplace. Right up inside the chimney where we found the baby's shoe and the witch bottle. It should be there forever. Well, if not forever, at least until the house falls down. A reminder, *in memoriam* for two people who shared one name. Our secret.

Anamnesis

Carley Drake
USA

A SINGLE BLINK, and you have made it to the library.
It is as if the light warps, the space beneath your feet falls away, and you are blank-faced and barefoot back where you began. This is no great surprise. Within the space beneath your breastbone, you feel relief. Homecoming.

Yet as the seconds stretch, confusion blooms in your mind like an inkblot. The plush library with its messy, copious smattering of books feels familiar in a way you cannot place. Footsteps mirroring yours wear dents into the soft shag of the rugs. They cross the room leading to a small desk piled high with papers and books.

It is altogether a rather small library. High shelves border the walls to either side of you, thick with spines you do not recognise. The room is shady, the air stale.

The longer you stand there the deeper your confusion grows. You realise you do not remember your name. Cannot recall your face or identity. Absent of proper language, a singular question consumes you. What had you been doing the moment before appearing in the library?

In your mind there is a flash of memory bright as a fish's eye. You are a young father tracing riverbeds downhill fetching water. You remember the guttural rumble of avalanche and a drop so deep it swallows you whole. Then darkness. Then silence. And finally waking within the library feeling as if you have come home.

As soon as you recall this, it leaves you and you are again absent of identity. Although you cannot picture your body, you do not feel tall and muscular as you once had been. When you look to your hands you find them pale and stubby and pruned with wrinkles. Palms flat, you feel your new body, discovering your soft belly and the heavy globes of your breasts. Your face is square, your teeth dull, your hair long and gray and wild.

In the library, you are an old woman.

And this is good enough.

Cold daylight shines from a large window at the opposite side of the room, casting the place in blue shadows. You walk slowly closer, glancing at the books for direction only to find their spines blighted by scripts you do not understand. This body is slow and aching yet you still approach the window. Outside, the landscape is heavy with winter, the faint trees sagging and frosted. No footsteps sink in snow, no driveway reveals tire tread. You cannot even see other parts of the building, as if the little library floats above a barren countryside.

You are completely alone.

Shuffling to the desk is difficult, but you make it. The sweet smell of fresh rot wafts through the room the closer you get. It is only once you can see around the stacks of books that you notice a large red mass twitching atop the desk. Fluid has rippled the wood beneath it and stained the pages of neighbouring books. Pinned beneath the wooden desk, the rug has grown damp with blood. You only realise this once you step closer to examine the gleaming heart and feel the carpet give and gush beneath your feet.

The closer you get the more frantic it pounds as if desperate for recognition. Without questioning, you know that it is human.

Taking the heart into your hands feels like an act of repetition. A muscle memory.

For a moment, you are not sure what to do. A bizarre thought rises in your mind and no sooner do you acknowledge it then you find a high glass jar of water perched on the rug where you had first opened your eyes.

Pain throbs in your kneecaps as you hurry to the jar and stoop, pausing to gently set the heart inside. Like a stone, it sinks to the bottom and clatters against the glass. Once there its pulse builds until steady, reminiscent of a normal beat had it a body. Despite the foreign books and confusion, you know you have done the right thing. Your body flushes with relief even as your mind questions your move.

You take the jar in your knobby hands and set it down atop the desk. The heavy rim hits the wood. A harsh clatter echoes from a high bookshelf. You turn to see a large flash of white hit the floor with a hollow crack and skitter across the rugs.

You only realise it is a ribcage once it stops moving. Even from far away you can see that it is small and unlike the heart is not covered in gore.

A large fire appears in an enormous limestone fireplace between bookshelves. There is no sound of spark and catch, no crackle of wood burning. You are not even sure the fireplace was there until the very instant you noticed the ribcage. Reaching forward and grasping the upper left rib and hauling the bones into your arms has the same hazy recollection churning in your mind. As if hugging a loved one, you clutch the ribcage to your own chest, finding it much smaller than your own. Instead of disgust you feel only tenderness, only mute, depthless compassion.

You drag the only chair from behind the desk and place it before the fire. No blood has marred the plush red velvet, so you plump the seat as best as you can and place the ribcage atop it. You tuck it in, make sure it will not tip over.

Without truly recalling, you know you have been a mother to several, to hundreds, other times just one child. At some point before arriving at the library, you had tended to children with bodies smaller than the bones against the velvet, and this knowledge fills you with whimsy and maternal heartache.

Time changes after that.

You are not sure how long you spend scavenging. You overturn books to send fingernails clicking against the floor. Coils of short golden hair loop in the drawers of the old desk. Delicate knuckle bones settle amongst the coals in the grate. A long spine rests in the bricked throat of the chimney and pulling it free feels reminiscent of clearing a long-clogged river channel.

You search and dig and shuffle even as your body aches. No matter how long you do this, the fire does not burn out, the snow does not stop, the light does not dim, and you do not grow weary.

You place your findings atop the rugs. The bones glint like the bellies of fresh oysters, almost opalite. Every large bone of the human body maps the fabric. Among them are fingernails, hair, and teeth, scattered like accessories on a grand tapestry.

You start with the ribcage, slotting each clavicle into place and stringing up the spine for balance. Same as before, you feel repetition in the movements, like premonition, like instinct. When the pelvis slides dryly into place to click against the tailbone, the bones seem to sing, humming a low tune you can't hear but can feel against your fingertips. You glide dual femurs into place, pin the tibias and fibulas with their matching patellas. From there, you fasten the feet, counting each little phalange. Once finished, you backtrack to craft the arms and roll them into hollow sockets. As careful as a mother, you kneel to piece together the hands and place them where they belong.

By the time you rise, a skull has joined the pile of bones before you. It sits connected to the spine as if it had always been there, as if you had fused it yourself. Sockets empty, it stares neutrally to you, yet that same tenderness has sweet sentiment singing through your veins as you drop each tooth into the vacant craters at its jaw.

It is only then that you realise your abnormal abundance of teeth. Along with the large jewels of adult teeth, you find milk teeth small as glass beads. Sorrow, sudden and deep, rolls in your stomach for reasons you do not have. The sentiment you felt moments ago is still there, still golden, but bitter with mourning. The adult teeth soon sit snug in their deep channels in the skull, the milk teeth plugging their descent like corks in tiny bottles.

A full human skeleton sits in the chair looking as if it had just settled in for a hearty conversation. Several other bones have appeared, filling the spaces your knotted fingers could not reach.

You wander to the heart.

Throughout your hunt, it remained at the bottom of the glass like a sunken stone, beating just faintly enough to ripple the water. Now it floats like a bobber, a round coin of flesh breaching the surface. It beats faster the closer you walk and when you finally dip your fingers into the water and take the slippery muscle into your arms, its pulse soars. Against your chest, the heart is hot and damp as if it were just born.

Water drips down your plain dress and across the rugs as you return to the skeleton. The heart is heavy in your hands as you slot it beneath the bottom left rib and shimmy it up and into place. The heart beats happily in its empty chest, like a single bat in a deep, empty cave. You release it slowly, afraid it will slip, but the heart sinks and settles.

No sooner do you wipe your hands onto your dress than a curious flapping gives you pause. Although the window is not cracked, the long curtains are rippling. Eager to continue the great puzzle, you approach fearlessly, yanking the curtains aside. Behind them you find long strips of creamy fabric, soft as silk and warm to the touch. Careful of the blood still slicking the rich grain, you climb onto the desk and unhook the material from the curtain rod, sending it falling to the floor. It hits with a familiar smack. Only then do you realise that it is skin.

You let the other strip fall to the floor, then haul them both before the chair despite the strain in the muscles of your lower back. When you tug, chunks of skin break free like damp clay. You mold them around the small bones at the feet, smoothing up the sides, and carving out the arches until a whole foot rests warm in your lap. You press the toenails into place. New muscles swell and flex beneath your touch.

You continue the easy work, gliding the smooth skin up and around. You reach the knee, begin at the other foot, press toenails into their spots and admire them in delight.

Time continues to bend before you, allowing you every second it has to offer. Still, the fire does not burn out, the snow does not stop, the light does not dim, and you do not grow weary.

Once you are finished shaping her lips, color rises in them, pink and brand new. You shape the button of her nose, the round caps of her eyelids, smooth the crown of her head. You trace your ears and mould hers after your own.

When no skin remains you step back and admire the young girl before you.

Her breath comes softly. Her cheek rests against the plush side of the chair as she sleeps. Although you are not sure of her age, you know she is young. No stubble graces the skin of her pubis. Her chest is flat with childhood.

You are smitten already.

Lastly, you uncoil the short loops of golden hair. It is soft in your hands and almost as opalite as the bones. Each strand you press against her scalp, watching as their ends sink and stick. Absent of the proper tools, you run your fingers through her hair, smoothing out subtle knots. She is absolutely, undeniably beautiful.

Her eyelashes flutter against the pale curve of her cheek. Your breath falters in your chest. You have a similar feeling to the brief instances precluding this visit to the library - a warping, a falling.

Only once she opens her eyes do you realise she is you.

Hers are grey as river stones. You have no mirror in the library, are not even sure of the color of your own, but as her eyes find yours and a smile splits her lips, you feel as if she has split you down the middle. You feel wounded by love. Identity and familiarity fog the air between you.

The young girl reaches out and takes your old, gnarled hand in hers as if leading you to memory. That simple touch acts as an unlocking. The subtle confusion you had felt upon first entering the library disappears as if absorbed and swept away by a quick tide.

"Oh," you say as understanding dawns. It is the first time you have heard the gentle lilt your voice. The girl grins as if proud.

The memory of your last life returns as quickly as you had forgotten it.

You were a young father swallowed by avalanche.

Before that life though, you were as you are now, an old woman in an empty library pulling parts from nowhere, creating the future body your soul will inhabit. Those bones had been larger, your frame thick with muscle. You had crafted your body's appearance based on the day of your death.

With clarity you can recall plenty of other visits to the library, moulding wrinkled skin around bodies more frail than yours, some so old they arrived with no teeth for you to place. In those lives, you had lived for many decades. Now that you are alight with memory, you cannot recall a single time your body has not survived at least until adulthood.

As if sensing your thoughts, the young girl squeezes your hand. The kind of peace found only in childhood softens her eyes.

Hot tears glide down your face. Although you know you will have plenty more lives after this little girl, ones filled with more sun and wonder and laughter, you cannot help but mourn for the life you will not lead. She will not grow into adulthood. It will be your very first time dying as a child.

The girl rises on steady legs to stand atop the seat of the chair, only then tall enough to take her golden hair in hand and blot at your tears. You nod, grateful, and tamper the grief. The girl leaps down and takes your hand once more in hers.

She leads you to the window.

The same grey light shines as you approach, but now you are distracted by the snag of it in what will be your golden hair. Along the high curve of the girl's cheekbone you spot a few of your own fingerprints as if pressed into dough. The sight of them makes a hot lump of emotion form in your throat, so you redirect your attention to the window, expecting to see snow and laden trees.

Instead you see only flat grey as if someone had thrown a cloth over the panes. Beside you, the girl shakes your hand and searches for your eyes. You meet hers to show you are watching. She nods and places her free hand flat on the glass.

Instantly, color explodes atop the window.

It shows a dense field laden with insects and wildflowers. Beyond that, you see a forest of thick trees. Sun shines high and blazing. The only shadows huddle between the trees. As if following a gaze, the scene shifts, drawing closer to where field meets foliage.

When you glance to the girl, she is eyeing the sequence atop the glass unflinchingly. You brace yourself once you spot a splash of red atop the mossy ground. The drizzle of blood grows thicker the longer you watch until finally you spot her body lying on the ground, head resting on the root of a maple, blonde hair fanned wide atop the grass.

She could have been sleeping if not for the ragged tear of her shirt and the deep cavern of her middle sliced open and empty. Frantic horror has you clutching your chest as if to calm your wild heart. When you glance to the girl she is still watching impassively.

Your view atop the window continues to shift, sliding up until you are peering between the high branches above her body. Shiny pink masses dangle between the leaves, glistening in the summer blaze. Dazed by panic, your mind does not comprehend what you are seeing until you spot the very heart you had just placed within her brittle chest nestled into a hollow spot of the trunk. Her organs are strung throughout the branches, already dry and withering in the heat.

Across the field, you spot a large man dressed in black lumbering away. You cannot see his face, cannot see any part of him but his clothes, and you know he is the one who will kill you.

As suddenly as it appeared, the scene vanishes. You are again staring out to the snowy landscape. Your own face watches you in the reflection of the glass. You are pale and ruddy from crying. When you turn to look at the girl she is already watching you with sympathy. She squeezes your fingers again and smiles when you squeeze back.

She returns her free hand back onto the glass and this time instead of flowers and gore you see the faces of your future parents. They are bright and happy and vague, hazy at the details. You hear the kind sound of your mother laughing. Your father's strong hands appear atop the window holding a small box turtle. You hear his voice next, soothing, instructive, *"Be careful. You've got to hold it like a sandwich. Like this- watch-"* A giggle follows and you realise it comes not from the peek into your happy future, but from the body you will soon inhabit.

The girl laughs at the vision of her father holding a turtle, her thin shoulders shaking. Atop the glass you see other pets flash by in a hurry. Several cats appear only to dart out of frame. You catch sight of dogs of every size, of horses and rabbits and chickens.

The final scene shows your body surrounded by bright hospital lights, a bundle of cloth and a small pink face in your thin arms. The voice of your mother asks, *"Are you so happy to be a big sister?"* She is answered by the same grin and a delighted nod of your head. You hear your future voice for the first time round with youth, *"So, sooooooo happy!"*

The scene fades. You stare at the snow.

The young girl shakes your hand. Without thinking, you kneel before her, grab her by those thin shoulders, and tuck her against your body. She wraps her arms around you as delighted as any adoring child.

When you pull away to look her in the eyes, she is smiling. You want to say something but no words rise in your throat. Instead, the girl pets your cheek, an understanding in the action. Absent of diction, she knows what you mean.

You will go into the next life together, one in the same, and once it has finished you will return to the library to rest and build your next body. Then you will begin again.

You rise and step away, knowing she must go.

With a last grin to you, the girl hooks her fingers beneath the windowpane and pushes. The glass slides up and frigid winter air swirls through the library, snapping at the curtains and extinguishing the meager fire. She climbs atop the ledge, her little toes dangling.

Without ceremony, she leaps and falls. You feel the familiar sensation of tugging, of darkness and the allure of *elsewhere* and, easy as a breath, you have melded.

You are laughing, wild and bright and so full of love, dropping straight into the eye of the world.

The Hour's Glass

Daniel Darwood
England

'THE USUAL WATERMELON VODKA, JOHN?'

'That was Mara's usual - not mine,' said John Buogoy, not taking his eyes from his half-empty glass.

The stocky man grimaced as if he had just stood barefoot on shards of broken glass; John didn't need to look to tell that the man regretted not awaiting his customer's request.

It was an anniversary of a sort. It would've been the fifteenth year since John and Mara Buogoy's wedding, if she were here. Some said no luck, not even the hardest of the kind, existed for the Bogeyman.

'Tell me, John,' Wilhelm said in a rush, 'how long have you been a customer at my establishment? Since eighteen eighty-three, I presume. And what year is it now? Twenty-seventeen?'

Regardless of the one-hundred and thirty-four years' gap, Wilhelm had not aged a day. John often imagined him as a sort of performer: his timid and panicked flourishing heavily contrasted his broad build, and often gave him an almost comical appearance. Any of that was negated, however, if you gave the man's eyes a thorough stare; anyone could identify that more than just being a bartender made the man.

'I know what you're going to say, Wilhelm, and you need not worry. It was an honest mistake - we're all still getting used to Mara's passing; I know that better than most, so don't give me any freebies, I'm not on the streets, I can afford--'

The clang of the freshly-filled beer glass against John's half empty was an action that outweighed any words John could say to convince the man otherwise. A generous, yet inconvenient gesture as he was still timidly supping his previous beverage as though under scrutinous supervision.

'This isn't an act of charity,' Wilhelm said matter-of-factly. 'I am giving my best friend a free beverage. If you insist on a financial contribution, then put some change into the jukebox and lift this mire of a mood.'

John stood up, his thick, handlebar-like moustache rippling with his sighing exhalations as he walked over to the jukebox. It was a small establishment - there just wouldn't be enough time for anybody to slip anything questionable into his drink before he was back to his seat again. The truth of the matter was, it was just too small of a bar for any kind of trouble; customers were too occupied trying to settle down at tables before they all became taken.

John thought he need not worry; nobody would think of robbing him this night.

He slid in a pound coin and chose *Fleetwood Mac: Little Lies*, and returned to his seat to find yet *another* freebie. He hardly paid it any heed, however. He thought of Mara dancing along in a happy place; just like she had when they first met.

'Give that extra to Spring-heeled Jack, if you don't want it. I think he said he was coming down tonight.'

When was Jack *not* coming down? If this place was not subject to closure he thought Jack would scarcely leave. It was because pubs such as this were a haven of sorts for Myths that blip the world. When you lived forever - or as close to the end of time as you could reach - you tended to expedite your allowed visits elsewhere. No amount of cosmetics could make your appearance blend in with the ageing mortals around you, and you couldn't disguise it as fine genetical inheritance from your smooth-faced grandmother, either.

Many Myths were seen here, as they simply had nowhere else to go for very long.

'Well, it certainly is picking up in here tonight,' said John, at an attempt to stimulate a conversation before Jack's arrival - to bask in the calm before the storm. 'No Featherman or Lady Red yet?'

'On business apparently. You wouldn't believe how much of a hassle it is to maintain the whereabouts of the lot; I want to accommodate them, not stalk them, but business will be just as it is.'

The Enclosure Guild, thought John: the owners of pubs, hotels, restaurants, gyms, and even reportedly brothels existing in unison to act as a secondary society and, however pretentiously, an omnipresent authority in which the reporting of activities is compulsory.

John was not a fan of the idea - he liked Wilhelm sure enough, and he was the only statutory member he would report his whereabouts to, yet this envisionment of a secluded society had limits to extreme proportions. John was aware that Myths can't die - yet humanity would not as a whole, either. Humans would always be more populous, making the idea of enclosure seem obsolete to him.

The effect of it on his life was just as much for Mara: contact with the police force prohibited, and any crimes committed against a Myth were to be reported to the guild, resulting in extreme identity secrets acts being utilised. The most heinous of all, in John's opinion, was the procedure of two weddings, one for mortal and the other for Myth. He had had to convey a sense of solitude - that he was a lonely man, with few friends in distant lands, and no identifiable family to speak of. He had not liked having to lie to his parents-in-law, yet, what was the possibility of them believing the truth?

A thought skittered across his mind that made him almost chip his teeth scathing: with Mara's passing, would the Guild not feel a sense of relief? The less mortal association the better, was their frame of mind. Would death really be a convenience for them…?

'At least Jack keeps an easy flow for me,' said Wilhelm. John was grateful for the intrusion on his negative thoughts. 'I don't know why he likes this place as much as he does, though, I keep saying I'll get him a stool he doesn't have to hover over, but what can I do about the size of his legs?'

* * *

Walking, spring-heeled Jack thought, hurt the pride of his legs more than having them run over.

There was always driving, he supposed. Maybe move to America and content himself with a life on the road like a spiritualist, but his fine, long legs would seize up in cramped transport. No. Without his legs, he was just Jack.

Leaping from rooftop to rooftop like a humanoid whirlwind - now that was worthy of the name "Myth." He felt a pang of lost opportunity walking these modern, and *lacking* streets: the buildings' height surpassed his belief - if only they were like that centuries ago. *Even immortals must grow old.*

At least he could walk fast - fast enough to ignore the temptation of the towers, the Devil's Fingers, he had taken to calling them. He pulled his hat low, despite it already concealing one eye completely. This way, he wouldn't have to look - would not be tempted to leap, with eyes seeing nothing but dark confinement, being all that was left for his kind.

The hat could be worse; a wheelchair would be his grave.

* * *

John felt a clutch of hesitation instead of *Hello, my friend,* while he shook Jack's hand. Wishing he kept a tally of how many times that had happened tonight with the locals, he passed his good friend a drink he had been given for free; he did not want to have too many, but Jack looked like he couldn't consume enough.

It was a part of withdrawal that all Myths must undergo since the enacting of the Enclosure Guild: Myths all over the world had to suffer deprivation of occupation; Jack couldn't jump; Wilhelm was resigned to selling mortal liquor; and John, the Bogeyman, sat there uncaring; any sacrifice made was for his marriage - the both of them.

An eternity of scaring children was not exactly a prosperous career, he thought. They had never troubled him, so why he them? He would much sooner integrate into the mortal society and build a life for himself by conventional means, yet the others would perceive his viewpoint with disdain, creating a healthy contention.

Despite whatever was spoken and thought about John, Mara was treated as an equal; sometimes more so, as she seemed to define him tonight.

Distasteful opinions towards his marriage were never spoken directly, or even insinuated. It was like everybody had lost their way, and were content with just getting by through the days as though there was an ending in sight. John wondered why this was any different to the mortals' lives - as everything had, or at least, appeared to have, an ending in waiting.

'I'll say, Wilhelm, this is one of the better steak and mushroom pies in recent history,' said Jack, with traces of his vigour returning and becoming visible like the steam emanating from his meal. 'A bit stingy with the gravy, though.'

'They are only small pies - you don't want to soak it, it's not a sponge. It takes me forever to mold the pastry just right - I should count myself lucky I have that long, or my customers would be subjected to soggy lumps that not even the worms would eat.'

John wasn't much into pies, or any pastry for that matter. He hated the way it would flake off like dead skin and make a mess all over his clothes. Retrospectively, he never understood why that would be a problem: he would eventually outlive his wardrobe's selection of clothes, and be forced to buy another century's worth. He thought about setting up a trade in knitting and sewing - Mara had taught him the basics, but he would most probably fiddle with a sewing machine until he made a half-decent-looking rag of sorts, and then, using his eternity, he would work his way up.

Jack handed over his plate and went back to hovering over his stool like it had just bitten his backside, and then decided to content himself by laying his feet across the counter, much to Wilhelm's protests.

The two chatted for awhile, John was looking at his watch surreptitiously as though it was a timer for a bomb and he was planning a mad dash to the exit anytime now.

He felt like ordering - anything perhaps, from the menu, but was worried that Jack would have something to say about the matter as he always did; if it wasn't a steak and kidney pie, or an amount of glasses of beer to equal a keg in contents, it was most certainly subpar.

It must have been an hour's passing, at least, though it felt like more in total. John decided ample time had passed to justify a late-night walk by the river which had seemed to become his new occupation. It loosened his thoughts - the good and the bad, but being an immortal, they would always be there to play on his mind; best just embrace and accept them as early as possible.

'I think I might go for a walk,' said John, 'I think I have had a bit too much, and it's getting quite late.'

'Why do they call you the Bogeyman, John?' asked Jack all of a sudden, with a pint of beer in each hand. 'Me, well, I'm just Jack now, but I *used* to spring about. I guess you could say I'm nothing without my legs, yet I never understood you, John, aren't you supposed to be a real spook? The epitome of horror for children? Yet I never recall seeing you in action. Me, I was all over the reports, but you were just a whisper.'

John got up and walked to the door, feeling the eyes of the punters searching him up and down, registering to their brains whether to cheer for a fight or ignore and look away.

'Easy, Jack, I think you've had enough. Here, another pie. On the house for good measure.'

Jack put both of his glasses down, gave John a half-smile, half-sneer, then started to eat his free meal.

'Right then. I'm off, gentlemen. I'll see you tomorrow, most likely.'

Wilhelm nodded, and Jack was lost in his food. John had one thing to say to the man, but he couldn't yet. Not right now, at least. So he decided to revise it in his head: *Well played, my friend. Well played.*

* * *

'Not just yet, Jack. I need a word. Everybody else, thank you for tonight. I hope to see you again before the next hundred years pass.'

The pub fell silent; not the creaking of a stool, or the chime of a moving glass to be heard.

'So then, did you pull it off ok? John told me you faltered slightly at the beginning but came around in the end.'

'I don't think anyone suspects us. It's all up to John now, anyway. Best we not meet here tomorrow; we should avoid each other for the time being. Though, it has been a pleasure, my friend,' said Wilhelm, shaking Jack's hand.

'Pleasure's all mine. Now, I'll be off as well. Thanks for the pie; the freebies are the best.'

They shook hands again, and performed a masculine gesture of pulling each other's shoulders together. Jack realised when he had walked halfway down the street that he had left his hat behind. He didn't care, maybe it was a subconscious act, maybe not, because if everything played correctly, he wouldn't need it any longer.

He spent his journey home eyeing the building he would like to climb the most. Because, however precipitant of him to declare it, he would do it anyway.

Spring-heeled Jack would spring again.

* * *

John spent a while walking by the river in the moonlight, and pondered how he was to greet his wife. The water rippled with little currents as though the fish were flatulating, and a few rats swam on by.

It had been over a year since he last saw her, and he worried whether she would actually be there at all. Had he imagined the whole ordeal? Was he too grief-stricken to accept the loss of his wife and created his own eternal hell in which she dictated from a throne inside his mind?

He could see her in the distance on the bridge regardless, glistened by the moonlight or the grave, John didn't know which was fitting to describe her, but she had retained all of her former elegance.

He picked up a purple-looking flower in which he intended to be a gift, though he felt like he would be placing it on a grave, and walked over.

He dropped it and left it behind.

'Hello, honey,' he said.

She turned around. The purple flower was a dark contrast to her pale skin; he didn't need it in his hand to know.

'Hello, John,' said a voice that sounded like it belonged in the back of his mind. I thought you'd be late - but I guess the Bogeyman always needs his element of surprise, now doesn't he?'

'I will do for the coming days - you're as good as a fugitive now, and I an accomplice. But I will protect you.'

She smiled and walked over to him, placing her hands on his. Real enough, for now. 'I know you will, pet. We can make it through this. After all, am I not a Myth? Have I not become one through your power?'

It was true. He couldn't help but smile: the Guild had tabs on all Myths, but not humans who became them; Mara was just a deceased mortal in their records, and if freedom could be obtained for one, then it could be done for all.

'Mara, what was death like?' asked John, unable to abate his curiosity.

'The rebirth is what is important, my love; we needn't fear any longer. Here. Put your hands there. Can you feel our baby kicking?'

He could. He felt a pang of guilt for his child whom he had used for the greater good - everyone's greater good.

'It seems the stories were wrong about you, my love. The Bogeyman never left his occupation - he instead expanded it. This child has already saved me - shared its power and brought me back as one of its own; one of our own.'

John couldn't help but smile despite his guilt. He now had a chance at freedom, as did all of his kind. One Myth living outside of the Guild is a symbol of hope to all.

'I suppose we will need some clothes for our newcomer,' said John. 'Now, I know I am not much good, but I think that with an eternity behind us, I may be able to comprehend that old sewing machine we have sitting around somewhere.'

Cold Dish

Dave Ashwin
England

THE BRAHMIN PRIEST, resplendent in his saffron dhoti, blessed the newborn child and his exultant parents. His gaze was drawn, almost by an innate reflex, to the neonate's lower body and his eyes, as if a switch had been flicked, lit up.

His smile widened as it dawned on him that his services had been more than adequately remunerated and, as his thoughts drifted to that torrid afternoon in the temple, he wondered whether it was his good fortune or Shiva's blessings that such munificence had been granted to him, especially after the tribulations of the last few months.

Some months earlier....

The bi-weekly state transport bus from Bhuj disgorged its passengers in the rapidly fading light of dusk. The journey had taken over three hours. One of the last to disembark, the Brahmin moved with great deliberation, in part due to an imperceptible limp and more so in trepidation at the start of a new phase in his life – to begin his tenure as a priest at the temple.

The near six-foot figure towered above all and his pale, fair complexion was barely tanned by the blazing heat of the dry summer. His athletic and imposing Adonis-like persona belied the roots of his profession. In a different milieu, he could easily have been mistaken for a Bollywood star.

Even in the fading light, he could discern the imposing façade of the temple, festooned with lamps. The faint acrid aroma of burning ghee became more prominent as he progressed towards his destination. The vibrant and reverberating tones of the temple bells foretold the impending nocturnal surge of devotees assembling for the closing puja (prayer ritual) of the day. The temple bells, sounds of familiarity, aided in calming his nerves, as did his silent rendition of his mantras. The thin patina of sweat on his brow was the only manifestation of his inner turmoil on the fast-approaching encounter with his future employers.

The young porter carried the Brahmin's bundle of possessions, delicately balanced on his head, as they approached the main square after meandering through the sand-logged residential lanes. The open courtyards of most homes, some with cows being prepared for the evening milking, were filled with the pungent smoke of cow dung-fuelled fires and the warm glow of lanterns as the evening shadows lengthened.

The village of Bhog, like many such villages dotted across Gujarat and, indeed, India, was a trading outpost to the market town of Bhuj. It comprised of a main square and a labyrinth of several dusty residential lanes. Sturdy brick built houses with tiled roofs nestled, cheek to jowl, with lesser ramshackle dwellings, representing the patent disparity between the haves and the have nots.

A few of the traders and farmers had cars and tractors parked outside their homes as an ostentatious exhibition of their wealth. The Rajputs showed off their regal lineage by shunning these modern contraptions and opting for stallions, an equine badge of honour. Some of these steeds could outrun the jeeps and the Massey Ferguson tractors on the sand-bogged trails.

On the outer periphery were verdant fields that grew cotton, peanuts and other myriad crops; so typical of the flourishing agrarian economy. Most of these farms belonged to large landowners, the Patels, who were mostly absentee farmers. The indentured labourers that were employed were on subsistence wages. Most were immigrants from the states of Bihar and Utter Pradesh, by far the poorest and most populous states, respectively.

The Kutch and its border communities were still reeling under the legacy of the cathartic upheaval that the partition engendered. The stigma and the trauma of one of the largest migrations in the history of mankind still festered under the veneer of communal harmony.

It was amidst this vibrant community that the Brahmin, a novice priest, arrived with an optimism that only youth exhibits; before the cynicism of age and impending mortality take precedence.

Probesh Chaturvedi, the novice, recruited by the Raj pundit (high priest) and the coterie of pujaris (priests) that managed the main temple had adapted to the temple hierarchy, however, acceptance by the majority would take time, especially as Probesh was a bachelor.

The pujaris all had their living quarters at the rear of the temple with ample room for spouses and family. Probesh was the only bachelor in the midst of a very family oriented, close knit community. The males, accustomed to the cosy interaction with other married pujaris, were irked by the Raj pundit's decision to engage a bachelor. The arrival of the dashing priest had not gone down well with the males; the females were all aflutter.

The main temple with its imposing marble and granite façade housed a pantheon of Gods from Ram, Krishna, Ganesh to Shiva, and a myriad other minor gods and goddesses.

There was a much smaller, decrepit Shiva temple on the outskirts, perched on a small hill. That temple was run by a solitary old Brahmin priest who lived in the residential annexe adjoining the temple. The entire complex had fallen into disuse primarily due to the rivalry between the two cohorts. The Raj pundit and the old Brahmin were adversaries in that each tried to protect their domain and power. The machinations of the pujaris to maximise their income and power tilted the balance in favour of the larger adversary.

The Shiva temple suffered as a consequence; the reduced attendance figures and the consequent decline in revenue were the harbingers that the old Brahmin recognised. He was resigned to this ever decreasing income and the dilapidation that the edifice exhibited. His only abiding hope was that the temple would muddle through and that he would not become homeless.

It was nestled amongst a grove of banyan trees with some trees so overgrown that a couple of them could be accessed from the temple terrace. The temple overlooked a nearby lake and the dhobi ghat (laundry site), used by the village women to wash their clothes and sometimes swim and bathe in. A motley crowd of cows and buffaloes shared the watery retreat, especially in the hot summer months.

Probesh, as an acolyte and a newcomer, had sparked a lot of speculation, for the rural location was to all ends and purposes a retrograde step for an ambitious priest. For a career-focused Brahmin it represented a lateral move at best; so newcomers and their motives were rich fodder for social gossip and vicarious innuendo.

There had always been a cloud of suspicion of a turbulent past and rumours abounded that Probesh's illicit liaisons with female devotees had become a modus operandi to feed his compulsive behaviour. No one really knew but there were persistent allegations that Probesh had either fled a matrimonial alliance or was exiled by an overzealous putative father-in-law who did not see any future for his daughter married to an indigent priest. The fact that the priest had a physical disability, a club foot, made the grounds for rejection compelling.

His detractors attributed his physical disability to divine retribution for past misdemeanours; whilst others pointed to a family history of inherited defects. The affliction had manifested and persisted through generations. His grandfather and his father, as immediate ancestors, had both fallen victim to the trait. Probesh had obviously inherited not only the ancestral profession, but the physical handicap as well.

His affliction was probably the reason why Probesh remained a bachelor, despite his Adonis like stature and his erudition. His mastery of Sanskrit and the title of a pundit (learned Brahmin) at such a young age presaged a bright future. However, the club foot had become a millstone; retarding his professional and social progress.

A few years of hard work and diligence had gradually built up his confidence and, whilst he thrived professionally as a priest, his finances were constrained.

His perfunctory analysis of the temple finances vis-à-vis the hordes of devotees that attended did not stand up to financial scrutiny. More so, if one took into account the fact that there was a higher ratio of the affluent attending; signs of a booming economy. His dissatisfaction became even more pronounced when he took account of the prosperity that his married colleagues seemed to be enjoying.

He started auditing the daily attendance and the potential revenue that he estimated to be a true picture of the temple's earnings. Probesh was convinced that his share of the spoils was being misappropriated by an unfair system based on arbitrary criteria.

Despite the poor wages, Probesh had managed to cope by doing extra work outside the temple. However, the seeds of doubt soon germinated and magnified into all kinds of imaginary conspiracy theories. This sense of betrayal festered and suppurated. The 'abscess' had to be lanced before it destroyed him.

In a fit of bitter frustration and rage, it all boiled over into a major verbal brawl with his mentor, the Raj pundit. Probesh's allegations and rancour did not sit well with the high priest. As neither party was prepared to give in, Probesh, in a moment of transitory madness, walked out of the temple and out of a job.

Although the Raj pundit had unequivocally stated his views and wished to draw a line under the matter, a few of the aggrieved pujaris saw an opportunity to settle scores by maligning Probesh. A litany of lies was maliciously circulated with the worst being that Probesh had been caught in flagrante delicto with a female devotee. It would seem that history was repeating itself and the past was stalking the Brahmin.

The Raj pundit, to his credit, when made aware of these rumours, took swift action to curb the gossip. He had no hesitation in reminding his pujaris that the repercussions would be far reaching if the devotees lost faith in the integrity and sanctity of the temple. The Raj pundit and, by proxy, the temple, could ill afford any adverse publicity if the allegations of impropriety were even investigated, let alone proved, by the village panchayat (a governing council of elderly villagers)

Probesh's hasty and misconceived notion to strike out on his own came home to roost in no uncertain terms when he realised that his lodgings had ceased to exist. Without a roof over his head, his only viable option was to go begging bowl in hand to the only other viable option – the old Brahmin at the Shiva temple. The shelter it afforded and the distance from the scene of his alleged crimes would be a blessing in disguise – he could lick his wounds, away from public scrutiny.

Fortunately, the old Brahmin, who empathised with the young priest, acquiesced and let him occupy the second room in the residential annexe. Although the wages and the potential income from other sources would be drastically reduced, the accommodation was sufficient recompense. He needed to recover his poise and confidence.

He soon realised that life on the streets for an upcoming Brahmin priest was no bed of roses and he struggled to keep body and soul together. A relentless battle to make ends meet became soul destroying.

His previous employer's influence was all pervasive and hindered his progress as most devotees cowered under the power exercised by the main temple. Most devotees decided to shun Probesh to avoid alienating the Raj pundit.

Fortunately the old Brahmin ignored the moratorium imposed by the vindictive pujaris and assisted Probesh in his fight to survive. It was intrepid and magnanimous of the old timer to go out on a limb for a stranger.

It had been several months since his abrupt and unceremonious departure from the main temple and he was just about keeping his head above water. His pride would not allow him to retreat and he decided to take on his detractors head on. Until he could break into the upper echelons of the landed gentry and the affluent middle classes, it was a fine act between subsistence and impoverishment. The real rewards would only accrue once he could break the monopoly wielded by the omnipotent Raj pundit and his pujaris.

It was during this spell of abject hardship that he had a summons from a rich businessman; a local wheeler dealer and a wholesale merchant.

The Bopal's had an imposing residence, adjoining the main temple, with enough room to accommodate an extended family. An open yard at the front not only housed a few dairy cows but also proffered enough storage room for the season's harvests. A staircase, without any bannisters, led to the terrace, which acted as an ad hoc dormitory for the family to escape the stifling nocturnal heat. The wooden rafters in the rooms below often gave refuge to rats and to snakes during the day. Cobras were revered as Shiva's presence, so were accepted as idols of worship.

Hari, the first born of the Bopal family, lived with his elderly parents and their extended family. Hari's second wife, Menaka, a demure, pretty eighteen-year-old, was his second chance at starting a family. Parineeti, his first, was unable to conceive after years of endeavour, and it was hoped that Menaka would offer an opportunity to safeguard Hari's lineage.

The matriarch's overriding desire to have an heir, a grandson, meant that Parineeti's marriage and her fate were sealed. Parineeti became a pariah; barrenness her stigma. She quietly returned to her parents in Bhuj. Hari was complicit by his silence.

Several years into the second marriage without a result compelled the matriarch to consider divine intervention; maybe an abhisek, a religious ritual, to propitiate Shiva. The longer Menaka's fallow period continued, the more she despaired at her husband's blasé attitude. The matriarch wanted to ensure that aspersions were not cast on Hari's virility and machismo.

Probesh was approached to officiate as he had been recommended. He was also an automatic choice on the grounds that the novice priest would be reasonable with his dakshina (fees). The matriarch had done her due diligence and realised that the services of the Raj pundit or his pujaris were not cheap and likely to escalate if the puja had to be repeated.

The price difference also gave her a valid excuse to engage Probesh and circumvent the tacit ban imposed by the Raj pundit. Besides, she could manipulate the young Brahmin with ease; whereas the wily Raj pundit would discourage any bargaining. She was also confident that the young Brahmin would exercise discretion if need be.

Probesh was aware of the double edged sword that was being presented to him – if he conjured up a beneficial outcome then word would spread about his fecund touch. As long as he did his karma, the fruits would follow.

Equally, any lapse on his part, would spell the demise of his embryonic career. The irony of his predicament was not lost on him; he was being coerced into pinning all his hopes on the couple conceiving. If he failed to invoke the gods his fate would be sealed.

Probesh referred to his panchang, an almanac of auspicious timetables, and selected a day in the lunar cycle which foretold a good result. An auspicious moment that would facilitate conception. On the day of the puja, he came well prepared with his crimson parchment bound scriptures and his paraphernalia of all things religious - turmeric, raw rice, betel leaves, incense sticks, etc.

Amidst an aura of religious fervour, incense and ghee fuelled fire, the couple sat in studious silence as the ceremony unfolded. The renditions of Sanskrit mantras in a baritone voice, the tinkling of a hand held bell, the haze created by the burning of ghee and the incense, captured the ethos of the ceremony; like a hypnotist inducing a trance.

The small audience and the matriarch watched and listened in rapt concentration as Probesh prepared some akshata (unbroken raw rice coated with turmeric) to represent prosperity and fecundity. The yellow turmeric stained rice was sprinkled liberally over the couple. Menaka was bedecked in her bridal finery with the end of her sari draped over her head and face as a veil. She felt like a new bride on her wedding day.

On completion of the ceremony, Probesh was careful to collect all the grains of the coated rice off the floor. Not to be trodden on as that would incur Shiva's wrath. He also instructed her to persist with the Shiv puja every Monday to maximise her chances of conception. Fasting on Mondays, for the foreseeable future, was also advisable.

He took pains to declare that if conception did not occur then the puja would need to be repeated; thereby, ensuring a repeat stream of revenue for his depleted coffers.

Probesh was expecting a payment as he gathered up his wares but the wily matriarch deferred the payment; ignoring the priest's protestations. The inference for Probesh was that she would only pay if success was achieved.

A payment in arrears was not ideal especially as he needed to replenish his dwindling finances but he was wary of squaring up to the matriarch, who had a formidable reputation of having her own way and a greater notoriety for maligning anyone who crossed her path. Reluctantly and with a heavy heart, Probesh departed with a promissory note.

Two months rolled by and then more, without any sightings of storks in the vicinity of the Bopal residence. Probesh, bearing in mind the failure of the first marriage, dreaded the worse and was convinced that Hari must be either infertile or impotent or both. He dared not even broach the subject of his outstanding fees.

It was then that he knew that he would have to repeat the puja and reprise his reputation. A second failure would be catastrophic for his nascent reputation and would entail losing his promised dues.

A second puja was performed in the absence of Hari, who was away from the marital home on business; the busy man that he was. Probesh repeated the rituals all over again, having secured, on this occasion, a promise of a payment. He made the puja more elaborate and took time to elucidate each Vedic mantra. Needless to say, the matriarch sat through the long-winded ritual with a look of stoic resignation and an incipient fear that history was repeating itself; a sense of deep dread and déjà vu.

When pressed for a payment, the matriarch admonished Probesh for his avarice and declined to pay even a retainer. Probesh retreated without further ado; his face an inscrutable mask hiding his inner frustration. Stoic resignation seemed to be the order of the day.

Months passed without any news of a fruitful outcome nor was the promised payment forthcoming. The matriarch had relayed that she would not pay until a positive result was guaranteed. Probesh was at the end of his tether and was deeply concerned that the matriarch may renege and go back to his rivals.

To avert such an outcome, he convinced the matriarch that his third and final attempt would not accrue his full fees. That tilted the balance in his favour and he retreated with a promise from the old witch that she would abide by the agreement. The matriarch, being very religious and superstitious, did not want to press her luck and incur the wrath of a Brahmin. The scriptures were full of the tales of retribution meted out by irate Brahmins.

This time, however, Probesh had decided to schedule the puja at the Shiva temple in the expectation that the matriarch would not be present. In her absence the couple would be more amenable to gentle manipulation. He would have to somehow overcome her reservations about shifting the venue away from her jurisdiction.

She seemed to be convinced by his assurances that the old Brahmin would be on site as he rarely left the temple. The omnipresence of a senior pujari swayed the argument in his favour. The usual planetary alignments were sought and the puja was scheduled a month later. Hari would ensure that business commitments were deferred so that he could attend.

Boredom and the lack of regular work led Probesh to while away a lot of his afternoons on the terrace of the Shiva temple, whilst the old pujari had his afternoon siesta in his room. His snores could he heard all the way to the top. Probesh got into habit of stepping off the temple terrace and perching on the nearest banyan tree – a perfect vantage point to spy on the village belles bathing in the blazing sun after laundry duty.

One such belle caught his eye, especially as she stood out amongst the motley crowd. As the area was secluded and away from prying male eyes, most of them frolicked with gay abandon; not worried about veiling their faces. All of them were modestly draped in their saris, albeit, the ends were wrapped around the midriff rather than the face.

Probesh became obsessed with this fair beauty with long jet black tresses and a voluptuous presence. He made it a point to access his usual perch and spy on the women. It became a regular afternoon ritual, almost an obsession. So much so, that he rearranged his appointments to accommodate his new found postprandial titillation.

On the auspicious day of the third puja, it came as a surprise when Menaka presented herself, with her face suitably veiled, in the company of her six-year-old nephew; a reluctant chaperone. Apparently, the matriarch was indisposed and the husband was again away on business.

Probesh was astounded that the matriarch had allowed Menaka to attend on her own. However, the alleged presence of the senior pujari and a chaperone, albeit very young, allayed her concerns. More importantly, the auspicious date and time could not be missed, hence the matriarch had no option but to relent.

With the afternoon sun at its zenith and in full blaze, the entire village seemed to be in a collective torpor of lassitude. Even the grazing cattle were minus their shepherds, who took refuge under the cooling canopy of the leafy banyan grove. The temple's proximity to the lake did not provide any succour from the searing heat.

The senior Brahmin had retired to his quarters, lost to the world in a somnolent 'do not disturb' phase. The young chaperone, bored with the unintelligible language and rituals, crept away to the lake where he was assured of the company of his friends and a cooling respite from the stifling heat. He was an accomplished swimmer so Menaka took no objection when she saw him stealthily creep away.

The puja was completed without any hitches and as the young wife bent down to pay her respects to the pujari, her head, luxuriant flowing hair and face, became unveiled, as the end of the sari fell away.

For a split second, the young Brahmin lost his poise as he realised that it was the same beauty he had been spying on; the buxom target of his voyeuristic fantasy - Menaka in the flesh!

Probesh was unprepared for this tantalising vision in front of him and was flustered. With images of his afternoon voyeurism flashing through his mind and in his haste to turn away from such glorious temptation, he lost his balance and unwittingly grabbed her to avoid falling over backwards. A pile of arms, legs, and intertwined torsos ensued on the floor. The cool temple floor did little to dampen his spirits.

His hypnotic eyes and attractive physique mesmerised her as she hastily averted her gaze and stood up. Her attempts to recompose herself were in vain as she felt his piercing eyes on her and blushed as she felt his proximity. Despite her inhibitions, she was drawn to him. She held his gaze for several moments and then lowered her eyes; signifying her submission. She followed him, lamb to slaughter, as he gently tiptoed towards his room. The stertorous snores of the old Brahmin could be heard from the adjoining room, through the thin plywood partition.

The ethereal spirit of Morpheus in the old Brahmin's room became an accomplice and aided the couple in their impromptu tryst. The figure on the stringy bed sank further into somnolence. His snores reached a crescendo of a cascading sonic medley. Eros prevailed in the lovers' room; muted sounds of passion and fantasy satiated.

After what seemed an eternity, Menaka emerged from the residential annexe with her head and face suitably covered. She rushed off instinctively towards the lake to retrieve her nephew and make her way home. Probesh left soon after, hastily rearranging his dhoti, to go down to the lake for his ablutions and to prepare for the evening puja. The tepid waters of the lake did little to staunch the afterglow of his serendipitous encounter.

With the village lights twinkling in the distance as dusk drew closer, Probesh started his preparations for the evening puja. It then dawned on him that the matriarch's absence may well have been pre-planned, to avoid settling his dues. She had again prevailed in not parting with her money. In any case, he decided to stay away from the matriarch and

Menaka for the time being, until his guilt had abated. The spirit had to regain ascendancy over the flesh.

After an inordinate period of total silence, Probesh decided to pay the matriarch a visit. His fervour had diminished and he was confident that his demeanour would not betray what had transpired.

His pulse quickened when he saw Menaka tending to the tethered dairy cattle. This was the first time he had caught a glimpse of her as she had kept away from the dhobi ghat and her friends. Menaka was quick to veil her head and face as she saw the approaching priest. The matriarch reclined on a bed nearby.

Despite his doubts and the matriarch's previous feigned indifference, a part payment was made with a promise of a full settlement once the baby was born! His quick glance at the young wife milking one of the cows confirmed his perfunctory appraisal earlier; she was indeed carrying a child. Menaka, meanwhile, fought the temptation to look anywhere but at the milking urn. Her blushes deepened as she too thought about that afternoon and the snores of the older priest in the adjoining room.

A few months later....

Probesh was jubilant on receiving word that he had to perform a puja to welcome the new addition to the family. His endeavours and patience had borne a result and he was more sanguine about his future.

Probesh blessed the first born and the parents and his gaze lingered over the torso and strayed to the feet of the baby. His heart missed a beat as he recognised the club foot. The thin cotton blanket, which had slipped off, was meant to cover the affliction.

He walked away with trepidation; his emotions in an upheaval. The anxiety in turn converted into a nascent smile at the sight of his son in the flesh; proof of his virility. He prayed that his son would not undergo the same tribulations as he had encountered. The joy of his birth was tinged with empathy and pain. With Shiva's grace, the affluence of his parents would mitigate any adverse consequences.

His dhoti had no pockets so Probesh clutched the crumpled notes of cash with gusto as he left the family celebrations. As he passed the main temple, his thoughts turned to the matriarch and her wily ways. She had manipulated him into a state of impotent rage, however, his pleasure at outsmarting her, albeit unwittingly, was immense.

It had been more than two months since the birth and Probesh's disappearance from the village. The old Brahmin had contacted the matriarch and the main temple when Probesh failed to return to the Shiva temple after the celebrations. No one had seen or heard of him. The police made cursory enquiries and had given up as an FIR (first information report) had not been filed.

A local reporter filed an extended piece with his editor, hoping that it may turn out to be a scoop and materialise into columns of print. The editor thought otherwise and printed a few lines on the penultimate page of the Bhuj Chronicle; buried amongst the classifieds. The disappearance of a priest was hardly significant as most priests were very peripatetic and led a nomadic life. Just as his arrival had sparked rumours, his departure led to initial speculation but was soon forgotten.

Parineeti fidgeted with the wedding ring that sparkled on her ring finger as she read the brief item in the Bhuj Chronicle. Her smile was mirrored in her soft brown eyes as she looked at Probesh reclining next to her on the double bed. A sigh of content escaped her pouting lips.

Her mind recalled the heartbreak she went through when her father had rejected Probesh's marriage proposal on the grounds of his uncertain future. She had been besotted with the dashing priest and had been carrying his child. Probesh had fled town fearing for his safety. Parineeti lost all hope after her parents forced her to abort her unborn child.

Her marriage was hastily arranged with Hari. Her vicious treatment by the matriarch and Hari on the presumption of her infertility led to the calamitous sequence of events culminating in her return to Bhuj.

When she bumped into Probesh before her unceremonious departure, the old flames of passion and love were resurrected. It then became a surreptitious collaboration to get even with the matriarch and Hari.

Parineeti snuggled closer to her dishy-looking husband and murmured, as she drifted off to sleep, '… revenge is, indeed, a dish best served cold…'

The Colour of Silence

Grace Gallur
Australia

~Red~

YOU USED TO TELL ME THE LONGER I lay on my back and stared at the sky, the more stars I'd be able to see. You'd say the sun rises in the east, and sets in the west. You used to tell me warm milk with vanilla helps quieten all my colours before sleeping, and that we cried different tears for sadness and happiness. But the best thing you told me was that if I held a shell up to my ear, I'd be able to hear the ocean.

"Earnest, take a look at this!"

Her silhouette was hunched, obscuring the low-hanging sun from the child's eyes. Earnest's gumboots crunched against the sun-dried seaweed, sounding to him like the colour yellow.

"See the little black ones?" she stroked the periwinkles. "If you turn them over fast enough, you can see the creature inside before he shuts his door."

The boy gently pried one from a crack between rocks and peered at the brown flesh underneath.

"He's looking at you!" His mother giggled. Small spots of thistle purple popped before the boy's eyes.

"What about that one?" he pointed to a cream-and-orange shell five feet away.

The pair spent afternoons crouched on their hands and knees, flaked in sea spray, and engulfed in the lemonade sounds of water.

I lie on my back, holding our cream-and-orange shell above my head. I've pushed the doona onto the floor. While I wait for you to come home, other families continue to eat dinner together. Other families go to the park and have picnics. *Other families* tuck their children in at night. The tide still crashes over rock pools, and the Earth still spins about the sun.

You used to tell me I could hear the ocean in our shell – that I could hear the crystal lemonade colour of that day captured inside it forever. My father told me it's not the ocean at all, but just *"an amplification of my own, confused blood rushing through my brain"*. Our shell isn't special - the same thing happens when I cover my ears with my hands.

"Earnest Walker, get back from there!" *Earnest gurgled indigo happiness as waves crashed against the rocks at his feet, filling his eyes and ears with cobalt blue.*

"But the colours, Mummy! The closer I am, the brighter they are!"

"What if you fall in? Be careful - or you'll get lost in the water and we won't be able to find you!" *Earnest's bottom lip began to tremble.*

"I didn't mean to scare you, sweetie! Just - please, come away from the edge."

Mother.

It's been 39 days. Last month, I blew out eleven candles all on my own.

(I was really hoping you might just...

come home,

for me.)

I stare into the sun as it sets, *in the west,* like you said. I stare at the sky until there are no stars left to wish on. I've drunk warm vanilla milk until I feel sick. I've held my shell to my ear to try and find you - *somewhere* - as if you'd be hiding in the sounds of the waves and rock pools. I've even tried praying, like the lady from school with the scratchy voice told me to do.

But my colours still won't go away.

I wish the lime green sound of the toaster popping, the tomato red sounds of cars honking in Sydney traffic, the green and canary yellow sounds of cicadas chirping in December, even the blue and lemon sounds of the ocean... I wish they would all disappear. I press my fingers into my ears as hard as I can - but that's no better.

Silence has a colour, too.

Silence is silky.

Silence is... *trickling.*

Silence is as hollow as the dark.

Silence is the worst colour of all.

Silence is the colour of you.

Silence is Violet. Like you, Violet Walker. Please, Mum. Walk back home.

~Orange~

I roll over,

peeling myself

out

of the world of the sleeping,

and into the world of the

living.

I reach for our cream-and-orange shell. When we brought it home, Dad called it a *conch shell,* and said you can make a sound by drilling a hole in the top and blowing through it. Mum went onto the internet to find videos. It was a resonant, brassy sound - curiously both breath-like and brilliant. It had the same colour as the letter "B"; carrots and tangerines and pumpkins, with slight streaks of powder blue. Dad used to say he'd drill a hole in mine *"first thing tomorrow morning".* When Mum reminded him a week later, she was *nagging.* The shell sat on his workbench for about a month before I snuck it back.

Mum bought me a big pack of crayons with fancy names so I could draw the colour of the sound. "THE SOUND OF CONCH SHELLS" was framed and hung next to the piano. Nowadays, the entire wall is covered in them. "THE SOUND OF BITING INTO AN APPLE" *("shamrock", "green-yellow"),* "THE SOUND OF SLAMMING DOORS" *("Christmas-red", "razzle-dazzle rose"),* "THE SOUND OF THE BIRDS IN THE MORNING" *("cyber-grape", "robin's-egg blue", "apricot").* I guess it was Mum's way of trying to understand, and my way of sharing, how I saw the world.

"THE SOUND OF SILENCE" was her favourite, because it was Violet-coloured, like her name. I drew oceans of *"lilac", "ultraviolet", "wisteria", "royal-purple",* by holding all the crayons in my fist and swirling them round and round. Dad took it down three weeks after she disappeared. He said he didn't want to be reminded of her.

And then, as I turn our shell over in my hands-

-Something happens that has never happened before.

An *envelope*

dr

o

ps

out.

"For Earnest" is typed on the front.

And I wonder-

I've held my shell to my ear to try and find you - somewhere - as if you'd be hiding in the sounds of waves and rock pools.

(could it be?)

(impossible.)

(don't be *ridiculous.)*

(but… could it be?)

All the muscles around my ribcage tighten. I slip my finger under the flap.

TOUCH

Dear Earnest,

It troubles me to learn you've not left your bedroom in over a week. I would like you to go outside and get some fresh air, so I've left a present for you on your father's chair in the shade. I suggest you look after it well, and with lots of water. Note: you are not permitted to wear gloves.

-Anon.

A voice floats up from downstairs in bubbles of indigo. *Aunt Josephine is here again.* I put my letter back in my shell, and crawl out of bed to the top of the stairs. I look down into the kitchen. They don't see me.

"You've got to acknowledge he's grieving too, Matthew," Josephine says.

"Hmm," my father grunts.

"You can't just shy away from talking to him anymore."

"Talking about it would probably upset him, and I don't want to have to deal with-"

"Don't give me excuses. Talking might just *normalise* our situation for him a little, and-"

"I don't *want* to normalise our-"

"You can't just let him lie in bed for over a week-"

"What do *you* suggest, seeing how *you* know everything?"

I heard Josephine sigh loudly. "Go up and *talk* to him! Sit with him, I don't know, be a *father* - God forbid, even *give him a hug!* It's nearly five in the afternoon and he hasn't even gotten up!"

(But I'm awake!) I peer over the balcony. They aren't facing each other – my father is staring into the depths of the pantry, all hunched over. Josephine is glaring fixedly at the back of his shirt. I stick my legs out in front of me and slide down the stairs.

Thump.

Thump.

"Okay, I know, I'm *always* wrong. You sound just like *she* did, always had to be *nagging-*"

"*Has* to be nagging. You can't give up and start talking about her like she's never going to come back."

Thump.

Thump.

"She *is* gone, Josephine. The police have given up, so maybe you should do the same."

I pause, and listen.

"She simply *walks off* the CCTV footage. I stared at the film on their crappy little computers for five hours. The only thing I saw? A *shadow,* in the bottom right corner at

12:33pm. Do you know what that's like for me?"

Josephine doesn't reply.

Mum always says that *"the key to expert eavesdropping is to absolutely never get caught!"*

"But just remember, Earnest – you might not like what you hear."
Thump-
-thump-
-thump.
"Matthew, do you hear that?"
They turn around slowly, spotting me in my pyjamas.
My father scowls as he stomps past. He slams the front door as he goes, sending sparks of red and white through the air.
"Hi, Earnest," Josephine says weakly. "Where are you going?" She looks too much like Mum, her hair all short and pinned back like that.
"Out." I close the door, so I can't see the scarlet-blueberry colour of her sobbing behind me.
I think it must have rained recently. The air has that clean, soil-like taste about it. If tastes had colours for me too, I'd say the air tastes like rich, dark green. I glance towards Dad's old wooden chair underneath the Jacaranda tree, across the grass. Nowadays, it's kind of rotten and mouldy-looking, the wood bloated and disfigured. The flowers have gone all brown underneath it. Today, a checked cloth covers some obscure shape sitting in the chair.
I've left a present for you on your father's chair in the shade.
I dangle my foot in the air, one toe touching the wet grass. Dad wouldn't be happy at *all.* He says I'll get sick if I spend time out in the cold getting wet.
(but Mum used to love it.)
(Mum used to run out into the rain,)
(sopping wet,)
(hair clinging to her face,)
(laughing and drinking in the)
(blue and grey colours)
(of the sky.)
"I spy with my little eye..."
Earnest held his breath with anticipation, trying to follow his mother's line of sight.

"Something beginning with… F."

The boy squinted around the garden as he gradually processed the world around him in search of solutions. Violet delighted in seeing the world tick away behind his eyes.

Reaching the chair, I pull away the cloth. And, to my astonishment-

"A flower! Mum, Mum - it's a flower!"

"Yes, Earnest - you're right! Go on, tell me what colour it is."

The label on the plastic pot says *chrysanthemums*. They are beautiful - gentle, pastel pinks, warm oranges, fiery reds, and feel like paper to the touch. I spot the shovel next to it, and I think I know what she wants me to do.

"Look at the label. This one says - full early sun. So you've got to plant it where it will get sun in the morning – that's east of the house."

"Over there," Earnest said. "It's sunny near the tree, now."

I look nervously over my shoulder, grab the shovel, and dig out a hole. I find my hands going through the familiar motions - squeezing the pot gently, separating out the roots, so they can grow in different directions. I lower mum's chrysanthemums tenderly into the earth.

I trace little circles of earth around in my hand, watching the smallest detail of every grain - all the yellows and reds and browns and blacks amplified in the quiet moment. I pull apart chunks of earth, to see how they are wet on the outside, but dry on the inside. Before I realise it, I've plunged my arms into the soil, and that rich, cold yet warm feeling envelops me.

I roll onto my back, dirt stained into the knees of my pyjamas, fallen rain clinging to my hair. As I laugh, bubbles of Thistle purple, indigo, Jacaranda - all *pop*.

As I see Violet, I can't help but imagine *you* here, planting purple paper flowers with me, lying in the sun.

~Yellow~

When I was five, Mum realised how intently I watched her play the piano. She went to buy one of those *Piano for Beginners* booklets, each musical note colour-coded to the black and white keys. Only, when I extended my chubby fingers forward and started to play, something was obviously wrong. As I struck "A", I looked confusedly between the sour orange colour on the page and the bright blue circles before my eyes. I pressed the ivory down over and over, loud, then soft, then quickly, then firmly. When it flatly refused to change colour, I looked up to my mother, my face scrunched in frustration.

"It's not working!"

"What do you mean?"

"All the colours are wrong!"

She was just as confused as I was. Mum searched the internet until she landed on a page about *Synaesthesia*. I could tell her that A was *"electric-blue"* and F-sharp was *"Granny-Smith-apple"*. E-flat was harder to describe, because it looked like one of Josephine's beef crockpot casseroles, and the crayon box didn't have a colour for that.

Only, I didn't understand just *how* different I was, until I started school a few months later.

"Weirdo!"

"Spaz!"

"Freak!"

"Retard!"

My kindergarten teacher tried to explain my *"unique perception"* to my father, but he wasn't interested. He found he was comfortable enough inside the warmth of his own perspective, and to brace the unfamiliar outside was to unfurl his limbs, and stretch into the cold. He preferred to say things like *try and see things the normal way,* and *get rid of this nonsense.*

My father was the first one who made me acutely aware of how alone I was.

Nobody

sees things

like I do.

So, when I got my *second* conch shell letter this morning, I wasn't sure how to react.

SIGHT

Dear Earnest,

Observe the veins that run through your hand. Stretch your fingers wide, then make a fist. Turn your hand over, and observe the lines running across your palm. Observe how fearfully and wonderfully you are made. Don't you think that your mind's ability to see the world in a way that is so unique is a marvellous thing?

Another marvellous thing takes place this Saturday, at 8pm. Find someone to take you into Darling Harbour, and enjoy.

-Anon.

Fine. I'm reacting the way whoever is leaving these for me *wants* me to. I'm curious.

I'm not going to admit it, but-

-What I'm *more* curious about, is-

-If, maybe-

-at 8pm, on Saturday-

-Would *you* be there?

Later that evening, when my father was out and Josephine was in a good mood, I approached her. I wasn't quite sure how to ask, without telling her about my letters, but I mumbled around the point until she helped me with the train timetable. With a tone that sounded a little like mock surprise, she said that there were apparently *fireworks* scheduled this coming weekend.

(She also said Dad didn't have to know.)

(I liked that she said that.)

And, so, now we sit on the train. I let the engine's gentle grey whirring fill my ears. The frequent caramel callings of *All Stations To Wynyard, Town Hall, Central* fade into the background.

And I begin to *wonder.*

What would it be like to be colour-blind?

Wouldn't it be lonely if every time you looked at the sky, you knew all day long everyone saw something totally different?

Would you hunger for nighttime to come, when there was no blue or red or yellow to look at, *at all?*

Most light is absorbed, never to be seen again - except, if it's lucky enough to be reflected back out. If it's perceived by a pair of eyes, then it turns into colours, like *BLUE, RED,* and *YELLOW.*

But does that mean -
underneath light's deflection,
everything is really
BLACK?
What if
everything has no colour
inherent in itself, until
someone shines something on it,
like a torch, or a sun?
It seems,
(to me,)
We're all just shining our torches,
probing around in the dark, our
minds working overtime to make
sense of
anything and
everything
our light touches.

What was *your* light touching, Mum, that day you decided to leave? Maybe the way you saw colours became different to how *Dad* sees them. Maybe your tongues taste sweet and sour and bitter differently – that's why you stood around wine tasting for hours, disagreeing on whether *the red is fruity* or *mellow* – and pretended to agree with each other when you got tired. Perhaps – your brains became so different, that you would see beauty and cry, *"Isn't this such a gorgeous, yellow-coloured day?",* but all Dad could see was *grey* and *brown* and *black.* What you saw as sunshine, Dad saw as rain. Maybe it was something like that.

We'll never know.

My fingernails drum against the window until Josephine nudges me to stop. I can't stop fidgeting. Some small part of me clings onto the unspeakable hope. Of exactly what, or *who* I might find there. Under the fireworks. At 8pm.

The world outside slowly… gradually… comes to a *STOP*.

"Attention, passengers: we are experiencing some delays due to a breakdown between Waverton and Wollstonecraft. This train must remain at a standstill until further notice. We apologise for any inconvenience and thank you for your patience."

Amber murmuring echoes up and down the carriages. One gruff old man paces and straightens his tie. A teenager scrolls through her phone absentmindedly, ignoring everything outside her headphones. I glance at Josephine nervously. She doesn't seem concerned. A man in a suit is asleep near the end of the carriage, and I don't think he's even noticed the train has stopped, let alone that he's going to be late for any kind of meeting-

-Wait.

We're going to be late.

Josephine sees me looking at her watch.

"I'm sorry, little E, but-" she looks over her shoulder, then out the window, then straight at me. "It's five to eight now. There's no way we're going to make it in on time."

I fold my lips over one another, and furrow my brow.

"But there *has* to be a way."

Josephine sighs and gets out her phone, like my father does when he's avoiding conversation.

I scan the horizon with my nose against the window. The tiny houses have their tiny lights inside lit up, their tiny red brick roofs glowing under a navy sky, cooling embers under a blue flame.

I'm not interested in them. I want to see the *fireworks*.

I want to see my *mum*.

Big, black blotches boil and bubble as fireworks burn and burst. Out of sight. Off in the distance. My breath leaves foggy condensation on the glass around my face. I press myself closer and *closer* into the glass, but no matter how hard I stare at the view that is fast becoming blackness, I can't see a single firework.

There is no *mum* to be seen, either.

And all of a sudden, I stop wondering about Mum being yellow and Dad being grey. I stop feeling eleven, and I start feeling five.

"*You should have* CHECKED!" I point at Josephine. "We should have just *driven* in… " I don't want to say it, but it's in my throat, and if I open my mouth again I'll say it and I'll say it and…

"*It's YOUR FAULT!*"

(Too late.)

Josephine breathes in. Josephine breathes out. Josephine is very obvious about breathing in and breathing out.

"We can go in and see the fireworks *next week.* "

"But you don't *understand!*"

"What, Earnest?" she crosses her legs.

"What if *mum was going to be there?*"

Josephine becomes extremely still. I look away. She probably doesn't want me to see her cry. I wonder if she's upset for the same reason I am. I *can't* see the fireworks and I *can't* see my mother and I *can't* get out of this train, and-

"Come on over here, little E," Josephine beckons for me to sit closer. I ignore the warning about having to pay a fine if you put your feet on the seats, and I lie with my head in her lap. All the blueberry and scarlet feelings bubble and bleed out of me as I splutter and sob and let myself feel five-years-old.

~Green~

My forehead has been pressed against the black body of the piano for a good half hour. My eyes are puffy, and have licks of purple underneath. I've got guilty red blotches all over my skin from where I haven't even realised I've been scratching.

I miss you.

And I really want you to come home.

They say that when you're angry, or upset, or scared, one of the best things to do is to create something. Josephine always says art is about

an *overflow of personal expression* or something. My father says *artists should stop being self-indulgent and contribute to society.* I don't really know what that means. Besides, I like my mother's description better. She says it's about sharing something - leaning in close and saying *"Do you feel this way too?"*

"No, Earnest - try again, but a little more like this," Violet said.

The colour of her voice was a royal blue. A perfect A. The boy bit down hard on his lip, watching the colour grow and spin in the air.

She says music is not just for you, but more importantly for who you're sharing your music with. She says I can come to music whenever words won't explain how I feel. Whenever I need relief.

"Your turn. This time, imagine where in your body you're going to sense it before you start."

He screwed up his face, trying to mimic his mother's sound, but his own colour wobbled like hot air on a mid-January freeway.

I'm sorry.

I'm not explaining this very well at all.

"It's all right, Earnest - I know you're trying."

"I don't get it. How do you feel a note on your face? It doesn't work like that."

"It's difficult to explain."

I remove my head from the piano, making a hesitant effort to play.

(Couldn't you have at least come home for my birthday?)

(Would you, if I had said… *please?*)

I hate to think about it.

But I can't shake this *guilt,* which

hangs

heavily

in the air,

and

sticks

like toffee.

For all I know,

It could be *my fault* she left.

I leave the piano room and tiptoe down the corridor. I want to make warm milk with vanilla. Voices begin to rise, so I press my body against the wall at the end of the corridor, and listen. My father's voice is the colour of straw, but Josephine's is indigo. Like mine, and like Mum's.

The key to expert eavesdropping is to absolutely never get caught!

"You know, there are many, *many* ways you could be making this whole

situation a hell of a lot easier, Matthew."

"What do you *expect* me to do?"

"Something!" Josephine becomes increasingly exasperated. "You go to

work in the mornings. You come home at night. Not a word to Earnest, or

me either, for that matter. And then, what do you do? You collapse into that

couch, like, *I don't know,* like its *quicksand,* and watch TV, for *hours...*

Then you fall asleep, then get up and go to work again, and-"

"Do you think I *enjoy* carrying on like nothing ever happened,

driving through Sydney traffic just to-"

"You do next to *nothing* to help me. You should know I've got no

obligation to continue preparing food that you're not interested in eating-"

"You don't think I can turn on the radio in the car

in the morning without thinking of her? Any music *anywhere,*

I just want to shut it out-"

That sounds just like me. I feel something turn over in my stomach and I swallow.

"She was my *sister!"*

"She was my *wife!"*

But just remember, Earnest — you might not always like what you hear.

"You don't even realise you're missing the point, do you?" Josephine stops.

Painful pulses of purple begin to fill my vision, in the absence of their words.

"It doesn't *matter* what she was to us. She was Earnest's *mother.* Earnest is

your child! I went into school last week to find out if he'd been able to talk

with a teacher or a friend or *someone,* but-"

"Maybe, he doesn't say anything because he quite simply has *nothing* to-"

"You can't honestly believe that, can you?"

I hear the kitchen stool creak and groan as he sits up. He doesn't say a word.

"I'm just trying to do the type of things Violet would have done. She loved playing games with him. She loved suspense, and fun, and quests,

and stories, and… You know why was *so upset* that our train was delayed

and he couldn't see the fireworks? He thought my letters were from *Violet.*"

My letters?

My dad starts to raise his voice. It's turning red. I don't like the colour of it at all. I screw up my eyes and try my hardest to think of Mum instead.

'I can't help easily as I can when you play the piano. If the shape of your hands are wrong, or you're pressing too hard, we can both spot the error and make it better. But I can't see the shape of your voice."

Their colours begin to soar and tangle, like purple and red kites battling in the wind. I close my eyes again. But despite myself, I can't help but shuffle *further* down the corridor.

"Try again, but a little softer."

He likened his voice to a shopping trolley rattling down a hill on uneven gravel. Perhaps, he thought, he would be better off sticking to piano.

"I just didn't think Earnest would ever believe the letters were from his *mother!* All right?"

I pause.

"I'm just trying to *help*, and that's certainly more than *you're* doing, and if putting little notes in his funny shell makes him feel better, than-"

I sniffle.

My father looks up.

Josephine freezes, and turns around slowly.

"Oh, little E," she says. Her voice cracks. "How long have you been listening?"

"Long enough," I mumble to my toes.

"What did he say?" my father grumbled.

"I *said*, long *enough!*"

I unconsciously return to the piano room, closing the door ever so *quietly*. I can't figure out what - but something inside of me begins to numb over.

You used to tell me if I held a shell up to my ear, I'd be able to hear the ocean.

I start to feel sick. My stomach tightens, churning like a washing machine. My head begins to throb. My hands begin to grow cold. Clammy. Something becomes tight in my shoulders and neck. My chest draws tight, too, and suddenly I'm finding it harder to breathe. It's almost like I can feel the Earth turning beneath my feet, as it spins about the sun. It's as if time itself slows down. Walking through minutes becomes wading through water. Pushing against the current. Dragging my feet through the sand.

Did you ever feel like this, Mum?

Is this going to be forever?

Unthinkingly, I move towards Josephine's vase. I hold it above the corner of the table. I hesitate. I tighten my grip. At the last moment, I realise the glass is *cold*.

Bright sparks of rich turquoise and lemon flash across my vision. As soon as the smash stops ringing in my ears — oceans of *VioletVioletViolet!* cascade around me in the silence that follows.

And the on ly thi n g I ca n n o tic e i s h o w m y h a n d s

j u s t

t r e m b l e.

I turn to face my drawings on the wall around the piano. "THE SOUND OF BITING INTO AN APPLE". "THE SOUND OF JOSEPHINE'S CAT". "THE SOUND OF DAD'S HEARTBEAT". Looking for you inside these memories - it's like holding a shell up to my ear to hear the ocean. All I hear back is my own, confused blood rushing through my brain.

"Think about it like this — you've got to dive into the note, like diving into an ocean. When you come up afterwards… there is no feeling purer, more exhilarating! Like you've had saltwater rushing through your sinuses. Like the air you breathe is somehow cleaner."

I grip *"THE SOUND OF CONCH SHELLS"* in my hands. I feel the wooden frame splintering beneath my fingers. I close my eyes, and watch in bitter delight as *turquoise and lemon* spots pop out from the blackness. The broken wood and glass lie discarded on the floor. Hardly knowing myself, I reach for another. And another. And another.

And, then — Violet began to sing. Her tone seemed… smooth. Effortless. He imagined he could feel her blue ripples on his skin.

And then, my eyes rest upon my conch shell. I gingerly tip-toe through shards of glass, so I can hold that, too. I feel — how *easy* it would be, how *thin* and *fragile* the calcium feels between my fingertips — how I could make it

I raise it above my head, AND-

~Blue~

"I'm sorry, Earnest."

I pause.

"You're sorry?" I reply. "Aren't I getting into trouble?"

"No," she breathes. I watch as she looks from me, to the broken frames and torn-up drawings on the floor, to my father standing in the doorway.

You used to tell me we cried different tears for sadness and happiness.

I reach for the blanket hanging over the back of the chair and drag it over my head. I grab onto my shins, and slowly curl up into

a tiny little

ball.

I wish I could disappear.

I hear Josephine stepping across the floorboards. She carefully puts her arm around the sobbing mass of *Earnest-and-blue-blanket*.

(The blanket smells like Mum.)

"Shhhh…" Josephine says, holding me a little tighter as I begin to sob more heavily. She lifts the blanket off my head.

"God, he's beside himself," my father's words hang weightless, like an unanswered question.

Josephine gives him a tired look.

"I had so many plans for things we could do," Josephine begins. "I wanted

to give you some kind of distraction – we could both go out and have some

fun and just *forget…"*

I look up. Josephine's face is just as tear-stained as mine, only hers is painted black with mascara.

"You didn't have to pretend to be *Mum* just so we could leave the house," I say, probably unfairly.

"I wasn't *trying* to, Earnest… It was an accident. I didn't guess you would

think my letters were from her. I wanted it to be a game."

She hesitates for a moment, pulling something out of her dressing gown pocket.

"I understand if you don't want it anymore, but… I have one more for you."

SOUND

Dear Earnest,

Please find three tickets for you, your father, and your Aunt Josephine stapled on the back. They're for the Opera House. I hope you enjoy the music!

-Anon.

"I wasn't going to give this to you for a couple of days," she says.

"The tickets are for next week."

I can feel Dad watching on as Josephine grasps my hands in her own. Her nails are painted the same *"electric-blue"* as my favourite note – A natural.

(The sound of an orchestra tuning.)

"What do you say, little E? Do you want to come?"

I nod. I wish she could see the soft Violet which falls around her in tiny snowflakes.

~Indigo~

I hold onto Josephine's beaded black sleeve and we apologise profusely when people have to tuck in their knees to let us past. As we settle into our seats, I notice everyone is *coughing*. I sneak a glance over my shoulder at a gentleman in a tweed jacket, spluttering over his program. I cough guiltily into my hand as well – of course, I understand how important it is to cough before the music starts.

And then, before I know it…

I feel my heart *racing*…

The lights go

BLACK.

Everybody in the concert hall *hhhhuuuuuusssssssssssssssshhhhes.*

The orchestra is illuminated.

I feel my pulse leap into my throat as I hear

the oboe commencing the tuning.

A perfect A.

440Hz. BpraaaAAAAAAAAAA…

Shortly answered by a sweeping rush of the strings, brass, woodwind, timpani… until the whole hall is filled with the *electric-blue* of my *A, A, A, A, A.*

And then, the music begins.

~Violet~

The night is cool, but Josephine's hand is warm. She has to stop in the middle of the path so I can gape upwards at the sky. Imagine if somehow, you could wrap yourself up in a blanket of velvety blackness, and disappear under a tapestry of stars.

The longer I stare at the sky, the more stars I see.

You know, you were right.

Josephine goes on ahead, and stares out across the midnight harbour. Dad stands beside her, his coat flapping in the wind. Lemonade, crystal, and cobalt blue sounds swell gently in the corners of my vision. My ears are still ringing with the thunder and lightning of timpani and cymbal. For the first time in months, their colours are something beautiful to me.

Perhaps we won't ever know why you left, Mum. We won't know what happened, or how it happened – or at least, we won't find out soon. I'd like to think that it wasn't your choice, and that you're going to come home. I'll *always* hope you'll come home. I'll always wonder where you are, and what you can see and hear and touch and smell and taste. But-

"Earnest."

It's Dad. He's got a strange, old sort of smile on his face. The corners of his eyes are pinched together, and he's chewing his lip, like I do, so that means he isn't smiling because he's happy. Before I can decide if the new expression suits him or not, he puts his bag on the ground, and bends over to reach inside it.

It's my conch shell.

"Why don't you have a go at playing it?" he says.

"See if you can tell me what colour it is."

I look briefly between my shell, my Dad, and Josephine.

I blow into my shell.

(Carrots! Tangerines! Pumpkins! Powder blue!)

I grin, giving my shell to Josephine, and hugging Dad around the waist. But, in between the sounds of the sea, and the tomato-coloured car horns and the amber-coloured chatter of clumps of people, and the golden-coloured guitar from the busker on the corner... Still, there are Violet pockets of...

Silence.

The Final Adventure.

Graham Buckby
England

HIGH IN THE GREAT TOWER OF THE CASTLE, the maid, Sagana, carefully put down her embroidery, and rose to her feet from the comfortable cushioned chair beside the crackling log fire. She quietly crossed the vaulted, tapestry-bedecked chamber and, worried, peered at the figure in the bed.

Almost lost in the vast comfort of the bed, a lady was sleeping. She was old, very old, shrunken and wrinkled by age, surrounded by a halo of long white hair lit silver by the spring sun shining through the tall windows. Outside the windows the snows were receding up the distant mountains, and birds were singing of the coming of summer. Sagana peered closer. The old lady's eyelids were twitching slightly, as though she was about to arouse, or perhaps was dreaming.

Sagana glanced at the open windows and frowned. It would be best to close the windows, lest the bird song woke her mistress, she resolved. She tiptoed silently towards them.

~

The sun beat down on me. I was laying on my belly upon a crusted slab of rock, high above all else; and the world was laid out before me, an endless expanse of jagged stone hills, all lit sharply by sun and shade, and speckled with blotches of living green. In the distance the hills blurred gradually into haze, and the haze blended into the vast azure-blue bowl of the sky. And, in all of that emptiness, nothing moved. I could be alone in the world. I could smell my own sweat, and the warmed wool of my cloak beneath which I was sheltering, and even the heat of the rock. I could feel the welcome touch of the desert breeze upon my skin and my tunic and breeks; and I could feel the hardness of the rock pressing against the softness of my body.

And all of that made me ache inside, a most peculiar ache that combined unease, an empty yearning, and the stirring of pleasure.

Oh, I thought, *I am here again, outside Braglin.*

'Attria?'

Eeek! I jumped.

'Don't sneak up upon me so!' I complained.

He was squatting beside me, young and handsome, my childhood sweetheart, my first ever love; and my heart pounded and ached with the sweetest pleasure at seeing him again.

'Oh, Adrell,' I whispered, 'it has been so long. I am sorry I was not there at the end.'

Adrell looked rather guilty. 'My apologies, I am sure I should have relieved you a half hour or more since; but I think you were just daydreaming, not actually asleep.'

He reached out and touched my forehead.

'I fear you have overheated some. Best you get in the shade now. I will take the watch.' He pivoted his sword out of the way and lay himself down beside me. 'There is no sign of Falgarin's men pursuing us?'

Falgarin's men? 'But that was so long ago!'

'It does seem an age when we have spent the whole day kicking our heels,' he conceded. 'Now go and shade yourself with Thales.'

He didn't know we were dreaming then. I was glad of that, but I was less than confident about standing up. I had not been able to do that properly for a while now.

I scanned the scenery before me once more.

'Tis a strange and wonderful view,' I said, 'and this was my first foretaste of what Ryaduran philosophers call the sublime.' I sighed. 'Tis a shame I will never come here again.'

He smiled reassuringly at me, a most curiously confident smile. 'Do not be so sure of that, Attria.'

What?

There was a peculiar squeaking noise.

~

The window squealed as Sagana gently drew it shut.

'Please don't shut the window, Pascana, I like to hear the birds singing.'

Sagana froze. The old lady had woken and had turned her head slightly to gaze benignly at her. Sagana released the window, licked her lips, and steeled herself.

'As you wish, your Highness. Your pardon, your Highness, but it's me... Sagana. I fear my mother can't be here now.'

'Oh... no, of course not. Forgive me, Sagana, my memory plays tricks upon me, tis not what it used to be. And you do look so like her.' The old lady smiled. 'And like him... you know?' She giggled, a surprisingly youthful sound from so ancient a frame. 'Oh, what a terrible brigand he was!'

The old lady's smile faded, and a sadness crept over her face. 'I never had chance to say farewell to either of them, you know?' She paused, her expression vacant. 'Not to any of them. They have all gone now, all of them. I never even said good bye to my lord...'

A tear trickled down the old lady's face. Then her eyes slid shut.

Sagana hurried closer. The old lady's breathing was shallower now. She rushed to the door.

'Call the Crown Prince and the priest,' she commanded the guard, trying to control the tremor in her voice. 'Make haste! It's close now.'

Then she shut the door behind her. Her composure collapsed and she slid down the polished wood, weeping helplessly.

~

The high meadow was covered in a profusion of bright summer flowers which scented the air. Ahead of me the hounds ranged along the tree line, noses down, tails wagging. Beneath me was Kalla, not my first, adorable Kalla who had travelled the world with me, but the pretty little dapple mare, which my lord had hunted the length of his realm to find, and had gifted me in remembrance of her. We were out hunting in the mountains behind Farcastle! My heart fluttered with excitement, and I turned my head.

There he was, tall and confident astride his magnificent roan stallion "Rascal", my second true love, my soul mate, my lord and master, my prince. I ached with pleasure at seeing him again, and I agonised. Did he know we were dreaming? I opened my mouth to speak... *Eeek! One moment! If we are riding Kalla and Rascal, then...* I glanced down, checking. I breathed out. *Phew!* No slave chain.

He was watching me, smiling that little dry smile of his. 'Not much game today, my princess,' he observed, then smiled more broadly. 'Though I'll wager that will not trouble you overmuch?'

I smiled back. 'I love to eat it, my lord, but not to watch it die.'

He laughed. 'Truly you have the gentlest of natures and the purest of spirits.'

'No, my lord, tis you who has the gentlest of natures to put up with all of my failings,' I responded.

'And I would leave you behind, to comfort those gentlest of failings, save that you enjoy the riding so much,' he smiled softly, 'and that I enjoy every moment of your company so intensely.' He gazed lovingly at me, making me blush, then he looked around the awesome vista of forest-clad mountains with their rocky, snow-capped peaks. 'And you see the sublimity of the gods as clearly as the most devout of priests, even more clearly than I do...'

I looked, and yes, I saw it; and my heart ached with that special pleasure that is mine alone.

Then a dark thought broke that most perfect of spells. *But, in your sixty-eighth year you will go hunting without me one day, and will fall from your horse... Should I try to forewarn you?*

'...and that will surely be the last delight to fade,' he continued quietly, 'for when you can no longer ride out to see it, still you can dream of it.'

What? How could he foretell that?

'It cuts both ways, you know, my princess, my Attria? If you didn't say it, then neither did I.'

What? 'Your pardon, my lord? Say what?'

'Fare you well, my truest love, my only love...'

I stared at him and opened my mouth to speak. The distant view around us was blurring now. I could hear bird song, and someone weeping.

~

'Sagana,' the old lady whispered, 'stop your wailing, I pray you.' She had not much voice left now, she realised. 'Dry your tears. There is no cause for sadness, for I have had the longest of lives, and have seen the world, and have had many fine adventures, and I have known love...'

Her eyes flickered and closed again.

~

The wind ruffled my cropped hair. All around me there was naught to see... saving for an endless sea of tall grass ripening under an equally endless blue canopy of sky. There was not a solitary tree nor a rock to break the monotony.

Oh, I am here, again, upon The Ryaduran Road.

Ahead of me was the long line of four-horse wagons creeping through the eternal emptiness of the Central Grasslands toward the distant mountain princedoms of Ryadur. I listened avidly to the rhythmic creaking of the laden wagons, the steady clop, clop of the horses, the wind hissing in the grass, and glanced up at the sun blazing down from the vastness of the sky. I soaked it all in, revelling in being here, being me. I lifted my head, savouring the warmth of the sun upon my face, and my heart ached with pleasure. I felt the sun and the wind touching my brand, and that did not matter at all.

'You look happy, my love,' he said.

I turned my head. My heart stopped. There he was, walking beside me, smiling, my first true love.

'Oh, Thales, I love you so much...' I whispered.

Then I remembered, where... and what... I was. '...Learned Sir,' I added like a dutiful serving girl.

'What has brought this on?' he queried, looking a little bemused.

I agonised. I truly did not wish to break this dream, but... 'Naught, Learned Sir, save that I should not miss the chance this time around, I should say my farewell while I can.'

'You are only going scavenging for groundnuts, Tria!' he chided me.

Oh! So, like Adrell, he didn't know we were dreaming then! I was truly glad of that. I thought as quickly as my mind would still let me. I licked my lips.

'Lest I should be trampled by a malhorn,' I quipped.

Thales shook his head. 'Still it does not matter, for, even then, it is not truly farewell, my love. We shall meet again.'

What? I knew I was dreaming! He was not supposed to know this was a dream! Anyway, it was my poxy dream! *Er... Just one moment! You always claimed not to believe in any gods at all! Ha! I have you!*

'Aha! Then you accept that there is an afterlife!' I cried gleefully. 'Confess it, there are indeed gods!' My mind shifted track. 'I wonder if they serve eggy-fries?' I mused. *Oh, eek! I said that aloud, didn't I?*

Thales frowned. 'Not exactly gods, my love, though very close. They are immortal, I think, or nearly so. It is most enlightening to converse with them. They find us amusing, you know? It is all a game to them, and we are like dogs watching their masters playing chess. We can see the chess board, see them moving the pieces, but we can discern nothing of their purpose, nor of the conduct of the game. We watch for a brief while, then we lose interest and go to sleep. They carry on with their game. They were very pleased when we arrived, for they had become extremely bored by then. They had already been stuck here for an aeon, you know, with nothing more intelligent than malhorns and nerwolves for company?'

He fell silent, pondering upon that.

What? I thought. I pondered in turn.

'What do the gods look like?' I asked.

'They do not look like anything, and please do not call them "gods"!' he scolded me. 'Gods don't crash their... er... no, I do not believe you could actually call it a spaceship, not like Jason's...' He focused upon me once more. 'Now *you* they find particularly interesting!'

Once more the distant view began to fade. I could feel breath puffing hot upon my cheek. There was something urgent I had to say before I woke.

'You blow yourself up, you know?' I warned him.

'I know, but at least I went out with a bang.'

'Hey, I do the bad jo…'

~

Sagana was leaning close over the old lady when her eyes suddenly flicked open once more, making her jump.

'Boo!' the old lady gasped, grinned weakly, then smiled reflectively. 'I have said that before, you know...' Her brow furrowed. ''Tis just that I cannot remember exactly when.' She sighed. 'I used to have a passing good mind, you know, discovered secret... things...'

She studied Sagana with her watery eyes. 'There will be one more dream, I think, just the one more before I set out upon my final adventure. This one time I shall manage to say it.' Her eyelids flickered. 'Fare you well, my most faithful maid...'

Her voice tailed off into a sigh and her eyes closed.

Sagana laid herself across the body of her beloved mistress and wept with helpless abandon.

~

I awoke. I was floating in a black void. It was dark, truly dark. This was not the partial darkness of a closely shuttered chamber, but the formless, absolute blackness of that other place, the place between life and death, the place which the priest Kevran had called "The Otherworld". I had been here before... more than once, but this was the final time, I knew that.

Ah, so I have actually managed to die then? It was almost a relief. *It took long enough!*

I looked round. I did not have to call her this time, she was waiting for me, as she had promised so long ago; a willowy, blond-haired, teenaged girl wearing a long, embroidered gown in the fashion of a Bakkomite noblewoman. I looked down at my hands. They were still gnarled and wrinkled. I sighed. I suppose that is the price of such a fine long life. But still wearing my bed gown? For eternity? *Oh, pooh!* That truly was not fair!

'Hello, Nescia,' I said. 'I am sorry to have kept you waiting so long, but you were right, I did have much to accomplish.'

'Hello, Attria. It has not been so long a wait, a mere flicker of the eye in the passing of eternity. You think you have accomplished enough then?'

I smiled. 'I have been called a heretic, a whore, and a heroine. I have been a thief, a slave, a serving girl, and a princess. I have founded three dynasties. Is that not enough?' I smiled sadly. 'I fear I can accomplish naught more. I struggle even to stand now, and my hand is too poor even to write my own name.'

'But you are still a fine wordsmith, and the gods appreciate a really good tale.'

Oh... more pooh! Do I have to go through eternity retelling my own tale? To the gods? In my poxy bed gown? Tis not my idea of paradise!

I smiled ruefully. 'I thought in paradise I could be excused telling my own tale?'

Nescia smiled in return. 'But the best tales are worth retelling, Attria, and what better way is there of passing eternity?'

Now that was a disturbing thought! Eternity is a very long time... *Er... what do you do for that long? Even in paradise?*

Nescia was watching me benignly. 'Tell me,' she asked, 'before I lead you into the light, is there no other place you would first like to revisit?'

I thought hard. 'Oh, yes,' I said.

~

Dusk was falling, casting deep shadows across the narrow stone street. I found myself hesitating before the door of The Three Crowns, smoothing back my waist length cascade of raven hair and tugging my cloak around me over my best linen tunic and breeks to hold back the chill of the desert night while I nerved myself to enter...

Er... What? I stopped and inspected myself.

Hey! My hair is black again! And all the wrinkles have gone from my hands! And my fingers are not stiff any more! And no poxy bed gown! And I am walking!

I tried a little skip. Yes, my legs were definitely working as they had done seventy years ago. And my mind felt wonderfully sharp too, as though an imperfectly glazed window had been flung open to let me see the world properly.

Happiness coursed through me. So, my last dream was going to be the best of them all then! I bowed my head and gave thanks to the gods for their generosity, then the excitement overwhelmed me.

My hand trembled as it slid to the latch. My heart was truly racing now. Beyond this door were my companions of old, our original company of thieves, Adrell and Dorrak and Vordan and Thales! I was back at Singlehill, back to the very night when all of my adventures had begun. The exhilaration was so exquisitely intense that I wanted to cry my delight aloud, and to weep with joy... and both at the same time.

Very nervously, I entered the alehouse. The Three Crowns is a haunt of those who owe fealty to no particular guild, so, as I expected, I found the long, dingy, smoke-filled chamber full of rough and disreputable characters. What I was not expecting was to find three such characters at

Adrell's table. I was piqued by that. I had thought this to be some adventure for just the two of us...

Er... What? Why did I just think that? I knew they were here, who they are, what is going to happen...

Adrell beckoned me to join them, then turned to his companions.

'Allow me to introduce Attria, an old and trusted friend, and an essential part of our company.'

'Not so much of the "old",' I muttered under my breath as I studied the others. Dorrak I recognised.

'Good day, Attria,' said Dorrak, beaming happily at me.

'Good day, Dorrak,' I responded glumly.

Dorrak is long on strength and short of wit. The sort of "adventurings" that included Dorrak invariably went wrong... horribly wrong...

What? Why the pox am I thinking this? Tis so very good to see trusty old Dorrak again after so long...

'This is the Percussor Vordan.'

I smiled weakly at Vordan. Even if I had not known the meaning of his formal title, his long black cloak told me exactly what his craft was. Vordan was an assassin. His hook nose, cold, deep-set eyes, and swarthy complexion fitted the part over-well, and he made me feel horribly uncomfortable. He scowled darkly at me. I gulped and looked away. An assassin as well as Dorrak? That boded very ill indeed! Inside me something squirmed. The only reason I could think of for including an assassin in this scheme was that people were going to get killed; and that was not my idea of an "adventuring" at all. It was time to find a half decent excuse and take my leave, I resolved...

Just one moment! There is something very wrong here! This is exactly what I thought then, what I wrote down afterwards, all those years ago! Vordan is the most honourable and compassionate of men, and becomes such a good friend. Tis as though...

'This is Thales.'

Thales? I mused. I seemed to vaguely remember coming across that name in my scrivening, as the name of some minor Oldlore god or spirit or suchlike. *That is truly his name?* I doubted it.

"Thales" was different, a rather pleasant looking young man. He had the pale skin and long blond hair of a southerner, very different to the deep desert bloom and raven hair of us Singlehill born. His garb was nondescript and gave me no clue to his craft, but he had more the look of a poet than a warrior.

He smiled shyly at me. 'I am honoured to meet you, Attria.'

One moment! I already know him, and his craft... don't I? And Vordan...? But how the pox can I know an assassin and a thaumaturge? Er... and how do I know that Thales is a thaumaturge?

The last echoes of the old memories were dissolving now. A strange girl was saying to me: 'But the best tales are worth retelling.'

The truth dawned upon me. *Oh!* I thought. *OH!* My heart burst. *Oh, sweet pity, what a good game they play!*

Now I knew what paradise truly was!

Er... was someone playing a game?

I was poxed if I could remember.

~

Vordan was summing me up scathingly.

'I can't see what use a tart will be,' he stated coldly, addressing himself to Adrell.

'Tart yourself!' I snapped, reddening...

The beginning...

They Had Done It

Helen Jackson
England

A S I LOOKED AROUND, the trees engulfed me. It was almost like the forest had swallowed me whole.

"The trees are your friends!"

I could hear the commander's words ringing in my ears. I bet that's what their commander told them. The honest, brutal truth is that they are nobody's friends. In this sick game of brutal aggression they are simply an added obstacle assisting and hindering both sides equally. My vision was just a blur of green and brown blinding my judgement; my next enemy was likely waiting just inches away. A sharp snap broke the deafening silence that the forest isolated us all with. My head spun on my shoulders to face the direction of the noise. One thing was clear. Someone was behind me. Whether friend or foe, someone was following, and close.

I ran as fast as my feet would carry me, my heart pounding out of my chest with every beat. A sweet, bitter sting of sweat and blood tormented my tongue, repulsing me to my core. Twigs and branches slashed, ripped, and bit my face as I staggered through the infinite forest. Another snap echoed around me. Only this time closer. Despite my efforts to run they were catching up. My only option left was to hope, to pray to the heavens, that the trees favoured me in this forlorn situation. I swerved to the left behind a tall tree and stopped dead in my tracks. Large splutters of air poured and blundered out of my mouth, forcing my lips apart. I tried to slow my breathing, to be as silent as I could. I bit my lip so hard it bled, the warm metallic liquid filling my mouth. I remember this next part as if it were still happening this very moment. A hand slithered around the tree, crept up on me, and wrapped around my throat. Squeezing. Gripping. Crushing my air supply. I coughed and spluttered. With that, I saw him. He emerged from behind the tree and looked me dead in the eye.

His eyes were steel grey. They lay in his head cold, emotionless, and contained no sign of humanity. Like a blanket of snow his hair was pure white, and his face boasted a fresh wound. Blood seeped out and his skin had began to curl at the edge. Yet he showed not an ounce of pain. With his free hand he reached up and inspected my name tag, his other hand still firmly gripping my throat. Intrigue swept over his face. His grip loosened but didn't fully release me. He began to shout and scream in a language I didn't recognise yet his face lay perfectly still. The voice behind this man, if that's what you would call him, matched his eyes in every way. Cold. Emotionless. Dead. That is when I saw the wires spark beneath his wound. This was him. Their secret weapon. Shock paralysed my body.

They had done it; they had built a cyborg.

The Boy with the Red Hair

Henry Ohaegbulam
Nigeria

THE BOY HIMSELF WAS A SPECIMEN to be ogled at; black studs, long wavy red hair, partly hidden under a black beanie and slightly tanned skin. His face; probably the reason why I wasn't the only one staring, he looked like he could have been a movie star or a celebrity singer with those hazel eyes of his.

Samson Cameron scoffed before looking down at his paper. The boy started coming three weeks ago. Sam at some point spaced out because he hadn't noticed anyone sit down in front of him for a long time till a muscular hand waved in front of his face. Looking up slightly, he saw the boy with the red hair.

"You alright?" The boy asked in a hushed tone that was careful to avoid disturbing the awkward silence in the library.

"Fine," Sam said.

He nodded briskly and started to get up, then stopped and sat back down like he had forgotten something.

"Your name," he said.

"What?"

"What's your name?"

"Oh, I'm Sam, Samson Cameron."

"I'm Clarence," he said before getting up, grabbing his books off his table, and heading to check out.

***

Sam hadn't seen Clarence at the library the following weekend, so he ended up walking to the hostel alone. He stood in front of the mirror attached to the back of the door and watched his reflection. He was honestly just another face in the crowd; blonde hair, blue eyes, average height, small feet.

"Sam, open up," his African roommate, Guy Nyabiba, called from the corridor outside. He was two years older. Sam opened the door to see him and surprisingly, Clarence too.

"Do you have ten pounds?" Guy asked hurriedly.

Sam shook his head shyly and looked at the floor. Clarence's gaze was burning deep into him.

"You're not very helpful anymore. I'll be back, Clarence. You can stay with Sam if you want till I get back; warning, he's about as fun as a bundle of twigs," Guy said, heading towards the stairs at the end of the corridor.

"Depends on who's holding the twigs," Clarence called out to him just before he disappeared. Again, his gaze returned to Sam.

"Didn't know you were his little roomie," Clarence said, his voice rising.

"I didn't know you were his friend too," Sam replied, fell silent.

"I am constantly creating myself," Clarence said, breaking the silence after a while.

"What?"

"You were observing me in the library the other day, most likely thinking what I was doing there. I'm creating myself, reading."

"Why so?" Sam asked perplexedly. "Isn't the library meant for students' use?"

Clarence looked away quickly, and peered briefly at his cell phone that had just vibrated.

"See, Sam, when you read a good book, it reflects on you, teaches you lessons. You get what I mean?" he paused, walked to the window, and peeped out. "What's the point of living if you don't leave behind anything extraordinary. You have to live and not just survive."

Sam didn't understand this explanation. He didn't even see how it came into the conversation; he just nodded and narrowed his eyes like he understood the idea. Then they sat and stared at one another until Clarence grabbed his phone and began typing in his contact information, and then handed it back to Sam.

"I gotta go. Tell your roomie I'd see him later," he said.

"Okay, I'll... text you?" Sam asked, staring at his phone with Clarence's number on it.

"I'd rather hear your voice than read your text," he said before hurriedly walking towards the door while still peering at his cell phone.

Sam was sitting in front of his desk, scribbling dreamily in what seemed to be his diary. He had just finished talking to Clarence who claimed he had to attend an important class even though it was a Saturday. Classes were hardly ever held on weekends. His eyes were narrow as his lips moved slowly to the rhythmic dance of his pen. He was writing about his crush, Clarence Price, the new student, if he was even a student. About the times they spent together touring London and admiring the old beauty of Buckingham Palace, the kisses, the romantic moments they shared, the summer nights they stayed out late gazing at the stars from the balcony, and discussing their future after Presley College. Now, these things never really happened, or perhaps they did, but only in Sam's introverted mind.

Sam first noticed his attraction to the other boys at age nine in Leeds where his family lived, but never did he take those queer feelings serious until after his thirteenth birthday and his glands began to break loose. Sam confirmed his sexuality after he began to read newspaper articles on same sex relationships and gay marriages. Still, he wasn't comfortable and was careful never to display any signs that could tell on him, but he couldn't control the situation whenever his mates, suspecting nothing, took off their clothes or unzipped their pants to pee.

The door flung open and Guy rushed in with a large, paper bag, the kind that usually contained borrowed books from the library.

"Hullo," he greeted, his black face dripped with sweat.

"What's in the bag?" Sam asked nervously as he closed his diary and placed it on his lap.

"Just groceries and a few clothes."

Sam watched as Guy emptied the bag on his bed and some packs of red meat fell out.

"Where did you get those?" Sam asked, pointing at the meat.

"Borough Market, of course."

"You know the rules," Sam said picking up the meat and placing it inside the mini refrigerator on which another large mirror was placed. "Did you sneak out again?"

Guy scurried over to Sam. "Shhh!" he hissed. "I know it's forbidden to eat meat here but I'm not a veggie!"

"You know the rules," Sam repeated, "you could get suspended."

"They'd never find out," Guy scoffed, "but since it's here already, you can as well join the feast."

"Savage!" Sam frowned. "You talk as if you don't know that I'm veggie."

"Presley is just one old dump, too bad I got accepted by the strictest Christian school in Great Britain," Guy complained "It's like saying Jesus never ate meat but He did on several occasions and I know He still does in heaven."

"That's not funny," Sam pointed out.

"It wasn't a joke."

Guy bent over to take out the other contents of his bag; a bunch of bananas, some noodle packs, tomatoes, a pair of ripped jeans, and some tank tops. He faced the mirror and began to unfasten his belt, afterwards, he removed his shirt and trousers, bare except for his red underwear. He faced Sam and noticed that he was observing him closely.

"What?" he asked, puzzled.

"Nothing," Sam sighed, his eyes wandering from Guy's face to his crotch and back. "You haven't shaved?"

"Too busy," Guy said. "I hardly have the time these days." He raised his hands up. "At least I did my armpits last weekend."

"You shouldn't be too busy for personal hygiene."

"Who cares about my grooming choices?" Guy smiled. "I can do anything I want to do here, and that's why it's called private."

They both laughed at the joke while Guy began to try on his new clothes. Sam watched keenly. His hormones were beginning to move.

Stylishly, he picked up a Presley Times Newspaper from the desk and placed it with the diary on his lap.

* * *

The weather was unusually very cold and everyone wore thick clothes even though it wasn't winter. Sam's was a blue and white striped turtle-neck sweatshirt. That morning, he had woken up to the sound of Clarence's soft knock on the door. Guy himself had slept out and his bed was empty.

Lazily, Sam left his bed and staggered to the door, expecting to see Guy but instead, Clarence stood there grinning. He said he was bored and needed some company. Sam had suggested seeing some new horror movies he had but Clarence insisted on them driving to the coffee shop for breakfast, as he had brought his vehicle. Sam didn't object, in fact, he secretly welcomed the idea of free breakfast. He hurried to the bathroom and in a few minutes, he was out, wearing a T-shirt and a pair of white shorts.

"It's pretty cold outside today," Clarence had warned. "I wouldn't wear that if I were you."

Clarence himself was dressed in purple overalls; beneath was a brown shirt, and round his neck was a Presley baseball scarf.

The duo were having doughnuts and milkshake at the coffee shop while they joked and gossiped about teachers. It wasn't a boring moment as Clarence seemed to have so many humorous jokes that made Sam laugh so hard until he spotted Anil Joni Mitchell from a distance. He was sitting alone at the far corner. Anil never sat alone. When he did, it meant trouble; his eyes were constantly fixed on them. He wasn't eating or drinking, only watching keenly like he was learning the basics of some modern experiment.

Sam felt nervous from his gaze. Anil had never liked Sam though he often visited the room to see Guy, who wasn't much of his friend either. On several occasions, Sam had caught Anil trying to read Sam's diary, which he thought contained the secrets to Sam's successful science essays.

"Let's leave, please?" Sam whispered.

"Why?" Clarence asked between mouthfuls. "I'm enjoying your company."

"Same here but I just want to leave."

"To my apartment, then?"

"Anywhere but here."

Sam got up and Clarence followed. They walked to the parking lot where Clarence's truck was parked; nothing fancy, just a white, two-door truck. Not the one that was unnecessarily large or small but somewhere in between. They got in, and Clarence started it up and drove off. At the main gate, Sam looked out for Anil but he wasn't there anymore. *Loser!* he thought.

While they drove, Clarence asked Sam about his family.

"They're not very supportive," Sam said.

"How can you say that?" Clarence asked, "After they have sponsored you this far at Presley."

"I do not mean monetary."

"What then?"

Sam meant his sexuality but he wasn't so sure if he was ready to disclose that to Clarence or anyone else.

"They treat me like I'm not a part of them."

"Well, I must say your family is better."

"What?"

"Mine threw me out when I got involved with marijuana," Clarence said, and laughed silently.

"You smoke that!" Sam exclaimed.

"Not anymore though."

"When did you get out of rehab?"

"No, I didn't need rehab."

"I learned it's very difficult to break drug addiction except after going through rehab."

Sam had wanted to ask how easily Clarence had learned to quit smoking marijuana but at that moment, the truck made an abrupt halt. He looked around and realised they were in an unfamiliar lot. Moist leaves and twigs littered the ground and dusty park benches stood here and there. Wild plants had grown all over them in spooky spirals. Not far from the truck was a clear, small pond that ran slowly into the bushes.

"It's running to River Thames." Clarence laughed as he stepped out of the truck, walked to the pond, and began to douse his face. "Lend me your handkerchief," he spat after raising up his head.

"What's this place?" Sam queried as he passed his white handkerchief to him, but there he stood with a smile, wiping his dripping face and hair.

"Ready for an adventure?" he asked, passing back the handkerchief.

"Where are we going?"

"To some place where no one knows our names."

"What do you mean?" Sam looked around. "There's no life here!"

"Exactly that; to go somewhere where no one is, to have some privacy," Clarence said, and began to lead the way through, a smile spreading across his face.

Sam couldn't help but stare. Clarence smiled so much so he decided to study him. The more he looked, the less real his smile seemed, and the more dead his eyes appeared.

"What is it?" he asked, looking at Sam through the corner of his eye.

"You smile a lot."

Clarence's face fell, turning into a void that was dark, dry, and sad. His eyes focused completely on the road, and then he began to scratch his red hair.

"Yeah, I know," he muttered, his voice almost inaudible and cracked. He cleared his throat. "I just want to show you where it all began."

"Where what began?" Sam asked curiously.

* * *

As soon as Sam got home almost four hours later, he went up to Guy who was working on his PC.

"Tell me all you know about Clarence," he demanded.

"Clarence? Well, he's complicated. It's not really my place to tell you. It's his, but Sam," Guy explained, "he's sad; he is in fact, miserable."

A heavy sigh escaped Sam's lungs and slowly, he turned and made his way back to his bed. He tossed and turned, lost in thought, then he took out his handkerchief, the one Clarence had used earlier. It was slightly stained, like someone had tried to clean up a rusty surface, but looked more like red dye. *Who is he?* he thought.

The next morning came quickly and just as planned, Sam had to run over to class. He hadn't thought of meeting Clarence after what happened yesterday but he watched out for every redhead he saw, just to make sure. In class, Anil himself had already taken his position and was working on his iPad when Sam got into the room.

The prickly silence sickened him; everyone was doing something that kept them busy and consequently quiet. He walked to his seat and checked the time; twenty-four minutes more and the lecture would begin. Just as he let up his eyes, he saw Anil standing in front of his desk and peering down at him. That wicked smile slowly darkened up his face.

"Where's your friend?" Anil scowled.

"Who?"

"Your new friend, Mr. Red Hair," he joked.

"He's not my friend."

"Oh!" Anil jeered. "He's your lover then?"

Sam looked quite nervous as he made a cross face at Anil.

"I'm not gay," he managed to say, "and if I am, I don't think Clarence would go out with me. That would be a bad idea."

"You're right; I don't think going out with your traitor is a good idea."

"I don't understand," Sam said uneasily.

"Clarence is a robot, my robot."

"I don't understand," Sam repeated.

"Come," Anil said. "I'll show you,"

He grabbed Sam's arm and led him quickly, past the classrooms and the library into the locker room and then, into the bathroom.

"Why did you bring me here?" Sam asked confusedly.

"To reach a reasonable agreement with you," Anil said, and began to scroll through his iPad while Sam just stood still like a scarecrow and observed.

"Look at this," Anil announced after a while, and handed over the iPad to Sam.

"Oh, my God!" Sam exclaimed.

"You know what that is?" Anil mocked.

"Yes," Sam stammered shivery, "it's my… um… my diary."

"And you think writing fantasies about boys is a good idea, right?"

Anil suddenly got serious.

Sam was speechless; his heart raced as he thought hard about how Anil could have possibly got scanned copies of the pages of his diary. It hadn't been missing for a moment, as he remembered writing in it last night before bed.

"Surprised, aren't you?"

Sam nodded sheepishly.

"Well," Anil explained, "you don't believe Clarence would do this to you ,right?"

Sam's head ached, and he suddenly felt weak. He bent down and leaned on the tiles as a tear escaped from his left eye.

"I thought you were keeping some interesting stuff in that diary of yours, you know, passing all the courses with no carryovers, so I hired him to find out."

"Hired Clarence?" Sam was doubtful; Clarence had seemed too real, too good to have been hired.

"I paid him to get me your diary but you never took a break from it, so we came up with a new plan," Anil explained. "He stole the keys from your satchel, then I sneaked into your room while you two were having fun at the Old Pilgrims' Park."

Sam was puzzled. "You know about that too?"

"Yes," Anil smiled mischievously. "Clarence tells me everything. I thought you said being lovers wasn't a good idea but you allowed him to do that with you. Now you're not only a liar but also a sodomite."

Anil laughed so hard his ribs twitched.

"Anil please," Sam begged as he got up from the tiled floor, "buggery has a penalty of expulsion here; please keep my secret and I'll do anything you say."

At this, Anil's eyes widened. "Anything I say!" he exclaimed.

"Anything, I promise."

"Be my lover then," Anil said and turned his face away, obviously waiting for a positive answer.

"That's not possible," Sam said in utter disbelief. He moved closer. "Are you gay?"

"Bisexual."

"Wow, I didn't know."

A new excitement descended after hearing this news. Sam seemed to have forgotten the situation he was in.

"Happy to hear that?" Anil asked, suddenly becoming friendly.

"Uh... perhaps," Sam replied timidly.

"I've been up against you because I liked you," Anil said, opened up.

"Seriously?" Sam asked.

"Yes."

"You have a funny way of showing love."

Anil smiled and stopped when he noticed Sam staring awkwardly.

"I know that stare," he said.

Sam had never imagined Anil Joni Mitchell to be so nice, he had known him over two years but never had he seen that friendly smile he was looking at. Steadily, his introverted mind gave way as he moved closer and closer towards him until Anil's back brushed against the wall.

"Do you think so?" Anil asked timidly.

"Perhaps," Sam replied in the same manner.

Slowly, Anil spread his right hand around Sam and gently caressed his neck with the left. Then he raised Sam's head slightly and their lips met. Anil couldn't remember if it had ever been longer.

"It's my longest," he said when they finally let each other go.

"I liked it," Sam shyly admitted.

He went closer and reached up to have a second round of the tongue wrestling but barely three seconds after their lips met, the door burst open.

Sam looked up sharply; his heart skipped a beat.

"Jeez!" Anil exclaimed and hurriedly stepped aside for Robert Clark, the senior prefect, and his assistant, Elvis Mbuya, to come in. They were obviously shocked to their bones.

"We saw you pulling him all the way and so decided to follow," Robert said, gesturing agitatedly. "Sorry if we ruined the fun."

"How long has this been going on?" Elvis demanded.

He was looking at Sam. It seemed like they had arrived too late to have heard the earlier conversation.

Sam was speechless. He looked at Anil, whom he had expected to be braver, but was shivering even more.

"Please, Rob, Elvis," Sam begged. "It's actually the first time."

"And undeniably your last within Presley," Robert said.

"Please be kind," Anil said, shivering.

"Homosexuality is not welcome in this school; you know it."

"You'd have to beg the administration," Elvis said regretfully, like there was nothing they could do to save the situation.

"That's true," Robert confirmed in the same tone.

* * *

It was a cool summer afternoon and Sam had just left the counsellor's office. He and Anil had been advised to go through the traditional one-week psychotherapy procedure that was mandatory in Presley after students committed such offences. Unfortunately, theirs was the first offence of its kind, and the counsellor wasn't qualified to handle homosexual teenagers. Sam's parents had already booked his flight back to Leeds and the press club had published the news of the two boys expelled for snogging in the bathroom. They had never been more excited about releasing an issue of the Presley Times Newspaper; news like that sold the most. Anil himself had left campus the day before without saying a word. Guy was still very mad; not so much about the cause or Sam's depraved crime, but about Sam's expulsion.

Sam came into the room and looked around; it seemed like a dream that he would have to give up his education at the prestigious Presley College; the same education that his parents had spent thousands of pounds on. He sobbed as he began to pack his bags. His flight was scheduled in four hours and he had to get to Gatwick on time. A soft knock on the door startled him; he had almost forgotten that there were still more people living in the world.

"Come in," he said, quickly wiping his eyes with the yellow socks he was about to put in the bag.

The visitor hesitated for a while before turning the knob and pushing the door open It was Clarence, but not exactly the same Clarence Sam had known; it was a new version of the old one; dark hair, straight, and pulled back. There were no waves anymore, no black studs, no tanned skin, no brown contact lenses.

"Hello," he said, still hesitating at the door, probably scared of an angry blow from Sam if he came any closer.

It was the first time they were meeting since after the incident at the Old Pilgrims' Park.

"Hey," Sam said, still shocked by the changes.

It seemed like Clarence was now a total stranger; he looked so different. Clarence himself wasn't surprised; he wasn't expecting a warm welcome.

"I'm sorry that you have to leave," he said, gradually approaching.

"Don't be," Sam replied, trying hard to hold back the tears, "it wasn't your fault."

"I liked you as a person but what happened in the park wasn't part of the plan."

"It's okay," Sam insisted. "I have to leave now; I've got a flight to catch."

"Can I drive you?"

"No thanks," Sam managed a smile. "You've done enough damage already."

"I thought you said it wasn't my fault?"

"It was in some ways; not entirely though."

"So who else is to be blamed, Anil?"

"No, me."

"You?" Clarence asked "But how?"

"I trusted you too much. That was my mistake and I regret that."

Clarence looked sorrowful. "Sam, I'm sorry, I needed the money Anil offered and it wasn't anybody's intention for this to happen." He waved towards the bag. "But it happened anyway, and worse still, everyone knows who I am now, even my family."

Sam couldn't hold it anymore. He began to sob.

Finally, after the sobbing and the comforting and the pleading, Sam left for the airport in Clarence's truck. He recalled the last time he was in that truck; if only that day would return, then he could have been able to avoid the disaster right then. He had never imagined flying back to Leeds so soon; he had two more years to spend at Presley, two more years of fun and education. Worse still, his dad wasn't very liberal when it came to homosexuality. What if he never even bothered about an education for him? Sam could remember hearing his father condemning homosexual people whenever he read about them in the daily papers or when one strolled into his delicatessen to eat. He had so much disdain for them, yet inadvertently, what he hated fell hard upon him.

Hours later, while in the air, a hostess came up to Sam with her trolley and handed him the menu card. It didn't seem like he could ever regain his appetite again, but he had heard that people who rejected food on the plane were drug couriers who didn't have extra space in their stomachs to accommodate food. He wasn't so sure if this was true but he decided to eat something, just in case it was. He peered into the trolley and his stomach tightened.

"Lacto-ovo-vegetarian meal, please," he said to the hostess.

"Euh… I'll see wat we'ave left for yiu, Son," she said with a gentle French accent before hurriedly leaving for the first class cabin. Sam hoped she didn't find any vegetarian food and would return to say, *"Sorry, Son, zis is all zere eez,"* but rather, she returned with a medium-sized plate of squash soup and whole grain bread, *"Oui! Tomato or vegeetaybul jiuz?"* she asked.

"That, please," Sam replied pointing at the tomato juice.

He managed a few bites and soon began to doze.

He sprang up as soon as the pilot announced the landing, and when the plane touched the ground, he disembarked. After checking out, he walked to the parking lot where Walter Mann was waiting for him. Walter was his family's chauffeur. His father must have been very mad, as when Sam returned from past trips, his father had always made it his joyous duty to pick him up from the airport himself. Sam wished Walter hadn't heard about his expulsion and everything else that had happened in London, but he already had. While they drove home, he began his one of his boring sermons, occasionally stretching his skinny old neck to peer into the rearview mirror.

The car finally reached Mutton Drive. Everything was still the same, just like it had been the last time Sam had visited. The streets were still clean with beautiful white and cream coloured buildings. Very few of them had gates. The only thing that had changed was the different atmosphere in Leeds. Sam knew something else wasn't quite right, and it had nothing to do with what had happened in Presley.

The first person he met was Audrey, his older sister, who had just graduated from an American college. She was holding a white, unfamiliar, miniature dog. She seemed happy, emotional, and almost tearful when she saw Sam approaching; no doubt confused and surprised that the brother she had grown up with was gay. Before Sam reached her, she looked away and hurriedly walked into the garage.

In the living room, his mother lay quietly dozing in the corner while his father sat on the sofa. He was holding some brown documents. On his lap was an old, bulky envelope. Sam recognised it. It was the same envelope that contained birth certificates and other documents that his father thought were too confidential or irreplaceable to be kept just anywhere. He wore his white-framed glasses and peered at one of the birth certificates - Sam's.

"Hello, Dad," Sam managed to say, obviously not expecting a reply or even any form of acknowledgment, but shockingly, he did.

"Hello, Son," his father said, and waved at the chair opposite him.

Sam felt dizzy. His father had never been one open discussions. His eyes roamed to where his mum sat, legs crossed, sleeping peacefully. It was as though nothing extraordinary had happened, as if he had just returned to Leeds for a short school break, and she hadn't received the shocking news of her son being gay.

During his past visits, she had always welcomed him with the best homemade vegetarian dishes, much better than those from the British Airways and Presley College kitchens put together. He couldn't focus; everyone was acting strange and he couldn't imagine why.

He sat down and sighed regretfully. "I'm sorry, Dad," he said.

"Being sorry doesn't change anything; you're still going to be homosexual." His father shook his head. "You've been expelled from Presley. Being sorry doesn't change that."

"I know, Dad," Sam paused and sighed again. "I was set up."

Mr. Cameron stared hard into his son's face. "I want you to have this, Sam," he said, and handed him an old sheet of paper. Its four edges were dog-eared with folded marks here and there. Sam stared at the paper, and back into his father's face.

"Read it," his father whispered.

Sam bent his head and began to read the fading letters. While reading, his heart raced, and then he discovered that he could read no more for tears filled his eyes. He raised his face and faced his father. He had never seen him look so sad; his eyes were filled with tears too.

"Tell me it's not true, Dad," Sam sobbed.

"I'm sorry Sam, but it is."

Sam buried his face in his hands and began to sob hard.

"We should've told you since," his father said, looking looked towards his wife who had just stirred awake, probably from the sound of Sam's sobs.

She approached them, and when she reached Sam, she took the old letter from his hand and frowned.

"We talked about this!" she exclaimed before hitting her husband on the shoulder.

"I'm sorry, but he needed to be told the truth," he said.

"But why now?" she asked. "He's going through so much already. Why did you have to tell him now?"

"I'm sorry," Mr. Cameron repeated, "someone had to tell him."

"You're so evil!" Mrs. Cameron screamed. "You're telling him now because of his mistake, right?" She bent over and held Sam tight. "I'm so sorry, Son," she said. "Its God's will for all these to be happening."

"Is it true, Mum?" Sam asked tearfully, his face flushed. "Was I really adopted?"

"I'm sorry, Sam. You'll remain the only son of the Camerons for as long as you live."

She was crying too.

* * *

In the train, Sam tried to remember what growing up was like. He had been the vibrant, young, and adored only son of Mr. and Mrs. Cameron. His aunts and uncles too had been very nice to him, always tugging at his rosy cheeks whenever they came visiting. Sometimes, Uncle William and Aunt Adriana brought him homemade cookies and pear juice from their small shop, and by the afternoon, they would all gather round the large dining table in the kitchen and eat lunch together. He could recall once, when granny Louis made everyone upset by calling to say that she wouldn't make it to dinner because she had gone out on a date with her dentist.

Uncle Jake, granny's last child, had joked about how bad it would be if granny made him an older brother. But granny's joke came to an end after the doorbell rang and she showed up holding a freaky, large pizza, 'generation sized', like Mum had jokingly said. Granny had been delayed because she had to wait to monitor the chefs while they made the pizza to her specifications.

Sam smiled at those memories. He had grown up thinking they were all family, his older sister, Audrey, had been avoiding his eyes since he arrived. Perhaps she too was feeling the shock, but Sam wasn't so sure if he could identify why she was shocked; his sexuality, the expulsion letter, or his adoption. He had made plans with his mother to visit St. Gregory's Orphanage in Manchester. At first, she had been reluctant to approve of his decision to find his biological family, but his adamance left her no choice. He copied the address from the letter his father had left with him and looked forward to the trip. He hoped he would at least find someone related to him, maybe an aunt or grandmother who would make him feel at home again.

On the train ride, he visualised himself beside his father in his car, on the road from the airport, discussing his needs for the next academic session. Then he recalled his mother's vegetarian delicacies; he almost smelled the food right from the streets as they drove. Sam was depressed; those discussions would never happen again, and worse still, he would miss his mum's food. Somehow he thought he would have remained the timid, normal boy in Presley College, living with his ridiculously defiant black roomie, Guy. In fact, he thought his father wouldn't have exposed the secret, if only he had never met or trusted Clarence, the boy with the red hair.

Three and One Seventh

Hugh Riches
England

THE HOUSE LIGHTS WENT DOWN in a packed theatre. The audience fell silent as the curtain rose to reveal a parabola of mirrors behind the proscenium. Each pane reflected the light of a magnesium flare in the pane opposite. The front row was dazzled, squinting to see a dull figure step to the centre of the glare.

"Ladies and gentlemen," said Nicholas Droste in his silken voice, "behold the greatest wonder on Earth, the apogee of arithmetic, the genius of geometry, the apex of algebra."

The crowd well knew what they had come to see. Some had travelled hundreds of miles. Nobody doubted the scale of the spectacle.

"Put your hands together for a man you will never forget, a man of incredible proportion, a man of phenomenal recollection."

A young lady on the third row screamed her delight. An old gentleman in the balcony knew, smiled on a life now content.

Nicholas was almost singing, extending the syllables, shouting to the gallery.

"Welcome, if you will, Marcellus Mercator, Master of Memory."

A spherical man in a round brimmed hat strode on as Nicholas slipped backstage. He turned to the audience and asked: "What do you want?"

His loving fans inhaled as one and simultaneously screamed their answer.

"Pi," they yelled. "We want Pi."

"What do you want?"

"Pi."

"You want Pi?"

"Give us Pi."

"You really want the circumference?"

"As ratio to the diameter."

"The true ratio?"

"Give it to us."

"How much Pi?"

"All of it. We want it all. Give us the whole thing."

Marcellus Mercator signalled for silence. He lowered his head in contemplation. When he looked up he appeared to his loving fans a man transported, beatified by the glory of his knowledge.

The ice cream girl in the aisle felt the vibrations of the cheers. The ticket seller in the foyer booth pulled down the shutter against the roar. A silver snake on the theatre steps was irritated by the noise as it scared off her prey.

"You want it all?" asked Marcellus. "You want the whole thing?"

"The whole thing," came the tumultuous reply followed by a silken voice from the stalls: "And don't leave anything out. I'll be checking."

"We have plenty of time," said Marcellus, "but what sort of show would it be if I don't leave you wanting more?"

The voice from the stalls spoke up silkily. "We've paid our money. We want a million decimal places."

A rhythmic chant filled the room. "One million decimal places. One million decimal places."

In the wings, a police inspector sighed and told his sergeant to put the emergency services on red alert.

"Very well," said Marcellus, "if you will be satisfied with a million decimal places I shall do my best to please you. I promise to give you Pi to one million decimal places."

The theatre fell quiet. The sudden silence startled the ticket seller as she unpacked her sandwiches. The snake snoozed in the corner of the steps. Nicholas Droste crept from the stalls and reviewed the ticket sales, happy to be rich, worried, as ever, about the stamina of his friend.

Marcellus drew a deep breath. He was proud of his timing so he paused to notice the plaster peeling from the balustrade of the royal circle and the tear in the velvet of seat 1F.

The audience was tense, eager, adoring their idol as he gathered his strength for the challenge to come. Seconds stretched to minutes before Marcellus began. Breaking the enchantment, he spoke.

"Three."

Some gasped, others cheered. After a few seconds they all rose in applause.

Marcellus hesitated, enjoying the adulation.

"Point."

Lovers clasped each other as if for the first time. The snake heard the clamour and noticed the moonlight on a tastily twitching morsel.

"One."

Old enemies shook hands. The ice cream girl stepped smartly from the fall of a fainting man.

"Four."

A lady in the royal circle had an unnoticed stroke. A boy in the seventeenth row disgraced himself.

Marcellus picked up speed for an arpeggio of ratio.

"One. Five. Nine."

Coiled and confused by the noise, the snake tried to focus on the flickering silver in the corner of her eye.

For three days and one seventh of a day Marcellus Mercator recited Pi. His pace varied with his voice, pianissimo and allegro, forte and crescendo. He felt the pulse of his listeners. They shared their mood. He manipulated the joy and fascination. They wept and swooned. He comforted and excited, calmed and elated. They swayed to the beat of the number.

He welcomed participation, gesturing for them to join in the more famous sequences. He knew their favourite digits and lingered over the popular places. He waited for ovations after the best known runs. They stopped him for six minutes after the third line of nines on the second day.

As they reacted, he responded. As he responded, they reacted.

On the step, the snake was dazed by the cheers and the roaring. She made an effort to lunge for the silver flesh. As her fangs moved forward, the shiny skin moved back. *Clever beast*, she thought, tantalised, trying to shake the echoes from her ears.

The inspector and his men worked through six shifts on stolen sleep. Lorries brought food for the enraptured listeners. Tankers brought beer and wine. Ambulances were called to tend victims of exhaustion or euphoria. Some cases were more serious.

The audience suffered three deaths, one tragically young but expected, one unexpected, and one expected but not by the person who died. Numbers remained constant after three births, two expected.

Other than the recently dead and the freshly born, the audience fell in love once more with the Pi of Marcellus Mercator.

"He's the only one for me," said a man to his wife, "I just don't believe in it unless I hear it from Marcellus."

Three hours and twenty-four minutes into the fourth day the millionth decimal place was spoken. The Master of Memory had stepped into the focus of the parabola, blocking each mirror's reflection of its partners. The stage was darkened by his image. Every pane bore a slanting file of spherical men in round hats.

Marcellus slowed for the last twenty integers as if regretful to depart the number. He wasn't. He was exhausted, looking forward to food and drink and rest, but he knew what his people wanted. Before the last word, he waited. The crowd stood, silent, transfixed, mesmerised.

"One."

The ice cream girl was already hiding beneath the stage. The ticket seller clapped on her earphones.

The snake on the step struck at silver prey. Her venom worked fast, tranquillising, a local anaesthetic. Her eyes closed as she swallowed, her long throat swollen by the size of her tail.

Nicholas Droste walked into the bar with a smile on his face and a bag full of money.

"A good gig, Marcellus," he said silkily, pouring himself a drink. "A full house, mostly old regulars. These people can't get enough. They'll come forever. Have you recovered?"

"I'm rested, refreshed, and ready for more."

Marcellus rolled off his chair towards the bar. He was designed to roll.

"Why do they come?"

"To hear something true, old friend. No where else can they be sure of hearing a truth."

"But not the whole truth."

"You speak for more than three days, Marcellus. Nobody has time for the whole truth."

Marcellus picked up his hat and idly drew a finger across the brim.

"I'm a little bored of it. The same number every time. It was comforting at first but I'm tired of Pi to the millionth decimal place. I could do with a challenge."

Nicholas sipped his drink. He did not relish a bored master of memory. "I like Pi. It's a good round number."

"I could try another number," said Marcellus.

"A bigger number?"

"Can you think of one?"

The two men sat in silence, Marcellus searching for ideas, Nicholas counting the seconds.

"We could adapt Pi for the next show," said Nicholas.

"Yes?"

"Instead of a million decimal places, how about a million and one?"

"That's brilliant," said Marcellus, "but what do we do after that?"

When the Madonna Returned to San Veronica

Ingvar Hellsing Lundqvist
Denmark
Translated by Anders Bellis

THAT THE LOOSE-LEAF BINDER did not immediately see the light of day was due to something as trivial as the key to a drawer in a chest of drawers not being found straight away. Thus, it was not until much later that a bundle of documents was found among the things she'd left behind. Most of them contained ideas, drafts for speeches, plans, and other kinds of outlines. But one of them was a prayer to the Madonna. The paper was folded in four equal parts and the text was not printed out like the others, but written by hand.

"Holy Mother of God, your spirit suffuses me. Each and every night, I hear your voice. I am small and weak. I need your strength and wisdom. Let me walk towards an eternal dawn.

Teach my hands and my mind to preserve what you have created. And sharpen my hearing, so that I constantly hear your voice.

Let us care for what we have got and what we have inherited. It has not been given unto us by our ancestors, it has been lent unto us by our children.

Teach us all that we have responsibility, not power."

In a little while his mum would leave him at school. One of the schools in the big city. Ángelo - he was named after his maternal grandmother - held his mum's hand. In his lap, the school bag. They turned into the last, long, narrow street. A bit further ahead in the misty dawn, a few heavily loaded gravel-cars. They were rolling towards a construction site. Every time one of them lurched on the bumpy, hot asphalt road, some gravel spilled out. The swirling dust clouds devoured the morning light between the blocks of flats. As the last lorry had turned off the road and disappeared in the haze, and the dust had begun to settle, the sun-quivering air was permeated by a downpour of glittering sand particles. Pebbles and gravel whirled as the large van appeared from a by-street and stopped ten yards in front of them, on the other side of the street, wheels spinning.

Before she saw the rhythmically blazing muzzle flares from automatic weapons, she thought that the windscreen had been hit by whirling pebbles. Large, white, broken roses bloomed brutally across the windscreen and the driver's shirt collar was stained red. In the hail of splinters and rattling metal, she glimpsed another car, which had stopped alongside theirs. She crouched, cowered, and pushed the boy down onto the floor. Shouted at him to stay there while she, in the unexpected silence, forced open the door and ran out with her hands in the air. She understood what this was all about. She had expected it, hadn't she?

"Take me! Leave my son alone! I beg you! Leave my son alone!"

She threw herself down in front of them. Two of the darkly clad, masked men grabbed her and, kicking and hitting, shoved her towards the van. The large side door was pulled shut and the car lurched away, leaving behind an acrid smell of burnt rubber. There was no one about. A stray dog who'd been hit by the fast-moving car was lying still on its side in the gutter, whimpering. The hissing sound from a broken radiator and the stifled screams from the little boy echoed between the facades of the houses. The sun broke through and sharp shadows chased each other across paving-stones and asphalt.

The Castanedas had, as long as anyone could remember, been one of the wealthy families of San Veronica. Vicente Castaneda, the family's patriarch. A sturdy man in his sixties, sporting an enormous moustache. Owner of one of the largest areas of land in the village. On his estate, he grew beans, corn, fruit, and vegetables. All of which he exchanged for money in the nearby city.

And today was a feast day. The table was set. Ángela, one of his daughters, the fourth child, would celebrate a christening. His grandchild, a girl, would be given the name Maria, and friends, relatives, and villagers came streaming into the large garden. They walked around in a circle. The men were carrying large baskets full of gifts on their shoulders. The women had their arms full. They walked up to the child and placed the gifts on a table in the sun.

The uninvited guest kept well out of sight. He had asked one of the dexterous boys in the village to sneak in and steal one of the gifts from the table, now in the shadow of the big tree. He wanted a sign. A sign to cherish. And the boy had handed him a small silver necklace. A medallion hung from the necklace chain, a medallion in the shape of a cat. He gave a few coins to the boy, who greedily clenched them in his dirty hand and disappeared among the swaying shadows.

When the guests left the garden, Ángela Castaneda remains in the mild evening breeze. She stands together with her child in front of the gift-laden table. She holds the sleeping Maria up towards the approaching dusk. She smiles at the little girl and she smiles into the future. Not until her mother has called her name several times does she leave the garden.

Night falls and the stars begin their eternal dance across the heavens. A few buzzards dawdle among the tables in the garden, rummaging among the food scraps. The uninvited guest slowly dangles the silver chain in the darkness before disappearing among the trees. He walks straight into the dreadful night which, to him, seems endless.

What long thereafter happened in the remote little mountain village will probably never be fully known. The authorities have their version, the peasants another. Ángela Castaneda moved to the city, where her daughter grew up, and the girl then went to school in the big country in the north, returned, and began a campaign against blind violence, a campaign unparalleled in the small villages of the countryside. A campaign against blind violence. A campaign against corrupt police and military, against ruthless drug cartels - all of that is known. That she disappeared is also known.

But what happened then is to a large extent shrouded in mystery. The poor peasants in her remote village, who knew the mother and the family well, tell different stories. According to some, she was the Holy Virgin Mary come for a visit, while others are convinced that Jesus

Christ himself appeared in her guise to visit their homely village. And some say that it was Mary Magdalene, the follower of Jesus. Yet another notion is that it was Veronica, the saint who had given the village its name. Now she had returned with a message from God. Some contented themselves with calling her The Queen. Before long, the stories and the testimonies became increasingly outlandish.

Carlos Mendez, the Acid Man, was at work among his pits and his large barrels. There had been a problem with deliveries, but now the barrels were full. Today they had appeared with a further three bodies. He had fires going beneath the barrels. The acid was boiling and smoke billowed as he immersed the cold, stiffening corpses. He cursed the syndicate for not giving him even larger barrels. On the other hand, he was grateful that he didn't have to dismember the bodies with a splitting axe, which he knew that others had been forced to do.

Many had told of the executions. How the victims were lined up and in a sort of short court hearing declared guilty and proclaimed disdainful traitors. Then an axe in the head. Arms and legs cut off. One after the other were thrown into these barrels. He was glad not to have to bother with that, at least. And it all became routine. The syndicate delivered and he did his job. The remnants - and there were some - he poured into pits he'd dug. Then he filled them up with sand and no one would suspect what was hidden underground. As he sat down, exhausted, in the late afternoon sun, he wondered how many pits he'd dug. For some reason, it frightened him every day when he counted to far too many. He had to stop counting.

Once in a while he had to take care of someone from his old home village. Somebody who had disappeared. Sometimes someone he knew. And that was the worst part. All the video clips, interviews on TV, desperate appeals from parents seeking lost sons and daughters. When he pushed one of them into the boiling acid, he felt nauseated. He had to throw up. And every night, as he was all alone in the darkness, he fell to his knees and prayed. Begged God for forgiveness.

He had to toil over the pits under constant threats. They had emphasised, clearly emphasised, that if he didn't put people in the barrels, he would himself be put therein. And the sharp-edged sights of an automatic carbine had cut his chest. Weren't the cuts still sore? He tenderly felt his chest. May God forgive him! He repeated this time and again. If there was a God, he must be forgiven!

One evening, when he'd collected some new barrels, he was stopped. Military men shoved him into a large van, handcuffed, his hands behind his back. Blindfolded. Before they tightened the blindfold, he saw them unloading the barrels and rolling them up along sturdy planks, into a canvas covered lorry.

The following day he is brutally awakened and shoved out into an open space. Still blindfolded. He hears the echoes of their voices. Suddenly his blindfold is torn off. A motley crew of policemen and armed soldiers. A few of the soldiers are aiming automatic weapons at him. In front of him, piles of packages wrapped in plastic, lashed with brown tape. Hundreds of small packages of cocaine. He could already see the headlines in the newspapers, proclaiming that the police had caught one of the ugly customers.

When in custody, he was beset by both big and small thoughts. When he killed one of the fat flies crawling along his arm, he wondered if he would have to account for that, too, in the eyes of God? He also wondered what it was in human filth and faeces that attracted these winged insects. That was one of the small thoughts assailing him as one of his fellow prisoners had emptied his bowels on the dirty cell floor. As he moved towards the wall on the opposite side, where he had a yard or so to himself, the heavy thoughts hit him. If this was the end, at least he retained the pictures. And he had kept close track of her, ever since she'd returned after her studies up north. He had read all the newspapers. Saved and hidden the cuttings.

"Whom do you work for?"

He kept silent. The plastic bag was tightened around his neck. Spots flickered before his eyes, darkness creeping in. He got spasms, felt nauseated.

"Who is your employer?'

He still kept silent. Now he convulsed until it all went dark. But the darkness was a blessing. It became deeper, until he saw a weak light - the city, which he glimpsed in the heat haze of the large valley. Once upon a time the city of the sun, La Solana. But the sun had gone out and the pictures were soiled. Already a few minutes after three in the afternoon, darkness descended on streets and alleys. Shops were closed, houses abandoned. Planks nailed any which way across windows. The cartel's pick-ups roared around, heavy weaponry on the loading platforms aiming this way and that. No one was safe. They could kill and loot freely. Sated and drowsy police officers looked the other way and contented themselves with waiting for the next wad of banknotes. Terrified families hid their daughters in holes they'd dug in the ground. Some were found and hauled off, thrown on loading platforms and driven away, never to be seen again. People were sitting indoors, fearing that their front doors would be broken down. They were hiding. The previous mayor had been threatened and was hiding in an abandoned shed outside of town, where he felt safe. He and his son were found murdered. Two chopped off heads, lying on the stairs to the entrance of the police station.

He couldn't take it any longer, he wanted to surrender. He sucked in air that wasn't there. Only sticky plastic. But the pictures flared up again. They surprised him and pumped new blood into his aching head. Because it was on that day, at exactly three o' clock in the afternoon, that the light returned to La Solana. The young woman was being sworn in as mayor. "We are all afraid now. But we must not be ruled by fear … "He saw her standing there, in front of the assembly. Her lips were moving, but he didn't hear what else she said. He only heard himself, choking and screaming, trying to catch his breath.

At the same moment as one of the soldiers tore the plastic bag off his head, a rifle butt hit him. Everything was slowly turning black again.

"We know that you work for the cartel. We want to know the routes and the names of those you work for. Who are your employers?"

He kept silent until the pain from a sharp-pointed gun barrel made his chest explode. And then again. And again.

At last he heard himself hiss:

"You are a bunch of swine! I don't deal in such matters. I swear! I'm no bloody cocaine courier. You are making a mistake! It isn't true. You know that it isn't true. You planted that shit!"

The soldier in front of him once again gripped the butt of his automatic carbine and raised the weapon.

"Stop!"

The interrogator stopped the soldier with a gesture. The mobile phone had rung. He stepped aside, took a few steps away, and stood with his back toward them. The soldier lowered his carbine. There was silence. The interrogator came back. Now the thin line of his twitching moustache was right in front of Carlos's face. He talked in what was nearly a whisper. Stinking of sour wine and old tobacco.

"We know that you don't deal in cocaine. We know that you handle far more delicate matters. But we don't want to broadcast that. A bloke from the security service will come here and take over the interrogation. He is dressed in civilian clothes; he doesn't sport tinsel, like me. Looks civilised. But you'd be wise to answer his questions. Just because he looks civilised doesn't mean his questions are civilised."

He chuckled smugly at his own witticism and disappeared.

The prisoner sat quietly, staring at the floor. He couldn't trust anyone. The cartels had infiltrated several prisons. They even had people working as guards and policemen. They could appear as commissioned officers, without anyone daring to object or even care. He knew the game and would be on his guard. At the same time, he wondered what they wanted, what they were after.

They took him back to the cell. Right now, the only thing he had to look forward to was the night. And she returned - her face was once again there.

The first catastrophe occurred. Her brother at the wheel. He accompanied her everywhere. The youngest sister had been looking forward to coming with them. They were on their way to a convention. She would present her programme. Give a speech. A car ahead of them. One behind. And from the wound-down side window of the car beside them, a rain of bullets. Her car overturned, ending up in the grass beside the road. Wailing ambulance sirens. The lives of the brother and sister could not be saved. A miracle steered the bullets away from her, but she felt how something broke as the car wheeled around in the grass.

He remembers the headlines. Remembers every word she said, already from the hospital bed. He had, after all, saved all the cuttings.

"My loss is so great that if the Holy Virgin couldn't help me, I would't be able to bear it. But, despite the horror and despite constant threats, the one thing I can think of is my responsibility towards my people. Towards the children, the women, the old, the family men who break their backs earning their families' daily bread. I will rise in the morning and thank God for every day, every hour, every minute I can continue my struggle. That is whom I want to be."

She disappeared through the bars, up towards the starry night sky. He couldn't see the stars, but he breathed the fresh air from the sleepy breeze outdoors.

The new interrogator appeared in the company of someone looking like a general, dressed as he was in a uniform full of tinsel and wearing dark sunglasses. Since one didn't know how long the man's belt was, one couldn't judge how fat he was. However, it was obvious that the buckle was fastened in the very last hole available. Beside him stood a prison guard with rolled-up shirt sleeves, exposing tattooed arms. An anxious ray of light, full of shimmering motes, found its way through the small window. The room was very hot.

The interrogator was probably in his early forties. Dark, bristly hair. Long nose with a pear-shaped tip above his meaty lips. Dark grey suit, blue tie, and chalk white shirt. Before opening his mouth, he gestured to the man looking like a general to leave them. The man quickly went out the door.

The interrogator turned towards Carlos Mendez, who didn't know what it was he saw in the man's face. Something. Suddenly he realised what. The man had one blue and one brown eye.

"The police are out digging in your little backyard. They've already began rummaging around in about ten pits. Nice ..."

The prisoner jerked out:

"But it isn't me who ..."

"Ah, ah!"

The interrogator waved his objection away, flashing golden cuff links.

"Let's stop playing hide and seek. We know who you are. You are an acid man and your name is Carlos Mendez. And we believe that you've magically made more than 150 bodies disappear in your boiling jacuzzi cauldrons. And the pits are practically devoid of DNA ..."

"I haven't ... They were the ..."

"Ah, ah! Watch it!"

Carlos resignedly kicked the floor. He had immediately noticed the chilly, formal attitude.

The interrogator, who had been bent over his laptop at the desk, rose from his chair, walked over to Carlos, and stopped a few steps in front of him.

"Strangely enough - and that's your good luck - we aren't interested in the stockpots. We are interested in something else entirely. This is about a woman and the whole thing is startling or shall we say ... rather remarkable?"

The interrogator handed him a cigarette and made a sign to the guard to help the prisoner light it. Carlos Mendez watched the suit's face again. He didn't see any kindness there. Just ice-shimmering coldness in those small, deep set eyes.

"We have heard strange things about your former home village. Yes, we know that you hail from San Veronica."

The prisoner once again stared at the floor in resignation.

"We have been asked to investigate this, as there are strange, widespread rumours about some Christ or Madonna figure having appeared or returned to Earth, and to your former home village! It is, of course, sheer madness and utter nonsense. Totally ridiculous, as a matter of fact, even though we are naturally aware of the exaggerated religiosity and superstition people sometimes harbour and express. Especially in isolated mountain villages. But in spite of this, we do have our reasons for trying to get a clear picture of what has happened."

Carlos, the Acid Man, fidgeted as if he wanted to be free of the chair they'd forced him down on.

"I want some water."

The interrogator nodded towards the guard, who moments later had fetched a glass of water. The guard handed Carlos the glass, but jerked it away as he tried to take it. The interrogator glared at him in irritation. Carlos got the water. He gulped it down.

"It could, of course, in light of what you've already heard, appear somewhat odd that we bother with this thing at all. All I can say for the moment is that it is of great importance that you give us whatever information you have. If you cooperate, we'll forget to look into what you've done. As a matter of fact, you as a person are of no interest to us. We are out to get the syndicates. The cartels. Not you. I will explain in more detail later. The supposedly strange events in your home village may - I might add - be of extraordinary importance. You will understand."

The guard had pushed the table towards Mendez, who put the glass on it. Stared at the table top. But didn't say anything.

"We want to hear you talk. We want to hear you talk now."

The interrogator nodded to the guard, who grabbed Carlos Mendez' shoulders and pulled him to his feet. He staggered as the rough hands pulled him away from the relative safety of the chair. He was dragged to the other end of the room. There was a high frame with a bar, tackle, and ropes. On the floor, a few broken razor blades and some trampled cigarette butts.

The guard shoved him all the way back again. He stood in front of the interrogator.

"I think that you realise how serious this situation is. We'll continue tomorrow."

Carlos was taken back to his cell.

The face was there. La Solana was there. A wonder - a miracle had happened! People were once again out on the streets after three o'clock in the afternoon. Fear and apprehension were gone. People had begun letting their daughters out of the deep holes in the ground. The street cafés were open again, the awnings out. The large parasols were up. A constabulary consisting of women patrolled the streets together with male colleagues.

People turned to the women for protection. They inspired new confidence. They were easier to trust. People who had fled the city began returning. Street orchestras replaced the rumbling pick-ups and the rattling automatic weapons. The older people called the new mayor "the blessed queen", sent by God.

And she had accomplished a lot. Cleaned up the city. Expelled corrupt police officers and soldiers. Dismissed bribed bureaucrats. Instigated the education for young girls who wanted to become police women. Renovated schools and hospitals. Subsidised overcrowded orphanages. Quite a lot had been done.

Carlos got the peculiar impression that every good deed of hers atoned for some of his evil doings. And in spite of the disgusting odours from his fellow prisoners in the draughty, frigid cell, and a constant fear of being beaten up or killed, he felt the warmth as he saw her in front of him in the darkness. She appeared like a fairy in a children's tale and he heard her voice. And every time he saw and heard her, he became all the more convinced that God had sent this being of light to mitigate his terrible guilt.

When he lay down to sleep the following night, he noticed that the fellow prisoner next to him on the floor had stopped breathing. It was very noticeable, since he had been badly beaten and had thus been wheezing loudly all evening. Carlos got to his feet and stumbled over some other prisoners to the bars, where he found an empty space. He sank to the floor. He abhorred stiffs.

Without previous warning, she was hit by the bullets again. Outside of the city, alone in the car. Pierced and shot to shreds, she was operated upon time and again. Outside the hospital, crowds gathered, waving placards. They sang silent hymns to "the Queen". Badly wounded, and cut by countless operating knives, she returned. And he remembers her words. This time he had been truly worried. A worry more corrosive than the horrible contents of his barrels.

"It is true that they hurt my body and wounded my soul. I am in constant pain. But I also know of many other innocent people who have been likewise afflicted."

Carlos Mendez continued digging among the notes and cuttings in his memory. They came fluttering, one after the other.

"Freedom means responsibility, and time is short. I don't dare fall behind. I must hurry. My journey is not yet over. Better leave footprints from battles lost than no footprints at all."

He nearly felt her physical presence. Reached out to grab her in the darkness.

But the spell was broken.

It all bubbled up.

"I am a poor peasant. I fled the village, but they caught me. They threatened me and my family. They would abduct and harm my pregnant fiancé."

Carlos Mendez pulled his trouser legs up above his knees, exposing wealed, pitted burns.

"We are listening."

"What am I supposed to say?"

"You are to tell us about Castanedas. What do you know about the Castanedas?"

"Everybody knew about the Castanedas. They owned a lot of land in the village. And they had six children. Most of them worked on the grounds, but a couple of the daughters worked in town, in the homes of some wealthy, American families. But what is this all about? Good grief! I haven't been in the village for... God, I don't know how many years!"

Carlos Mendez was lying. He had been back to the area several times. But always surreptitiously and in darkness. In a neighbouring village, he still had some friends he could confide in. He was always welcome at their homes, and he wanted to keep up to date and inquire about his family. He raised his eyes but did not meet the interrogator's gaze. The interrogator loosened his tie, undid the top button in his shirt, bent forwards toward Mendez, and lowered his voice. The guard wiped some beads of sweat from his brow.

"We got a tip that an acid man had been seen in the vicinity and that he has friends there. We followed up on that."

The interrogator punched some keys on his laptop and read from the screen: "Gilbert Morales, Manolo Chavez, and Ramón Castellanos ..."

Carlos froze. How the fuck had they found that out? And what had they done to them?

"One of them showed us the shed and your soup kitchen. Very unwillingly, I might add."

For the first time, the interrogator steadily met Carlos Mendez's eyes, and now he spoke in a very low voice. Mendez wondered how his voice, which had been so metallic earlier, could sound this kind and suave. He would once more be on his guard.

"You are an acid man. The acid man of that area. Area, by the way. More like a region. But they turn to you, right? The cartel wants to get rid of the body. Why? Because a grave would give rise to martyrdom and pilgrims. People would gather in large crowds. They would come from near and far. Martyr! Martyrdom! That is the last thing the cartel wants. The police are manageable. The military are manageable. Authorities are always manageable. But an entire people ... Nobody can handle an entire people! So they want bury this thing forever. Therefore they will contact you and ask for your services. You understand?"

The interrogator drummed his fingers against the tabletop.

"You don't seem to understand."

Carlos Mendez stared at the floor.

"Maybe you'll wake up if I say the name Maria Castaneda!"

It all welled up inside him. The corners of his mouth began twitching and there was not a thing he could do about it. This would soon be too big for him to endure. The unexpected signal saved him.

The guard's mobile rang. The sound cut the air and reverberated through the room. The interrogator grabbed the mobile, threw it to the floor, and stamped on it, crushed it.

"We will soon release you and we count on the cartel getting in touch with you. We want you to inform us when they do. They made a mistake not taking care of the body immediately. That mistake may prove fateful. But it gives us an opportunity to act and also to arrange for the funeral and bestow the public honours Maria Castaneda deserves."

Mendez looked at the guard, but the man didn't even bat an eyelid at the destroyed mobile. Then Mendez met the interrogator's gaze.

"What more do you want?"

"We want to know everything about the body. It was taken to the village by one or more people. We believe that you know about this. We want to know exactly what happened then!"

The interrogator shut his brown eye and stared at Carlos with his blue one.

"Tomorrow we want to hear you talk!"

The interrogator left the room. The rope and the tackle dangled in the draught from the door. A knocking, rattling sound followed him as the guard roughly shoved him across the threshold.

Carlos Mendez was to spend his last night in custody. He was not afraid of being brutally awakened and placed on a chair with his hands tied and subjected to heavy blows and burning cigarettes. What frightened him were his memories, the pictures in his mind. The memories that had attacked him and been so chillingly painful during the last interrogation. Some farm

workers on their way to work had found her in a ditch. Stab wounds, burns. Tape over her mouth, tightly wound several times around the nape of her neck. Contusions on her head. Visible marks of tightly tied ropes on wrists and ankles. The body had been taken to San Veronica, where the old family grave was situated.

He wondered how much she had suffered.

"What happened? What happened to the body? The reports we've had are incomplete and confusing."

Carlos Mendez decided to tell them what he had heard during the nightly conversations with his friends.

"They must have stolen it from the mortuary at night and brought it to the square."

"Who did?"

"Some villagers, I presume."

"And?"

The prisoner fell silent and stared at his hands.

"And?"

Carlos Mendez spoke with difficulty.

"They brought her to the square ..."

"Yes, sure. But what happened?"

"They got her up on a cross. A big cross!"

"A cross?"

"Yes. Made of sturdy beams. And it was high. It is said that it was very high!"

The prisoner fell silent.

"They tied her to the cross?"

"Yes, with ropes round wrists and ankles. She hung there with the shroud around her hips and sideways across one shoulder."

The prisoner fell silent again.

"And?"

The interrogator punched the laptop's space bar. Hard, several times.

"And!"

Carlos Mendes stared at the ceiling, in a slanting angle, past the interrogator and the guard.

"Her upper body was naked. And she had ..."

He straightened his back. Smacked his knee with one hand, and then, turning his head to one side, raised the hand to his chin.

"She had big scars and horrible wounds. Her legs were ... I can't ... And she had a large hole in her side. In the light of dawn people started pointing ... falling to the ground ... And her eyes. They were closed ... but it was claimed that they were glowing, as of some strange light ..."

"I think I can picture it."

The interrogator flipped back and forth on his screen again. But his gaze was somewhere else. He loudly forced air out through his nostrils, and his eyes shot rays at Mendez.

"Is that all? All you have to say?"

The man with one blue and one brown eye stared incredulously at the prisoner and raised his arm towards the guard. The prisoner quickly resumed his account:

"Everyone fell to their knees ... To their knees! To the ground. Heads lowered ..."

"And ..."

"It has been said that more and more people arrived. That people made pilgrimages from nearby villages, that the rumour spread like wildfire. People started arriving in cars and buses. Both men and women were crying. Hymns were sung. People prayed, Our father, which art in heaven ... The village priest, who had been woken, rushed out on the square, started shouting thanks unto God, and raised his arms towards heaven. And then everyone did the same. It has been said that the sky was torn asunder, as if to let the song in ..."

The interrogator listened without batting an eyelid. He stared suspiciously at the prisoner.

"You were there! You sound as if you were there."

"I wasn't there. But God knows that I would have given my right hand to be there."

"Whatever. It does fit some other information we've obtained. And then what happened?"

"The jeeps with the soldiers appeared and a commander came running and ordered the body to be cut down."

"How long do you think the body was hanging there before the army jeeps appeared?"

"From dawn, I would think, until ... well, about nine p.m. the following day."

"What became of the body?"

"It is said that it was taken back to the mortuary. But I don't know. It was never recovered!"

"And you are certain that it didn't end up in one of your pits?"

"As God is my witness, that did not happen. I swear by the Holy Virgin!"

"Something makes me believe you. But you shall be aware that there are rumours and echoes! Fanciful rumours about some sort of epiphany. Some sort of mass psychosis. They seem to be spreading."

"Yes, but I don't know anything more. Just that ..."

"What? Just that what?"

"Well, that thunderstorm. There was talk about the thunderstorm."

"Thunderstorm?"

"Yes. On the evening of the following day, the landscape was lighted by peculiar, enormous flashes of lightning. It was like daytime. The elders say that they'd never seen such a thunderstorm. Several villagers swear that she disappeared in a hissing, blinding light."

"Thunderstorm ... but ... Nonsense! Probably some army helicopter out searching for something. Their searchlights are pretty dramatic. Might have looked like the clouds were blazing."

"But the elders swear on it! And there were hundreds of people gathered in the square ... They swear that she disappeared in an enormous pillar of light! And that the shroud shimmered like large, white wings. And that the cloud cover opened up between the flashes of lightning. Then it stopped raining and the weather cleared!"

"But you said that the military cut her down. How ...?"

"Yes, but this was the next evening. There was still a crowd in the square. And the mortuary ... you couldn't ..."

The interrogator slammed the lid of the laptop shut.

"Don't forget what you are to do! We are waiting. And we'll watch you."

The interrogator cast a sideway glance at the guard.

"Remove the prisoner!"

When Carlos Mendes was shoved across the threshold and out into the corridor, he got a final glimpse of the interrogator. He was talking fast, agitatedly, and apparently in short bursts, on his mobile phone. In the noise and commotion, Carlos didn't hear what was said, though.

It is likely that no one could have anticipated what happened during the following days. Like small circles and then like increasingly larger and steeper waves on the water, the echoes began rolling across mountains and plains, and found their way into streets and squares in town after town, village after village. Carlos Mendez perceived the force, could nearly feel it at his back as he sneaked about on the paths up in the mountains. He travelled by night and was determined to try and just disappear. But first he would meet with his friends.

They told him about beatings and the interrogations. Ramón had recognised one of the men. He belonged to the cartels. They had also mentioned what they'd seen as an unimportant detail about the interrogator. They couldn't help but notice that his eyes were different colours.

Carlos pulled the heavy front door shut with such force that it reverberated through the big clock on the facade. The heavy yoke had cut into his shoulders. He hadn't been able to carry it any longer. In the centre aisle he ran into the priest, who hurriedly came stumbling.

"My son, you want to open your heart. The Lord will listen ..."

He pushed the dark-clad priest aside and hurried up to the altar, looking at the figure hanging there.

"She served you, spoke in your name, and the Virgin's. Asked the people for love. Asked them to do what you said is right and true. But where were you? Where were you when the bullets pierced her body? Where you there when those devils burnt and stabbed her? Where you there when those beasts crushed her skull? No one saw you. You stayed away! Didn't you? Just like him who once betrayed you!"

As he heard his own words echoing among the vaults, he saw the glass cupboard with the relics in it. He glimpsed a small piece of cloth, which he recognised since childhood. It was supposed to be a piece of the cloth with which the holy Veronica had dabbed the saviour's forehead and cheeks as he walked to Golgotha.

He formed his lips to a dark hole and like a bullet from a rifle, the squirt shot out. The viscous liquid slowly flowed down the pane. In that moment, Carlos Mendez sank to his knees, his gaze convulsing in darkness.

When, a moment later, he opened his eyes and looked down on his hands, he discovered that they glistened like transparent, flowing pearls. They glistened in the light from the one hundred fluttering flames of the altar candles and looked like small, shining blotches on the marble floor at his feet. His arms began shaking.

As he hastily left the altar and hurried towards the exit, the priest once again approached him, hands half raised.

"Why in such a hurry, my son? I will pray for you. The Lord hears prayer. The Lord rewards and takes care of his people ..."

Carlos grabbed the fluttering, black cassock, dragged the priest outside, took his arm in a hard grip, and forced it skywards. The dismayed man of God clenched his teeth and gasped. Carlos hissed in his ear:

"Him about whom you speak is not here! All these tapering towers are pointing at a heaven which is desolate, frozen ... Empty! Empty!"

Carlos ejaculated the word with all his might at the terror-stricken father confessor, and then stumbled away along the gravel path. He had not gone far when he suddenly felt burdened by doubt and regret, gnawing inside him in time with his heavy breathing. Behind him, the priest, massaging his arm, still stared glassily at the sky. Carlos had to get up into the mountains, fast. It was dangerous to remain in the village. It was dangerous to be in church.

He had to continue along the road. And the cuttings he knew by heart flared up in his mind again:

"It is impossible for me to give up. I have children. I have to bring them up, serve as a role model. You, too, have children. And you, too, must bring up your children, serve as role models. I can't give up. And it is not for you to give up either." The words had been burnt into his mind. One couldn't know how long one would have to go on. And one could lose every battle. One just had to continue, every single day. He didn't care if he got caught any longer. Of course they would catch him. But no one could take the Virgin away from him. His Virgin!

As he made his way through the dry brush vegetation towards the mountains, he squeezed the little silver chain and the charm in the shape of a cat which he kept in his pocket. He remembered the farewell and the pain. How they had forced him into the frightful duty which had become his. She had left the village to begin working at the large hospital. The child had been born in that same hospital. The Castanedas had supported her.

Maybe providence had actually meant that he should be the instrument and that the girl should be the meaning of his life. How many people ever got such a gift?

He thought he heard the sounds behind him. The sounds of hooves and breaking twigs. He wasn't sure.

When he saw the first rider with his rifle held aloft, he raised his eyes towards the high mountains in the distance. He immediately realised that there was no point in going there. Hadn't he already reached the highest possible summit?

The people one saw walking in endless rows along the main street had no graves to go to. Not even a memorial grove where they could put their flowers.

Even so, the women are wearing large, white shawls over their heads, shawls flowing down over their shoulders and their beautiful evening dresses. In their hands, bouquets. At the front of the procession, a small orchestra with horns and folk music instruments. Behind them, a pick-up. On the loading platform, a large portal framing a blue-clad female figure with a halo. The car's bonnet is covered with a light blue cloth strewn with flowers. A plethora of children in white attire, with red bands around their waists. Running around with innumerable balloons in a variety of colours. Some of the women carry censers on long poles. Light grey sheets of smoke billow towards the sky. The parade passes two flagellants on their knees, lashing themselves. The face of Christ is tattooed on their backs. A group right behind the pick-up carry large, flying banners. They hold them high and the banners are dark red and in the middle of each banner there is an oval photograph in a glimmering, golden frame. Maria Castanedas' face shines everywhere.

And in nearby towns and soon in the whole region, processions are walking along the main streets. In the capital, they decided, after a few days, to proclaim a minute's silence.

While the country held its breath, some peasants from San Veronica buried the body in a nearby but unknown cave. They then rolled a large boulder in front of the entrance.

This is what has in strict confidence been told by a few people claiming to have insight.

Six Feet Under Down Under

Jeff Taylor
New Zealand

'DAD? I'M HERE.'

Danny looked around and shuddered. Nothing much had changed for as long as he could remember - the stainless-steel benches with drains that still gave him nightmares, trays of terrifying instruments, tubing that looked always reminded him of human entrails, bottles of embalming fluid, and God-knows-what other obscene stuff. There was no sign or sound of his father so he stepped through to the display room.

'Hey, Dad!'

Still nothing.

The line-up of coffins was much more extensive than he recalled from his last visit. For his mother's funeral it had been just that fleeting visit. What was it – a year ago? Before that he hadn't been back for all those many years. There'd been a range of just a few caskets then. All standard, nicely grained veneers. From light teak, to medium mahogany, through to a dark oak. Sensible colours, *proper colours to die for!* This new selection stopped him in his tracks. My God! Did people actually get buried in stuff like this now?

There was one made out of what looked like driftwood planks, and bound with old fish netting and anchor rope. *For a beloved who loved the sea,* the handwritten sign said. Danny stepped close and sniffed it. It ponged of dead crustaceans and rotten seaweed.

He was a bit happier with one that was made out of untreated pine – *For the conservation-minded* it read. *No nails. Plant-based glue only used. That reminds me,* he thought, *I must renew my Greenpeace subscription.*

Shaking his head, he took in another casket in shiny, metallic red enamel, with flames down each side, and mag wheels painted on. *For the motor enthusiast.* Bumpers at the front and back. For the pallbearers? Surely not!

Beside it was one *For lovers of the bush* – tree trunks with fern fronds spouting that looked like they were still growing! He reached and touched it. It was damp! For God's sake, his father was watering it to keep it alive! What sort of insects might be living in the wood? Still, he supposed, the incumbent wouldn't know that he or she was being nipped or bitten anyway. Or, heaven forbid, having orifices occupied for nesting and breeding. Earwigs came to mind, and he shuddered. *Slaters. Worms.*

There was a stack of what looked like assorted plywood pieces in a corner, and in front was a display of the most basic looking coffins he'd ever seen. Five-ply with so many knots it looked like leopard skin. Maybe for a big game hunter? No, his father had stooped to selling flat-packs for home assembly! *Complete with screws, handles, hinges, and all instructions. Kitset - or pay seventy dollars extra for assembly.* The sign also advised that it came in five sizes – *From infants to adult.* Danny examined the smallest, about the size of a box you'd get a pair of gumboots in. The sign read - *Stillborn, to newborn.* Well at least, he supposed, his father hadn't written *From cradle to grave.* Be thankful for small mercies.

Danny had to sit down; this was a lot to take in. He flopped onto a bench that looked suspiciously like a church pew his father might have pilfered from somewhere? He took in a few deep breaths. After a while he regained his composure, and went back into the preparation room, where all that horrible after-death stuff happened.

His childhood was coming back to him. He could remember when he was pre-school, playing and clambering in and out of coffins. They were perfect huts. In fact his father had made him a special one, with little windows in the side. No lid though, that was asking for trouble with the lack of air in there. Later on he'd made him a tree hut from a large *Custom Oak,* a reject that had been measured and made for a terminal thirty-stoner. They were a difficult, oddball family who wanted the casket made well in advance and insisted on a roomy fit. The huge man took some time to die, and had gradually shrunk from a mountain to a hillock. Then they turned around and couldn't accept the thought of their loved one rolling about in an oversized container, even though his father had offered to use plenty of packing. They'd been happy to pay up for the jumbo one anyway, and also for the smaller model as well. More money than sense, and the tree hut had been a perfect retreat from stuff he had to put up with at school each day.

That constant bullying. He would never forget one hurtful taunt from Curly McRae when he was twelve. 'Ha, ha. Your old man has sex with dead women!'

That was going too far, and Danny had always been proud of his quick reply. 'Yeah? So that's why he was in your old lady's bedroom last night.' He'd had to run for his life, but just for once he'd stuck it to that prick.

And the coffin-trolley his father had once made for him that time had been great too.

'I'm here, Dad!'

Where was he? Maybe he should have phoned ahead with his exact time of arrival. Stuff it, his father knew he was coming sometime today and he'd better be here. Well, he should be here, because it was asking for trouble leaving the place wide-open like this. Coffins weren't exempt from the criminally minded. He could easily see the souped up hot-rod in a gang headquarters being used as a bar leaner.

Where was he! All this fuss. Just like the old man, all this bloody drama, expecting him to drop everything. He'd had to pay top rate fare as well, no special deals with just a couple of days to book. Maybe he should hit the old bugger up for it? After all, his father had practically demanded that he came running and refused to say why.

'It's a matter of life and death, Son,' he'd pleaded. 'Can't tell you on the phone.'

Danny had presumed that financial things had finally caught up with his old man. Well, he wasn't in any position to help there.

'Dad! Where the hell are you?' It was always such a mission getting back here to New Zealand. Aotearoa, the Land-of-the-Long-White-Cloud, was what the Maoris had named the small country at the bottom of the world. This last toilet stop before Antarctica. The flight had been crap. Whenever he flew south, it always felt like his life was sliding downhill from the equator on. He'd left London in clear air, but they'd struck bad turbulence over the desert areas as they headed down to Dubai for a stopover on the way. Economy class of course. He'd tried a bullshit sob story at check in hoping for an upgrade. Might've known it wouldn't work. He'd flashed his father's business card, and implied a family funeral that he was desperate to attend. No joy. He guessed they'd heard them all before. The airline served nothing but Middle-Eastern crap food as well. And no alcohol!

Something wasn't right. There was an eerie feeling in the place over and above the smell and the coldness. His skin was crawling and the hairs on the back of his neck started to stand to attention. The stuff of his childhood was back big time. The atmosphere of it, the creepiness of the whole business that still permeated his mind even after all these years. He opened a door to look in the extra sluice room, and what he saw surpassed everything.

A corpse, a middle-aged male, naked, obese, and pink-skinned, was lying on its back on the floor beside a stainless steel bench. There were a number of bruises along one side, and he surmised that it had rolled off somehow. It seemed to be grinning. Danny's heart and lungs paused, and the rest of his organs went out in sympathy. The shock almost moved his bowels as well, and he had to clench his buttocks. The dead man was bald, but made up for it by the biggest thatch of pubic hair that Danny had ever seen. If he had a male organ, however, it was missing somewhere in the bush and finding it would need a rescue party prepared for some serious searching. Hardly daring to breathe, he went cautiously up to the cadaver, and touched a shoulder. It was warm! He jumped back, and made a quick exit from the room.

Just then the refrigeration room door opened and his father peered out. 'That you, Danny?' Soundproofed. No wonder he hadn't heard.

At last. 'Y… yeah. Hi, Dad!'

His father came in and they man-hugged awkwardly. Tall, thin, and sparse-haired, the sixty-year-old man in a long, rubber apron, clutched his athletically built thirty-one-year-old only son, who looked spoilt somewhat by the pallor of the recent London winter.

'You better take a look in here.' Danny grabbed his father's arm and pulled him through into the other room. 'This body looks like he fell off the bench. He's got some damage.'

'Oh, don't worry about that. It's okay. We can cover that, as you know.'

Danny recalled the tricks of the undertakers' trade, and the stuff they used. What was it called now? Restoration Remedy, that's right. The undertaker's version of Pollyfilla. Covered a multitude of things, from the bruises of domestic violence, to serious trauma damage. He remembered that worse 'accidents' sometimes happened in the funeral parlour as well, with bodies occasionally tipping off gurneys, and limbs getting broken and marked from being straightened or bent while being squeezed into caskets. He shuddered with the memory of one particular difficult incident that had involved bolt cutters. Horace Denton, his father, mortician and owner of Denton's Quality Funerals, suddenly convulsed and was consumed by a rattling cough, the ferocity of which would have cleared a doctor's waiting room.

'Take it easy, Dad.'

Danny suddenly noticed how gaunt his father had become. His jaw, jowls, and chin seemed to be sagging as if his skin was now too big for his head.

'You're sick? Is that why you wanted me to come back?'

He was now suddenly worried about why he'd been begged to come home urgently. The body was forgotten with concern for his father's health. He noticed Horace's teeth as well. They were looking like something appropriate for an undertaker - lopsided tombstones in a gum graveyard.

'Didn't want to worry you, Son. But you're here now, and we'll talk later, after a cup of tea, eh?'

Danny had to get it in early, get things straight.

'Yeah, well, don't start on again about me coming into the business, you know I hate it. I spent all those years overseas to get away from all this.'

His father said nothing. Danny was beginning to feel nauseated as more recollections flooded back. His after school job had been preparing the bodies, which included sponging and cleaning dead flesh, and turning the taps on the clear tubing to flush the embalming stuff in or out. Out was always worst, the colour, and the thought of what now contaminated it, had always worried him. He'd pleaded for a paper delivery job like the other kids, but his old man insisted. Times were tough and the new franchised chain parlours were starting to make inroads into the business. Independents like theirs were struggling and everyone had to pitch in.

His mother had hated it as well, and had put her foot down – she would only handle the business side - reception, the accounts, the advertising, liaising with the families. Eventually though, the proximity of all that death finally consumed her those twelve months ago. A stroke caused by emotional stress.

It had been Horace and his only son who had done the hands-on stuff, and every day death had oozed into Danny's skin and permeated his mind. And while Horace seemed to revel in it, Danny had made his run for overseas the moment he'd left school.

He followed his father to the sink in the corner of the main embalming area. There was no separate staff tea room, and the bench was the same as the one in the centre of the room. In fact it was used for back-up when things were busy. Shiny, stainless, big enough for a body, with those revolting channels to drain the exudates into the sink. Horace lifted the top off a plastic container and took out a couple of teabags.

Danny stared at it. The receptacle was the one that they'd always used to store the personal items of the dead until they were needed to be re-inserted for viewing – like false teeth, and prosthetic eyes. His father then filled a jug with water from a flexible hose that Danny was sure he could remember using to wash down scaly flesh and spilled body fluids. And the nozzle that he had inserted so many times into those dark places where the sun never shone. Two enamel mugs were removed from a drawer that contained a selection of the implements of terror, and rinsed with the water from the same hose nozzle. The cloth with which his father dried the mugs, came from the pocket in the front of his work apron, and was stained with what just had to be assorted body fluids.

'Sugar? Milk?'

Danny nodded in a daze to both. The sugar was in a jar marked *waste* and the milk was in the fridge amongst assorted plastic containers with mysterious, dark contents. It was in a beaker that could have once contained anything. The spatula to stir the sugar was probably one he'd used many times to scoop pus and blood off dead customers for all he knew. It was almost too much, but he needed to humour his ailing father, who was wheezing noisily.

'Good trip, Son?'

The words came in a rush followed by another death rattle cough.

'Yeah. Dream flight.'

He closed his eyes to the scum on his tea, and took a little experimental sip. 'That's good. How's your love life? What's her name? Alice?'

'Alicia, Dad. We're… going through a bit of a rough patch. But all good.'

'That's a shame. I like her. You've been together a few years now.'

'Yeah. Three years.'

He likes her? He'd never even met her. Spoken a couple times on Skype, that was it. There was no way he'd tell his father that there'd been the nasty bust up. That she had taken off to Europe with an old boyfriend. That it was all over. He needed the old man to believe that there was a good reason he couldn't stay in New Zealand for long. That he needed to get back pronto. If Horace got a sniff of it there'd be all sorts of pressure to stay. There was also no way he'd let on that he'd been laid off his job at the bank, either. No, he'd stick to the story that he'd had to get special leave to come out.

Thank God Alicia hadn't still been with him and come down as well. He'd never talked much about the family business, with his shame of it. How would she have handled all this? She only knew his father was an undertaker, and that he hated attending funerals. They'd had a bitter argument a couple of months ago when he'd refused to go to her mother's service. *Her own mother!*

'I get nausea,' he'd pleaded. 'I faint. The past just comes and grabs me.'

'Surely for my Mum, though?'

He'd shaken his head, and she'd festered and fumed that much about it she almost forgot to grieve. And afterwards there was just resentment. Maybe it was this that had started the decline of the relationship? Well, now, if she had come here, and seen what he had grown up with, maybe she'd be dizzy and vomiting as well.

'Okay Dad. Let's have it. And no bullshit please.'

Horace knew there was no point now in beating around the bush. 'You might as well know the truth then, Son. My lungs have packed up, and they've only given me a couple of months.' To accentuate the severity, the old man coughed up a wad of thick, black sputum the size of a small rodent, and spat it into the sink.

'It's the fumes from embalming fluid. The old formula. They're saying now that it's going to be another asbestos. Maybe it was just as well you didn't take up the family profession after all.'

Danny looked at his father, stunned. 'There must be some treatment?'

'There's nothing, Son. I've been to doctors, lung specialists.'

Danny had his head in his hands. 'I just knew that handling corpses was a deadly business.' *Oh, my,God! His father was dying and he was making sick jokes!*

'The modern embalming fluid is clean and safe now. They've refined it. Too late for us older ones though. Alby Jones of Eternal Rest passed away six months ago, and Norm Wilkins of Resthaven is on his deathbed. Anyway, come through, I want to explain it all to you.'

They went back through into the small room. As they entered, the silence was broken by a sudden, gurgling sound from the corpse, which also wobbled slightly, as if it had been taking all this in and wanted some attention. Danny jumped with alarm, but Horace took no notice. He was used to cadavers being in on the conversation, it seemed.

'What the hell?' Danny indicated the body.

The corpse's face seemed to be registering some pleasure at them finally getting around to it.

'Help me get him back up.'

Horace took the feet, and Danny, with his eyes averted, took the shoulders as they struggled and heaved the corpse back onto the bench.

'This is what I want to tell you. My special project.'

'What?'

'It's a huge breakthrough. Never been done anywhere before. Ever.'

'This guy must've just died then? He's still warm.' 'That's just it son. He's been dead for three days. It's my new secret technique.'

Danny's brain was spinning. 'How come?' He knew that three days should mean stone cold.

Horace went on. 'I've been quietly experimenting, trying it all out.'

'Like what?' Danny mumbled, reluctant to ask.

Horace was racked by more coughing, and Danny grabbed his shoulders with concern.

'Just breathe slow, Dad, and take your time.'

'Are you ready for this? You know we work on maximum one week expiry for open caskets? Well I've developed this new procedure. It's a big breakthrough. Wait for it, Son! We can now extend the cadaver use-by date indefinitely! My first prototype has been dead for twelve months now, and it's still in perfect condition.'

Danny could hardly speak. 'No decomposition? You deep freeze them?'

'Cryogenics? No way. They can stay at *room temperature*, Son. More importantly, no rigour mortis, all joints remain flexible, and no smell.' He leaned closer and whispered hoarsely. 'It's all in my new embalming formula and the temperature, and so simple it's a wonder no one's thought of it before. We install a small pump in the heart, all wired in with a heating filament, that keeps the fluid circulating - *at normal body temperature*. Thirty seven degrees celsius. There's a thermostat. As long as the body's serviced every six months - fluid top up, check for leaks, skin rehydration, battery replacement - that sort of thing,' he said triumphantly. 'Just two AA batteries inserted in a flap under the armpit.'

'How come you never told me any of this? How come you're not on the news? CNN? Graham Norton? The Ellen show?'

'Kept it hush-hush, Son. Until I could tell you all about it. The fluid has nutrients, hydrating, and lubricating stuff in it. I spent a long time perfecting it, and I got it all patented. Think of the possibilities. A family can take their loved ones home forever. A widow can keep her man about the house for security. Forget about just leaving men's boots outside the door. Passengers. There are the road lanes reserved at peak times for cars with at least one passenger.' He put his hand on the corpse. ' Anyway, Jeffrey, meet my son Daniel. Danny, this is Jeffrey Johanson, our local butcher. Recently deceased from sudden heart failure.' Horace chuckled and coughed simultaneously.

Danny was so numbed he started to reach out for a handshake, but recovered his composure just in time. He realised it would have been the most limp -wristed handshake of all time.

'Now, luckily, his family want a closed coffin, so we can play around with him. The pump's already installed, but I've waited so you can see how the rest of it's done.'

Danny closed his eyes and swayed for a few seconds trying to prepare himself.

Horace gave the corpse a sharp slap on the belly, and pink flesh wobbled like a jelly.

'We have to lower the centre of gravity so we use these for ballast.' He pulled out a tray containing a selection of what looked like large fishing sinkers. 'Rectal weights.' He produced a tape measure and measured from the head to the toes, did some calculations on a calculator, and took out one about the shape and size of a large cucumber. The selection seemed to range from about medium carrot to extra large marrow in size.

A lead vegetable garden, Danny mused, not amused.

After pulling on long rubber gloves, Horace sprayed some lubricating oil on the weight and proceeded to thrust it up into the rectum. Using the measure again, he adjusted the position of it once or twice until he was satisfied at the distance of penetration. Danny was sure he saw the corpse's face wince. 'The size and the placement are very important. We need the backside always pointing down, and the feet on the ground. The final result needs to be about that of a big stuffed teddy bear.'

'Lead suppositories?'

Danny stared open-mouthed at his father who, despite his shortness of breath, almost seemed to be enjoying himself.

Horace withdrew his arm with a soft plop and Danny's anal sphincter contracted in sympathy. 'I've also been super-gluing the anus shut. We don't want him to accidentally pass a lead motion. And leakage is the last thing we want. He proceeded to squirt some glue in and pressed the cheeks together for a few minutes until it set. He winked. 'Now, watch this,' he said.

Even in his weakened state he handled the body as effortlessly as a large stuffed toy. He bent the legs and sat Jeffrey Johansen in a chair, folded the arms, turned the head from side to side. Then he turned the lips up into a smile. 'Best to have 'em looking happy. Eyes can be open or shut.' Finally he bent both arms in the air, thumbs up in victory. 'The perfect companion, and it can't answer back,' he cackled. 'In the past they were stiff as a board, and perishable, as you know. Now you can keep 'em and take 'em anywhere. All for a substantial fee of course,' he winked again. 'It'll be a niche market, and we can corner it. Makes a change from boring old cremations and burials, eh?'

'You think there'll be a demand?' Danny asked cautiously. 'I reckon. Oh, we'll still offer the regular bury and burn stuff. But there's huge potential. What about this as well? We can build up a store of the unclaimed bodies, the John and Jane Does, and market them for zombie films? *The Walking Dead?* For the crowd scenes. Specially the face and head damaged ones. You got a mob of them lurching down the road? Well, you have half-zombie real actors, and half our guys. Our cadavers are in the middle roped together and the real zombies are jerking them along like a big bunch of store dummies. The heads'll flop around, and the viewer'll be none the wiser. We can send 'em anywhere around the world in shipping containers.'

Horace hacked into a sluice bucket. When he had regained his breath, be proclaimed proudly. 'I'm calling my invention Denton's Alternative to Grave System. DAGS for short.'

Danny was appalled. '*DAGS?* You want to name this after something that hangs off a sheep's bum?'

'Well, why not? It's a New Zealand invention, and we're known as a nation with forty-million sheep. That's our international image. Thousands of Japanese and Chinese come here every year just to pat one. The tourism people might even give us some advertising funding.'

He had a point, but it was almost too much for Danny.

'So, you want to promote this for tourist junkets? What, we entice the terminally ill down here for the sheep, the geysers, Lord of the Rings sites… and… to become… *undead?* 'Why not? It'll be cheaper. The families pay one-way fares, and they can be shipped back as check-in freight.'

'Have you done any proper trials for this, Dad? Other than Mr. Johansen here?'

'Jeffrey's actually my third with the full DAGS treatment. The other two, Son, are… well, first was your…,' he hesitated. 'Your mother,' then he went on quickly. 'And George Adam's wife was number two. You remember him?'

Danny nodded numbly. George was an old family friend. The enormity hit Danny. 'Mum? You preserved Mum?' Not Mum!'

Just that one year ago he could recall attending his mother's funeral, and had watched her casket roll all the way into the flames!

'You mean she wasn't in that coffin?' he asked incredulously.

'No, Son, she had a more important mission in life … I mean death. That was a bundle of old books in there. Her favourite ones, mind you. I kept her hidden in a cupboard until you'd gone. I started to experiment on her the moment you left to go back. Couldn't tell you about it, you would never have agreed. She's upstairs in the bedroom right now, in bed, you can go up and check her condition. Smell her - she's fresh as a daisy. Now George, he's more than happy,' Horace said quickly, trying to divert the subject. 'He and Molly used to argue all the time. He still argues with her, but now he always wins. Ha, ha, just joking. He's sworn to secrecy, of course. Anyway, as far as your mum goes, it'll be up to you how long you keep her around. She's our mark one prototype, though, don't forget. Hey, where're you going?'

Danny took the stairs three at a time, but hesitated at the bedroom door. His mind was whirling, and he needed to take some long slow and deep breaths to prepare himself. Slowly, he stepped into the room and straight away saw that one side of the marital bed was occupied. There was an inert form lying where his mother had always slept. He advanced at the pace of a handicapped snail to the bed and stood still, rooted to the floor. It was his loving mother's head that rested on the pillow all right, and she looked exactly like he remembered. Like she was in a deep sleep, her eyes closed, and with healthy pink-coloured cheeks. He placed his lips on her forehead and she was warm.

In a daze, he made his way back down, and stared at his father, his mouth open and his eyes wide.

'It's… true. Oh, my God!'

Horace looked at Danny, begging with his eyes. 'How about it, you'll carry on the business? Make your dying father happy? Your marketing degree will come in handy.'

Danny was quiet, completely overwhelmed by the day's events. But, then, *why not?* he thought. Jobs in London would be hard to find with the recession, and he had just broken up with his girlfriend. There was nothing back there for him. This could be an exciting challenge. He could become rich. And famous too. This was world-shaking, Nobel Prize stuff, even. 'Okay, Dad,' he said slowly. 'Maybe I'll give it a crack. But there'll have to be some rules. No using them as scarecrows. Or crash-test dummies. Or window mannequins. And forget the zombie idea. There must be a level of respect.'

Horace coughed, hacked, coughed again. 'Fair enough, Son. But the families should have the opportunity to rent out their loved ones if they want to. It can be listed in a last will and testament as well.'

'Rent? What the hell?'

'Yeah, it's another option to taking them home. They can get an income from them after they've gone.' His eyes were far away. 'Rent their dead kids to childless couples. We can store 'em here, handle everything and get a commission. Act as agents. They get their payments. Their loved ones live on in a way, and help to go on supporting the family. We can market it on-line. We insist they take out our maintenance service contract as well.'

Danny had been thinking. There was already a potential marketing name in his head Forget DAGS! Maybe *Never say Die?* Might have to check with the James Bond people over copyright though. He was silent for a while, then spoke slowly and quietly. 'Okay, Dad, I'll do it.'

'Great! It's all yours then, Son. Everything you need to know is in the safe. The formula, everything. Here's the combination, and I'll run through it all tomorrow.' He handed Danny a slip of paper. 'I just want out now.' His voice was breaking. 'I know it's all in safe hands. And, I can still be around, of course,' he managed a wink. 'If you want, that is. And by the way,' he wheezed. 'I've done the calculations for you. I'll need the size number seven weight, inserted exactly sixteen centimetres. I'm going upstairs to lie down. I feel the end is close.' His head slumped and his eyes started to droop. 'And for God's sake, when the time comes, make sure you use plenty of lubricating spray, and insert that ballast weight carefully.' His voice was fading. 'And warm it up a bit first. Just in case I haven't quite completely gone.'

Mr. Reginald's Last Encounter

Jo Else
England

SEVENTY-FOUR, A SMALL AMOUNT OF HAIR remaining; he brushes it forward each morning to cover the bald spot. He never forgets, standing before the mirror like one performing a sacred ritual. Mr. Reginald is overweight with an arthritic hip; he has a pot belly and occasional trouble with his prostate. The boys hanging round the ruined cemetery won't meet his eyes these days; about ten years ago they could be induced to give him a hand job. But now they avoid him; old age is contagious.

Early summer. He drinks whisky at the Old King, then heads off to the cemetery, the light just starting to fail. May too the cruellest month: memory and desire and hope fumbling around inside you like a feckless drunk in a soiled raincoat. But it's just no good, no good. By the Victorian mausoleum in the centre of the cemetery two men fuck noisily against a railing but Mr. Reginald walks on, eyes front. Like the soldier he'd hoped to be, but hadn't.

'Hopeless to come here,' he whispers to himself. 'I shan't come again.'

He sees suddenly his mother, imagines her looking at him now; him sweaty, overweight, rumpled in his clothing and his manner. Tiny wisps of hair falling over a hot seamy forehead, limping undignified through a leafy cemetery in the vain hope of sex. Sex with men. 'Jesus, Mary, and Joseph,' she would have exclaimed, and the knowledge would have killed her sooner than the cancer. Though that took long enough.

The last few days, lying in the hospice bed with its raised sides.

A dying old baby in a terrible echo of a child's cot. Then her flattened corpse in the tiny, scruffy room at the funeral home. Face stretched out like a waxwork, red lipsticked; they'd smudged a bit. Her coffin lid had been propped against a wall with peeling paper and a picture of a sunset. He'd stared at her, hoping to feel something other than grotesque tiredness; nothing had come. Instead he had walked round her body and straightened the picture of a sunset on the wall over her coffin. It was on crooked - he couldn't stand that.

'She was a lovely lady to do,' the attendant had said. She smiled up at Mr. Reginald. He believed her name was Donna.

Donna bent her head again to her laptop.

He had trampled home in the snow. His mother had been very green, he had thought, despite the make up. Not lovely. She had never been lovely. She had been forceful in her ways and devout and only occasionally kind. She'd never had an idea, and he'd worked hard to keep it that way. Even now, walking through this churchyard, he wanted to protect her.

Mr. Reginald begins to make his way out of the cemetery, noticing that from around the bend of the path leading to the gates, a boy approaches. A boy to Mr. Reginald anyway - Indian, late twenties, beads around his neck, white open-necked shirt. His black hair is long and hangs down his back - Mr. Reginald has never seen such long hair on a man.

They pass each other on the gravel overgrown by weeds. At close range, Mr. Reginald sees that the man's long hair is not only long and black but thick and wiry. Mr. Reginald feels what he thinks is ivy or some undergrowth brushing his shoulder but it's the fingertips - very light - of the Indian boy on his left arm. Startled, Mr. Reginald looks down at his arm and up into the eyes of the boy. Two tranquil brown spheres: not judging, not appraising.

'Come with me' the boy says in an English accent tinged with Indian.

Mr. Reginald can barely speak.

'What do I pay you?' he stammers.

The boy laughs. His face creases pleasantly.

'You think I charge? Don't be a fool!'

He gestures to a secluded spot behind a stone angel, wings outstretched over a child's grave. Maria Edwards Farrar, born December 1911, gathered on May 2, 1918. Jesus took a little child. The sex is brief but satisfying and, incredibly, accompanied by kissing: the boy kisses Mr. Reginald gently on the mouth, seemingly without repugnance. Mr. Reginald is surprised. The Indian is a good actor, perhaps.

'Where are you from?' Mr. Reginald ventures afterwards, mumbling into the man's white shirt.

'The Punjab, originally. I am a Sikh.'

Mr. Reginald is slightly shocked.

'Isn't this against your religion?'

The Sikh leans back his head and laughs.

'Maybe. But it's not against *my* religion.'

He pats the older man's hand.

Shocked unbelievably by the friendliness of the touch, Mr. Reginald's eyes begin to fill. But he returns the pat on the boy's hand, casually. To seem as casual as possible is important; he must assume nothing. The Sikh detaches himself, smiles. His mobile bleeps; he takes it from his pocket and looks down at it, frowning.

He lifts up his face to Mr. Reginald and smiles. 'I have to leave. I am sorry.'

Abruptly, the Indian heads off towards the dark blue gates of the cemetery, now turning purple in the war paint of evening sun. He turns again at the gate, raises a hand to Mr. Reginald, smiles, and disappears.

No names are exchanged, but nothing strange in that. Dazed, Mr. Reginald wonders if the boy was ever there at all. But, tracing the burn of the Sikh's stubble on his face, he knows that he was. But he does not expect to see him again.

A small miracle for a May evening, that's all.

Mr. Reginald cannot sleep.

He is burdened by tightness around his chest, a shortness of breath. Sheba, his old black Labrador, rests at the end of his bed, both reassuring and disturbing him with canine sighs and grunts.

In the morning, feeling no better, Mr. Reginald makes his way to the doctor, heading first for the local chemist, three streets away, to pick up a prescription for his hip. At the shop, he enters then halts, dumbfounded, by the door; the boy from last night, now turbaned and white-coated, is behind the counter.

Rooted, inanimate, Mr. Reginald sees under the fluorescent light of the shop what he only felt the previous evening; a stubbled chin, dark but barely registering in the Sikh's brown face.

'Can I help you?' the man asks.

He doesn't smile or show recognition.

It takes some minutes for Mr. Reginald's mouth to grind open. He asks for his prescription, falteringly, in a voice dry with shock.

Winces as the chest pain returns. The boy notices.

'Pains in your arms? A tight band across your chest?'

The tone friendly but professional.

'No. Just a tightness, no arm pain.'

The boy nods, still unsmiling.

'Perhaps indigestion, muscle strain. But see the doctor, or go to casualty. I'll get your prescription.'

The pills are handed over and Mr. Reginald thanks him, imagining that there is a mother or sister in the back of the pharmacy. Something to explain the man's seriousness, something to inhibit him. Mr. Reginald is halfway to the exit when a clear, loud voice behind him calls out.

'Sir? Sir?'

The Sikh stands in front of him.

'Your wallet.'

He hands the brown wallet back to Mr. Reginald. Mr. Reginald is embarrassed.

This is always happening - the senility is kicking in. Mr. Reginald turns from the man, heading for the exit. The shop is temporarily empty.

But the Sikh touches his arm, like before in the cemetery, and with a rapid movement pulls him round to face him. Glances quickly to the office behind the counter.

'You never told me your name,' he whispers.

'There was no need,' Mr. Reginald mutters. 'You were being kind. Anyway, you didn't ask. You rushed off. What's your name?'

'I am Adarshpal and I wasn't being kind; I liked your face, but I was already late. My father owns this shop - I've come to work for him. I was abroad but they needed me. And you?'

Gently, with the same smile.

A smile in relief against evening sunlight, against a stone for a dead child; against ivy, close to earth.

'Paul, Paul Reginald.'

Suddenly Paul starts to gabble, words falling out on top of each other, like starving children tumbling out of a cupboard they'd been locked in.

'Before it was Paul O'Donnell; my mother changed the surname when we came over looking for a place to stay. They kept turning the Irish away, you see. My father was a labourer on a building site; he couldn't get work in those days and… '

Mr. Reginald trails off.

Boring, I am boring, and fat and hairless and disgusting. In a minute, I will start to tell him about the army, how I wanted to be a soldier but how they would not let me in because of my astigmatism. He will despise me, hate me for the accumulated failures stacked up like pointed sticks behind me.

But Adarshpal does not seem impatient. Or bored.

Mr. Reginald rallies himself, looks at the boy, straight into the centre of his pupils.

'Adarshpal. Does that mean anything?'

The Sikh smiles. A stretching of his face, one last time; Paul feeds on it, treasures its outline.

He will not return to this chemist's shop.

Not ever.

'Adarshpal? It means the keeper of ideals.'

The Sikh shrugs.

'I do my best. But I think for myself. My father is dying. I will not hurt my parents - not while they both live.'

'Will you marry?' Mr. Reginald whispers.

Adarshpal considers.

'I may have to.' He lightly touches Mr. Reginald's face, as though to examine him. 'But I will see you again?'

Mr. Reginald laughs.

'Do you know how old I am? How little time I have?'

There seems little point in hiding the truth.

The boy laughs, touches Mr. Reginald's face again. Speaks gently to him.

'Believe that good can come to you. Believe it.'

Mr. Reginald will remember this, always.

But right now, he mustn't embarrass himself with tears.

A woman's voice from the back room. Adarshpal leaves him again, raising his arm in farewell, returning to the counter to serve another customer.

Glancing back just once, as if to say, 'We will speak again.'

Mr. Reginald cannot get an appointment at the doctor but by then the pain has vanished anyway. Adarshpal was right, probably indigestion.

Paul spends the rest of the day weeding, raking, and scarcely feeling his arthritic hip. Putting down seeds for the cabbages that will sprout later in the year. He is empty, rested in spirit; Sheba sprawls on the old garden chair watching him, yawning deeply.

About six, he wanders out again for some shopping, contriving to walk past the chemist's he'd sworn he'd not visit again.

Back home Mr. Reginald eats, then works in the garden again till late, watching the new moon rise with cryptic dark markings along its surface. It pleases him to think of the markings as water. Not empty craters but deep, peaceful rivers stretching endlessly across the lunar surface. A shadow of cloud passes over the moon's glow, and Mr. Reginald lifts his head from the earth and his trowel to watch it. A dense bliss moves over him; turning back to deep earth smells, he works to the moon's illumination until he is almost too exhausted to stop.

Finally, Paul lifts himself up from the earth goes back indoors, staggers up to bed to lie full upon it, not bothering to take off his clothes. Sheba lies beside him; he strokes her silk coat with an absent, calm hand.

Sometime towards morning, the old dog wakes unusually cold, shakes herself, and jumps off the now comfortless bed. Dragging her body to the window, she lays herself down, watching with her one good eye the rows of fading dawn stars.

Head on her paws, ears up, she waits: waits for the warmth to return.

Waits for her master's voice, her master's whistle.

Adam Butterfly

Joe Else
England

DUSK IN ADAM'S STUDIO as he sits cross legged in the centre of the room. The ending of the seventh day and no Takumi. Seven days of wiping the dust from the white orchids in the grey stone bowl his lover had given him; wiping in hope of Takumi's return.

Adam has been doing the same exhausted calculation all day. If Takumi came back when he said he would, then he's been in England for seven days. Three days to recover from the flight - Adam's of a generous nature - the fourth day to come. But it's the seventh day and there has been nothing.

No call, no text, no email, no posting. No visit.

Possible explanations had been comprehensively mulled. Takumi's father was worse, and he had not returned at all. Or he had been snowed under with doctorate work almost from the moment his plane touched down.

Or had gone for a further interview with Portland Down. Perhaps Takumi himself was sick. Less likely was the option that he was shyly awaiting Adam's text, unwilling to make first contact. That made no sense. Takumi had the edge, the power from the beginning. He had known it.

'I am in your hands completely,' Adam had whispered in the middle of the last night.

Takumi's eyes had gleamed in the darkness, a beautiful demon.

Adam shivers and rises, back stiff, frowning slightly at the thin hairy legs sticking out from under his short dressing gown. They look ridiculous and ugly, he thinks.

Takumi will not come because I am ridiculous and ugly.

He sighs, switches on a lamp on the top of the green bookcase, and picks up his favourite children's book, *The Borrowers*. Opens it a few pages into the story, to lines he has remembered all his life.

'Now breakfast rooms are alright in the morning when the sun streams in on the toast and marmalade but by afternoon they seem to vanish a little and to fill with a strange silvery light, their own twilight. There is a kind of sadness in them then.'

His studio in the morning - just a few weeks ago - with Takumi, the both of them munching down on toasted cheese sandwiches in bed, happiness splattered everywhere like yellow paint. Sunlight forming a puddle on the golden carpet, the faded green armchairs that came with the flat welcoming and charmingly retro.

But now, afternoon slipping hopelessly into evening, Adam notices the black scuff marks on the cream walls of his studio, the springs coming through the green armchairs. The depressing orange glow of the ancient black angle point lamp inherited from his dead father. Not retro, really, just sad. Adam recalls his father typing under the light of this angle poise in the kitchen at the back of their 70's semi, wearing an off-grey jumper with holes in the elbows. Typing and whistling and making tea in cups without handles.

Adam sighs. Everything is darkening outside and inside of him. Darkening down for evening and November. Maybe forever, if he never sees Takumi again.

In the fruit market outside his home, the stallholders are closing up their stalls and benches and shouting to each other. Pushing aside the curtain, Adam gazes down onto the street. As the stalls shut down, a few hesitant old people of indeterminate sex are buying fruit and veg for what Adam suspects will be solitary dinners. The Three Golden Sisters Chinese restaurant on the floor under Adam's flat has switched on its door lights and red lanterns. Its owner stands fag in hand on the steps whilst the smell of roasting duck begins a gentle upward waft.

They had takeaway one night, ordered up from the restaurant. The owner's son had brought it; Takumi had been unfriendly to the son.

Adam had noticed but not cared much; his arms had been around Takumi, his eyes engaged and delighted by him. Later he had fed Takumi pieces of duck with his bare hands, stroking his arm.

Eight days and nights. Alternately fucking, sleeping, and eating. Takumi, twenty-nine, looking twenty-one, a little grey starting to bleed into his jet hair, almond-shaped eyes and features, a small tight body, hairless.

Takumi had been fascinated by Adam's hairiness, running his hands over Adam's thighs, muttering something in Japanese. Softly. Presumably words of admiration.

Takumi, one of the top ten young scientists named by New Scientist as winner of the magazine's scientific talent competition. A ferocious brain, pursuing doctorate chemistry with molecular physics, headhunted by the MOD for work on anthrax and chemical weapons.

'But you're not that kind of a chemist, are you?'

Adam had laughed, nibbling his lover's neck on their last night together.

'Why do you want to work on weapons?'

'I have top qualifications' Takumi had declared confidently. 'I can work anywhere. On anything. Weapons are work, like anything else.'

Takumi had apparently not cared about Adam's lack of comparable status.

'My father worked as a guard at Tokyo Station all his life. You're a good man. Like him. You have gentleness.'

Takumi's father grew vegetables. So did Adam, on a small Hackney allotment he had had since coming to London in the nineties. Mostly he grew courgettes, carrots, potatoes; recently he had branched out into broccoli and raspberries. But he was not overambitious. They had eaten in bed, on that last night, before Takumi's return to Japan, and then Takumi had leapt out, pulled on his jeans and gone to the kitchen, where he had filled two buckets of water from the taps. Armed with a mop, dusters, some cloths, and housecleaner, he had begun to clean every inch of Adam's flat, including the toilet.

Adam had seen this as a declaration of intent rather than a Japanese fastidiousness. Takumi would return to him and he wanted the place they would spend time in together to be immaculate, beautiful. Adam, security guard, forty-three, would hover gently at the corner of Takumi's brilliant career, providing him with vegetables and small pieces of wisdom. It would happen at last; the thing he had crushed all belief in having. Like's a pretty child's head plunged again and again into the depths of a cold bath and then, almost unbelievably, retrieved, brought back to life, its hair dried.

Finally, Takumi had leaned the mop against the kitchen door and smiled.

'Adam, you are a good man but you're not a clean one. Now this place is clean!'

He had handed Adam the mop and went to take a shower. When Adam took his own shower later, he found two packs of anti bacterial wipes in the bathroom. They had not been there before.

Adam had been delighted.

The next day Takumi had texted Adam of his father's sudden illness, and taken a flight home. One month ago.

Ten days ago he had emailed Adam and gave him details of his imminent return to London.

Then silence.

Adam had cleaned and dusted every other day since Takumi's departure. Now he moves his fingers over the bookcase. There is still too much dust on them when he examines his finger in the light. Takumi is right, I am dirty. I am an unkempt old man. What I had hoped for could not possibly have happened. I dreamt, that is all.

I dreamt.

The eighth day dawns. Adam drags himself from bed and decides to visit the British Museum; he must do something with his day. Try not to assume the worse. Distract himself.

There's an exhibition of Renaissance art; Mantegna, Veronese from a small museum near Mantua. Lesser works damaged during an earthquake in 2012, but restored and well preserved. Adam loves art - anything, from installation art to Warhol to Van Eyck.

Takumi had shown no signs of being interested in art of any kind; the boy had looked blank when he had mentioned Hiroshige, Hokusai. But Takumi was a scientist. Why should he have an interest in 18th-century Japanese art? Or any art. Adam had not blamed him, but had felt an unreasonable, inexplicable disappointment.

Adam takes the tube to Kings Cross, walks the short distance to the British Museum, stopping briefly for a coffee near at a small kiosk near the entrance. When he finally enters the museum a security guard indicates for him to place his bag on a table for searching.

At a table on the other side of the entrance, another guard is searching the handbag of a Japanese woman. A man whose face Adam can't see crouches by her, his back turned, tying up his shoelaces. His frame is slight, hair black. The man stands up.

Takumi.

Adam is at the bottom of a lift shaft, his stomach leaping like a mad frog. Takumi - thinner, tired looking but smiling at the woman, taking her arm and heading off with her in the direction of the cafe area on the right. Its tables and seats are open to the hallway. Adam watches them join the queue for drinks and food.

Adam, almost unable to breathe, pulls up his green hoodie over his short grey curls, and taking his bag from the guard follows Takumi and the woman to the same area.

Letting several people go before him, Adam ends up seventh or eighth down in the cafe queue from Takumi and the woman. Close enough to get a good view, far enough away not to be seen.

Adam can make no decision about the items behind the plastic food holders. He can barely focus on the type of sandwiches available, on whether there is sparkling as well as still water. He cannot breathe.

So it is a woman. Because he, Takumi, young, cosmopolitan, but with the values of traditional Japanese society still ingrained within him, cannot bring himself to choose the man. Adam, trying to hold back familiar crumpling panic within himself, makes himself scrutinise his rival.

Early thirties, petite, dressed conservatively in black and gold suit, patent shoes. Hair in a shiny black bob, her garb is that of a much older woman, maybe a senator's wife. She isn't pretty; her nose is large and her chin juts forward. A few years older than Takumi and half an inch smaller. No stunning Asian female. But she is listening to Takumi silently with her head bent towards him deferentially.

He beams back at her; she pats his arm gently, intimately.

Another rush of pain, and then a gush of coldness. Like anaesthetic.

And then the true shock.

A tall man, red curling hair and a rangy walk, rushes past Adam in the queue, close enough for Adam to smell the cologne, observe the neat goatee, the springing confidence. Observes how the man takes Takumi clearly in his arms and places a brief but proprietorial kiss full on his lips.

In the middle of the British Museum, on a Sunday afternoon. People stare though they're angry at themselves for doing so; but one man kissing another is still so novel.

Adam grabs the rail next to the cafe counter, his heart pounding too fast for his ears to keep up with its racket.

'Hey, hey!' the redheaded man says loudly to the cashier in an American accent.

'I'll get these, yeah, and a cappuccino for me.'

He lays down a twenty pound note in front of her, smiling broadly. Pulling his headphones from his ears and ruffling his hair. The cashier smiles back. Everyone smiles back at this man. He's used to it.

Takumi and the Japanese woman let themselves be guided by him to a nearby trestle table. The cappuccino arrives, Takumi starts to tackle pasta. The woman unwraps a chocolate brownie slowly, carefully, ritualistically; she takes an age to pick away the plastic.

The American chatters on, whilst Takumi, fork to mouth, suddenly lifts his eyes and sees Adam. Adam, still in the queue, grasping the handrail. Takumi's mouth is open but he seems frozen. The Japanese woman, seeing Takumi, also turns her eyes to Adam. Then the American too, glances his way

Takumi gets up from the table, approaches Adam. Stretches out his hand into a shake.

Adam is too surprised to do anything but respond with a limp grip of his own. A handshake, how extraordinary. How painful.

Takumi leads Adam back to the table where he is introduced, hesitantly, to Dana, manager of Takumi's doctorate programme at Imperial, and to Masoko Ito, an old college friend of Takumi's working in London as a marine insurance underwriter.

Dana immediately takes charge.

'Hey, bud, sit down. Have a coffee?'

'No thanks, I had one earlier. I was just after some water but it doesn't really matter.'

Adam scarcely knows what he is saying. Takumi had extracted him from the queue as he was about to blindly reach for some Evian. But Adam sits down anyway, on a bench opposite Ms. Ito and her slightly surprised face. Ms. Ito's forehead is awash with blackheads, Adam notices. Dana sits on the same side as Takumi. Close up Dana is nearer to late than early thirties with deep lines in his cheeks and forehead, and hair that is taking on the whitened look of the ageing redhead.

But he is beautiful, no denying that; long legs that clash with Adam's under the trestle: a broad, defined chest in a check shirt, green eyes. He opens the conversation.

'So you're doing the Renaissance thing today? It's not really Takumi's and my stuff, but Masoko likes it, don't you Masoko? Takumi decided to take her.'

Masoko nods, but does not smile.

Adam turns to her. Recovering a little, he decides he may as well play this scene through.

'Van Gogh said everything he did was based on Japanese art. What's your opinion of Hiroshige, Hokusai?'

Ms. Ito frowns. Lifts her eyes from her chocolate brownie for a second.

'They are generally clichéd. I prefer the Renaissance. Especially the Mannerists. The Great Wave is on too many student walls. It's embarrassing.'

Her English is good, idiomatic, her voice scornful. She's been here a while.

Dana stretches his long legs out; his feet briefly brush Adam's. There isn't really room under the trestle for such vast extremities; both Takumi and Adam have to draw in their feet.

Dana regains control of the conversation.

'So, Adam, you're teaching somewhere, I guess?'

'Sorry?'

'You're teaching, at school?'

'I'm a security guard in the city.'

There are other jobs than university academia. The world does not just consist of app developers with unforgiving ruthlessly manicured beards, or, brainy but unscrupulous scientists and their fixers. Dana is fumbling visibly for something to say.

'Must be interesting, I guess you get a lot of annoying Americans. I know a lot of bankers from NYC,' he finally ventures, winking at Adam.

'I don't know if they are annoying,' replies Adam. 'But the American visitors generally always ask how I am and then walk on without waiting for a reply. It's like they are compelled to do it, even though they don't care what my answer is. Why is that, you think?'

Adam is made of ice now, happy to put the American on the spot.

Dana laughs uneasily. He ignores the question.

'So how you know Tak?' he queries, his eyes sharp.

Tak. Adam would not have dared. Dana puts his arms round Takumi, in ownership. Takumi seems tense, perching on the bench stiffly, uncomfortably. He glances at Adam pleadingly. He looks a little afraid. Adam feels terrible familiar boredom and disappointment. The fearfulness of others. *I've never known a man who wasn't a coward,* he thinks. *Nor a woman neither.*

Adam finally responds to Dana.

'Takumi and I spent eight days together. Or should I say, eight nights.' The words sound flat now, dead.

Meaningless. Adam has lost. He knows it.

Ms. Ito's chocolate brownie crumbs rest pre-lick on her mouth. Dana looks from Adam to Takumi.

Dana's features are still organised into a smile. Adam guesses that he is assessing what a penchant for hairier older security guards says about Takumi, if anything. Is Takumi the rock solid proposition he seemed to be? Older men are clearly not Dana's' thing. A young slim boy of around eighteen is clearing the tables, loading cups onto a tray; Dana stares at him, half smiles, and looks away. The boy is flattered but flustered.

Adam watches as Dana's assessment of him spreads into his features. He's decided that Adam is just a slightly extended pickup that won't interfere with him or Takumi. He can be dealt with, expertly managed, like everything in Dana's life and the satellite states that revolve around him.

But Adam will not be problem-solved. He will walk away. He gets up, the bench screeching as he moves it.

'I have to go. It was nice to meet you, Dana. And Masoko'.

Adam makes a half bow, turns, and begins to pick his way through the crowded café area.

Dana calls him back. He's unused to people striding away from him.

'Hey come have lunch with us, we're going to a pizza place later. Come on, stay. I like to meet Takumi's friends.'

Takumi's friends. That's how he's playing it.

'Thanks', says Adam, turning his head just enough to be heard. But I have to be somewhere.'

Adam walks quickly to the entrance lobby, past the large donations chest awash with five pounds notes and scatterings of dollars. He heads down the broad stone steps leading down into the courtyard and the evening November gloom. A guard seated in the porter's lodge looks bleakly out as Adam heads into Museum Street. The guard - so close to beautiful expensive things and he cannot live on the pay.

Not with three kids.

Ms. Ito, perhaps deprived of some expected excitement, looks down onto her unfinished brownie with irritation.

Sorry, Masoko. Not this time.

At nine, Adam's intercom buzzes.

'Adam? Takumi. Please let me up.'

Adam lets go of the buzzer. In a few minutes, a knock.

Takumi, pale in the landing outside against the yellow flickering of the one remaining corridor strip light that works.

Takumi wastes no time. The words, in good but occasionally broken English, peppered with Americanisms, fall out of him. He almost gabbles.

'I meant to come to you Adam, to explain, but Dana took me to a conference in Brussels. I was going to end things with him before I went back to Japan, when I met you. But here's the thing Adam, Dana is very influential - he knows everyone - all the important people. I need him. Do you understand?'

Takumi reaches out his hand to touch Adam's shoulder. Adam both flinches and relishes.

'But he is cool about us going on seeing each other.'

'He feels you have a function in my life. He still wants me but he wants me to have you too. Let's make things easy, good for us. You're awesome, you're a good working man. Like my father; he is better you know, a small stroke. You're not clean though," Takumi adds, familiarly, certain Adam will take the deal.

Yeah, thinks Adam, *I'm a good working man. The salt of the earth.*

And no, it's not a bad deal. A lover he shares - better than no lover. Almost more than a forty-three-year-old security guard with a shitty rented studio over a Chinese restaurant has any right to expect.

Pretty awesome.

But you have a nerve, Takumi, you and your fierce intelligence and your antibacterial wipes. You have a nerve.

Looking into the almost black irises of Takumi's eyes, Adam has the strongest desire to touch him. Desire will pass. It passed before - it always does. And you are back where you started; back to the boredom and the end of things. Takumi is talking on, repeating himself.

'I wished first to continue only with you, Adam, But Dana has so many contacts. He got a starred first from Cambridge in my field, then an MSc, and doctorate at Imperial. In a few years he'll be a professor. I am not from a rich family. My father worked as a guard and grows vegetables and I... '

'Yes,' Adam interrupts Adam harshly. 'Your father was a guard and grows vegetables. Your uncle put you through college and an American taught you English. I know. You told me.'

Silence.

If Takumi is startled by the sharpness of Adam's tone, he tries not to show it. Then Takumi's voice begins again, a little plaintive. Maybe he is afraid, afraid of being controlled and organised and owned and one day abandoned by Dana. But probably more afraid of returning to what he was - the bright but poor working class boy from Asakusa.

'Adam. Please.'

Adam takes in Takumi, one last time, standing in the dirty corridor, with its buzzing and garish strip light. Takes in Takumi in all his gorgeous demon-eyed confusion.

Adam closes the door on him, not rudely but firmly. He turns off the room's central light and sits crosslegged in the middle of the room.

'Adam, Adam. Please... '

After a few minutes of persistent knocking and calling, Takumi's footsteps going downstairs.

Then Takumi's' voice calling up to him from the street. He calls up for a few minutes more. But his voice seems to be fading further and further away with each call; a vague chirruping, disappearing bird-like sound.

A sound from another age.

Adam remains still; he hears his own calm breathing, feels the movement of his rising and falling chest. Closes his eyes and opens them onto the silk green coverlet of his bed, and above his bed, Hiroshige's' Japanese bridge in rain, *Sudden Shower Over Shin-Ohashi Bridge*. Eighteenth-century Japanese men are crossing the bridge in a downpour of sheet rain, their umbrellas held high above their heads. Adam closes his eyes again. Feels the rain pattering on the slats of the wooden bridge, the clatter of the men's pattens as they traverse it. Hears the slopping sound of the boatman's pole navigating his log raft downstream of the rainy river.

Adam breathes deeply, his hands making an imaginary trail through the water under Shin-Ohashi Bridge. Sloosh, sloosh. A falling sound of herons calling over the river. The falling sound of a silence growing great within Adam.

Mr. Liu in the 3 Golden Sisters also does fish and chips. The chips are too skinny and the battered cod tastes of stagnant water tinged with disinfectant. When he is certain that Takumi has gone, Adam will go down for some.

There is no greater strength than never to care again.

Before White Angel

Joe Fuller
England

THE OLD MAN SLOUCHED, groaned, and moaned as he crossed the dust road.

His tweed coat was moth-eaten. Hair, uncut and unkempt. Mind suffering from sickness.

Cars saw the old man whilst the old man saw suicide. His pinewood cane rocked and knocked on the earth. Like a friend on a door. To him, it was the same music he heard everyday. Flies lay in his beard - a grey, busy mess. And the cars whistled close. But the time was not now.

First, for a burger. The last... a bloody slab of beef. Each knock brought him closer to the Blue Sparrow diner, a 50's-style joint equipped with checkered tiles and a vinyl player. It was his favourite place in the world.

When he breached the door, the scents of fresh pepper. Spices. Meat. Greeted him.

They said, "Come sit, weary traveller. Take a load off."

The Blue Sparrow was in a subtle swing this afternoon. Red balloons hung high. Grills pumped out food. Men and women dressed in quality suits awaited meals with rich contempt. The drink flowed free and no baby let forth a cry because there was no baby to cry. Always a plus. He hated those screechy, fleshy baubles and their redneck parents.

In the background, Dean Martin was having a ball.

"Can I take your order, Sir?"

Suddenly, a teen with greasy hair and bad breath crunched into his personal space. He was grinning and drooling. A dog.

"You must be new," the old man tried a sweet smile. "I usually take a seat before you serve me. Is Bob here today?"

"Bob?"

"He knows my favourite."

The teen looked taken aback, almost disarmed. Behind his face, a new kind of ugly brewed.

"I'll go fetch him for you."

The old man breathed easy at that - no stench and no rudeness would intrude upon him today. The Blue Sparrow had certainly let it's standards drop… ditching a slick, black-haired waiter and his bonny blue-eyed assistant for a young man who had algae grow in between his teeth.

The old man sighed and let his knocking stick pave the way.

A booth in the corner, semi shadowed against the sun. The destination for good eats. He limped over to it, leather shoes slipping and sliding on the buffed floor. To the booth, once splintered and cracked, but soft on the behind. Homey. Soft wood. Squishy, rose cushion. Replaced by a backbreaker of a chair.

He lit a cigarette to alleviate the pain. Although, he figured, that was probably obsolete as well.

Then they'll let the minorities in. Animals. Insects. And he sure as hell guaranteed that a black man's cigarette would be lit and stay lit. The old man loved all skins, colours and creeds, but The Blue Sparrow had to stay 50's. It had to. For his sake. For his sanity.

"I'm gonna have to ask you to put that out, friend."

The old man looked up from his rolled-up poison and into the milky, warm eyes of Bob Redbridge.

He was a cowboy in modern life, enveloped in a black blazer with red cuffs. Scrawny but confident. Greying but almost not grey at all. A picture of a warm grandpa who drank malt liquor on many a porch. Womaniser and rascal turned to working cog.

"You're joking…"

"'Fraid not, times have changed." Bobby held out a palm, clawing for the smoke and upon seeing the old man's distasteful expression, his tone softened. "Listen, I don't like it either. I'd happily go back to the days of smoking indoors and drinking from the taps... Hell, I'd even love to be able to kick shady characters from the premises-"

"But you can't."

"Exactly, It's bad for business. You're a good fella. You understand."

That claw came back around again. Fingers like sickles. A palm that would shred his vice. His last cigarette. The old man let it fall, fire and all. Ash and a stink that clung to Bob's hand.

"The bloody beef and cheese burger with extra onions?"

"You know me," he grinned through gritted teeth.

Or would you take that from me too?

The old man let Dean drown out... The babble was gone... The hiss of the food... the smells were all gone...

He turned his attention to that horizon through the pale window: watched the sun dance through the skyline, possessive and all encompassing of it. And to the desert, dust and dry. The carpark in which couples made out over burgers and fries. A pink Cadillac that had a woman lolling in the backseat, dressed in ketchup. Back to the long and lonesome road - onto the blurs that rocketed by.

He wanted to be hit by a pink Cadillac.

When the burger crashed onto his table, the old man wasted no time. He sank his teeth into the brioche bun and split the cow into bits as the blood poured out from a gaping wound. The burger was charred, bloody, and the bun crumbled into a soft mache whilst his choppers went to work. Fitting. He was one Cadillac away from being a bleeding, dead animal. He spat seeds. He licked his crinkled lips as they became doused in red. He even slurped the juices. A vampire in the day. The affair was messy: ruby puddles coating the wooden table, seeping into the cracks. Cheese splattered. A slasher movie. He reached for a drink to take the overbearing edge off. The dryness. When fate slapped a Pepsi in his lap.

"I bought you this," exclaimed the shadow.

The old man looked up - taking in a dark-haired bachelor, purple shades, and a walking stick that outshone his own. He was clean-shaven and young with eyes that could make ice crack.

"May I sit down?"

"Mhmm," came the mumble, fighting against a mouthful of cool soda.

The bachelor took his place opposite, resting his walking stick against the table. Smooth, black marble with a silver lion head. Mesmerising.

Thoughts bounced from: *Where did you get that fine cane from?* to *Sorry, I'm preoccupied with sugar and sweetener.*

The bachelor simply stared. If staring was a sin, he'd stare all the more. Deadpan. Not a wrinkle, blemish or scar in sight. His eyes could be seen through that purple glass. He leant, elbows on the table. Into the pile of cheese and blood. Dutifully waiting. Unfazed.

"Thank-" the old man managed.

"No need, no need," came a sharkish smile. "I watched some guy crush up your cigarette, thought I'd reimburse you a bit... If you fancy a smoke now, he won't dare stop you. Here, I brought my own."

His wrist flicked and from the sleeve came two cigars - both wrapped in ebony paper with a golden band hugging the tobacco in place.

The old man took one tentatively. "I don't want any trouble."

"Nonsense, I'll even light it for you."

The bachelor fished in his pocket and produced a golden dragon lighter that breathed fire from it's maw. The dragon glared, singing his whiskers as the cigar burst into flame. The old man took a rich puff and sighed in contentment, the smoke running down his throat like cough syrup.

"This is fine; finest cigar I've ever tasted."

"Sun-bleached and burnt paper..." the bachelor mused. "Those son's a bitches cost me two-hundred dollars a piece."

"How much do I owe you?"

The bachelor chuckled. "Do you really think I need anything in return?"

"To be honest… no. You seem well off. Dashing. Just a few girls short of what I'd expect."

The bachelor shrugged as if he knew all this to be true. As if it was fact, rather than opinion. Ego thoroughly massaged, he gestured to the outside world.

"I have girls." His finger pronged the glass. "They're in my car."

The old man followed the bachelor's perfect pointer - to the pink Cadillac and the ketchup lady.

Her legs now, split. Resting on the driver's headrest. Shoulders lolled back. Eyes open. The white of an egg whilst her pupils boiled a yellow yolk. Golden hair. Hints of a white dress. Mouth agape. Sneering. Dead. And something else. A ruffle in the car, a disturbance from her breasts or perhaps betwixt her thighs. Two faces retracted from the woman: ruby-dressed chins with fangs. Droplets of blood peppered their hair like snow… And they headed back down to tear more flesh.

"What is this?"

"I bet you'd do immoral things to get home. Maybe, even disgusting things."

The bachelor picked at his nails, cigar hanging slack from his jaw. And spoke once more.

"I present to you, a choice. I've ordered another fat burger. All yours if you've the appetite. Free. On the house. Finito. But at the cost of time. I watched you chow from afar and reckon you'll finish in about five minutes. That's great. That's good. Though, it's five minutes to escape. Five minutes you'll wish you had. Because in five minutes, you'll die by my hand and my girls will simply eat the evidence."

The old man looked around, struck by the moment. And the upcoming moments, what they would entail. He almost locked a look with the staff members. One of desperation. One they'd understand. His hands shook. He felt bile burn away his throat.

"Turn back or I'll blow your goddamned head off." Comply. Comply. Comply. "That's better. Basically, if you eat the burger, you're fucked. No two ways about it. You have to get from the Blue Sparrow to home. A hidey-hole. An apartment. I don't care much for where. If you get there like a good person, I'll just be running after you with a gun. Get away from me by screwing people over and I'll hunt you down like an animal. Hell, I'll be level with you, the second way is slower for me."

"Has it ever occurred to you that I want to die?"

"If you did, you'd have done it already. Now make a choice. You're burning daylight, baby."

He tried to question morals.

But was given four minutes.

He tried to reason with the Bachelor.

But was given three minutes.

And so, the old man hobbled back into daylight - glaring at the shadows of death that sped by. Finding that. For once. He didn't have the stomach to take his own life... In this moment, he decided, he wanted to keep on living.

To actually live. To choose. To make the wrong choice. Should he be scared? He was, yet pulled his tweed jacket tightly around him. To keep the ghosts, spooks, and doubts from his core. He soldiered on. Knocking dutifully on the pavement without so much as a glance to the pink Cadillac or the rich psychopath. Heart beating. Vision misty. A body that creaked and cracked in the wind. He knocked towards the sun. The sun flipped him off, descending fast. He stuck out a blackened thumb and felt whispers at his back.

"They won't stop for a scruffy tramp."

The old man waited for a sure minute... his arm tiring, whirlwinds of dust gathering by his feet before he made the choice. 50/50. To tuck that blackened thumb back in and leap like a lover into the path of a car.

The RV caught his fragile frame like a catcher's mitt caught an old ball. He hit the grill and cracked the windscreen. Tumbling. Turning. Spiralling. Hopefully into a soft sleep. When the old man hit the ground, he saw a gun and the sharkish grin behind it. As he came to a stop, the vultures circled.

"Oh, shit. You alright, Mister?"

He didn't stop to acknowledge the one who helped him up. Man? Woman? Maybe even a child at the wheel? He shoved them off, grabbed his cane from the side of the road, and whacked the person, half-baked. The person resisted and was gunned down like a dog. His kneecaps burst open.

"Bang, bang." The bachelor laughed. "Just thought I'd help out."

The old man spat in his direction and clambered over the howling mess on the floor. He felt hot tears run down his cheek like gasoline. People would be watching. Cops would be here soon.

But he wept for the mess… He wept for the misery he'd caused them.

"Taking that car is a very immoral thing to do."

His fingers ripped open the door and he fell into the RV - crawling up to the driver's seat. A baby in awe.

"You're awakening the animal."

Gaze settled on the keys in the engine. As a magpie, he was drawn to them. Shiny keys. Shiny car. Shiny glass that splintered his toes. His arm shot out to catch that big red monster of a door. To drown out the bachelor. To crack his skull if he followed.

He did not. The old man shut the door with something close to malice and looked deeply into the rearview mirror as he tweaked the keys, making the engine chug on.

The ground swelled. Pulsating blood. Though, the man with the busted kneecaps shrieked on, no help came to him, and his death would be agonising.

Even worse - was the bachelor, who simply licked his fingers free of white powder. Whispering. A dozen times.

"It begins. And so, it begins."

The old man stomped on the tiger's tail… leaving behind a trail of dust in the wind. His mouth, slack-jaw. His eyes still looking behind.

Like black holes, they swallowed the scene. Wide as the bachelor leaped onto all fours. Wider as the bachelor ran that way, as a clumsy animal or deformed dog - barking and laughing in a torrent of madness. Widest as the bachelor bent over his pray. Drooling. Slobbering. Stupid. He sunk his teeth into those busted kneecaps and chewed until the bone snapped. Until the face caved in. Until liquid life force and flesh flowed in great abandon and screams became music.

Poor fucker. I'm dead aren't I? I'm dead.

The old man didn't let up on the gas pedal. His foot stamped and pressed relentlessly, spurring the RV into demonic speeds. Tumbleweeds shot by like bullets. Cars became lights-peed. In the cracked glass of the windshield, he saw four futures and four slow setting suns - even as the glass continued to dribble out - plinking upon the shoes. Rebounding off the rim, inside to claim flesh as a basketball would… He squirmed. For what deft, daft hands had delivered him to this fate. His feet were probably shredded meat. Raw. Cut. But better, he admitted, than succumbing to flashbulb eyes and vampire teeth. Where was home again? Where was love again? Perhaps it was time to dust off the mothball jacket, buy some aviators, and look to the moon. The horizon was fast becoming a blushing mistress. The old man turned his thought train to strip clubs and alcohol. To love and drugs. To burgers and cannolis.

He pulled over on the old highway. Sweat covered and cold in the growing of early night. To pick up a thumb and a face. How foolish, right? Normally so, the old man was anxious enough, even without a glimpse of a pink Cadillac. Even without a rabid man-dog sniffing for his scent in the cool western breeze. But he digressed… The fleshy pointer belonged to a small Thai boy, barely out of his double digits. Dark ringlets around his eyes. Black unkempt hair with streaks of whiplash blue. Clothed in despair; namely a yellow blazer with a sunshine tie. He waved gratefully at the RV, skipping towards it, childlike and simple in contrast with his steel glare and hatred of all things beautiful. The door trapped them in awkward conversation.

"Where are your parents?"

"Hmm?"

"It's not safe to be out here alone."

"Okay."

"Where are you headed?"

"North."

"Well… we'll be going fast. You might wanna get buckled up in the back."

The boy shrugged, letting his feet play with the glass and heeded those words without further thought. He clambered into the back, scratching the leather on the way past, and opening the chair up. A chair that spilled it's guts of white stuffing. Within moments, he was curled up and strapped in. Eyes stapled shut as The Old Man took five to think.

You don't ask questions, I like that.

He took this time to quietly sift through the glove compartment and paw at the goodies within… Pack of Cubans. Box of matches. Pound of pills.

Take the pills. Light the Cuban. Strike the match.

And relax.

The old man expected the sweet lift of an LSD tablet but (like many things in his life) was met with bitter disappointment as the serene sleeping tablet washed over him.

Mr. Sandman was a' calling. Mr. Sandman would see him eaten. And Mr. Sandman would take full effect in fifteen minutes.

Time to get out of the limelight. Away from the stars. Far from engine and road. Into soft sheets and deep sleep. With a locked door, barred twice. Give the little one a shotgun or something? Can't find one… You'd better goddamn find one!

He rubbed his eyes free of grit, taking a deep gulp of aromatic smoke and pushed down onto the tiger's tail. Making it roar under his feet whilst the RV vibrated with power. Windows open, ready for the sobering cold air to hit. Praying for adrenaline or an energy drink. He took to the road once more.

I'll even break the speed limit to get away from you fuckers.

He went fast… Faster than man and saw only sand on the horizon - an oasis of dry dust, bones, and slim pickings. The air made his face burn like fire; it blew his smoke out. Ripped into his eye sockets. Amplified his buzz. Kickstarted his heart. Caused the boy to tremble. But kept him awake and awake meant alive. For maybe twenty minutes now, his eyes fluttered like the wings of a butterfly and bore holes lazily into the rear view mirror - weighing up options. Pull over and die? Keep driving and hopefully kill them both in a painless blaze of glory? He felt a pleasing shiver run through his beard… that, even though he no longer craved death, there was a thrill about riding that tightrope.

The old man fought his tired eyes away from whites and snuggled into the seat, threatening to explode the vehicle with each pump of the gas. More straight road. It was like an eternal highway. He gave his brain a cosmic pump in this moment of calm and clarity… *I have things to do before they bring me before the Lord.* A coyote cried from beneath the wheels, spewing a fountain of blood. *I want to lose my mind. I want to bathe in liquid love. I want to get revenge on my ex-over. I want to eat like a king and get this guy to his family. I want to massacre these bastards. Most of all, I want to sleep. Let me sleep.*

"You hear me? I'm sick of running from the clock! Let me sleep! Let me sleep!"

The boy was out cold for the tirade, otherwise he might have just bailed out. But the Old Man yelled and flipped off the desolate wastes undisturbed. He'd found a new emotion. Anger. And it burnt at his insides like napalm. He loved that too. When the tears came, he refused to look in mirrors. Vulnerability was for the weak. He'd cried his fill. Even so, he felt them drip as silent ghosts from the strands of his beard.

I want a hotel room. he decided. *And that little boy better learn to kill.*

They happened across a hotel just when his vision began to fade and wane - it was a watermark of existence. And he didn't overshoot it either, but he did leave grilled tire marks when pulling into the carpark. The smell of burning asphalt rose and fell. Calm waves on a bed of black.

"We're here, little one," he said gruffly, shaking him. "This is north. As north as I aim to go, for now."

Boy mumbled and yawned, showing bloody teeth and a maw stuffed with crispy flesh… though he rubbed his eyes ravenously, the image did not fade. Even if his wits knew otherwise. False fears continued to breed. The old man rode the frequency of paranoia.

"I don't like this place. It's slimy. Do you feel?"

"Yeah, it does give me the creeps."

"No… I mean, do you feel anything."

"Brave. Bright. Happy." This was a lie of course, a lie spent on the innocent.

"I think you're scared. That's what I feel."

He handed him his walking stick and leapt out of the car. Still a pixie but with eyes of stone as he regarded the hellhole in the pale moonlight.

It loomed over them: a shoddy giant that seemed to sway a death march, balconies speckled with pigeon shit, moss and weeds growing demonically. The thing withstood five stories and each was probably more harrowing than the last.

The sad thing is, we'll have to spend money to stay here. Money that I don't have.

"Why aren't you getting out?"

He was at the door now, peering and shivering in the cold. Crinkled nose. Confused.

"It doesn't matter… Listen, no matter what happens, you need to get us inside. Make sure we're safe and locked away. I have to drive this round back but I won't be able to come back. I need you to get me back. Keep in mind, use your wits and you'll have to do some immoral things to get home."

He smiled at the irony in his sleepy daze and drove off without a further word.

Round the corner. Into oblivion.

The little boy watched him disappear, unaware he would be alone for the next several hours. Unaware of the coming danger. His feet felt concrete. His mind was addled. And himself doubted… himself. He wasn't the sharpest or the cutest. The fastest or the funniest. But he was damn sure expected to drag the old man front and centre before a receptionist and waffle on about some bullshit story. Worse still, it had to work. Even if they could survive a night on four wheels, the night gave him the jitters. He couldn't take much more of the manifested monsters, scrabbling around her brain. Sinking their needles into his knowledge. Couldn't have it. Wouldn't have it. The bastards only came out at night time. Mosquitos of the void.

He unfroze but felt the cold cling to him as he took those tentative steps to the corner… each one feeling important and weighty. Eyes down. Dejected. He took the corner by the hand, flipping the world with ballerina grace. He took it in with baited breath - expecting little and unsurprised when little came to him. The RV was wrapped around a black, dead tree. It was crying smoke and hissing angrily; the smoke itself billowed ankle-high and was consuming all. He sprinted now, across the concrete, past a garbage can that ate seven flies by the second. To the old man who drew air quietly. Slowly. He pressed a cheek into the car, against his breast and listened to the soft, butter like draw of his heart. It ticked and tocked well enough. Sigh. Safety. He began to root through his pockets, digging deep into the money farm. Finding squat.

"I thought all adults had money," he muttered. "I thought they all ate pizza whenever. I thought they all loved me enough to stay."

He was glad to see him… possibly indifferent enough to leave him out in the chill. Hell, he could have easily stolen his shoes and sold them on for petty cash. To go north. Forever going north. The little boy sighed, tightened up on his tie. He tried to remember. Tried to be the good guy.

Immoral… The word haunted him.

Tiny eyes entered a hotel so large. The wallpaper peeled around a great, wooden desk that was rotten and stained with coffee marks. The ceiling pissed on said desk every few seconds… droplets diving from the cracks above. The smell of damp was overpowering. To the left, a bellhop - ugly and grinning, pushed an empty rack down the hallway. The orange carpet squelched underfoot, and the receptionist watched him with cool interest.

"I need a room."

"You got money, lad?"

His furrowed brows regarded the boy; he was far too young to need that walking stick.

"My grandpa can pay you in the morning - I just need help getting him inside."

"Not gonna happen, lad… you've got death in your eyes and copper fingers that have never seen gold. Magic up something shiny or leave my home."

"I told you, we can pay tomorrow-"

"I don't give a damn. The willing find a way." The receptionist's laugh crept slow and dark. "You see, I knew a guy who would let you stay for free. Unfortunately, for you, we ain't even in the same ballpark. He's outback. Head bashed in. Gargling. The only language he can speak is blood… And I'm here. Your little miracle. The man who did the swinging."

He was a big bear and he advanced now… hands hooked into the hoops of his belt, brandishing a sickle. Taking it to thick and stubby fingers that carved off the yellow nails. He hammered it into the desk, causing a shiver through his spine.

"You may not know this yet. But this ain't Earth."

Bang!

"This is the place where they come from the walls."

Bang!

"This is where the devils roam free."

Bang!

"Home."

Bang!

"Flesh."

Bang!

"Food!"

Bang!

Boy felt the bullet slice his cheek and watched as a geyser of blood erupted from the bear. His stomach took the brunt. He smiled widely.

"Sorry, Grant. Old chum. I was aiming for the boy."

He spun round to face the trio. Shellshocked. On the left, a blonde-haired woman slouched and pouted. On the right, a brunette adjusted her breasts and flashed from grimace to smile. Both were dribbling. Hungry drips. And both wore red - fresh and metallic scented. Ugly perfume. In the center, the gun toter blew the smoke from his pistol. His shades didn't quite cloud his pupils whilst his lion-topped cane seemed to bite into hands that shone.

"No harm." Grant grunted. "I was only showing off my sickle."

"I'm glad you didn't gut him just yet." The bachelor pulled out a wad of money, throwing it at Grant.

"What's the reason?"

The bachelor shrugged. "Do I need one? Be reimbursed for your bullet hole… use it to advertise. Attract new meat or whatever. Say- I wonder if you've seen an elderly chap. Screwball hair. Wearing tattered tweeds. He owes me dinner."

The little boy bit his lip nervously… *If he sees the walking stick. He'll come after me. He'll go after grandpa.*

All he needed to do was study it. Because, without a shadow of a doubt, this walking stick belonged to a dead man. And it lay dormant, in the hands of a dead kid.

"Can't say he's checked in. But you know how cockroaches are, some get through."

He analysed the wall of feet. Heels were adorable, though they couldn't run for shit. That left boots and shoes.

"We have to search, that cool with you?" the bachelor asked, leaning forward. Slack.

"Sure. You'll only find bones, if anything. My residents, you know? A guy like that wouldn't last an hour pent up in here."

"Nor do I expect him to. This is the only rest stop for miles… he ain't much of a fast cookie but he might be a clever one. Got anything planned for Mister, here?"

"Hell, he was almost a fillet in my hands." Grant huffed. "As far as I'm concerned, he's all yours now. I ain't that thirsty anyway."

The little boy tried to stretch his neck. To peak round corners left and right. All he got was the sickly fragrance of flesh. Images of kitchens. Boiling pots. Cutlery. All clanging against his brain. They'd want that. Fast food for the ages.

Three gunshots shattered his thoughts, slicing through the silence like a white knife. The cheese holes. The gouts. The pools. They weren't lathering his body. They didn't leak or open skin.

He almost wept. He almost wished for it. And when he fixated on the broken blonde - who spat bullets, keeled over. His hands quivered.

"We'll let you go if you eat the blonde."

The bachelor was shark-grin serious. The little boy was shark-grin shitless. He chose this moment to bolt: darting under the arms of Grant and his meathook hands. Almost skidding on the carpet as he took the hard right, water sloshing underfoot. Away from the kitchen. Down a hallway with no doors - except a singular metal marvel. An elevator. His fingers jabbed frantically at the button. He waited for those to give chase. He was met with the brunette who had shed her heels.

"Eat, my friend!" the brunette howled with a palm full of brain. Racing. Bounding. Sprinting. Gaining. The little boy clawed at the doors. Prying. Pushing. Pounding. Mind whirling and wired. He fell into the box, flailing at the house of options. Lighting them all up. Before slumping and praying as the doors began their closing ceremony. Groaning. Stuttering. Slapping footsteps that slowed to a crawl. A running psycho became a walking one. Sparks from the doors. Flickers from the lights. Silence. They were almost shut… a minuscule hint of the ugly wallpaper remained. And a wicked laugh from the outside echoed like the bark of a thousand dogs. A pencil elbow filled the gap.

"You ain't leaving us!"

The brunette scrambled into the lift and screamed in glee. Trapped with fresh meat.

Meanwhile, Grant and the bachelor heard the doors grind shut.

"Don't you worry about him getting away." Grant chortled, pacing over to the wall and tugging a lever. "He's only going to one floor… and we get to watch."

"You'll be better without skin baby, it'll keep you hush."

The brunette loomed over him as a scary skeleton, fishing into her pocket for the switchblade whilst the little boy whimpered. Walking stick frozen to his side.

"Aww. Please don't cry. This won't hurt none."

The brunette unhooked her coy weapon, the blade. A little flipper of red with a streak of silver.

She advanced. Intentionally snail-paced as the lights flickered. Mouth curved upwards like a zombie. Relishing the moment. The little one wanted that back wall to swallow him… Or at least for the noise. The ping. Safety and clarity in one charmless note. Better than being in this reeking square, smelling sweat and old sex. Being stabbed wasn't great either. He watched the brunette come closer. Forever closer. A soft hiss escaping cracked, blackened lips like the woman was trying to laugh. And swiped. The little boy lashed out with the walking stick, catching the brunette off guard. Robbing her of legs. She fell, cutting wildly at the air, and nicked the little boy's fingers. A sliver of blood creeped from the wound. The doors pinged happily. Batter up! The little boy stumbled to his feet and took a grand swing… Splintering a jaw into mushy foam. But his drive. Rush. Adrenaline. Slowly dissipated when he emerged into the hallway from hell. Shiny blue sheets of reinforced glass covered the floor, foreseeing a drop that could kill - it was interspersed by a bed of nails. Shiny little demons. Inches apart, turning every step into a dance. The ceiling and skirting boards had a disease of barbed wire which wove and spun. Intricately. Doors were sparse but each appeared bolted, thick slabs of wood. Light bulbs hung from fraying cord, the walls wore mirrors - giving only a break to those doors.

To the right, a naked corpse stripped of all gender, lay against the dead-end wall. Pinned by nails. The little boy dashed back into the elevator, noticing the glowing number five that buzzed in the silence. Jab. No change. Jab. No change. Jab. No change. He whirled, over the brunette, and into the corridor. A feather on the glass. Still, taking care for placement of feet. Slipping occasionally but making strong progress. To a door. Any door. Any room of substance that had a bed he could hide under. Who would want to fight these maniacs?

"You're so cheap." The elevator growled, churning out a crawling hand. "We're gonna gut you! Maybe he'll let me take off a few pounds, keep you alive while I crawl into your chest."

The little boy didn't even give any satisfaction to the rising brunette… refusing to look back, he continued on steady progress as the woman. Now hobbling. Seemed to breathe down the nape of his neck.

"I'm coming for ya!"

He hammered against the closest door, avoiding the curves of wire.

"Let me in!"

"Little pigs don't get in, sweetheart. When they do, sometimes they'll wish they hadn't!"

The brunette barked like a dog, in hysterics. He picked up the pace.

The door began to shake under every punch. Dust and rubble cascaded from the sky. Pebbles fell. Hammering became frantic. It groaned open. Not enough to scramble through. Nor would he want to. The gormless, gummy faces showed no teeth from within… their pale, dead hands reached for the boy. Some half-eaten. A man with four faces scuttled forwards, eager to feast. The little boy gasped - feeling bile burn away his throat, he lurched away and narrowly avoided the grabs of his pursuer. But he felt the air. It was a close call. Every step or two, he banged the walking stick against the floor... The nails felt precariously close. The glass itself spat at his efforts and the brunette finally found long, black hair between her fingertips.

"You ain't much of an escapee," the brunette spat, twisting the strands into thin pasta. "I could throw you in with those fuckers. I've seen them swallow guys and gals whole. Not for a long time though… I ain't seen true humanity for miles. It don't exist out here."

The little boy felt his hair strain and snap under the pressure.

"They frown upon us outside, ya know? We got our own black markets. We got our own underground. But we're always creatures of the dark. Eating people to live an extra day. Opening ourselves up. Selling our spare parts."

The little boy turned his head sluggishly to the woman's whim. His blazer felt like a choking vice and he could see things on the periphery. Hands that groped. Mounds of skin that could have been anything. They oozed from each door. They said hungry things.

"Let me go!"

"No can do. You've seen things, sweetie. We can't let you leave and go blabbin' to the cops. I came here as a babe. I left as a savage. Shit, it'd be a blip on my conscious. I'll always know. We created another animal."

The little boy felt his walking stick arm go limp. He was choking on yellow. Succumbing to a black fade that ended with a bed of nails, a stomach stripped of skin or… nothing. Death was a siren song, calling. A cold phantom who gave free hugs. He had but one thing to say to death.

Not today, dummy!'

His arm shot down. Last ditch. One call. And the walking stick thundered into the brunette's foot. Crunching. Sinking. The brunette gasped. Incapable of words. Her parting gift was a smile. A well done to the brave hero. Before she lost footing and was impaled sixteen times. Moving nevermore. The little boy took off and the fresh blood chased him…

"He'll find the medical room, Grant."

"Ain't nothing in there but a few rusty needles."

"And a window."

"And a window," Grant agreed, rubbing sweaty hands on his dirty smock. "But I figure we have more chance of him catching something' fatal than jumping out into the night."

"Here's hoping."

"You look worried."

"I've never been usurped by a little boy before."

Both men stared at the crackling screen; it painted a picture of black and white. Of a small killer, trying his luck with every door.

"I give the bastard three minutes before he's dog food for the undesirables." Grant chuckled. "Look how he bangs and begs."

"I disagree; there's more to this one. Your sickle ready? I have to go replace my ladies… "

"You're not seeing this one out, Mister?"

The bachelor removed his glasses to reveal purple, batting eyes. Contacts. Not even a friend like this could see his true soul because he would find true lies with false intentions. The bachelor planned to swirl his mouth out with gin, hit the road, and wake up next to a nameless stranger.

"You're better at this killing business." The bachelor shrugged. "Besides, I've got to go take a quick whizz." He tapped his nose with a pinky that trembled. The coke he craved. The vials and the injections. The potions and the drinkables. The powders and the creams. All lay, tightly packaged, in the pink Cadillac. He'd drag a few bags clear. Stab them. Bleed them dry. Scratch teeth. Lick papers. Spark up some sunshine. All in Grant's motel bathroom… ironically, the driest room in the house. Better that than chancing a condom-crawling toilet in some B-movie splatter-fest hostel. He spun on his heels. Hearing a sickle drop and the roar of a thousand engines crammed into a box of blades. Grant had a chainsaw. He'd look forward to the screams but he'd be too buzzed to care.

A yellow blazer caught on further nails, he danced carefully. Ballerina in distress. Could have been on fire. Forever lost in highways and hallways. Eventually, the little boy gave up on doors. He leant against the far wall. To the right, a boarded up blockade that seeped paper and plastic concrete. To the left, red paper that leaked dust on a wall of bloodstains and suppressed memories. His fingers thought about the right but they knew they'd be at it for days… They settled for left hand trigger. He swept over, almost tripping, and embraced the wall. To fall. The walking stick almost jammed in his jaw. The paper split. He crashed through like a newborn.

"Damn!" came the muffled curse, a grownup word for grownup times. It was mumbled into the new floor. A white tile. Growing. Spreading. He saw what it ate up. A gurney with sheets piled high hid behind a snowy curtain. No monitors but trays and shelves of curious bits ran around the room in groups of three. A window, slightly ajar, let forth a breeze just behind the gurney. And his ears pricked up at a raw, primal noise. A noise that had just entered the airspace.

"You sure did a number on this one," he whooped. "An' now. An' now, I'm gonna do a number on you."

It was Grant. The vile receptionist had come calling.

His brain wanted the window… to fall into the dead of night. A broken neck would still be welcome. His limbs however, scrambled to the paper trail behind. It was a clear rip. Even this numbskull could catch on. He poked his head out, just enough to edge a peep at the metallic monster. It grinned. The little boy watched as Grant stepped on the brunette's head and caved it like a beer can. His chainsaw did the rest, painting the floor. He saw him bathe in the red. He could see no more. For his legs started climbing and running. His hands started searching. He swept every shelf clean, finding chemicals unknown. Sharp objects. Smashing each in an act of God. Something flammable. Please. Something flammable.

"Do you like our little collection? We got a white-haired angel who adds to them sometimes. Maybe she'll come for you too."

He giggled in madness, letting his shoes soak in the fluid. Unhooking his tie to dip in the waters. Swinging it surely. Skidding over to the window. Digging further for his spark. He found nothing but sorrow on the gurney. No match. No love. But he wheeled it anyway, pressing his back to the window, opened more to the western dark, giving the universe a good look.

"Leaving without a kiss goodbye?"

Grant stood in the passageway, caked in a fragrance of metal. The chainsaw roared on. His smock held blurs of black, white, and red.

Boy shrugged, starting a backwards trot.

"Come on, lad. You're not that crazy. That fall… That'll kill ya worse than I ever could."

He was daydreaming, jumping back, pulling the gurney with him as the window gave way to a small body. The little boy met the brick wall and it greeted him with a snarl. A puckered kiss of pain. Still, he hung from the metal bar. Trying low while he heard the nightmare above. Creaking metal and a chainsaw.

The bachelor watched his pink Cadillac drive out of sight, wearing a cocaine moustache. The flames behind him burnt fresh nirvana. But he saw that crash of yellow blazer, a farewell flag in the trapped door. And knew Grant was burning in that fire behind yonder. He rested on the cane, knowing not to move on till morning. This place would smoulder long before the firefighters took note. He could enjoy the cornucopia of drugs… Then again, alone was so lonely. His phone hand gave a good twitch.

"You coming, White Angel?" came the drawl of drawls.

"You're circa north. You're at Grant's place. You're off your face."

"Damn right, you wanna come gunning with me?"

"Would Bonnie turn down Clyde?"

The phone buzzed dry.

For Ever This Moment

John Bunting
England

A S USUAL, THE COACH LEFT Victoria Bus Station on time. Jack had arrived early, and managed to get his favourite seat; upstairs at the front, where other people would be the least bother. Thankfully, no one had sat next to him. He'd made this journey many times before without incident, and was not to know that today's would be very different!

It was a beautiful summer's day. As the coach drove along Buckingham Palace Road, Jack relaxed, put his jacket on the empty seat, and spread himself about. But then he heard the dreaded sound - someone huffing and phewing up the aisle behind him. His heart sank. Sure enough, a few moments later an out-of-breath woman, all hot fluster and bags, plonked herself down beside him.

"Gosh, that was close," she gasped. "This is the coach to Leicester, isn't it? I was in such a rush."

"It is," Jack said tersely. "And I don't wish to be rude, but you're sitting on my jacket."

"Oops, I'm so sorry." The woman stood up, and brushed it down. "Shall I put it on the luggage rack for you? And while I'm up, I'll put my things on here too." With more huffing and phewing, and leaning over and generally getting in Jack's face, she did. As she sat down again, she said, "My name's Sophie, by the way."

"Jack."

He glanced at her quickly, in that way quiet people do in such situations. He got the impression of a middle-aged, slightly overweight woman; not unattractive.

"Why are you off to Leicester today, Jack?"

Jack sighed, resigned to talking. "I'm… um…" he paused; for some reason his mind had gone blank. To hide his confusion, he waved at the open laptop on his knees, and said, "Look, I'm sorry, I've got a lot of work to do."

"Of course, forgive me. I've got something to do too." Sophie pulled a notepad and pencil out of her handbag, and started writing. But after a while, she looked over at Jack's laptop, and said, "Sorry again, and I know I'm being nosey; what are you writing?"

"Oh, it's nothing really," said Jack sheepishly. "Just a science fiction short story about a teenager who runs away from a broken home, and joins a space mission to explore Mars."

"My goodness," exclaimed Sophie.

"That's very kind of you, I'm afraid the plot's not exactly original."

"No, that's not what I meant. I'm writing a short story too. I'm an English teacher, and I've asked my sixth form pupils for a two-thousand-word piece of fiction; I thought I'd better have one of my own ready for them."

"What a coincidence," smiled Jack. "I retired recently from the Merchant Navy; went round the world nine times. I read a lot of science fiction on my rest days, most of it very bad, so I thought I'd have a go at writing something myself."

"Well then," laughed Sophie, "happy scribbling to both of us."

For the next twenty minutes, Jack sat silent writing his story. As was his way, he thought about things, wrote something down, scratched his nose, made some deletions, and wrote some more. He noticed that Sophie was more ordered with her story; thinking for longer, and seemingly happy with what she wrote first time.

But, as they joined the motorway, she muttered, "No, no, this isn't right," reversed her pencil, and started rubbing out furiously.

At the same moment, Jack felt a violent pain in his right foot. "Ouch," he yelped, and reached down to massage it - *but it wasn't there!* Then he felt the same pain in his left foot. "What the hell…" He pulled his legs up in front of him, only to find that both his feet had disappeared. He watched in horror as his legs started to fade away too. "What's happening to me?" he screamed.

Sophie looked up. "My, God, what's going on?"

"I don't know. When you started rubbing out your story I started to disappear!"

"Don't be silly. Look…" Sophie rubbed out some more - Jack's knees faded. "Goodness, you're right. What on Earth?" She put her hand to her mouth. "Heavens, surely not… how can that be? Jack, I think I know what's happening; you must be him, the man."

"What are you talking about? What man?"

"The man in my story. He's on a coach journey too. When I started to rub him out, you started to, I don't know… not exist. But that means you're not real; that you only exist because I'm writing about you."

"That's rubbish. I'm me, I'm Jack Branding."

"Is it rubbish? Where do you live?"

Again, Jack's mind went blank. "I… err… hell, I can't remember."

"How did you get to the bus station?"

"…I've no idea."

"And you couldn't remember why you're going to Leicester, could you?" Jack was silent. "You see. That's because I haven't written those bits of my story yet."

Jack shook his head. "No, no, I don't believe you. I've caught this coach before, I know I have. And I remember being in the Merchant Navy."

"So does my character. You have those memories because I wrote them."

"Oh, come on, that doesn't make sense. I've had those memories for years, and you didn't know about them until we met today." Jack slapped Sophie's notebook angrily. "You only started writing them down after that. The timeline isn't right."

Sophie put her hand on his arm to calm him. "Isn't that the point about a short story? Anything can happen, including time being twisted inside out all wrong. A moment can last forever, or vice versa. Time can be whatever we want it to be."

"But what about the other people on this coach?" asked Jack, still confused. "How come they exist? You haven't written about them, have you? I know I haven't."

"No." Sophie glanced behind them, and then back at Jack. "See for yourself."

Jack turned round, but instead of the expected coach load of travellers, all he could see was a grey, swirling confusion of… nothingness; an absence of anything. "I don't understand, where are they?"

"Now take a look outside."

Jack peered through the panoramic window in front of them. There was the motorway he knew so well, disappearing away ahead of the coach. "And?"

"Keep looking; tell me what you can actually see," said Sophie quietly.

After a while, Jack realised something was wrong, something he'd never noticed before - there was no other traffic. No cars, no lorries; nothing. And on either side of the motorway was that grey, swirling emptiness. Slowly, he turned, and stared open-mouthed at Sophie.

"That's right," she nodded. "Apart from mentioning the motorway briefly, and the nice weather, I haven't written anything about what's outside the coach; as far as my character's concerned there's no such place."

"All right," groaned Jack, "one final test. Rub out some more of your story." Sophie did so, and his left hand faded away.

There was a long silence as the terrible truth began to sink in to Jack. Eventually, he mumbled, "I don't exist, do I? I'm a figment of your imagination."

"You do exist; you're in my story."

"Are all my memories and thoughts yours?"

"Your memories are. But I haven't written anything for several minutes, so you're probably having your own thoughts now."

"What…" Then Jack paused, an extraordinary idea growing. "Wait a minute, if I'm only a…" He pressed the 'backspace' button on his laptop. This time it was Sophie who screamed - now *her* feet were fading away. "There," shouted Jack, "I knew it. If I'm just a character in a story then the only way you can exist to me is if you're a story character as well. You're disappearing, so you must be the woman I'm deleting." Jack held his finger down on 'backspace', and Sophie's legs started to disappear.

"What are you doing?" she yelled.

"I'm deleting all of you. Maybe then this nightmare will end, and I'll get my legs back."

"No, stop. *Stop!*" Sophie reached over and pushed Jack's hand away from his laptop. "Don't you see? If you delete me, my story will cease to exist too; and so will you, because that's the only place where you… are. Gosh, this is complicated." She giggled. "You know, I wasn't going to rub out my title." She showed Jack the front of her notepad; it read 'Race to the Bottom'. "That's all there would have been left of you."

But Jack was not in the mood for humour. "So, we're saying that we're characters in each other's stories, and that the only way we'll survive is if neither of us deletes the other from them."

"It would seem so."

"Does the opposite apply? That if we don't delete each other we'll live for ever?"

"Jack! One minute you're asking me if you exist, now you're asking if you're eternal. What do I know? I guess it depends if the stories we write are eternal."

Jack took a slow, deep breath to calm himself. "OK, try this; is there anything else except our stories?"

"What do you mean?"

Jack pointed out of the window at the empty greyness. "Are you and I… our stories… all there is? Or are there other characters, other stories, out there somewhere in all that?"

Sophie shrugged. "Now you mention it, it does seem odd I know about things like Leicester and the Merchant Navy. I wonder if they exist in another story, which is somehow leaking into ours." She sighed. "Or maybe I made them up. Whatever, I think we should write each other back into our stories properly; make us whole again." She looked Jack up and down quizzically. "And I could make some improvements while I'm at it."

"Me too," harrumphed Jack.

Jack and Sophie redrafted their stories, and slowly their legs and feet returned. Eventually, Jack stopped typing, and said, "Done it."

"Me too." Sophie looked Jack over. "Mm, not bad. Here, take a look at the rewritten 'you'." She took a small mirror out of her handbag.

"Hey, I look like Johnny Depp."

"You wouldn't believe what he and I get up to in my dreams. Last night, we…" Sophie stopped as Jack grinned at her. "What? Oh I see, you wrote those dreams." She smacked his arm. "You're a naughty man. Give me the mirror." She took a look at herself, and burst out laughing. "Madonna?"

"When I was a teenager, I had rude posters of her all over my bedroom walls. At night, I used to shine a torch on them, and—"

"Please, enough." interrupted Sophie, "I know!"

Jack blushed. "Who's the naughty one now?" When he'd recovered his composure, he said, "All right, what happens next? What are the next chapters in our stories… our lives?"

Sophie looked coy. "Well, seeing as we've created sexual fantasies of each other, I think we should write about a hotel bedroom, and see what happens."

"That sounds like fun."

"And we'd better write ourselves a long-term affair."

"A *very* long one," laughed Jack. "We don't ever have to leave the bedroom. Imagine, never-ending sex!"

Sophie smiled. "Nice idea, but there'll surely come a time when we'll want to move our stories on."

"Then I'll rewrite you as someone else. Or maybe a threesome. Me, Madonna, and Kylie; now there's a thought and a half."

"Who's Kylie?"

"Um… good question. But I like the idea of her!"

"Stop it, I'm being serious."

"All right. Actually, I've written that I'm in love with you, and always will be, whoever you are."

"Why, Jack, that's so sweet." Sophie scribbled on her notepad. "There, now, I'm in love with you too. I suppose if we're right about all this, you're the first man I've ever fallen for."

"If we're right about all this, I'm the first man you've ever met!"

They laughed, happy just to be with each other in all this confusion, and Sophie snuggled into Jack's shoulder. "But after your fantasy threesome, *then* what do we do with our stories? We can write anything we want."

"And we've got all the time there is to do it - assuming unwritten stories are eternal too."

Sophie glanced up at Jack, a strange look in her eyes. "Do you think they are?"

"As you said, my love, what do I know?" Jack scratched his nose. "One thing is certain, though, it will take a lot of thought."

The coach journeyed on through the grey, swirling eternity of stories written and unwritten. Upstairs, Jack sat hand in hand with Sophie, wondering about their future together. It wasn't clear to him any more quite who was thinking what, or writing what, about whom, and it didn't much matter. He knew they were bound together forever, each not able to exist without the other, living lives limited only by their imaginations. He leant over and kissed Sophie. "Maybe we should go looking for those other stories, see if they exist, and write their characters into ours."

Sophie sighed deeply. "Maybe, but…"

"…But?"

"…I've been thinking. I've never written a story much longer than two thousand words. I don't…" She paused, choosing her words carefully. "I don't want to turn our lovely short stories into horrible long ones."

Jack looked at her thoughtfully. "So?"

Sophie stroked his cheek, his eyes, his lips. "So why don't we stop writing? Finish our stories right here, right now; with you and me the only characters in them, just living in *this* moment." She put her notepad and pencil back in her bag. "Forever."

They kissed again for a long time. "Forever gets my vote," whispered Jack. He pressed 'save' on his story file, and closed the laptop.

Shapeshifter

Judy Levitz
USA

I

TRUE, I AM A SHAPESHIFTER. But shapeshifters have feelings too - feelings as fluid and infinite as the possibilities one's body-container can achieve. My present container is a male form, chosen because it seems to be somewhat privileged on this planet, and I have adopted one of the presumably pleasant countenances popular to North American culture: I stand 6 feet tall, with sandy-blond hair, layered short and tapered with a block neckline. My eyes are Cerulean blue, (chosen to match the waters our ships landed in) and my skin is fair which blends with many of the populace in this area. I have a tiny cleft in my square chin -- somewhere I read this indentation is unique and desirable in the human species. It still feels strange though, since on Mir there is no set base shape – we usually maintain our "elemental" selves, existing in states of energetic auras, but take a desired form to serve any function necessary. On Earth we must keep our human shapes for prolonged periods, since it is vital for our survival that we assimilate. But this business of *feelings*? Let me tell you Earth Folks, it is quite the enigma! Back home, we experience consonant and dissonant charges of varying intensities, that are much more electric in nature. We pulsate a little, or we pulsate a lot. But here the experience is mystifying and complex. When the feelings are negative, it seems like your whole existence is in jeopardy. (You Earth Folks refer to this as "feeling down". Like closer to the ground?) When positive, there is a pleasurable sensation that pervades all molecules and makes you want to keep repeating the behavior attached to it regardless of what else you have to do or whether it is purposeful. (You refer to this feeing as "up" or "high". Like closer to the sky?) I sort of get it.

Case in point, as I approach *Cybar*, my favorite local hangout, I'm thinking it "lifts my spirits" that I might finally connect with someone special, though I never imagined it would be anyone other than another shifter. At the top of the stairs to *Cybar's* roomy loft space, the brass fixtures and mirrored walls reflect just enough light to let me spot Sharon, sipping a margarita, talking to a nice looking man with his baseball cap on backwards. He is leaning casually against the highly polished mahogany bar rail. Perched on the barstool to Sharon's right, is Amanda, the Earth woman I am looking for. She is swaying almost imperceptibly to Al Green's "Love and Happiness" and seems lost, staring down at the bar counter. Her short, stylish jet black hair and energy aura just about make me vibrate. As I get close she comes out of her private reverie, looks up from what I see is a small sketchpad upon which she is making tiny doodles of Earth puppies. She smiles, big brown eyes sparkling with smarts and sweetness.

"Here we are again," I say, meeting her smile.

"Hi! Adam, right? Yes, here we are. How are you?" She adjusts herself on the stool to face me more easily. I try to send thought waves to the guy on the seat beside her to get him to leave. (No, I cannot really do that, but neither can you people and I believe you wish these kinds of things all the time.)

"I am pretty good. How bad can it be with love and happiness in the air?" (I wonder if that was a good flirtation. There is a big learning curve down here for me.) "How are *you*?"

"I'm just fine. It's a nice night, and should be a nice weekend too."

I am rather nervous at the moment, not being good at small talk, so I inhabit more relief when the bartender moves down my way and catches my eye. I try to remember to speak in contractions. It seems a more familiar form of your communication.

"Verjus and soda, please. Thank you. Umm, thanks."

"Not a hardcore fan?" Amanda asks. I like that she notices but does not judge.

"Not so much. It makes me headachy and like there's a plexiglass wall between me and the rest of the planet." I felt for a split second like I had given something away, but realised that was just paranoid.

"Same here," she says casually. "Also, I'm the perennial designated walker."

"You mean for Sharon? Do you live close by?"

"Yeah – we share a place on Mississippi just past Fremont."

"So what keeps you busy when you aren't not getting drunk?" she asks with a sparkle in her eye.

You know what it is like to hum along with someone, and when you get the pitch just right you feel you are part of a bigger, empowering whole. It just happens. That's what it felt like to be near Amanda.

"I am, uh, well, I'm kind of the I.T. person at Ground Kontrol. I can fix their games and equipment and keep things running smoothly. I love the hands-on repair part, getting to see these big machines chime and hum. But the best part is when the children's faces light up and they can get back to an aborted match. Playing the games themselves is a bit too frenetic for me."

I do not care for the 'what do you do' question but I knew it would come soon enough. It always does. People on Earth are overly defined by what they do, that is, the thing that they make money from. Where I come from we don't exactly have work. We need not eat or drink and need no specific place to inhabit therefore no need for goods or currency. But we take the assimilation process on Earth very seriously, try to fit in as good human citizens, so gainful employment was imperative, and this work was indeed challenging and enjoyable.

As though she read my mind, Amanda said, "Sounds like a good fit. It's not so much what we do, it's how we feel."

I like that she is reflective, and soft. She periodically adds a remarkably lifelike feature to one of the paper canines.

I am falling into her.

"And what do you do when the sun is up?" I keep sounding like some kind of alien, I fear, but I wanted to keep the exchange going. "Artist?"

"I'm a photographer and I love to draw. I do a lot of my own work, hoping to show someday – but for paying the rent, I work at Blue Moon Camera and Machine. We specialise in old school film development and repairs. One of the only businesses left that does. I guess I'm a little anti-digital at heart, and like the feeling of having my hands get to tinker with gadgets." She is attractively tremorous, if you get my drift.

"Blue Moon," I muse, Earth ironies not being lost on me. They still have typewriters there, right? I've passed it a few times. Very cool. Well, the world is getting away from us a little, so it's good to have things slowed down when we can."

"Understatement, that."

I love how succinct and easy she is.

A few moments pass, and trying to sound more casual than invested, I venture, "Um, I haven't eaten so I'm going to order some nachos or something. Care to join me?"

At that same moment, Sharon's conversation with baseball cap man has just fizzled out, and she turns to Amanda. Her speech is just a tad cottony.

"Let's get out of here and go to *The Lounge.*"

I can sense Amanda feeling torn, (which is good) but her first loyalty is to her friend (which is good too), so I know what is coming, (which is not so good).

"Sorry, Adam. I'm gonna head out with Sharon, but I'm sure I'll see you again."

"Take care. Have a great rest of the night, Amanda."

At this moment, I am inhabiting a feeling of disappointment.

II

Saturday night, my routine is to head over to *Inn or Out.* It's close to where I now live on Beech Street, and has the best blend of blue note jazz and Motown that I thoroughly resonate with, but my version of a heart is not really into it. I like the place, though. They know me because they have several pinball machines from the same company that sells to the arcade, and they call me to service them on occasion when they jam. Kenny is on tonight behind the bar, and slaps a napkin down right away as I slip into one of their high-back chrome swivel stools.

"How're ya doing, Adam." It was more of a statement than a real question. Kenny is nice but busy as ever and goes right for it. "What can I getcha?"

"I would like a Rock Shandy with O.J., Kenny, thank you. Oh, and can I get a few hundred nuts to go with it?"

Kenny raises and eyebrow and shoots me a funny look. He whips together my drink and gives it a good shake. I asked him to add orange juice so I get an extra blast of Vitamin C as well as some D, nutrients we need more than any others. (Being human works out well because it so happens that by assuming the shape of an Earthling, we are clothed in the skin that produces mass quantities of D when exposed to the sun.) Kenny sets the drink down in front of me and reaches under the counter for two small bowls of nuts.

"A few hundred? You ok tonight?" He swipes the bar top around me with the white bar cloth otherwise flung over his shoulder.

"Yes, thank you." I smile weakly. If the night were slow maybe I would get into it with him, but no point tonight. In the meantime, the nuts fuel my human form and give me something to do with my hands.

"Ok. Start with these, I'll keep 'em coming."

He disappeared to the other end of the bar. I settle in a bit, pop peanuts in my mouth, and survey the dim-lit space. A small group of shifters arrive and take a table in the corner. (Another thing I like about *Inn and Out* - its clientele includes the occasional shapeshifter -- and a good number of your own sexshifters. It makes for a very relaxed, inclusive atmosphere.)

The shifters order some Belgian beers on tap and the one in female form takes hers over to the two-tone jukebox with plastic translucent pilasters. Inside the pilasters are rotating color cylinders flashing red, green yellow, and purple lights as they turn. She flips through her choices, slips in several coins, punches buttons, and country music starts to play. As she leans against the box sipping her beer, she scans the room for a bit and her gaze lands on me. She comes towards the bar.

"Hi. My name is Colleen. I just came in with some friends and thought you might want to group." We can tell when we encounter others of our kind -- we sense our unique matter composition independent of its form, you see.

"I am Adam." I greeted her back with a friendly lift of my drink. "Um, thank you. I think I am good here for now. Maybe in a bit."

"Do you mind if I join *you*?"

"Not at all, please. Have some nuts. Can I refresh your beer?"

"Absolutely!" She downs what's remaining in her glass and places it on the bar counter.

"Kenny?" I get his attention and point to the almost empty nut bowl and Colleen's beer mug.

He nods in acknowledgement. A brew and fresh supply of Planters appear in an instant.

You might wonder what shapeshifter small talk looks like. Well, it is not all that different from what you would imagine people from anywhere discuss when running into a fellow clansman in a foreign country. "When did you land? Have you joined any particular coterie? Do you keep shape (that is, human) most of the time or do you shift?" The usual. If you happen to get less superficial, it might go to: "Have you found an Earth imperative? What is your assimilation narrative?"

Colleen and I got into it all. And though her atoms moved a bit more quickly in her kept shape than I comfortably resonated with, she had very agreeable vibrations.

I told her I landed with the first expedition (hence, Adam) in 2014 and my imperative was atmospheric testing and homeostasis. (To clarify, Earth-person, the totality of our species is driven by "imperatives" of evolution, which for us means the refinement of all life and life forms. This is different from your survival of the fittest doctrine in that we don't believe that any life form has a hierarchal position over another. Perhaps the infinite morphing nature of our cores enables us to see ourselves as inherently a part of the whole in a way that you cannot.)

Anyway, I described some of the responsibilities the first landers had, and the tests we performed to determine if we could survive. We hope, if Earth works out for us, to be wholly relocated a good fifteen years before we solar combust in 2040.

"One of my shipmates was charged with analysing morph stability," I told her. "I think his was one of the more scary imperatives since Mir was on a rapid trajectory towards our sun at that point, we only had time for five years of study. Happily the results were quite satisfactory." (Our dwarf planet is known to you by a long number assigned to KBOs – Kuiper Belt Objects, but Mir is the name we call our home. You can't see it when you look up at your sky, but it is at the very edge of the Kuiper-Edgeworth Belt, beyond the orbit of Neptune, and it is, that is - was, quite beautiful there.)

"I can't believe you were on the mother ship itself!" Colleen says excitedly. I notice she speaks informally too. I seem to be behind the learning curve in this regard. "That's so interesting. I came in 2017 and my imperative is studying the effects of maintaining kept shapes over time. An offshoot of what your friend was studying, I guess. There are animate and inanimate organisms on this planet that we may morph into that don't exist on Mir so we don't know if that is going to effect us. We don't expect any problems with this, but there's no firsthand knowledge of any of it. So I'm in charge of developing interview protocols so we can design useful studies."

"Assimilation shifting research. Very gratifying I would think, Colleen. Any specific protocol you are working on currently?"

"Well, one basic study we're starting is having shifters describe the experience of shifting on Earth as a way to collect subjective narratives which we might be able to objectify. So we know that generally speaking, shifting is not an unpleasant experience... One shifter imagined that to us it feels just like what breathing or digesting is to an Earthling, presuming nothing is wrong in the core plexus. Another said it might be somewhat comparable to sensations Earthlings feel when they are swimming — there is at once a weight, pressure, and buoyancy as the corpus moves and is moved by the water in directions it might not ordinarily seem to go. Most agree so far, that the morph does not require effort so much as clarity, so we're concluding that we must have certainty of thought to facilitate the transformation. Then we are in a different configuration, just like that. Too much shop talk? Let me ask you: do you keep your male form 24/7? Have you shifted into other forms since you have been here? I keep my female form when I am out amongst humans, but I also morph to other forms when I am alone or privately grouping with shifters."

I say, "Actually, I have kept shape as a male human for a long time. I have had little, if any, social contact with other shifters once I completed my initial imperative. At that time my cohorts dispersed and I do not recall a time I have morphed since then."

"Oh, well maybe that will change if I become a new part of your social network!" Colleen jokes.

I do not pick up on the invitation right away and I think she senses my hesitation.

"I should get back… would you like to group at all now?"

"I am happy to say hello to your friends, but I do think I am going to head home shortly. Thank you. I have enjoyed our talk."

I go with her to her table and there are quick introductions. Her friends seem very nice. Come back some time, they say. We are here late most Saturday nights.

Though I found real pleasure conversing with Colleen, something is nagging at me and I can't wait to get out into the cool Portland night. I head up North Shaver for ten blocks, loop around Denorval Park to North Haight Ave, and down to Beech where I reside. I can't really concentrate on anything but missing Amanda.

I begin to inhabit a feeling of deep longing.

III

Counting the sunsets until I will return to the *Cybar Café*, time has been going slower than it usually does. When end week finally comes, I am jittery in anticipation of seeing Amanda again. I realise I have thoughts of gratitude towards Sharon who, as the more reliable drinker, will likely be there this evening.

I arrive at *Cybar* around 8pm. - not too early or late so as to not miss them. It is not crowded yet, and I have my pick of seats at the bar. My view of the entryway is unobstructed so I need not keep turning my head every nano-minute to see who is coming in. Al Green is back, singing "Take Me to the River", which reminds me of the conversation with Colleen. I start feeling unsettled again. It is hard to have two different entities whose matter matters to you.

The stars finally align and in walk Amanda and Sharon a bit after 9pm. I smile at Amanda from afar and she waves warmly. They both come over to the bar and I relinquish my stool in an Earth-like gentlemanly gesture. The seat adjacent is still empty, so they both perch and affix their bags on the hooks beneath the glossy wooden bar rail.

"Can I start you both off with something?" I notice that Sharon seems very un-cottony tonight, so I presume *Cybar* is their first stop. This might mean there won't be much time for Amanda and I to resume getting acquainted.

"Thank you, Adam. That's very sweet," Amanda replies. "I'd like a virgin mojito I think… "

"Yes, thanks Adam! Let's see. A Moscow Mule for me! I love the mugs they use for those." Sharon really appreciates her drinking experience.

I place their order just as the lights dim another notch, and the music volume goes up. When the bartender returns with their drinks, Sharon says, "See you guys in a bit. I'm going to take this over to the pool table and see what's doing." She hoists the heavy metal copper zarf which is already dripping with icy condensation and saunters over to the back where people queue up to play billiards.

When Amanda and I are alone, I inquire, "How was your week at Blue Moon?" I've reclaimed the stool Sharon just left.

"Pretty good," Amanda says. She whips out her sketchbook and opens to a page where there is a detailed charcoal rendering of a typewriter.

"I worked on this old Underwood today – from 1935! I straightened her keys, cleaned her platen, replaced her ribbons on the original spools. Very satisfying." Her face just beamed with delight.

"Our jobs have a lot in common," I ventured. "I was doing something quite similar with three of our pinball machines. Replaced seventeen rubber bumper components, and eight cracked flippers. I love that there's not a digital bone in their machinery."

"I know, right? Gosh, I haven't played pinball since I was maybe eleven or twelve," she thought aloud.

"Well, you'll have to let me take you to see it sometime." My throat is experiencing mild contractions and I think my voice has gotten higher.

"That would be fun!" Amanda replies bouncily.

She turned the page of her pad and started to sketch a pinball machine. I un-tense a little, and offer to refresh her drink along with mine.

"No, Adam, let me get them this time." I accept and we sit quietly enjoying the mocktails and music, content not having to talk at all. By 10:30 it is getting pretty crowded, and I am contemplating asking if she would be interested in going for a late snack, or if she will need to wait for Sharon.

On cue, Sharon returns with a guy on her arm and chirps, "We're gonna go over to *Crow's Nest.* Come everybody!"

"I'll pass, Sharon, if that's ok. See you at home, then?" Amanda says.

"No prob, I'm great!" Sharon flings a smile at her new friend. "See you later. Maybe!"

She laughs and they head out, totally entangled, to their next stop. I think, great – Amanda would rather come with me to get something to eat, and we can be alone for the first time. Some confidence starts to set in.

"So! A reprieve," I say. "You need not be the designated walker tonight, so how about getting a bite to eat with me?" I lightly put my hand on her hand.

Amanda gently slides her hand out from under mine. She looks down, clearly uncomfortable.

"Um, Adam. Listen, I just… don't want you to get the wrong idea. I mean, I like you, I think you're terrific, but… "

I cut her off, to save her and myself both.

"Hey, no problem. Don't give it a second thought. But you still have to come to the arcade sometime, just for fun."

"Thanks, Adam. I know it sounds lame, but you really are the nicest, nicest guy."

She is relieved, as I let her off the hook. But I am not so comfortable now to just continue being friendly.

"Would you like me to walk you home?" I manage, trying to find a way to get out of the moment we are in.

"No, I think I'm going to stay just a little longer," Amanda says. "But I know you're hungry so please don't let me keep you. I'm fine, really. Thanks again, Adam, for understanding."

I nod to her reassuringly, and leave as quickly as I can without looking like I'm rushing away.

I proceed to take full occupancy of the state you would call heartbroken.

IV

On Mir, our equivalent to your coupling process is functional pairing. It's when two electrically charged molecules sustain an attractive interaction that results in a stable association. It is extremely rare for the breakage of bonds to occur: everyone on Mir strives for irreversible, eternal covalence. When we first landed in the northeastern quadrant of your North Pacific Ocean off Cannon Beach, which is eighty miles east of Portland, pairing was nowhere on our minds. There was no time to delve into all the benefits or calamities of living amongst you, and perhaps I just assumed that if we came to a point where survival was no longer an issue, I would simply link with a compatible shifter of my own kind.

But now, I really have my quandaries laid out for me: First, I am attracted to an Earth woman, but I cannot bond with her though she is the one I sense would provide me with my eternal union. Second, I could bond with Colleen, but right now I don't foresee the force between us being exceptionally strong. Third, Amanda might be willing to remain friendly and to do that I must overcome my deep sense of destabilisation. (This would be most evolved scenario, enabling us to share energy in some form. However, I am not "feeling" evolved at all, I am feeling something more akin to your sulk.) Fourth, though I do not want to stop going to *Cybar*, I will see Amanda there if I go and that will reactivate problems one and two. Fifth, right now I am supposed to be mending an electrical short in the Asteroids video console, and my attention is anywhere but on my task. I notice this when my voltmeter's current-probe tip inadvertently comes into contact with my com-probe tip, and the entire arcade loses power.

Suddenly, dings and bells and flashing lights are replaced by darkness, moans, and groans.

"Adam!!!!!!" my boss bellows across the game floor. Saturday is prime time and he will not be happy to lose any players.

"I am on it!" I yell back.

I run to the breaker panel, quickly flip each circuit and everything comes back on, except of course for the Asteroid game. I return to it, resolved to bring my usual laser-like concentration.

After work I take my time getting home. I have decided that I will be sensible, that is to say, I will invest my energy where there is no resistance. I will go to *Hip and Soul* tonight, just for a little change of surroundings, and maybe return to *Inn or Out* later in the evening. If Colleen is there, we can continue our interesting dialogue. Still, I find I am moving as if I had morphed into molasses.

I read somewhere in one of your magazines that "clothes make the man". I never understood this, but tonight I think I am getting a glimmer of its meaning. I don a nice jacket, button-down shirt, and dark denim jeans, and for some reason additional energy emerges within me. As I put on my North Face coat, I survey my place a little. It is a small, cozy one-bedroom apartment in a two-family structure, with a window that frames a Pacific willow, of which there are many in this area. I feel resonant with its bent, but sturdy substance, and this too improves my mood. In the scheme of things I am quite fortunate to be here, and must put my dating dilemmas in the proper perspective. I make myself an inch taller and walk out into the neighborhood.

Hip and Soul is off Mississippi Avenue near Mason Street and occupies two stories that they loosely divide by having more food upstairs and more drink downstairs. I didn't have lunch due to the small incident at work, so I order their fried chicken, andouille sausage, poached eggs with grits, and a few glasses of milk. (I know the face you are making, Earth-reader, I saw it in the countenance of my server as well. But do remember that I don't gain weight, and I shouldn't *have* to remind you of my fundamental relationship to vitamin D supplements or my newfound Earth relationship with emotional eating for that matter.) Once sated, I head down to the lower level where I will switch to peanuts and a Moscow Mule, without the Moscow.

The bar is already extremely packed, but there is a garden with some high tops out back, and since it's getting cold they are not all taken. I pay for my drink, snatch a bowl of nuts, and start to walk outside. As I move through the crush of bodies to the patio, I see two women sitting and holding hands. One has a sketchbook on the table next to her drink and she looks like Amanda. It is Amanda. Oh. Amanda is sitting with a woman who is holding her hand. Yes, that is definitely her. No wonder she was not comfortable having my hand on her hand.

At first this improves my state further, since maybe it means she did not *not* like *me*, but in the end I am still left with the fact that she is unavailable. Nonetheless, I harness the natural force with which I am drawn to her and walk over to say hello. The situation, along with the number of times we have been friendly, makes it acceptable, I think, to lean down and kiss her on the cheek, (which makes me quite dizzy if you must know). I quickly extend my hand for introductions to the woman she is with. Surely this will be rightly construed as both congenial and affirming.

"Adam! Hi! This is Tracey. Tracey, this is my friend Adam. I mentioned him to you actually. He's the guy who works at Ground Kontrol. I think we should do a pin-ball night sometime, right, Adam?"

Amanda smiles brightly and shakes open her sketchbook to the pinball drawing. It pops off the page with extraordinary detail and multi-colored accents.

"Wow. That's beautiful!" I exclaim. I am moved and surprised by the amount of work she put into it. "You should definitely both be my guests sometime, you will really enjoy it. It would be my pleasure to arrange some complimentary beverages and a discount package to our best games." I add, "Next time we run into each other, let me know some good times and I will take care of it. Enjoy your evening. Nice to meet you, Tracey."

I linger a bit longer in the garden, watching people, seeing Orion rise into the sky, and spot an Earth plane crossing right through his belt on the way to somewhere. Sipping my Mule, I replay the image of my first viewing Amanda with Tracey. I replay it over and over until it comes to feel all right. The sadness, the disappointment, find a place to live. My thoughts turn to Colleen and I have a new eagerness to talk with her.

I begin to inhabit a sense of possibility.

V

It is quite late back at *Inn or Out* but I have no desire to rest, only a strong urge to connect with Colleen. There she is with her friends, and I approach, asking if I may group. Of course, they say, and I ease into their discourse. (Some of it is out loud in Earth English, and some of it is in our native language, which is something like a cross between telepathic and empathic.) One of the male shifters has been describing his imperative of researching a correlation between economic growth and presence of minor life forms.

"Right now we're only looking at non-mammalian vertebrates just to get a sense of the ratio of fish, birds, and reptiles to humans in various countries," said the shifter named Christopher. (He must have come in the craft that adopted names of human explorers, like Columbus, Magellan, Armstrong, etc.) "Once we get that data, we'll expand to spiders, insects, and so on. So far we see a starkly inverse balance. It's so unlike Mir!"

"But seriously, Chris, did you really expect *any* other macrocosms in the solar system to replicate Mir's bio-climate? Name one moon, one comet, one minor or major planet in the galaxy that does," the shifter called Marco paused for effect. "See, you can't because it doesn't exist!" As Marco gets excited, he lapses into silent intensity, continuing the argument in Mirean. His eyes blaze, and occasionally he sort of flickers as if he's going to morph on the spot.

"Look," Christopher continues out loud in English. "The fact is, we're here now. What better imperative can there be than to try to observe how things work first, and then see over time if they can be more like Mir?"

Colleen chimed in. "You're venturing into gnarly territory. How do we know that our way of doing things is better for Earth just because it was our way?"

"Come on, Colleen," Marco insists. "It isn't that complicated to choose balanced over imbalanced existence of all forms."

"Hey, I totally agree. I'm just saying that is our imperative not theirs."

They debate a bit longer until Colleen says, "How about we try not get too polarised the first time we have a new friend."

"Please, do not change anything on my account," I say. "I find this all of great substance. In fact, Colleen, I have been thinking about your work since you described it to me. Are any studies being done of what variables determine what makes us choose which form we are going to morph into, and what effect does it have to be occupying one kept shape for so long? And should we keep a particular shape because of our own needs or the needs of others? The benefit is the prime mandate, is it not? That's both Mirean and like Earth's Tibet when I think of it. Well, no, not really Tibetan since they are more about enlightenment than benefit, but the concept of benefit for Earthlings is not a contradiction to our..."

"Whoa, Adam! Slow down! What are you drinking, man?" Marco laughed.

I too had begun to vibrate and flicker. Without thinking, I conveyed an ongoing stream of curiosities and dilemmas that I hardly knew I had myself. Recouping, I said, "Please forgive me. I must seem quite over-activated."

"Hey, no problem. Let's take a little walk and talk more where there is less stimulation. Ok with you all?" says Colleen.

Lewis and Christopher nod in affirmation. Marco adds, "Sure, but please group again with us, Adam. I like your energy!"

Colleen takes my hand and leads me outside. We head south towards Irving Park, just a few blocks away from the bar.

Irving Park has everything: enough grass to make you feel green yourself - gently sloping hills, walking trails, trees, trees, and more trees. Flowering dogwoods and Scouler Willows rim the fields and provide shade on the side of the baseball diamond. We talk and stroll unhurriedly, Colleen holding my hand, towards one of the trails that is closed after sunset. We have already wordlessly communicated what we plan to do but must find a private place so as not to be seen by passers-by. Once we are sure the path is clear, we turn towards each other. Simultaneously, we each transform into what I can best describe as a magnetospheric plasma of electrons and protons, otherwise known as an aurora, just like your Aurora Borealis. We lift up gradually and commence to sweep over the park in arcs of electric blue, green and yellow, lofted by variations in air pressure and soft breezes. Higher up, we glow crimson, pulsating and radiating in trajectories not imaginable in our kept forms. Minutes or hours go by, and for a time we are completely free.

Back on the path behind an ageing, sprawling oak, we resume shape and sit on the ground, leaning back against its immense trunk.

"Beautiful, yet mutually non-covalent," Colleen says softly.

I take her hand and squeeze it. "I am sorry."

"No Adam. It's fine. This is how we know."

"However," I say tentatively, "Would you be willing to be my new best friend?"

"Adam, I would love that. Truly. You've made my sunset."

My night with Colleen did not end after we morphed. We sat at the foot of the old oak tree talking all night. We questioned all the mysteries of our Earth lives. Her assimilation narrative was fraught with elements of emptiness and mourning for Mir. She experienced waves of void that had lessened over the years but had not gone away completely. She thought maybe they never would. In the foreground of my narrative was the conundrum of wanting to be with someone I could not be with.

I did not know what I was going to do. Perhaps the problem was now simply moot since Amanda was involved with Tracey. But I did know I had found a special friend in Colleen. So despite my penetrating disquietude, by the time the sun was came up and turned all the rooftops golden and all the grasses damp with dew, I inhabited a feeling of gratitude towards her.

VI

Weeks pass and I have not gone to any bars. I have left Ground Kontrol, I see Colleen for dinner Wednesday evenings, and we talk or take walks to pass the time. But otherwise I have retreated into myself. I am untethered. I thought a great deal about Colleen and how she morphs as she pleases when she's not at work. I don't know why I kept my human shape so rigidly without letting myself go these last years. I go to Irving Park on alternate nights and morph by myself on the walking trail after dark. It had not occurred to me how centring it could be to glide through the Portland sky, looking down at the gold glittering lights and tracking the Willamette River as it wends its way through North Portland towards Vancouver. When I first re-took to shaping (I admit to you sheepishly), I assumed the configuration of a 1900 Underwood Typewriter 2 and stayed on my desk at home imagining Amanda was assigned to refurbish me. I went to all my bars several times in different human and non-human forms -- including a copper-hammered zarf -- in the hopes that Sharon would order me and I could be close to Amanda again. These days I remain in varying forms for a while, just to see how it feels. One week I kept shape of an American Kestrel. Another week I morphed into the same Pacific Willow that is outside my apartment. I just planted myself along the walking path in Irving Park and shaded the hikers who ventured past. My essence has remained intact irrespective of my form and that has enabled me, once again, to inhabit a feeling of feeling better.

VII

It is 9:30 Friday night and I am going to *Cybar Café*. As is customary, Amanda and Sharon are there, this night Sharon is at a table near the bar in deep conversation with a man in medical scrubs. It's likely he has just finished his shift at Legacy Medical and is done for the evening. Amanda is cupping what looks like a coffee mug in her hands, and lost in her sketchbook. I approach the bar where she is sitting and give her my best upbeat hello.

"Hi!" She says back, cheerful and related as ever. I order a coffee too.

We ease into conversation. It was always effortless to talk to her, but tonight she opens up more and I learn about her family of origin, her childhood, her life with men, her struggles coming out as a gay woman, her recent breakup, her love of animals and art, and more and still more. I tell her about my love of nature, what I like about kestrels and willows, my desire to hold onto my inner core, my hopes and fears about the future of the planet. The night flies by.

The bartender calls for last drinks. I don't know where the time went. But Amanda says, "I had one of the best evenings talking to you and I don't even know your name! Mine is Amanda."

"Eve," I say. "Nice to meet you, Amanda!"

At this moment, I am inhabiting a state of what I think you Earth folks call love.

When the Bough Breaks

Justine Bothwick
Italy

WHEN HER PARENTS DIED IN THE ACCIDENT, Ester ran straight into the arms of The Great Gombar. The circus had been in town all season and she had often seen the horses exercised along the soft, palm-lined sands of the beach, and the elephants, slick as wet tyres, bathing in the river. Andreas – he of The Great Gombar fame – was a stocky, blond Hungarian with eyes that scanned you like a searchlight across prison grounds. He galloped past her on his dappled steed, kicking up spray from the waves as they hissed and foamed and expired on the shoreline around her feet, and she – angered the first time and amused thereafter – would laugh and wave until one day he slowed his horse, jumped down beside her and asked her name.

Ester's brother was a violent, jealous man. When their parents' car crashed over the edge of the road, down the hillside, tearing a swathe through the green velvet of the tea bushes on their way home from the plantation, Ester knew she could not stay with him. When he learned of her involvement (at that stage purely platonic) with Andreas, a man neither Indian nor British, and who, moreover, *ran a bloody circus,* he had gone for her, hands encircling her slender throat and a swift bash of her head against a doorframe. It was the family bearer, a taciturn man named Prakash, who saved her, picked up her inert body from the floor, and took her to the hospital. The next time she went home, it was to pack a few belongings into her bag while Andreas guarded the door. Her brother arrived just as they were leaving, and for a moment the two men faced up to each other on the path, and she thought then that she was safe.

The two of them made an unusual couple: Ester was slender as a bamboo leaf, with her mother's sleek black hair, full lips and dark eyes, and her father's fine nose together with the height that came from his Scottish ancestors. Andreas was a muscular little gnome in comparison. However, he gazed upon her adoringly, followed her as she walked from tent to tent and caravan to caravan to discover her new world. People smiled at her as they groomed horses, swept up elephant dung, hammered pegs into the iron-hard ground. Everyone from everywhere: Hindu, Sikh, Moslem, Anglo-Indian, European. While the radio reported riots and massacres and crowds baying *blood for blood* across the country, here there was no division, no partition, and no one was untouchable. She was drawn to the arena and the circles of coloured light that bloomed across the sawdust, and clapped her hands in delight at the acrobats and trapeze artists as they practised tumbling and falling from the sky. She felt Andreas watching her, felt she was being assessed.

The next day he asked her into his office. He pulled a roll of paper from a large cardboard tube, unfurled it across his desk, lit a cigarette and sat back in his chair, giving her that searching look once more. Ester studied the plans in front of her that looked like the designs for a large weapon. But the war had only just finished, although it didn't exactly feel like peacetime, she had to admit. Still, what this had to do with the circus, she couldn't fathom.

'It looks like a cannon. Why are you designing a cannon?'

Andreas stood up and came round to her side of the desk. He leaned in close to her, put one arm around her shoulder, and she felt his rough cheek against hers. Something pulled at her insides, down in the pit of her stomach and lower, and she heard her own breath: loud, roused, and quickening.

'It is a cannon. But it is not a weapon. This…' and here he stabbed at the paper with his cigarette, 'this is why I am truly the Great Gombar.'

He had, he told her, already designed one cannon back in his native Hungary, and there had been a woman whom he had trained to fly from its mouth.

'A human cannonball!'

Ester could hardly believe it. She had thought he was just a Master of Ceremonies, an overseer of elephants and acrobats, and that would have been enough for her. But this was something else indeed.

The detail about his former protégée, she preferred not to think about. The next day, he asked her to marry him.

First, Ester mastered the trapeze. There was a practice bar where she learned to support her weight, hanging by her knees and with her back perfectly arched. It was easy to pull herself back up, and locking her arms as she hung seemed natural to her. Then again, she'd always been an athlete, running rings round the other girls on the lacrosse field at the expensive boarding school her father had insisted she attend. Not that she had ever really belonged. Not like here, where her mixed blood was no more unusual than a piebald pony. After a week of training, Andreas nodded in approval, and then pointed up into the roof of the tent.

'You have the sequence. Now try up there.'

Up on the tiny platform that shuddered and swayed with the least movement, Ester willed herself to look down. The net seemed far away and far too flimsy to provide much in the way of safety. Ravi, a member of the troupe, stepped onto the platform beside her, placed the bar into her hands, and steadied her with his hands on her shoulders. From below she heard Andreas shout.

'It's all in the mind. Turn off your mind.'

Momentum and timing. Breathe in and breathe out. Legs forward, legs back.

The walls of the tent and the lights above moved in a blur while she let unseen forces push and pull her, push and pull, like a lullaby, like rocking in a mother's arms, her lost mother's arms.

After, she stood on the ground and felt electrified, sparks jumping in muscles, tendons, ligaments, and jolting through her cells and across synapses. Andreas took her in his arms and kissed her until she didn't know what was happening to her body, so many sensations were there running over it and through it all at once.

The cannon arrived shrouded in secrecy and tarpaulin, delivered from the back of a trailer one night into its own tent. The next day Andreas invited her inside and, under the gloom of the canvas, unveiled the machine, tugging away at armful after dusty armful of material until it was there, squatting like a giant toad: a solid dark presence with an even blacker heart.

Ester placed her hand on the surface; the metal felt cold and pockmarked under her fingers. Andreas, sitting astride the far end of the cannon, was watching her. He seemed amused. Without thinking, she stuck her head inside the opening. There was nothing to see, just a cramped space disappearing into the darkness. She pulled herself away, momentarily unable to breathe.

'It's not really gunpowder, is it, that launches you?' she asked, with her hand on her chest. 'I mean, that just wouldn't be possible. It would kill you.'

Andreas jumped down, took her hands, and placed them on the surface once more.

'Feel it. You are perfect for this. As if I summoned you with my design. But we never discuss how it works. You have to agree to that.'

The circus was struggling. They needed a new town and new audiences but there were so many reports now of violence across the country that they were afraid to move the cavalcade of staff and animals. The cannon, however, would cause a sensation, from the cantonment to the villages and even as far as Bombay. People would be sure to come to see a human cannonball.

And so, resolute, Ester trained. Every morning Andreas had her lifting weights and stretching and bending until her body was as hard and as explicit as the cannonball she would ultimately purport to become. She continued with the trapeze, making ever-higher and more daring launches and catches, with somersaults mid-air and a firm, assured grip on the bar when it smacked back into her palm for the hundredth time of the day. Each evening, Andreas would take the callipers, the tape measure, and the scales to record all her physical details – height, weight, circumference – in order to perfect the dummy he would use to establish the angles and distances of her jump, the position of the cannon, and the net.

The permits arrived from the Governor's office and soon after, the printer from the bazaar delivered a sack of posters. Ester took one and studied it. *Look who's here: The Great Gombar and his cannon. Ready to thrill. See his amazing flying lady soar a hundred feet and more from the mouth of the monster. The sight you'll never forget. Boy?? It's good. This is something you have been waiting for. The spectacle of spectacles! Book your tickets to avoid disappointment.* There was a picture of Andreas astride the cannon and over the top of the page flew a cartoon of a person being fired amid a cloud of smoke and flames.

With two weeks to go before the day, Ester asked when she would actually get to practise with the cannon. Instead, Andreas passed her two brown paper packages. Inside the first she found her costume – shiny, tight and scarlet, decorated in spirals of sparkling gold that would wind around her body like a spring. There was a matching helmet and a red satin half-mask to disguise the goggles and complete the outfit. In the second lay a mass of creamy lace; when she lifted it up, she realised she was looking at her wedding dress.

Andreas had explained the position she had to take, with total rigidity required in the flight phase. Aiming for the net was crucial. Above all, a complete commitment to the act. After dark, alone in her bed (for Andreas respected her wishes to wait for their wedding night) Ester dreamed of that dark, suffocating space willingly entered into. A hundred times a night she reversed inside the tube, pushing herself backwards with her hands until she felt obliterated. As she lay, listening to the elephants whispering down their trunks and chinking their chains outside her caravan, she told herself over and over: be determined, be strong. Be metal. She knew she couldn't afford even the smallest hint of doubt.

The dummy would indicate the calculations needed for a successful flight. It hurtled through the air, falling short, over-shooting, rebounding too vigorously from the spring of the net to crack its skull on a rock or twist its body into the trunk of a tree. Andreas watched each trial, expressionless, and Ester watched him. *Turn off your mind* she repeated to herself. By now it had become her mantra, a talisman to be invoked any time troubling thoughts might begin to surface.

And so, in no time at all, the day arrived when she would commit to the act and her new life in perpetuity.

The show would begin with men juggling torches and breathing fire, followed by dancing horses and tumblers and contortionists creating a confusion of changing patterns and formations. From the entrance gate, people streamed in to take their places around the field. The Governor and his officers seated straight-backed under gazebos, their wives with fans colourful as butterfly wings flapping in desperation against the heat. On the other side of the field, with no canopy to shelter them, stood the villagers, the fishermen, the farmers and their families, noisy and expectant.

Inside the tent Ester waited, ready in her costume, adjusting the strap of her goggles and pushing the helmet ever more firmly onto her head. Through a gap in the canvas she could see the sun descending into apricot clouds over the horizon – she would glitter like a golden coil in this light. Like the thin band of gold that Andreas had placed on her finger that morning. She tugged at the buckle of the helmet once more, and then Ravi appeared at the entrance. It was time.

She stood, shimmering against the white tent until she saw Andreas stride into the centre of the field and raise the megaphone to his mouth. He began to incite the crowd.

'Ladieees and gent-le-meeeeen!'

Ester walked with slow and even steps towards the cannon, noticing the grass, sun-browned and flattened beneath her thin ballet pumps. Her mind returned to those words she had spoken earlier, of sickness and of health, and being parted by death. The church had been empty, save for a few members of the troupe, dressed in their eccentric Sunday best.

There had been a polite round of applause when it was all over and outside the women had thrown handfuls of petals.

'Welcome, welcome, welcome to the grrrrrea-test show on earth!'

She kept on walking, drawing closer to the cannon now. As she appeared in view of the crowd, a cheer went up. She stopped next to Andreas and raised her arms, facing each different section of the audience with a gymnast's salute.

'The sensation of the century!'

Florence gave one more wave, her body arched and tense. A bow stretched by an arrow.

'For your entertainment and pleasure, for your delight, delectation and diversion…'

Now it loomed over her, a giant machine of war.

'The astonishing, the amazing, the astounding flying lady!'

More cheers as Ester climbed the ladder and stepped backwards into the jutting column. Down, down and reversing until the light faded and she was sucked into the dark.

Muffled now. 'Shooting from the mouth of a monster…'

The platform solid against her feet. Arms firm against her sides. Pressure building. The dreamy, underwater echo of the crowd chanting. 'Ten, nine, eight, seven…' Breathe and prepare to brace. Fists, thighs, buttocks, stomach clenched, and chin tucked in. 'Six, five, four…' Lungs too – filled with air and held ready for… 'Three, two, one!'

Violence. Punched forward and up and out. A flash of light, and through the smoke and she must, must aim straight, with body exact and unyielding. Her vision starts to speckle and darken but she cannot blackout. Time has become meaningless – these four seconds as long as the life she has lived. And the life she has yet to live, and whatever comes beyond. She is immortal, infinite, boundless. A kaleidoscope of pictures turning and encircling her, in and out of focus, all the colours of the rainbow. Departed love and extant hate. Future grief and former joy. A mother and father, a brother, all gone. A husband with eyes that will not let her hide. And then a woman, unknown, lying broken in bed, turns her head, mouths words that cannot be heard. She pleads pity, reaches a raw and blistered hand towards hope. Then twisted, mangled, and dragging herself across the floor, dragging a shroud of darkness around her, and Ester, horrified, starts to disintegrate. No longer metal, now she is nothing but granular doubt, fine sands of fear blowing in a storm. And all at once, there is the net zooming into sight – a somersault required as she plummets towards it. A flip, a turn, and then she must land in its bouncing cradle, and she must grab and hold and cling as it bounds and rebounds around her, determined to hurl her to the ground.

Drip Feed

Karen Cogan
England

DON'T THROW UP BRENDA, don't throw up, for fuck 's sake.
You know that feeling when you are doing the absolute wrong thing but you keep going, like, as you go to do the thing your whole body says: Stop. Don't Do This.

I feel like that a lot. I can feel the No's rise up in me but I'm so used to them I just let them wibble up and then ebb away and press on regardless. Like now . No! I'm just visiting.

She might want to see me. You don't know.

She might bloody be delighted to bollocking see me. This time.

She wanted to see me when my head was between her legs.

Look at me Brenda, keep looking while you do it.

I thought I was going to get lockjaw trying to do the deed with my mouth and make sultry eyes at the same time. I looked demented. But it did the trick. She was delighted with me then. So, maybe she'll welcome me with open arms.

Come in, come in, you gorgeous lunatic, what are you loitering out by my bins for? COME IN.

This woman I live with is my hired help, not a long -term lover.

Help. Ignore her gleamy mirror hair. I've no interest. It's you.

It's always been you, Brenda.

No. Ok.

She is unlikely, realistically, to welcome me with open arms.

She is Olivia, she is my girlfriend, kind of and I am hiding in her bin hut, balancing on a wheelie bin.

Who has a house for their bins? She was always immaculate; she would line up all her toiletries in the bathroom in order of size and make sure that the labels were facing the right way like an army of hygiene.

Frizzy hair, Brenda, is a curse. You're so lucky with yours.

Her hair wasn't frizzy at all like, it was perfection but that's not relevant.

What is relevant is her attention to detail so… no wonder her bins have a house.

Three different bins. I can't work out what the square blue one is for? Blue bin is a bit far to go investigating and I'm already in real danger of my rain -soaked converse sliding me off the one I'm on. But I am very curious now to know what's in it. Should never have started thinking so deeply about the blue bin but here we are. What is in it?? I thought we were only supposed to have one bin. She's always extraordinary, always different from the rest of us, a bit… better.

Fuck it. I have to know. If she sees me I will…

Ok. Be wide and stay low. Crouching as small as I go, I slant my whole body to the right, clinging onto the timbered wall for balance, the smell of my feet and the bin rot creeps deeper into my mouth but , *but*I just manage to grab the lid of the blue bin and launch it upwards. It whacks against the back of the bin house and I teeter and then the bin totters underneath me. I freeze. If one of them comes out to me I will be in such shit. But. Silence.

I'm ok , I think.

And

The blue bin is full of paper, it's full of paper, oh.

But thick paper and kind of coloured canvasses. I pull one out, just about and hold it up to see, and it's her.

My girlfriend, a picture of her in thick colourful crayon strokes and she is knotted laughing and she has no top on. Laughing in the nude, all the colors blurred together and beautiful, it is beautiful in fairness but It's signed, Sam.

Sam.

Why are you painting my girlfriend naked , Sam?

Why is Sam painting pictures of Olivia naked if she's just the help??

But. She's not just the help. She is his girlfriend. Sam is Olivia's Girlfriend, new long-term girlfriend, English and an artist apparently , which is…

They're naked and having the craic together right now: laughing or riding , don't know which is worse.

The notion of them sitting in silky pyjamas, drinking something, tea or beer with their legs interlaced like an ad for SuperValu, y'know, where there are kids and puppies and gorgeous couples, not gay couples, obviously.You'd never see gay couples in an ad for picking up eggs and bread in the morning. But, if you did.

Fuck it. I'm taking it. She threw it away. Olivia is more mine than hers. I've known her longer.

I shove the bright colours of her down the back of my pants and edge out of their garden, swift and damp and careful.

Walking through Cork, streets on streets of badgering memories, I used to have salami and cheese rolls with Olivia from that Spar deli, by the river. Garlicky salami always defeated me, so I had to eat the whole big slice at once instead of spreading the bites through the roll.

She laughed at me and called me an idiot but she kissed my nose, very intimate to kiss a nose. She was always kissing my nose. Even though I look like Barbra Streisand without the cheekbones.

Barbra Streisand is in a film called *The Mirror has Two Faces* and she is ugly as anything in it and she falls in love with this fella who only likes her for her personality because she is a brilliant teacher. I am not a brilliant teacher.

I'm not teaching no one nothing. I am on the part - time dole, queueing on Tuesdays in a clump of people I know who don't say hello to me.

Over Nano Nagle Bridge and down the Grand Parade. Nearing the Coal Quay and my loins start to twist. My feet go shivery and I walk slower, half expecting her to pop out of Flat 19 over the pub and go.

What are you out here for? Come on in and we'll bunker down out of this rain? I got a new Angelina Jolie DVD and a pizza.

The feeling of her is kind of insidious. Like, my ears miss her. It's not all vaginas. It's the sad eyes she makes when she's half asleep and the way she cocks her head to the side like a Fraggle. It's the anxiety, like the constant crushing in my chest, the sense of falling and of my mind resetting and forgetting she doesn't love me. And her. The artist. Sam. Cunt.

I shove the painting further down the back of my jeans as it starts to ride up and out attempting an escape. I fold it in four and shove it between the waistband of my knickers and my skin and tie my belt tight.

What are you doing Brenda, girl - are ya alright?

Grand , yeah , John. How are you?

Fucking John Morley, in his cream tracksuit staring at me like I'm a zoo monkey.

Grand altogether. I saw your sister on Tuesday and I said —

Ok. Mind yourself. John. See ya, now.

And onwards.

John Morley's one of the lads from around who was obsessed with me going out with girls; the questions he used ask while he collected white bits in the corners of his mouth.

But he was the least of my worries in Cork when I was going out with Olivia. She's fierce, dramatic looking, long mad curly hair in about twenty-seven different shades of brown and black and huge dark eyes , and we used get a lot of comments on the streets. But me and her rose miles above everyone.

Even when the skinny man in the saggy jeans spat in my face. He smelt like last week's tobacco and I could see his pores for a split second as he leaned it to our faces. We were close together on Popes Quay, bent laughing at something she had said, can't remember what but... she's very funny. And I could see the

crinkles by her eyes and I thought why would anyone fight the seven signs of ageing if they're this divine?

Then.

DYKES. And spat. I sniffed his spit as I wiped it away with my bare hand, couldn't help it. It was almost yellow; that's not right. He'd be better off down the doctors like.

Olivia didn't do anything except hold my hand tighter and take me for a brandy in Loafers pub. What could she do?

We didn't tell anyone in Loafers; not that there was many in there at 4 o'clock on a Wednesday. Just skinny camp Finbarr on his usual stool smoking and welcoming us into the smell of last nights farts and Tanora underfoot and beer taps that always needed changing. Lovely Loafers. A welcome escape from comments and spit.

This one, Katie Watkins , right, used to do maudlin lesbian poetry readings in there every Monday night and me and Olivia were obsessed with them. Our favourite was the one that started: ' *I want to wear you on my fist like a shield*' .

We used to say it to each other instead of 'I love You'. *I want to wear you on my fist like a shield, Olivia.'*

' *Oh , thanks , yes. I want to wear to wear you on my fist like a shield too, Brenda.'*

But.

Yeah.

The comments.

They're the only thing I don't miss about being with her.

Alright ladies can I get in between ye? How are ye girls? Heading home for some fun? Can I get in between ye? I know what yer up to. Can I watch? Can we watch? Can we film it? Room for one more? Oh, to be a fly on the wall? What I wouldn't give, boys.

Anyway.

Onto North Main Street, it's all foreign shops now. That's what people say. Foreign.

Ya, they're different I suppose 'cause they didn't grow up here. They didn't live in tiny two up two downs with aggressive, pretend plants in the living room and glossy wallpaper masquerading as expensive.

Upwardly mobile: my sister Rita and my Mam , Orla. Upwardly mobile sums them up alright.

What does she have? Where did she get the money for that? That's fake I'm sure, there's no way she can afford that. State of your wan, who does she think she is, did you see what Aisling Sullivan's daughter was wearing in the Echo last night? Why is she always on the Echo? Why do you never get in the Echo? What bars do you go to that you never see the Echo photographer? Maybe if you dolled yourself up a bit more, you've nice breasts, shove them up and hide that stomach and just put yourself out there. I'm not trying to be funny like , but time is ticking.

And then she died. My Mam. Dead Mam, very sudden, her heart went.

She had a chocolate eclair three times a day every day and had done since she was a waitress in in her twenties. Thirty odd years of three eclairs a day, that must be... hundreds of thousands of eclairs. No wonder her heart gave in.

And after she was in the ground: sisters doing it for themselves in the two up two down. Rita and me.

My sister is a bulldog in white jeans but beautiful eyes, green and kind. We'd a lovely time, chatting and thick sandwiches with utterly butterly and hunks of cheese. And beers from Galvin's, dancing to 96fm in the kitchen.

We had a good thing going until the Gay Epiphany.

I see her in town all the time of course, officious in leggings. Storming down Patrick Street with a Nike bag in her hand and Dunnes stores bags full of groceries. I launch myself into doorways and round corners to avoid her now.

I thought she was going to melt into ground when she finally caught me with Olivia.

We'd had daytime white wine down the alley by the Roundy House pub the day we got caught. A bottle each, downed and then sexy squabbling through the streets, in a different time zone to everyone else.

I was trying to apologise for whatever I'd said wrong to Olivia so I caught up with her on the Coal Quay and grabbed her waist and then her hands and I kissed her hard on the mouth and from behind her head.

Rita.

White face frozen, like that *Scream* painting.

Hissing.

Get. Up. Home.

I didn't have the bravery to say no.

So home to:

Lesbian this, disgrace that.

I love her , Rita. I'm just gay. That's all.

Gay? Gaaayyyyy?

You're about as gay as the dog.

Why do you always have to be different? What am I supposed to tell the girls? Jesus Christ, who else saw you mauling each other? Bold as brass in the middle of the day! Do you not think about anyone except yourself?

Get out , Brenda. I'm sorry.

You're not welcome. Get Out.

I begged her. To let me stay in the house.

Mortified in hindsight. But. No go.

I stayed on a bench Fitzgerald's Park for two nights with the winos cause Olivia had to go away working in England.

But then: Veronica, my ferocious best friend , rescued me. She bumped into me looking like a junkie on Sullivans Quay, stringy hair dripping into my eyes from the constant constant rain, even in June. Pissing Ireland.

Veronica installed me on the couch in her tiny one bed flat, then she put me on the back of her bike and drove us over to my Mam's house, Rita's house, and stood outside, looking like a policewoman from a porn film in tight jeans and a leather shirt.

Go in and get your stuff and I'll take you back to ours.

I'll just see if she's calmed down…

No. Go in, get a bag, and leave.

Skulking around the bedroom shoving random bits of underwear and letters into a rucksack and Rita walked so we exchanged shit pleasantries and it was awful, until I looked up and Veronica was standing over us with her hand outstretched.

Give me the bag and get on the bike.

Just a second , Veronica.

Get on the bike, Brenda. She doesn't deserve your company.

Ah , now.

She doesn't deserve your fucking company. Outside.

Like a dykey Indiana Jones.

Rita didn't know whether to kiss her or call a priest. Veronica is so unapologetically gay. She is gay out the door, gay all day. Never let a man go near her.

We sat in her flat later on, looking down at Cork, drinking powdery hot chocolate and Baileys and she exploded in rage.

How dare she judge you because of who you kiss, how dare she, like! It's her loss, you're a champion and she's a fucking amoeba.

Anyway. She's not around at the moment.

I'll go see her later.

Rains is pelting itself at my head now so I readjust the painting and tackle the massive hill to Veronica's house.

I peel my jeans off the second I get into the house and leave them on Veronica's floor like I dissolved. The painting falls out, on the ground, hot and crumply.

A bit of blu-tack and it's up on the wall of Veronica's room with a desk lamp trained on it so I can see it in its full glory. She looks incredible. I can almost, almost forget who painted it.

It's comforting to lie underneath the shape of her.

Christ.

An hour later and I bolt up late for work. Jump off Veronica's drooly pillow; I'll make up her bed later. I don't think she cares, she won't know anyway.

She's… She is in the hospital at the moment. She's 'not well in herself'. In the trunk by her bed, there are hundreds of small teddy bears from when we went round to every charity shop in Cork buying all the teddies.

We can't leave them, Brenda, they've soulful eyes.

And she dragged me around for three days until we had bought every teddy bear in Cork and spent every penny of both of our doles. We lived on stale cornflakes and sweetcorn from a tin for seven days.

I go once a week to see her but God, the state of that place they have her in. No one chats to her.

The Lithium has her mellowed but tears come out of her eyes constantly so you're not sure when she's crying and when it's just water.

I should bring her up a few of the teddies , actually.

The only thing is, the sight of them might remind her of all the new ones that would have been donated since she got put up above and she'll have me all over Cork.

One time we went to Midleton on the bus because she overheard an aul wan saying 'there are grand second hand shops below in Midleton'. We didn't get back til all hours 'cause we had to sit in rush hour traffic.

We had teddies and dolls and butterfly toys, fat snails and smiling cows and even a furry penis left over from a hen night, falling out of our every crevice and people thought we were absolutely off our heads. Well, one of us was , I suppose.

I don't think of her as sick. I just think of her as my best friend. Sick , yeah , but brilliant too. They're not mutually exclusive.

I only learnt what that meant recently. So like ok, mutually exclusive. It's that two things can be the same and still not… no. It means that one thing is not necessarily. No so, like, if I say to you: I am living up in Sundays Well but I also… No. FUCK. Ok , maybe I need to work on that a small bit more.

Can I help you?

No that doesn't come with peas. They're a pound extra.

Well , why don't you go buy a tin of peas yourself, so?!

Fucking work. Tiny cafe, smells of ass. No matter how much we bleach it, deep dirt.

We sell sandwiches and cakes with bright pink icing, the kind of colour that does not occur in nature and Malcolm , my boss , is a bit of a downer, like.

It's all a bit: *Tut— ah , sure.*

His son Martin fell into the river and died after he took seven E's and Malcolm makes everything about him. He references him in every second sentence and it is draining.

Egg mayonnaise
Oh , Martin's favourite, well, he preferred egg mayonnaise and ham, but still.
He loved sandwiches.
You could offer him a roast dinner and he'd take a sandwich over
it any day.
Sandwich mad
He's gone now o' course.
But sure, look.

It's not worth the seven pounds an hour, like, but I have to live.

And the day presses on with a constant stream of gobshites looking for chocolate slices and chips and beans and stew, God help them; the stew is violent.

Six hours ahead. Dragging crumbs around tables and Olivia.

Olivia haunting me.

I just want to cradle her velvety neck and say:

Whatever it is making me not good enough for you, I will change it. If it is the nose I will break it and get a man to rebuild it. If it is the flab I will do the cabbage soup diet , and properly this time, better than the time you caught me eating a whole sliced pan with jam on Day Two.

Is it cause I won't ever watch the news?

God, its agony .

Phone is going and going.

Constant ringing.

Malcolm, the PHONE!

Whenever I answer it, he acts affronted as if I'm stealing his personal business.

Excuse me girl I'll answer me own phone if you don't mind!

BRENDA!

Phone for you.

Oh.

And I hear her exhaling smoke and coughing like an exhaust pipe.

Oh, my God.

Veronica?

I'm out , Brenda. I'm up home.

And… are you better?

I'm great, girl, out the other side, finally.

Come on home. I've a bottle of vodka.

YESSSSSS!

My pal is back.

Malcolm. I'm dying. I'm faint. I'm dying like. I'm very bad. I'll have to rest. Sorry, Malcolm. Malcolm , you'll be grand. I'll see ya Monday, Malcolm.

Out of there and up to her. Panting at the hilltop but Cork is laying out, shimmering a bit below, goldfish on the right, and river in front. Want to bask in it but can't wait to clap eyes on Veronica back in residence

And there she is, throwing open our yellow door, and her face is shiny and she's herself again. Like she climbed back into her own body and it is actually her looking through her eyes instead of some dreadful stranger.

Who are we meeting, Veronica?

Everyone! It's Saturday night, like.

And she downs another tumbler of vodka 7 -Up.

We sit in the empty bath holding each others knees. That's our favourite spot, with the bath curtain closed and the lights off.

It's better now, is it? Your… head?

Much better, dote.

Sorry I didn't come up to you more.

Ah , it was fucking depressing. Let's have another one.

Two of us dance to the Indigo girls holding hands and twirling; we're nothing if not cliched but I fucking love the Indigo Girls. Their voices harmonising together, they make an unbelievable sound , and we sing and pound our feet in every room of the flat.

We go to Loafers first for pints, then the Other Place for shots and a dance downstairs and then to Sir Henry's cause it's Saturday and there is nowhere on the wide Earth like Henry's on a Saturday night.

Even Nirvana played here in '91.

So.

Not 100% sure where everyone is exactly.

But I know I am delighted.

I can't see that well and the wine is making all my aches and pains fuck off tiny shots of green Apple Sourz on offer; ten for a fiver so I buy another round and keep adding them to the swirling mixture in my gut. I feel very healthy and free . Tomorrow will be different , yes , but tomorrow is not here; tomorrow didn't come out for a drink . I did . Now. With my pals, with my pals Veronica and Annie and Jean and Liz and other good women. They are good people . They are different and ferocious and Jean is kind of sexy sometimes but no one, no one holds a candle to Olivia.

To my girlfriend.

My girlfriend is in event planning. S he plans Huggee events; the whole events from start to finish and people cannot get over her, like , people think she is unreal altogether. They can't believe she's Irish cause she's better than all the English girls at it . She used live in England, yeah, London, yeah , Camden,

but now she's back it was very hard. Long distance, ya. Fierce strain on the two if us but she's back now reunited and it feels so good, y'know? Do you want a shot? Have a shot? Get her a shot. Have a shot. You're only young once.

Moving on, onwards and dancing to No Diggidy and Teenage Dirtbag and Puff Daddy and hardcore house.

Different tunes clashing from all of the rooms of the club, y'know, they should sound bad all mixing together but it sounds amazing it sounds like someone should record the mix of them and make it into its own song Good idea Brenda Beautiful sound.

I have a pint of Heineken that a man put a shot of tequila into I told him to piss off but I grabbed it from him anyway and the taste is grand Mingling with all of the strangers but no one is really a stranger in Cork I see Sarah Murphy's brother Michael chatting to Laura Hanley from my class Alright Laura

Dull as a wall that girl

And Jessica Bradley grinding herself up on Veronica There you are Jesus

Veronica looks langers but shag it She deserves it She deserves a bit of a celebrate after everything she's been through I'm proud of her I'm proud of Cork I'm proud of everyone

I climb up on a round table with graffiti all over it and I

scream to the crowds:

UP CORK

GO ON CORK

LETS FUCKING DANCE LADSSSSSS

And a few scream back and a few don't but that's grand

It's all grand and I'm floating on them then everyone is lifting me up with their words

I love your top, girl

You look fierce , well

What are you up to

Olivia

Olivia is up

Olivia is what I'm up to

Me and my girlfriend , Olivia, are

Me and Olivia , my girlfriend, are going to Mauritius

Me and my girlfriend are actually thinking about New York in the
Spring
As a couple
My girlfriend
Olivia
Events
Girl
Woman
Olivia
Friend
And I
Not sure
Exactly
Where
Four
Paracetamol
Slamming
Head
Shots
Headache and thump
Small
Rest
Lie down
Cold tile
Toilet
Lovely
And
Maybe
Tomorrow
Will be
Kinder.
Death.
Murder.

I am dying.

My gums are thirsty and my tongue is a husk.

Dust ball lodged in my throat and making me gawk.

Vomit escapes out of me before I have a second to think about where to aim it.

Clean it later.

Vommy chin though.

And the smell makes me go again.

This is a bad one.

I'll drag myself to the shower in a minute.

I just can't warm up.

VERONICA CLOSE THE WINDOW

Unstick my eyes from the tarry sleep to see how bad things are this time.

My lips are old balloons and I'm pretty sure I'm cut but I can't face looking. Not yet.

Why am I outside?

Fuckkkkkkkkkkk.

I am outside Olivia's house.

But not in the bin hut today.

At her front door.

Lying on the step.

No wonder my side is killing me.

Quiet my breathing.

I can't actually cope with this.

Sssh.

Fuck.

Drag my carcass up

Off a mat that says welcome.

Doubt it.

Then.

Madam

Madam can you come away from the door , please

Shiny black shoes and a cheap navy trouser.

Can only be:

I'm from Sunday's Well Garda Station. There's been a complaint of disturbance. Is this your house?

It's

Its my girlfriends house.

The lie comes easy.

Never trained my mouth to stop saying it.

People must think I'm loopy.

A long line of all the faces I've said it to over the years.

How many of them knew?

That we weren't long - distancing, she was just distancing

Herself

As far away as possible from me

And now

How am I here?

I've done a pool of boozy puke on her welcome mat.

My left breast is flopping out of my bra in a bid for freedom and I threw my holdy in knickers in a bin somewhere last night and I've a heavy period and my mouth is thumping with pain. And I am about to come face to face for the first time in Three Years

With

My girlfriend

My Ex -Girlfriend.

Guard knocks again

And she unhooks a bolt from inside. Keeping intruders away.

And there is the shadow of her behind the door.

God, I even fancy the outline of her.

But.

It's not her.

That's not Olivia.

And.

Her voice, all English and gentler than I imagined.

Garda Flynn goes:

Is this your girlfriend?

She makes a noise

No.

She says.

I can't look at her. I look at my knees, bleeding.

Brilliant.

Brenda? It's Brenda is it?

My name sounds like a potato in her accent.

Pathetic.

Hello it's Sadie, is it?

I attempt.

It's Sam actually.

Whatever

I'm sorry. I had no choice but to call someone this time. You turned up at half five in the morning screaming and singing Joni Mitchell songs and throwing your shoes at our window.

I feel my bare feet on the ground and know she's right.

BUT. Where's Olivia?

Why didn't she come to the door herself?

I want to ask your one but my mouth is glued shut with mortification.

Guard is getting bored of this Sunday morning domestic and wants to go for a cup of tea.

Sam is not impressed but Olivia is not coming to the door. Even now and I suddenly know it's because

Olivia did not want her to call the police!

Pounding shuffles to the back of my head to make way elation, for the joy of Hope. The joy of her. Not wanting me to get in any trouble. Because Olivia sees me. She knows me.

She still cares about me.

I won't be any more trouble. I apologise , Garda. I apologise , Sadi…Sam. Honestly.

And.

Free.

Of her, venomous manipulative stick of an English bitch, trying to convince Olivia to distance herself from me, calling the law. Because I just what? Turned up?

Turning up is not actually a crime in this country,Sadie , so tell Tony Blair or someone to send a plane for you and just fuck off.

As I reach the Opera House it's clear that the elated adrenaline was just a stand in for the absolute Horrors that are starting to seep into me.

I need a beer and a sandwich but no money.

Nasty old flashbacks of Olivia as I cross into town, past Supermacs.

Memories of the day she left me in there with curry chips going soggy from my tears.

Her words from that day are coming in and into my skull.

Telly and Drinking. Telly, drinking. Stuck. Stagnant. Sad.

Expanding into your own sofa.

Don't you want to do better than this? Is this it for you?

There's a whole world out there, Brenda.

No! Can't handle this.

Stabby pains in my ears and very badly needing a loo.

I dive into the Gingerbread House and lock myself in the disabled loo in the back staircase. There is a smell of coleslaw and burnt toast and appalling coffee and it sneaks up my nostrils and my stomach starts to go again. Jesus, what did I eat?

Vaguest recollection of a stale breakfast roll.

Centra. Yeah.

I throw up, black pudding and old egg, barely digested.

That would have been sitting under the heat lamps since half seven in the morning. They shouldn't have sold that to me at all. Not on.

I gawk and gawk and gawk again until I can gawk no more. There's a reflection of me watching me. She's in the full-length mirror next to the toilet. Who wants to watch themselves going?

Sitting on the loo and I'm staring at the mess in the mirror.

I'm like a drunk Michael Jackson song.

Mouth looks worse than I thought, slit lips and (*she notices*) chipped tooth. Balls.

Flab plopping over the waist of my low slung jeans with the chain on the pocket. *Makes me look edgy*, I thought when I bought it in Paul's Street shopping centre but now it just looks embarrassing.

I'm 32.

I thought that by now I'd… NO.

I consider staying on the cistern and hoping I eventually drown in it but

ANYWAY! Onwards and upwards.

I skulk out of the cafe avoiding the aul wans having midday ham sandwiches. They stare but I duck out the side door and down towards Patrick Street.

Veronica must be dying if I'm this bad; she was annihilated by half 7. She didn't know her name at 3am when we danced to "Unfinished Sympathy" in a mad clump of people.

It's always "Unfinished Sympathy" by Massive Attack at the end of the night in Henry's. Everyone fucked and best friends with everyone.

Poor thing. I'll bring her a Lucozade in a while. Lucozade and a bag of Tayto will sort her out.

Not yet though.

She's like a poltergeist with a hangover, weeping and scratching at herself or worse; catatonic, staring at home improvement programmes for hours.

I'll go up to her shortly.

On Oliver Plunkett Street I realise I stink, pungent. And I badly need to change my tampon now.

I'm digging in my deep pockets for one, among hard tissue paper and chewing gums and hair clips when I can just feel her, in front of me, appalled.

Rita .

Normally I wouldn't come down Oliver Plunkett on a Sunday cause I know Rita goes for a cooked breakfast in Scotts bar with her horrible friends.

Hi Brenda, how are ya keeping? You're looking lovely in your... big shirt, aren't ya?

Judgy girls with spite and cheap blusher coming out of their nerves.

I'm in one of my no -go Rita zones but I'm not thinking straight 'cause of the booze and the pain in my face and the tampon swelling inside me and I fucked up and here is my sister. She takes me in and I see a glimmer of soft in her.

Jesus, Brenda.

Are you alright?

Do you know you're bleeding down your top?

My mouth is filling with blood. I've split it afresh, trying to smile at her.

She reaches for my hand and her eyes are filling up.

Mother of Christ, I've never seen her like this. She didn't cry at our Mam's funeral. I was like a hose.

I don't know what to say to her. I love her cross face but I am dripping old blood and my gut tells me I should leave her alone before anyone she knows sees us together and she bristles again.

So I let go of her hand and walk past her down towards Grand Parade.

I can feel her standing behind me, watching me go but I keep moving, stomach empty and body lagging until I settle in the record section at the back of Cork City Library.

I put George Michael on the listening station and settle into a big chair; the red wool on it is prickly but otherwise it's womb comfortable.

I have to picture Olivia next to me to go to sleep. My head is swimming and soon I'm out for the count.

Tribes won't let me in 'cause of my 'attire'. Tribes like. It's a cafe for 15 year -olds to shift each other on sofas with security outside in the middle of the day. I said to your man on the door:

Oh, God, you'd wanna have a look in the mirror , love.You're a bouncer at a sandwich shop!

Turn the corner fast in case he comes after me.

The Oval isn't open for some reason and I can't go into the Spailpin Fanach because my uncle drinks there.

I'd still be safe in the library if it wasn't for dopy Paudie, with his hands in his pockets, standing over me. I woke up and he was shuffling and humming with both of his hands deep in his pockets. He has a simple enough face but there's something very creepy about his crotch. So I bolted.

I'm sitting on the footpath outside the Beamish brewery and tears are pooling on my collarbone, and if anyone sees me I will actually liquidise and flow down the drain like.

I don't know where to go. I want to kidnap Sam or Sadie or whatever and dump her in the sea so I can lay with Olivia and fiddle with her thumb and talk about how clouds happen.

I need a sausage sandwich with ketchup and mayonnaise mixed together and a slice of cheese on top. I need a cup of tea. With my sister.

I want my sister and the way she used to be.

I want the comfort of her, the warmth of pyjamas , and the Superser in the kitchen and the kettle on constant boil for cup after cup until we feel better. Tiny telly on the countertop and we watch something and not say anything.

She looked pure upset on the street when I walked away.

Maybe she was about to invite me up home.

Maybe.

Ok.

Outside her door and I'm doing deep breathing. Can't knock.

I'm 99% sure Jacqueline next door is staring at me through the curtains but I can't knock. Can't bring myself to.

Are you alright Brenda , love? She's inside alright. Just knock on the door.

I know how to get in, Jacqueline. Thanks.

You're in an awful state, aren't ya, girl. What happened ya?

Fucking Jacqueline.

I pound on the door and dash to the side window and pound that too to escape Jacqueline's chin hairs and nosiness.

And there she is. Rita.

A bit puffy -looking, holding a washing up sponge.

Come in.

You sure?

Just come in, love.

Relief.

But Inside.

There's no cup of tea.

Just.

I'm worried, Brenda.

Are you on drugs? Are you in trouble with the law? Are you … a prostitute?

No telly and sausage sandwich just.

Why are you bleeding? Who saw you in town like that?

Do you need to go talk to someone? Something isn't right with you.

What are you doing for work? When did you last visit Mam's grave? Who knows about the gayness? We need to do something about you.

Endless and my stomach is in my shoes. Shouldn't have come.

I'm focussing on the smell of Air Wick and the six -pack of beans on the floor, not put away yet after the shop. Thats a lot of beans for one woman living alone.

All this space and I'm back on the old couch under the window now Veronica is home.

Couldn't she just get over it?

Just process it and move on?

I'm gay, get over it.

And I feel my head rising up from the beans to face my sister.

And I say:

I'm actually leaving. I came to let you know. I'm moving to Paris. I leave this evening.

Paris?

Yes, Paris.

What are you going to do in Paris?

I'm not sure Rita , but I'll bloody be in Paris.

Thats a big expensive city, dote. You get lost in Clonakilty.

Just….PARIS, RITA.

Bye , Bye , now.

And I'm out. Again.

Jubilant at the lie but hollow from the welcome.

She's right like. Imagine me in Paris. State of me.

VERONICA! Are you up? I got you a surprise.

I passed a St. Vincent de Paul shop on the way home and I saw a minuscule brown lump of fur. It was a little lump of bear with a flat face and black eyes that are just stitches. He is peculiar and I knew she'd love him.

Look, Ron, he's ridiculous.

Into her room and she's STILL asleep in her clothes from last night, a Debbie Harry t-shirt and leather skirt, cropped hair and about 97 earrings. She looks great, even in this state.

Cheekbones.

Don't ask me to get you Lucozade after I've a shower. I'm revolting. I'll get you water and a Nurofen first.

Dizzy in the kitchen, I hold myself up, gushing water into two Heineken glasses, soaking me , and diluting the blood on my top. Water drowns the unwashed plates and glasses I let pile up while she was away sick , and as I stand there I know that Veronica is dead.

I bring the water and headache tablets into her.

I hold her waxy hand lying useless on the mattress.

She has short nails and veins near the surface , which I always thought was attractive but there's nothing much moving through them anymore.

I move the packets of pills from under her, one tablet left, and a half empty bottle of Cork Dry Gin.

I lost count of the amount of times she rescued me.

And now…

And her skin is almost purple.

And that's the end of Veronica

And as the police and the ambulance finally pull away and before her terrifying Mother arrives…

I kind of know that no matter how long I live I won't find another one of her. A pure one-off like, as they say.

And

Em.

I stay on her duvet for twenty -four hours or so.

I sit in the empty bath with the curtain closed and hope her ghost joins me.

Nothing.

And.

I call Olivia's house from the landline, a few times in the night, and on the sixth time she answers but the sound of her voice after so long flummoxes me and I'm frozen.

And I don't say anything. I just listen to her questioning and tutting until.

Brenda?

If that's you

Will you

Just for once and for all leave us

Alone.

Will you?

Do you hear me?

My friend … do you remember Veronica?

But she's put the phone down.

Back to Sam, Sadie, England , and art and and all.

I look up at the painting of her.

But.

It's not there?

Where is it?

Oh

I took it dancing.

I wanted her close to us when we went out. God. I showed it to randomers and boasted about her.

And then.

Later.

Oh, God.

Blurry feeling of scrawling on the painting in black marker, borrowed from the bar I suppose.

Scrawled hate.

You better lock your doors. I'm watching you. Stupid bitch.

Liar. Whore.

And now it's?

Where is it?

It's

Under the Welcome mat on her front door.

Hand - delivered.

Threats on her naked body.

Can't go to get it.

Obviously.

So. That's.

Don't know what time it is.

Light and dark stream in and out , one by one , and cover Veronica's bears. I pack them all, but one, in a suitcase with her My Little Pony pillow and a letter for her Mam.

I pick up the phone to call Olivia again but I don't dial.

I spot a sharpie behind the phone book. Thick black, smelly lovely ink.

I mark my hand with it.

And sniff, mark , and sniffing deeper and deeper into my arm until it can't go any darker.

And then I stick a pin in my skin; from a brooch of a St. Bridget's cross that is on a calendar that was here when we moved in.

St. Bridget is one of Ireland's patron saints, y'know, very important and she was…kind to everyone and she used sleep next to a younger woman in her bed, and when Bridget died, your one died exactly a year after her, which is, you know.

And I dig the cross into the top of my hand and follow it up with ink from the pen time and time again. Pen and pin. Pen and pin. Till there's blood and Sharpie ink deep in me. It's messy but you can read her name.

So I know it'll be there till I can afford to get it done properly.

Prison loyalty.

So she knows I will never stop thinking about her, no matter what anyone says. She is the best woman I've ever met.

I stare into the mirror at it, backwards but fantastic.

I think she'd like it.

Veronica.

Eight letters of fucking defiance.

The sound of Veronica's Mam howling is in my skull as the bus pulls in.

The small flat bear is at the top of my handbag, watching the world go by. Everything else in a fat mound in a backpack digging into my shoulders.

Overnight to Paris.

I hear him from the bridge and I fly to make it in time.

My heart is thumping, my face is flaming, and my eyes streaming from wind.

And I can hear Veronica saying:

That's it, girl, go for it. This place is stultifying. Fly free, like!

Just…if you don't go for any reason, will ya pick me up a packet of Marlboro lights on your way back ?

Unlooping the knots in my stomach at the thought of her and half-skidding , half -falling down the street, I make it.

And when I get there…To Paris.

Maybe I'll get a job in a cafe. Or a pastry shop.

And maybe I'll put a bunch of daisies down for Veronica in the famous graveyard where Oscar Wilde is buried. And I'll live a shiny life for both of us.

And after a few weeks, maybe five…

I'll call her, when I'm sure she's alone and I'll say

Olivia, I live in Paris now, and I work with pastry , and I am a size eight, and I am writing a book about women and our hearts and lives, and I am very centred , and very very thin, and I have the skin of an infant.

Maybe you could come and see me. I'm not desperate for you to but…

Maybe , nonetheless , you could pop over to Paris and we could have a wander and just…see.

And she will arrive and and she will see me in floaty rose-coloured trousers and a little vintage top that says , 'Nice Girls Do'.

And we will …

Hold hands…and…

Maybe

Just…

Just. Be. Together…again

There

Will we?

Maybe.

Or

Not…

Maybe

Not.

Maybe Not.

The Haunting of Emily Whitechapel

Kurtis Fagg
England

IT'S NOT EVERY DAY A VACANCY is displayed for the countries most haunted house. Around twenty-six years had passed since they last hired new staff and this wasn't an opportunity Emily was going to pass up. A job at Silvergrave Manor was a job for life.

"No thank you, Emily. I don't believe I've seen a more darling presentation in all my years here. You are truly splendid."

"Oh, you are too kind, Ms Featherstone. I'm just really glad you're willing to give me an opportunity to put all of my years of acting school to good use. To work so hard and feel like it was all for nothing has been pretty heartbreaking, you know?" Ms Featherstone met Emily's defeated expression and nodded apologetically. She reminded Emily of her own grandmother in many ways. A woman that seemed mentally and physically strong for her age, yet she also had a real warmth and kindness to her. Reaching to the right, she proceeded to pour yet another cup of tea from the teapot - this must have been number four or five within the space of an hour. While the number escaped Emily, the same couldn't be said for her bladder. There was no way she could handle another drop.

"Oh, yes, another for me please. I'm so glad I share your love of tea Ms. Featherstone, and your tea set is simply divine," Emily said reaching for the refilled cup, the smile on her face doing its best to hide her unrest. As she stared into the cups golden brown depths, Ms. Featherstone's eyes flicked to the hands of the mantle clock sat atop the fireplace.

"My apologies, Miss Whitechapel! Me and my little old teapot have kept you far longer than I had intended. I still have one final interview to conduct. Following that I will be calling back those on my shortlist for an overnight trial. Now it wouldn't be proper for me to promise anything, but I would certainly say it's not worth straying too far. I would thoroughly recommend the Manor's grounds at this time of year."

Both Emily and Ms. Featherstone rose to their feet and exchanged pleasantries. Emily's tailored dress still looked pristine despite her fidgeting through the closing stages of the interview. Her appearance had clearly impressed Ms. Featherstone too. Being complimented on her long flowing blonde hair and bright blue eyes wasn't something she had ever experienced mid-interview. It was a nice change from having every nook and cranny scrutinised in her acting auditions and the boost in confidence it gave her may have just secured her the job.

"The toilet is just down the hall and to the left, dear," Ms. Featherstone warmly joked as she opened the door.

"Thanks again!" Emily replied trying to hide rosy cheeks as she shuffled away.

Silvergrave Manor was an impressive sight. Its tall 16th-century walls were a beautiful faded red with patterned cream accents lining its windows, while the network of corridors and staircases were as difficult to navigate as its large garden maze. Emily's thick jacket was keeping her cosy as she sat outside with her head in a book about the manor's long bloody history. She wasn't a horror movie fan. Supernatural teen fiction didn't remotely interest her and she wasn't there to search for ghosts or the undead like the majority of the hotels guests. She wasn't against the idea of ghosts existing though, in fact the idea of having ghosts to keep her company sounded nice. She reached into her bag and rattled out a small translucent orange container. As she flicked open the lid, she remembered exactly why she wanted this position. After eight years filling the cracks in her head with medication and living solely to impress everyone around her, this job was the one thing she needed to do for herself.

"So, the interviews for the four candidates you selected all went well?"

"Oh, yes, very much so. Especially Emily Whitechapel. She was just splendid. So eager to please and that smile, that smile could light up any room," replied Ms. Featherstone, a touch of sadness in her voice.

"You didn't regret your decision, then? They all seemed themselves, nothing unusual?"

"There are few things I have ever regretted in my time running this manor and this wasn't one of them. There were many other applicants. If I wasn't one-hundred percent sure about these four I would not have selected them," the hint of sadness turning to irritation in Ms. Featherstone's reply.

Two hours had lethargically passed since leaving Ms. Featherstone's office. The bar and restaurant areas had become a crowded safe haven away from the rolling coastal fog that often blanketed the manor without prior warning. As she stood staring out into the white, Emily was greeted by a buzz containing an invitation to the boardroom. As per her usual luck, the room was located down the hall at the opposite side of the room. Thankfully, Emily succeeded in quickly traversing the horde with minimal casualties, which was always a plus. The rewards for her efforts came in the form of a locked door and another female applicant that had beaten her in the race there. The woman seemed to be a similar age to Emily. She was probably mid-to-late twenties and had a unique style painting her head to toe. Clearly the sort of person that could put her own twist onto any outfit or hairstyle to make it her own, or both as was the case today, with a gothic black dress and jacket combination that perfectly complimented her long wavy hair. Thankfully her bright facial expression was a stark contrast from her dark aura.

"Damn girl! You nearly added to the number of ghosts around here in that sprint," the woman said trying to hold back her laughter.

"I wasn't that bad, was I? Oh, God I go need to go back and apologise!" replied an embarrassed Emily.

"Nah you're good. They'll probably run into scarier things than that later tonight and wish it was you."

Emily could feel an instant connection to this girl. Not the usual co-dependent connection but something more like that of seeing an old friend. It was an odd experience, but a welcome one. Having only moved to the area recently, Emily was a little short on the friend front.

"I'm Emily by the way. I'll be the one embarrassing myself for the rest of the day," she replied with a smile sneaking from the corner of her mouth as she held out her hand for a handshake.

"Embarrassing Emily. Got it. I'm the ever-sarcastic Lexi Sparks," replied the woman as she ignored Emily's outstretched hand and went straight in for the hug.

Their embrace was broken awkwardly by the swift appearance of Ms. Featherstone and another two members of hotel staff dressed in their distinct burgundy and gold uniforms. As they approached, they greeted the pair with warm smiles and congratulated them on their interview performances. With a clunk, the door was unlocked and the pair were ushered inside. Ms. Featherstone remained by the door, and with a last look in both directions, stepped into the room allowing the door to close behind her. It had only been shut a moment when another young man and woman burst through abruptly.

"Nice of you to join us, Mr. Carter; you too, Miss Kennedy. My apologies if I interrupted the pair of you becoming better acquainted." Embarrassed, Mr. Carter quickly wiped away the hue of his lips, the colour of which was an unmistakable match for Miss Kennedy's glossy pink. Emily and Lexi sat back contently as the late arrivals offered up paper-thin excuses much to the disapproval of the assisting staff. Emily had a pretty clear idea about what personality to expect from Mr. Carter. Wearing gold-rimmed sunglasses indoors quickly saw to that. With all eyes focused on Mr. Carter's questionable fashion choice, Miss Kennedy attempted to quietly slide past and into her seat. A good idea executed poorly, as she stumbled past the waste bin with a clatter.

"Didn't realise we had a day tripper in the room," joked Lexi, who expected more of a reaction from the room than just her own amusement.

"I'll have you know that I didn't trip. I think you'll find I gracefully misstepped!" replied the agitated Miss Kennedy.

With much of the room struggling to hold back their laughter and in Lexi's case, tears, Ms. Featherstone took it upon herself to defuse the situation and proceeded to distribute paperwork to the four applicants. The documents were a seemingly standard mix of contracts, health and safety procedures and non-disclosure agreements. Emily looked through more of it than the rest but even she didn't fancy reading it cover to cover. Four final signatures and was time to move on.

"Excellent!" exclaimed Ms. Featherstone, who clearly had as much love for legal procedures as the rest of the room.

A laptop and projector sat on a desk in the centre of the room. In many ways, they looked out of place against the classical wooden decor. Ms. Featherstone looked equally out of place trying to use the machine, with one of the younger staff members having to step in at regular intervals. She ran through more of the building's history, in particular, its connections to the paranormal and the many televised investigations that have been conducted on the site.

"Whether or not my staff believe in ghosts and the paranormal isn't something that concerns me, though I have the utmost respect for their opinions. What concerns me is keeping those that do believe they exist, coming in OUR doors, staying in OUR rooms, and putting money into OUR pockets." Ms. Featherstone's honest words pleased Emily, though she didn't want to upset anyone in the room by letting a smile show it. Lexi's face didn't change from its relaxed position either but it was clear the other two applicants were a little uncomfortable with the revelation. The young man in particular looked as if he was about to speak up but was cut off, open-mouthed by Ms. Featherstone's voice.

"Now I know I have not been particularly clear about the roles you have each applied for. This was by design as the details must never be known to the public, but as you have all put your faith in me, allow me to put mine in you."

The man opted to escape his awkward expression with a fake yawn, one that did little to convince anyone in the room.

"Wow..." Lexi countered with a muffled cough meeting his glare.

"Ladies and Gentlemen, you are invited to join Silvergrave Manor as 'Supernatural Effect Artists'."

The news brought a mix of intrigue and confusion to the room. Ms. Featherstone went on to explain the details of the role. The position, for which Emily could barely hold back her excitement, required them to add to the entertainment of the manor guests. They would have a range of equipment at their disposal to provide paranormal content for all of the human senses. This would range from visual aspects such as makeup and period costumes, to environmental controls for lowering the temperature, and introducing scents into the manor.

"So, we can be as theatrical as possible? Like acting as the ghosts of murder victims?!"

The excitement in Emily's voice drew a laugh from Lexi and shocked, disapproving looks from the less than impressed man and woman whose names she still didn't know.

"To an extent, young Miss Whitechapel. You are here to create an atmosphere for our paying guests, not perform a play for them," Ms. Featherstone replied in a tone that conveyed both warning and respect for Emily's desire to perform.

"No disrespect to Emily. I'm Terry by the way, but am I the only one that has a bit of an issue with pulling the wool over the eyes of these poor fools like this? It's pretty messed up. Am I right?!" Terry replied pleadingly to anyone in the room that would listen.

"Now Terry, Emily, Lexi, and Mary, I understand you all have different beliefs BUT, I am a firm believer in everything happening for a reason. You all found your way into this room today with only the most minimal information about the positions you had applied for. Surely you don't want to let this opportunity go without at least trying? What is the worst that could happen?"

The firm words rolling from Ms. Featherstone's tongue had a calming, reassuring effect on the rooms occupants.

SLAM! The room's door flew open and crashed handle first against the solid wall behind. Everyone in attendance jumped out of their skin, with Lexi almost falling from her leaning chair. Ms. Featherstone in particular seemed particularly flustered by the event.

"Well, that was unexpected!" announced Lexi to the still shaken room. As she spoke it became apparent that the temperature had also dropped with fog accompanying each word that flew from her mouth.

"Don't worry folks, the wind does that in here sometimes. These old doors aren't what they used to be, you know?" one of the assistant staff members offered up as an explanation.

There were subtle glances between the staff members and Ms. Featherstone. Emily noticed her reassuring one of them with an arm on his shoulder. She then turned back around to face the new starters.

Ms. Featherstone addressed the room, speaking in a quicker manner, "Well, I don't know about you but I think that's enough excitement for the time being. Each of you have a room prepared with some additional information about what you should expect tonight and what we expect to see from you. Of course, I would also recommend that you get some rest. Shall we say, reconvening in this room at 9pm?"

Everyone in the room nodded their heads and offered words of agreement. One of the assistants distributed keys and directions while the other briskly helped Ms. Featherstone to the door. The group left the two assistants studying the door and its frame and headed up to their respective rooms as Ms. Featherstone quickly vanished into a distant corridor.

Glad for the opportunity to take a breath and relax, Emily slid her key into the lock and stepped inside. All colour faded from her face, leaving only a pale imitation in its place. As she inched warily backwards across the suddenly ice-cold floor, her eyes remained transfixed on the movement in the darkness before her. The stalking black shadow matched her stride for struggling stride. Her heart began to beat louder and quicker, her stumbling pace increasing to match. She didn't want to break eye contact but was forced to turn her head to find the handle of the heavy door blocking her path. With her attention momentarily elsewhere, the figure lunged at her in chaotic black blur, knocking her through the doorway and to the corridor carpet in a crumpled heap. Even the glowing, golden hallway lamps above began to flicker in fear.

Disorientated and paralysed by dread, Emily's legs refused to acknowledge her plea for any kind of movement. Spying a gathering of guests at the far end of the hallway, and knowing her life may depend on it, she let out a piercing scream for help. A scream soon cut short by the cold dead grip of her assailant's fingers wrapping around her trembling throat. Clawing desperately at the carpet threads, Emily could do little to prevent the figure from dragging her helplessly towards the tall staircase. She could hear the onrushing rumbling of feet heading her direction, though she also knew they would not reach her in time. With her feet leaving the floor and the ceiling becoming suddenly closer, she lost her fight to break free. Uttering one final shriek, Emily watched her short life flash before her eyes as she plunged over the balcony, crashing to the ground below in a bone-snapping thud.

The onrushing guests could do nothing to prevent the event that had just transpired. Calling for help as they continued to sprint the length of the corridor, they reached the staircase no longer than ten seconds after her impact. Fearing the sight of the scene below, they nervously peered over the ledge and down to the floor below. To their bemusement, there was nobody in sight. No victim, no attacker, and only the dragging marks along the carpet to indicate any form of activity at all. They continued to survey the area and found nothing but an icy chill to the air and spiking electromagnetic frequency readings on their handheld devices. Had they just witnessed an incredible ghostly apparition? It was the only explanation that made any sense.

"Damn girl, you sold the hell out of that scene. What a show!"

The excitement radiating from Terry was clear as he embraced Emily, his moral objections to the role seeming dead and gone.

"Hey, I can't take all the credit. It was a team effort, so well done, everyone!" she said, her beaming smile doing its best to spread over the lips of her colleagues.

It was apparent as the congratulating continued that Mary wasn't feeling the love. Perhaps it was jealousy, spite or hurt pride, but whatever it was, she felt the need to outdo Emily.

"It's my turn now! Goth girl, pass me that white wedding gown and try not to crease it. I've got a masterpiece to perform," proclaimed Mary, instantly draining all of the positive energy from the room.

With a vibrating buzz, the group received an urgent message from Ms. Featherstone, who apologised for interrupting their excellent work thus far. Apologetically, she needed the assistance of Terry with another task temporarily. Not wanting to disobey his superior on the first night, he obediently agreed and departed after ensuring the remaining three could cope without his 'manly' skills.

"We'll be fine, Terry. I'm pretty sure Mary's the biggest man here anyway," replied Lexi, to Mary's utter disgust. "Tell Mrs P. she ain't seen nothing yet!"

"So, all morals aside, the group were successful in making a first impression in their roles?"

"It was a sterling performance. Everything I could have asked for and so much more. If you had only seen the faces on those poor guests. Horror, despair, and intrigue all around," replied Ms. Featherstone, pride filling every wrinkle of her face.

"And requesting the presence of Terry Carter immediately afterwards, what was the task you needed assistance with?"

"There was no task. It was simply a test to see how well the three ladies could cooperate with each other on their own."

The reply from Ms Featherstone was flat and final as she began to rise from her seat and head for the closed door.

"Just one more question, Ms. Featherstone, if I may."

Ms. Featherstone washed the frustration from her expression and turned her head back towards the desk, the door handle still firmly locked in her hand.

"Did Mr. Carter EVER reach you that night?"

Ice filled Mary's lungs as she glided soundlessly through the garden labyrinth, her ivory dress trying its best to dissolve into the swirling mist. Very few guests dared to enter the maze after dark, mostly due to the fear of getting lost. Many would instead set up night vision cameras, motion detectors, and proximity sensors around the green walls during the day. All actions designed to catch a glimpse of the fabled 'White Lady' that stalked the area after dark. As she strode onwards, the beeping and blinking red lights were clear indications that the plan was working perfectly. Her journey's end was the second of the manor's fountains, one that greeted only those accomplished enough to reach the maze's heart.

"Mary, we're picking up a lot of audio-visual signals around that fountain. Should be perfect for the show. Lexi is standing by with the signal jammer ready for your escape as soon as you make the sign. If you understand and are good to proceed, raise your right hand and run it along the hedge," requested Emily who was enjoying being the one behind the curtain after her earlier excitement.

As the leaves trickled through Mary's pale fingers, Emily took a deep breath.

"All eyes are on you now. I'm sure you will do great!"

All Emily and Lexi could do now was sit back and watch. Lexi had taken the watching part one step further, going radio silent until the end and tagging along with a group of investigators in the main hall, purely to see the looks on their faces. She clearly had faith in Mary's ability, though she was also perfectly happy take that fact to her grave rather than say it aloud for anyone else to hear.

Mary collapsed down to the fountain, turning her gaze towards the image of the invisible. The trailing motion sensors blinked into life again, broadcasting the news that she was not alone. As she lay against the cold damp stone, she wished she had worn something a little thicker under the dress. She raised her outstretched hand to grip the fingers of her unseen guest. In a swift silky movement, she rose back to her feet and into the assailant's heartfelt embrace. The shocked confusion in her eyes quickly dissolved into calm comfort. As the silent symphony began to play, their embrace became a slow dance with the lifting fog revealing their starlit dance floor.

"Hey, guys! Get over here," called Lexi to the surrounding crowd of investigators.

Though it had not completely dispersed, the dissipating fog had provided them with a brilliant view of the gardens from the enormous window in the upper hall. It all felt so easy. Like moths to flame, and Lexi had a big box of matches.

"Have you ever seen anything like this? This is incredible," proclaimed one of the ghost hunters, whose words were echoed around the buzzing room.

"Are you getting it? ARE YOU GETTING IT!?"

"We are green across the board," replied the agitated videographer, clearly mistaking the excitement as a lack of faith in his filming ability.

Lexi took out her phone and also started recording, though her lens was firmly focused on the events on her side of the window, and the entertainment it would provide to her new colleagues.

Outside, the dancing had increased in pace and aggression, to the point that Mary had become unwilling to participate. Feeling the firm grip of her partner's hand around her neck was the last straw, with her spinning around and shoving them back. That was followed with a clear gesture that they were through dancing and with her beginning to pace towards the exit. As she strode forward, she was sent tumbling to the floor with a strong thrust to the back, her head impacting with the stone border of the fountain. Groggy, and with a cut above her eye, she struggled back to her feet. With her vision all over the place, she had no chance to block the impact that seemingly came from multiple directions and sent her tumbling backwards into the ice-cold water.

Lexi watched on in frustration knowing she was next in line. How the hell was she going to follow this up? It was like watching an Oscar-winning performance from an actress. From the dancing, to the fighting, and now the being pinned under water and drowned, it was all flawless. If she didn't have any prior knowledge of the events, even she might have believed that ghosts were real. How she had managed hold her breath for so long was impressive in itself. *Maybe she was part fish* thought Lexi. At least that would provide her with another good insult.

As the splashing subsided and the last kicks flew from her legs, the show had reached its conclusion. All that Lexi needed now was the signal to proceed with recovery. She waited and waited, but after five minutes, it didn't come. As the investigators began to mumble about heading outside, Lexi burst out the hall.

"Emily! She didn't give the signal. What the hell is going on!?"

"What the hell happened out there?" asked Lexi, her feet rapidly carrying her through the doors and to the chilly outside.

"Oh, my God, Lexi. I don't know what's going on! Everything was going fine until the she shoved the guy away. After that there was a screech through the comms, then nothing but static. Oh, God, oh, God!"

Panic overcame the inconsolable Emily, instantly absorbing all the blame for the situation.

"Okay, okay! Kill the video feed and take a breath, Em."

For once, Emily's need to satisfy everyone else's feelings over her own was actually beneficial to a situation.

"Someone is gonna have to get to Mary before the ghostbusters do and it ain't gonna be Terry if he's still servicing Ms. Featherstone. I'm already out the door but can't get through this stupid maze without you to guide me. Think you can help me with that?"

Lexi managed to lock away any hint of fear to prevent it from escaping her mouth.

"Y-yeah, I'll try. But y-you need to be careful! You hear me!?"

Lexi heard her. With a two-handed shunt, a bar of rusted black iron came loose from the maze's ageing gate. Being careful was handled.

Unlike Mary, there was nothing graceful about the way Lexi moved down the path. Emily read out the twists and turns as quickly as possible in an attempt to keep up with her aggressive pace. Even the motion sensors had trouble keeping up. Despite the returning fog's best efforts, it took under half Mary's time for Lexi to near the fountain. She swore the temperature was getting lower and lower as each chilling breath stabbed deeper into her lungs. As she turned the final corner, she immediately caught a scent in her nostrils. She could smell the pool of red along the fountain's stone edge. She could smell the dragged trail of red leading through the opposite route of the maze. There was nothing fake about the scent of blood that filled the air.

"What's going on, Lexi? How's Mary?"

"She's not here, Em," Lexi replied, her voice torn between worry and confusion.

"Well that's good, right? She must have made it out after we killed the cameras. Yes, that must be it. Don't you think?"

Maybe optimistic Emily would have been a more fitting name.

"Yeah, maybe," replied Lexi as she surveyed the scene further. "Maybe not. Either way, there's another pathway out of here with a trail blood leading down it."

"Probably the blood pack Mary used in her show! So, your gonna follow the trail, then?"

"That's the plan. I'm going to need to go radio silent though. I can hear the ghost squad getting closer and I don't want to give away the game. I'll speak when I can."

Lexi decided against mentioning the fact that it was real blood so that Emily wasn't worrying. The investigators weren't nearby either; that was a lie. Lexi didn't want to admit the real reason for killing the radios was purely for her own safety. Whatever or whoever dragged Mary away could be around any corner of the web of greenery listening to her every word.

"Sounds like a plan. I don't want to sit here feeling useless though, so I'll go look for Terry. Surely Ms. Featherstone will understand we need him back. Just make sure you let me know when you find her!"

"That's more like it! I've got a feeling were gonna need more of that spirit before the night is out so keep it up. I'll see the two of you later, hopefully."

"Ah, Millie. Thank you for coming back in. Please allow me to apologise to you for my earlier behaviour. I am sure you can appreciate how terribly difficult a time this has been for myself and my staff here at Silvergrave."

Ms. Featherstone appeared to be speaking from the heart.

"It's completely understandable, Ms. Featherstone. No apology required," replied the smartly dressed, early-thirties woman once again entering Ms. Featherstone's office. Her smile was almost as superficial as the bright purple dye in her long hair.

"I lost my sister very recently so I know the feeling of loss all too well. I just want to make sure this story is told correctly, that's all. I saw the footage of poor Mary Kennedy. A truly horrifying watch. Can we go a little further into your impression of Mary and what you think happened to her?"

Ms. Featherstone appreciated Millie's honesty and nodded back in agreement.

Emily gingerly exited the safety of the control room, the LED light of the lantern in her hand helping to illuminate the dark corridor. The manor was transformed throughout the early hours with all but the main hall's lights turned off for paranormal investigations. Emily didn't quite understand why they needed to operate in darkness. Did ghosts have an issue with lightbulbs? Maybe they just didn't care for the ambience of modern lighting? That was a mental sight to behold.

"Candlelight or nothing!"

It was at the point those words leaped from her tickled mouth that she felt a crack and crumple under her foot. Placing the lantern aside, she peeled her foot back to reveal the damage. It was the crushed wreckage of Terry's gold rimmed sunglasses. There was no doubt about it and that terrified Emily. There was no way he would have left them willingly. It was enough of a challenge to prise them from his head before their performance earlier to realise that much. Her trembling hand shot straight for the radio attached to her waist. No reply. Both Mary and Terry going missing, within an hour of each other, in the country's most haunted building? The word coincidence didn't quite cut it.

"Ms. Featherstone," Emily said, as if needing to reassure herself.

Tracking down Ms Featherstone felt like the most rational decision. It was she that Terry was heading to after all. If anyone had an answer to what was going on, it would be her.

As Emily once again found herself in a hallway she didn't recognise, it became abundantly clear. She was lost. The manor was a hard-enough place to navigate in the light, but this was getting ridiculous. It was beginning to feel like the directional signs were deliberately sending her in the opposite direction from where she needed to be. Thankfully, upon turning the next corner, the unmistakable burgundy uniform of a male member of staff sent a wave of relief washing over her.

"Oh, thank God. EXCUSE ME. SIR, EXCUSE ME!"

Her words seemed to fall on deaf ears as the man continued to stride on down the passage with Emily in pursuit. Her stumbling feet picked up the pace as she began to close on her ignorant co-worker. She continued to call for his attention through a number of left and right turns before losing sight of him thanks to a final turn and the creak and slam of the closing door at the bottom of path before her.

The temperature seemed to have dropped during the pursuit. Emily's breath struggled to force its way through her chattering teeth as she pinned her hands into her pockets in a failing attempt to keep warm. She continued wearily towards the final door and paused as she gave herself a pep talk. She hadn't had anywhere near enough sleep or coffee to deal with anything else the night had the nerve to throw at her, so whomever the staff member was that had given her the run around was going to have a lot to answer for!

Following a moment of persuasion, her right hand conceded the fight to stay in her pocket and met the ornate door handle before her. Its icy surface froze the blood in Emily's veins and only with the help of her left hand was she able to provide a sufficient twist to release the door from its frame. As she passed through the room's entrance, the frost in her veins passed through her whole body down to the tips of her toes. There was nobody there to greet her, and no alternate exit found her shocked eyes. The man had simply vanished into the stacks of newspapers and luggage littering the lantern-lit room. Behind the frozen Emily, the door slammed shut, sending layers of dust soaring uncontrollably into the darkness at the back of the room along with the shattered soul of Emily, who collapsed into the leather chair to her right.

She felt alone and abandoned. If she were to stay in the room forever, would anyone care enough to look for her? Even Lexi, with whom she felt she shared a connection, hadn't contacted her in over an hour. She had probably found Terry and Mary, then the trio continued having fun working without her. No, the closest thing Emily had to a friend right now was the newspaper stack beside her, which rudely refused to resemble a person no matter how much squinting she did.

Removing the top broadsheet reacquainted her with the familiar face of Ms. Featherstone. A familiar face but an unfamiliar name. Ms. Featherstone hadn't actually used her first name at any point, but Emily's interview preparation had revealed it to be Rosaline, a name that didn't marry up with the Gwendoline Featherstone captioned in black and white. Upon further reading, the article spoke of Gwendoline passing ownership of the manor over to her younger Rosaline following a terrible accident involving her staff.

"That resemblance is incredible!"

A breeze rolled through the room in response to Emily's words, carrying another newspaper from the stack into her grasp. As her eyes scrolled through the ink, she was once again greeted by the face of Rosaline, or was it Gwendoline? It was neither of the above. Intrigue had rebuilt the shattered pieces of Emily's spirit. Maria, Vera, Madeline, and

Sylvia were just a few more of the names pinned to the same face as the dates and fashion changed from cover to cover.

"What the hell is this?" Emily asked herself aloud, only to be answered by another tower of ink and paper toppling towards her from the darker end of the room. Upon closer inspection, this pile of papers was different. Each served to highlight the various accidents, murders, and suicides that had transpired at the manor, for which Emily recognised the dates. It couldn't be another coincidence, could it? In her left hand sat the printed face of Morrigan Featherstone, made owner of the manor in eighteen thirty-five. In her right, the murder and subsequent suicide of three staff members. They all matched, right up to Rosaline Featherstone in nineteen ninety-one and the tragic poison gas leak that killed five.

Emily couldn't explain the how or why, but it was all there in black and white. Terry and Mary had disappeared. Lexi's radio silence probably meant she was gone too. There was only one person that would have the answers, and Emily was sick of seeing her face. As she dashed from the room, rolled up broadsheets under arm, she was greeted by a sight that startled her. The lamps flanking her on either side were flickering. There was nothing new about that but they appeared to be flickering in sequence, as if to show the direction she should go. Given the two options were being lost there forever or taking a chance in following the illuminated route, the latter felt like the only option and if someone out there wanted her to find the answers she was seeking, all the better.

Emily was tired, dusty, and breathing heavily. Her night of ghostly encounters, flickering lights, and graceful misstepping had all led to this moment. Ms. Featherstone's door sat directly in her line of sight. The corridors and halls had emptied with even the most hardened paranormal investigators retreating back to their rooms ahead of daybreak, which was a stark contrast from the last time she had stood in the same spot. Looking down to the seats where she first saw her fellow applicants added fuel to the fire burning in her gut.

"Here we go!"

"HOW DO YOU EXPLAIN THIS AND WHERE ARE MY FRIENDS!?"

Emily threw her words and the broadsheets across Rosaline Featherstone's desk.

"My my, haven't you been a busy little bee, Miss Whitechapel. If you take a seat, I will happily to tell you everything you want to know, over a cup of tea?"

The calmness in Rosaline's response dampened the burning within Emily, while the pouring tea extinguished it completely.

"Oh, no. Oh, no. I didn't piece this together all wrong did I? My friends? They are all fine, aren't they? Frick!"

Emily ran everything back through her head in an unmedicated panic. She had forgotten to take her tablets with so much happening around her, and while hallucinations hadn't been a symptom in the past, she didn't put anything past her splintering mind.

"I will be happy to reacquaint you all shortly but first, I would very much like you to tell me what you think you found out instead of doing the job I assigned to you. It was no sugar, wasn't it?"

Emily answered with a nod as she sunk down into her seat. The negativity in Ms. Featherstone's voice sent her head into a torrent of disappointment and hopelessness. Barely able to hold back her tears, Emily recounted the nights events in full, paying special attention to the latter stages. The longer she went on, the more ridiculous the whole story sounded in her head, though Ms. Featherstone's expression remained unmoved as she absorbed every last word. Emily felt numb as the concluding sentence fell from her mouth, while her tired eyes awaited any shift in Rosaline's stone expression. As the final drop of tea rolled down Emily's tongue, the porcelain cup slipped from her senseless grasp, cracking as it collided with the desk.

"Do you know why I chose you Emily?"

Emily sat paralysed, unable to offer an answer to the now rhetorical question.

"It was because much like the others, nobody would notice if you dropped off he face of the Earth. Your family doesn't want you. Your so-called friends don't need you." Rosaline's venomous words burned deeply. "Who would bat an eyelid at the death of a poor girl with a list of mental issues exceeded in length only by the list of names I have been known by over the years."

The smug Rosaline refilled her cup and continued to gloat unopposed.

"You were so close to figuring it all out. There was just one crucial ingredient you managed to overlook. The one simple key to the lock that is the Featherstone mystery." Rosaline rose to her feet and ambled over to the painting of herself mounted above the fireplace. "Ghosts, spirits, the supernatural, and magic. It's real. All of it. Magic has kept myself and my business alive for over three-hundred years. Immortality is a wheel, Emily. My wheel. Killing people such as yourself every twenty-six years returns my youth twenty-six days later, while in turn forcing the very same victims to wander the manor for all of time. You and your dear friend Lexi Sparks will be the newest attraction for all of the pathetic psychics and mediums walking through my halls and into my bank account."

Ms. Featherstone watched as the tears rolled down Emily's increasingly pale face.

"If you had only been aware of the otherworldly aid you had been receiving all night long, maybe things would have worked out differently. Killing off two off my sacrifices was a commendable idea, but clearly my long-dead attractions made a mistake in trusting you to finish me off rather than murdering you themselves."

Emily could feel the light disappearing from her drowning eyes as Ms. Featherstone found the perfect eulogy at the bottom of her teapot. Victoriously, she walked around the tables edge and took Emily by the hand.

"Emily Whitechapel. The girl forever lost within her own head. Friend to none and enemy to one. Told all the answers but couldn't hear a sound, took her own life as she fell to the ground."

"And it was you that found them both on the ground that morning?" asked Millie remorsefully.

"It was. A moment that haunts me every night and I am sure it will follow me to the grave as well. The pain that would drive such lovely girls to leap from my manor. It's unimaginable to think this is the end of their story," replied Ms. Featherstone, her overwhelmed expression showing no sign of her internal delight.

"It's just such a shame for two young girls to have their youth ripped away from them."

Millie's statement cut a little too close for Ms. Featherstone's liking.

"Just one last question before I leave you in peace, Ms. Featherstone. I've heard you may be considering stepping aside and passing the business over to your daughter? Is there any truth in that?"

"I... I... May I ask where you heard such a rumour?" answered Rosaline, whose rattled words sounded far too defensive.

"Just something my sister and her friend mentioned to me late last night," replied Millie, taking great pleasure in seeing Ms. Featherstone's face shift as her words set in. "Oh, forgive me for not fully introducing myself earlier. My name is Amelie Whitechapel and you are going to find out first-hand, that this is only the start of Emily and Lexi's tale."

Sisters in Time

Lina Nicklin
England

I KNIT. THAT'S WHAT I DO. I KNIT CREATION.

Once, the energy was soft against my young fingers. It flowed and teased and sighed when I twisted and purled, or picked up and mossed its delicate pulses. Imagine picking a thread, a surge of energy, or a flash of light and shaping creation with it.

Sometimes, when I am feeling mischievous I might tell you that I have knitted since time began, but today, I'm in no mood for jokes. No, today, I will tell you the truth. I have knitted since the potential became the actual, through the before, the now and I am afraid that I shall have to knit the after. Where there was once a silken thread of purpose, of intent, a sigh of recognition that this is at last what it shall be, I sense a giving.

I'm sure that I've knitted it right. The gossamer clouds of gas, the rings of dust, spirals, and holes were perfect. There are no gaps, no spaces. You see, everything is connected; there is no nothing. How can there be? It exists.

I knitted the atoms, the quarks, the dark places. I've never had to unpick, never dropped a stitch in time, or out of it. But I fear that I might.

Because, now it's a red-hot sulphurous, writhing, barbed wire of a yarn that I must knit. It knots and clumps; sometimes it frays down to a single thread of gas.

Atrophy is next.

I've seen the pattern.

It's been well over three seasons since it happened. There was a big search, and an appeal for sightings. According to the papers he cried on TV. Begged me to go home. I had to get away from him before I disappeared entirely. I just ran, and here is where I stopped; it felt right. Sometimes I think that I got washed up here by some cosmic tide, or fate, or magic maybe.

I never gave this roundabout a second's thought before; I just drove past. The passers-by don't pay any attention, they drive around me … I suspect that I may be invisible.

I like living here. There's a kind of stillness, in the middle. Like the centre of an old vinyl record… if you listen hard you can hear the hiss.

Sitting here watching is hypnotising. There's a rhythm to the day and the night; weekends are different of course, and the seasons change. It's like a song; one of those chants that slows your heartbeat. I suspect the whole world is circling around me. Like I said, there's a stillness, and a calm here at the centre…

I'm building my place, piece by piece. I collect things… food, water, things that get thrown out of car windows. Something fell off the back of a lorry once.

I did laugh! I found some good-as-new, green tarpaulin and pitched it underneath the bushes. I think I've got pretty much everything I need here. Life is so much simpler when you stop wanting...

A year or two ago I watched a TV programme about living out of skips. I must have stored it away in my mind, not realising it would come in so handy. It's surprising what you can find in the bins and anyway I need so little.

I'm a watcher… or maybe I'm a witness. One thing I do know is that this is my calling… my reason is to be here. I feel quite safe on this roundabout. I've got my finger on the pulse.

I check the traffic… going this way and that, although nowadays it's more often that. I patrol the Edge and make sure the two sides stay apart.

You see, birth is an anomaly. It's like the mother's womb is in another dimension. You hold her close to your heart and give her life, but a child must be given up… cross to this side and take a breath… before she is 'here'. There are always anomalies of course. Some folk hold their breath… and stay there in the middle, in the in-between, but that's a story for another day.

Crossing didn't use to be so complicated.

My sisters and I have done this through space and time. The Edge demands a witness. I can feel the hiss of a crossing. Humanity rises and falls. A first breath and a last breath. We fear the rise and rejoice the fall, or rejoice the rise and mourn the fall. Scream or sleep, the crossing requires to be known. Without a witness there is no name, no line to cross, and what would we do without a crossing point? There would be no this side or that. Just chaos.

In times gone past, I lived in hedgerows or on the edges of forests to guard the boundary, between the known and the unknown, between safety and danger.

I knew the herbs; I made their salves and poisons. I eased their path. Hedge witch… Haegtessa is what they called me; although, it wasn't really the hedge that I walked. Nowadays I have no name and I'm invisible. They don't want to see me anymore. But the Edge is there, none the less.

There was always a rhythm, a pattern. The tide came in, and the tide went out. But something's changed. I sense it. It's the metallic tang you taste when you bang your head. A sneeze aborted. The heart that missed a beat, then fluttered on. A presence behind you in an empty car. Something's not right… something's happening.

It's been two days, five hours and ten minutes since you left me, my love. No, let me begin that again. Civilisations have risen and fallen in the aching, leaden centuries that have trudged past me since you slept your death away.

How could you?

Don't get me wrong, heart of mine; I don't begrudge you the potion. I only wish that there had been some for me.

What on Earth am I supposed to do now?

It's three millennia since you went out the door to work. I waved from the bedroom window, my hair was wet, and I was running late.

A breath.

I turned the record off to answer the door. He had his hat under his arm… the policeman. I fell. I blinked. I was at your bedside. You we're perfect. Serene. They gave you drugs to calm you down. And then you ceased…

I was kissing your cheek when you gave your last sigh. I could not let you go.

So, I breathed it in.

Everyone knows about the meridian but do they realise that it strikes true north, thinner than a shaft of hair, right through this promenade and on through space and time?

If you get really, close you can see a shimmer. There it is… see? Just to the right of the line, on the tomorrow side. The light's got to be just right, though. You need this rose-pink kind of light that you get just as the sun goes down.

Remember, Harry, when we were children, how we used to pretend to be tightrope walkers. One sandy hand stretched towards tomorrow, the other pointing to yesterday. We used to balance and wobble and scream when we fell, then we'd collapse into a heap and hold each other 'till we'd stopped laughing.

Some days, the dusk-shimmer takes me right back to our best times. We're together, walking hand in hand along the promenade, courting, laughing, teasing, chasing. The wind off the sea can slice right through me, but in your arms, Harry, I was never cold.

Once, I saw a rainbow arc right over it and I swear it split in two, spliced by this line of universal time and place. My every-days are getting spliced now, Harry. They think I don't know it, but I do. They're starting to bother about my walks. Last time I took a shortcut, only it wasn't.

Listen to me wandering! I've come to talk to you because I had another one of those dreams last night. I could hear the hiss of shells. One was really close… too close. The soil, it smelled of guts. I saw you going over the top, walking the line between the bomb craters; one arm stretched out to yesterday the other holding your rifle. You fell... I couldn't get to you.

--

I know it's cold but I'm wrapped up well. They've got me on some dream-stealing pills. They say they stop me wandering off, but I spit them out when they're not looking. I'm sure they mean well.

--

I'm building a special place for my memory of your last home leave, Harry. I've made a kind of snow globe around it. So many of my memories are slipping their moorings. I wonder where they go?

My memories of our last time are so sharp, just like it was yesterday. I wish it were tomorrow. You were so thin, and jumpy. It took till our last night for you to talk. I could tell that you were protecting me; there was a different world behind your eyes.

I have something to confess, Harry I seem to have lost the mizpah brooch that you gave me before you left ... I'm so sorry.

When I concentrate really hard on my globe, I can hear something. Is it your heartbeat, Harry? Are you near?

--

I had that dream again last night. It was different though, this time you called my name. Then you said something but I didn't quite catch it. I tried so hard to get to you that I woke myself up. And then, I have to admit; I had a little cry.

--

I cry a lot, nowadays. I'm scared, Harry. My globe is getting scratched; I'm frightened that it might break. They think I don't know where I am, and maybe I don't some of the time. They've walked me here under sufferance and gone to have a cup of tea. I don't think they'll bring me back again.

So, this is my last look at our beautiful meridian; this silver thread we made. Even after all this time, it still links my heart to yours.

I'm at a loss about how to live this next bit, Harry... I wonder where I'll go?

Wait a minute while I come closer; I've got something important to tell you. I need to whisper it to you. Oh, but it's such a long way down… I can't quite do it…

And I think I've put the wrong glasses on. The shimmer is strange; it's on the yesterday side of the line. It's darker too.

Now, there's a throbbing in my head. It's getting louder; it's beating against my chest so hard it hurts.

Our line, it's glowing, Harry! Cold and hot at the same time, how can that be?

Oh, I do feel strange….

Look, something's moving in the yesterday light! It's bright, not pink at all… and it's hissing.

What's that sparkle? It looks just like my brooch… is that's where it went? If I stretch down maybe I can reach it.

The light is changing shape. It's a … it's a hand.

Harry, you have my brooch!

Will you catch me one last time?

I'm not quite sure how it works, it just does. If you asked me to explain, I would say that I taste a colour… then it happens. I've always had the power; I was born with it.

When I was little I used to play with it, bring a flower into bloom a day or two early, ripen a blackberry if I wanted one. Birds used to stop and listen to me walking by, then sing their hearts out when I had gone past. That was back when my power was a crazy, swirling tangle, like a ball of wool after a kitten had played with it.

A few of the kids at school sensed it, so I showed them this and that, made an apple ripen, healed a mouth ulcer. Some of them were even friendly for a while. Then one of them said that I smelled different, and then they all decided that my different smell was bad. I didn't mind not having anyone to talk to. They came secretly if they needed something, but all together, they were a cruel and jagged wall that took away my child-life.

At first I tried to wait them out; I can be quite patient, when I want to be. But when I found that some of the boys were pulling wings off flies so that I would fix them back on… and worse… things began to change. I tried to talk to them, to ignore them, I even cried once, but nothing that I did stopped it; everything that I did made it worse. I'm not going to tell you what I found nailed to my door one morning, suffice to say it was the last straw. I decided that I would do the same to one of them. It didn't matter which one, I just needed it to stop.

I could feel my energy building as I strode to school. The first one that I saw was going to get it! As it happens it was Nathan, not the nicest boy but not by any means the worst. I watched my hand reach out to grab his shoulder, but it wasn't a hand it was a ball of crimson energy. I paused for a second - I'd never felt such a rush - and then I flung it at him. Horrified and fascinated, we both watched as the embodiment of my rage and pain and roaring grief spun around him like a comet around a sun and hit me square in the chest.

I woke up two days later, exhausted and expelled from school.

Since then, I've learned from my sisters-in-time about how the world works, how to make my energy wide like sunshine or focus it thin as an atom. I've seen the seasons tick and heard molecules of sap rise up inside a waking oak. I've felt the pull of planets and watched new rock spitting from its bed then rise and fall to dust.

Above all I've learned that I must do no harm; it magnifies and bounces back at me. But there is no pure goodness, because everything carries a consequence. This is a gift that keeps on taking!

--

I've lost count of the seasons that have slipped through my fingers: I couldn't cup then in my hands if I wanted to. My hands and feet went first: my earth and sky connections. Then my brittle bones failed me one last time and here I lay.

Clouds were my consolation for a while. But this new phase is a terror; my sleep is robbed. I'm not even sure if I have eyelids; oh and how the rain smarts in my parched sockets!

--

For the longest time I saw nothing at all. And then I probed deeper and began to hear stardust dancing. I caught a beat, a hiss, and then it grew into bronze, beating, swirling clouds of dust like bonfire sparks against a blank night sky. A breeze shape here, a face there exploded into whirlpools of glowing pulsing synapses, stretched beyond my senses... so I followed them.

We played.

The hiss became a hum, a drum, a heartbeat, a cosmic body... unravelling.

I read her pain... then I reached out... lay my body down... and healed her.

The Princess and the Chariot

Linda Chafer
England

PRINCESS GWENNIKKA WAS A COURAGEOUS, undaunted warrior and, like similar wanderers, she felt a thrill of excitement at returning home at long last. With her came her entourage. On her left, the High Queen dressed in dazzling cloth of gold, and to her right the giant Aelfried, with one hand on her shoulder and the other grasping a mighty battle trident.

She saw them now perched precariously on the edge of a precipice. In front of her she thrilled to see mountain peaks, a raging river far below, and above, screaming eagles. Gwennikka laughed out loud. She soaked up the brilliant sunshine and tossed her flowing black tresses out into the wind.

She then imagined a verdant, emerald valley leading to her home estates, her reward for persevering through many battles and great pain.

The High Queen, or rather Mrs. Bedlow (as she insisted Alfred call her), was momentarily caught off-guard by her daughter's embarrassing, rather eerie giggle. As requested, she had been trying to imagine a warrior princess in a chariot surveying her vast domain. Unfortunately, Mrs. Bedlow (shivering in a thin orange cardy), could only see poor Gwennie as she teetered on a visitors' dreary look-out point.

She glared at Alfred, the nurse, who persisted in dragging everywhere that humiliating drip-stand-thingie, and she was annoyed at him for filling her daughter's head with those silly notions of dragons, witches, and fearless princesses. Absently, Mrs. Bedlow stroked Gwennie's warm woolly hat and its tossing pompoms.

You see, Mrs. Bedlow was a contrast to her delightful, brave daughter, by being constantly fearful. It was not that she was a totally unimaginative person but simply that she had found the past months terribly draining. She couldn't understand either where in her mind Gwennie had gone to cope with the operations and her pain. In fact, Mrs. Bedlow had been unable to visualise anything except the day when she could drive her daughter safely home from hospital. So she struggled every day with the adventure stories Gwennie told her and what Mrs. Bedlow actually knew.

Nevertheless, every now and then she did try to see the world through Gwennie's eyes. As today was a very special occasion, she had fought hard but sadly saw only grey dumpling hills, a muddy gravy-coloured brook and crooked, wilted, broccoli-shaped trees. Not a towering mountain, nor raging river, nor soaring eagle in sight, just that annoying black crow chattering and grumbling and spoiling for a fight. Feeling she had failed again, the High Queen sighed.

As Princess Gwennikka's protective cloak wafted in the cold breeze she felt her mother and nurse race each other to smooth it.

Their fingers touched. One of them felt a heavy fur cloak and the other, a thick hospital blanket. But our happy, returning warrior merely smiled, lay back in her golden chariot, and was content to let the High Queen pull the wheelchair away from the edge.

Swallow Chick

Lucy Grace
England

2nd place in the 2017 International Literary Prize
University Centre Grimsby

I SMILE WHEN I HEAR MY GRANDDAUGHTER downstairs, her tread in the hallway and her voice on the phone. How I wish I could greet her. I could, except that I died half an hour ago, and now I'm dead.

I hear her step on the kitchen floor cease and the stiff wooden cutlery drawer scrape open. She's wearing her work shoes. My guess is that she is making a cup of tea, passing the time until I appear. How wrong she is, expecting movement from me. Only my mind is alive now, swooping, young and freed like a baby bird.

The back door grinds open with a clatter of chain rattle and then undefended silence. The wood swells in wet weather and makes it stick – she'll have to learn that. I know by each careful sound where she is, what she is doing; I am certain of it. She is sitting on the step of the yard. How I long for that step, just one more time, to sit on the warmed stone in the sun and rest my head on the red brick feeling the heat in my temple. I think of the women that have rested there and their different trials and tribulations. Only women of course – the men are too busy being and doing to trouble sitting there. I imagine swimming darkly inside my mother as she sits taking a rest from the laundry and all the other lonely hard work of being a young wife in the war. I wasn't the first child but the middle one so I add my elder sister into this picture, a toddler in cotton layers scrabbling in the yard, bringing my exhausted mother unwanted treasures of pebbles and petals.

I see my granddaughter now in her work suit, pulling the narrow pencil skirt over her knees, pressing her shined shoes together to admire them on the step. How tired she must be, I think, to actually sit on the step in that expensive wool. I hear her again on the phone in a different tone now, murmuring familiarity with her other half. Her partner. The words around me are transforming – once upon a time partnership inferred serious business deals of lawyers or doctors or funeral directors, their trades written high in gold paint on solid black signs - now it relates to ones nearest and dearest, another half, an other half.

Her tone has become softer, quieter, at home, with love. The contrast sharpens like a paper cut exposing my antique marriage as one more of function and survival than of hearts and flowers. I put myself on the step, in the dusk, waiting to hear the end of shift siren. I had to be ready – if I missed them walking home he'd be straight in the pub, or sliding on past with his mates hoping not to be seen. Tough luck, my friend. Every penny counts in this life and that means your pennies too. It wasn't as bad as for some of the other women; they had to wait defiantly outside the factory gates with their pinched faces and bitten nails, but all the same I ran the money in this house, in fact I ran the house, full-stop.

Partnership seems a good term for what we had, in truth. Longer a widow than a wife. What a relief that had been – now I was the man in manager and I was great at managing. It must run in the family – the expensive wool and pencil skirt downstairs said as much.

I hear her step in the kitchen again. She is still on the phone, mentioning a hospital. Suddenly I feel a wash of worry for her, why this talk about appointments and scans? Is her body now hiding an illness? Hadn't it given enough? When she was visiting the clinic regularly a few years back she used to come and tell me how she was chasing her fertility as if it were a spill of milk slipping silently over a surface edge. I'd lean in and listen, enthralled at the information she held, the dates, the history, the terminology, the expectation. As if a baby was just something you could order to specification with a delivery date. A delivery date – that had made her smile. I loved to hear these secret stories just shared between the two of us, so intimate and exposing and so difficult for my ninety odd years to catch hold of. The thought of all that knowledge about making babies; she had no idea, she wore it so casually slung about her shoulders like a cape and swirled around words like ovulation and in vitro and sperm count without a blink. No idea how mysterious it had been for me, for other women, in times past. Now it was so out there, apparent.

But it hadn't worked out for her, that was the brutal truth. The cape had done her no good, it had only shielded her from the stork who had not seen her need and desperation and had flown on by. Now, aged forty, she had put it away in a box with a lid, discarded the fertility jabs and regained her body as her own not to be given as a vessel for another. The shoes became higher, the skirts narrower and the eyes more tired and resigned.

I listen from my bed. Love was made and unmade here, as was life. Through the nights where I shared both bed and room and fought for mirror, fought for love, fought away from the frozen icy feet and fought under the pink-bobbled blankets the colour of thick medicine, this room always held me - such a lot of fighting for space and a place, first with siblings, and then with a spouse. And then at fifty, when my husband's new bed became a mortuary slab, it was suddenly all mine. Longer a widow than a wife - this was where my life began. Nearly another half a century without him, how is that even possible?

Once my body began to arrogantly disobey me and reduce me to the essence of the elderly, shrunken and bowed, I wished for the end, but I had been insolently kept alive by my mind and its love for mathematical symmetrical comfort in numbers and their roundness. It would have liked to have worked to one hundred, just for the neatness, but my brittle bones and thinning blood will not allow it.

One hundred has a solidness like binary code, like decimalisation and the metric system and probably mobile phones. My headstone and funeral order of service will not be neat and precise in black and white type, 1920 – 2020; it will carry the untidy edges of oddity.

I can hear her now on her phone downstairs, talking, not worried, not frantic, just calm in that work way she has. I know that she's on her mobile as I measure the metronomic beats of her step across the kitchen floor; it's the only place she can get a signal out here in the sticks. Of course, it's not the sticks, it's a town – there's a Tesco and everything now, but I suppose if you work in a place where the people run about like ants, where there are so many buses they are different colours and you need to use a lift to get to the desk you sit at to work, then this might seem like the sticks. But not to me. I know every street, every name; I know the grand facades that remain solidly crouched behind their contemporary shop fronts, and the new parking spaces where there were once roses and every wall railing cut off in its prime leaving black stumps bubbled like pimples. I can recall places that are not there anymore, the roads rearranged, the buildings removed like troublesome teeth, and the families vanished.

It's like having an alternate world view in my head. If I knew of such things I would be able to say it was like wearing virtual reality glasses that change scene as I turn, or like switching from Google Earth Map View to Terrain, but of course these are the unknown to me. I am ninety-seven, and I am dead.

I listen carefully to see if she will stop talking soon and come up to see me. She knows that I have a nap each afternoon and that since the stair-lift arrived I've been coming upstairs for it instead of napping in my chair, but I'm usually up and about by 2pm, and now it's nearly half past. Maybe the hospital conversation is distracting her.

I see her dolls and teddies, all lined up with bandages and medicine spoons and plasters stuck all over them, their illnesses and ailments simple, mendable complaints such as breaks and spots and cuts. No messy blood, no tears or fluids or difficult emotions pouring out and flowing untidily over everything, staining and changing things forever. I was never required to help play much, she was always the director: "Do the blanket, put them overneath, Granna", and they'd be tucked up snug as broken bugs under the same blanket I am now lessening beneath.

I consider the solid knots and raised whorls of this crochet as I think about the other things we have done together. The interminable casting on as she learnt to knit so clumsily, and the casting off for her every time as she had forgotten how to do it by the time she had reached the end of her indiscriminate rectangle. Only straight lines, really, I'm probably being too kind calling it a rectangle as that would infer some kind of regular edge and repeated stitch count. Her knitting was like her speech – rapid and irregular and often off at tangents. After concentrated effort she would return with pointed tongue tip to where she left off and try again, but then her brain would fire up with something else and the tension changed, the stitches dropped, and the knitting suffered.

I remember reading something about Native Americans creating journey sticks or something, wrapping leaves and fabric and objects around a stick as they journeyed through the landscape to use as an aide-memoire when they returned to their people to tell their story. My granddaughter would not have done this. She is someone who doesn't want anyone to have her story but herself. She is unaware that it seeps out through her into the light and will not be hushed. She is loved.

The house is quiet now. The rattle of the door chain tells me that she is back on the step. Through the open curtain I can see the sun sharing the last of today's warmth with this house before it moves into next door's yard to shine on them. I am glad that she has this place, that it is a place she can find solace and comfort in her memories. She will find out soon that it is now hers. She reminds me of me.

The click of the hall door discloses her journey to my room. I do not want this – although I know that I have chosen my best nightdress, that I am safe in my own bed covers, and nothing is too distressing. I do not want to be here when she finds me. I fly out of the window and down into the yard and onto the step, where I sit next to a small black and white wraithlike presence swimming in a hospital scan photograph, warming on the red bricks, with the time and the date stamped at the top, fragile bones pressing into existence.

"Hello, little one," I breathe, finally. "Welcome to our step."

In the Hands of the Gods

Marc Hall
England

MY FIRST DEATH WAS AT WATERLOO, 1815. We were at Mont-Saint-Jean under Wellington and he had decided to stand ground against the attacks we knew were to come since the Prussians had managed to offer support. Hopes were high and spirits weren't as low as they could have been. We all thought victory was inevitable but battle is still battle. We were scared. I was nineteen; too young.

It was early afternoon when the French first advanced against us and the Prussians hadn't reached us yet. The word was given and we charged, cavalry first, us infantry next, muskets roaring. Many men have written and remarked that the worst part of battle is the noise. Not of the guns that is, but the screams. The endless yelling, emanating from the souls full of holes, with their lives being carried along the tide of blood escaping their mortal forms. Personally though, I didn't hear a thing. All around me, deafening silence and that was the scary part. I see could the men with their mouths agape and I knew what should have been there. I could see the bright flare of guns erupting and I knew each flash equalled a short sharp bang. I could see the dirt on the ground spontaneously drive upwards as a shell hit home and I knew the bang of that hit would be longer and louder. The scariest part though were my instincts. Young men I didn't know ran towards me and I shot away, taking out my fair share of the enemy. I didn't think, didn't strategise, I didn't feel any uprush of pride when my bullets found their marks. I just saw someone run at me and I killed them. I have never considered myself a violent person but I took lives without any hesitation at all, and that is what truly terrified me. Soon enough the French let up and backed away. They kept coming throughout the afternoon and every time we turned them back, especially as more and more of the Prussians showed up to swell our ranks. As evening fell, Napoleon threw his last troops at us.

Darkness was drawing in around us but so was the fear. We knew the last throw of the dice would come soon. I prayed to God that I wouldn't have to kill any more people but it seemed to be inevitable. We sat in small circles staring at our feet. We couldn't much find the will to talk and fires certainly weren't allowed, so altogether it was a dismal affair. That was until the first guns started to go off; heavy artillery and huge shells dropping. Nothing wrong with my hearing this time. We scrambled together, some lacing up boots, others buttoning tunics, and all of us loading guns. This time we had the numbers and we could smell the desperation on the enemy. I don't know what happened but a sort of blood lust fell upon me. Maybe it's because I knew this was the final push but I needed to fire my riffle at someone. God help me, I wanted lives, souls, death at my fingertips and smoke in my nostrils. I drove myself to my feet and rushed headlong into the night, ready to send some Frenchmen to hell. The gun came up, the iron sights lined up with my hungry pupil, my finger, holding the power of life and death wrapping itself around the trigger like a snake, its soul brimming with malice; then darkness. This darkness wasn't like the deep blue of the night and there were no flashes of gunpowder. This was a comfortable darkness, as if the black was a pillow enveloping me, consuming me, putting me to rest. For the first time, but not the last, I was dead.

When my eyelids finally opened a crack the sudden brightness of the day caused waves of pain to crash through my head. Then, once my eyes adjusted to the light, I lay unmoving, staring upwards. Nausea washed over me and I couldn't feel any of my extremities. At the time, I had no idea what had happened nor did I know how long I had been there, but soon, little flashes of memory started to return to me. I had been in a battle at Waterloo against the French. We were charging, then nothing. I must have been shot. But how could that be? Surely I was alive? I could see clouds; I could hear birds, and I could feel the gentle breeze rustling in my hair. Eventually, after what seemed like hours, I mustered up the energy to move. Sitting up revealed a wealth of horrors surrounding me; men, young and old, lay dead all around me, resting in a myriad of positions in puddles all a mixture of evil red and dismal brown. A mist clung to the ground and the air was chill. I realised I was sweating; it must have been the anxiety for it certainly wasn't warm. Guns and body parts littered the ground, strewn about like so much detritus after a tropical storm.

Looking down at myself presented the worst sight of all. My tunic was torn to shreds revealing my undershirt, a garment which had been white now stained with paint from the palette of war; crimson, black and brown. More tears allowed my pale flesh to peep through, which itself was caked with dried blood. I couldn't be sure at the time whose it was but I'd later realise it to be mine own. I had not a scratch on me, there was no pain aside from the pounding in my head and altogether I was simply confused. Rising to my feet, I saw some soldiers stood not far away. Their livery revealed them to be British officers but I didn't recognise any of the faces or voices. I decided that I must have taken a blow to the head and fallen unconscious and remained so for the length of the battle, a battle I assumed we had won owing to the fact that the four men I staggered towards were my own, and no one else around was alive to say otherwise.

Staggering toward the four men, they turned to see me, their faces frozen in horror as if I was lumbering about without a head. I turned my attention to a sergeant, the highest ranking among them.

"What news sir? Have we won? What of the French? The Prussians?"

My questions were met with silence and still their mouths hung agape, though after speaking, their eyes seemed filled with terror. The sergeant stood at around six feet tall with a barrel chest and a thick neck. His full, brown moustache looked wild and unkempt and completely covered his mouth. He had the kind of eyes that would hold a weaker man still as granite, locked in place, but I had been through too much to be scared of men such as this. Stranger still, on each of his shoulders sat perched a huge, jet black raven, their eyes sad and their beaks dripping with blood. The four men stood still in silence.

"How is it you're up and about soldier?" the sergeant finally replied.

His voice was thin and quiet as though it struggled to escape his throat

"Why sir, I feel fine. Well, besides a belly full of aches and a head full of pain. Might I ask sir, what's the matter with you all? You all seem as though you've encountered a ghost!"

"We...rather think we have, Sir, if you don't mind my saying so," said a private stood to the sergeant's right, looking worriedly at his fellow soldiers.

"I don't understand" I replied, confused.

My head pains were getting no better and I was in no mood for riddles.

"We took you for a dead man. Not an hour ago you lay over yonder, blood dribbling from bullets holes. Four we counted all together. Your chest was still as I recall. You were dead as they come and yet here you stand, talking and all! We may be forgiven for being rather disturbed, Private."

The sergeant sounded irritated now. He seemed to be the kind of man who held a firm core of beliefs and what he was seeing violated all of them.

"Well I can assure you all I am alive and well, Sirs! And as for bullets wounds, there's not a one on me as far as I can tell. Are you quite sure you aren't mistaking me for someone else? There are rather a lot of dead men about and to me they all look one and the same. With all due respect this seems like some jape and I am in no mood for it! And could someone please tell me why this man has two enormous ravens perched on his shoulders?"

For some reason, that outburst seemed to confuse them further.

"Ravens? I see no ravens anywhere. This man is mad!" said the private, looking about him.

"That's it; I've had quite enough of this! I assure you, Sir, you were as dead a man as I've ever seen! Now I've no idea as to what's going on here but it seems frightfully ungodly to me! I've been in enough conflicts to know a dead solider when I see one and you, Sir, were dead. Private Davids?"

"Sir?" replied the private to the sergeant's right.

"Shoot this man."

Davids' musket was up and pointing at my chest in a flash. I tried to plead, to reason with these madmen, but I couldn't seem to get any words to form. My eyes landed on one of the ravens, its feathers like oblivion and its beak and claws slick with red. I still couldn't tell if this was my imagination or not but that raven looked straight at me and said "Death" in a voice that was not of this world. Deep and loud, thin and quiet, all at once. Lightning escaped its beak, the muzzle of Davids' riffle erupted and the world, once again, went black. For the second time, but not the last, I was dead.

The next thing I remember, I was alive and well and living in London. The year was 1888, seventy-three years after Waterloo but as far as I could tell I hadn't aged a day. I never considered myself the most handsome of chaps, my hair was a thick nest of black tangles, my chin and cheeks were always rough with stubble and no one had ever remarked how beautiful the blue in my eyes was. I was the epitome of average. I spent my days driving various things around by horse and cart. I took food to markets, drinks to pubs, and people to wherever they needed to be. It wasn't exactly glamorous but it paid a fair wage. I had a decent enough room in a house in Whitechapel, I even had a couple of friends to speak of. One such friend was Charles Cross. I recall one occasion in which we sat in a bar in Brick Lane. It was August 31st and Charlie was in a bad way. His eyes were blood shoot and open wide, his skin sallow and crusted with grime. The whole night he didn't go without a drink or a cigarette, held in a hand wavering in an ever-present tremor and he hadn't spoken since I arrived.

"Charlie? What's up fella?"

"Nothin'," he replied, seeming as if he was holding back a river or tears. His tremor worsened.

"Ok, though something's troubling you. I can tell. Talk to me."

Charlie took a long draw of his cigarette and sighed. "It were the wee hours of this morning. I were going about me' business, startin' work. It wasn't full dark but a kind of dank, grey light. I'm making me way down Buck's Row when I see somethin' on the floor in the gloom. I couldn't make out what it was but it stopped me short in me tracks. I started to walk up to it when I saw it were a woman. I ran up, thinkin' her in trouble. There were this huge black bird perched on top of her and blood were all around her, dribblin' down the street. She were dead. Dead! Her throat all cut up and that weren't the worse of it. Someone had gone to hackin' up her stomach. I never seen anything like it."

"Christ, Charlie. What a scene that must of been. I'm sorry fella, truly I am." I paused, not knowing what to say. How do you respond to that? "Does anyone know the woman?"

"Aye. Mary Nichols."

"No suspects I assume?"

"Can't say I know, to be fair. Police spoke to me and I was done. I couldn't stick around no longer, not with her lyin' there like that… I'm done for the night. I need sleep"

He forced himself to his feet and lumbered towards the door, drunk. I stayed around long enough to finish my drink, thinking on one detail about Charlie's ordeal. The huge black bird. Something about it stuck in my head. Of all he said, something about the bird stood out.

Roughly a week later, I was driving my cart down Hanbury. A small group of people on the pavement caught my attention, and as I slowly made my way past them I couldn't help but overhear mention of another murder.

"Aye just down there it was. Number 29, right in the back yard they found her, poor ol' Annie. Throat and belly all cut open, I heard."

I've never been any sort of detective nor have I ever claimed any sort of intelligence but I couldn't help but note the similarities between this killing and the scene that Charlie told me about a week earlier. Probably a notion best left to the police, I thought. As I gazed at the clouds, and as I looked skywards, I saw them. Two massive jet black ravens circling above me. For around a minute or so they seemed to size me up before wheeling away into the blue.

On the afternoon of September 30th I was hired for a job I hadn't even considered I'd ever be doing one day. A body had been found in Dutfield's Yard opposite the International Working Men's Educational Club on Berner Street and I was needed to move it to the mortuary. I turned up not quite knowing what to expect and found a large crowd outside. I pulled up, hopped down from the cart, and strode over to the young copper minding the door, taking my hat off as I approached.

"You here for the casket?" asked the young man.

His skin had a slightly green tinge to it. If I had to guess, I'd say this was his first time at a murder.

"That I am, Sir."

"Well, I'd brace yourself if I were you. It isn't exactly pretty in there."

Death held no fear for me. I'd been a soldier. I'd seen and dealt my fair share of killing. Nevertheless, I nodded and made my way into the yard.

The officer was right, it wasn't pretty at all. I've seen men in their hundreds cut down by gunfire, their entire bodies jerking as the backs of their heads exploded in clouds of pink mist, skull, and viscera catapulted backwards. But this? This was a woman laid on her back with a slash across the throat. In war, you die with men beside you; people you've bonded with and offer some sort of comfort, but this poor woman had died alone; her life stolen away by an unknown man the papers had dubbed 'Jack the Ripper'. This was the third murder attributed to him at least and I must admit I had spent many hours in my bed awake thinking about what sort of person could not only kill a person in cold blood but mutilate them further, post mortem.

Stride. I overheard an officer call her Elizabeth Stride. Her eyes were open, facing the sky. I looked up, joining in her gaze. The clouds floated pure white, dangling gently against the pale blue. Suddenly my attention was monopolised by two black points racing across the heavens. Round and round they circled and danced, descending with terrifying speed towards me, two enormous ravens, screeching a bloodcurdling scream, like death itself had become a sound.

"You, there! You the cart driver?"

The voice belonged to an old policeman. He struck me as too old to be working. He leaned on a rough wooden cane littered with splinters and an eye patch drawing attention to his deeply wrinkled face. He seemed as though he'd been alive since the dawn of time.

"Yes, Sir, that's me." I replied, slightly in awe of the man, though I couldn't work out why.

"Right, then. We'll get her boxed up and load her up for you. You know where you're goin', eh?"

"Closest morgue as far as I've been told, Sir."

"Aye, that's right. You'll pick your pay up there. Awful business having to get you in, you just being a citizen and all but most of the horses have come down ill. Damnedest thing. They don't breed 'em like they used to, not like old Sleipnir. One horse left untouched and he's off collecting another victim."

"Another, Sir?"

"Aye, another. Jack's been busy tonight, it would seem."

With that he hobbled off, giving orders here and there as poor Miss Stride was loaded onto my cart.

Over a month had passed since Elizabeth Stride fell victim to Jack. His next attack came in early morning of November 9th, 1888. Mary Jane Kelly was her name. She lived in the same building as me, a decent enough woman. I didn't wake to her screams. I couldn't tell you what woke me, let alone what drew me to her room but I felt compelled to see if she was alright. The hour was ungodly but there was a faint glow emanating from beneath the door, which opened at the slightest touch. The sight before me stole my breath away. The thing that had been Miss Kelly lay on her back and barely resembled a human at all. Her abdomen was completely ripped open, organs missing, her face beyond recognition, but most disgustingly of all, the entire part of her body that was between her legs had completely disappeared. Blood soaked nearly every square inch of the room along with small chunks of flesh and skin. I am not ashamed to say I vomited immediately. Even the strongest stomach could not have withstood the sight.

"You're later than I thought you'd be." The voice came from behind me but as I furiously wheeled around there was no one there. "I'm here, lad." Behind me again. There, seated on the windowsill, a man. Robed in black, hood drawn, shadow hiding his face.

"Who are you?! What have you done with Miss Kelly?"

"You probably wouldn't believe me if I told you who I was, and as for the girl? Well, that wasn't me I'm afraid. Ol' Jack did that."

"I ask again, Sir, your name!"

"I've watched you since you were a babe at the breast, my lad. I'll continue to watch you as well. You'll die and live again for eternity."

His head leaned back enough for me to see a deeply malicious grin.

"Enough of this."

I reached for a letter opener on a table to my right and prepared to slit the wretch's throat. I couldn't though. Something stayed my hand, some invisible force. From nowhere my hand began to turn on itself, the point of the small knife facing my exposed throat. Fear held me tight in its grasp. My mind screamed at my limbs to move but nothing happened. The hooded man forced a small grin and with a wave of his slender hand, the knife I held thrust upwards, plunging into my neck. As blood streamed down my chest, mingling with Mary's on the bare wooden floor, I wondered where the ravens were.

For the third time, but not the last, I was dead.

I awoke in 1912, twenty-four years later, still in London. I recall being frightfully confused and scared. I had no idea what was happening to me and I was too afraid to go to anyone, not that I had anyone to go to. Somehow, I'd fought as a fit young man in the Battle of Waterloo in 1815 nearly one-hundred years ago, and yet here I was, not looking a day older than I did that night a century before. I tried to cast my mind back to the room of Miss Kelly, her disembowelled corpse laying forlornly in front of me, the voice surrounding me and then him, the stranger. I had decided he must have been a ghost; he certainly wasn't in there when I entered and there's no way he could have gotten past me unless he was possessed of some unnatural ability.

I wandered around from town to town, taking work where I could get it, when I eventually ended up in Southampton. I took up service with a company called White Star Line tending bar on one of their new ocean liners, the Titanic. She was the biggest passenger cruise ship ever built and truly a marvellous sight to behold. Impossibly long and painted in white, black and gold, she had four smoke stacks where all other ships had only three; the fourth was fake, however, and only there to give a grander impression. Her interior was nicer than that of any building I'd ever seen. It oozed class and elegance and the attention to detail all over was astonishing; even the plates were specially made.

I worked in one of the first-class lounges and was bowled over by just how well the other half lived. The men with fantastically tailored suits, top hats, and smooth smelling cigars, and the ladies in exquisite gowns, fur scarves, and not a hair out of place. I myself was dressed better than I ever had been before in a pressed white tuxedo with a black bow tie, my short hair slicked back and my rough stubble had given way to a chin and jaw smoother than the day I was born.

We left Southampton just before noon on April 10th. Masses of people were there, not only to see off loved ones but simply to see the ship itself, the pride of Britain. The crowds dominated the docks, proudly waving red, white, and blue streamers above their heads and singing "Rule Britannia". As we sailed, we felt like kings and queens, as though nothing could go wrong. The upper echelons danced the night away, ordering fine cocktails, and eating food of the highest class; a good time being had by all, even us serving staff. We were all so proud to serve on the mighty Titanic.

It was the fourth day of our historic voyage and I was laying in my cabin, reading peacefully. I can't recall the book but I can remember the time was 11:40pm when suddenly an unearthly chill ran down my spine and in my head I heard a horrible shriek of laughter. The next sound I heard was utterly terrifying. There was a tremendous crash and a horrifying scraping noise, like nails on a chalkboard, only on a much more biblical scale. The entire ship listed violently to port, sending me hurtling across my small room. My head struck the corner of a small table, sending my mind spinning and leaving me incapable of grasping what was happening. As blood dribbled down my head and into my eyes I snapped back to my senses and realised that we had to have hit something. But what? We were in the middle of the Atlantic, what could have possibly stood in the way of the largest vessel on earth?

After coming to my senses and ignoring the rising nausea in my gut, I pulled myself to my feet, determined to find out what was going on. Bursting through the door of my room, I entered the hallway, which was teeming with men and women running this way and that in blind panic. I inserted myself into the flow of human traffic heading towards the stairs to try and make my way up on deck.

"What on earth has happened?!" I asked the man running beside me.

He looked haggard, petrified. The stress in his eyes was palpable, accented by the welling tears I could tell he was trying desperately to fight back.

"We've struck an iceberg! Starboard side!" he screamed before picking up his pace ad racing ahead.

As I reached the end of the corridor, I took a right and entered the hallway at the end of which were the stairs. Only, when I looked ahead I saw nothing. The stretch of corridor was still there but it led nowhere, only a black void yawning at the other end. Turning around I was shocked to see that I was alone. The press of people that had surrounded me only a moment ago had all vanished. The entrance to the hallway I had just passed through was a smokescreen of blackness, matching the other end. In my state of utter confusion I hadn't noticed the light start to grow dimmer and dimmer until I was stood nearly in pitch blackness.

"Help! Someone help! Please!" I begged.

Blood still dribbled down my face and my head was pounding in agony, my stomach still in knots.

"No one can help you now I'm afraid," came a voice from behind me as the lights snapped back to a searing brightness.

Silence descended as the sounds of the failing ship and the distant screams faded into nothingness. I wheeled around to see a man stood calmly before me, a raven black as tar perched on each shoulder.

He wore a simple robe of light brown wool, tightened at the waist by a cord that shone as if it were spun of gold. In his face he seemed to be both young and old at the same time. There was a living light in his flesh, crowned with gentle wrinkles, lines carved by both laughter and anger. His hair was long and a bright white as was his beard, which was braided and held together with ornately carved rings of silver, bronze, and gold. He leant on an old staff carved of ash and wore a leather eye patch, undecorated and understated.

"All Father," I said.

I had no idea how those words had come to me but I felt compelled to address him in that manner.

"So you know me then, son of Midgard?" he replied in a voice that could crush mountains whist soothing a fevered baby to sleep.

"I confess I do not. Though I feel I should do. Who are you? And what is Midgard?"

"I am as you said, the All Father, and Midgard is the realm in which you stand. You call it Earth."

"What's happened to all the passengers? And the hallway? Did you do this? Are they dead?"

"You mortals have always been the same, asking a thousand and one questions and none of them relevant. The people you saw a moment ago are still here. I have suspended this hallway in a different time and space, just for a moment."

"I don't understand."

"I don't expect you to. I am come to shed light on some of your troubles."

"I see." My confusion didn't improve. "Please, Sir, tell me you're aware of the ravens perched on your shoulder? I see them everywhere. They haunt my dreams and I've no idea what they want of me."

"These two?" he said, motioning as if carrying two huge birds around was as normal as drinking tea in the morning. "They are called Huginn and Muninn. They circle the world for me, gathering news and whispering it in my ear. You have nothing to fear from them, boy. They have watched you for a very long time."

"But why? I don't understand any of this? Why me?"

"I'm afraid I cannot answer that. I know a great many things but why you're being subjected to this is something beyond even the wisdom I sacrificed my eye for, can tell. What I do know is that one of my brethren has taken over control of your mortality. He watches you die and gives you life again so that he may watch you die again. You are always brought back around pivotal moments of violence in human history and… "

"Who?! Who is doing this? And if he truly is your brethren why can't you stop this?"

"He is Laufey's son, Fenrir's father, and the master of lies. He can change his shape whenever he wishes. He is the eternal trickster. I understand your frustration, human, but it is not in my power to stop him. Thousands of years ago we became blood brothers. If I were to lay hands on him in anger, the world as it is known would end. My time with you grows short, boy. I must return and I fear you shall not see me again."

"Why did you come here? If you cannot help me, why show yourself?!"

"I heard the confusion of your mind through the depths of time and space and sought to shine whatever light I could on your plight but his power over you is stronger than I realised. If I have not given you any comfort, I apologise, mortal."

He vanished in an explosion of light in every colour imaginable. The carpet where he had stood seemed scorched and faint, and fragrant smoke arose from it. I was more confused than ever. Nothing was adding up in my mind. I thought maybe I had died at Waterloo and I was in hell or perhaps even in a deep sleep, dreaming.

With the stranger's disappearance, all the sounds that had evaporated moments before came flooding back to life. The thrum of the engines, the hideous creaking of heavy iron and steel, the distant popping of rivets and the terrified screams of men, women and worst of all, children. The throng of people rushing by me reappeared as if from nowhere and when I came to terms with what was happening, my sense of urgency returned. I had to reach the deck.

As I climbed, the crowd became more and more dense. People congregated around the doors to the open deck, trying desperately to get out to the life boats. There were around 1,312 passengers on board, not to mention crew, and at the moment, I couldn't see how any would survive. Even if there were enough lifeboats for everyone, who would have picked us up?

Panic intensified as people were told they weren't allowed through the door and somewhere, a gunshot fired, sparking a frenzy of terror and the herd of people to break their way through the ornate wooden doors.

Out on deck, the air was frigid, the sky an oblivion of black, decorated with the stark pinpricks of the stars hanging above us. The moon shone brighter than I'd ever seen, its reflection dancing on the ripples in the water in a hue of graceful silver. My breath danced in front of my face like a ghost, dissipating into the night. The air, though freezing, was entirely still. For a brief, fleeting moment I experienced a few seconds of peaceful serenity.

The moment ended and chaos reigned again. The water was foaming and roiling around the ship. Screams penetrated the stillness of the air and people ran terrified in every direction. The unsinkable ship was sinking. The bow was starting to dip lower and lower towards the icy Atlantic, the stern steadily rising up as water rushed violently into the gaping hole torn into the hull. I had already made peace with the fact that I was going to die again. I knew that some force was willing my death but what I didn't know was why. An unusual calm washed over me, maybe because I knew there was no stopping what was coming. No saving myself. Only death.

Slowly, I walked towards the sinking prow, paying no mind to the frenzied throng that surrounded me. I reached the point where the water was creeping slowly up the deck. Its stabbing cold washed over my feet. I gazed up to the moon, still beguiled by its brightness and beauty.

Let's get this over with.

Walking into the freezing water I couldn't help but notice the absence of the ravens.

Oh, well.

For the fourth time, but by no means the last, I was dead.

I awoke roughly two years later; the world marching towards 28th July, 1914, when then whole world was plunged into war following the assassination of the Archduke of Austria, Franz Ferdinand. I managed to stay out of the affair and largely unaffected by it until the Military Service Bill came into force in January 1916 and forced us to sign up. I found myself stationed at the Somme come July, sat deep in the trenches. The waiting was oppressive and morale was non-existent. The rats crawled around in the thick mud at our feet, getting into the rations, and gnawing at our toes in the night. Most of the day we spent sitting around, staring at the wooden boards on the floor or the muddy walls of the trench wondering when we were to lay down our lives to gain a few yards of ground. Looking to the sky, I saw hundreds of black birds. I didn't know whether any of them were ravens but they sent a chill down my spine nonetheless. Given the events of my past, I wasn't a fan of birds in general any more.

The orders we had all been waiting for came in. The Germans were to suffer heavy bombardment and after we were sure there wasn't anyone left in their trenches alive, we'd advance over. Only, Field Marshall Haig had specifically said that we were to walk across the dreaded space between us and the enemy. Walk. Not charge, but walk. So sure was he that the shells would take care of our foe, we were commanded to slowly advance towards our goal rather than charge, though God knows why that was.

And so the shelling began. Hundreds upon hundreds of bombs flung at our enemy, raining down with hideous whistles and landing in a plethora of explosions, illuminating the darkness with a hellish, orange glow. The constant booming of the guns themselves made sleep difficult but it crept upon us anyway. After all, war certainly does take it out of a man.

After a few days, the guns finally fell silent. Everything seemed silent in fact. I could hear the breath of the men next to me raggedly escaping their frightened lungs, I could hear the fires crackling and spitting in no man's land, but then came the worst sound of all; the whistle. A long, shrill blast and over the top we went. We didn't scream to encourage our adrenaline since we were led to believe that all of the Germans would already be dead in their trenches. We walked in total quiet, our feet dredging though the thick, sticky mud. Closer and closer we crept, trepidation hanging over us like a heavily laden storm cloud when suddenly I realised, I was the only man walking. I turned about to see what had happened to the rest of the battalion to find them all stopped like statues mid-stride.

Running up to the closest man to me, I found myself unable to move him. He was as strong and stoic as granite, his eyes completely glazed over, his muscles tense and his chest, as with the rest of him, was completely still. I tried to rouse him to no avail. I tried the others as well, man after man, all the same. As panic set in I heard a voice in the distant recesses of my mind attempting to calm me down. It was a voice I was sure I had never heard before but at the same time, it was a voice I felt I knew. I turned to face back towards the German trenches to see a man with long black hair, a long, pointed chin, and a crooked nose. The corners of his mouth curled up in a sinister grin and there was a deeply malicious look in his small, shining eyes. He wore a dark green velvet tunic, woollen trousers in the same colour and a golden belt from which a dagger hung from a black leather sheath, its handle encrusted in jewels.

"It's you, isn't it? You're the one. Laufey's son," I said to him.

I was sure this was my tormentor, the being that had kept me living and dying for so long. He let out a cruel laugh.

"You are a perceptive mortal. My reputation precedes me it seems." His awful eyes shone brighter and that terrible grin still stuck to his face. "Indeed I am Laufey's son, father of the serpent, the wolf and of Hel herself. You may call me Loki."

"What have you done to these men? Your quarrel is with me. Let them go."

"I will, fear not. But as soon as I do, you're all bound for sweet, sweet death. That trench you walk so slowly towards? Full of enemies, all very much alive." He had started to slowly circle me, trying to intimidate me. "You're walking into a trap."

"Why? Why do you play with my life? Why constantly kill me only to bring me back to life?" What is in you that makes you so evil?"

He stopped circling.

"Why? I have lived for countless years. I came into being not long after creation itself. I am bound to live for eternity and do you know the bad thing about eternity? It's boring. I watch years slip past like seconds and I hunger for sport, something to hold my interest. You think me evil? All evil stems from boredom. Any man who does horrible or unspeakable things does so because his life is empty and cold."

"Boredom?! I live in constant anxiety! I watch over my shoulder night and day wondering what my next death will be like. Every time I close my eyes I see the horrible things I've been through. The war, the murder, the disaster. I hear the screams of children and I know that even when death comes for me it isn't the end! I have to do it all again and again and it's because you need sport?!"

My anger overtook me. I pulled out my knife and charged at Loki head on, though as I reached him, running as fast as I could, I passed straight through him as if he wasn't even there. I heard his uncontrollable laughter as I lay face down in the mud.

"You really think there's anything you can do to hurt me? I am a god, you ape! Your actions, just like your entire life, is an exercise in futility!"

I struggled to my hands and knees, seething in anger.

"I will find a way to beat you. God or not. I will exhaust every avenue of research. I won't exist this way. Even if it takes the rest of eternity, I will end this murderous cycle."

"Heh... eternity it is then."

He vanished with a cloud of smoke and a sinister laugh. Clambering to my feet, I heard gunfire roar to life. It was though the play of my life had been resumed, my fellow soldiers had started to advance again, released from their purgatory but no sooner had their life returned to them (if indeed it had left them in the first place) they were being mercilessly mowed down by heavy German machine guns.

Never in my life had I seen so many die at once. For the Hun, it was like shooting fish in a muddy barrel. They had been clever enough to let us advance far enough that escaping back to our trench was inconceivable. Men ran wild about me, some screaming towards the enemy in a last ditch attempt at glory, others backwards, their faces slick with tears, shouting for their dear mothers. Mothers who would never again see their sweet boys. Me, however, I dropped my riffle and stood perfectly still. I knew there was no escape. I closed my eyes and felt the explosive pain drive through my chest, knocking me flying through the smoky air onto my back. As I lay, staring listlessly at the sky, blood seeped from my mouth, warm and oddly comforting. And then I saw them.

The ravens.

That was my fifth death. I sit now, writing this account of my life to date, the date being March 28th, 1942. Tomorrow, we set out on

Operation Chariot where we attack a dock at St Nazaire in German-occupied France. I know I'll die. I can feel it. That's the funny thing about eternity, you can never quite grasp it, the vast concept that it is. I'm not prepared to live like this for that long, forever. I've not been idle waiting for my next death, though. I've practically lived in libraries, read hundreds of books, I even visited Scandinavia in my search for a solution. One word continues to jump out at me everywhere I look, a word that could be my salvation. A lasting, permanent death. After all, eternity is boring. My studies surround this one word, this one, final event: the end of days. Ragnarok.

The Wish

Mary Brown
England

TEN-YEARS-OLD HAD BEEN YOUNG for her age, milky-white. Twenty had been mouse-brown. Thirty had been blue-green, a late blooming. Forty had been the blood-red of the last chance saloon.

Fifty was grey. Even before Julie hit it, she could see the greyness ahead blowing back over the water. 'Swim upstream…' the words came to her, and kept coming back. *Swim upstream, swim upstream…* like a shoal of silvery fishes flowing the wrong way through her thoughts.

A flyer landed on the doormat. An Italian artist was going to run a course of *light art* workshops at the local adult college. Stefano Rossi. His photo was underexposed, with pools of shadow round the eyes that overflowed down the side of his nose and up into his ears. It was like the woodcut of a villain in one of her childhood books, one she used to open up, thrill to, and slam shut again.

Was *light art* something she could perhaps try with her doddery Sunshine House clients, whom she helped do hopeful things with old photos, haberdashery, and glue?

She signed up for the course.

Stefano in the flesh turned out to be merely good-looking. If any of the students talked too long, his eyes emptied out, and his fingertips drew impatient patterns on the table. Understandable, when time was so short. Julie made sure she never said more than five or six words in one go. The photo stayed in her head though, vaguely translucent, and she projected it over his real face like film. And it was amazing what he could do with wet rags and a torch in a darkened room, and how he made sparkles of silver light look like rain. And rather charming how he muttered *'Eccolo'* whenever he was pleased with something he'd produced.

He gave them leaflets. He was going to open with his *light art* in the Spectra Gallery, near Chalk Farm Road. On the thirty-first of September. She nearly cried out, 'My birthday!', but bit her tongue.

Walking home from the workshops, Julie sometimes forgot and imagined she was back in her blue-green years, until she saw Henry coming up the street to meet her, stiff-legged and fearless, with his carrier bag of pamphlets and papers. He liked to do that, walk the last few blocks home with her. He liked for them to amble along, her right arm hooked through the crook of his arm, which made it ache after a bit, while he talked about his book. A history of the cooperative movement. It was at a crossroads. 'Same crossroads we were at fifty years ago…' he told her a couple of days before her birthday '…fifty wasted years…'

Fifty wasted years. It chewed away inside her as he talked. After a minute she interrupted him.

'I wish I wasn't going to be fifty…'

They crossed a road. She was used to waiting a long time for his replies. Sometimes he was thinking about what she'd said. Sometimes he'd forgotten that she'd ever spoken.

She nudged him with her elbow. 'Fifty. If you can remember that far back.'

He shot her a glance over his bony, sixty-one-year-old nose.

'Don't be silly, we'll have a nice day. We're going to walk the canal, remember?' His far hand reached across to pat her aching arm. They plodded on, not quite in step, while he returned to the subject dearest to his heart. '…way before his time, Robert Owen, ahead of Marx…'

She woke early on the Saturday of her birthday. The bedroom was dim and still asleep, but something had invaded it. A long, slender cone of light had squeezed in through a chink in the velvet curtains and transfixed the gloom. More than light. What? She knelt up on the bed, twisting towards the bare back wall, and saw leaves stirring, faintly green. A tree stood on its head there, gently breathing, its upside-down branches spreading down the wall towards the floor.

The ash tree. The one outside the window. It had floated onto the bedroom wall, turning over as it came. The room was a pinhole camera.

Henry would love that. If they'd managed to have children, he'd have had them all making pinhole cameras out of old boxes. Or at least starting to make them for him to finish off.

She looked over at the other bed. He was fast asleep, his mouth in a tight O, snuffling rhythmically. As he did. Probably dreaming about his hero, Robert Owen. She knew he was extra tired this week, but it wasn't a good look. It made her think of all those words he kept using these days – *cooperative societies, mutuals, credit unions* – queuing up inside like grey moths, waiting to wander out whenever he woke up.

In the wardrobe mirror, at the back of the looking-glass room, an upside-down pigeon flapped its wings and flew down into the floor. The door opened wrong way round. An alternative world lay beyond the wrong-way-round door.

And silvery fish were swimming the wrong way through her head. She swung her feet off the bed. Out, out, swim upstream. And back before you're missed.

Quietly, she dressed and went outside.

The sky was an exquisite, anxious blue. Cut upstream. Which way? She crossed the Heath and chose the streets she knew the least, but they kept leading her downhill instead of up, and sooner than she expected, she'd turned onto Chalk Farm Road.

She found it on the second side street, halfway down. A deep blue neon sign in joined-up writing, dangling at a tilt behind a bare shop window. *Spectra.*

It was today he opened, and here she was. With something interesting to report. The pinhole camera room. It was light, wasn't it? If he was there.

The gallery was closed, a notice said, but would open at eleven. The opening bash had been the night before, with wine and a short 'light show'. They hadn't been invited to that.

She killed time, too much of it, in a bookshop and café. Then used up more time in the Ladies, parting her hair the other side. Approaching the gallery again, she saw a little group beyond the glass, holding mugs and laughing. One of them was Stefano. As she pushed at the door, the silver fish dived from her head into her belly.

A man with a pointy beard was telling the group something in Italian which made them all guffaw. There was a hush as the door whined shut behind her. Because she'd come in. She smiled vaguely at everyone's chest, then turned to stare at a giant lump of glass.

One of the group broke away and came towards her. A glossy-skinned young woman with a scarf woven through dark curls. She was smiling, but it was the smile that was left over from everyone laughing. 'Good morning.'

'I just came in,' Julie said, 'to look at Stefano's… the… light art.'

'Please. You are welcome.' The woman swept her silky hand towards an archway leading to a blacked-out room. 'And we have two other artists also.' Her eyes flicked back to the group by the door, and Julie's eyes followed hers, crashing smack into Stefano's. She flashed on a grin. Her emergency grin. *Just came to looked at the installations, like you said we should.* He didn't smile back; what he did was he winked at her. A fancy wink, with those black eyebrows, that dissolute hint of pink in the cheeks. She could see him brooding moodily in a rotting Venetian palace, and flashing such a wink at the besotted maid-servant. Already he'd turned back to the man with the pointy beard who was making them all smirk.

The floor sucked at her feet as she walked through the archway into gloom. An oblong haze on her right took its time to come into focus. Pillars of green and purple light. She counted them. Twelve green pillars, thirteen purple, floating in the dark. The wink blinked on and off in her darkened head. Thirteen green, twelve purple. Each time she counted she got a different number. This artist was called Estella Verdi. Green star. Lovely name.

A wink was a sort of light art too.

She followed a blue flame into a black box and watched a tumbling river of light. That was Stefano's. Clever. If he came through to say hello, she might not even mention the pinhole camera room. No one did come through. She counted the reflections in two angled-together mirrors until the sight of infinity calmed her down. Jamming on a smile, she walked back out through the archway.

All had gone, except the girl with the headscarf, who was reading a book at the desk.

'Thank you so much,' Julie said, yanking at the heavy door.

Uphill now, really uphill this time. Things would be different back under the trees.

They were different, and different from the morning too. The trees had darkened; the air had cooked. Now, spread across every clearing, there were picnic parties. You could hear the buzz through the trees before you came across them. Extended families. Colleagues letting down their hair. Australians.

How did so many people collect so many friends, and family, all in one place?

She must head home. What would Henry be...? Too late now. It was the far side of lunchtime. It was the hunger of the afternoon. She wandered between trees. It wasn't lunch she wanted. She didn't know what it was. She tried lying down on the warm grass, but soon got to her feet again and walked on. Far, far too late to go home.

On the slope between copse and pond, there was a picnic too. Late, like this Indian summer. The perfection of it clawed at her belly. Two little girls rolled around in a hammock strung low between copper beeches. Adults of various generations sprawled on rugs, waving wine glasses and chortling. What was the joke? She'd never know. But yes, she would, because it was their friends playing football with... her eyes squinted against the low, splintering light. They were kicking around a hat. The bearded man facing her kicked it high and the black-haired one facing him caught it on the side of his head, hand on hip, to hoots and whistles. Julie grinned too, though the slivers of light were blinding her. One of the lolling-about ones waved his glass at her. '*Ciao!*'

Ciao? The hatted one twirled round to see who it was, doffed the hat at her as he twirled, and, all in the same graceful spin, kicked it back to his friend.

Tripping on grass, she turned sharp left, away from them, the grin fossilising on her face. That had been Stefano. That had been him. Or someone horribly like him. Mustn't look back. Mustn't look back to check. *Had* it been Stefano? Most improbable. She glided down a woodland path, balancing herself like a cup of tea she mustn't spill.

The clouds overhead had deepened to coral. The air was grainy pink. Anything remotely russet glowed.

'Like through rose-tinted glass,' she wanted to cry to someone, but there was only a crow of unsullied blackness stamping on a crisp wrapper in the fairy-tale grass.

A just-before-sunset moment. No light-art show could match it. A soothing thought. And the trees around her now were soothing too somehow, tentative birches, almost invisible in the long grass, and a few squat, gloomy oaks.

A man appeared down in the hollow, head and clothes in shadow. He skirted the fallen oak, heading towards her and got waylaid by brambles. She couldn't make him out, but that moody, crooked gait could easily be Stefano's. Stefano, coming after her… why?… with an invitation… to join them by the hammock… really?… to make up for the wink. A mad idea… a mad, mad, bad idea… and she didn't want to go and she'd be tongue-tied. And they'd be bound to find her boring. Though she wasn't, to herself.

Because she had light in her head too, *and* art. Because just now, with this pinkish light and that figure silhouetted against the thorns, she was back in the witchy woods of childhood books, caught in a spell, or undoing one, or, simplest of all, making a wish.

She pressed her palms against the nearest oak tree's furrowed bark.

A wish. Not a crazy, impossible one either, just the wish that was hurting inside her. She brought her forehead to the trunk and breathed in living, listening wood. The wish didn't come in words. Picnics were in there, and having one. And talking, easily, about... whatever... upside-down trees even, and everything simple and clear. Her palms pressed harder against the bark ridges. A crazy, impossible wish after all. Scraping her ear against its furrows, she listened for the tree's heartbeat.

Too deeply buried to hear.

But the shadowy man had picked his way out of the brambles and was coming closer, and the last thing she wanted to do was wait or watch or let that stuck-up Italian see her wishing. Ducking under a branch, she ploughed through undergrowth.

'Julie!'

She turned. The magic light had drained away. The world was shades of nearly grey.

Grey-bluish, carrying a grey-greenish plastic bag, Henry climbed out of the brambles towards her. Slightly crooked, slightly stiff.

'Hello.'

He'd got the look he had when working something out, eyes pointy in the corners, mouth clamped shut, like when he'd been studying her broken bicycle gear. Which he'd fixed.

'I was waiting for you in the flat,' he said. Not a reproach, a fact. 'I thought you might want to do something today.'

'I thought you'd prefer to be working on your book.' That was dishonest. That was devious.

Legs apart, fingers in the pockets of his old jeans, he stood and studied a spot ten inches from his nose. 'I did work on it, but I was wondering where you were.'

She didn't answer.

He peeled a curl of silvery-grey bark off the birch branch she'd ducked under. There had to be reproaches chugging round between his two big ears. There had to be. There were. Of a kind. 'I thought we might have done something today,' he said. 'We were going to explore the canal route, weren't we? I looked at the map. D'you know we could have had a picnic in Kensal Green Cemetery… where Robert Owen's memorial is…?' He tailed off, watching her uncertainly.

'Robert Owen.' She couldn't keep a childish singsong out of her voice. 'Course. Robert Owen. Because if the credit unions hadn't been *mutulated*, and if…'

'Demutualised.' He couldn't help it. He clamped his mouth back shut, obviously wishing he'd kept it clamped. She saw that, but she didn't care. Her voice rose.

'*Mutulated*. I said *mutulated* and I meant…' Her voice dropped again as she realised she'd said it wrong. '…mutilated. Like when a leg's gone. Or arm or… other thing… that's missing…' For one off-balance moment, the real missing things went scampering through her, faceless but scampering on until his voice cut them off.

'What're you talking about?' He was bent forward, shoulders hunched, a skinny old dog bracing for a fight.

She stared down at her tired toes and shook her head.

'Sorry…' at last there was anger in his voice, '…sorry I'm such poor company.' He started on past her up the path. When she looked around, he was gone.

She plunged deeper into the woods, and straight back out again, because they'd got too dark. She reached the weeping willows by the dog-pond and flopped onto a bench, mouth not quite closing. Because of the nausea seeping from her belly.

Someone sat down on the next bench. She peered. It was Henry. Henry, who'd been waiting in the flat all day, not knowing how to get angry. He was staring straight ahead at the dog pond. Like her. Each staring at the same pond, watching the same light fade, from different benches.

She walked over and sat down beside him. He kept on staring straight ahead.

'I'm sorry,' she said. It wasn't enough. 'Sorry…' Not enough. She wound her arm round his.

He cleared his throat. 'Happy Birthday.'

She kept her arm wound tight round his, all string and bones that it was. 'I'd something for you in the flat,' he said.

Her voice sank. 'Sorry. I don't know why I did it, going off like that.'

For long moments, he neither moved nor spoke. Then, with a sigh, he pulled the plastic bag onto his lap. 'Are you hungry?'

'What's in there?'

'Sandwiches, cake, ginger beer. For our picnic. That we didn't do. I thought I'd come out here and eat it.'

Her fingers began trembling, and went on trembling till she was halfway through the chicken sandwich. When nothing was left to eat, they stayed on, sipping the ginger beer, watching the dog-pond darken. Uncannily quiet, now he was trying not to mention Robert Owen.

'Guess what the bedroom turned into while you were asleep,' she said.

'I give up.'

'A pinhole camera.'

She sensed his spine straightening up beside her. This was his sort of thing. 'D'you mean literally?'

'Literally.'

She told him about the upside-down tree. They talked about light. He tried to explain about its constant speed. She tried to understand. Her arms were tight around his arm again, hugging the stringy, bony lifeline to her ribcage. She wondered if this was what she'd wished for. A round moon rose over the trees, pouring pewter and silver into the pond, over the whole park, turning it monochrome, unreal, as under dark silvery waters, her stretched-out legs and feet pale as underwater marble, all still, perfectly still, so no one could tell which way was upstream or which way downstream anymore. Or if there even was a stream.

Life

Mathew Brummond
USA

I CUP THE PILL BOTTLE, my hands soft but unyielding, as if cradling a wounded animal. Turning it around, I look down with a revolting curiosity, as unwilling to cast away the small vial as I am to continue holding it. For a moment, I consider the thought process of removing the lid, taking out a pill, and placing it on my tongue until I forget it requires no thought process at all. The movement, that is.

Breaking my trance, I force myself to look up. How long have I been in this motel room? A week? Must be close, and the do-not-disturb sign hasn't come down once. Discarded carryout containers and used towels litter the floor wherever they happened to fall. I like that. It feels less like home. Not that there's anything wrong with my home – all the researchers connected with Project Lazarus have done quite well for themselves. But right now, I need to be somewhere unfamiliar, somewhere dirty.

And alone.

Clouds are gathering outside and I can taste the inevitable rain. Either I've had too much to drink or not enough; everything feels like a sign or metaphor. The storm is my brooding mood; this cramped room is as claustrophobic as my mind. Or is that a simile? I'm stalling. Despite my liberal education, I was never any good at soft subjects.

The hard sciences always called to me. I glance involuntarily at the worn, pocket New Testament lying open on the writing desk. Well, at least since college. In my sophomore year, I joined Project Lazarus – not that we called it anything so grandiose at the time. It was simply "Dr. So-and-So's Study" or, less formally, "a tremendous waste of time." The graduate students relegated me to data entry and any other menial tasks they could foist on an undergrad desperate for time in a real lab.

I wonder if I would still be in this position if I'd picked a different major? I grab the cleanest glass at arm's length and pour a few fingers of Johnny Walker over the dregs from my ice bucket.

Modest as my rank had been in the beginning, there was a certain camaraderie born of our collective pipe dream. Science, by nature, is slow; even if our lab had all the talent and all the funding, all we could expect would be a paper explaining a non-insignificant correlation. Or, more likely given our limitations, a non-significant one. You don't get a cure for something as complex and inexplicable as progeria – the genetic disorder characterised by premature ageing – by swirling random chemicals between beakers. It would take years of research, by countless scientists, each building off the incremental insights of the past, before anyone might add a few extra years to these kids' lives. Despite that hard, unassailable truism, I doubt I was the only one harbouring secret, unscientific fantasies of curing the cruelest of childhood ailments.

Imagine my surprise, then, when we did.

I give the glass a swirl to help circulate the ice and take a sip. A real cure – not extended lifespans or help coping with symptoms – against all reason, our underfunded university lab cured progeria by slowing sufferers' ageing back to normal rates.

That should have been the end for me: a named author on our paper and bragging rights for my CV. However, if that were the case, I would not be in this grungy motel room facing the most difficult question of my, or anyone else's, life. I take another sip.

As if success wasn't shocking enough, nothing could prepare us for how quickly our discovery escaped academia. Good as the cause was, we could barely scrape together enough funding to keep our equipment running. Yet, once we succeeded, the popular press picked up the story of our breakthrough almost at once. They applied the name "Lazarus," giving the lead legs as well as paving the way for my current predicament.

Christening the research project for the man Jesus raised from the dead must have seemed innocent enough at the time. So did the late-night TV jokes that the drug could replace Botox. But, then an anonymous investor, presumably a rich guy with everything he could want besides the future, gave Lazarus a new direction.

Taking a drink, I let my mind wander back to that last life-altering choice I made. Not that it felt like much of a choice at the time. I eagerly followed the project. It meant leaving school with just my Master's, but after three years of instant noodles and cheap beer, I was ready for a steady paycheck.

I wasn't alone, either. Nearly everyone followed the project from the public to the private sector and its resources. With new facilities and a host of staff at our command, it took months instead of years for us to succeed again – this time in creating the impossible. Deemed Elixir Vitae, for obvious reasons, our creation did far more than eliminate wrinkles. It ended ageing altogether.

More than that, even.

No, in fact much more. Early clinical trials showed a curious regenerative effect. Cancers vanished, immune systems restored themselves, and arteries cleared – there seemed no end to the ailments the Lazarus drug might cure. Even bones healed faster, the breaks realigning themselves cleaner than any doctor could have managed. By all outward appearances, save for the most sudden of catastrophic traumas, Elixir Vitae could put an end to death itself. Only time will tell, and everyone opting for the treatment will have plenty of that.

I take another drink.

In retrospect, it seems inconceivable not to have realised the full consequences of our research. We … *I* wasn't merely prolonging the human lifespan; Elixir Vitae could change the very meaning of humanity. As we worked, though, the process itself felt unreal. I never considered the whole, just each incremental, abstract step. Find a problem and solve it. Repeat. That focus made everything so much easier. Back then, anyway.

I'm not sure whether the government shared my lack of foresight, or fully understood our drug's potential. Either way, in a rare bit of nonpartisanship, the powers that be decided eternal life was too important to be sold to only those who could afford it. So, the State stepped in to manufacture and distribute the drug in discrete gel cap doses, available to everyone over the age of thirty. All of which brings me back to my present circumstance.

Happy birthday.

Happy birthday to me indeed. Eying the last of my drink, I take a longer pull than usual and wince. I pick the pill bottle back up and resume my inspection, but there isn't much to see. Just a plain, brownish orange vial whose most striking feature is the complete lack of warnings or contraindications (there aren't any) or marketing material (it doesn't need any). Holding it up to the light, the translucent blue orbs stare back at me, black through their amber prism. For a moment I imagine the liquid elixir swirling around inside, but the pills are of course inert.

Dead.

I look away quickly. Searching for a new focus my eyes drift back to my Bible sprawled out beside me. My body reacts slowly, reluctant to discard the dangerous bottle in order to retrieve the tome. I finally make the exchange, and turn to a badly dog-eared page in *Deuteronomy*.

I know that once I found comfort in my faith, the same way a visitor to a planetarium knows the distance to the nearest stars. However, after years of pursuing other interests, first academic and then pecuniary, faith hasn't seemed as … pertinent. I suppose it was always there, somewhere tucked conveniently out of the way. Otherwise, I wouldn't have this problem. Consciously, though, I have not thought about it in... I don't remember how long.

All the same, I have 30:19 memorised, and likely always will. I just find comfort flipping through to the page, fragile as tissue paper, to take in the printed words.

"This day I call heaven and earth as witnesses against you that I have set before you life and death, God's blessing and God's curse. Now choose life, so that you and your children may live..."

It was always so simple in the abstract.

Now, though, my choice is very real. Do I forsake the elixir in favor of eternal life in the hereafter, or do I not risk being wrong? If there is no afterlife, wouldn't it be better to live forever on Earth? Of course, by erring on the side of caution, I give up on a world surpassing this one in ways I can only imagine. Is it worth that risk?

I shake my head. Too many thoughts, too fast. I have rehashed this same line too many times, and I know the arguments all too well. I have to force myself to be methodical. Clinical, detached – just as I trained.

With a sudden swell, the wind finds every fault in the room's facade. A break in the curtain reveals a few dozen feet of threatening sky separating me from the ice machine. Looking from it to the empty bucket, I realise it is now or never. Standing to the side, I peak through the front curtains to check the dark parking lot, but of course, no one is out in the ominous weather.

Heat lightning plays on the horizon as I slip through the door. The same wind whips at me, even stronger than it sounded from inside. My skin prickles from the chill and electricity in the air; I quickly make for the small fluorescent island of vending machines. Aside from the wind and my dry footfalls on the parched pavement, there is no sound accompanying my foray outside. Even the crickets have retreated. Filling the bucket to the brim, I walk quickly back to my room and duck at the first sound of thunder rolling in from the west.

Right now, I wouldn't mind just erring on the side of caution and having it over with. How, though? It would be silly trying to label one side or the other as "cautious." If I could do that, the choice practically would make itself for me. But what is cautious? I cannot definitively, deductively, indisputably know whether my beliefs have grounding, but I know *this* life. Is taking the elixir cautious, then?

With a soft click, I close the door behind me and deposit the ice bucket beside the bed. Of course, I have also experienced my faith in ways just as immediate and personal, even if not so easily explained. How do I ignore that, and what I stand to lose if there *is* a God? Besides, if I pass on Elixir Vitae and it turns out there isn't an afterlife, it isn't as if

I'll ever *know* I was wrong. So is that erring on the side of caution? Though if there is an afterlife and I never die to see it, I won't know what I'm missing, either.

Running my fingers through my unkempt hair, I pause to consider how long it has been since I last showered. Maybe it'd have been better to get caught in the rain. What time is it? I don't even know what day it is, but it's getting dark and --

I'm cut off mid-thought as the once-simmering storm reaches a tipping point. In an instant lightning and the deluge spill from the sky, assaulting my cramped quarters. The lights flicker, and when I locate the clock radio it's flashing "12:00" unhelpfully. I've always said irony is proof that God exists, and has a sense of humor. Sometimes it's just hard to appreciate the punch lines.

I may have had a bit too much to drink; I could almost nod off if the now-raging storm would only let me. Rain pummels the building, lashing out at each window while thunder rattles everything in the room. Good thing I got more ice when I did. I pour myself another drink and return to my well-rehearsed conflict.

I think about that tempting prospect, of having real proof that God exists. Something a bit more solid than my little irony joke. But, then I think of Milton's Satan and his fall from grace. Satan could never receive forgiveness because he knew God, knew he was omnipotent, and rebelled all the harder for it. It would seem uncertainty affords us mortals a bit of leeway. But just how much?

If not proof, then what?

I upend the bottle, letting the round gel caps pour out in front of me onto the bed. I spread them over the blanket, sowing them into the weave as neat little rows. Counting my crop back into the vial one by one, I pause at the last pill and roll it between my thumb and index finger until it deforms slightly. Ninety pills. A three-month down payment on eternity, and an endless free supply after that. I give the pill a final, gentle squeeze and return it to the bottle as well.

What of the stakes if I am right and a loving God has prepared an afterlife just for us? I wish I could tackle the problem mathematically, as easy as counting to ninety. Pascal tried. He weighed what one stood to lose if there was a Christian afterlife versus if there was not. He concluded the trade-off of following a few rules for even the slightest possibility of everlasting happiness was worth it. Rationally, it only made sense to believe in God. It's a sandy foundation upon which to build one's faith, sure, but you only need a mustard seed's worth.

Of course, Pascal did not have the fountain of youth to grapple with.

Would I ever tire of life? All Ovid's Sibyl wanted was to die, but Elixir Vitae promises more than her handful of sand – we get immortality *and* youth. Still, if I take the elixir and then change my mind, in oh, say, 940 years, I could simply discontinue my daily dose. Would that be tantamount to suicide, though? Damnation? How unscientific, my advisor would be disappointed. Nevertheless, even if I cannot articulate it, a drug regimen like Elixir Vitae feels like a commitment. After I start it, wilfully abstaining would mean choosing death: surely the wrong choice regardless of whether God exists.

Maybe the opposite, then. I could decline the drug now, and then start it later. That seems safe, but… no. That won't solve anything. Whatever decision I reach now must be final. Otherwise, I could agonise over this dilemma every day of my potentially *very* long life. Self-doubt is a funny thing. For all I know, I may reflect on this decision, even if it is final, forever.

Forever.

It doesn't help my cause that I can't even conceive of what "forever" really means. I've always felt that time passes not in constant intervals, but relative to what I've already experienced. This is why young children talk about "forever" so much – to them it's forever until their next birthday. Now, a year is all too short. The unfortunate downside is that the longer I wait, the harder it will be to understand it.

All the more reason to decide now.

Forever means eternity. A world without end. I shake my head, its mass sloshing side to side. I might as well say, 'Forever means forever.' It doesn't tell me anything about what that would mean, what it would be like. A world in which only those who choose to, ever die? Elixir Vitae has only been available a few years, how long until the population spikes? Thanks to my success, I'll be well off, but what of everyone else? We still wouldn't have enough resources to go around, the consequences just won't be as fatal. Would the State step in again, this time to control the birthrate? Would it decide who could reproduce? Would it dictate who must die? Or does only our fear of death make us think there isn't enough to satisfy everyone's needs? Would fear of suffering replace fear of death? Would that make us better, or worse?

Maybe stagnant.

Now my own fears are getting to me. It's easy to picture dystopias. With or without Elixir Vitae, we always have misgivings about the future, and dire predictions carry more weight precisely because they're pessimistic. Or is that what the Lazarus drug will change?

Or is it the final surrender to fear?

Does Elixir Vitae itself represent the end of history true believers are awaiting, each generation as certain as the last that they'll be part of it, seeing and participating in the final days? I shrug. Hell, with Lazarus they probably will, someday.

I can't help chuckling at myself. I'm getting carried away again. Whatever this drug may promise, no one could really live *forever* forever. Only human short-sightedness and hubris keep returning me to this point, after all. Someday I'll accidentally step out in front of a bus, an asteroid will collide with the Earth, or the universe will end in heat death. For that matter, something more banal may happen and Elixir Vitae simply won't be available anymore. So eventually, I will die and face whatever awaits us all, be it judgment or oblivion.

But that doesn't solve anything if the impulse itself is the transgression. Whether the reaction is wanting to die or live forever, the motivation is still despair over the finite conditions of life in the here and now. For why would someone seek immortality, regardless of whether it is attainable, without a lack of faith? The desire to seek permanency in a world where everything good and significant is ephemeral? That itself could be the fatal sin. Though, for that matter, so could my indecision. Maybe I'm assuming too much about what sort of afterlife awaits me.

I look around for a distraction from the unpleasant thought. My drink is nearly finished, as is the fifth. I take my final sip, letting the ambrosial libation warm my throat. For a moment, I let my mind wander and I think only of the storm. The howling wind and pounding rain drown out all other sounds and for a few seconds of bliss there are no choices, no thoughts, no consequences...

Nothing.

...but it only lasts a few seconds. This is getting me nowhere; I'm tired of thinking. Wouldn't it be wonderful for Judgment Day to just arrive and take this choice away from me? Is this laziness, or wan hope? Hard to say at this hour, whatever time it is --

HURRY UP PLEASE, IT'S TIME

I awake with a start, and thunder rocks my room to make sure I don't drift off again. Where have I heard that before? In any event, it *is* time. I have had this same conversation, contemplated the same arguments and refutations *ad nauseam*, and if I wait a moment longer, I may lose my mind. Not that I'd miss it, it's scarcely helped me so far. Thinking is out then. Picking up the bottle in one hand and the pocket Bible in the other, I gauge their weight. Enough is enough, time to throw caution to the wind. I discard the contents of my left hand, that I might hold life in both – as if cradling a wounded animal.

The Shelter

Miguel Lopez Bohorquez
Colombia

Y PARENTS AND GRANDPARENTS have told me lots of stories. Encounters with fantastic beings, anecdotes, dangerous situations that they hope I'll never experience, impromptu comedies, and well, all that stuff. But I want to highlight one that one of my grandmother's shared a couple of times about her first encounter with my grandfather. More than talking about a romantic moment that came before the couple as a shooting star, my beloved grandmother emphasised the place where love arose. A magical place where the world stops.

It sounds very poetic, I'm afraid. When we are in a sublime moment we want time to stop, basically because we don't want to go back to the sad world that shelters us daily. This occurs in many activities that we like, but what takes us to that state in an absolute way is love. We become idiots and long to be like this forever. It's so typical.

At twenty-five, that perspective continues. Unfortunately, let's say I haven't been able to get into that ... let's say, state of mind. I'm single and an only child whose parents, who gained recognition thanks to literature, longed to put my heart to work by giving meaning to the systolic movement. Yes, I'm young and there is a lot of road ahead, but I also know that sooner or later fate takes a stand and pushes us along. As can be deduced, everyone expected a special person to make an appearance in my life, because there is a feeling in the air that the other details of my life are practically settled.

I have used several places of "hunting" to find them: online dating, parties with friends, events, bars ... even the university. But I want to share my experience about a particular bar: the KOR bar. Curious name, to begin with.

It all started on a Friday of a certain month; I cannot remember if it was a Friday in mid-June or November. That would not matter, really. I was accompanied by a cousin and my group of friends composed of three men and four women, all about my age, whose main motivation was to provide support in this sort of search.

We entered. The access price was a relatively small sum. My first task was to examine the place. Occupying the ground floor in a three-story building, it was a clean, soberly-decorated place. Scarcely a few pictures of famous people, strange phrases, and apparently abstract figures decorated the walls. The ceiling was a generous height. I was struck by the lighting, much greater than usual in this class of establishment. More than a bar, I believed to be in a kind of auditorium before the beginning of some event. As for the rest, there was a clear line of elegance and simplicity, highlighting the design of the furniture.

"Well, more, let's say ... an exotic place. Was that how your grandmother described it?"

"Grandma did not give me much detail about the set, but I guess it has not changed much."

"If your granny found the love of her life here, then something special must have happened in this place, right?"

"I don't know, but well, let's move on."

Without further dialogue we sat at one of the large tables, ordered drinks, and started to party. We talked a little about everything. One of the girls looked at the clock with a gesture that worried me.

"Hey, guys, what time did we get there? Does anyone remember?"

"I think we got here at around seven-forty-five. What time is it?"

"Seriously?"The girl looked at her watch again. "Look, it's seven-forty-five. Something is wrong with my watch, or you're teasing me."

"No, no, I'm telling you the truth. Let's see; show us your watch."

The others looked at my friend's watch. The second hand wasn't moving. Maybe the battery ran out. It wasn't a big deal and we continued the conversation.

After an hour or almost an hour later, we began to examine the people around us. There were adults of all ages, and the gender distribution was more or less balanced. I specifically watched the girls. In each conversation the typical judgments were present: this may be, that one seems married, the other does not seem to be a good person ... those kinds of perceptions. During my observation I noticed a woman sitting at a small table. She was alone and wore a blouse of a blue silk with black trousers. She had a brown complexion, curly hair, and a warm expression.

Without hesitation I left my friends and approached the other table. Respectfully I asked permission to join her, and she accepted. I started to talk about what I found in this place, emphasising curiosity. She agreed to continue the conversation, noting that she had heard a story of a friend who had come here to get drunk out of spite, and when he left to go home he had learned that his ex-girlfriend had died, not by an accident or an illness, but by natural death. Before she told me the ending I asked whether this story was real or was an urban legend. The truth was that she had sensed something unbelievable about the story, and noticing the sincerity in which she spoke, I urged her to give me details.

Our conversation continued for a long time. I looked at my table and noticed that my friends and my cousin were gone. I asked the girl if she wanted to meet again. She accepted almost mechanically, gave me her phone number, paid her bill, and left.

At that moment I didn't know what to do. There were other girls sitting alone at several tables, several at the bar, and a few accompanied by a large group of men. At one point I thought of approaching someone else, but the shortage of prospects instantly dampened my enthusiasm. I opted to go to the bar, order a beer, and wait ... for something. After several minutes I checked my phone. There was nothing new, except for something out of the ordinary regarding the time.

The clock on the phone indicated seven-forty-five, the time we came here. It was te same thing that had happened to one of one of my friends. I could not think. Mechanically I finished my drink, paid the bill, and went home.

In my room, I checked the phone again: the clock now showed ten-thirty. How was that possible if the journey from the bar to my house barely took half an hour? Did the phone break down or what? I worried a little. I went down to see my parents. I greeted them with normal affection, but immediately I noticed their strange behaviour.

"Mom, what's wrong?"

"Nothing, Bob, ... just that you were gone a long time."

"But it was only a few hours."

"I know, but it felt like an eternity."

I didn't give too much importance to the conversation. I said goodbye to my parents and went back to my room. I had forgotten about the incident with the clock and decided it was time to rest.

A week went by. A week of absolute normality. My romantic interest had declined a little. In its place came curiosity about the inexplicable behavior of the clocks. Over the course of those days I investigated the possible causes of that particular event, but my task didn't bear fruit. I talked to several people about it, but no one managed to give me a convincing answer.

Without further options I agreed with my group of friends to go again to the bar on Friday. At first they resisted, arguing that there were other places to try, and trying to talk to them about the issue with the clock was a waste of time. After heated discussion, I managed to persuade them to accompany me.

We arrived at the bar at approximately eight-thirty in the evening. Reminding everyone of the purpose of our visit, I asked everyone to consult their watches for a minute or two to see if the strange phenomenon occurred. Indeed, all phone clocks and watches stopped. I expected my companions to be surprised and talk about it, but their amazement was rather trivial.

"There must be some type of disruptor here," one of them said sharply. "Maybe it's some weird signal or there's a hacker who's interfering with the phones to stop the clocks. It must be some joke or something."

Such was his sharp tone that nobody dared to contradict him or even continue with the subject, so the incident was practically forgotten. I chose to follow the flow.

After all, what could be wrong if the clocks stopped?

We proceeded with the same motivation of the previous visit, but this time there was more "work". We all dispersed, some dancing, others talking, and I speaking to a few women about different topics, seemingly unimportant. In the middle of the "operation" I was approached by a thirty-year-old woman, tall, white complexion, and a look that inspired confidence.

"So you're looking for someone to share something with, be it life or bed?'

"How is that…?"

"Please calm down. I saw you last week with a young woman at the table over there." She gestured to her left. "Apparently it went well for you, but then I noticed something that upset you a lot."

I was going to explain the clock, but I restrained myself.

"Yes, there was something special, but nothing to worry about. I'm here, having a good time and yes, as you say, 'looking for'." A boost of courage came to my aid. "Do you want to continue talking at a table or are you with someone?"

"You're with me now. I accept the invitation; come with me."

I could not hide a smile. Apparently I found at least one way. The spontaneous woman led me to the second floor of the bar, which consisted of a huge hallway with several rooms with open doors. We walked together as I examined each room. In one there were video games. In another, ping pong tables. Another room looked like a small restaurant. You could find different things in those rooms. The woman and I walked into one of them. The room in question had a table, two sofas, and huge furniture crammed with books. The place was free, which allowed us to sit on the couch.

"What kind of place is this?" I asked, slightly confused.

"Well, I don't think you know what you saw in that hallway, but hey, this is not a common bar."

"Yes, I see that. Come on, tell me more."

"Well ... it's difficult to explain, but believe me when I tell you that this place is special." The woman spoke with absolute confidence as I nodded almost inwardly. "Do you want to stay here or walk around the rooms?"

"You'll come with me?"

"You'd better go alone, but don't worry, I'll wait here."

I agreed to go to the rooms, but before I did I went down quickly to find my friends. I didn't find them. This didn't seem to be good. I was getting nervous, but then I remembered that coming back to this particular place was my idea. I regained my composure and returned to the hall.

I began to rush through the rooms and noticed many people in them enjoying the elements of each "theme". I saw guys playing video games, families dining in the miniature restaurant, and young people improvising in the room equipped with musical instruments. In the midst of the eagerness I noticed that all the rooms had something in common: huge windows that clearly showed the street. The only relevant novelty was in the room that was located down the hall. It had a massive brown door, which was closed. On the door was a kind of white circle. On the left side stood an intimidating-looking man. I assumed he was a guard and the room was an exclusive place for VIP's or the KOR's owners. I ignored that room.

I continued my hurried examination, but fatigue made me stop. I decided to go back to the library, where the woman was still waiting, sitting, and looking at me. Without a word, I returned to my place beside her. She just stared at me. I quickly took a closer look at the room. Just like the others had, it had those large windows.

"Seriously, tell me what this place is. You know that you know."

The woman was was slow to reply.

"I could say it's an universal place. I bet you saw that it's not just a bar. There is everything for everyone. Yes, everything."

"Don't get me wrong," I said. "The place is very good, but I think that there is more to a bar than what you told me a while ago. But…"

"But you expected more, didn't you?"

"To tell you the truth … yes."

"Well, let's go, then. Come on, let's take a look, but first I want you to look out the window."

I frowned, but under the circumstances I chose to listen to her. We held hands and stood in front of a large window. We saw a street, several shop windows, and people passing by.

"Do things happen on this street?" I asked skeptically.

"Easy. Just watch."

I stared for a while trying to calm myself down, but I couldn't. At one point, the events began to take place more and more rapidly: people were walking at a greater pace, shop lights were turning on and off at a higher frequency, the sky brightening and darkening faster ... The picture started to scare me. With effort I restrained myself and asked the woman to show me the other rooms. In spite of my growing fear we calmly visited some of the rooms.

We basically entered each room, got to know each other, and watched people. We began to notice that people were talking very loudly about various issues. Some talked about how fast they saw their children grow. A young girl was talking about an apparent encounter with a well-known philosopher who had died decades ago. Several men presumed to have been with beautiful women to whom "the years never passed by". In some corners we could see various objects that people brought and carried, like mirrors, pictures, packs of clothes ... all different and apparently inspired by elements of other times.

After several minutes we opted to go to the restaurant. We were hungry, and ordered several dishes. In the middle of dinner, we began a normal conversation, despite the enormous task of concealing my fear. I didn't dare look at the window.

We finished dinner and paid. She hoped that together we would leave that place to go elsewhere, but she said she had to go home. I asked her if wanted me to accompany her, but she didn't, and said goodbye with a kiss. I kept thinking. Left alone at the table released my fear. My heart felt like it would jump out of my chest, and my stomach churned. My hands were sweating. In the middle of despair and acting mechanically, I looked out the window, which showed an alley and a park. I watched as I did earlier in the rooms and the result was the same: increasing speed of events.

In a state of panic, I hurried away, but a male voice stopped me.

"Bob Gestalt? Is that you?"

I turned and saw a middle-aged man sitting at a table apparently with his wife. His face was slightly familiar.

"Yes… I am. Pardon me, Sir, do I know you from somewhere?"

"Young Bob, it's Roy, Roy Patrick. I work with your father. Do you remember me?"

"Yes, yes, I remember." The information refreshed my memory. "You used to visit us when I was about eleven. What a surprise to see you. What brings you here?"

"What makes me come here almost every day. To keep me, let's say … young."

"The food, I guess."

"Not just food; this place slows me down."

I didn't understand his last comment, but I decided to continue.

"I understand, Mr. Patrick. Anyway, I have to go. A pleasure to see you."

"Same here. Please say hello to your parents and grandparents for me."

"Hold on, Sir. My grandparents died several years ago. Did you know?"

"Oh, seriously? I'm so sorry. Please forgive my presumption, lad." Roy was suddenly sad, almost bursting into tears. "I'm really sorry."

"I'm the one who must apologise, Mr. Patrick. As I said that was a long time ago." I regret that he found out in such an awkward way. "I'd like to stay, but I really should go. Please do not be angry with me."

"I'm not upset, Bob. Do not worry, this was coming." I winced as I shook my head in frank amazement. "You can leave without worry. We'll talk another time, maybe tomorrow."

"It's okay. Have a nice day, Sir."

After saying goodbye I ran down. I didn't think of anything else. I was about to reach the front door when a familiar figure stepped in. My friend, Ana. I noticed the she looked older. She greeted me, but I could not respond because i was already terrified and paralysed with fear. Summoning my courage, I remembered a detail: Ana had been the first to notice the apparent malfunction of her watch. I quickly looked at the phone. The clock showed eight-forty-five, the time I entered the bar. Panic overtook me and I ran back home.

I entered the house almost knocking down the door. I checked the clock. It was eleven-eighteen at night. I sneaked into my parents' bedroom, finding them asleep. I noticed they looked the same; they did not seem to have advanced in age as opposed to Ana. That reassured me enough to plan what to do about it. I had a chance: tomorrow I would go back to KOR, look for Mr Patrick, and ask him. I was sure he knew exactly what this is was about.

Saturday. I was free, which gave me a chance to go back to the seemingly magical place to clear things up.

I was ready to leave when the doorbell rang. I opened the door to two of my friends and Ana, who started to scold me.

"Robert, what happened to you last night? Did they do something to you? Because you did something to me. You're not so rude."

"Forgive me. Something happened to me last night."

I stared at Ana. She did not look as old as yesterday. She looked normal.

"If you knew what I saw, you'd know there's something strange about the bar."

"What are you talking about? asked Dan, one of the men. "We did not see anything strange. Did you do that?"

"Yes," I answered, sorrowfully. "Last night I met an older woman. We stayed for a while, walked the second floor where there was a game room, a restaurant, and other things. I looked out a window and it seemed that everything was moving fast, as if time passed faster. I was scared. Then I saw Ana and she looked like she was older. I was scared out of my mind."

Ana gave me a sharp look.

"How so, older? Were you hallucinating? Did that woman put something in your drink or what?"

"Not any of that, I swear. I'm fine, but trust me."

My friends gave me looks that confirmed they didn't believe me. I decided to end the conversation. I told them that I had to run errand, but I didn't give them anymore details. We said our goodbyes and went our separate ways.

I hurried back to KOR and went straight to the restaurant, where I spotted Mr. Patrick, as I expected. I decided to be blunt.

"Listen, Sir. Yesterday you told me that this place keeps you young ... well ... literally. Please explain this to me."

"Take it easy, Bob," Patrick said, somewhat frightened." Just as you say, this place keeps me young. Do you want to know the secret?"

"I hope you're not taking me for a fool," I said angrily. "I don't know what's going on here and I hope you have a good explanation. Apparently several here also know what this is all about. So what's going on?"

Patrick did not answer. He got up from the table and beckoned me to accompany him.

We planted ourselves in front of the window of the restaurant overlooking the street. Unlike the meeting last night, I was not displeased to see the increase in "speed of time". I stared at my grandparents' friend. He began to explain.

"What you're seeing, Bob, are events that happen at an accelerated speed. As your grandmother would surely have told you, in this place time stands still, in every sense of the word."

I was going to ask how this was possible, but he interrupted me.

"Do not ask me for explanations. I don't know how this works either. I suppose it's magic, but a common magic. I don't know if you have noticed them, but many of those who come here behave naturally. So what does that tell you? Simple: they know the same thing I'm telling you. In short, the point is that this place allows us to experience eternity; that time passes for others, but not for us. We can do several things: play dominoes, eat here, get drunk, dance, read ... many things. Here we have the possibility to stay doing something forever, or several things forever. Do you get the idea?"

It took me a while to assimilate the explanation. Eternity... so this is a place where we become eternal while the outside world follows its course. What if a disaster or event occurs that compromised the site, such as a fire or an earthquake? Was there ever an assault? Does the place work legally? Have politicians, policemen, mob members, journalists, and other people come here to expose the bar in one way or another? There would be time to answer these questions. I told Roy that I understood.

"Very well," Roy continued. "There is a detail. What you experience is a simulation, but it can become real. The events you see out the window are speeded up, therefore, this is your life in real time when you're here. Is that right?"

I nodded.

"Good. I call it a "simulation", because when you leave the bar you return to the outside world just as you left it. You should have experienced that last night."

How right Mr. Patrick was.

" Yes, I did."

I awaited the final revelation.

"Now here's the fun part. Come with me."

We left the room and headed for the closed door. Roy approached the guard and spoke a word in a strange language. The man nodded and opened the door.

The room only had a table to one side and a sort of lectern with a glass-shaped sphere the size of a basketball and almost transparent. What kind of artefact was that? Would that thing make me immortal?

"That's the most important part," Roy said as I watched the object. "All you have to do is look at the sphere until your reflection appears. With that, the events that have passed will have really passed. If you do that and you leave here, you will notice that you will be the same as always, but from what you will see you will know that you were eternal at least for a while. Ah, but before that you have to give a very valuable thing to the watchman in order to receive the password, which is the word I said to let us in."

At first I thought it was absurd. That room was a sort of time machine. What person in his right mind would want to witness events at one speed in this place, while possibly losing many things, including loved ones, in the outside world? Well, Mr. Patrick may have his reasons, but what about the others? They must have compelling reasons to make such a choice. Now I was clearer, but something made me wonder whether I should follow in Patrick's footsteps and become a being that will never disappear, who will witness events without being affected by events in the outside world.

I didn't want to tell that person my wish, but an idea arose.

I said a terse goodbye to Roy. I left KOR and took out my cellphone to dial. Fortunately I had gotten the phone number of the thirty-year-old woman who approached me last night. She should also know the truth of this place. We did not talk long, but long enough to arrange to meet at the bar. After half an hour she came.

I decided to tell her what I had experienced after her departure, the meeting with my grandfather's friend; the journey through time; the strange, guarded sphere; the possibility of taking that road ... absolutely everything.

The woman listened calmly and attentively. She clearly knew what I was talking about and believed me.

"I understand you perfectly. Many have experienced the same uncertainty," the woman spoke calmly. "Not everyone needs to experience the power to live forever. It's like when others decide to take drugs or take a sabbatical for a year under the pretext of wanting to start over. It looks tempting, yes, but do not feel obligated. But before you go, answer me the following: for you, what is eternity?

"What a difficult question. I have always thought that eternity goes far beyond our understanding. It means to exist forever, to be the same forever. Not to change. Through the windows I saw that the rest of the world changes, but I don't. Everything else will disappear except me. Not being able to perish would allow me to live things that others would not; not just see everything happen, but ...

"I see you understand. But be very careful. The possibility of intervening makes the matter more tempting. Time will not affect you, but fatigue, boredom, and the desire to transcend will. They told you that you could live a "temporary" eternity with the sphere being here. But they did not mention that you could become immortal in a definitive way. It means to live forever both here and outside. I don't think it's a good idea to explain how."

Her explanation frightened me greatly. This had already gone too far. I was tempted to ask how that would be achieved. In my mind I drew the possible requirements to reach that point, which would surely require elements such as the sphere, or something else hidden in the enclosure. I finally asked if she was a real immortal. With some sadness, she said yes.

There was a feeling of old, open wounds. We both decided not to touch the issue anymore. Her muted gaze hinted to me many things: surely she chose the eternal, enjoyed the eternal, and now it became a sentence. I also felt that she appreciated me and did not want me to live the same way.

With nothing more to discuss, we said goodbye, hoping that we would meet again very soon. The impulse to taste eternity had not died at all.

I returned home. Bravely, In I told my parents what I had experienced over the last few days. I could not hide my surprise at the knowledge that they knew about the "building where no one dies" and had gone through an odyssey similar to mine. My parents had hidden this fact from me throughout my life, but their motive was simple: they did not want to expose me to such a double-edged sword.

A long and tortuous conversation ensued between us. My parents confessed that they also wanted to live eternally to be able to do things, enjoy and assume the state of stillness, and be remembered for what they had achieved thanks to their work as writers. Thanks to their work they learned that there are many forms of eternity, and not all are inherent to physical existence.

It was necessary to end the matter, given the emotional and existential charge that I had been acquiring. One decision: my parents and I started a process to assume eternity in our own way. Thanks to this choice I can tell this story.

Eternal

Nicola Maasdam
England

SHE TRIED TO OPEN HER EYES. She hurt everywhere and wasn't even sure if opening her eyes was possible or indeed wise. They were slightly stuck together like the morning after a heavy night on the tiles, when you didn't bother taking your makeup off before falling into bed - that's if you got that far. Mascara and tears of laughter melting together to form a sticky glue. But she knew the night before hadn't been a fun night out with friends. She knew that much - those nights seemed so far away now.

She tried to lift her head off the floor but it felt heavy and it hurt. She realised the left side of her head was wet. She put a hand up to her face to try and rub her eyes open, then blinking through the morning light, she put her hand to the wet side of her head and felt a bump. Pulling her hand away she squinted at her fingers now sticky with some sort of liquid and congealed blood. She looked at the floor and saw more blood and a puddle of something else…

She recoiled in horror and pulled herself up on the kitchen cabinets and realised every part of her body ached. Managing to stand, she looked at the clock on the oven. 9.27am. She stopped, so confused. The house was quiet. She then remembered it was Friday. Rowan should be at school by now. Greg was probably at work. Automatically her mind kicked into gear. She had to get Rowan to school. Act normal.

Wincing and taking it oh, so slowly, she walked to the stairs to get to the bathroom. "Rowan?" she called, feebly. "Rowan, darling?"

"You look awful."

She turned round and saw Greg. "Good sleep?" he asked, with a smirk. She started to speak but he interrupted, the smirk replaced with a snarl.

"As you couldn't get yourself ready in time I've had to take Rowan to school," he shouted in her face. " And now I'm late for work thanks to you and I've not even had a coffee yet."

She prayed her son hadn't seen her lying on the kitchen floor. He had already witnessed far too much in his six short years. She tried her absolute utmost to keep him from the "stuff" that went on, as she privately referred to it.

Greg bent down towards her as if to kiss her but stopped short and looked at her left eye. It had a large bruise breaking through from the bottom of the cheek all the way up to her eyebrow. Megan instinctively pulled her head back away from his sharply.

He laughed.

"I'd put some ice on that if I were you," he whispered.

He turned to go back up the stairs.

She turned to go back to the kitchen to put the kettle on. He wanted a coffee.

Megan Markham met Gregory Thorne when they were both studying at different colleges and when they were both just eighteen. She was working in town at the Milkymoo Milkshake Shack. She loved the cow-shaped aprons with the silly corporate name on it. Her friends thought it suited her nature, slightly quirky and fun. Greg came in one Saturday with a group of friends. He stood just in the doorway. He thought the name was silly and the product childish so wouldn't go further inside to sit down. His friend Clark shouted over to him,

"Sure you don't want anything, Greg? They have Milkymoo Malibu shakes today?"

Greg scowled. *Pathetic,* he thought. He heard his friends laughing with the dark-haired shop girl in the daft apron. She had a pretty smile. *She was flirting though,* Greg thought. Tart. She glanced over and saw him looking and Megan smiled - this time just for him. He thought they were all making fun of him so he stuck two fingers up at them and walked out.

What an idiot, thought Megan. Then she served the next customer forgetting all about the boy at the door.

"We never actually met at the milkshake shack," Megan would later explain to friends, "we saw each other there for the first time but didn't meet as such."

This is where their stories started to differ, and Greg seemed to have a different recollection which involved Megan poking fun at him, despite her protestations.

Megan and Greg properly met when her college was playing his at netball. Megan and her team had gone into the canteen after the match for a drink.

"Hey! It's my little milkshake moo girl!" Clark shouted across the canteen.

Megan blushed and her girlfriends laughed.

Clark moved towards the girls, tray in hand. Greg sighed and walked closer but stopped at the table to their left. Megan saw Greg and she remembered the two-fingered salute of their last meeting. Greg looked bored to be in the same company as the girls, something which didn't go unnoticed by Megan's friends.

"You ok? Look like someone's farted under your nose."

Everyone laughed. Callie was unashamedly loud and didn't suffer fools. She didn't care. She stared hard at Greg.

"You too good for us?" she continued, smiling wryly at the girls.

"Yes," replied Greg.

He got up glaring at Callie and walked away.

"Your mate is a dick," said Callie to Clark.

Clark laughed a funny half-laugh all the while not taking his eyes off Greg as he watched him leave the hall.

"Best not to wind him up."

Clark glanced at Callie then looked away when her eyes met his. He moved his lips as if to say something but thought better of it and walked away.

The next time Megan and Greg met was on a date organised by their families. They were both members of the same religious organisation and although Megan didn't attend church as often as her parents thought she should, the one thing she knew was that she had to marry into the organisation. Megan's parents were honoured when Greg's father approached one day and told them he thought Megan a good match for his eldest son (besides, she was the only available girl of age within the organisation at the moment. Greg was getting older and his father wanted grandchildren. But Megan's parents chose to ignore these facts).

Greg's family were wealthy and very influential not only within the organisation but also the area they lived in. Megan had no choice but to agree to the date. And eventually to the marriage for fear of being outcast. Love didn't come into it. It was agreed so had to be.

Megan remembered her vows as she was on her hands and knees scrubbing the blood off the kitchen tiles later that morning.

"To love and to cherish. Till death us do part," they had promised each other.

She had made her vows in the presence of God and of course their family and friends. Her parents had made it plain to her the first and last time she had left the marital home after Greg had hit her, just three days into their marriage.

"You, my girl," shouted Megan's dad, "you have made a vow and it would be a mortal sin to break that vow! What did you do to provoke him? You will bring shame upon this family! Go home to your husband NOW!"

Megan had gone home; her dad drove her there. He marched her back up the pathway and made a grovelling apology to Greg for his daughter's behaviour.

"Remember your vows" was her dad's parting shot. She remembered…

"'Till death us do part… "

The words Megan had whispered to herself almost in disbelief as Greg leant towards her for their first kiss on their wedding day. It was clear his heart wasn't in it, nor hers. But from now that was how it must be. She made a promise. Love is Eternal.

But true love eventually appeared in the form of Rowan, all 6lbs 4oz of him. As soon as Megan held him in her arms she finally knew what real love was. She held his face close to hers and breathed his sweet newborn scent in and she whispered, "For Eternity, little man. This love is Eternal."

The following years were tough and all Megan wanted to do was to run away and take Rowan with her. Greg was never violent towards him - yet. She was thankful for that. But she knew Rowan saw "stuff" and that upset her. The one and only person in the world she loved was hurting; he must be. He was quiet and withdrawn and it pained Megan more than anything but if she did leave Greg her church would without doubt track her down and take Rowan from her as they saw that he "belonged" to the father in all circumstances. And when she was found she knew what the consequences would be. So she had to make the best for Rowan and get on with it. As much as it pained her, he would be worse off without her, she reasoned.

Megan had just about finished the list of jobs Greg had left her. The last job wasn't the last on the list but she had left it as long as possible as it was a job she hated. She went into the garage and got the pond vacuum. The large, crystal clear fish pond in the garden she used to love until it became her job to clean it. The pretty orange, red, and silver fish flitting around with the sunlight glinting off their backs was a relaxing sight and Megan used to love lounging by the pond wiggling her fingers in the water attracting the fish.

But that was then. And rare days they were, usually when Greg was away on business. Now, the pond job was such a smelly thing and she had to get down into it to clean it. Even in summer the water was freezing and as she was barefoot, inevitably a fish or two would swim between her ankles or nibble her toes. It never failed to make her jump, which wasn't safe as the floor of the pond was slimy and slippery and a sharp movement would mean Megan would wobble, skid, try to regain her balance, and fall, her whole body unceremoniously splashing under the water.

On this day that was exactly what happened. She slipped right under taking in a mouthful of putrid water. She quickly regained her feet and stood up. Right there and then she decided she wasn't going to clean that pond; sod it! Why should she? He worked, but so did she! Well, at least she did until he put a stop to it. But wasn't the house and the care of Greg and Rowan a full time job?

She waded to the edge of the pond shaking the water from her hair and tipping her head to clear her ears. She heard an excited shout, "Mummy!!" Rowan was coming up the path waving a painting in his hand. It was then she saw Greg. She hadn't realised the time. She hadn't even got tea on yet. She felt the familiar butterflies of dread and fear. He was striding towards her looking mad. She could see he was already shouting but couldn't hear what he was saying.

"… just so you can take your own sweet time and do the heck what you want? You lazy bitch!"

The speech became all the clearer as he got closer to the pond. Megan realised she was still standing waist deep in water. She looked to her right, horrified that Rowan was standing in the garden watching, pure fright in his eyes that were wide open, darting between his Mum and Dad.

"I had a call from the school because you forgot your own son! Do you know how embarrassing that was? It's a good job Miss Hartnett knows what you're like," spat Greg.

Miss Hartnett. All blonde hair and big boobs. Megan hated her. So did Rowan.

"You are the worst mother and poor excuse for a wife there has ever been!"

Megan was fixed to the spot with terror. No words came from her mouth although in her head she was explaining what had happened to Greg and she was screaming at Rowan to go inside. Greg had a look on his face she had never seen before. It was contorted with rage and the loathing and pure anger etched across was something else. He was lunging at her, garden spade in hand. What… ?

The last thing Megan saw was Rowan running up to his dad, mouth open but no sound coming out.

Three months later

"Greg? Greg?"

The blonde woman called out through the kitchen window. "GREG?! Will you come and help me or not?"

She was rifling through the drawers searching for something. Greg hadn't heard. Or he was ignoring her, one or the other. She cursed under her breath then opened a lower drawer.

"Aha!!" she exclaimed, holding a sheet of paper up triumphantly in front of her face.

"They're Mummy's things, Miss Hartnett."

Rowan had come into the kitchen and he made the woman jump.

"What do you want?" she barked, slamming the paper down onto the work surface, "Go away and leave me alone. Brat."

Rowan laughed and walked away. He hummed to himself as he ran his toy car along the dado rail. He got the the end of the hallway.

"I'm telling Mummy," he whispered to himself, looking back over his shoulder.

"Why is there still so much of her shit around here?" the woman muttered to herself, referring to the contents of the drawer but casting an eye towards Rowan.

She carried on rummaging through the drawers despite apparently already finding what she was looking for. She was just being nosey now. She saw a crumpled few sheets of newspaper shoved under a framed photograph of Megan with baby Rowan. She cast aside the photo frame and pulled the papers out. It was the front page of the local paper with the headline "Woman Dies In Tragic Pond Accident." Why he had kept that she had no idea. The paper told how Megan had been playing chase with Rowan round the pond when she slipped and fell, banging her head as she fell into the pond unconscious. Greg had tried to resuscitate her but because the useless child hadn't got help quick enough (her words) it was too late despite Greg's heroic efforts.

"Tragic…" she said, pulling an insincere sad face then screwing the paper up and throwing into the bin with a flourish.

She went back to the drawer which was proving so interesting. Reaching in, her fingers then touched something at the very back of the drawer. She grabbed it and pulled it out.

"What the… ?!"

The blonde woman threw open the back door and stormed over to where Greg was busy knee deep in water, pond vac in one hand and radio in another.

Her lips were moving but his headphones meant he hadn't the foggiest what she was saying but she looked angry. He considered taking out his headphones but didn't have a spare hand. Plus he didn't really want to hear her whining voice going on at him. He had disposed of one pain in the neck and quite frankly was beginning to regret moving this one in so soon.

She was waving something about and was clearly shouting. He looked at the object in her hand and he smiled. Why was Megan's wedding ring box causing so much anger? It made him laugh seeing his new girlfriend in such a state. *She looks an idiot,* he thought.

"You can't afford that handbag for me or an engagement ring but you've still got these in the house? Are you for real? You'd better not be thinking you'll get away with proposing to me with these pieces of tin…
"

Greg looked behind her and saw his son standing there looking bemused. Greg waded closer to the edge of the pond and turned off the vac. Removing his earphones, he looked up.

"What?" he asked.

"Why haven't you sold these?" she asked.

"Because I'm keeping them for Rowan. He can do what he wants with them when he's older."

"Oh, my goodness! You cannot be for real, Greg! You tell me we haven't got enough money to go on holiday or go out for a meal even and you're sitting on these! Sod the kid, especially after he is the reason she's not here anymore! What do you owe him? Sell them!"

Rowan frowned and looked at Greg.

"They're Rowan's," Greg repeated, slowly and deliberately, leaning towards her.

Her face shrivelled as she twisted it into a grimace.

"You're always saying he's just like his useless mother!" she carried on. "He even looks like her. Just like her. Nothing of you there at all. How can you be sure he's even yours?" Her eyes narrowed and she spat as she spoke. "Why let him benefit from them in the future when we can benefit now?"

There was a rather large diamond in the engagement ring and the gold wedding band was heavy. They would be worth a bit. Not her style whatsoever but the cash from them would be nice.

Greg sneered and laughed at her. He muttered something that sounded like "Stupid…"

This just served to enrage her even more.

"You want him to have them? Do you? You think more of him than you do of me? Well he can go and get them, then!" she screamed as she pulled open the lid of the box and grabbed at the rings.

She hurled them into the middle of the pond, then turned on her heels and walked back towards the house calling over her shoulder with venom, "Don't slip and fall while you're finding your rings, Rowan. You never know what might happen."

Now it was Greg's turn to contort his face, and rage spread through his body. That "thing" inside him snapped and he jumped out of the pond, ran towards her and lunged, grabbing for her hair. She gasped in shock and tried to dig her nails into him. This just made him even more furious and he put an arm across her face. She tried to bite him to no avail. He was already pulling her towards the pond and her eyes widened in horror at the realisation of what was to come.

"No, Greg! Stop it! What are you doing?"

Panic gripped her and she glanced across to Rowan.

"Help me, Rowan!" she cried, her fingernails digging into the muddy grass trying to gain a hold with which to stop the relentless dragging of her body across the garden.

Rowan just looked on, expressionless. Greg carried on pulling her thin body towards the pond. She was now in such a panic that no sound came from her mouth. Every ounce of effort was focused on trying to get loose from Greg's grip. They had reached the edge of the pond.

Greg, with still one handful of blonde hair, grabbed the waist of her jeans, lifted her up, and launched her into the pond, her top heavy chest landing first. She went completely under and the cold shock caused a sharp intake of breath.The pond was green, cold, dark, and deep. She couldn't swim.

Greg sat on the edge of the pond and let himself down into the murky water. She bobbed up just in front of him, coughing up putrid liquid from her lungs, splashing, trying to regain her foothold. Greg leant forwards and put his hands on her head, pushing her back down.

Suddenly, Greg felt a heavy pain running down from the top of his head through his spine. He instinctively pulled his hands from her head and put them to his. The pain was excruciating.

Thwack.

His fingers had lessened the blow this time but the force had shattered his knuckles, and he brought his hands down in front of his eyes. He tried to look at his fingers, to make sense of what was happening. Everything was going dark. He felt his legs buckling beneath him. The last thing he remembered was seeing her face, blonde hair matted with pondweed, eyes wide open in terror, staring at a space just behind him. Then she disappeared slowly, back down into the water as if she was being pulled.

Greg felt the cold water flooding his lungs as he lost consciousness.

Rowan ran his car up and down the hospital floor all the time humming to himself contentedly. The doctor stood up, sighed and left the room, leaving Rowan alone. Rowan heard the door lock with a big "clunk".

As soon the doctor left, Rowan looked up and smiled.

"Am I a good boy, Mummy?" he asked, looking at a point in the space across the room.

He laughed, happy with the response. He fingered the two rings on the chain around his neck. Mummy had got them back for him. After all, they were his.

He was happy now that things were back as they should be - just him and Mummy.

As Mummy always says, Love is Eternal.

At the Lunar Path

Nino Memanishvili
Republic of Georgia

I WAS A STRUGGLING, aspiring journalist working in the city's respectable newspaper. My editor was terribly unhappy with me, and nothing to be surprised about! Throughout the whole year I was not able to write even one typical article.

One day, Barbara, my editor's blonde assistant, informed me that my boss wanted to see me. Nervous sweat poured from my face. I already knew what he was going to say, that our edition is one of the most prestigious and people do not work here by chance. Unfortunately, my intuition did not deceive me. Mr. Schmidt was sitting comfortably in his huge leather armchair smoking a pipe and nervously typing on his old IBM computer. He started to lecture me without glancing at me.

'So, one year has passed and you are still tapping in the same place. The time has come to make a choice. I'm giving you one month; either you write an article that meets our standards or you can find a new job. I think everything is clear!'

'Yeah, Mr. Schmidt, I … ' I whispered.

He returned to his typing, which meant that the lecture was over. I was able to exhale only after I left his office. I knew it; I knew it from the very beginning that this day would eventually come. Here I was, sitting in my narrow but comfortable office, and I could not stop thinking what the hell I could do to save my ass.

I was looking around my office, which I was definitely going to miss. I would miss this old goddamn company, perhaps I am even gonna miss Mr. Schmidt with his always grieving face and of course, his always confused secretary.

I am in the shit! It is time to get used to the fact that I do not have a job anymore. Thus I can avoid false expectations. Most of all I was worrying what I would say to Professor Hawkins. He always had high hopes for me. Actually I got this job thanks to his recommendations; otherwise I really could not make it here. He wrote to Schmidt that if he did not hire me, he would make a fatal mistake. Yeah, Schmidt made a fatal mistake when he fired me and now he was thinking how to fix it.

If I really am going to lose this job, I do not have more prospects beyond writing eulogies. Excellent! This is why I studied for four years at the university and drilled my brain writing colloquiums. And how desperately I need this job! My parents are still paying off my tuition fees, and the flat rent costs too much. I am fucked up! Going back home and living with my family is not an option. Do not get it wrong; I do love my family, my parents, my little sister, and my home, but I do not want to return a complete, empty-handed loser. When you are from a little town and make it into prestigious university, and then start to work for a notable company, everyone starts to expect something from you. Everyone was talking only about me, so just imagine going back and declaring that I just sucked! Apart from this I felt both regret and frustration, because this year I really tried my best. Maybe nothing was approved by goddamn Schmidt, but I really worked hard… that's why I felt discouraged…

It was already midnight when I left the office. I preferred to walk to my shabby apartment, which was not far from my work. It was the beginning of December; breezy rain was coming and it was quite cold already. I could not stop thinking. Frankly speaking, Schmidt was a real pig. He was ready to fire me for Christmas. I could not have dreamt about a better present. Tomorrow was Saturday and I promised Professor Hawkins that I'd visit him. He was the only one I could open my heart to, and maybe the only one who could save my skin.

* * *

Hawkins lived in the city's most prestigious district. He had a huge, duplex-type apartment with a gym, spa, and everything. His much younger, super sexy lover opened the door and led me to the living room, where the professor was resting. He was happy to see me.

'I thought you would not come. Good to see you kiddo!' he said.

'How are you doing professor?'

'I am fine… not to mention that I am getting old.'

'C'mon, man,' I said.

'Ok, leave it. How is your job?' he asked, looking at me in a way like he was examining me.

'I am in deep shit and everything is getting on my nerves.'

'Ha, ha, ha! We are all there. Tell me something new! Look around, dude! I am surrounded with pills and medicines; the doctor also forbade me to drink! And you know, my boy, alcohol produces such a nasty feeling of a physical revulsion that it is actually the best way to get rid of any shit you have inside. Now everything is finished for me. I'd be better off sitting in the mud. You are young and fresh. When you are young the whole world is at your feet…You should not worry. He kind of yelled at me."

'Um…. Sir … of course …I understand… ' I muttered.

I think he felt sorry for me after what I told him. He asked me kindly, 'Hey, tell me what's up?"

'I am not able to write even one fucking article. Schmidt does not like anything; he gave me one month.'

'Yeah, he is a cool guy; you know he was labelled as the godfather of journalism. He is an absolute heavyweight in his field. He used to compete with me, we had the stories… It is past now; we are not friends, nor enemies, but I respect him and he respects me, that's all.' He paused for a while and continued. 'He has rules and if you want to stay there, you need to follow them, so it's up to… '

'Yeah, I know. I understand this…I am suffering from writer's block; I assume,' I said.

'Shit happens.'

Hawkins' young companion brought coffee and candies in the room. She was very attentive to him and very friendly to me. Actually the professor knew how to inspire and attract people.

'You know, actually, once Mr. Schmidt advised me to interview one award-winning actor,' I said 'This literally killed me. In order to interview an actor of that scale, I needed some contacts, which unfortunately I did not have; and where could I find those contacts, when I was always sitting at my desk writing trashy articles that never made it into the newspaper.'

'Old man has a sense of humour!' he said, and laughed. 'Yeah contacts, this is the thing. Actors are like a tribe; you cannot come to them just because… you need to have some kind of reputation… You know… I think that we all live as 'nomadic tribes' nowadays: there are mountaineers, fashion people, painters, writers, lawyers, photographers… not to mention surfers and politicians. They are impossible… You cannot approach these people easily. If you want their attention, you need to get one of them… But I believe in you. Do not disappoint me, kid!'

'This is what I am afraid most,' I said sadly.

'Hey, look here, boy!' he cried. 'Do not even dare to surrender! Do not show this to Schmidt; he will devour you. I saw him a lot destroying people; young blood like you! And I want you to understand that I cannot interfere, because it is your fucking life and you need to deal with it, kiddo!'

'Perhaps I need to interview Graf Dracula or Doctor Frankenstein.'

'You need to surprise him! So if you think that you even need to visit an oracle for this, then you should not waste time,' he said, and smiled.

'Oracle…C'mon Professor, are you kidding?' I said, and laughed.

'Hey, I want the miracle to happen in your brain. I am trying to root it to you!'

'Sometimes, I even do not know what I want. I enjoy writing, but not what Schmidt wants to see. Sometimes I think that I should not have abandoned writing novels and short stories, sometimes deep in my heart I feel that I am not doing the right thing and I am not in the right place.'

'Schmidt represents the mass media! Whether we want to or not, we cannot get away from this. Everything and everyone moves around masses. I want to vomit on them, Martin, if we observe thoroughly mass does not create anything truly worthy. When you are different or think differently you cannot be related to masses any more. You are literally becoming the enemy to them, and when they see this, they start to panic. If you are not strong enough they will eat you alive. Mass selects the attack as the best method of defence. And elusive is the freedom of speech. Masses do not have freedom of thinking and speech, they do not decide anything; they live in illusion. Masses are obsessed with performance, they do not need ideas, views, opinions; mass is afraid of everything. They are like mice hiding in the walls; they obey those in power, which does not exist as a material substance.

We already exist in the 21st century. The universe has reached perhaps the zenith of civilisation, but people remain on the same level. They are not able to develop; they do not want to change. Sometimes I think that they are asleep and do not want to wake up,; maybe it is somehow related to the well-established dominance of social network and by over-activated mass-media outlets. This keeps people in virtually-induced comas; it's like being guinea pigs swirling in clouds of dust. Mass is obsessed with performance; they are like spectators who are watching a play without even asking if they like the play or not? It is not vital at all, no matter, they keep watching until they are told that now they need to watch the another play. They only change seats from where they are observing the performance; and this seat is only thing they have, the only thing they care about.'

So you can be poor, but doing what you love, or you can be rich and be soulless; be like a machine, be like a mass, so, you need to think about this, Martin,' he said and winked at me with a smile.

* * *

I stayed at the professor's until late evening. When I went outside it was terribly cold, but I was so overwhelmed and taken by thoughts that I did not care about the weather. In the street there was winter silence; the city was getting ready for Christmas, and thousands of lights hung everywhere. Shop windows were decorated for the holidays. And here was the first snow, which would last for several months, almost to the beginning of spring. I was thinking, *Well, that's winter ... how quickly time goes by...!* Like it was yesterday when I was still a student, full of hopes and expectations.

And now everything seems so fake compared to those student days. That is something that deeply pains my heart. I walked a lot, but I did not feel tired at all. I enjoyed walking in the winter silence. The road was lit well by the moon; everything was perfect, not to mention that I was on the verge of a nervous breakdown.

My wandering took too long. Frankly speaking I did not even want to go back to my apartment as I was struggling with insomnia and tossing and turning in bad had no appeal. I passed by the old cinema. They were showing a Christmas film that I watched as a child with my parents and little sister. For some time, I stood in front of the ticket office wondering if I really wanted seeing this film.

Finally, I gave in. The cinema was almost empty; only several amorous couples sat in the back seats. I sat in front. The film started and I was back in my memories, back to my home town. I remembered my dad, who is a bus driver; I remembered his hands gnarled from forty years at the steering wheel, and I felt sorry. The film was halfway when I went outside for a smoke. I puffed a French cigarette and inhaled the smoke deep into my lungs like this could smooth my fucked up emotions. The moon was shining brightly and snow fell lightly. I could see my own shadow on the ground. It was already midnight. The silent city was plunged into deep sleep, and cars passed infrequently.

'In several hours I will not be alive anymore!'

I turned around to see an athletic, elegantly dressed man before me.

'What? I am sorry, Air, are you alright... ?' I asked in confusion.

'Heh, I never felt as good as I do knowing that the end is close.'

'I am sorry. I cannot understand you!'

'And, you do not have to!' he said and paused, then added, 'Perhaps you do not know what to do with yourself and the time you have!'

'Is it written on my face?'

'You know, since you are here… I guess I'm here for the same reason or… '

I did not respond. I just lowered my head; perhaps I agreed with him despite the fact that I did not want to…

'Maybe you will listen to me. I mean…. when I told you that I will not be alive in several hours, I was not joking!' he told me seriously.

'I am sorry for saying this, but either you are very smart, or just crazy,' I said.

'Neither one nor the other! I am the one who asks you to give just couple of hours to a man who has something to tell… I do not want to die without this… '

'I… I do not even know what to say, Sir…'

'Do not … Do not say anything! I only ask… listen to me!' he begged.

Still I did not want to believe whatever he was saying. I was completely sure that he was insane, and he was … Just in another way…. It seems crazy, I know, but I agreed… I agreed to listen.

'I was born in April in this city. My mother was gentle and sensitive person. My father died in car accident when I was six. My mother raised me alone. She tried her best to give me happy life full of bright memories. I attended a French boy's gymnasium a few miles away from home. I was studying well and got excellent marks; I was very communicative and was on perfect terms with my teachers and classmates. I was a promising adult, but my world was soon shattered and then… what happened… changed everything.

'The days of my youth fled like early morning snow. I never wanted or planned to become a cold-hearted motherfucker, but the road of life took me in different direction. The story I am going to tell you… it's my life. I feel that death is close and I want to confess. I do not believe in any religion. I do not believe in God, I especially do not believe in priests. You are complete stranger to me and I feel that it will be easier for me to talk to you. I found out that strangers are less prone to judgment and criticism, and trust me ,these are last things I want to hear.'

'When you are young sometimes some bad things happen in wrong time. You do not have experience and easily get influenced. Now I hate myself for this, but it is too late... I cannot blame anyone. I could always choose the better way, but had preferred the wrong... and you know it is strangely ridiculous that it is always easier to be wrong than right... maybe being right is a luxury, which only few can afford...

'I know I am a sinner! I have done more bad things than good. I already told you that I am completely faithless, perhaps this is my greatest sin! You know, I realised that man should have a belief in something or someone. I do not mean Buddha or Jesus Christ. It is important to believe in love and kindness, which I always lacked. And you know why? Because love and mostly love is a type of faith, which gives you the ability to believe in your inner self; and somewhere, somehow, you can be better than you are, but unfortunately I always lacked this.'

'Do not ask me questions; do not try to interrupt me! Just listen! Do not ask my name; anyway I won't tell you, for you and for everyone I am Nameless! Get ready; get ready to listen to me! Prepare yourself to listen the confession you have never heard before, to hear the most terrible thing you could ever read or see somewhere! Here I am, the man whose soul and body is heavy with terrible guilt. Get ready to listen to the road of life, which did not leave me even one human close to my heart. Listen and do not live like me, do not turn your back to yourself, do not live to be disgraced! And you know, my stranger, we are not born alone, but we die in complete loneliness. This is the only truth; the rest is an illusion!'

'And you should remember one thing; every person has some kind of mission, or role or call it as you wish. I do not know what my mission was, maybe that I had to tell you the story of my fucking life! Maybe the story of this miserable unnamed man is going to change your life, maybe it will help you to make the right decision, and decision-making is the greatest burden! But remember that you can always chose the right way, always. It is difficult as I said, and I do have experience in this, but the more correct your decision, the more accomplished you are going to feel! I was always too weak for this despite the fact I thought that I was strong.'

'I was only eighteen, fresh from studies, when the war broke out with fascists. I volunteered in the army. My mother opposed it but I believed that it was my duty. I had to be there, so I went; whatever I saw there, it is not possible to express with words, so I will be as brief as I can. I was following the flow of the war, which took me to Anzio, Italy, where I was severely wounded. Actually I did not remember anything. When I came to, I was in the military hospital. I stayed there for one month. There and exactly there I felt what type of beast was hiding inside my flesh. I longed for massacre. I did not want to remain at the hospital any longer. I could not stand seeing my compatriots dying in the walls of the old hospital. Men should not die in a bed; warriors must be killed on the battlefield. I wanted to be back in combat as soon as possible. The desire to avenge my comrades kept me on the hop. Fortunately I was soon released and was back on the field. I sent a lot unworthy and worthy opponents to the afterlife and frankly speaking, I did have any regret, moreover, I LIKED it....'

'The war was over; I returned as a hero. Everyone was expecting something extraordinary from me, but I had no idea what I wanted. I knew only that I missed battle, I missed the blood of enemies, and the sound of the bullet. Once I was driving back from a war friend's late at night. I had driven a few kilometres when I saw some stranger on my way. I stopped the car. He said that he was feeling bad and asked me if I could drop him at the local hospital. I did not refuse. We drove a few kilometres in silence. The car started making a strong noise. I stopped and told my passenger that I had to check the engine. When I got out of the car, my passenger followed, said wanted to smoke. In a nutshell, he wanted to kill me for the purpose of robbing me. He did not know whom he had come across. I killed the son of a bitch and left him there on the road. Not caring about the consequences, I quietly drove on; the beast inside me was satisfied. Killing him was just a matter of choice. If I did not kill him then he would kill me. I could see clearly that ordinary life was no different from war.'

'So, what to say. Of course I could continue studying at university, however, I preferred being the member of criminal gang. As I told you, I was young, my war friend suggested that it was a good way to good money. We made not only good money, but a lot of it. I realised that the criminal world was attracted to me like a magnet. I realised it was my fate. I was a good shooter, a good fighter, and I drove like a a professional racer. I could fit in socially at any level; with boozers, I was the boozer, with hooligans I was the hooligan, with killers I was the killer.'

'I was earning huge amounts of money mostly by robbing, stealing, and racketeering; if I had to, I killing without batting an eyelid. I was getting rich and living the high life by being evil. I liked gambling and won and lost lots of money, and I could leave whatever I won at a casino and never gave a damn about it. I liked woman, and I could spend my last cent on them. You'd be surprised that they loved me back; well, I dined in luxurious restaurants, drove expensive cars, wore the last fashion, always looked good. How could they imagine that behind this mask was a completely evil man.'

'The thing is that a rich man is loved and liked by everyone, not only by women. The main thing is that you have money, how you earn it, what kind of soul and heart you have; no one is interested in this. Interest in your personality is only determined by how much you are ready to pay. Fortunately, wealth is not the universal 'illness', if so we would have been overwhelmed by it. Wealth would have absorbed, strained, sucked the soul from us.'

Actually, women are strange creatures, to their misfortune they are attracted to the worst. So was the case with HER; you know she was somehow special. First of all, she was not related to the world I belonged to; her family was intelligent and respected. We were seeing each for a year, then I got bored and left her. We had son; he was named after me. Then she moved somewhere and I eventually completely forgot about her ….until …'

The nameless stranger paused for a while, took breath, and continued.

'You cannot be lucky forever. We were robbing the central bank when my friend, who introduced me to the crime world, was seriously wounded. We could not take him to the hospital. Instead, we went to one of our conspirator's flat. The doctor working on us did what he could, and I gave him my blood twice through transfusion, but unfortunately he could not be saved. His death destroyed me and made me more despicable and impatient. I mourned him for forty days; losing a best friend could have been a wakeup call for me, but I did not even try to think about my life, only about the crimes I committed. I was the one who was building his own happiness on behalf of someone else's suffering.'

'Soon, my mother died; luckily she did not know anything about my life. I was seldom at home; I was like a steppe wolf. I am happy that she left this world never knowing who I really was. Deep in her heart she knew that I was troubled. I know she felt that I was not ok. She never asked about anything, but I could read the questions in her eyes. However, she was my mother and could not tolerate to the fact that her son, a war hero, could so absolutely evil. I stepped in the world of mud and as the further I stepped, teh deeper I fell into it. You know, it's like entering a dense forest. You go and eventually you are lost; this was what happened to me. The life I chose for myself had been so fierce that it made me rough and coarse, killing the little humanity I still had inside. I lived in the world of boozers, the depraved, criminals, and robbers, a world where no one thinks about feelings and emotions …'

'I founded the crime cartels throughout the country. Everything worked with clockwise accuracy. I felt like the lord of the world and in my world of crime, I was indeed. From being a gang member I controlled an entire network. Believe it or not, I was considered by many authorities to be the most dangerous man alive and I was wanted for acts of crime in more countries than any other man in the world. But I had many faces, many identities; I was a citizen of many different countries, illegally of course, having at least twenty fake passports. I was changing my appearance and locations quite often, so it was practically impossible to locate me.'

'People in my crime cartel, not all of them were from the street or had a criminal background. You will be surprised that some of them were lawyers, doctors, people who were true professionals, but injustice and disappointment caused them to choose a different circle of life. My case was different; as I told you I realised quite quickly what my calling was. I was doomed from the very beginning, and believe it or not, I felt sorry for people who were not inclined to lies and crimes, who gave many years to studies and perhaps had hopes and expectations that they could achieve something, but they were let down so many times by governmental machines and absolutely unreasonable rules, that finally they were ready to pass the most terrible verdict on themselves. I really do not want you to think that I considered myself to be a messiah or someone to whom all the frustrated people were coming. I just somehow could relate to them,. Maybe I was cold-blooded motherfucker, but I could understand people. Certain people are not born to be villains; it's the environment that compels them to get on the wrong side.'

'Perhaps I need to explain my philosophy, my attitude, and understanding of my vision of life, being... maybe then you can understand this Nameless man. For me existed only anarchistic wisdom - the strong dominates the weak! I was completely sure that being strong gave me the absolute right to oppress the weak, like a wolf dominates a lamb. I thought that the lamb is weak because it should be attacked by the wolf, but it is not so ,of course. There are those of us who contribute to evil and praise and worship violence.

Many kings, emperors, and commander-in-chiefs are buried in tombs, and millions of people visit to pay homage to them. Astronomical sums are spent on the maintenance of and protection of their graves. Does anyone think what most of them have done? Why does no one think of how many people have been sacrificed to their ambitious ideas? Why are their ideas justified? And all these leaders, starting from Alexander the great to Napoleon Bonaparte, are called the greatest ruler. They oppressed the weak, forced hundreds of women and children into slavery against their will, they killed people, poor people, trampled their faith and ideology... and us? Maybe we do not rule the whole world, but what do we do? We are cutting the throat of a helpless lamb; we turned this sinless creature into human consumption for food. Why does mankind not eat the meat of a wolf or lion? Because they are strong; the wolf does not give up easily, it is not possible to tame him... So who are we now? Tell me! We are all oppressors, and an ordinary farmer does not differ from me. We both kill, we both justify our actions through vocabulary.'

'Captain Ahab was defeated by Moby Dick; he was defeated in the battle by something stronger than he, but he had fought against evil, and at least he tried. Unfortunately Ahab's are rare in history or in literature. Nobody glorifies them, and and you know why? Because they lost the battle. Humanity counts only winners, no matter what value was obtained by the victory; and history is written by the winners not looking on the other side of the coin. So now you know that I just did not want to be the loser, I did not want to be an ordinary nothing, but to my misfortune I failed and all my castles crumbles.'

'I am not a believer, as I told you, because religion is the biggest evil to control the masses. They do not want the idea of God; they want only ceremonies. I am evil, but I am not hypocritical. If Jesus and Buddha walked barefoot and were poorly fed, why it is so that today's clergy drive Cadillacs and wear gold and silk? Where is humility and simplicity?

After all, is not it the basis of all religions and philosophies. And you know there are many people in my circle who are financing the construction of golden temples for the redemption of their sins. They confess and receive communion, they pray to their 'gods' and their 'gods' 'forgive' them everything. Indulgence and inquisition changed the surface, but the core remained the same.'

'This is what I believed and how, but now I am done with my philosophy. Now I do not know anything and I do not care. My ideologies crashed, like they did not exist at all. What I knew and know is not important any more; I am just a human, wish I this or not. I want you to know, and this is word of a man, the man with tortured soul, that I never used force on women or on honest and simple people. I was stealing from those who stole from the masses. I was killing the ones who truly deserved this; I thought it was totally fair. You may ask who gave me this right; I will answer you – myself.'

He paused. All this time we walked side by side. He seemed very nervous. Nameless man was smoking, not just smoking, but literally eating cigarettes, puffing madly one by one. Then he took the deep breath and continued.

'And now, my story is coming to the end. I do not have much time. November 31st was the most fateful day of my life. We were out on a job; perhaps you are surprised that the head of powerful criminal cartel would do this. Sitting in an office has never been my cup of tea, despite being the boss. I thought that it was right to be on the street and, moreover, this was boosting the motivation for new recruits as they could fight with the general! It is so ridiculous now! I was the general of false expectations and dreams.'

'Actually it was not typical job. My presence was vital; we had to deal with one guy called 'Turk'. He owed me a lot; you perhaps have heard something about gangster divergence; that was it. His house was protected by hundreds of security guards. I did not want to involve a lot of my people in this so we found a simple solution. You have heard the saying, 'fortress breaks from the inside', so we did, however, unfortunately for me, I could not properly assess my enemy. Some of my guys were killed in bilateral shooting. I was enraged and ran into Turk's office all alone, fielding bullets like a crazy man. I once again felt like I was on the battlefield, taking revenge for my gang members. Turk and his personal guards were dead; the blood and malice was taken. All of sudden I heard a woman scream. She ran down from the upstairs. I could see her mad face and crazy eyes, yet she seemed so familiar, like I had seen her somewhere, but I could not remember when and where. Perhaps she was Turk's wife or lover; I had no idea and was not interested either.

The entire room was drenched in blood. She was looking for someone. Suddenly she stopped, fell on her knees, and cried with agony, 'My son, my son!' I slowly started to move towards her. She was hugging a bloody little body in her arms, squeezing tightly. I came closer. It was a child, a little boy. I could not believe that I had not noticed him. How could I do this! It was against my rules. No children, no women could be ever hurt. But I did this. I looked at the boy; his face seemed familiar as well. I was looking at him, trying to remember something, and I remembered he looked exactly like me when I was gymnasium student. Holy Shit!

Now I recognised the woman, it was HER, women I dated many years ago, who had a son by me, whom she named after me. It was my SON. So, she and Turk? How? How could I miss this? My son lived in Turk's house. My vision blurred. I was looking at little boy's face; it was my boy, my flesh and blood, part of my soul and spirit. I could not hear anything; I was still holding the guns in my hands, standing frozen in one place. It was deadly silent, only the woman's cries could be heard.

Here I was in my forties, beaten by life, and he, my son in his twelfth year, young, pure, spotless, life still unseen, brutally killed by his father, by ME. I dropped the gun, then looked on my hands, hands which killed this innocent soul. I could not stand the evil spirit that had fallen into my body that enslaved, oppressed, and subdued my mind. I wanted to run away from that place. I do not remember how I got outside and got into the car. It was already dawn.I was driving crazily down the narrow, slippery road. I remembered old tale about the shepherd and lamb. There is such thing - if the flock is well guarded by skilful shepherds, the wolf is no longer dangerous. My son was the innocent lamb and I had to be the shepherd who would have protected him, but I was the wolf that thought it was justified to kill the weak.'

'I was driving as though in a daze; indecisive and as helpless as a newborn. Mountains were covered in snow and the breeze was cold. Nothing was moving on the road. On the left there was a ravine and on the right, a canyon. I stepped on the gas. In front of me was a turn; I do not even remember how I tumbled down the canyon. Shit! I was alive and unhurt. I fell into a river and the water turned red from the blood on my son. I was fighting the strong currents. The water was ice cold, and I felt like I was losing my mind. Though the current took me to the riverbank. Unfortunately for me, I was still alive. I was not even worthy of death.'

'I barely reached my flat, unintentionally stopping by the huge mirror hanging in the corridor. How I hated my appearance, hated these hard-hearted strong arms, muscular body, long neck, dense chestnut hair. My body was fuelled to take revenge. How I wanted to cut in pieces this unholy hated man looking dishonestly from the mirror. I roared like a beast and shattered the mirror with my head. I could not stand looking at myself anymore, looking at the hands that killed my own son.'

'I was not in the mood to take chances, so I called the loyal doctor. He injected me with the poison; it's an old but proven and very painful method, and I deserved this pain.'

During all this time, I could not see the eyes of my mysterious Nameless. His hood was pulled over his head do that his eyes were not visible. Only time after a while could I see sparkles flashing from his eyes. The eyes are the mirror of the human soul. You cannot look into the heart of human, you can never know what excites and worries him, but the eyes will soon show you that. When he finished his story, he took off his hood, and in his glance there was so much grief and sorrow that I could not bear the sight anymore and lowered my eyes. I am not ashamed to admit that I felt sorry for him.

'And now, my stranger, the time has come. The poison will work soon! Leave me!' he said.

'Sir, please let me…'

He interrupted me. 'I told you already that we die alone. I never was a man of illusions; I beg you to leave me with my past shadows. This is between us only, but before you leave, let me ask you one question.'

'Sure, whatever you want.'

'You think that I am terrible person, yes?'

'Judgment is not my business; I am just thankful to you!'

'What for?'

'That you helped me with my decision.'

'I hope you do not want to become a criminal?' he asked with slight smile.

'No, on the contrary, I was on the verge of turning into someone I do not consider myself. You did something genuinely good for me. Thank you!'

'One good thing does not count. This is eternal, trust me! However, I am happy if it so; now go on your way and do not look back. You know, sometimes I want to be back in my childhood when I was studding at gymnasium, when everything was still ahead, when I could choose the right way, the way of love and kindness,' he said regretfully and turned his back.

Walking down the road well-lit by the moon, he went to take his final step at the lunar path. He asked me not to look back, but I did. He was moving slowly, then he started to collapse and eventually fell down. The man considered by many authorities to be the most dangerous man alive was now fossilised for ages, and somehow I felt something deep in my heart flutter, like my heart skipped a beat.

I went to my apartment. I knew only one thing - I had to be honest with myself. I know I never could be like a nameless stranger and I know I do not want to be a slave to the rat race, I just want to be me.

* * *

'Mister Schmidt.'

'Yes.'

'Martin sent this parcel for you.'

'What parcel?'

'The article. He met the deadline.'

'Yeah, hand it to me. Let's see…'

'……………hmmm.'

'Mr. Schmidt, what happened?'

'Heh…. Hawkins was right…this guy has a future.'

'So, he wrote a good article?'

'The best I have seen so far.'

'May I have a look?'

'Sure.'

'But, Mr. Schmidt…these are blank sheets.'

'Yes, Barbara, these are blank sheets. Paper bears everything, a death sentence or confession of love, cursing or congratulations, dismissal or promotion, everything…blank paper means new life, a fresh start, and new opportunities…heh, this kid definitely surprised me.'

'Do you want me to call him or …?'

'There is no need. He made his decision; he choose his way. It took time, but it was worth it.'

END

2017

A Matter of Life or Death

Paul Hale
England

SHE LOOKED IN THE MIRROR and noticed, with satisfaction, how much older she was looking. There were more wrinkles and the fresh-faced appearance, thankfully, was starting to wane. In her head, she knew she ought to be grateful for living an extended and eventful life. In her heart, there was only one further experience she felt any enthusiasm for and was ashamed by it. Wanting to die went against every natural human instinct and, for months, she had tried unsuccessfully to nurture a desire to live that might override her unnatural wish to die.

She had not always felt this way about her appearance or about life. The first hundred years had been marvellous, despite a hint of boredom around the centenary. By the end of the second hundred, the novelty value had well and truly worn off. Now, after three-hundred years, there seemed barely any point in living at all. While everyone she had ever known could hardly bring themselves to think about death, Patience dreamed of it. Normal people regarded longevity as a blessing. For Patience, even her own name now sounded like a curse and the irony of it grated on her. Most people, on occasion, chat with friends and muse over what it would be like to have the chance to live their life over again or even to live forever. How wonderful it must be having a second go at things using wisdom acquired over the years. Patience would excuse herself from such conversations. For her, it was not hypothetical.

The 'Black Death' plague in 1665 was a significant memory. Patience remembered getting married a year or two before the outbreak and having two young children by the time the first bubonic cases were reported. Her own mother and grandmother had been born during the previous outbreaks of 1625 and 1603. They had both survived and passed down stories from her great grandmother about the original 1593 episode. Her mother's warning words, spoken often, had made a deep impression on her: "Patience, at the first sign of plague get out of London." In part, she had heeded this advice by taking her children to relatives who lived on the Suffolk coast but she had then returned to London to stay with her husband who dared not leave his place of work. A fear of plunging his family into abject poverty due to loss of employment outweighed his fear of disease, and Patience would not abandon him.

Against all odds her mother, grandmother, and great-grandmother had survived successive outbreaks of the plague, but Patience did not expect to do so herself. Yet that was exactly what happened. Her husband was less fortunate. He died in her arms and she had walked along in sorrow with the cart that took his body away. After exposure to the burial site, the authorities regarded her as doomed and only fit for collection work. Consequently, she was designated the job of helping with the removal of the dead. During this period, she made many friends due to her kindness and disregard to her own well-being while collecting persons deceased.

When, finally, the outbreak was declared to be over, Patience went to collect her children and returned to live under the protection of a wealthy lady who had lost all her own family to the plague. This benefactor, Mrs. Fareham, felt a debt of gratitude to Patience having several times watched, grief stricken, while her Collections team came and went with a promise to see her nearest and dearest buried "decent, proper and dignified." That promise, although unlikely, had been her only consolation upon finding herself the lone survivor in a big, empty suburban house. Inviting a fellow survivor and her children into her home was not just a one-way benefit. For the ageing Mrs. Fareham, the young mother and her offspring became a new family, and she drew comfort from seeing other children blossom into their teenage years.

Naturally, Patience pondered on her own escape from the plague and the similar improbable achievement of her ancestors. Such reflections were private. She did not boast or seek opinions about her plague-beating luck. On the contrary, she steered well clear of the topic. These were still dangerous times for females suspected of witchcraft. For this reason, she dared not talk of the matter with others in case she found herself gaining a dangerous reputation. She was baffled but, as time went by, became less preoccupied with an explanation and more inclined simply to savour her good luck and enjoy her family.

As her children grew older something else began to preoccupy her thoughts - she was not ageing. Her wealthy patroness owned a good mirror so Patience could view her own image with accuracy. Fortunately, Mrs. Fareham's eyesight had started to diminish so she was unable to see Patience with the clarity required to notice anything unusual. Her children did not pay any attention to the matter as, to them, she was simply 'mother' and the natural constant in their lives. Meanwhile her raven hair continued to frame her symmetrical features and her youthful skin radiated good health.

The children were in their early teenage years when a male shopkeeper remarked to Patience, "You're a lucky woman Patience, the way you keep so fresh looking, it's amazing." To most women that would have made their day or even their week. For Patience, the compliment felt like a blow. In that instant, she knew her life was going to change. She muttered a quiet "thank you" and left the shop hastily without buying anything. The only thing she took from that shop was the clear message that people had begun to notice. It was a wake-up call.

The next day she set off with the children to her sister, Elizabeth, on the Suffolk coast. She selected her clothes carefully to produce a mature look and tied her hair back to create a more severe appearance. Her brother-in-law opened the door upon her arrival and greeted her cheerfully with "Patience, come in, you look healthy as a herring." She knew this dubious assessment was high praise from Jack who was a fisherman but at least he had not made any specific reference to youthfulness. As for the children, they were delighted to be back again with their 'seaside' relatives.

Patience returned to London after staying only two nights having explained that Mrs. Fareham was unwell and needed her back in London. This was not a lie, because her benefactor had indeed become unwell lately. The lie was claiming she had brought the children to Suffolk so she could care for the old lady. The real reason was to get them away before they, too, noticed their own skin not looking much younger than their mother's. The childless Elizabeth and Jack were secretly thrilled to have Daniel and Katie to stay again. It felt like a ready-made family. Furthermore, Daniel showed an immediate interest in matters of fishing. This was gratifying to Jack, though it took him a while to adapt to the fact that the younger Katie seemed just as interested! In no time, they were both getting involved in a hands-on way with the various chores of a fishing family.

Upon her return, Patience found Mrs. Fareham to be noticeably worse than when she had left a few days before. The doctor was called for and became a regular visitor but Mrs. Fareham steadily deteriorated. Patience found herself in a turmoil. She loved dearly the old lady whom she had come to regard as a beloved aunt yet, at the same time, yearned to leave the neighbourhood and could not but help appreciate the convenience of an impending death. One day, Mrs. Fareham was visited by an officious and imposing stranger accompanied by a younger assistant, whose development of these professional traits was well on track too. After they left, Patience went straight upstairs.

"I've updated my will, Patience," spoke the frail lady sitting up a little in bed, "and I have no relatives except you whom I regard as my own kin. Everything goes to you. No questions just now, Patience. All that legal talk and form signing has exhausted me. I must have a little nap. We can chat about it later if you wish."

The chat never took place. Mrs. Fareham's little nap lasted almost two days before she entered that longest of all sleeps. Later the same week, Patience was barely out of her funeral clothes before arranging the sale of the property. She needed to live somewhere else where she was not known. Already she was adapting her lifestyle and walked further afield to do shopping to avoid meeting people she knew. She placed the sale of the house in the hands of the imposing solicitor and left the area for rented accommodation twenty miles away. This marked the beginning of her new way of life. It was characterised by invented tales about her past, present, and even her plans. She knew that she could only stay in one place for a limited amount of time; a few years at best, before moving on. Accordingly, she became adept at inventing stories about where she had just come from, why she had moved to the area, and what her intentions were.

People were not at ease until they felt they had 'thoroughly' established these basic 'facts' about her when she arrived anywhere as a newcomer. In truth, their enquiries were anything but thorough and rarely were there any genuine facts. Patience developed her abilities in this area to such a high level that she could work on her next story whilst living out her current one. By the time she felt it necessary to move on, she would be able to start again seamlessly somewhere else in an environment and situation she had pre-prepared. Faced with such a charming open-faced person such as Patience, folks were perfectly happy to accept her stories as valid.

She had gone back to visit the children after six months, having first taken considerable trouble to buy an expensive wig with a few greying hairs and applying makeup to show signs of ageing. She pretended to her sister that Mrs. Fareham was still alive and needed help and "could the children stay just a little longer please?" Jack and Elizabeth could scarcely believe their good fortune as they had grown attached to the children and felt their lives enriched. They felt guilty not making efforts to encourage the children go back to their mother and even more so when Patience insisted on leaving money towards their keep. Daniel and Katie had their share of conflicting emotions too. Though very pleased to see their mother, they inwardly felt a sense of relief at not having to go back just yet to what now seemed a comparatively dull past life in London.

Patience maintained regular correspondence for a year before visiting again, this time with more grey hairs added into the wig. By now, her two children were firmly established as part of the Suffolk fishing family. Not only were they clearly feeling at home with their aunt and uncle, they radiated health, contentment, and happiness from their current life by the sea. Jack had grown to rely on the help and energy of the youngsters and Elizabeth had started to regard them as her own. Patience was astute enough to see all this and deemed it time to arrange matters on a more permanent basis. She revealed that Mrs. Fareham had recently passed away, which meant the children could come back to London, "at least I'm assuming that is what everybody wants?" she had added without looking anyone in the eye.

After allowing a few moments for an awkward silence to develop and for their obvious disappointment to take root, she had skilfully turned the conversation around to how they could, after all, remain in Suffolk while she returned to London. She left a forwarding post box style address for communications stating, by way of explanation, that the London house was to be sold under the terms of the will. She avoided going into any more details about the legacy but did say Mrs. Fareham had not forgotten her and she would be fine. In this way, she stopped short of telling any direct lies and even her original white lie regarding Mrs. Fareham still being alive could now rest in peace along with the venerable lady herself.

Just as her children enjoyed their new way of life, Patience found her adopted lifestyle grew to her liking and it seemed full of excitement and potential. Financially, she was secure. Much of her inheritance was made up of investments which periodically would boost her available spending funds. In addition, she would often take on paid work, partly to fit in with whatever tale she was spinning at the time and partly for day-to-day expenses. She enjoyed dalliances with unattached men of 'her own age' and it was this aspect of her life that was the first to reveal the down side of her unusual situation. She realised that she could never develop a serious relationship. Marriage was unthinkable for how could one marry a man who would become gradually old and infirm while looking across the fireside at a permanently youthful wife?

She began to see that she was literally wasting the time of young men in forming relationships. In effect, she was stealing a part of their precious youth merely for her own temporary amusement. Knowing this preyed on her mind and she deliberately kept any relationships as short as possible. There were even times when she had to move away just to extricate herself from clinging admirers - for their benefit rather than hers. Worse still, she began to find their comparative immaturity tiresome. Before long, she began to avoid any form of dating as there seemed no prospect of real fulfilment for either party. She avoided cultivating close friendships with female friends too, knowing they could only be short-term.

She turned her energies instead to developing her own accomplishments and set about learning a musical instrument. She did not begrudge the time needed for practise. On the contrary, she welcomed any activities that filled her time. The clavichord was the chosen musical instrument and she took great delight in being able to produce tunes - albeit a little haltingly. As time passed she became disillusioned with her keyboard efforts as she discovered that becoming proficient was not simply a matter of time and application. It required some natural ability and/or affinity with the instrument and the harpsichord proved no better as a second choice. A different music teacher introduced her to the violin and yet another to the flute. The outcomes proved the same. Patience took satisfaction in having acquired a reasonable level of ability on several instruments but was frustrated by the discovery that being endowed with hands, lungs, and eyesight that remained free of strain still did not guarantee virtuosity. Neither did they make her a great singer, sketcher or painter as these hobbies were similarly tried and abandoned.

Although Patience had purposefully dropped out of the lives of her children and relatives in Suffolk, she had kept a watchful eye from afar through the occasional use of agencies whose services could be purchased for such monitoring. Her key interest was that they did not run into hard times without her becoming aware and able to help.

Fortunately, there was never a need for her intervention. She heard about the major events such as when her sister and brother-in law died and when her children married. Much later came the sad event she had dreaded. In real terms, she was well beyond old age when her children died though her appearance and vigour belied her actual years. She attended both funerals and no-one paid attention to the tearful young lady who kept to herself but lingered at the graveside long after the other mourners had left. She could pass easily for a relative of the deceased such as a niece. Certainly, no one thought in terms of a mother!

As the 18th century progressed, Patience read of developments in science concerning something called the 'immune system' and the work of Edward Jenner. She did not fully understand the scientific detail but did grasp the fundamental principle. Ever astute, she perceived a link between her maternal ancestry and this new concept of becoming immune. Successive and repeated survival of multiple plague outbreaks, she reasoned, must have created a stronger and stronger bloodline. It occurred to her that perhaps she possessed an exceptional level of this strange thing called 'immunity'. She came to the firm conclusion, without any tests to back it up, that she had acquired an abnormal level of immunity that somehow made her immune to everything - even the wear and tear of ageing. She was unable to verify her theory, but she felt now there was an explanation for her unique place in the scheme of things. Accordingly, Patience felt less concerned by her condition - but it did pose new questions. The most obvious were how, when, and indeed whether she was going to experience what should be the one certainty in everybody's life - death.

Nobody liked to dwell on such a thought and Patience was no exception. She brushed it aside and decided to live life to the full and enjoy not having any commitments. Her finances were healthier than ever as her inherited investments compounded in value. Over the years, at suitable intervals and using different solicitors, she made successive wills leaving everything to a 'favourite niece' who conveniently shared the same name as herself! Posing as the niece she would then open a new account at a different bank. She made a conscious decision not to follow the progress of her grandchildren or their children, for that was simply too much prolonged responsibility for anyone to cope with. So, she continued her life of moving from place to place. She became more adventurous and began to conduct trips to the continent, via arrangements made through monasteries, to embark on pilgrimages. Devising a suitable story, as a recently widowed woman needing time to get away for prayer, was simplicity itself to Patience. Her ability to make a generous donation quickly removed most obstacles to her travel objectives and she always kept her side of the bargain by ensuring payment was made in full.

Through travel, she discovered she had a natural flair for learning languages and soon became fluent in French, German, and Italian. It was a joy to discover this hidden talent. European journeys enabled her to make numerous acquaintances and she met many diverse and interesting people. Frequently, she would receive invitations to make a return visit, thereby expanding her travel options. These pleasurable activities occupied Patience for many years but there came a day when she realised, staring at another clutch of tickets in her hand, that she had no appetite for yet another voyage. Wanderlust, like everything else, eventually loses its allure.

Patience now entered a new phase of her life, namely that of the seasoned traveller and worldly-wise independent lady. Her long life, countless acquaintances, numerous homes, and foreign travel meant that she had accumulated a knowledge and perspective normally associated with people very far on in years. Wherever she went, folk were drawn to her because of her impressive general knowledge and apparent wisdom. Patience seemed to know something about everything and people sought her advice on a wide range of issues. She confounded the rule "you cannot put an old head on young shoulders."

More years passed while she enjoyed this flattering status as a person to seek out and consult with but eventually her popularity became a burden. Wherever she moved to, people gradually sought her company not for friendship and sharing, but to draw from her whatever nuggets of advice they could. Contact with others became a strain on her nerves. She began moving onward more frequently and, to her alarm, found herself re-treading paths used in previous 'escapes'. She could not keep track of when she had previously visited places and the risk of recognition was a constant worry. Resuming foreign trips was an option but, if anything, the risk was much worse. As a foreigner, she would stand out and might draw the attention of a previous acquaintance from bygone days. The acquaintance would now be well on in years - unlike herself. Feeling under considerable pressure, she took herself off to a remote Scottish isle to consider her options.

The loneliness of the near-deserted island mirrored the profound loneliness Patience had begun to feel inside. Each day she spent time attempting to convince herself that she still loved life and appreciated her 'gift' and would actively look for new experiences. An example was in the advances being made with flight technology. Patience started to use aeroplanes to journey to and from the island. Sadly, the excitement that her fellow passengers clearly showed from this sensational new technology was lost on her and increasingly, she became more reclusive.

Her attention turned to reading up on different religious beliefs and the concept of an afterlife began to intrigue her. Death offered a curious kind of freedom, even an opportunity! An eternal existence in a spiritual rather than physical form was promised to everyone. Logic dictated that this must, somehow, apply to her too so she started to seek out, almost furtively, books about salvation. The promise of a life hereafter represented an escape from the present world but the thought of possibly being denied this release would leave her depressed and sobbing over her books. Before long, without noticing, she fell into a pattern of praying daily for 'peace'. After all, this seemed a more appropriate petition than praying for death itself. As her depression deepened so did her prayers.

It was about this time she started to notice a change in the way she felt. She became tired more easily and her joints would sometimes ache.

One day she glanced in the mirror and felt both shock and joy in the same moment. There were grey hairs amidst the black. Each day that followed brought further signs of ageing. Joy of joys! She read newspaper articles about depression and how some doctors suggested this could adversely disturb the immune system to the point of making people ill. Others in the medical profession scorned the theory but Patience, astute as ever, saw a link between the decline in her super-immune system and her lengthy depression. A new worry seized her, that becoming aware of the cause might somehow bring about a reversal in the ageing process. She fretted over this but, far from reversing, this additional worry accelerated it. Day by day the images in the mirror finally convinced even her that the process had become irreversible. Along with this realisation came a peace of mind that flowed to the core of her being.

Patience's remaining days on earth were her happiest. It turned out there were still new experiences of genuine interest to be had such as eye tests, spectacles, and even dental work. The worse she felt and looked, the happier she was! She became something of an inspiration for all the islanders. Following home visits, her doctor would speak to other elderly patients and tell them about the remarkable old English lady who never let her illness and decline get her down. A visiting priest went to see her and decided he had never met anyone so eager to meet her maker. Such faith! The local solicitor was struck by the chirpiness of the frail old lady when framing her will - leaving everything to a charity in support of the elderly.

For her own part, Patience could not help but wonder if her increasing depression had been a peculiar answer to her prayers. She could not be certain about that but of one thing she was sure, for months she had experienced a lightness of spirit that formerly she could only dream of. Late one morning, feeling unusually weary, she put down her newspaper and spent an hour sitting in her favourite chair visualising the various stages of her considerable lifetime. She remembered with a strange clarity her husband and children, the numerous people known, the hobbies tried, and the various journeys abroad. For the first time in decades she fully appreciated what a magnificent life she had been blessed with. Feeling extremely tired but more contented than she had ever felt before, she settled down for a little nap.

Two Problems with One Bite

Peter Collins
England

I CAME AWAKE SLOWLY AND PAINFULLY. My head throbbed like a…. Oh, God. It was too early for similes. Just take it from me that my head throbbed. I lay on the bed and tried to piece together the events of the previous evening. I'd left the university about seven and stopped in one of the student bars. A few drinks there and I was on my way home when I met up with a crowd of post-grads going to a party. Oh, God. It slowly began to come back to me. A wild student party hosted by one of the well-heeled Hooray Henry's. Unlimited booze and enough white powder to line a football pitch. God knows what I did after that. No wonder I felt awful.

I lay there for a while in the darkened room as my senses slowly began to regain some sort of order. I was on my sixth or seventh *'never again'* when the door burst open and a high-pitched wailing fractured my delicate sensibilities.

'Morning Humphrey, rise and shine!'

A small bustling whirlwind, known to her friends as Anna, burst into my room. Anna had been in my undergraduate year. While I had stayed on researching for a PhD in the Haematology Department, Anna had gotten a job managing the Students' Union office. As most of the actual day-to-day work was delegated to the student volunteers, she only ever appeared in the evenings to brief them. Even then she seemed to have very little to occupy her time, and as a consequence, was always pestering me for something or other.

Anna always seemed full of life. She wasn't a classical beauty – small, with a mop of unruly blonde hair that flopped down over a pretty face with an almost permanent grin on it. But there was some sort of presence about her and she had, as the bard Meghan Trainor put it, *all the right junk in all the right places*. We'd been close friends for three years. At one point there was a serious possibility that we might take the relationship to another level. 'Together for all eternity' was how Anna had phrased it at the time. A throwaway remark perhaps, but it had struck me as unusual. Why say 'eternity' instead of 'for the rest of our lives'?

It turned out to be an academic point anyway. Anna was having a few 'complications' she wouldn't explain and so our relationship had stayed platonic. But I don't suppose it would have taken much to persuade either of us to change that.

She wrenched the curtains back with an evil relish and wrapped them around her, keeping herself well out of the sunlight. She laughed out loud as I took cover beneath the duvet.

'Have a heart,' I wailed, 'my eyes are so bloodshot I can barely see my own eyelids.'

With a disdainful sniff, she relented and let the curtains fall back in place. She stood menacingly over me as I emerged, blinking, from under the duvet.

'You're letting yourself go, Humphrey,' she said, blatantly inspecting my inert form with more than a passing interest. I opened a questioning eye and said nothing. We both knew that was far from the truth. When it came to getting first prize in the genetic raffle, I had been lucky enough to have the right ticket. I was just under six feet tall, with short dark hair and pale blue eyes. There was not a spare ounce of fat on my well-defined body, which was toned without being heavily muscled. The only thing that set me apart from the male models in Anna's 'lifestyle' magazines was my lack of a bronze perma-tan. But then as I worked in the north of England, spent most days locked in a windowless laboratory, and didn't earn nearly enough for regular holidays in the sun, there wasn't an awful lot I could do about that.

She pulled back the duvet to pay even closer attention to my body so I jumped from the bed and made to chase her away. She screamed playfully and scampered off while I attempted to pull myself together enough to get changed. By the time I had worked out how to get my trousers on, Anna was fussing about in the four-foot by four-foot cupboard, which my landlord laughingly referred to as my en-suite kitchenette, and soon the aroma of freshly-brewed coffee was forcing my reluctant senses awake.

She passed me a cup, which I took gratefully.

'So tell me why you are here at this outrageous hour.'

'We've got a mission,' Anna said mysteriously. 'Look!'

She passed me a copy of the morning paper. It took me a while to see anything of relevance, so Anna had to point it out to me.

'There, look. *University student found dead on campus.*'

Exasperated with my blank look, she launched into an explanation. Apparently, this was the fourth student who had been found dead in the last year. All had lost a lot of blood, but there was no obvious cause of death apart from minor puncture wounds on the neck.

I suppose I should have put two and two together to make five then, but in my defence, it was early and I was still hungover, and I was after all a scientist, not a comic-book writer. I continued to look blankly at her.

'Vampires, Humphrey, vampires!' she shouted with unrestrained irritation at my slowness.

'No such thing,' I said blithely, forgetting to my cost that Anna had been head of the debating society during her time as an undergraduate and relished an argument at every opportunity. I sat and cowered while she gave a twenty-minute speech about the history of vampirism, the widespread existence of creatures in nature that fed on blood, and the plausibility of human vampires.

I poured another cup of coffee. 'You sound quite sympathetic to them,' I said casually. I was surprised at the passion of her response.

'Vampires aren't monsters, Humphrey. They might exist in eternal night but they are people too!'

I looked curiously at her. If she hadn't been so pale I believe she would have blushed.

'Anyway,' she hurried on, 'we're going to go looking for them tonight and we need you to join us.'

It turned out that Anna and a couple of her equally looney friends had planned a vampire hunt that evening. Apparently, they had already decided that I was essential to the expedition due to my specialism in all matters blood-related. Quite how a part-completed doctorate in new approaches to platelet and neutrophil immunology was going to be of any use when confronted by a blood-sucking demon was frankly beyond me. But as I knew full-well there was no chance we would ever see even the faintest trace of a vampire, I reluctantly agreed to join in their lunatic scheme. Anna fussed and kissed me, and we agreed to meet behind the Student Union at midnight.

By that evening, my hangover had abated and I joined the small group ready to plan our vampire hunt. I knew one of Anna's friends already. He was a tall young man, dark-skinned and well-built. His name was Victor and he was one of the university's leading Footlights performers. I think he secretly had a crush on Anna, but most of all he was in love with himself. There would be no chance he could tackle a vampire without worrying about cracking a fingernail. The fourth member of our group was a slight, talkative individual named Carl. He wore wire-rimmed glasses and carried a small backpack over his shabby green parker. All he was lacking was a large sign over his head saying 'Nerd!'

After Anna had introduced everybody, Carl delved into his backpack and produced four small rubber hammers and some thin pieces of wood.

'Are we going camping?' I asked innocently.

There were blank looks all round.

'I just wondered why the tent pegs,' I said, instantly feeling Anna's toecap in my calf.

Carl frowned. 'Stakes,' he replied seriously.

He mimed hammering the stakes into a vampire's heart before handing them round. I inspected one of the stakes that was barely larger than a ballpoint pen. Using a rubber hammer, it would be difficult to force it into a tub of margarine, let alone through the breastbone of a deranged blood-sucking maniac. It struck me that Anna could not have chosen two more inept vampire hunters if she had gone out to do so deliberately. However, I kept my opinions to myself as the group split into two. Anna took my arm firmly and we set off towards the Chemistry block leaving Victor and Carl to head towards the sports ground.

I must confess to being something less than vigilant on our patrol. It was a warm evening and no hardship at all to be strolling through the moonlight arm-in-arm with Anna. Of course, we saw nothing and it was almost one o'clock when we met up with Victor and Carl back at the Union building. Not surprisingly, they had seen nothing untoward either. We decided on a fifteen-minute break before we set off again. We found a bench and sat down. Carl had had the foresight to bring a flask of coffee and some sandwiches with him, but he made no attempt to share them and as I sat there watching him, his cheese and pickle dripping down his chin, I began to feel the first stirrings of hunger myself.

Despite having his mouth full, Carl was in no mood to stay silent.

'What I don't understand,' he slobbered, ignoring the large trail of pickle that slowly cascaded down his parker like a small green lava stream, 'is why these people are ending up dead. I thought that if a vampire bit you, you were turned into one of them too.' He looked around in silent enquiry.

Nobody spoke until, somewhat reluctantly it seemed to me, Anna decided to answer.

'Vampires carry a virus,' she said. 'It's unpleasant and difficult to live with. It's nothing at all like the glamour or romance in films like *Twilight*.'

I looked up. Her voice was unusually flat, tired almost.

She carried on. 'The virus is how they infect others, but it needs blood to survive. If a vampire drains the blood of their victim, then the victim dies. But if a vampire only drinks part of their blood, then the victim lives but becomes infected and turns into a vampire themselves.'

'Why would a vampire want to miss out on a full feed and turn another person into a vampire? Wouldn't that make more competition for them?' asked Carl, with what seemed to be a surprising amount of insight.

'Love,' said Anna simply. Her voice was barely more than a whisper and we had to strain to hear her speak. 'You can't imagine how lonely it is living the eternal life of the undead; to have nobody to hold and care for; nobody to share your hopes and dreams.'

She seemed to realise that everybody was staring at her and she shook her head and smiled.

'Well, that's what my research says, anyway. Come on. Let's get patrolling.'

She picked up her stake and headed off. I was aware of Victor and Carl looking at me curiously. I shrugged and took off after Anna. We walked in silence.

'Do you ever feel the need to have somebody to share things with?' I asked after a few minutes.

She put her hand in mine. It felt cold and clammy. She looked up at me, pale and drawn in the moonlight.

'Yes,' she said quietly. 'Twelve months ago, I thought that it might be you, but then…' She trailed off. I looked questioningly at her. 'There were difficulties,' she confessed. 'I wasn't ready at the time.'

I said nothing, but my mind was whirling as we strolled on in silence. As we walked I noticed Anna becoming twitchier and twitchier. After a few minutes she said that she had to go to the toilet and disappeared towards one of the female hall of residences. I stood in the dark and wondered what to do. The sight of Carl's sandwiches had made me hungry, but I knew that most of the campus cafes would be long closed by now. I wondered if there was any chance of getting anything to eat while Anna was away. But my hunger had abated by the time I heard her return. Maybe it was the break, or perhaps she'd had a chance to wash her face. Whatever it was, she looked revived and refreshed. There was colour in her cheeks and her pale anaemic look had disappeared.

We were about to carry on when a panicked shout made us look up. Carl came crashing through the bushes near the hall of residence. His face was stained with tears and he could barely speak.

'Terrible thing…' he garbled. 'Monster… Victor… come quick!'

We followed him through the bushes as he led us to a small garden that was on the route Carl and Victor had patrolled. It was the closest point to our own route. In the daytime it was used by the smokers in the Chemistry department, but now it was deserted apart from Victor's body on the ground. He was clearly dead. Even with his dark skin, he looked unnaturally pale in the moonlight. There were two obvious puncture marks on his neck.

Carl was still in shock. 'He thought he heard something,' he shrilled, his voice wavering and high-pitched. 'He was only gone for a minute. When I came to look, there was somebody, or something, crouched over him. It ran over there.' He pointed his arm at the female hall of residence behind us.

I looked at Anna, who had shrunk back into the shadows. It was impossible to tell what she was thinking. I turned to Carl and put an arm on his shoulders.

'You're in shock, Carl. Go home and try and rest. Don't let anybody in apart from me. I'll call the police and we'll get it sorted. OK?'

He nodded and set off straight away, eager to leave.

Behind me, I sensed rather than saw Anna move in the gloom. She seemed bigger somehow, almost menacing, a strange smile on her face.

'I told you we'd find a vampire, didn't I Humphrey.'

I straightened slowly and turned to face her. As I stood, I felt the stake and hammer in my coat pocket. I remembered how I had derided them before.

'I underestimated you, Anna.'

She looked questioningly at me, but stayed in the shadows saying nothing.

'There was I saying there were no such things as vampires. Yet you knew, didn't you? You knew that a vampire was here all along?'

Anna nodded her head. She took a step forward. A strange intensity burned in her eyes.

'What was this, Anna? Some sort of test?'

'I suppose you could say that.'

'How long, Anna?'

'Twelve months maybe, no more.'

I nodded to myself. Looking back now, I could see that there had been a subtle change in her behaviour towards me from about that time. I took a step back from her, and looked around for any avenue of escape.

'Humphrey, don't,' she pleaded. 'I love you. Don't make me…' her voice trailed off and her eyes followed me as I brought my hand out of my pocket.

I was still clutching the stake and hammer. She took another step forward, almost gliding across the ground, her head held high, eyes shining bright.

'You don't need those, Humphrey. Trust me. I love you.' She held out her hands.

Almost against my will, I felt the stake and hammer fall from my fingers.

'Are you sure?' I asked, trembling.

'I promise, Humphrey.' Her eyes seemed to bore into me. 'I love you. I will love you for all eternity.'

I felt the final feeling of helplessness wash over me. I knew I would be bent to her will. Anna stepped close towards me, a triumphant look in her eye. I resigned myself to fate, leaned forward, and sank my fangs deep into her neck. She gasped, at first in pain, and then in pleasure as I drank deeply from the wound and then withdrew. Anna caught my eye and managed to mouth the words, 'thank you,' before she collapsed into a faint. I felt my heart sing. I had always hoped that she and I could be together. But we'd been friends for so long; I had never wanted to turn her without her permission. But now she would be mine for ever.

But our eternal happiness could wait for a while. I had more pressing matters to attend to. I took Anna into my arms and headed for Carl's house. Although I was sated from feeding off Victor, I knew Anna would be hungry when she woke and Carl would be happy to invite us in. It would solve two problems with one bite.

Sunset for Dolores

Peter Mallett
Japan

WHENEVER WE HEARD OF THE DEATH of a celebrity – and there were many of them that summer – Dolores put on a little show for us. Dressed from head to toe in black, iced in about a kilo of face powder, bleeding crimson lipstick and leaking mascara, Dolores might have been labelled a Goth had she been decades – many decades – younger. Thus attired she was guaranteed to receive the attention she desired at the funerals and memorial services she attended.

"Have you heard the news?" she would inquire as we met her putting out the garbage. "It's not righT," she complained, spitting out the final dental like an unsavoury pip. "It's not right. All that talent wasted. And so young."

Compared to Dolores, about a million years old – well, all right, eighty, if she was a day – some of the deceased *were* young, though many of them wouldn't have seen sixty-five again had they been spared.

She wasn't really Dolores at all but plain Doris, and the 'de la' she had inserted before her family name was an affectation she had no legal claim to. Doris Haye was the name to which she was born, and even the authenticity of the final 'e' was suspect. Letters addressed to Doris Hay were sometimes misdirected to our mailbox outside the converted villa we shared in a no-longer fashionable part of Hollywood. Judging by the modest size of the properties, I doubt Oleander Drive ever had been fashionable, but it was tree-lined and pleasant and the proximity of some minor studios where filming still took place lent colour to the neighbourhood. It was the studios that had attracted me to Oleander Drive during the year I spent in Hollywood trying to complete my screenplay. They added some verisimilitude, some atmosphere. That and the fact the area was cheap – or what passes for cheap in the most desirable belt of California.

The studios, so Dolores claimed, were the reason she'd chosen to live on Oleander Drive as well. They reminded her of her past. I suspected cost might have played its part in her decision too.

"Of course, this is a come-down for me," she informed us. "When I was big in the movies I lived in a mansion on Sunset Boulevard. Huge. Chandeliers, Italian gardens, a long sweeping drive, and such a lovely pool. It could have been the one where Billy shot the movie."

Except it couldn't. The mansion Billy Wilder used as Norma Desmond's home in his film was actually on Wilshire, long since demolished for some commercial development. We didn't spoil her delusions; we played along with the pretence. It didn't hurt us, and it gave Dolores some pleasure in her reduced circumstances to recall those glory days – real or imaginary.

"I'm on my way to the memorial service," Dolores announced when I bumped into her one morning in July. "The driver is picking me up at nine."

The 'driver' was usually a yellow cab she hailed herself on Santa Monica, unless the death demanded an added degree of grandeur. Such occasions were usually on a Saturday, I noted, when neighbours trimming hedges or washing cars, witnesses to the drama of Dolores setting out for the funeral, would justify the extra expense of a cab that had been called to the 'town house', as she liked to call her ground-floor apartment. On these occasions, she would replace the wide-brimmed straw hat she considered appropriate for B-list celebrities with a black crepe turban pinned with an imitation diamond the size of the Koh-i-Noor. She looked like a caricature of Gloria Swanson in *Sunset Boulevard*.

"Whose memorial?"

"Whose?" Dolores stared at me as though I had that moment arrived from another planet. "Why, Michael's. Surely you've heard."

Even I couldn't have missed the hype surrounding the unexpected death of the King of Pop at the age of fifty, though I couldn't for the life in me imagine Dolores' connection to him.

"So young. Such a waste of talent. Liz is devastated. Bereft."

Liz? Elizabeth Taylor, of course. Dolores frequently claimed first-name acquaintance with the greatest stars and dropped their names as though we would immediately know whom she was talking about.

"Liz and I are such great friends. Almost like sisters."

We frequently speculated on the reason Dolores was so attracted to these funerals.

"She's appropriately named," I said. "Doesn't Dolores mean 'sorrow'?"

"It's almost as if she's living her life vicariously through the deaths of others," my wife perceptively pointed out.

"Dead men tell no tales," I added. "Deceased celebrities can't deny they were ever acquainted with Dolores."

"But why?" Anna asked.

"Just a variation on the young generation following the famous on Twitter, I suppose. Makes them feel significant."

"Do you think she really knew them?"

"I doubt it. Why would she be living in a place like this if she'd really been big in movies? She's delusional – talks and dresses as if she were Norma Desmond putting on an act for Joe Gillis in *Sunset Boulevard*. She even claims she lived there!"

"Perhaps she's planning a comeback!"

"A *return*, you mean! *A return to the millions of people who have never forgiven her for deserting the screen!*"

We were no longer in Hollywood when Dolores' own funeral took place. Inevitably, the money ran out and I was nowhere closer to a completed screenplay or a contract with a producer. Nowhere closer to moving to a place with a pool. At least I didn't end up floating in one with two bullets in my back and one in my stomach. There's always something to be thankful for.

Never mind my undiscovered talent: I had to earn a living. We returned to London – if you can call the dreary northern suburb we lived in 'London'. The 'third most unhappiest *[sic]* borough in London,' according to a recent ungrammatical survey. Like Joe Gillis, when we hit Hollywood I'd been itching with ambition. But I needed inspiration, not ambition, and Oleander Drive hadn't provided it. Graham Greene set out for the Congo 'in search of a character' and wrote a masterpiece on his return. I'd never found my character in Hollywood and it wasn't likely I'd ever complete a masterpiece in Brent, a place like Norma Desmond's mansion, *stricken with creeping paralysis and out of beat with the rest of the world.* So times were tough and I paid the bills by marking English literature examination papers and editing barely literate soft porn for an erotic publishing house.

On a regular visit to my agent one day for a routine rejection of the script, I learned of Dolores' death.

"No!" my agent said, shaking the script. "No better at all. You've been watching too many old movies; your script's starting to sound like one. Flat, trite, full of clichés."

"Thanks. And you sound just like Betty Schaefer."

"Who?"

"Nevermind."

"Betty Schaefer? That name rings a bell. Where did I hear it recently? Oh, yes, of course." She rummaged through the pile on her desk and picked up a newspaper. "Have you heard the news?"

Now, that was a line that sounded familiar.

"You mentioned once you'd met Dolores de la Haye when you were in Hollywood."

"What?"

"Dolores de la Haye."

"Doris Hay? We lived right above the old biddy on Oleander Drive."

"The 'old biddy', as you so respectfully refer to her, has died."

"Dolores is dead? I thought she was immortal."

"So did her fans."

"Her fans?"

"Well, you were born too late to know, I suppose. Dolores was a great star in the forties."

"Good God!"

"It's all in her obituary. Here, take a look," she said, passing the article over to me.

Los Angeles

The black-and-white movie star Dolores de la Haye played her greatest role last Thursday when she starred in her own funeral at Forest Lawn Memorial Park in the Hollywood Hills, the venue of the funerals of so many other celebrities she'd attended.

In accordance with the explicit directions left in her will, an open white coffin lined with flaming red satin displayed her body, dressed in one of the Gloria Swanson costumes from *Sunset Boulevard* de la Haye had bought at auction. Billy Wilder, the director of the movie, originally considered de la Haye for the part of Betty Schaefer, eventually played by Nancy Olson. De la Haye later said it was her greatest regret not to have appeared in the film.

Born Doris Hay in 1925, the actress changed her name to Dolores de la Haye to avoid confusion with her contemporary, Doris Day. She enjoyed a brief period of stardom at the end of the black-and-white era, when reputedly one of the highest paid stars in Hollywood, in such epics as *Desert Princess* (1946) and *Jezebel* (1948).

Her career ended with a disastrous marriage to the producer Samuel Goldenstein, who used her fortune to finance a string of flops before disappearing to Mexico with the remainder of her savings. The star never recovered. The Sunset Boulevard mansion was sold and de la Haye retired to a villa she divided into apartments, living on the rental income. She was never to act again, nor did she ever remarry.

Despite having to sell most of the trappings of her former stardom, de la Haye refused to part with one object: a magnificent 50-carat diamond (Elizabeth Taylor is the only film star to have owned a larger one), the gift of an infatuated Indian maharajah. She also retained the loyalty of her former chauffeur who, after losing his job and becoming a cab driver, was always on call to drive the ex-actress wherever she willed. It is rumoured that de la Haye has bequeathed the diamond to him.

In later life, de la Haye enjoyed a bizarre restoration of her fame as a mourner at the funerals of all the stars she had known. No celebrity funeral was complete without her. The compliment was repaid at de la Haye's own lying-in-state last week: Elizabeth Taylor, in a wheelchair, led a huge crowd of A-list celebrities and minor royalty to give Dolores the sunset she deserved.

"Good God!"

"What's wrong?" my agent asked. "Did you know her well?"

"As I said, we lived on the upper floor of her house. Only we didn't know she owned it. We paid rent to an agent. We thought Dolores did too. I'd no idea she was really a Hollywood star. We thought she was a fake – we thought the diamond was a fake. Good God!"

"Why do you keep saying that?"

"What a wasted opportunity. All those people she could have introduced me to! And…"

"Yes?"

But I didn't need to say anything more. For it had dawned on me that I was the fake, not Dolores. I'd squandered a year in Hollywood and not produced anything. Dolores had been a star and lost everything through no fault of her own. I was no less of a hack screenwriter than Joe Gillis. Now I'd earned the life I deserved – marking exams and editing third-rate fiction in Brent.

I pointed this out to my wife when I told her the news at home that night. She wasn't sympathetic.

"Stop feeling sorry for yourself," she said, giving me a whisky. "Forget the people Dolores could have introduced you to. You're missing the obvious."

"What?"

"You know that bit in *Sunset Boulevard* where Betty Schaefer talks to Joe Gillis about someone helping a little old lady across the road who turns out to be a multi-millionaire and leaves them all her money in her will?"

"Forget it. Dolores de la Haye did not leave us a cent in her will."

"No, stupid. Not literally. But more than that: she left you her life. She's your subject. What a gift! Her story – it's your screenplay. I can just see the opening, a misquote from *Sunset Boulevard*: *Death, which can be strangely merciful, had taken pity on Dolores de la Haye.*"

I put down my whisky. "You genius! You could be right."

I'd been completely blind to what had been standing in front of me all along.

"Of course I'm right. Remember what Norma Desmond says about stars being ageless? Well, you can make Dolores de la Haye ageless. You can resurrect her. She'll be more famous dead than she ever was in life. In your creation she will live for eternity on the big screen. Now drag yourself out of that swimming pool of self-pity you're floating in, stop up those bullet holes in your pride, and start writing."

Acknowledgements

Quotations from *Sunset Boulevard* (1950), screenplay by Charles Brackett, Billy Wilder, and D M Marshman Jr.

Brent and Kilburn Times, 6 Aug 2015: http://www.kilburntimes.co.uk/news/brent-dubbed-the-third-most-unhappiest-borough-in-london-1-4183508

Always the Eyes

Peter True
England

ANIMAL EYES THEY CAN DO. But for some reason they can't replicate human. That's why I stick with dogs.

I work at the coffee bar opposite our city's *After Life* centre, so I see a lot of Facsimiles and the people who acquire them and their opinion of the results, and it's always the eyes that let them down. What's the point of growing to love a person if you can't get a good Facsimile afterwards? So, that's why I stick with dogs. Besides, they're cheap and if I ever find one I like, I'll know that when it gets sick I can get a good *After Life* produced that won't disappoint.

* * *

I walk Roscoe on the common field by the water purification plant. It's a nice open space and there are trees.

It's cold and grey. I turn up my collar against the drizzle. I don't mind really. The drizzle makes a mist that softens everything up. You don't see the rot on the trees, and the towers of the water purification plant sort of fade into the background.

However, the wet does make Roscoe's fur stick flat to his body. You can see he's getting thinner. He's not much time left on him. Not to worry. It's an opportunity to get another. I thought at first maybe this was the one I would feel something for; that maybe when this one got sick I'd take him over when the time came. But he developed a tendency to whine. I couldn't live with that for the rest of my life, it would get annoying. Maybe the next one will be the one.

Looking at Roscoe in the rain, I decide I should probably go to the *Animal Companion Centre* pretty soon. I'll work an extra shift or two to get the money. Like I say, dogs are cheap.

* * *

Roscoe died yesterday. The cost of animal disposal has gone up. Not much but I'll have to make a note for next time. Unless of course I take the next Roscoe to *After Life*. I have to give a wry smile at that. I think maybe the next will be the last Roscoe. After that I'll try something else. Maybe a cat. But I like cats less than dogs.

* * *

The *Animal Companion Centre* is as weary as it is smelly. I hate coming here. Everything's painted bright colours and the staff are always smiling their heads off. Some people really get a kick out of cats and dogs I guess. I used to try and get in on the act; pretend to be all excited and full of love for getting a dog. But now I'm pretty much, go in, pick a dog, fill in the forms, pay, and go. It's their job to provide me with a dog. I don't have to be all enthusiastic about it. Also, I don't want to make a new friend when I go there. You know what I mean? When I sell someone coffee I don't try to get their phone number and set up a play date or anything. It must be something to do with working with animals that are needy and full of outward signs of affection but the people at *Animal Companion* are overly friendly. I don't want to be your friend; just give me the dog.

"Ah, Mr. McCarthy, back with us so soon!"

See what I mean? The lady at reception is beside herself that she's recognised me. Well I'm on Roscoe number five, so what does she want, a medal?

"Are we looking for a friend for little Roscoe?" she asks. She asked me this last time. Doesn't remember *that*, does she.

"A replacement," I tell her. "Roscoe passed."

That just about spoils her week, you can tell.

"I'll just take a number," I tell her, nudging her in the right direction to do her job.

I sit in the waiting room, surrounded by families with excited children. There's an older guy waiting on his own, sitting opposite me. Some people get a dog or a cat for companionship because they can't afford a Facsimile of their husband or wife. Or maybe can't go through with the procedure; some people need to hold on to the bitter end. If they figure out how to make the transfer after death I guess that won't happen.

At least these people are either too busy with noisy kids or lost in grief to try and be pally with me. So, I'll be left to my own devices until my number is called.

I seem to be in luck today. The young girl dealing with me isn't that chatty. In fact, she's pretty much silent as she checks through the form I filled in about the kind of dog I'm after. Maybe a cat got squashed by something heavy in the back and she's worried she'll get the blame or something. She's obviously new; her blue scrubs are un-faded and crisp.

"You OK?" I hear myself asking.

"Hmm?" she says, looking up.

"Sorry," I say. I don't even know why I asked. I guess it's because she's pretty. In a small-shouldered kind of a way.

She looks back to the paperwork and sighs.

"You know," she says, "the more information you fill in, the easier it is for us to find you a suitable animal companion." She looks up at me and smiles.

I get the distinct impression I've just been told off and that I should be annoyed. However, she didn't say it in a mean way. And it's just such a relief not to have to deal with niceties and friendliness.

"I'm not overly bothered, really," I say. "About the dog, I mean. That is to say, what kind it is."

She gives a little shrug and invites me to follow her to the kennels with a slight nod of her head.

"Most people are very particular," she says, as she unlocks the chain-link gate.

I don't really know what she expects me to say, so I just shrug, even though she is in front of me and not looking my way.

"Makes a change I suppose," she goes on, as she opens the gate and walks on through. "I can see this isn't your first dog, so I'm sure you know the drill."

I follow her through to the corridor I know leads to the kennels and start to think about whether to get a smaller or larger dog than the last one.

* * *

The one I ended up with is a shaggy thing. He's definitely cute, there's no denying it. Not what I usually go for at all. Funny, he looks more like a Roscoe than even the first one did. He's bouncy and full of energy but not in an annoying way. I don't mind throwing the ball for him when he races back to me with it. We're on the common again. However, today the rain has cleared and it's actually sunny. Usually all that means is that you can see all the crud about; like the rotting trees and the water purification plant. But today I don't mind the sunny weather.

* * *

I'm at work and I find I'm missing the new Roscoe. Maybe this is it. It would certainly be a load off my mind to finally find a nice dog that I can get a Facsimile of when it gets sick. Then I won't need to worry about looking any more.

* * *

It's just over two weeks since I got the new Roscoe and, what do you know, I still like the little fella. We go out for walks all the time and he sits with me in the evenings when I'm not working. I wonder if, if I get him done, whether I'll back-date him to now. It makes me wish you could get the Facsimiles done when you like. But you have to wait until they get sick. Not to worry. Dogs can get sick pretty quick. He has this little trick where he stands on his back legs to get into the bin. He's so cute when he does that. I sure hope he gets sick soon. It costs more to back-date.

* * *

I'm working an extra-long shift today. Roscoe is definitely worth carrying over. So, I need to start putting money aside for the procedure. You'd think I'd get a discount. I practically work for *After Life* in this place. Pretty much everyone I serve is on their way there or coming out. So, anyway I'm pretty tired.

"How's the dog?"

I'm half asleep and I barely register that someone is talking to me. I look up and it's a youngish woman, probably about twenty. Kind of pretty.

"What can I get you today?" I ask.

She frowns, like I asked her a surprise question or something. Then I realise it's because I didn't answer her question. Then I also realise it's the girl from the *Animal Companion Centre*.

"Oh, hi," I say. "Sorry, it's been a long day. The dog, Roscoe, he's fine."

"Cool," she says. "Large black one."

"No, he was small and white," I say.

She wrinkles her nose like she's still smelling the stink of where she works.

"I'd like a large black coffee, please, to go," she says patiently, like she's talking to an idiot.

Which she is, I guess. I click back over our brief conversation and realise what I said. Like I said, I'm really tired. I shake my head and smile.

"Sorry. Long day," I mumble, a little embarrassed, I have to admit.

"It's OK," she says. "I've done a few all-nighters myself. Last week I nearly gave a cat vaccination to a Doberman."

"I can see where you'd get those two confused," I joke, turning my back to fix her coffee.

"Why the long day?" she asks.

Boy, she wasn't this chatty at the *Centre*. I don't mind though; she's helping me keep awake.

"I'm saving up for an *After Life*," I tell her.

"Oh, I'm sorry," she says. "Is someone sick?" she asks, whilst taking two sachets of sweetener.

I use real sugar myself. She holds the sachets at the top and gives them a little shake. Not strictly necessary with the sweetener but I do it with the sugar.

"No, it's for Roscoe," I say putting her coffee on the counter.

She stops shaking the sachets and looks at me with concerned eyes.

"You said he was OK," she says, titling her head to one side.

"He is," I clarify. "It's for later. You know, later. Got to save up now."

"Oh," she says and tears open both sachets together and pours them into her coffee. A pro move that one.

"He's not your first dog," she says, watching the coffee fizz. "You never got any of the others carried over?"

She sure asks a lot of personal questions. But she did it so casually that I don't feel interrogated.

"This one's different, I think," I tell her. "I think he's the one I'd like to keep."

"The others didn't come up to scratch?"

"Precisely," I say.

And then I tell her all about it; about the previous Roscoes and the Facsimiles and the eyes. Everything. I guess I must get chatty when I'm tired. I never noticed before.

"So, you found a dog to get carried over when he gets sick," she says when I'm finished.

"Yeah," I say.

"That's sweet," she says.

She snaps the lid onto her coffee, gives it a little tap on top, and picks it up.

"Well, I hope it all works out for you," she says and turns to leave.

Before she steps away, the door opens and in walks a smiling man. He's holding the arm of a brand-new Facsimile; presumably his dead wife. He's grinning away, making sure all the people in the coffee bar can see how happy he is pretending to be. The Facsimile is of a pretty woman. To his credit he didn't back date her to a younger representation; she looks about mid-thirties. She's tall and fair-skinned, with blonde hair. It smiles too and pats her husband's hand. From a little further away you might not even notice at first. But it's there. The pallid eyes, with the unfocussed stare.

The girl from the *Animal Companion Centre* watches them as the husband leads the Facsimile to a table. She turns to me, raises her eyebrows, then lowers them into a little frown.

I see what you mean, she mouths. Then she smiles, turns away and leaves.

* * *

"Oh dear," the receptionist sighs regretfully, "he didn't pass already did he?"

I'm at the *Animal Companion Centre*.

"No," I tell her. "He's fine. I'm just here for supplements."

I get my number and dutifully sit down in the waiting room. I'm here to check out the food supplements like I said. I noticed Roscoe's coat was looking a little dull. So, I figured I'd come take a look. I never bothered before. The other Roscoes just got my leftovers and the budget animal pellets from *General Supplies*.

My number gets called and I go through. Luckily I get the girl. That way I don't have to dodge any friendship overtures.

"Hi," she says.

She's filling a beaker up with some sort of green goo. She's doing that thing kids do when they're concentrating; the tip of her tongue is sticking out the corner of her mouth and she's frowning hard at the beaker. Kind of sweet I suppose; her nose all wrinkled and everything.

"Careful," I say, trying to make it sound like a joke but I immediately realise there's nothing funny in what I just said. "You don't want goo on you," I add lamely.

"Umm," she agrees distantly and finishes her work.

When she's done, she seals the beaker and goes out of the room to put it away. Then she comes back and tidies up – you know, no rush or anything; customer waiting.

She turns to me and says, "Oh hi, it's you." She gives a little smile. "The man with the eyes!" she says with a wink.

"Yeah," I say. "Don't tell me I have a convert. Have I spread my message?"

"You raise a good point, that's for sure," she says, washing her hands. "That *After Life* woman looked freaky!"

"You never noticed before?" I ask.

"I've not seen that many of them. And like you say, it's only when you actually look," she says taking a paper towel from the dispenser on the wall.

"Yeah," I say, "fine to walk by in the street but imagine waking up next to one."

"Urgh." She gives a little shudder and covers her eyes with one hand, leans her head back dramatically. Smiling, she says, "Ooh no, take it away!"

The way her arm is raised up tightens the blue fabric of her top, and I notice she's slim. I remember I haven't been to the *Conjugal Drop-In* for a few weeks. Perhaps I should swing by on the way home.

"Can I help you?" the girl asks.

I'm snapped out of thoughts of sex and focus back on the girl.

"Supplements," I say, "for the dog."

"We're going all out on this one then are we?" she says as she heads to the filing cabinet that holds the forms required.

"Well I don't want a dull-coated dog forever," I say.

She opens the top draw of the cabinet and selects a form.

"You know, for when they make the Facsimile," I clarify.

"I know," she says casually, looking the form up and down.

"They could add the shine, afterwards, as part of the procedure," I explain, "but it would cost more, even taking into account the extra cost of the supplements. It's cheaper this way, in the long run."

She's still studying the form. She seems a little distracted. Maybe she still has goo on her mind. Or perhaps there is a riveting quiz on her dog supplement form. Boy, she's pretty inattentive today.

She looks up after a second or two, smiling, as if she found the answer to a particularly tricky question. "Well you're here now," she says in a suddenly jolly sort of a way, "so let's get you fixed up."

We go through the rigmarole of selecting the correct dietary needs for the dog. The form turns out to be a lengthy analysis of breed and environment, activity and living conditions.

"He'll be eating better than me at this rate," I joke.

"True enough," the girl sighs, distant again.

"Look at this," I say, pointing at the pack. "It has cabbage in it! I can't remember the last time I had any vegetables."

"Well it's only dried… " she says.

"I'd settle for a dry cabbage leaf over the muck I get issued," I say, putting the pack down.

I look at her. She's looking at the form and I swear she's about to do the tongue sticking out thing again. She seems pretty lost in thought. As if she's deciding whether or not to say something.

"I... have a friend," she says, staring even more intently at the form. I guess she decided to say what was on her mind. "He," she continues sheepishly at the form. "He has contacts. Out city people. He sometimes gets things in."

"Sorry?" I ask.

I don't think I'll ever understand what goes on in some people's heads.

She looks up at me. Then takes a conspiratorial glance around the room in case the paper towel dispenser is listening in.

"Fresh produce," she whispers and looks back down at the form.

"Oh," I say. This could be quite a score.

"He has these dinner parties..." she says. I swear she's going to look the ink right off that bloody form at this rate. "He's having one next week and well… "

Oh, no, I think. I hope this isn't going where I think it is. I can spot a potential invite a mile away!

"… I'm always invited and I always go, for the food, but I never take anyone and everyone else is always with someone and I always feel sort of… "

It *is* going where I thought it was. I begin to prepare my excuses.

"… I mean, seems as you mentioned it, the food thing, I thought… " She looks up nervously and says, "I mean, I never really know who I can tell. You won't tell anyone, will you?"

"Well, no, of course… " I tell her.

"Good," she says, before I can add the beginnings of a get-out to my sentence. "There's a fine you see," she goes on. She relaxes and smiles. Then she gives a little shrug before continuing casually, "Anyway, if you want to come you can."

"Well," I begin. And then, to my surprise, I think, *what the hell.* "OK," I say.

Looking back to the supplements packet, I say, "Is it cheaper to get a big bag?"

* * *

I load the big bag of supplements into the boot of my small car. It takes up most of it.

I head west on the motorway. The *Conjugal Drop-In* is only a twenty-minute drive away.

I'm pretty happy with my purchase. It's definitely cheaper in the long run if I present the *After Life* team with a fit dog with a shiny coat. Well, when I say fit, he'll obviously have the sickness. But they just need to test positive to qualify – stage one. That's always been the policy at *After Life*. Some people feel that they don't want to suffer unnecessarily, you see. Naturally the rules apply to pets too. So, Roscoe shouldn't be showing any outward signs of being sick when I take him in, if I take him as soon as he's positive. Every modification they have to make carries with it extra cost. And the cost is high, believe me. So, by presenting them with healthy looking dog, with a shiny coat, it'll make for a far lower price for the Facsimile.

I take the exit that leads to the *Drop-In*.

I think the thing that made me change my mind about the dinner party wasn't just the promise of fresh vegetables, but the fact that she didn't really seem to care whether I said yes or no. Her nervousness was more about my reaction to the illicit food stuff. So, our acquaintance promises to remain casual. Still, I should probably give the *Animal Companion Centre* a wide berth for a while. After I make contact with this friend of hers.

I turn into the car park. Our *Drop-In* is a good one. Always different girls; always a fresh face.

* * *

Roscoe fucking died didn't he. The little shit got hit by a car. There's no carrying *that* over. Now I have to start all over again.

* * *

It's the night of the dinner party. I'm looking forward to the food, I have to admit. However, the 'social' aspect of it is filling me with... boredom.

The light flickers above my mirror in the bathroom before staying on. That will need changing. Everything in my apartment needs replacing. Getting hot water is a game of chance. My Single-Issue domicile is basic and outdated. This block has been due for refurbishment for two years but Single-Issues are always low priority.

I'm bored already at the very thought of having to spend the evening with all these people. People I don't know and who I have no interest in getting to know. I suppose it'll be worth it.

I wonder if I should take some money in case this friend of hers has fresh food to sell tonight. Or will tonight just be about setting things up?

* * *

I pick the girl up at her building. She's waiting outside. Looks pretty nice. I'd say it was built about the same time as my building block but it's better maintained. It's closer to city central so I guess they just got to it first. It makes me hope that perhaps they'll get to mine before I get shipped to a retirement hall. I'm a low contraction blood type. I'll most likely not get sick and live until I'm fifty or something! Which is why it's important to get a good Facsimile with which to while away my time.

I pull the car up in front of the girl.

"Hi," she says.

She's wearing this massive coat that makes her head look like a peanut.

"Nice building," I say as she opens the door and climbs in.

* * *

We pull up outside Mick's house. Yeah, you got that right: his house! This guy is obviously crazily wealthy.

Mick is a little chubby. He's short and his hair is a lank lattice of a few carefully arranged strands. However, he smiles warmly at us on our arrival. He shakes me firmly by the hand, but not in that macho proving-a-point kind of way.

"Welcome sweetheart," he says kindly to the girl. To me he says, "when she told us she was bringing a guest we didn't believe her!" and he laughs so hard his hair very nearly moves. But not quite.

I'm introduced around. There's Andy, who's a doctor, and his wife, Sharon. The tall skinny guy, whose face has the complexion of a towel, is called Richard. There are others but I stop even trying to remember their names. They're all loving the fact they have someone new to 'make friends with'. I hate being social.

I get sat at the table between Mick and Sharon. Opposite me is the doctor, Andy, who's been pretty opinionated about most things all night. Some people are like that. I don't really hold with people's opinions when they have an opinion on everything. They're too spread out.

Turns out he's not a real doctor. He works at *After Life* as a 'biological transference technician' something or other. I don't know. He got pretty pissy when I twigged he wasn't a proper people-doctor.

"No, you misunderstood," he argues, getting defensive as hell. "It's an easy mistake to make. People often do."

"Oh, well it's very interesting," I say, consoling. "It's a shame you can't do people right." I say, trying to move the conversation on.

"I beg your pardon?" he says.

Boy this guy is tetchy. I mean, I don't get all worked up when someone tells me the coffee at the bar tastes like crap. I know it does; it's nothing to do with me what they put in the mix. No need to get snippy about it.

"Well, just the eyes," I say, trying to placate the grumpy fucker.

"I assure you," he says, "our work is the finest in biological representation this sector of the world. The human eye contains millions of densely packed photoreceptors. The biology of the eye, in order to simply function as a perceptive devise, is a staggering undertaking.

Besides which, the emotional range that the eye of a human Facsimile is expected to replicate is astonishingly complex… ”

"Oh," I say politely, in the hope that he'll stop talking to me, "so that's why you can't get them to look right. I'm sorry. You're right. I apologise."

Andy, starts to splutter a bit and looks to Mick for a way out. He obviously doesn't take criticism very well.

"He has a wonderful plan," the girl says. She's smiling at me enthusiastically.

"Sorry?" I ask.

"The dogs," she prompts.

"Oh, I don't think they want to hear about all that," I say.

I mean really, I don't want everyone doing it. The price of dogs will go through the roof.

"On the contrary," Andy says with a strained look on his face, trying to get his embarrassment in check. "Please do tell us of your wonderful plan."

"Well, I wouldn't call it wonderful," I say, trying to play it down.

I wish she'd not brought it up. I mean, all this talking? I just came here for some fresh vegetables.

"He's being modest," the girl says.

Then she tells them all about it. Spills it all.

Resigned to it all coming out I wait to see what Andy says to it. He looks at the girl incredulously; his mouth slightly open. I guess he's not too pleased that his work just got trashed. He looks at me.

"You…" he says slowly, in sort of a whisper. Then he clears his throat and starts again. "You judge everything on its potential as a Facsimile," he says, frowning like he's not quite getting it. I mean, I'm not sure this guy really does work for *After Life*. It's not that difficult a concept. "You've ruled out people because you say we can't make a good *After Life*," he goes on.

"Yes," I answer patiently.

"So you buy a dog and wait to see how it performs," he continues slowly.

"Yes," I say. Boy t

his guy really has to have it all spelled out.

He goes a bit red in the face. "Do you have a score system?" he says, his voice a little raised.

I don't but it's a good idea actually. It'd be more empirical. I mean at the moment I guess I'm too sentimental. I just generally give them a thumbs up or down.

"You're auditioning things for when they pass!" Andy's still trying to get it. "Everyone and thing you meet you're judging based on what kind of Facsimile they'd make. Every living thing you see you imagine if it'd be worth the trip across the road before you get too 'attached'."

I don't know why he's shouting.

"That's not what they're for!"

I smile politely as Andy continues to make a spectacle of himself.

"They're supposed to stop you missing someone," he goes on. "You're supposed to love the living, not look forward to the *After Life*!"

The vegetables finally arrive. They look a little disappointing. If I'm honest I can't really believe it and I'm struggling not to show the disappointment on my face in an attempt not to be rude.

"So if they got the eyes right, you'd be able to love a person?" Andy persists.

Talk about a dog with a bone.

"I guess so."

I'm not really paying him much attention. I'm too distracted by the vegetables. I mean, it's a pretty poor showing; three carrots and some things that look like small cabbages. That's not each! That's between us all. They're placed round the edge of this silver platter thing like they're the showpiece to the world or something. It's crap, really. I'm starting to get myself worked up to tell you the truth. It doesn't help that Andy is still banging on about the bloody Facsimiles.

"You're sick in the head!" he shouts, thumping the table to get my attention. "Your whole purpose is to find something living, that you can have feelings for, based solely on whether or not you can accept it as a Facsimile. If we perfected the eyes and you met someone you could fall in love with, you wouldn't be able to wait for them to get sick so you could settle down with their *After Life* product – you'd prefer them *dead!*"

Well, that did it. You can talk about death all you like. But you can't use any of the 'd' words. It has to be 'passed' or 'taken' or something like that. Everyone looks away from Andy, which is pretty much the same as everyone looking directly at him. It makes him the centre of attention. The centre to be ignored. Anyway, who mentioned anything about 'love' in my plan?

Maybe he's so uptight because, like I said, he's not a real doctor. He's probably sick of being introduced at parties and people assuming he's a real doctor and then when they find out he's just a Facsimile technician he has to explain. That would bug me I guess; having to constantly explain to people that you're not as impressive as they first thought you were – especially if you think everyone should think you're amazing and your opinions are the best thing ever.

* * *

"Well that was interesting," the girl says to me as we walk to my car.

"Yeah," I say, noting the intonation in her voice and knowing exactly what she's referring to. "Three grubby carrots between the lot of us. We may as well have stayed at home."

She laughs and playfully punches me in the arm.

* * *

I pull the car up outside her building, noting again how well maintained it looks.

"You can come up, if you like," she says, noticing I was looking at her building.

"Sure," I say, wondering what it'll be like inside.

* * *

Her apartment is pretty modern. Facility-wise.

"How'd you swing this?" I ask, taking it all in.

"I'm lucky", she says. "My mother died last year. Full sickness. So, they did a full deep clean. They gutted the place. After they were done they replaced it all. I got new everything."

"Cool," I compliment her.

"You really made an impression tonight," she says with a smile.

"Oh, you mean Andy?" I say. "I don't get why he couldn't understand it. It's pretty simple."

"Would you like a drink?" she asks, disappearing into the kitchen.

"Yeah, sure," I call after her. "I just think you're setting yourself up for a lot of hurt with a person," I go on. "The Facsimiles don't work. People die and you're left with a dead-eyed thing that can never reflect the person you lost and serves only as a reminder that it isn't them; that the real 'them' is gone."

"What if you couldn't tell the difference?" she asks, coming back into the living room holding two coffees.

"That'd be great," I say. "But the technology just isn't there and it never will be."

"You can only miss what you had in the first place," she says, handing me one of the cups of hot black coffee.

"Exactly," I say.

I never thought I'd meet someone who got what I was saying like she does. Nice coffee too.

* * *

I'm at work. I signed up for all these stupid extra hours before Roscoe got flattened and now I still have to do them.

The front door swings open and the girl from the *Companion Centre* walks in. Sort of jaunty. Is that the right word? You know; bouncy?

"Hey, I was talking to someone about the eyes!" she says all smiles.

I really do wish she'd stop telling everyone about it.

"Gee, swell," I say, all sarcastic.

"You want to hear what they told me or not?" she says, giving a mock pout; her fuller lips making her face sort of prettier.

"Go on then, if you must," I say, casual as can be.

She laughs and sticks her tongue out.

"There's this new group," she says, like she's talking about what's on at the cinema or something, "and they offer a service."

"Oh, yeah?" I say.

I think she's dyed her hair a bit blue to match her eye colour. You'd think they'd be against that sort of thing at an official city facility.

She hops up on the counter. Her arms straight and by her sides, like a schoolgirl on a wall. I half expect her to start chewing gum and twirling her hair.

"People go to them when one gets sick, you know, couples. And they," she puts her forefinger to her head and strikes down her thumb in the mime of a gun, "they top each other."

She takes her finger and puts it inside her mouth and then does that pop sound thing.

"Cute," I say. "Now kindly get your ass off the counter will you?"

People are starting to look over.

She sticks her tongue out again and hops down.

"I'm going now," she says. "You said a naughty word!"

She smiles, turns, and walks off, pausing to give a little wave at the door. She's an amusing one, I'll give her that.

It's an idea. The killing themselves thing. That way you don't have to suffer the crappy Facsimile. Funny though – Andy would have a fit – that's the sort of thing *After Life* was set up to discourage.

* * *

I finally got a day off yesterday. I didn't know what to do with myself so I popped round to the girl's place. We talked for a bit about this and that. Then she went to work and I went home. Well, first I went to the *Conjugal Drop-In*.

So today I arrive at work all happy and rested and all that. But there's a queue a mile long. Sam, the guy who works the shift before me, is blowing more steam out of his ears than the damn coffee machine.

"Where's Tom?" I ask, putting on my apron.

Tom is the other guy on the shift before me.

"He's in the bloody back with the Great Boggle Face," he says.

That's what we call the boss, on account of her huge ugliness of body and mind.

"He's not in the shit is he?" I say as I chip in to help deal with the line of grumpy citizens in need of their brown infusion.

"Not him, mate," he says. I don't like it when people call me 'mate'; it's a bit familiar. "She had me in earlier too," he continues as he wrestles with the machine.

"What can I get you?" I ask this fat woman with a big spot thing on her forehead.

"A large coffee, when you have the time," she says in this really unpleasant nasal whine.

"Certainly," I smile back professionally.

I turn to start the machine off and Sam leans close, all conspiratorial.

"Boggle was asking me about you," he says, turning to give a short bald man his coffee.

"I don't mean to interrupt your obviously important conversation," whistles the fat woman, "but I am in a hurry."

I fill up the coffee and turn to pass it to her. Boy, that thing on her forehead looks about as angry as she.

"I presume she's asking Tom the same questions," Sam whispers to me.

It's kind of gross. If I had a throbbing thing like that on my forehead I wouldn't go out in public. I certainly wouldn't draw attention to myself by whining my head off in coffee bars.

"There you go, Ma'am," I say, all pleasant and smiles to the spot-creature and she pays and waddles off with no 'thank you' or anything. Some people are just rude.

"I don't know what shit you've been up to," Sam says, pouring a large coffee for the curly-haired woman he's serving, "but she's mega pissed about something. She was asking about you talking to customers."

"That's me," I say, all whimsical, "Mr. chatty."

"I wouldn't joke about it, man," he says, putting the lids on six takeaways.

He always snaps them on whilst I always twist them on. Drives me mad, to tell you the truth.

Just then, Tom comes from out back where the Boggle has her cave. He sees me and gives a nervous smile. I guess the old boss really is on one today.

"She said if you were here," Tom says, "you should go right in to see her."

"Sure thing, Tom," I say, giving him the full smiles, "was just serving your customers for you. You're welcome." I can be pretty sarcastic.

I give the door to the boss's office a nice little knock, being all pleasant, and open the door wearing the same toothy smile I gave Tom.

"You wanted to see me?" I ask, all nice and polite.

She's sitting behind her desk, leaning back in her chair with her hands together like she's having a little angry prayer. Only her eyes aren't closed. They're on me like two cannons ready to blow my head off. I reckon I've really been dropped in the shit by some little grumpy fucker; probably someone in a bad mood with no patience, like that wart-head woman. Someone who's taken their bad day out on me. I'm always polite with customers and treat them with respect.

"Close the door, Mr. McCarthy," she says.

I close the door gently in case it explodes or something. Suddenly everything looks like it's made out of gunpowder. It's not my bloody fault if some fat woman with a crater on her face is in a rush and has a strop. I best steel myself for a tough ride before I get back to work.

"We've had complaints."

Here we go.

"I assure you… " I begin.

"Quiet," she barks. Shit, this is going to be a real chew-out, I reckon. "Your conduct has come into question."

"I'm always polite to my… " I say, trying to keep my smile on but it appears to have left my face and hidden under the table or something.

"Quiet," she interrupts.

This is what happens when you put comment boxes in places. I was against them when we first got them. They're open to obvious abuse; little fat angry women chucking slips in as if you get a free cake with every hundred or something.

"You have been behaving inappropriately," she goes on. "This is not a place for inappropriate conversations."

You'd think this was a *Church Centre* or something. And anyway, no place is a place for 'inappropriate behaviour' or 'conversations'; that's what makes them inappropriate. Stupid.

"I don't see what I… " I start, but she's off again.

"You will vacate the premises and return only to bring back any property pertaining to this place of work," she says coldly.

"But… " I say.

"I won't say it again, Mr. McCarthy," she says, looking down at some paperwork on her desk. I think it's my employment file. "You are fired."

"But… " I say.

"I'm sorry," she says. "It's out of my hands."

And that's that, then, I suppose. I stand up. I turn around and I'm heading to the door.

Crazy fat lady!

I guess I'm going to have to find something cheaper than dogs.

* * *

"What do you mean they fired you!" the girl says.

"This morning I had a job and now I don't," I say. "That kind of fired."

I stopped off at the girl's place on the way home. Her sofa is pretty comfortable; I'll give her that.

"I'm glad you came here," she says, "you shouldn't be on your own at a time like this."

"That's what I thought," I say.

I knew she wouldn't be at work this time of day. So, I went to her building to see what I could get for cheaper than a dog.

"You need companionship," she says.

"Yeah," I say.

Her place really is something, you know. Not a single flickering light.

"I'll get you a drink," she offers.

"Yeah, thanks, that'd be nice," I say. "Not coffee though," I joke.

She disappears off into the kitchen.

"You can stay as long as you like," she calls from the other room.

"OK," I call back.

I mean, I didn't think I was on the meter or anything. Did she think I was expecting her to turf me out after precisely five minutes or something?

The decor's not exactly to my taste around here. All cushions and frills. She comes back with two drinks.

"Here you go," she says, passing me the drink. I take a sip. It's not water. It's alcohol. "I was talking to my friend some more yesterday," she says, sitting down next to me, "about the new group."

I don't twig what she's on about at first. But then I remember what she was saying the other day at work. At what *was* work.

"There are surgeries too."

"Hmm?" I mumble after taking another sip of the drink. Boy this is good stuff.

"It's interesting, don't you think?" she says, in an effort to get me talking, "to know that there are alternatives available?"

"Yeah," I say, not really paying all that much attention.

She leans forward and puts her glass on the little table in front of the sofa. The table has a little frilly doily on it, obviously. When she leans back her shoulder brushes on mine. I start to think about the *Drop-In*. I could go after I'm finished here. I think I will. After all it's been a pretty tough day.

"Would you ever consider it?" she asks. It might be the alcohol – I've drunk all mine – or it might be that she's boring the crap out of me, but I think I've missed something out of this conversation.

"I guess so," I tell her, not wanting her to think I hadn't really been listening.

And with that, she kisses me.

I know. I don't know where the hell that came from either. But there you go. So, I get up with a start, like I got an electric shock or something.

"I should probably go," I say.

Boy she's got me all worked up. I mean, like I said, she's slim. And I didn't mention it, but she's wearing this top that shows just the top of her breasts. Not too much like. Not tarty or anything. Anyway, now I definitely think I want to go to the *Drop-In*.

"I'm sorry," she says, "I just thought… "

"No, it's not that," I say quickly.

She looks like she's going to cry and I really really don't think I could handle that right now.

"I mean," she says, looking down at her hands.

I look down at her hands and notice her top again. Boy, I need to get out of here and to the *Drop-In* so badly!

"What with all that's happened... and, you know..."

I don't have a bloody clue, to be honest. But I don't want her to cry, I really don't. I don't want her to feel bad.

"Don't you find me attractive?" she asks.

I don't know what to say. I mean, of course I do. That's why I'm so desperate to get out of here. I'm turned on so much all I can think of is getting out of here.

"I do, I do," I say, trying to get her to smile or something.

"You're just saying that," she says. I thought she was different, you know. I thought she knew I didn't want to get involved with any people. I thought she got the whole plan. "I can tell all you want to do is get the hell out of here and never come back," she says with a slight wobble in her throat.

"Well, yeah," I say and that just about does it. I know she's going to cry any second. "But that's because you *are* attractive," I blurt out, stumbling with the words. It's the first thing I could think of to stop the tears.

She looks up. Man, she looks so sad. I feel really bad, I do. This is a horrible situation to be in. Really awkward.

"I mean," I say, just to make her feel better, "you made me, well... that top, and your... well... breasts." Boy, this is embarrassing. But I want her to feel better. "So I wanted to get out of here, to go to the *Drop-In.*" She's still looking at me sadly, like none of this is helping. "You know, the *Conjugal Drop-In?*" I go on. "You turned me on, so I wanted to go there."

There, I said it. I didn't want her to know. I didn't want her think I was coming on to her or anything. Trying it on. But I had to say it so she felt better about herself. Then maybe she'd let me get the hell out of here.

"Oh," she says.

I don't know if it's working or not, but she definitely looks less like she's going to cry.

She smiles. Actually, smiles. Great, I think, I can go.

"You don't have to leave," she says.

She stands up and steps towards me. "Why go there, when you can stay here?" she says and reaches out her hand and places it on my chest.

My heart is going a million miles an hour.

"Stay here," she says again.

She moves her hand down the front of my shirt. I've still got my uniform on from the coffee bar and I think about that stupid fat woman, with the spot, that got me fired.

"You don't have to go to any old *Drop-In*," the girl says, as her fingers touch the top of my trousers and the button there. "You have me," she whispers, "why go there?"

And then I get what she means. Of course! Why go there? Why spend my money? She knows I just got fired. She means I should stay here and save my money. Why go to the *Drop-In* when I can use her for sex, for free? She *does* get me after all! I knew it wouldn't be a problem hanging around with her; that she didn't want to be my friend.

"I thought, for a moment..." I start. Then I smile. "I knew you were different," I say and I reach out and touch her left breast. It's firm and the nipple is hard. She's in much better physical condition than the girls at the *Drop-In*. I can't believe my luck. This arrangement should work out great. Just when I needed to save some money.

* * *

It's the morning. She lays next to me, sleeping quietly. She looks like a crumpled thing, all wrapped up in blanket and hair. She's dyed it green. I hadn't noticed last night.

I get up and walk over to the bathroom and, well, you know, do the usual morning sit-down meeting and I think about last night. Her bed is comfortable. It must be newer than mine. I had a good night's sleep. It's funny she's dyed her hair green. I thought she'd dyed it blue that other time to match her eyes. I can't even remember if they *are* blue now. I'll have to look when she wakes up. It's supposed to be an indicator; eye colour. Though there are various opinions if it really is or not. I know I'm low risk of getting sick. Because of my blood. Which is really the only way to know. But you can't very well go about asking for people's blood type, can you?

I leave before she wakes up. I figure, if she's at work today, she'll want to get off without any fuss. I'd only be in the way.

You have to smile, though. I mean, there you are, you hang around with someone for a bit and then you convince yourself that they're pretty. I mean prettier than they were when you first met them.

I suppose I'd better go to *Employment Allocation* today. What a hassle. I sort of liked my job at the coffee bar.

* * *

I'm pretty sure I was right the first time. I think they're blue.

* * *

Employment Allocation is a grey and uninviting sort of a place. I get on fine here, though. Everyone just goes about their business. What some people might call curtness or rudeness I call, 'no fuss'. It's brilliant.

I get called through and I follow the little green line on the floor to the right room. I think all life should be like this. Get given a number and a little coloured line to follow. No fuss. Except, you can bet that the Andy's of this world will still spend all their time trying to convince everyone that their line is better than yours!

I sit down at a metal desk in a small room with motivating posters on the wall with slogans like, 'Work Makes You Free For Travel!" and "Serve The People In Retail". This place makes my apartment look jolly. Behind the desk is a man in a wrinkled suit who does nothing to brighten it up.

"We'll begin with forms A through to Six before we make a mandatory break for lunch," he says, lifting a wad of forms onto the desk.

This is going to be a long day.

* * *

It's that promised 'mandatory break'. I thought it would never come. I step out to the street and dust off my phone.

I dial enquiries and get the number for the *Companion Centre* and get put through to the girl.

"Hi," she says quietly.

She probably has someone with her; some young family after getting a Labrador or something.

"Hello," I say. "I'm at *Employment Allocation*."

"Oh," she says, practically whispering.

"Yeah, it's a real fun-fest," I joke.

"I'm glad you called," she says.

"Yeah?" I say.

She probably wanted me to know she got to work OK or something.

"When I got up and you weren't there, I thought..." she says, sort of trailing off. One of the kids from the family is probably touching something they shouldn't, or the dad is being all tutty about her being on the phone.

"I just didn't want to disturb you," I tell her.

"It's nice you called," she says, her voice sounding normal, not giving a damn whether Mr Impatient Dad tuts his head clean off. "I was going to go to that place..." she says in a smiley sort of a voice.

"Oh, I'll be quick then," I say. She must be going on a supply run for the *Centre*, or something. "It's just, I need a character reference, for the *Employment Allocation* people."

"Oh," she says, quiet again.

The dad must have turned it up a notch. Boy, some fellas can just be insensitive, you know?

* * *

Back in with Mr Wrinkled Suit. Lunch didn't do anything to lighten his demeanour. We've moved on to the bit where we actually start looking at possible employment vacancies.

"Do you have anything in retail?" I ask.

I mean, I was pretty good at the old coffee bar.

He taps away at his computer like he's stabbing a dead bird with a stick.

"Hmm," he says, frowning. And I realise he hasn't been frowning all along. Which is strange, because, a man like that, you assume would frown all the time. "There appears to be a restriction on your account, Mr McCarthy."

"Oh?" I say a bit taken aback.

"We have a restriction on you working anywhere that involves the public," he says. "Due to the nature of your previous employment termination," he explains insensitively.

"What?" I splutter. "Just because one fat woman complained?"

"Says here," he goes on, reading the screen, "that the complaint was made through official channels by the *After Life Corporation*."

* * *

I pull up outside the girl's building. It's times like this you want to be comforted. And, seeing as this is the new *Drop-In*, I ended up here. This restriction has got me pretty worked up, I don't mind admitting. The coffee bar was the only job I had. I don't really know how to do anything else.

"I have something to tell you," she says, smiling her head off.

"Me too," I say. I sit down on the sofa next to her. "I've got a damn restriction on my employment account," I tell her.

"Oh?" she says, tilting her head to one side like a stupid Roscoe or something.

"Yeah," I say, getting tetchy, "*After Life* complained! Through official channels!"

I get up and walk about a bit.

"They say I've been spreading inflammatory propaganda!" I say, waving my hands about at the absurdity of the whole thing. "I'm not anti-*After Life* or their Facsimiles! I just know their people are shit!"

"Not the whole people," she says, pedantic-like, "just the eyes."

"Yeah, the eyes," I say. "Always the eyes."

"Maybe if you got one," she says, smiling again. What is it with this girl? "Maybe if you had a Facsimile – a people one – they'd remove the restriction?"

I look at her. She's obviously lost the plot. She knows I couldn't have a Facsimile of a person. And there she sits, smiling like a mannequin.

She stands up and walks over to me. Sort of like she did the other night. Boy, I really don't think I'm in the mood anymore.

"My news," she says, "my news will help solve everything."

She puts her hand to the side of my head and gently holds my cheek. She's beaming with joy, a tear sparkles in the corner of her eye.

"I got in to see them," she says, almost a whisper, "they've agreed to do it."

As I look at her, wondering what the hell she's talking about, I smile.

"I'm stage one," she says, laying her head on my chest. "I'm sick."

Blue. I knew they were blue. High contagion risk.

* * *

Her skin is still clear and soft. She looks good. She should stay that way for a good few weeks. Long enough for me to become accustomed to how she'll look after the surgery. I can finally start to let my guard down. I can have feelings for this one and the Facsimile would match. It's a great new plan. It took me a while to catch up, I'll admit. But once she explained it, it made perfect sense.

She's lying on the hospital cart. Is that what you call them? A metal bed on wheels that they take you places on. Anyway, she's on one of those, all wrapped up and ready. This isn't strictly a hospital. But they seem to know what they're doing. I wasn't really paying that much attention whilst they were explaining the procedure. We had a hell of a time finding the place, all hidden away like it is and I was fretting about the charge in the car's motor. I just know what the end results are going to be and I don't see how it can go wrong after that.

She's pleased as punch, I'll tell you. Who'd have guessed it? I didn't know she felt that way. But hey, she figured it all out so that it's OK for me to feel that way back too.

"I love you," she tells me. And I know she means it. I can see it in her eyes. I'll miss them, I suppose. But I'll get used to them not being there. Like she said, "You can only miss what you had in the first place," and by the time she's stage two or three, it'll be like she'd never had them. Then the Facsimile will be perfect.

I realise it was shallow of me to reject the notion of getting close to people. Once you take the eyes out of the equation, there really is no problem.

Siren

Prudence King
England

THE PUB WAS KIND OF SLEAZY. The furnishings were all glass-ringed dark wood, casually wiped with a damp-smelling cloth, and redundant glass ash-trays – the type that are used as murder weapons in cheap crime novels. The carpet, which looked as if it had been ripped straight out of a hotel lobby, had been inexplicably upholstered onto the booth seats and bar stools. Bald men nursed beer bellies in shady corners, as they discussed euphemistic business 'down the market', and a television, mounted precariously on one wall, relayed the latest football match in mute flares of colour. In a lone corner, a fake-retro jukebox and fake-retro pinball machine flashed showily. The landlady, who was a frizz of blonde perm, neon-pink lipstick, and a jaw that never stopped chewing invisible gum, plopped a pint in front of Paul and shook her head when he offered his card.

"Machine's dead."

Paul rummaged in his wallet for a note and smiled to himself as the landlady tottered off to the till. Yeah. The pub was sleazy, and dated, and harbouring the odour of smoke from days before the ban, but it was the last place anyone would expect to find an Indie rock star, which was exactly why he had chosen it.

The landlady returned, placed Paul's change in front of him, and went back to reading her magazine at the far end of the bar. Paul slipped the money into the back pocket of his jeans and sipped his drink. The pub might be tasteless, but the beer was good. This was just what he needed to clear his head. It had been an intense week. The album was coming along nicely, but being stuck in a basement studio with six other people sometimes got too much for him. Today, after eight hours of recording, unproductive discussions, and the repetition of 'let's just do one more take', he just had to get out, find some fresh air, and have a few feet of space to himself.

He rested his elbows on the bar and rubbed the back of his neck. A movement to his left caught his attention and he glanced across to see a girl sitting along the bar from him. Paul hadn't noticed her come in, but she had a drink in front of her already. A second later, the jukebox clicked on and music started blaring out of the speakers. Paul winced at the tinny quality, but appreciated the song choice. A classic: Soundwave's 'Didn't See You Coming'. Spent twelve weeks at number one in '86. Winner of five awards. Covered countless times by almost every famous artist. Somewhere, he had a recording of his own version, from before the band got together.

Paul eyed the girl with mild interest as Davis Sunday's voice soared through the pub. Her shoulder length, strawberry-blonde hair was tucked behind her ear, revealing three piercings, which winked at him as her head bobbed a little. She was wearing black jeans, boots, and a black bomber jacket, which was open to show a simple white t-shirt underneath. A silver charm bracelet jangled against her slim, pale wrist, as she tapped her thigh.

She didn't look like she belonged in this sort of pub.

She took a sip of her drink and then turned her head and caught Paul staring. He smiled awkwardly. "Nice choice," he said, trying to indicate the music.

She smiled back. It was almost a conspiratorial look, as if she appreciated that he shared her good taste. "One of my favourites," she replied. "Though you should hear him live."

"Yeah, I wish I had," Paul admitted. "I bet he was amazing. So sad that he got throat cancer."

She gave a single nod, as if in agreement, and that seemed to kill the conversation.

Paul took a long slug from his beer and tried to wriggle the knots out of his neck and shoulders with one hand. He needed a hot shower and about ten hours sleep. As the track came to an end, he looked round to find the girl had shuffled up next to him. Up close, he could see grey-green irises and a delicate dotting of freckles on her nose. The scent of warm sea air and honey perfumed the air between them, reminding Paul of a meadowed island in the Mediterranean Sea.

"Your turn," she said with a lift of one eyebrow. "Pick a song. Make it a good one."

Paul glanced behind him at the jukebox and then at the other six punters in their dark corners. He shrugged and slid off his stool. Pulling the change from his back pocket he critically eyed the options on the jukebox. He felt like he was being tested: should he play it safe or go for something a little more out there? Too predictable and he'd come across as boring; too obscure and he'd come across as pretentious. He threw the girl a look over his shoulder and she raised her eyebrow again in a challenging manner. With a quick, nervous smile, he slipped a coin into the machine and hit a button.

The girl began nodding her head in approval as the track started. "Jazz," she said. "Nice choice."

"Sadie Terrone is probably my all-time favourite jazz singer."

"Favourite song?"

Paul thought for a moment. "Summer Tears," he said eventually. "Or Romance the Moon."

"Perfect songs," she agreed. "'Romance the Moon' isn't that well known, but definitely one of her best."

"The sax solo is something special."

"Mmm…," she mused. "But I like it best when it's just her voice and the instruments are pulled way back. 'Honey, Hold Me' always makes me cry. Sadie's voice is so pure and there's this beautiful vulnerability to it – like she really means the words and isn't just performing."

"Everyone thinks that song's about a love affair," Paul said automatically, "But it's actually about her younger sister… "

The girl smiled, parting her nude-pink lips to show small creamy-white teeth. "You're right," she said, as her eyes widened with surprise.

"She lost her sister to a genetic disease. They were really close and it broke Sadie's heart, like no romance ever could."

"I guess that's why her songs are so full of sadness," Paul added. "You can hear it through all of them – somehow it's just there – this underlying poignancy."

The girl flicked her hair slightly as she looked at him with a curious gaze, and then held out her hand. "Agla," she said. "Nice to meet you…"

"Paul." He took her hand and hoped she hadn't noticed his blush.

"Well, I didn't expect to bump into another music nerd here," she grinned.

"Do you come here often?" Paul asked.

She wriggled her shoulders vaguely. "The jukebox has some great tunes on it. After a crappy day, I like to come and listen to some decent music."

"You don't have decent music at home?"

She laughed. "All right," she conceded. "I like to come and have a proper pint and listen to some decent music. And sometimes meet other geeks." She swivelled round on her stool and her knees lightly bumped his. "I bet I could out-nerd you though," she said with dry playfulness.

"I accept that challenge."

And so they began a game of music mastermind. Sometimes the jukebox was utilised, sometimes their phones, as each of them tried to impress the other with obscure artists, song lyrics, and cultural references. They were fairly evenly matched, but at one point she had him on a Molly Joy song.

"I've never heard of her covering that song," Paul admitted reluctantly. "She only did two albums, didn't she? Before that thing happened… "

"She definitely covered it," Agla insisted. "Right at the start of her singing career, before she became famous. It's how I discovered her… " She stopped at Paul's gentle laugh.

"Discovered her?" he said. "You weren't born then."

She just smiled. "It was the first song I heard her sing: 'So Sighs the Wind'. It's a really old folk song…"

"Written nearly two-hundred-years ago," Paul said.

He inwardly winced at his own obnoxiousness. Why did he have to come across as such a know-it-all?

She slapped him lightly on the arm. "All right, smart-arse. Molly Joy did this totally original arrangement of it – completely acapella, but like you've never heard before. It's one of the most enrapturing things I've ever heard."

"I've never come across it." Paul shook his head. "But I wish I had. I can't believe she never sang again after… you know… There's obviously a recording of 'So Sighs the Wind'?"

"I have it," Agla said, starting her third – or fourth? – pint.

Paul wasn't really keeping up with the numbers - or the time.

Agla pursed her lips as she savoured the beer. "You'll have to come and listen to it," she added casually.

"Well," Paul said, flushing a little and confused as to why he should suddenly feel so self-conscious. "You're a real connoisseur of vintage artists – but are you up to date on the latest talent?"

"Who've you got in mind?" she asked.

Paul slid his phone towards her and brought up a track on his playlist. "This guy," he said. "They call him the Soul Man. He's been doing the small gig circuit for a while now, but he's just picked up a record deal. We did a collaboration with him for our new album… " He stopped. He genuinely hadn't meant to mention the band. When he glanced up to check her reaction, she was giving him a half-cynical, half-questioning look.

"I knew you had to work in music," she said. "I thought I recognised you. You're a musician?"

"I'm in a band."

"Called?"

"In-Dependence."

She grinned, obviously a little amused. "Of course! I've heard of you guys. I liked your first album."

"But not the others?" Paul joked, a little embarrassed by her apparent indifference.

"I just mean that the first album is great. First albums are always the best."

"I could think of a few artists who would disagree with you."

She wrinkled her nose and waved a dismissive hand so that the charm bracelet jingled. "Real artists," she clarified, "always produce their best stuff on the first album. It's when they mean it the most: when singing is still a personal, raw act – and when it's not become about record deals, or fans, or trying to stay 'fresh and relevant'." She met his gaze, which was fixed on her with a sort of charmed interest.

It was rare to meet such an enthusiast: someone who seemed to know everything there was to know about music across such a broad range of history, genres, and cultures. Her main obsession seemed to be with singers and from what he had heard; she had impeccable taste. He wondered what her voice was like.

"Anyway," she continued, with a slight twist at the corner of her mouth. "First albums are the best. Second, third, and sometimes even the fourth are usually satisfactory – but artists should stop after that. It's all downhill from there."

"Davis Sunday recorded five more albums after he left Soundwave," Paul argued, "And all of them reached the top ten in the charts."

Agla rolled her eyes a little, but the reproach was friendly. "The charts are hardly an indicator of true art," she said. "Which songs of his do people still dance to at parties? Which ones get requested the most? Which ones do people choose as their 'couple song'? Or play on repeat when their hearts get broken?"

"His Soundwave stuff, I suppose."

"Exactly. And they're primarily from the first album."

Paul nodded thoughtfully, went to take a swig of beer, and realised his glass was empty. How many had he had? How long had they been sitting here? He looked at Agla, who was running her fingers through her hair, and a sudden thought occurred to him.

"His last single was worth waiting for though."

"'Grey Horizons'?" Agla's smile became a little dreamy. "Possibly his best." She sighed. "When I heard it for the first time, I felt like…"

"You'd been waiting to hear it all your life?"

She nodded and, for a moment, Paul was tempted to believe in kindred spirits.

Agla gave him a little sideways smile. "But you know when he wrote it?"

Paul narrowed his eyes. "When?"

"Before he even formed Soundwave."

Paul laughed at her triumphant look. "All right – you may have a point," he conceded. He tapped his phone. "But you should hear this guy, the Soul Man, and tell me what you think."

They sat in silence for a couple of minutes, hunched over his phone, and reeled in, like fish on a line, by the sonorous tones of the Soul Man. There was a time-stopped moment, after the track had finished, where they both continued to listen to the melody as it travelled beyond their ears and into their consciousness.

"He's incredible," Agla breathed eventually. "That voice!"

Paul felt a wave of pride, tinged by a touch of jealousy, as she turned shimmering grey-green eyes on him.

"Thanks," she said. "I will definitely check him out." She downed the dregs of her pint and then arched her back in an elegant, feline stretch. She tugged at her jacket and tucked a loose strand of hair behind her ear. "I reckon I owe you that Molly Joy song now."

"Yeah?" Paul watched her slide off the stool. Another waft of honey-sweet air tingled his senses.

"Yeah. Come and listen," she said casually. "I'm only round the corner."

Paul hesitated slightly, but she was already walking to the exit. He had to make a snap decision. He was a little worried for his own safety and reputation. Going home with girls was a precarious business these days - which was why he never did it. Such seemingly simple situations became complicated and fraught with danger when you were famous. Not that he was really famous. The band was well known and so was their music, but he rarely ever got recognised on the street. That didn't stop people taking advantage of you though. You'd think that a certain amount of fame would provide security, but since they'd 'made it', he felt increasingly vulnerable. But he didn't have time to agonise over that right now.

He joined her out on the street. Perhaps the drink had softened the edges of his inhibitions, but he felt quite excited and daring. It helped, somewhat, that Agla hadn't been impressed by his Indie rock star status. And she clearly wasn't attracted to him. It was easy to relax in to conversation with her because their interaction was purely platonic: just two music nerds sharing an obsession.

He felt a moment of nervousness, though, as Agla opened the door to her flat; but she gave him that same conspiratorial look as before and he shook off the feeling.

"Have a seat," she said, indicating the sofa.

Paul forced himself to sit all the way back in the depth of the sofa, hoping he looked nonchalant, though he seemed unable to put his hands anywhere except his lap. Trying to distract himself, whilst Agla took off her boots and jacket in the bedroom, Paul glanced around him at the interior of the flat. It was a streamlined place of neutral hues and plush textures. There didn't seem to be any electronic devices or CDs, but Paul guessed those were probably neatly hidden in the wall cupboards. On the wall opposite the sofa was a delicate little wooden cabinet of tiny square drawers and a shelf, which had a collection of white crystal-like stones lined up on it. Paul shifted self-consciously and smiled as Agla came into the room. She smiled back, touching a gold chain that peeped through the neck of her t-shirt.

"Before you hear Molly Joy," she said, with a teasing raise of her eyebrow, "I have to admit something."

Paul widened his eyes slightly.

She smiled and tossed her hair. "I was a bit coy earlier about your band. I did know who you were and I'm actually very fond of your music."

"But mostly of the first album?"

Agla laughed lightly as she turned and ran a hand over the line of crystals on the shelf. "Mostly of your voice," she admitted.

Paul felt his heart jump a little at her honesty.

"And I was wondering – before you hear Molly Joy – if you would sing something for me?"

Paul's eyes widened even further and he shifted uncomfortably. He was glad that she still had her back to him. "Sing?" he repeated. "Now?" He laughed nervously. "Here?"

Agla picked up a crystal and turned to face him. She bit her lip as she idly rubbed the white stone between her palms and then raised that challenging eyebrow again. "I dare you."

Paul shrugged. "Okay. What do you want me to sing? Something old? Something new?"

"From your fifth album?" She wrinkled her nose.

"I know. It's all downhill after the fourth..."

"The last song," she suggested, "On your first album."

Paul's forehead furrowed slightly as he thought. "'Shipwreck'?"

"Yes. It's indescribably beautiful."

Paul was embarrassed and amused. That song was always a fan favourite. They had never released it as a single and it was right on the end of the deluxe version of the album; it wasn't even on their set list for tours, but, if they were ever taking requests at a smaller gig, that was the one guaranteed to come up. He was pleased; it was one of his personal favourites.

"Well," he agreed tentatively, "I'm not sure I'll do it justice without the rest of the band."

"It's your voice that makes the song."

Her frankness made him feel hot all over with abashment. He hoped he wouldn't disappoint her. He nodded, swallowing a little and suddenly very aware of the fragility of his throat. The silence of the flat seemed to intensify and that usual twist of nervous excitement, which he got before any performance, gnawed at his stomach. He tried to focus on the first line and let his eyes flutter shut as he found the melody in his memory. As usual, when he opened his mouth, his voice did not let him down and struck out into the expectant air with clarity and ease.

Feeling his body begin to relax, Paul opened his eyes and locked them on Agla, who was staring at him as if he were an exotic, mythological creature. As he started the second verse, she stepped forwards, her eyes never leaving his and her hands still moving softly over the stone. Paul caught a flicker of golden light flaring between her fingers. Her shins touched his legs, and then she leant forward and planted her knees either side of his lap, sinking down into the luxurious padding of the sofa until they were eye to eye. Even though his pulse kicked up a step, Paul kept singing. It was as if his voice had become a separate entity from the rest of him and would finish the song, even if he pressed his lips shut. He couldn't draw his gaze from the grey-green eyes, even when he felt something cold touch the hollow at the base of his throat. He felt as if he were in a spell, where time had stretched and he had lost connection with reality. His body became perfectly still, in some sort of stupor, but he didn't feel frightened.

As he started the last chorus, Agla pushed herself back up from the sofa and stood with her neck stretched back, allowing the dying wave of his voice to wash over her. Paul stared at the line of her lovely white throat, and his eyes skimmed irresistibly down to where she held her hands to her chest, like a prayer. He felt a sudden, unnerving twinge as he saw the golden glow of the crystal between her fingers. As if waking from a dream, he realised something strange had happened to him.

He tried to move and speak, but discovered that he could do neither. His body had become like lead, though he was alert to all the usual sensations: the press of the sofa on his back, the cooling air on his neck, and an itch on his right wrist. But worse than that, when he moved his lips to speak, no sound came out, even though he could hear the last of his voice trailing to the stone at Agal's breast as it finished the song. He tried a couple of times, feeling the panic rise, as Agla lowered her head and watched him with the same fire she'd had in her eyes when she had talked about her favourite singers. Paul attempted to find even a sound and managed to send out a strained cough from his throat. That was it.

"It's all right," Agla said matter-of-factly, but not unkindly. "You're going to be okay." She turned to the cabinet of drawers and placed the crystal inside one of the tiny boxes, closing it with a sharp snap.

Paul felt something inside of him evaporate. His eyes, the only part of him that could still function normally, followed her as she went in to the kitchen. For a minute, there was a clattering sound and then she reappeared, sliding something that glinted thinly into her back pocket.

Paul was still trying to move, and the effort was making his eyes nearly pop out of his head. Agla went back to the cabinet, opened another drawer, and took out an identical glowing, golden crystal. She saw Paul's frightened look and gave him a gentle smile as she walked back to the sofa.

"Oh, sweetie," she said. "I can see it in your eyes – so many questions! But there's little point in explaining it; you won't remember any of this in the morning: not this place, what's happened to you, or even me." She caught his gaze flickering to the cabinet. "It's gone, Paul. I have it now. It's so perfect, I just had to have it."

The reality of what she was saying hit Paul like a punch in the lungs, and he couldn't stop the tear that rolled down his cheek. Agla came forward and settled herself back on the sofa, with her knees either side of Paul's thighs. Paul wanted to shiver as she ran a hand through his hair, down the back of his neck, and over his collar bone to the dip at the base of his throat. But his body made no response. Her hand cradled the side of his head as she stooped to catch the trickle of tears with a compassionate kiss.

"You're going to be okay," she said again. She pulled back to look at him whilst her thumb stroked his cheek. "When people realise they'll never hear you sing again, their appreciation for your music is going to double. Trust me. What-might-have-been is so much more desirable than what-has-been. You'll live forever now, in your music. And you'll still write songs – you write beautifully. You'll be offering a new generation of talent the chance to fill the void."

Paul could feel his heart breaking. The bile rose in his throat as he began to fully understand their earlier conversations in the light of this moment. Sadie Terrone, Molly Joy, Davis Sunday. Countless other artists. And now him. How many of those drawers had glowing crystals in them? And there was still that whole shelf of white quartz…

"I am sorry about tomorrow morning though," Agla continued with her typical bluntness. "I like you, Paul, but I've had to become quite creative these days. It used to be simpler: no one needed a medical reason to lose their voice. And then there was the smoking. When they clamped down on that, I had to find other convincing reasons. So, I am sorry. When you wake up in hospital, it's going to be a shock for you. It's horribly tragic that the tracheotomy that saved your life also irrevocably damaged your vocal chords. You just shouldn't walk home alone from the pub these days…" She pulled on the chain around her neck to reveal a shell-shaped locket hanging on the end. She gave him a brighter smile. "But I did promise you that Molly Joy song. It's the only thing you *are* going to remember."

Paul willed his muscles to resurrect themselves. He tried to lunge forward, push her off his lap, and run for the door. But his body remained inert and the tears flowed more freely. He could do nothing: nothing at all, but watch, as Agla slid the glowing crystal into the shell and then ran her hand over his hair again. She parted her nude-pink lips, showing those small creamy-white teeth, and a melody, so haunting that it stabbed Paul straight to his heart, flowed into the stillness of the room. His vision started to swim. The achingly beautiful sound began to fill his whole body and the world merged quickly into a strawberry-blonde halo, swirling with a golden flame. And then, eventually, there was nothing but Molly Joy's voice, singing him into sweet oblivion.

At a Junction

Rhiannon Lewis
Wales

3rd in the 2017 International Literary Prize
University Centre Grimsby

THERE WAS A HORRIBLE, RUBBERY SCREECH and Emil Stein, concert pianist, was catapulted forward so hard that he ended up being pasted against the back of the driver's seat like a splatted cartoon cat.

'Oh, my giddy aunt!' said the driver, Gregory, once he'd wrestled the car to a stop.

Emil was just peeling himself off the plush black leather when another car flew past them, taking out a bollard. It came to an ungainly stop, perched on top of it. A second screech, behind them this time, was followed by a delicate, almost musical release of broken glass. There was a bump, and their car was shunted forward, narrowly missing the one in front.

'Bloody hell,' said Gregory. He wasn't normally one to swear. 'Did you see that?'

Emil had been too busy checking his recital schedule to notice anything going on in the outside world. 'What happened?' he asked, sweeping his wavy blonde hair back over his forehead. Through the clouds of dust and smoke, and the sickly glow of orange street lamps, he could see that a van had somersaulted on to the central barrier, wedging itself up against a lamp post and something that looked like a hanging basket.

'A lad on a bike, came out of nowhere – came right across… what a mess!'

Emil looked around and tried to work out where they were. Some dog-eared part of the city, by the look of it. They appeared to have stopped in the centre of a huge five-way junction, with traffic lights in every direction.

'You stay here,' said Gregory, 'I'm going to take a look.'

They both knew Emil wouldn't be venturing out himself. Not that people were likely to recognise him. People didn't generally recognise him, thought Emil. But that was more a reflection on their level of education or lack of musical taste rather than how famous he was. Besides, the car windows were blacked out, thank goodness. And in any case, he had plenty to do while the road was being cleared. Emil craned his neck to see if he could spot Gregory. He couldn't. There were a lot of people running around. He wasn't sure what they were doing.

Emil's diary and paperwork had slipped and scattered in the sudden stop. He leant forward to pick them up. He put the loose papers on the seat next to him then turned his attention to the pages in his diary. Earlier on, his PA had told him about a last minute invitation to play in Stockholm. *Stockholm in January! I don't think so.* This time last year he'd been performing at an amazing festival in Rio de Janeiro. Now that had been worth the flight. It was a new development for him – South America. The audiences had been very appreciative and surprisingly knowledgeable. He flicked through the weeks ahead: Lucerne, Boston, Vienna – such a stunning auditorium, Berlin, Paris – the best venues in the world. He swiftly passed over the words 'Carnegie Hall!!' which had an impatient thick line drawn through them. Carnegie wasn't the best auditorium by a long chalk, but he had always had a hankering to play there. Being passed over for a younger, 'more marketable' female pianist still rankled. She wasn't exactly playing fair either. When she performed she seemed to wear less on stage than most women he knew wore to bed. His team was still working on it, though. Although he was damned if he was going to turn up in a backless shirt or trousers cut down to his bum.

'But look,' he'd reminded the team, 'I'm not desperate. Only if it fits with my schedule. I've got to work around all my charity stuff and there's Jeremy's holidays too to consider, don't forget.'

Jeremy. He hadn't seen him for weeks. He would be getting pretty grumpy by now. *Mental note: ask the PA to order a consignment of that hideously expensive cologne.*

Emil looked over the passenger headrest to see whether there was any progress on the road. Everything seemed to have gone very quiet. He scanned the sad looking Victorian terraces. The people up front could have chosen a more scenic place to have an accident. The street lamps made the scene look garish, like a man in drag. But, to be fair, the city's concert hall had been rather impressive. It was still new and a little shiny, and had none of the gravitas of the more established venues. But it had a promising feel about it. Nicely placed on the harbour. A smartly dressed audience. He liked that. He liked to think that people made the effort. It was a mark of respect for him, and for his art. He had no patience with these people who turned up in jeans, looking like they'd been dragged through a hedge backwards. Even less patience with musicians who did the same, expecting audiences to take them seriously. It was laughable really. Would the prime minister turn up to work in a set of overalls? And the Queen – now there was a smart lady. He'd been introduced to her at the South Bank. No flies on her.

Emil set the diary down on the seat next to him and picked up the pile of paperwork. It was a jumbled mess of performance notes and press releases. There was fan mail too, but only a small sample. His team must have selected the most interesting ones rather than waste his time. He flicked through them: *Stunning. Delightful. Exquisite. Pleasing.* Pleasing? Emil re-read the sentence. 'Your rendition of Beethoven's piano concerto number five was very pleasing, and although not as eloquent as Kaspar Volkov's performance which we saw in Sydney last year, it was nonetheless masterfully done.'

Pleasing! In the same breath as Volkov! Emil tossed the letter aside and peered again over the top of the passenger seat.

Oh, hurry up, will you?

Gregory had left the driver's door open and there was strong smell of traffic fumes. People's engines were still running. That was a good sign at least. It meant that they weren't going to be there long. Mingled with the fumes was the faintest smell of fish and chips. *Fish and chips and mushy peas.* He quite fancied that. Jeremy wasn't there to tell him off with his acerbic macrobiotic, vegan-cum-gluten-free guilt trip. Perhaps Gregory could do a detour once they'd got moving? He was from around here, wasn't he? This was his patch?

Then in the space of three minutes, a police car, a police motorbike, and an ambulance turned up. Everything was a swirling cacophony of flashing blue lights and sirens. There was a lot of activity up ahead, and some of the drivers returned to their cars. A police officer was weaving his way between the vehicles, updating people on progress. He peered in through the open door.

'Alright, mate, where's your driver?'

Emil's mouth dropped open. There was so much wrong with that sentence. But before he could think of a clever riposte, the policeman added, 'You can't leave a car unattended with the engine running you know,' and to Emil's horror, he leapt in to the driver's seat.

'What have we got here, then? BMW, seven series. Nice. Let's put it out of action for a bit, shall we?' The officer made sure the handbrake was on, then switched off the engine.

He removed the keys from the ignition and tossed them back over his shoulder towards Emil.

'Don't want anyone kidnapping you, do we?'

Emil was pretty sure that the officer had absolutely no idea who he was, so could only assume that the comment was some kind of policeman-y joke. The officer got out of the car.

'We're not going to be here long, are we, officer?' asked Emil in the most obsequious tone he could muster. The officer sighed and leant back in through the open door.

'Mate, we have a distressed teenager who seems to have broken most of the bones in his legs, and who is currently depositing a significant percentage of his blood supply on the central reservation. Not to mention a bloke who's cleverly got himself pinned between his steering wheel, a lamp post and a hanging basket – although that doesn't appear to have diminished his ability to put the world and the entire police force to rights. The traffic's already backed up as far as the city centre. So you may be here quite a while. But don't worry. If you're stuck any longer than two hours we'll bring you some bottled water.'

Two hours! Emil watched the officer as he sauntered off towards the other car. Nice arse he thought, resentfully. But the man was clearly a bit of a joker.

Emil groaned. Why did he have to spend so much of his life feeling like a prisoner? Blacked out cars, empty hotel rooms, private hire cars. It was one of the reasons he liked coming to Cardiff. He always used Gregory's company and it was great to see a friendly face. He and Gregory had chats about all sorts of things. Cooking, gardening, novels. He was a very nice man. Emil had even met his wife Marjorie. She was very sweet.

One by one the engines became silent. There was a brief flurry of excitement as the fire engine arrived – presumably to extricate the van driver from the hanging basket – and then everything became even quieter. Emil drummed his fingers along the top of the seat in front. He couldn't even hear distant traffic. They should have been on the M4 by now, speeding their way back to London. He had three days at the Kensington flat, then he was off to Ghent. *Ghent? Who's idea was that?* He couldn't remember agreeing to sodding Ghent. Still, it was a nice enough place. *Mental note: check with the team that they haven't put in that grim dog-hole of a place like last time.*

He rubbed his hands together. It was getting chilly. Perhaps he could risk getting out and shutting the driver's door? He was hardly likely to be bombarded by autograph requests just here, was he? Massaging the joints in his right hand, he thought they felt a little sore. The Prokofiev always took it out of him. And it was getting windy. A sheet of newspaper fluttered by along the pavement. He could really murder a bag of fish and chips.

Just then, he caught the sound of something on the breeze. Two notes. D flat,

D major, repeated for three bars. He recognised them immediately – the beginning of 'Rach Three'. He wished Gregory had left the radio on so that he could listen to something too. It would help to pass the time. He wondered if he could reach forward to the front of the car and switch it on, but he had no idea how the system worked. He would probably have to turn on the ignition. Knowing his luck he would probably set off the alarm. For a moment he toyed with the idea of creating enough disturbance to attract that police officer back. Wasting police time. Public disturbance. Maybe not.

He heard the music again, clearer this time. It was definitely the 'Rach Three'. For a long time he had considered adding it to his official repertoire. It was fiendishly difficult. People's reputations had been made or broken by it. He had vowed not to perform it until it was utterly perfect. After all, Volkov had tried it, and look where that got him. A promising start then, *quelle catastrophe!* Every now and again, usually when he and Jeremy were on holiday at their villa in Cap Ferrat, he would return to it. He could play it, but there was something about it that was completely unnerving. It was like a beautiful shoe that didn't fit. He knew it was a thing of beauty but invariably it caused him pain. He and Jeremy had come back early from the villa that time precisely because of it. Emil had been practising for hours every day, getting increasingly dispirited, and Jeremy had been particularly unsympathetic.

'Perhaps it's just not your thing,' he'd said, flicking the latest Christie's auction catalogue in his direction. 'There are plenty of other amazing pieces. Why do get so worked up?'

Emil had tried explaining but it was no use. Jeremy was decorating again. There were 'mood boards' all over the place, which pretty much summed it all up, in Emil's opinion. Predictably, they'd ended up having a hellish row and got the PA to book return flights for that very evening.

Emil strained to hear the music through the open door. He wondered who the recording was by. They were good, whoever they were. Ashkenazy perhaps? No, it didn't sound like him. Emil reached for the electric control on the door and opened the window half way, just enough to let in more sound without revealing himself.

The music was clearer now. It seemed to be coming from a terrace of miserable looking 1960s' houses to his right. *What an architectural abomination*, he thought. There was a window open on one of the oddly shaped bays. *Some people have no idea about interior design*, thought Emil, looking at the untidy configuration of curtains. Despite all his quirks, he was lucky to have Jeremy. He really did know how to create a lovely environment.

Emil concentrated on the music. The recording was intriguing. He didn't recognise the style, but it was quite lovely. *Mental note: ask the team if there have been any recent recordings.* Maybe *Deutsche Grammophon* had released something new without sending him a copy? He found himself tapping his feet to the repeated theme.

There was a pause for the piano section. The clarinet entered along with the strings. It was exquisite. Then he realised that he knew the piece so well, he was imagining the orchestra. All was, in fact, silent. Perhaps he had imagined the whole thing? Then, perfectly on cue, the piano tumbled back in, like a waterfall of notes dashing themselves on to the intricate rocks of a cliff.

No orchestra? Who on earth would record without an orchestra? Emil sat up and stared at the row of peculiar houses. The sound was definitely coming from that one with the open window and the bizarre curtains. He listened. It was masterful – and at such a pace! Only Rachmaninoff himself played with that kind of speed. A remastered recording? Without an orchestra?

The music continued. It was technically perfect, which was a gargantuan feat in itself. But, oh, there was so much more to it than that. Listening to it was like looking at a vast landscape – if you stood back you could see it in all its immense majesty. Then, here and there, the playing drew you right in to the detail, to the living, breathing heart of it. It was tiny and exquisite. It was monumental and astonishing.

The theme returned again. Emil knew there was no orchestra, yet the pianist was making him hear it – somehow. How? It was extraordinary. Now the horn weaved its way through the theme along with the strings – they drew together, then parted. A drum roll, a simple series of notes – so easy to misjudge. Another pause, a playful interlude, and a sudden charge, like a storm breaking. The piano was an orchestra in itself. There seemed to be half a dozen melodies all playing at once.

Emil pressed the window controls. He didn't care who saw him now. He was transfixed. Whoever was playing was a master. How could the sound be coming from that tiny, miserable rabbit hutch? He sat forward and squeezed his eyes shut. He planted his forehead against the back of the seat and concentrated. It was breathtaking.

Eventually they came to the finale. Emil ran through all the recordings he had ever heard. No one had this skill – the delicacy, the nerve, the colour, the guts. It was spellbinding. He pressed himself against the car door. It was beyond perfection. It was transcendent. It was joy and delicious pain rolled together – the joy of hearing something so beautiful and the crushing realisation that such art was utterly out of his reach. He could never, ever, in a million years play the piece like that. He was in awe. He was transformed. He was utterly alive in the world. *Oh, my God!* He was in love! It was a *coup de foudre! Bravo! Bravo! Bravo!*

He also wanted to die. Emil shoved open the car door and made a beeline towards the odd-looking row of houses. He swept his fingers through his hair. So what if someone recognised him? He had to know. It had to be some old recording, surely? He would find out. He would get his hands on a copy and study it. There might yet be a way to learn from this person. This genius. He could feel his heart thudding as he walked up the path and pressed his finger firmly on the doorbell. It made a hideous, shrill sound. *F sharp.* There was a light inside the house, but no movement. He knew he hadn't imagined it. He was quite certain it had come from this house. He drummed his fingers against his thigh. He could still hear it in his head. *Oh, God, don't let it fade.* He wanted to lie in its majesty, bathe in its glory.

Nothing happened. He pressed the doorbell again. *Where are you?* He was about to press the bell a third time when he heard a woman's voice from the interior.

'You can stay outside! I'm not playing any more of your silly games!'

Emil turned around. He was the only one at the door and he wasn't playing any games. Whoever they were, he wished they'd let him in. He was feeling rather on show, standing there, not getting any response. *Come on, come on.* He tried the doorbell again. He looked at the letter box and considered shouting through it. But then a shadow appeared in the hallway from the direction of the room with the window. It lingered, then seemed to reverse and slither backwards out of sight.

Emil went to the bay window and tried to see in through the curtains. The window that had been open earlier was now shut. It was all very odd. He couldn't believe that anything so exquisite could have emanated from such a dump, but he knew what he'd heard. He wasn't going mad. Emil pressed his nose up against the glass. There was a tiny gap where the curtains didn't quite meet. He squinted and wondered whether he should knock on the window, or whether that would be a little rude. Once his eyes adjusted to the light he saw the top of an anglepoise lamp. He twisted his head around to get a better look. There was sudden movement and then, without warning, an eyeball appeared in the gap. Emil sprang back.

He returned to the doorbell, pressed it again and held his finger there. *I know you're in there.* The doorbell screamed horrifically, then after a few moments it was joined, by means of accompaniment almost, by a woman shouting. It was difficult to make it all out. There was something about childish behaviour, a mathematics degree, and frozen peas. This time the illusive shadow – which was connected, Emil presumed, to the alarming eyeball – returned at speed to the front door.

The man who opened the door was quite small, around five foot tall, mostly slim but with a little pot belly. He had very little hair, but what he had was a fair sandy colour and it was making a valiant effort to cover the top of his head. But in Emil's opinion, the most striking thing about this man was how angry he looked.

'Yes?' he hissed, as the door opened.

'My apologies for disturbing you… '

'Yes!'

'Yes?'

'You have definitely disturbed me!'

'I'm sorry. I don't like to impose, but would you mind giving me the details of that recording?'

The man looked terrified. Emil noticed that he was dressed formally and neatly in suit trousers, white shirt and functional navy tie.

'We don't have any recordings here,' replied the man. Then to Emil's surprise, he began to close the door. No door had been closed in Emil's face for a very long time.

'The music,' said Emil placing his hand forcefully on the door frame, 'the Rachmaninoff, if you please – all I want is the name of the pianist! If it's not too much trouble, I would be very grateful!'

The little man's response was to push harder against the door, and Emil was embarrassed to find himself responding likewise.

'I just want the name! I heard it with my own ears. It won't take a moment – who was it?'

'You've made a mistake. There are no recordings here. Go away.'

Emil protested. He explained that the traffic had come to a standstill because of the accident, and he had heard it quite clearly. There had been no doubt about it. Emil pushed as hard as he could but the little man was stronger than he appeared because he was putting up a good show and the door was closing.

In desperation, Emil gasped, 'It wasn't just me! We all heard it! All the people sitting in the cars heard it. We want to know who is in the recording!'

The little man faltered and through the gap in the doorway, Emil could see him glancing past him, scanning the cars, making a mental calculation of how many strangers were likely to bombard his front door.

Seeing his chance, Emil added, 'In fact, if you don't give us the details, we'll all be at your door, all one hundred and fifty-three of us. We just want the name!'

This specific number clearly made an impression on the man because after a pause, he stepped back from the door. The fingers of his right hand fluttered nervously to his forehead, and he pushed away an imaginary strand of hair with a little backward flick of his head.

'Oh, dear,' he said.

'Look, I promise you, they won't come in. I just need the name of the pianist. Then I'll leave you in peace.'

'Oh, dear me,' said the man, and he stood aside to let him in, closing the door firmly behind him.

Emil entered the sitting room but no sooner had he gone through the door than he realised that most of the room was taken up by an ebony baby grand. Unless the sound system was hiding under the piano, he couldn't see how there space for anything else in there. There was a lingering smell of cooked vegetables, and for some bizarre reason a large brass umbrella stand had been placed on top of the piano. He sidled around the room as far as the bay window. The curtains were creased and hanging untidily. Near the keyboard there were three misshapen paperclips. But apart from that, the room was clean and neat. He stood behind the piano stool and felt a shudder as if the tremor of an earthquake had moved through the room. On the stand in front of him was a copy of Rachmaninoff's third piano concerto.

'So, you see… ' said the man, fiddling with the imaginary strand of hair, 'No recording.'

Emil stared at the sheet music.

'Do you mind?' he asked, gesturing to the stool.

The little man flicked his head in that haughty manner of his. Emil wasn't sure whether this meant it was alright to sit or not, but as his legs were giving way in any case, he presumed to sit.

'What's your name?'

'I don't see why that's… '

'What's your name?'

'Mr. Wagstaff. But I really don't see what… '

'Do you know who I am?'

This man, Mr. Wagstaff, didn't need to reply. It was clear from his response that he had no idea. Emil thought he'd tell him all the same.

'I am Emil Stein – concert pianist.' The man's face did not alter. 'At the moment, I believe I am ranked ninth amongst the world's most successful pianists. Some highly eminent critics would have me placed much higher – but whatever. I am up there – among the best, the highest paid classical musicians in the world. I have houses in Paris, Geneva, the Hamptons… '

The little man's attention was wavering. His eyes flickered to the window and back, then to a hideous sunburst clock on the wall.

'What I mean to say,' continued Emil, 'is that I know something about this piece. I know how it is supposed to sound.'

The little man's attention returned to Emil.

'I play for my own amusement. I am not trying to impress anyone.'

'Who taught you?'

'No one.'

'Who?' asked Emil, a little more aggressively than he had intended.

'Well, Aunt Margaret, if you must know. Not any more, obviously. She died and gave me the piano. I did Grade III.'

Emil couldn't help it. He began to chuckle. At least it started as a chuckle. It was a strange kind of convulsive attack that took over his whole body until it began hurting his diaphragm. Then, what started as a release of tension, turned into a sob, and tears began streaming down his face. He could sense Mr. Wagstaff looking at him with distaste. The man must have been disturbed by the whole turn of events because he started to babble.

'I practise every Tuesday and Friday, mostly Fridays because my mother goes out to the film club that night. Or bingo. Mostly film club. Usually, I don't disturb anyone. It's certainly not my intention. That neighbour is deaf,' he said, pointing to one side of the room, 'and that one,' he said, pointing to the opposite side, 'is hardly ever at home. Apart from the traffic lights, it's very unusual for the traffic to be stationary out there. Very unusual indeed. In fact, this evening is the first time it's happened in twenty-two and a half years. No one stops at Ainge Terrace, not unless they want a parking ticket. Not unless they're mad. There are double yellow lines – everywhere.'

A tectonic plate was shifting underneath Emil's feet. He placed his hand on the piano's glossy veneer to steady himself.

'Please don't touch the piano,' said the little man.

Emil wiped his face with the back of his hand. 'I promise, I'll go away.'

'Good.'

'Only…' whispered Emil, 'I need to hear the piece once again. Then I really will go.'

Mr. Wagstaff glanced at the curtains and sighed.

'I promise they won't come in.'

By the time Gregory returned to the car, Emil was already slumped in the back seat. He'd thrown the paperwork and diary aside and was dialling the PA.

Someone answered.

'Hello?' said Emil.

There was a response, but they were obviously in a busy place because they were having trouble hearing him.

'Can you hear me?' asked Emil. 'Listen. I don't want you to arrange any more venues. No. No more venues. Yes, I'm absolutely sure. No – no, not even the Carnegie.' There was a lot of hysterical screaming in the background. Emil hated having to repeat himself. 'The Car-ne-gie! Oh, it doesn't matter. If they want me, they can always come back.' There were more incoherent noises on the end of the phone and Emil only caught the last word. 'Fine?'

'Yes, of course I'm fine. Well, we're stuck in a traffic jam as it happens, but otherwise, I'm fine. No, of course not. No, I didn't say anything about retirement. Who mentioned retirement? I'll decide about retirement when I'm good and ready.' There was a burst of laughter somewhere. He really wished his team was a bit more mature. Did they have to get so thoroughly plastered every Friday night?

'I can't hear you! Phone me in the morning! NOT before eleven!'

Emil hung up and slumped back in his seat. Telling Jeremy was not going to be so easy. He was pretty sure he'd ordered a new car. Something low and shouty in electric blue.

He leant to his left and tried to see if anything was happening up ahead. Everything was very quiet now and although there were flashing lights, the sirens had been switched off.

Gregory was back in the driver's seat.

'All done?' Emil asked.

If Gregory did reply, Emil didn't hear it. Perhaps I'm going deaf he thought, feeling slightly aggrieved. 'Are they off to hospital?'

Gregory made a noise of some sort but it was incomprehensible and just as he was about to ask why they were still being held up the driver added, 'Poor bugger. Kept saying he could hear angels. Delirious, I expect.'

'The van driver? The hanging basket?' ventured Emil, desperately trying to remember the policeman's words.

'Oh, no. He's alright, the chopsy bugger. Couple of broken ribs.'

'Oh, good. Well, not good, but … you know. Not dead.'

Gregory made an odd sound. Something halfway between a grunt of frustration and a groan of disbelief.

Up ahead, there was movement. An ambulance was driving off slowly, its lights flashing but no siren.

'Looks like we're moving,' said Emil.

He'd had enough of this junction. So had Gregory by the looks of it, because he was slumped forward, cradling his head with his forearms.

'Fourteen … with a new bike,' said Gregory, his voice muffled by his jacket sleeves.

Emil was thinking of a response to his driver's cryptic comment when his phone pinged. A text from his team.

'Kaaaaarnnnneeeeeegeeeee!!' it said, followed by a series of silly faces making weird facial expressions. Emil tossed the phone aside in disgust and looked out of his window. Everything was starting to move, thank God. It was also starting to rain. The light from the lurid orange street lamps fragmented into a million shards as raindrops fell on the windscreen. Each drop of water clung desperately to the glass here and there until other bigger droplets ran into them. Emil watched as they streamed and collided at random.

He sighed. He had imagined that the end would come in a blaze of television appearances, lifetime contribution awards, and retrospective specials on Channel 4. He thought it would be like a slow climb to a magnificent crest from where he would be able to look down with pride on a lifetime's achievement. There would be applause, plenty of it, and deep heartfelt bows. Tearful kisses blown to the balconies, huge bouquets. Large blousy peonies. Months of standing ovations. His name would be etched on granite plaques strategically located in smart public places. He would be embedded forever in the world's consciousness, like Julius Caesar, Einstein, and Elvis.

But he'd been kidding himself. He could see that now. His career had been stuttering, like a candle that had been burning too long, the wick slowly drowning in its own molten pool. *This is where it really ends*, thought Emil, the whole bally shoot. It ends on an ugly junction in some random town. It ends with a gift and a curse.

He watched the raindrops on their giddy downward paths, veering from side to side, slowing now, then rushing on. They made him think of Rachmaninoff's beautiful tumbling notes.

The car moved off. Emil reached for his phone and switched it off. When was the last time he'd done that, he wondered? He leant back against the headrest and closed his eyes. Eventually, he fell asleep.

The Shrouded Madonna

S.T. Taylor
Netherlands

A HUDDLE OF PIGEONS cool in the shade of an old headstone, nesting in a bunch of collected garden flowers as they wither in the heat. The grass is dry and brushy there and scored with yellow veins. A breeze blows in and hisses through the grass like a rough broom over concrete; still the pigeons stay put, faces to the wind.

'David, hold up. We're not going through there.'

David stops and turns back to his sister, the birth of a coy smile wrinkling his eyes. 'You all can go round. I'm not forcing you either way.'

'David.'

But he's off. As he nears the pigeons they lift and fan grey overhead like a plume of ashes scattered to the wind.

'Shit,' says Harriet.

Tommy squirms about on her back. 'You can't say that.'

She twists to set him down but he locks tight to her neck. Hiking him higher she takes her schoolbag in hand by the top loop and looks after David where he's disappeared behind a crypt.

'Are we going in?'

She shakes her head no. 'We go round like we're supposed to.'

No fence borders the graveyard. Where the grass grows wild the land becomes public. It tickles Harriet to the knee and folds as it brushes the underside of Tommy's school shoes. Earlier that year Harriet and a friend had stumbled upon an old headstone broken at the base and hidden by shrub. That was on the far side where the graveyard borders bushland. The name had read Stein, no date to be found. They didn't know of any Stein, not alive nor dead. It must have been an old headstone.

The breeze rustles treetops and takes some sting from the mid-afternoon sun. Light dances purple on the trodden path siphoned through a canopy of blooming jacaranda. Dangling seed pods smile overhead like gaping scallops. Harriet and Tommy have circled the graveyard and are beating the bush for home, he still clinging to her back, pack set to his shoulders. Harriet's steps are heavy and jar the round-brimmed school hat free of Tommy's crown. Secured to his chin by a loosened drawstring it trails them, flapping behind his head like a drunken halo.

'Think he'll wait for us?' Tommy asks.

'Has he ever?'

'Could be he does this time.'

'Why do you even want to walk home with him for? He'll just poke fun at you for being a baby.'

'He doesn't mean nothing by it.'

'And don't go saying things like he might wait this time.'

'Could be he does.'

She shakes her head emphatically and sunlight blinks ephemeral as it catches in the beaded sweat.

'People are who people are. The things they've done, that's what you have to expect of them. It's how you get by.'

'You mean like when I ask can I do something but I already know you're going to say no.'

Harriet hikes Tommy higher, her dress-back beneath him heavy and wet. The calls and movements of insect and animals bring the bush to life around them. Harriet's heavy footsteps supply tempered percussion to the track of the outback. Her breath comes faster and harder and rises and falls to the measure. It exists there unobtrusive and complements the afternoon song until a note of no musical value cuts through the soundscape.

'Still lugging him around like a tired mule?'

David appears at their flank from his spot in the hollow of a tree.

'You want to carry him for a bit?'

'How you holding up, bud?'

Tommy's grip on Harriet's neck eases. He slides down her wet back, the instep of his shorts damp so that he takes his first few steps bowlegged and awkward. He looks up to his older brother.

'I'm doing good.'

Harriet stops to watch the boys as they continue ahead of her.

'Race you the rest of the way?' David asks.

'No, guys.'

But Tommy's nodding enthusiastically.

'Drop your bag, Harrie can take it.'

They leave their bags in the middle of the path.

'Go.'

And they're gone. Tommy stumbles after a few steps and his feet scratch desperately to keep up with his body. He rights himself and follows his brother's big hat in tow. Within moments he's lost to the bush. Harriet sets her own pack to one shoulder, Tommy's on the other, and takes David's by the arm-strap in the crook of her elbow.

-

The screams arrive as a faint chorus when she is still a distance from home and it's that very faintness which obscures their origin. Clambering up the path as it gradually rises, the cries are carried to her on a welcome breath of wind. She closes her eyes both to enjoy the respite and consider the sound.

Nearer the house she spots him coming down the path toward her, arm held crosswise before him, and still in a state of bother. It's red and puffed and his eyes are too, and the reaction looks to be coming up out of his collar.

'What is it?' she asks dropping the bags.

He tries to talk but his breath is hitched and he can't pass words. She lifts the shirt from off his back. There's no connection between the outbreaks on his arm and neck and he stands sobbing, white-chested, and childlike in the middle of the path.

'Put this back on.' He takes the shirt and they walk. With each step the sobbing recedes. 'How do you feel? Can you tell me what happened?'

'I fell,' he starts. 'I fell,' he says again. Pauses for breath. 'Some stinging nettle, I think,' he hitches.

'Where's David?'

Tommy shakes his head and the tears return.

Their house is found in a small clearing bordered the way round by a fence of scavenged bush timber. Inside the fence a shack rests in the shade of a great eucalyptus. A rainwater catchment of corrugated iron sits atop the structure like a pauper's crown. The shack is their father's toolshed. Harriet leaves Tommy to wait outside. She comes back with a role of duct tape, taking a measure with her teeth and tearing it there between. She then wraps it around her fingers, adhesive side exposed. With the tape she dabs at the affected areas using the stick to collect any remaining plant matter. Tommy pinches his eyes tight squeezing off a few last tears. He doesn't make a sound.

'Good,' says Harriet. When he's undressed she sets him up under the outdoor shower and opens the catchment. Water sputters from the shower head. 'Is it too hot?' she asks. He shakes his head and she uses the warm rainwater to wash him clean. 'Good,' she says once again.

-

'What happened to you lot?' Nan calls from the porch.

Crossing the lawn, Harriet is laden with bags. Tommy skips along behind her, dripping wet in his undies, clothes bunched in his fists.

'What are you doing here?' Harriet asks.

'Nice, Harriet. Hi to you too.'

'Hey, Nan,' says Tommy.

'Your mother's a little under the weather today.'

'Still?'

Nan bends to kiss him as he comes to the landing. 'Yes dear,' she says warmly, holding the screen door open. Harriet follows Tommy inside while the door's still ajar.

The kitchen is a clutter of heat and mess. A large pot of stew simmers on a stovetop burner and vegetable scraps and animal offcuts line the bench to the left. Blood-red sauce belches like a lanced boil from up out of the pot and tattoos the wall there behind in a pattern of arterial spurts.

The kitchen thick with heat, they take dinner on the porch where they watch in silence as a family of lorikeets hunt fruit and nectar in a cluster of shrubs out beyond the border fence. On the porch their collective quiet need not be contained to four walls. David and Harriet are yet to make nice and in Nan's unusual reservedness, any conversation is perpetuated by Tommy who has happily forgotten his subsiding welts.

The meat is chewy and their jaws ache from the effort; the sauce devoid of any flavour at all as they've come to expect of Nan's cuisine. It's not until they finish eating and Tommy mentions dessert that Nan finds her words.

'You lot won't be off to school in the morning.'

'Yeah?' says Tommy.

'No arguments here,' David agrees.

'Why?'

David leans forward to look past Nan and Tommy.

'If Harrie wants to go I say okay, sure. But me and Tommy, we plan to enjoy a day at home. Here with you Nan. Don't we, Tommy?'

Tommy nods enthusiastically.

'I won't be here,' says Nan. 'I'm taking your mum for a little bit. A little break.'

'Where are you taking her to, Nan?' asks Tommy.

'Not far, dear.'

'And who'll be here with us?'

There's a tremor in Harriet's voice betrayed by her effort to still it.

'Your father's coming home early. Should be in by sun up.'

The boys holler and cheer, and the screen door claps shut behind them as they take their plates to the sink and scavenge the cupboards for sweets.

Harriet rises and takes Nan's plate in hers. 'Thanks for dinner.'

'Did you enjoy it?'

Harriet's halfway to the door and doesn't turn back to answer. 'Always,' she says and leaves Nan on the porch alone to enjoy the quiet they'd all been sharing moments earlier.

-

The boys lie on a double bunk pressed up against a clapboard wall. Tommy is restless with excitement. The bunk cries in protest and raps on the wall at every turn. From below David slips his feet up through the slats and lifts the mattress clear off them. He then quickly withdraws his feet to let his brother drop and bounce to a still on the groaning bed.

'Will you two quit it?' Harriet hisses in the dark.

'He keeps shifting.'

'And you poking your feet at him won't help nothing.'

'I can't sleep on this bunk with him shifting about.'

'Then you come here to the floor. You can take the swag.'

'Yeah, that'll happen.'

'Okay, then.'

The room briefly settles. It's Tommy who stirs it once more.

'You think he'll bring us presents?'

'Of course he will,' says David.

'He'll bring you a present,' says Harriet. 'Something for your birthday.'

'He'll bring us all presents,' says David.

'You think that's why he's coming back? For my birthday?'

Out in the night the cooling wind has fallen still and cicadas percuss the darkness with a heightened trill.

'Could be it is,' she says.

'Didn't come back for yours or mine.'

'No, he didn't. Now hush up and get some sleep. You know we can't be up all night till he gets in.'

The boys toss about restlessly and the bed calls them out but as the still night weighs heavy and the bunk slowly settles, the boys' breathing dies to a lull. Harriet on her back feels the gaps between the floorboards. The swag bunches there and she struggles for comfort. She stares at the ceiling, which hangs overhead in endless darkness, and it's an age before the dark makes its approach.

The curtain in the boys' room is rough and porous, and the morning is as still as the night that preceded it. Somehow in spite of this, the curtain ripples in gentle waves. Morning light is sundered there through in parts red and orange and scattered alive over the timber floorboards like a fistful of discarded saffron. The movement skirts soft over Harriet's drawn eyes and pulls her like a chord, an umbilical connection, from her deep reverie and into an unbridled state of sobriety.

The boys lay dead to the waking day and Harriet slips from the room without disturbing them much. She pads barefoot down the hall and spots Nan asleep in the sitting room chair. A cup of tea steams on the floor at her foot, teabag string coiled around the mug handle. She eyes the rising steam and notes Nan can't be long at rest. Back-stepping gingerly, her foot finds a whiney floorboard that groans low out into the morning. Nan lurches to life as if pulled from the precipice by the hand of God.

'Morning dear,' she says in breathlessness.

'Hey.'

'You're up early.'

'So are you. Well, sort of. Can I have my room back then?'

Nan shakes her head. 'Your father's in there.'

'He is, is he?'

Nan rises. 'You want a cuppa?'

She says she doesn't and goes back to the swag and lays awake until the boys stir. Nan puts on a breakfast with Harriet's help and they eat eggs fried in fat on thick bits of toast. The skillet cackles and spits and the smell claims the kitchen and seeps slowly down the hall, coating the walls like a hardening artery.

If the smell of frying fat reaches their father in Harriet's room, it's not enough to draw him. The boys get restless and David begins tormenting his brother. Nan suggests they go out for a while and enjoy the day while their parents' rest.

'But I'm already dressed,' says Tommy, standing in his nicest clothes.

'Well go and get undressed,' says Harriet.

'It's alright dear. You can go like that. Just take care.'

Harriet stares at her grandmother.

'You know he's not careful. Couple weeks back he was wearing school clothes round the clock cause he'd gone and ruined all the rest.'

'I'll be careful.'

'You see,' says Nan. 'Now run ahead and brush your teeth.' David thumps up the hall and Tommy runs after him.

-

Harriet waits for them by the gate. Observing the makeshift fence that borders their land, she notices oddities in a thing of such familiarity that she'd never before given it much thought. At some conjunctions lengths of orphaned timber are butted one to the other and held firm with a length of string. For others, her father used chicken wire. One joint is held to place by nothing more than a solitary rusted nail.

She considers his work with ironic admiration and in full understanding of the fence's integrity but as the weight of a restless sleep sullies her patience, Harriet leans momentarily on the gatepost. The fence shifts in full and moves as one, budging the circumference of the house. She rights herself in shock. It seems the world and everything in it has turned a peg while Harriet managed to keep her place so that even though her two brothers crossing the yard are entirely familiar, as is the house from which they come, she feels she's seeing them through a grainy filter. Something in the image is not as before and it puts her at odds with her surroundings.

-

They venture deep into the bush and follow a familiar stream until the landscape develops a sense of unfamiliarity. Exploring the area unknown they come across a house where no house should be. It's old and abandoned and made mostly of stone and has a chimney shaft ascending from a partially collapsed roof. Like something borne of the European woodlands.

Tommy is fascinated and wants to explore and David offers to lead the expedition. Peering inside the eaves are thick with web and hung with dead insects. Harriet warns them off.

'You can't go in there.'

'Sure we can.'

Harriet doesn't bother reasoning with David and turns on the younger boy.

'Take one look. It's teeming with crawlies and covered in webs and dust. You going in there with your good clothes on?'

Tommy stands in the cavernous doorframe and shrinks a little.

'You know how Dad is about looking after what's yours. You return with your good clothes all sullied and you watch. That lump in his throat'll go dancing about like crazy. Then you know you're in for it.'

Tommy is nodding in thought, wide eyed and curious.

'You're scared,' says his brother.

'Can I talk to you a second? In private?'

'Anything you got to say we can say right here in front of Tommy.'

'Jesus, just once. Be an adult and come along.'

Harriet marches off around the side of the house, unsteady on the carpet of decaying plant matter. David turns to Tommy and offers a helpless shrug of the shoulders, and Tommy watches as he stalks off after her.

Left alone he shuffles up to the house and leans in through the fissure. The air is heavy and damp and coarsely textural in the sunlight that stretches from the cleft roof corner and crosses the darkened room like a silken veil. A timber crossbeam supports what roof there is and the floor is littered with all further remnants. Eyeing the crossbeam and judging its integrity, Tommy begins to edge into the house, but as his foot crosses the threshold he's held to place by his brother's voice that comes vociferously in with the silken sunlight and echoes endlessly about the room.

As Tommy rounds the house he keeps close to the wall for fear of being seen. He first spots David, a malevolent smile corrupting his brother's features. Harriet stands fronting him, her face strained in frustration.

David shakes his head and turns from her briefly. As he comes back around he says, 'No,' his voice deepening without explanation as though sourced from some furious well within. 'You couldn't stop me if you wanted to,' he rumbles, and straightens his back getting a few more inches on Harriet. Lurching boldly forward, he shoves his sister. He moves in closer but Harriet raises a hand and holds it lock-elbowed before her, the action instinctive and keeping him briefly at bay. Then he bats her hand off and comes closer still.

Tommy presses himself into the wall. Harriet retreats but backs into a tree then David's before her, breathing heavy and eyes flat. Harriet curls around the tree but he takes the back of her hair in a ball in his fist. She cries out of instinct, and in spite of herself and the sound, scores the moment as the bush about them ebbs into silence. The breeze has fallen still, the animals hold their breath, and the stream running in the distance seems to gossip in a cloud of reprobate whispers. David eases his grip and his eyes slacken. He holds up his hands by way of innocence.

'No,' says Harriet.

She shoves him once with both hands and he takes a half step. When she shoves him again he remains firmly in place. The innocent arms fall to his side and he offers a warning. 'Don't.'

She makes to shove him a final time but he snatches her wrists and twists at her arms. This time she doesn't cry. Her struggle goes unnoticed and it's with ease that he casts her away. When she hits the tree and falls to the side he moves in to catch her, but the timing is off and his position awkward so the only purchase he finds is on her dress shoulder.

Lying on her back and propped up on elbows, her breathing comes in fits. Dirt and dead plant stuff cuff her forearms thick as shirtsleeves and there they remain held to place by a thin film of sweat. She looks up at her brother who blushes and softens and is unable to hold her eye. He turns. Her dress strap is torn and the chest has come open to one side, a pubescent breast exposed to the sun as motes of unsettled dust dip and eddy about her.

Harriet's eyes flare white as she rolls to her chest and buries her face in the crook of her elbow. 'Go,' she cries muffled into the ground. He does.

She lies there a while then rolls slowly over. She pats at the dirt caked to her breast and notices it dance a little when touched. More so than before. Her stomach lurches and turns over, and she blinks at a tear.

She gets to her feet and circles the gutted house. The calls of the boys come from within its four walls. She walks on to the clear running stream. Under the surface is a mud-coloured fish holding its place in the quickening water. She stands tall above it. It looks distant and distorted as though seen through an overturned telescope. The water surges and shifts and still the fish remains, thinning and bulging as water toys with the perception of light. Then the it turns and is carried away, and Harriet sees what had been there before but remained unnoticed. Her reflection stares up unrecognisable and subject to the shifting water surface. It's a curious image. She puts a curled fist through her face and cups tepid water up to her body.

-

Harriet has tied her dress at the shoulder and is sitting feet to the water when the timber crossbeam comes down inside the forgotten house. A column of dust rises up out of the hollow where a roof once existed and rises high enough for her to see from a distance.

She jumps to her feet and claws wretched up the path but when she gets to the house the boys are fine. David stands tall and clean and hitches in silent laughter aside his little brother who is coughing and covered in dust. Tommy looks to his sister and away again.

'We're going,' she says.

On the walk home she gathers they'd been leaving the house as the crossbar fell. David was outside and Tommy climbing through the door as dust blew out after them. Tommy in the doorframe had faced the worst of it.

'When we get home we try to sneak in quiet. Dad can't see you like this.'

Tommy had rinsed himself in the stream but his shirt is still fouled with dust. They come upon the house from the side, see their father sitting to a cigarette on the porch. The boys get excited but Harriet steadies them. David looks to ignore her and run off after his father, but is held to heel by her gaze and nods in reluctant admission.

Harriet slips around back and in through the boys' window and comes back with a new shirt.

'I didn't want that one,' he says softly.

'Then you should have stayed out of that place like I said.'

He grabs it and throws it over his head and makes with his brother for the porch. A chorus of laughter greets Harriet as she arrives at the landing.

'Got a hug for your father?' he says through squinted eyes. She steps between the boys and complies.

He collapses back in the chair and looks drained with fatigue, as if he hadn't slept at all. She asks how he is and he tells her he's fine; the smile breaks his face open and keeps further inquiries at bay.

'Did you bring us anything?' David asks.

Dad rubs at the back of his neck and looks down and away.

'Look, I didn't have much time, guys. The ship came in and I rushed through the port. Had to be quick to make the bus.'

David is deflated. Tommy too.

'Not even for Tommy?' says Harriet. 'It's his birthday in two days.'

'I know when your birthday is, bud. Look, tomorrow we'll go out, get you something. What do you want? A cricket bat?'

'Yeah.'

'Okay.'

'A cricket bat, shit. When I was his age I got... ' says David. 'I got... Oh, I don't know but it wasn't a bloody cricket bat.'

'Hey. Calm down, son. We can.'

'No. Serious. Tommy here, he's out in the bush and ruins his good clothes. Then we see you when we get to the fence but Harriet has us sitting in the shrubs like a couple of bloody wombats so she can fetch him some new ones and you don't get mad. And as soon as you're back it's Tommy this and Tommy that. And I, well I… '

His eyes are puffy; he's swallowing tears and his words fall away. The bush rustles softly about them.

Dad puts forth a knee and the point bobs in his throat like a rotten egg in water. When he swallows it disappears altogether. He blinks once or twice and Harriet watches him closely. Then he takes both their hands and sits Tommy on his knee and pulls David in.

'They're just clothes, son. Just clothes,' he whispers. 'Tomorrow we'll get something nice, for the both of you. But first we'll go visit your mum.'

-

Harriet leaves them be. She goes to the room she once called her own. Her bed is slept in and her father's travel bag lays yawning at the foot. It has little inside. A toiletries bag and a couple of t-shirts, all white, and each one pressed sharp of edge. She bows her head a moment, forehead to the doorframe, then looks back over her shoulder and down the hall. The boys can be heard outside bothering their father and the house is quiet but for their voices.

She slips down the hall to her mother's room. The door is slightly ajar and she pushes it tentatively. The room is empty. The bed is made. Curtains drawn muting the shine of the midday sun. She steps full into the room. Hasn't been there for months. The floor is carpeted and soft underfoot, and the silence it offers pervades her presence there and sullies it by association as an act clandestine in nature.

Leaving the curtains drawn she crosses to the bedside table and picks up the sole framed photograph, a pastiche in black and white paying homage to her parents. In it her mother's hair, long and waved, is the focal point. The trappings of black and white photography do little to humble the life in her image. She smiles not at the photographer but rather the husband on her arm who appears to lean away from the camera as though in hope he will lean right out of frame.

She puts the photo down and crosses to the wardrobe that cries as she draws the door. The sound is sharp in the quiet room but is quickly lost to the soft carpet and curtains. The wardrobe is full, not a hanger to spare. She pulls out a drawer and in it lie folded sweaters stacked five deep. Crowning the pile is a green one, thin and worn. Harriet's favourite. The neckline frayed and a hole in the underarm. Harriet lifts out the sweater and points a finger up through the hole. She then bunches the sweater in a ball in her fists and presses it to her face. Something wells from within, a playground of memories that come rushing warm as sunshine. And the family is together for a moment once more. And then. Well then…

The screen door calls like a gunshot down the hall and draws Harriet from another place. In spite of the dry heat she pulls the sweater down over her head and wears the memories like mail. She pushes the drawer shut on the other sweaters and the wells of memories there attached and leaves them forgotten in the wardrobe to rest undisturbed like the unknowable Stein under his broken headstone.

-

Another still morning and the curtain hangs limp. Harriet finds her father outside where she knows he'll be. She heard him in the night wearing a path in the porch, a trail of ashes and spilt beer stretching from end to end. By morning he's sitting, a bottle of spent butts between his feet. His eyes are glassy and laced red.

'Morning,' she says.

He simply nods.

'When are we off?'

'When the boys are up we'll go.' His voice is raspy and shallow.

Harriet looks him over as he rises from the chair.

'You developed a taste for coffee yet?'

'No.'

'Suit yourself.' He sidesteps her and she jumps as the screen door claps behind her. From the kitchen, he calls, 'What about brekky? Still got a taste for that?'

His eyes begin to clear over breakfast and by the time the boys wake there's some light behind them.

They walk off together, the four of them to pick up the truck from a neighbour. Harriet brings up the rear.

The truck seats are soft and comfortable; the cab is spacious and the country around them blurs in an earthy pallet of rushing greens, browns, and yellows as they take to the freeway. The bitumen rises in the middle and tapers out from there. The truck naturally drifts to the left. A loud buzz fills the cab as the tires run the audible lines. Dad adjusts the steer but the boys hold him to account, humming and buzzing away until he shuts them up with a look. He doesn't run the audible lines again.

The late morning sun climbs high overhead and the road before them distinguishes itself from the horizon with a band of air warped by heat. A wind kicks up and the sand it carries reveals it for where it is, crossing the hot bitumen ahead. They plow through the sand cloud like a train through morning mist and the cab rocks gently on its suspension as they look out over the day, each in their own direction.

Trees sit atop their own shadows in order to cool the very ground on which they stand. As countryside becomes suburbia, then city, Harriet notices the houses and buildings do the same. The hospital when they get there casts no shadow she can see and looks big, stale, and unwelcoming. She can't shake the unease that infects her gut and sits heavy like spoilt food as they drive around the carpark in search of an empty spot.

Nan had been at the bedside when they arrived, watching as the doctor ran small tests. When she sees them come in she says her hellos and leaves her daughter with her family in peace. And the doctor. He palms off Dad's questions and confuses them all with words that mean nothing. Doctor jargon. Harriet pays him no mind and looks out through the door to a room across the hall. A family of ten gather around a bed she can't see pawing at a patient who doesn't notice them there.

With a smile and a turn the doctor leaves them, his white coat trailing him out. He has a pile of steel folders in his hands. Pulls the one from the bottom and puts it on top burying the truth of her mother's condition. He enters the room across the hall and the gathering turns as one. Hope breaches their teary eyes and reaches vainly forth. Harriet thinks she sees the doctor hesitate at the door.

Mum is tired and weak and the boys consider her through sunken eyes. Harriet struggles to watch as they rally what strength they have simply not to shy from their mother's touch. Their father looks as lost as his offspring. The three boys wading at her bedside, holding to the bed. Trying to keep their heads above water.

Harriet gets up and says she'll be back. Before she goes she kisses her mother's forehead. The skin is slack and cold.

She pushes through the glass turnstile and out into the blowing heat. Her breath can't be found. She puts palms to her knees and folds in the middle, sucking at the air and looking about herself in shame. Further along the wall to her left Nan sits at a bench, hair blowing about in a Medusa tangle. She dabs at her eyes with a tissue. It's a moment before she notices her granddaughter and puts the tissue away. Harriet moves to go back inside but stops short. Nan pats at the bench seat beside her.

Across from them over the carpark is a cafe. A young father with tired eyes sits at a table under a great white parasol, his child climbing all over him. A man who has given his body for the life of another. The boy's mother is in absence. The father looks out at nothing and sits perfectly still, still as a ladder, and there he sits until a waitress comes with his coffee.

'We don't agree on much, the boys and me,' Harriet says. She's near yelling to be heard from the wind. 'But there is one thing. We've never argued this.' Nan sits in wait. 'We don't like your cooking at all. On that we can agree.'

Nan nods a little and begins to laugh. 'I can't be certain of what you lot are thinking most of the time. We differ in age. Greatly. You've had to deal with some things I didn't. I certainly dealt with things you'll never have to. But there's one thing I'm sure of. I'm a terrible cook.'

Harriet wrestles her eyes from the man and his boy to look at her Nan for what feels the first time in a while.

'What I don't understand is why you lot always tell me my food's good.' Harriet blushes. 'I never did the cooking in our household. That was your Pop.'

'Really?'

'He did. The cleaning too.'

'What were you doing?'

'I made the money. I had to work.'

'You made the money? I thought Pop was a farmer.'

'Oh, sure, Pop was a farmer. Funny thing about farmers. Seems all you need to be one is to own a bit of land. Pop did that. Didn't seem to matter much to anyone at all that he didn't have clue one what to do with it. Didn't want any livestock. Couldn't stand the smell, though I think he feared the work's what it was. So I took the barn, used it to make clothes. Got a couple machines and that's how we fed our family. How we got by.'

Across the way the boy spots something on the footpath. He climbs down off his father and stumbles a bit. The father rises an inch in his seat but when the boy stops a short way along he sinks back down and takes up his coffee again.

'Did you ever make clothes for me?'

'Made most of your clothes. The boys' too. Well, that's till you got to an age where you started caring what you wore.'

'Which ones did you make?'

'Most of them. Till a couple years ago. That sweater you got on there. It's your mum's.'

'Yeah.'

'I made that for her when she moved to town. Left me and Pop alone on the farm. Must be nearing twenty years back. Can't say I know what you got it on for. It must be pushing thirty-five out here, even with all this wind.'

Harriet pulls the frayed neckline up about her mouth and breathes in the warm scent of her mum. Looking out over the carpark she spots the waitress saying something to the man. The parasol above him cracks in the wind like a slacking sail, the mast developing a warp. He nods to her and gives her some money, then collects his boy from off the footpath. Together they cross the carpark and enter the hospital.

With the terrace cleared of customers the waitress tries to drop the parasol but it's heavy and stubborn in the wind. The barista comes out and together they get it down and tied off, leaving it swaying about like a shrouded Madonna keeping watch over the carpark.

Something Biblical

Sam Woods
England

WITH VERY LITTLE LIGHT POLLUTION, the night sky was often a sight to marvel settling over the Serbian border. Adam's torchlight flashed along the ground; his uniform of vast camouflage and webbing gave him the appearance of a much broader man and his boots gifted him an extra inch. Some men were grateful for such enhancing elements, while some men just took comfort in their own skin. He wrestled at his tunic, engulfing him as he patrolled the perimeter of the fence.

Stopping occasionally to inspect the barbed wire above the steel, he felt himself convulse at the images from his training, rushed photographs on an old projector of torn flesh and cartilage from a war concluded long before he was born.

He walked back towards the sentry cabin; a lamplight in the window meant Max had woken. Though forbidden to sleep on duty, they each stole precious hours most nights. Even after several months together, friendship had never quite surfaced. It was just easier to let each other sleep.

Max was lacing his boots before standing, blocking the light from the stove behind him. Adam nodded in acknowledgment and settled in to a chair opposite, pulling a small book from his jacket.

"A little early isn't it, even for a Sunday?" said Max motioning to the book in his colleague's hand.

Adam looked up and smirked. "It's a habit from childhood, my parents were devout."

"Do you believe it?" asked Max.

Adam shrugged. "I don't know; it just reminds me of home."

"So you don't take anything from it?"

"I read the passages and I'm a decent man, so maybe that's something," said Adam.

Max frowned. "Something biblical?"

"That may be for a higher judgment," Adam replied irritably.

Max suppressed a laugh, lit his torch, and walked into the darkness of early morning.

Adam looked down onto the open page, defiant against the heaviness of his eyes.

'Therefore, *let us stop passing judgment on one another. Instead, make up your mind not to put any stumbling block or obstacle in the way of a brother or sister'*. His lips moved to the passage but no sound formed. Before very long the page dissolved into sleep.

Jolted into the morning by the sound of sirens, he registered daylight and shouting outside.

"Back! Back away from the fences, you will not be passing through."

Beyond the fences were a thousand faces, a foreign language, and a harmony of protests he could not understand. Women were pleading against the barriers and children's exhausted eyes looked to their fathers united in a pathetic war cry of begging. Max ran towards Adam, his face written in panicked lines.

"Didn't think they would make it this far; Syrian refugees."

He placed a heavy baton in Adam's palm and edged towards the gates to beat at the hands that passed through the steel.

Adam's feet were rooted, his lips moved to object, but no sound formed. A glaring sunrise looked down upon him.

Pop Goes the Weasel

Sharon Dormer
England

SO - I'M SITTING IN POP'S tiny front room. Just sitting, and waiting. It's a bungalow in Lewsey Farm Estate, just outside Luton. It's a practice coffin, really. The houses get smaller as you get older. Until, in the end you get one of these pensioners' places. Next step… A box. No space for odds and sods. A tiny little room, square, beige. It used to have a small cottage suite, a sideboard with little crocheted doilies. A television in a walnut unit. A smoked-glass dining table and matching chairs. Not any more though. Now it's just got pictures. Pictures of me and pictures of Mum. Mainly me though. Pop loves me to pieces. That's why I knew he'd take me in.

Pop and me - we're close. When Dad died Pop took over. Became the glue that bound us together. Me, Mum, and Pop. I remember once, he took me up Dunstable Downs. We walked for ages. It was freezing and the mist was about knee high and the air was wet and cold on my face teasing the streams of snot from my nose. Pop tied this big rope to a tree on the top of the hill and we were swinging on it and yelling out like Tarzan. "Aaaaarrrrgh!" Oh, my God, it was exhilarating. Swinging on the rope so far and high that you could see all of Luton and Dunstable lying before you. Like those little model villages you get in theme parks sometimes.

Afterwards, we rolled down the hill. Over and over until we had no breath left in our lungs from laughing and the effort. When we stood up we were dripping wet. But best of all, Pop had rolled in dog shit. He was covered in it. It was hilarious. I skipped in front of him the whole way home crying out, "Stinky Pop. Stinky Pop!"

That's who Pop is to me. My Grandad. My Dad. My best friend - and look at him. Look at what I've done to him. He's sitting on the chair opposite me. I think I see now for the very first time who he actually is. What age has wrought from him. An old man - vulnerable. Full of love and family loyalty. Ready even now to die for those he loves. And he may just do that. Unless somehow, I can protect him. If once, just once in my miserable life, I can stand up and be half the man he was… is. I shake my head with the effort of trying to think of some kind of strategy. Pop must see me struggling internally. He smiles bravely at me.

"Don't worry, Son," he says. "It'll be alright, you'll see."

Even now – waiting for the hell to rain down on us, he only thinks of me.

He's holding that photo. That picture that he has, of him - him and that lad that he saved when he was a soldier. A gunner in the Royal Artillery. He was in Northern Ireland during 'The Troubles'. He's told me about it so many times. He was in Theipval barracks, just outside of Belfast. He always talks about his army days with a kind of longing. But then, maybe he is just wistful for the days of his youth, when he was strong and virile.

He thought at first, that he was supposed to be there to help the Catholics. They were being almost persecuted at that time. It turned out in the end that the only people he was there to help was the man standing next to him. Shit was flying at them from all sides. Everybody just wanted them gone. They were thrown into a maelstrom of hate and got caught up in it all, good and proper.

Pop was nineteen. Just a kid really. He had no idea of the political history of the place. How deep the hatreds ran. The old prejudices. He told me once that he and a group of his men were sent to protect some young kids going to school. All these little girls, five, six or seven, walking to school, holding their mothers' hands with tears running down their faces. Meanwhile, on the other side of the road, stood a different bunch of mothers, from the Protestant side. Hurling abuse and condemnation and threats at them. At kids! It was terrible. Grown people throwing bricks and balloons filled with piss at little girls. Why?

Because they were Catholic and their school was in a Protestant area – that's why. Holy Cross, it was called.

Terrible times. Pop always drummed it into me. Hatred breeds monsters. That's what he says and he's right.

Anyway, this one time, Pop was with his mate just outside the barracks. They'd gone to the chippy van. It was against the rules but there was this young girl serving the chips that Pop had his eye on. She was a real cutie, Pop said. A looker. Anyway, they heard a ruckus going on, just down the road a way. It sounded bad. If they had been more experienced they would have reported it and waited for instructions, but they were both young and headstrong. Also, Pop said, he wanted to look good in front of this girl.

They went to investigate and came across a young black guy. He was being set upon by a group of kids; there was about twenty of them. The thing was, there were Catholics and Protestants together. All of them were kicking the living crap out of the black lad. He was dying right in front of their eyes. That's the thing about hatred - it can change the rules, jump the barriers. The Catholic and Protestant hatreds could be put on the back burner for a bit, just long enough to allow them to gang together to stamp out the life of this black lad. Good old-fashioned racism. If the Protestants couldn't go into the Catholic areas, and the Catholics couldn't go into the Protestants areas, the blacks could go nowhere. They were never safe. Not even in their own homes.

Pop and his mate – Willy, his name was, they ploughed right in. The trouble was, someone had a knife. Or, more probably, more than one someone. Willy got stuck twice. Once in the leg and a deeper one in his side. These kids were only about ten or twelve. They were like demons, snarling and hissing. Pop said he has a clear memory of a kid with blond curls and huge periwinkle blue eyes. He spat in Willy's face, wiping the blood that splattered on to him from the spurting artery on Willy's thigh.

"Feck off, ye fecking British bastard! Just feck off and fecking die!"

All the violence of that day, and it was this that had shocked Pop the most. Such vitriol coming from the lips of that angelic little face!

It spurred him on into action. Somehow, without injuring any of the demonic little brats, he swept them aside. He grabbed the black guy with one arm and Willy in the other. He kicked and pushed and stumbled his way out of there. For some reason, his leg kept giving way but he held onto his charges and got them to safety. Behind him he could hear the kids' insults flying first at him, and then toward themselves. Deprived of their common enemy, they had returned to the comforting familiarity of baiting at each other over their differences.

Pop limped into the barracks and collapsed on the ground with his charges. It turned out in the end that he himself had received three knife wounds in his leg, which was the reason it was failing him. Pop said he wasn't even aware of any pain until they had taken the other two guys off to the hospital.

Willy recovered physically after treatment, but had to be medically discharged in the end. He suffered terribly from post-traumatic stress. They just said it was nerves. They may as well have called him a coward.

The black guy, Thomas, was in hospital for some weeks. The kids had kicked his ribs so hard and for so long that they had shattered and pierced his lung. He was so grateful to Pop. Kept telling him he had saved his life, which he had, but it wasn't in Pop's nature to need thanks. He treasured the photo, though. It showed him and Thomas, both in flowered hospital Johnnies – arms round each other and big grins on their faces. Pop said any decent person would have done the same as he did. It was just the human thing to do. I'm not so sure.

The kids were never caught. Pop said they didn't really even bother trying too hard. It was one of those things. The police even told Thomas that perhaps he should think about taking his wife and their young son and move away. Perhaps to England. How did the police put it to him? "Your sort often can't settle." It's disgraceful but that's how things were then.

Pop recovered fully after treatment and some physio. He got a medal for that. The Military Cross. He got other medals, too. The five service medals for his tours of duty, but it's the military cross that he is mostly proud of. I suppose I should say, *was* proud of. He hasn't got it any more. Another sacrifice he made for me.

It stood to reason that I would come here to Pop when Mum had finally had enough of my lazy ways and kicked me out. She had no choice really. I loved her, of course I did, but I ran rings round her, as they say. I couldn't keep a job down. Just couldn't seem to get up in time. After I lost my sixth job in as many months she just lost her temper and threw me out. Trying to teach me a lesson, but we both knew that Pop would always have an open door for me.

It went well, for a while. I mean, we were cramped, but Pop appreciated my help and we had a kind of routine going. Every Sunday Mum would bring dinner round in one of those Tupperware box things and I would heat it, then I would do the dishes and we'd go to the Legion for the afternoon.

It's good in the Legion. Pop has a load of good friends there, some were even in his regiment. They all like me and we get on really well. I often play dominoes with them but they always win. They call me Downer. That's because I can down a pint in just less than four seconds. It's not much of a claim to fame but it's my party trick and it seems to entertain these guys for some reason.

Anyway, I wasn't here for long before I blew it. It was inevitable, I suppose. I overslept and missed an appointment with my key worker in the job centre. They sanctioned my benefits for three weeks. Three weeks with no money. Pop went ballistic! I honestly have never seen him so angry. I thought he was going to hit me. I just stood there like a stupid oaf while he called me all sorts of horrible names. Said I was good for nothing and he was ashamed of me. I was devastated.

After, it calmed down a bit. I really believe it's the first time in my life that I had apologised to someone and actually meant it. I was gutted. It felt like my heart was broken with the shame that I felt. I promised him that somehow, I would make things right. Pop just put his hand on my shoulder.

"We'll sort it, laddie," he said.

After that we went to the Legion. I got talking to this guy called Gibson. Anyway, he offered me a job. A good one. I really liked the sound of it. He runs a small chain of independent off licences all round the Bedfordshire area. A couple of them were local to us, in fact. Anyway, he had this huge warehouse for storing all the booze. Trouble was it had been broken into a couple of times and he was looking for someone he could trust to act as security for him. Like he said:

"I've tried dogs, but I got attached. They've ended up moving in with me and the missus. She's spoilt 'em rotten. Like two big slobbering kids just wanting belly rubs now."

Some bright spark shouted out, "Yeah Gibson - you're best off with Downer. No bugger wants to rub his belly!"

Everyone laughed. Like I said, it's a good night in the Legion.

The only problem was I would have to get an SIA licence. That was going to cost money. Gibson made some enquiries and it turned out that he could book me on a course starting at the end of the next week. It would be two-hundred and fifty pounds for the course, and a further two-hundred for the actual licence, which would take about three days to come through. Then I would be set. So, four hundred and fifty pounds altogether. At that point it might as well have been a million.

Of course Pops came to the rescue. He went out the next day for a few hours and came back with two-hundred and fifty pounds, which he put on the table.

"There you go, laddie," he said.

I looked up wonderingly. "Where did you get that?"

He looked stern. "Now then, Downer, don't you be worrying about that. I just did what I had to do is all."

I thought for a while, then it came to me. The only thing that Pop had of any kind of value to sell … his medals!

I felt absolutely devastated. "Oh, Pop! Why? We could have found some other way. Not your medals. They mean everything to you."

He sat down then and took my hands in his and looked at me seriously.

"Now then, laddie," he said, "Those medals, you know what they are? I'll tell you. Those medals are bits of pretty metal and that's it. A reminder of my past. Now you – you on the other hand, are my future. My much loved, only grandson. D'you understand? So I will do whatever is necessary to ensure that future."

He got up and walked into the kitchen to put the kettle on. I followed him in and just grabbed him round the waist and gave him the biggest, strongest hug that I could without actually squeezing the life out of him.

All this was fine and good, but we were still two-hundred down. I had no idea what we could do. Pop was more optimistic.

"Keep the faith, laddie," he said. "Something will turn up."

And so it did.

A couple of evenings later - out of the blue, a knock came at the door. This bloke stood there, all friendly and smiling. He looked smart. All suited up with shined shoes. Pop has always been impressed with that sort of thing. Before I knew it Pop invited the bloke in and was introducing him to me.

"Downer laddie," he said, "This here, is Mr. Weasel. He's from a place called Weasel & Co. Financial Solutions. He says he can help us. Why don't you have a wee listen to what he has to say?"

Pop was beaming and went into the tiny kitchen next door to make Mr. Weasel a cup of tea. Meanwhile, full of friendly enthusiasm and chat, Mr. Weasel explained to me and Pop how he could lend us the money we needed. No problem at all. I was surprised. I didn't think people like me who had zero credit rating could get cash loans. Especially with no collateral.

"That's normally true," explained the guy. "But you see, as an ex-military man myself, I've recently been putting together a package for service men and their families."

He looked over at Pop who was sitting at the table sipping at his tea. After Pop reassured him with a smile that he was listening, he went on to explain that we didn't even have to worry about going into town to pay monies in at a bank or anything. He offered a personal service where he would come round every Friday evening and collect the payments. All we had to do was to make sure we paid the instalments in time.

"In fact, I tell you what," he said, leaning back and lighting a cigarette, "I think that to be on the safe side, you ought to borrow two-hundred and fifty pounds. After all, you'll be needing some lunch money and that."

Pops was getting a bit worried. "What if, say for some reason we miss a payment, what then?"

Mr. Weasel explained that if we missed a payment then there would be an extra fifty pounds interest put on the loan, but not to worry as if it got to three missed payments, then special measures would be put in place.

"Special measures," asked Pops, "what does that mean?"

Mr. Weasel came and put his arm round Pop's shoulder, as if he had known Pop all of his life. I didn't like it much. I thought it was too familiar, but he was just reassuring him after all.

"Now then, Pops," he said. "Don't you worry about that, 'cos that's just not going to happen is it? Payment is fifty a week and like I said, I'll come round personally to collect it so no worries there. And young Downer here, well he'll be in a job - so he can easily afford the payments, so no problem. Okay?"

And that was it. Mr. Weasel counted out the money, two-hundred and fifty pounds, note by note, making a big show of it. He took one last swig of his tea and showed himself out.

Me and Pops just sat in silence for a while, looking at the pile of notes on the table. Even then I had a feeling – you know, like we had just walked out of the frying pan...

Thursday came and I went off to the college. It was only a couple of bus rides away so not much problem there, and the course itself was really easy. I was relieved.

The not so nice surprise came about five o'clock the next evening. Me and Pops had just finished dinner and were in the middle of watching TV, when a loud knock came to the door. It was Mr. Weasel. Pop was a bit taken aback but he invited him in and sent me to the kitchen to make tea.

Mr. Weasel sat at the table without waiting to be asked and he took a small red bound book from his pocket with a pen. He looked up at Pops and smiled broadly.

"How are you, Pops?" he asked. He turned to me; I was standing in the doorway. "And you, Downer? How's the course going? Well, I hope."

Pop glanced over at me with bewilderment.

"We're ok, thanks. Doing well. Downer's enjoying the course, aren't you Downer?"

He didn't give me enough time to answer, but I gave a feeble nod anyway. Pop carried on.

"Er, can we help you in any way, Mr. Weasel?"

He responded by leaning back in the chair and blowing smoke towards Pop's face.

He said, "Well, yes, you can help me out, Pops. You could pay me the first instalment of the loan if you please. Fifty quid."

Pop looked alarmed. I expect I was looking a bit pale as well. I was certainly feeling a bit panicked.

"Now?" I questioned.

Weasel nodded slowly. "Yes, now. Now indeed. It is Friday, is it not?"

I could feel the blood draining down into my feet. Weasel was smiling. He really did, right at that moment, look just like a weasel.

"So, if you could just pay up, then I will write it in my book and be on my way. Leave you good folks in peace to watch your programme."

Pop realised that we had left the television blaring. Quickly turning it off he turned to Weasel and tried to reason with him.

"We thought you understood," he said. "Downer just started the course yesterday. That lasts for a week and then its three days before he gets his licence. He won't start work till a week on Tuesday. Even then, he'll have to ask for a sub to be able to pay you on that Friday." He trailed off. "So that's two weeks today."

Weasel shook his head sorrowfully. "Of course. I understand," he said in a low voice. "It's you that doesn't understand. You see, I don't give a flying fuck about you – your job, or anything. What I care about, the only thing I care about, is the money that you owe me."

Pop's mouth thinned. He cleared his throat. "I'm sorry Weasel," he said. "We don't have it."

Weasel stood up abruptly. I think, I'm not sure, but I think me and Pop both took a step back. There was no doubt about it. We were both scared.

"Okay," said Weasel. He wrote something in his book then put it back into his pocket. Stubbing his cigarette out on the saucer, he finally turned to go. "As discussed, that will be a further fifty pounds added to the interest of your debt," he said.

Pop was automatically walking him to the door, relieved to be seeing the back of him, but before Weasel left, he turned to Pop and pushed his face right up close. Quietly he said, "Of course, just so you're both clear, that's strike one. Two more weeks - and Special Measures!" He walked away whistling.

We asked about it at The Legion. It soon became clear we had made a terrible mistake. Weasel was a well-known loan shark, apparently. He had a thug that did all the strong arm stuff for him. They called him Treacle because he was as black as treacle. He was a bully. A mountain of a man. Rumoured to have beaten some people so badly that they had later died. No evidence was ever left and everyone was too scared to speak out. Even more scared now, we tried to sell furniture, clothes, kitchen equipment, anything and everything to make the payments.

But - in the end, it's come to this. Me and Pops sitting in his front room. Me on a wooden box and Pop's on the only chair that we kept. He is holding the picture that reminds him of his past, when he still felt like a man and not a victim and I'm just trying to summon up some courage from the empty pit inside me. We wait and we know with dreaded certainty that for us, there is no escape.

A loud knock at the door. We sit there - not moving. A crash. Weasel bursts in. There is a black mountain of muscle looming over from behind him. It's a blur. Weasel moves to one side so we can fully appreciate the doom that he has bought upon us. I have only one thought. Try to live long enough to protect Pop. I get up and run towards the thug, Treacle. I clench my fist and punch as hard as I can to his face. I have to stand on tiptoes and it puts me off balance. There is a noise.

Someone is shouting. It could be me? Then there is a whoosh and pain explodes behind my ear. It sends me reeling to the floor. There is more pain, but I don't register it. Nothing is getting through. Maybe I have already died. No, I can't have – because my arm is wrenched out of its socket and the pain in my ear now seems almost pleasant compared to the screaming agony that used to be my shoulder. I lay, broken. Defeated and bleeding. All I can do is gaze up at Pop and pray that it's quick. Pop is crying. Weeping like a baby. All I feel is shame.

But Treacle is not hitting him. He has taken the picture from Pop's hand. He shouts. "What the fuck are you doing with a picture of my dad?"

Pop is crying and just looking at Treacle. I think I'm crying too. I don't understand what's happening. I just hurt. Treacle has got Pop's picture in his hands. He keeps looking at the picture, then at Pop.

"Are you him?" he asks. "Are you him?"

I still don't get it, but Pop does. I can see the light in his eyes. He takes the picture from Treacle. "Yes" he says quietly. "I'm him. I'm Pop. And you're dad is Thomas. Me and my best mate, Willy, helped him out that time, when you were just a tiny babe in arms."

Treacle picks Pop up. I draw in a deep breath. I think he is going to kill him, but he wraps Pop up in his great meaty arms and hugs him.

And that's it. Over. Just like that. Happy days!

Treacle comes round a lot now. He helps us out. Tries to pay us back. It's Pop he owes, not me, but you can't tell him that. He just wants to make it better. He does as well, not just money, he helps us out in lots of different ways. He took Pops over to see his dad. That was good. Pops was well happy.

No one has seen Weasel round here for a long time. I wonder if Treacle has got anything to do with that, but I'm not going to ask him.

Sequence

Shelly Rahman
England

WAKING UP, RUNA WENT STRAIGHT to the window next to her desk. She drew the curtains, opened the windows, and looked at the garden. The red hibiscus was spotlit in that morning's sun. Holding two iron rods of the protective grilling and leaning forward, she stuck her nose out. The air was fresh. She drew in a long, deep breath. It was good she was invited to Flora's for a chat otherwise this would have passed as yet another unmemorable weekend.

And yet she was not sure if she should visit Flora's house particularly after all those teasing remarks from her friends. This was because Flora's brother, Bashir, was staring at her nonstop during their elder sister's boubhat reception, which took place three days after the actual wedding. Did Bashir really like her? Her friends thought he did. He was certainly paying her a lot of silent attention. How embarrassing and fascinating!

She wanted to find out the truth. This was the first time Runa visited Flora in her house even though they had been good friends for the past couple of years. They chatted for a while about their school life, about their college life, about the wedding.

'Would you like some tea?' Flora said.

'If it isn't too much trouble.'

'Not at all.'

'Shall I come with you?'

'Not necessary. I'll be back in a tick.'

Flora, on the way to the kitchen, wondered where her brother was. He forced her to invite Runa and now he didn't appear.

Sitting alone, Runa thought she was worried unnecessarily. Bashir was nowhere near her. *Good,* she told herself.

She looked around the sitting room and saw some nice paintings and a bookcase along a wall. She knelt down in front of the books to look at the titles. Right then, Bashir came in the room quietly and saw Runa on her knees. Her curly black hair was spread all over her back.

'You are alone? Where's Flora?' he asked.

Hearing a male voice, Runa startled. Turning her head slightly and seeing Bashir, she jumped up. She straightened her kamiz, made sure her scarf was in the right place, turned around fully and looked at him. He was wearing stone-coloured trousers and a black T-shirt. His muscular arms were exposed and he had a black beard that looked bristly. It reminded her of some heroes in Hindi movies.

'Flora has gone to get some tea. How are you?' Runa said with a nice little smile.

'Fine. Let me introduce myself.'

'You are Bashir bhai, Flora's elder brother. One of the girls told me when I saw you at the boubhat reception.'

Runa gently walked to her chair, sat on it, kept her head down, and eyes fixed on the floor. Bashir started to pace up and down. Runa felt him staring at her.

Let him look. And what can he see? I'm well covered, she told herself.

'You have nice curly hair.' Bashir's voice again.

'You think so? I don't like it at all.'

Runa then grabbed a bunch of hair, brought it over her shoulder in the front, and bending her neck towards it, stared at it ostensibly to examine it.

'Were you born with curly hair or do you do it using a machine?'

'No, I don't do it with a curler. My hair has always been like this.'

Runa said it with an affectionate voice as if the curly hair was her baby; whether ugly or artificial, it was hers.

Bashir was about to say something when Flora entered the room carrying tea and samosas. 'Oh, good! Bashir Bhai, you are here. Glad that Runa wasn't on her own. But why are you standing? Do sit down. Let me introduce you properly …?'

'I saw Runa before from a distance; today we've met face to face.'

Runa looked at Bashir bashfully. Her lips developed a momentary crescent-like smile. Flora gave her a cup of tea and offered some samosas. She took one and then Flora offered them to Bashir.

'Bashir Bhai, would you like one?'

'Not really. I just had tea and stuff at Alam's.'

'Still, do take one.'

Bashir picked one up and started to scoff it. Runa had a sip of her tea and put the cup down. She recalled that while waiting for lunch at boubhat, the boys were standing in a group not far from where the girls were chatting.

'We had lots of fun at boubhat celebrations. It seemed that you boys were competing with us girls to see which group could laugh louder,' Runa ventured with a lovely smile.

'Now why should we be doing that? As a matter of fact we also enjoyed ourselves very much. It was pleasantly cool,' he said, having swallowed what he had in his mouth from his second samosa.

'Was it only because of the weather? Could there be other reasons, for example, the girls were nearby?' Runa's face was teasing.

The taunting was melody to Bashir's ears. He thought it conveyed a message of interest.

'A close friend of mine, Alam, the friend whose house I've just come from, was telling us funny stories. Perfect humour for the occasion. I hadn't laughed so much for some time.'

Because he did not have a witty response ready, he tried to be genuine.

'Let's hear some of the jokes,' Runa said.

'I actually don't remember any.'

'Or is it that you can't possibly share those stories?'

'Truly, I'm not good at telling stories.'

There was a pause in the conversation. Runa bent forward, picked up one of Flora's hands, and began to examine her glass bangles.

'These are new. Perfect colour for you. You know, if I wear glass bangles, they will definitely break, cut my arm, and my mother will scold me.'

'Yes, that's the problem with these bangles, and that's why I almost gave up wearing them. Just because you are coming today and we'll be at home, I wore them,' Flora said.

'I like the jingling sound of glass bangles,' Bashir said.

'Yes, boys generally say so. They also say that we girls intentionally make more jingling sounds to attract boys' attention.' Runa was still teasing.

Everybody was silent again. She hadn't hit the right tone; she could feel the embarrassment.

'I have to go now,' Runa told them.

'Stay a little longer,' Bashir said.

'I have to go, Bashir Bhai.'

On the way back home, Runa recalled how incredibly simply Bashir had said, 'You have nice curly hair.' There were no excesses, no pomp or grandeur in the language; it was plain and simple. He really liked her hair. Runa felt good.

That night, lying in bed, Bashir thought about Runa. That innocent curvy smile appeared in front of him. He remembered how Runa's breasts danced as she jumped up from kneeling. He couldn't forget the way her thick, black, curly hair swung as she stood up. He felt an irresistible attraction to touch her hair and smell it. Everything about Runa he could remember seemed to draw him nearer to her, invited him to be closer.

Flora was compelled to invite Runa to her house the following Friday. Initially Flora didn't want to.

'Last Friday when Runa visited us, you two enjoyed chatting, didn't you? Then why are you complicating everything? Let me drop you by car,' Bashir tried to encourage her.

Runa and Flora were talking to each other in Runa's house when Flora said, 'Bashir Bhai seems to be in love.'

'Truly? With whom?' Runa enquired enthusiastically.

'Could be with you.'

Runa was afraid of this. Was she too friendly to Bashir the other day? She didn't think so. Still, perhaps she shouldn't have talked to him in the way that she did.

'He probably loves you.' Flora continued. 'But I don't wish to be involved in the relationship. This is a matter between you two. I have already put this clearly to him several times. I told him that it has to be him to tell you personally what he wants to say. And yet he forced me to come here.'

Signs of Flora's annoyance with her brother were visible on her face.

'Leaving aside the question of your particular situation, he doesn't know me. The only thing I know about him is that he's your brother. I've only ever talked to him for a few minutes in your house. How can he fall in love with me?' Runa said.

'Somehow he likes you very much. Flora said. 'Doesn't it happen, love at first sight? Maybe, that has happened. I could escape having any responsibility for this if you two talk. It's belittling to act as a middleman.'

'I'm sorry for you, but I can't talk to him.'

'Listen, if you don't talk to him, I doubt whether he can get out of his depression. And I won't have peace at home.'

Inside, Runa felt a delightful sensation. Her face brightened up a little, but only momentarily. Then a rush of anxiety and embarrassment occupied it. She decided that it wasn't right to get involved in this way. She told Flora most emphatically that she couldn't do it. She was sorry.

Flora didn't give up. Because of her repeated insistence, Runa felt that she had to visit Bashir one more time. So she went to their house, but always in the presence of Flora. Runa came to know that Bashir never passed his matriculation examination even though he took the exams twice. So he'd given up studying, took a loan from his father, and started a small stationery shop in the New Market. Runa felt convinced that she shouldn't see Bashir in this way because she couldn't see any future in the relationship. But she was unable to make Flora understand her inner conflicts. Neither could she leave Flora because she was one of the few close friends she had.

On her way back, she thought of her father, who was the joint secretary in the government social welfare department; he would never marry her off to a half-educated, petty businessman. Her father and all her uncles were professionals. Besides, her father wanted Runa to continue her studies in the university, as she firmly planned to do. She decided to avoid Bashir.

Next Friday, Runa did not visit Flora's house. On Monday, Flora made sure to see Runa at the college campus. She said to Runa, 'Bashir Bhai waited for you the whole afternoon. You should've come.'

'I'm not committed to come to your house every Friday. I told Bashir Bhai too. Hope you don't mind my saying this but I don't see any future in this relationship. I cannot marry against my parents' will. I don't wish to hurt Bashir Bhai either. It would be best if you can explain this to him. If you don't accept it or your brother doesn't, then ask your father to send a marriage proposal to my father.'

But Runa felt compelled by her friend to go and see Bashir one last time the following Friday. Runa told Bashir about her worries and tried to make him understand the situation. Bashir refused to accept this.

'All right, since today is the last day, let's go and do something together that we can remember.' Bashir's eyes implored her.

Runa looked away for a moment. Then looked back. Showing signs of anxiety on her face, she listened to Bashir. With his eyes fixed on Runa's, he pleaded, 'Let's go for a short drive somewhere close. What do you say?'

Runa thought of the poem, "The Last Ride Together" by an English poet, Robert Browning. They read it in college last year. She thought 'a last ride' would be rather romantic.

'For a short while then. I need to return home quickly today. Do ask Flora to come along,' Runa said.

Flora did not want to join them on the expedition. She said 'I need to help mother in the kitchen. We have guests tonight.'

Bashir got his father's car out. For an Austin Morris 1954 model, the eight-year-old car looked immaculate. Runa liked being in it. Sitting next to Bashir on the front seat, she got an opportunity to see Bashir closely. She was aware of his bare arm. The scent of his aftershave filled the whole car.

His fast driving thrilled Runa as much as horrified her. 'Where are we going?' she asked.

'Towards Joydebpur. The roads are pretty empty there. It's nice to drive.'

'Joydebpur is quite far. I really don't want to go there.'

'Let's go a little bit beyond Tongi then.'

'Please could you drive slower.'

'You needn't worry if I'm driving.'

Runa thought he was driving like a maniac. She gripped her seat. They remained quiet but full of excitement and anticipation. Bashir suddenly pulled up by the side of the road. Runa jerked forward. Bashir leaning against the steering wheel a moment, sat back, stretched his arms forward, and cracked his fingers. He looked at Runa briefly. Then, without saying anything, he started the car and moved on. But not towards home.

Runa protested. He accelerated. She wanted to go back. He paid no attention. He continued to push forward. After a while he stopped in an open area and pointing towards a rice field he said, 'Look at this field, just beyond it we have a little garden where we grow all kinds of vegetables. There's a little pond with kingfishers and pond herons. Would you like to have a look? It's really pretty.'

'Just to visit and then we'll go back.' Runa said.

Bashir's garden had a hut in the middle. Runa liked the pond. A few water lilies bloomed and a kingfisher sat on a bamboo pole looking for an opportunity.

Bashir said, 'Let's go and see our hut.'

There was a bed in the hut but no chairs or stools. Bashir asked Runa to sit on the bed and rest a few moments while he freshened up in the toilet before driving back. Runa wanted to look at the pond and the garden.

But Bashir said, 'I saw a snake last time I came. I think it's safer in the hut.'

Coming out of the toilet, Bashir found Runa sitting on the bed, looking sad. While rubbing his hands together he said, 'It's a nice place, isn't it?'

He came and sat next to her. Runa felt uncomfortable and got up saying, 'Let's go back now.'

Bashir quickly got hold of her hand and pulled her back on the bed. He pushed her down and grabbed the waistband of her salwar. She slapped him, hit his chest with her fists, and screamed, 'Let me go. You're a wicked man, a pig. Let me go!'

Who listened to whom? Bashir was unstoppable.

Driving back in silence, all of a sudden, Bashir pointed with his index finger to the top part of Runa's chest and said, 'These are all mine.' Then he pointed to the space between her thighs and said, 'This is mine.' He looked at her and continued, 'No one has any right to these anymore.'

Runa was sobbing. She didn't want to stay in the car any longer. She put her hand on the handle.

Bashir said, 'Absolutely not. You'll cause an accident if you open the door.'

Runa was shaking. She gripped her seat. She couldn't control her trembling, neither could she stop crying. She sat there numb. Sad, disgraced, and devastated. Raped.

Runa felt that her soul had left her body. She wanted to jump out of the car. She wouldn't mind if she broke her limbs or if she died; then all her miseries and pain would end. She went for the door handle again. Suddenly, the car slowed down and stopped in the middle of the road. Runa panicked.

But Bashir only said, 'The engine is very hot. Perhaps there's no water in the radiator.'

'Now what?' Runa snivelled.

'Fortunately, there's a tyre repair shop not far from here. Look, you can see it. But we need to get out of the car and push it.'

She had been keen to jump out. Now she said, 'I'm not getting out.'

Bashir went to the shop and brought someone back with him. Together they pushed the car up to the shop. Runa stayed where she was. They had to wait until the engine cooled down.

On the way back Bashir said, 'Shall I drop you home?'

'No. Drop me in front of your house.'

Runa got out. She didn't call on Flora. She didn't look at Bashir. She straightened her crumpled clothes, then hired a rickshaw.

She managed to get back, suppressing her tears. She felt unclean and disgusted. Someone forcefully took away her virginity. She was wounded. She felt dirty, very dirty. She went in the bathroom to remove the filth. She washed herself time and again. She wanted to get rid of Bashir and his touch. She had a long shower. The parts of her body Bashir had declared as his own she washed with soap and water again and again.

Runa's mother wondered why Runa was having a long shower. She generally had a shower in the morning. Why now and for so long? She knocked on the bathroom door and wanted to know if everything was all right.

Runa shouted, 'Why wouldn't everything be all right?'

'Are you OK? You sound upset.'

Runa came out of the bathroom. Without talking to her mother she went straight into her room. She was angry, very angry. She was angry with Bashir. She was angry with herself. She was angry with Flora. She was angry with the whole world, the world which had been incredibly unjust to her, the world that she now hated. She shut the door almost in Ayesha's face, bolted it, and then went to bed, burying herself under the duvet. She wanted to hide. She didn't want anyone to see her, not any part of her body. Her sobs became louder.

Ayesha knocked on the door. Getting no response, she left. After a while she knocked again, calling her to dinner. Runa screamed, 'I'm not hungry. I want to sleep.'

'Why so early?'

'I don't feel well. I'm tired. Go away.'

Ayesha thought that perhaps Runa had started her period.

Runa couldn't sleep. She tried to analyse the situation. She thought she shouldn't have gone out with Bashir alone. She was angry with Flora who pushed her that way. But could she have ignored Flora's request? Bashir was Flora's brother. How could she have said no to her close friend's brother? Runa trusted him as much as she trusted her own brother. How could he have done this? Just because she'd agreed to the drive, that didn't mean she gave him permission to do whatever he liked. He'd done an appalling, vile thing. He'd destroyed her purity.

It was completely unfair.

She sat up suddenly. Bashir hadn't used any contraception. Was she going to be pregnant? She must talk to her mother. Then she dismissed the thought; getting pregnant was a chance occurrence. If she wasn't pregnant, then talking about this with her mum would create an unnecessary mental pressure. She didn't want to create anxiety. What would she do then? She covered her face with her hands and sobbed, rocking backwards and forwards. After a while she hit herself, and lay down abruptly under her duvet. She fell into restless sleep.

Next morning Runa felt very tired. Calm, she came out of her room and saw her mother approaching.

'How are you? Ayesha asked.

'Hungry.'

'You look tired.'

Without answering, Runa went straight to the dining table. The others had had their breakfast. She lifted the covers off the plates and saw that there was some dry flat-bread, fried potatoes, and eggs gone cold. They sat down to eat. Runa stalled her mother's questions with noncommittal answers and retreated to her room after breakfast.

Runa thought that she would have to marry Bashir. She couldn't marry anyone else. She believed what he said: her breasts and other parts of her body which Bashir touched belonged to him. She couldn't give these to any other man as these were no longer pure. She knew she was no longer a virgin. No man would marry her when he heard what had happened to her. And why should anyone? Therefore, she needed to tell her parents that she had to marry Bashir.

What if Bashir didn't want to marry her?

He knew that Runa was unchaste. But he was the one who'd made her so. He was responsible for it. And yet, he could hold it against her. He could question her integrity. He might ask why she'd got in the car if she didn't have hidden desires. Many men would think she shouldn't have gone out alone with any man. But she hadn't wanted to go. It was Flora who encouraged her by saying that her brother needed to be rescued. Runa had trusted Bashir; he was her friend's brother. Now she hated him.

A few days later Flora came to visit Runa. Runa let her in and then shut the door immediately and hissed at Flora, 'Haramzadi, why have you come?'

'Bashir Bhai loves you deeply. He wants to marry you.'

Runa was dead silent. After a while, she said, 'I don't know if my parents would accept this proposal. Ask your parents to get in touch with mine directly.'

Runa kept tightlipped about what happened with Bashir the other day.

'Do you want to marry Bashir Bhai?' Flora asked.

'I'm not sure. You should've come with us that day.'

'Why? What happened?'

'Nothing.'

'I thought if I didn't come with you, the two of you would get a chance to talk to each other, get to know each other better. The third person always creates a problem — do you remember we often used to say this?'

They sat quietly for a few moments and drank the tea that Runa's mother sent via a servant girl and then Flora left.

Runa noticed that she did not have her period when it was due. Another week passed. She panicked. Then finding her mother alone in the inside courtyard, with tears rolling down her cheeks, she said that her period hadn't yet started.

'Sometimes the period may start a bit early or late. Ayesha said. 'There's no reason to worry about it.'

'No, it isn't that simple.' Runa sobbed.

'What do you mean? Why are you crying? What's the matter? Is there something that you haven't told me?'

'Yes.' Runa's crying was uncontrollable.

Ayesha took Runa to her room and asked her why she was crying.

Runa said, 'Promise me that you won't tell it to anyone, not even Baba.'

'It depends on what you say.'

'I may be pregnant.' Runa hung her head in shame.

'You! Pregnant! How? Which man? When did it happen?'

'About two weeks ago. It was Flora's brother, Bashir.'

'Oh, Allah!'

Ayesha sat down on the bed and made Runa sit next to her, then said, 'Did you want to do this? Do you know what the consequences could be?'

'I know. That's why I didn't want to do this. He forced himself on me when we went for a drive.'

'You went where? For a drive? Alone with him in the car? Did you want to go?'

'No.'

'What do you mean?'

Runa told her mother the whole story.

Ayesha smoothed back her hair, then said, 'For about a month, your father has been talking to a prospective groom who wants to marry in a hurry before he goes back to Rajshahi where he teaches in the university.

Baba's practically fixed your marriage. Now I'll have to tell him everything.'

'What's going to happen to me?' Runa couldn't stop her tears. She said, 'Maybe I should marry Bashir. He wants to marry me.'

'What does Bashir do? How far did he study?'

Runa told her mother about Bashir. 'You sit right here,' Ayesha said. 'Let me go and talk to your father.'

When Ayesha told Mubarak everything, he jumped up. 'What did you say? He forcibly did this. I'll get him arrested. What does that bastard think? Is this a lawless country?'

'Do calm down. We need to do what is best for Runa. It's not wise to do anything when you're angry.'

The two of them sat and discussed what could be done. Then together they went to Runa's room to talk to her.

Mubarak said, 'You need to keep absolutely quiet about what happened with Bashir. You do not talk to anyone about this. Your marriage has practically been fixed. Do you understand?' Mubarak continued, 'The young man I chose for you studied in Tokyo University for eight years, got a doctorate degree in Pharmacy. He speaks Japanese fluently.'

Runa said, 'I knew nothing about this. When did you fix all this? Is he a Bengali?'

'Of course he's a Bengali. Haroon comes from Barisal. He has seen you and liked you,' Ayesha said.

'His name's Haroon?'

'Yes.'

Runa said, 'I want to see a gynaecologist. I want to destroy the baby if I have one. Besides, I want to see Haroon. I want to tell him myself what happened with Bashir. If he still wants to marry me, then I won't have any problem.'

Before Runa could even finish her sentence, her father said, 'Absolutely not. If you do this, a real calamity will descend on our entire family. Hearing this no man will ever marry you. So forget about it.'

With tearful eyes Runa said, 'How can I forget it, Baba? The whole thing sits on my chest like a heavy rock. I'm carrying this burden every second.'

'I understand that. Since an accident has happened, you'll of course suffer.'

'It is hurting a lot, Baba. '

'Who's responsible for this? You should've thought about it before you went for a drive.'

Runa began to sob. Mubarak Hossain changed his tone and said, 'You need to be patient. Your mother and I think that in time everything will be all right.'

Mubarak gently hugged Runa. He said, 'No one denies that you've had a terrible experience. We are all sad. That's why we want to get you married as soon as possible. If something new happens in your life, this nasty incident may gradually become a hazy memory. If you become busy with your life now, for example, if you get married, have a baby, then this would start a new life for you. And that ugly wound in your heart will fade in time and may finally disappear.'

Runa stood in front of the window of her room looking at the dahlias and spider lilies. She wanted to smell them. That morning's breeze moved through the leaves of the plants. On the star-fruit tree a few noisy parakeets were clambering from branch to branch and sucking the tasty juice of one fruit after another and dropping them to the ground wasted. Runa released a long sigh but watched the little black and white doel panicking on the branch of a hibiscus. She presumed that its nest was somewhere nearby. It might have left its eggs or nestlings unattended. The parakeets must have made it apprehensive and it gave its buzzing alarm call. Runa sat down on her chair. She still thought it would be immoral not to tell Haroon everything. Hearing her story, if he wanted to marry her, then she supposed everything would be all right.

Runa sank deep in the ocean of anxieties. What her father said was also right. If Haroon knew everything then he might accept her but might not fully trust her. Would the union then be one of unhappiness?

If that were the case, then she couldn't possibly marry anyone other than Bashir. But what about Bashir's mistreatment of her? Would she not hold it against Bashir all her life? Could she ever forgive him? If not, would the marriage be a happy one? The moment Bashir came into her thoughts, several other questions popped up in her mind. Had Bashir raped other women? Would he do it again?

Runa began to notice a few changes in her body. She had these feelings before, during her periods, so she felt relieved. She must be getting one soon. However, a few days before her marriage, she told her mother that it was nearly four weeks since her period had been due. To this her mother said, 'Don't worry. Insha'Allah everything will be all right. But do not talk about it with anyone else.'

'But Ma, I'm very worried.'

'There's no reason to worry. When you go to your husband's house, do whatever is necessary with him without wasting any time. Your father thinks that the next set of happenings will flow like a river does to the sea.'

But Runa didn't want to fall in the sea.

After all the celebrations of Runa's marriage with Haroon were over, it was time to say goodbye to the bride and groom. Everybody was standing on the veranda. Two steps down, there was a car waiting, especially decorated for them. Runa hugged her mother and cried and cried. Then she embraced her father, her eyes flooded. She was biting the end of her wedding sari train. Stream of silent tears were rolling down her father's cheeks. Close relations were surrounding them observing they thought, the traditional farewell tears. The driver opened the back doors. Runa gathered her sari and got in cautiously, then Haroon got in the other side. Two strangers were travelling together on an unknown journey to an unknown destination. The driver closed the doors.

Runa could hardly manage to remove the red and gold sari and hair and nose ornaments, she was so tired. When Haroon had said goodnight to his relations, he came back to find Runa asleep. He took his clothes off silently. He tried to wake her up with a gentle kiss, but Runa didn't open her eyes. He lay down quietly next to her and gently held her. The hard touch of the body and its warmth woke her up. She half opened her sleepy eyes and smiled. The moment she saw Haroon's naked body, her smile disappeared. She sat up quickly with a fright. That thing again! Haroon with fondness and affection made her lie down. To Runa, all this felt unbearable. The scenes of Joydebpur with Bashir rushed back. She pushed Haroon off, sat up again and covered her face with her hands. She started to cry. She gasped for breath and rushed to the bathroom. Utterly perplexed, Haroon sat there.

While in the bathroom, Runa recalled what her father had told her to do: to try and forget the horrible memories of the past, to create new ones and cherish them. When she finally came back to the bedroom, she found Haroon asleep. She looked at him for a few brief moments, sighed, and then carefully lay down next to him. Her pillow dampened with tears. She eventually fell asleep.

In the morning, Haroon tried again. This time he was successful although he didn't get any cooperation from her. She was like a rubber doll, lifeless. There was no excitement, no emotion. There was only distance.

There was the same coldness the night after. Runa neither expected this detachment from the situation nor liked her own passivity. Nothing seemed pleasing to her. Her period still hadn't started. Besides, she was showing signs of morning sickness. Everything appeared confusing. She didn't know what to do.

After all the obligatory visits, the bride and groom set off for Haroon's place of work, the University of Rajshahi. She was sick during the car journey. Haroon thought that it was car sickness.

The day after they arrived, Runa started to get the flat organised. It took them more than a week to make some sense of it but they still hadn't been able to fully equip the kitchen. But Runa was so tired.

On return from work a few days later, Haroon found Runa vomiting. The family doctor after listening to all the symptoms and a quick examination asked them to see a particular gynaecologist. That woman, Dr. Humaira Kamal, after examining Runa thoroughly, called Haroon in. She congratulated him and said, 'Your wife has been pregnant for nearly two months.'

Runa continued to look at the floor with her head down. The feelings of guilt, shame, and insult froze her. Her face didn't show cheerfulness. It expressed the disgrace and sorrows that shrivelled her.

Haroon was astounded. He looked at Runa once and then said to Dr. Kamal, 'Are you sure?'

'Of course, one-hundred percent.' Dr. Kamal turned towards Runa and said, 'This is good news. Be cheerful. Go home and celebrate.'

Haroon thanked her and then turning towards Runa said, 'Let's go home and celebrate this good news properly!' He left the room. With difficulty Runa followed him.

On their way back, a wooden silence fell over them. There were no more tears running down Runa's face. Oceans full of tears had all evaporated. Her insides were contorting. She was suffering from an unbearable inner ache. The ache was because she went on a drive with Bashir alone; the ache was because she should have married him but couldn't. The ache was because she didn't abort Bashir's baby; instead she deceived Haroon. And yet this chain of events could have been broken at any stage. But she hadn't done so.

When they went into the flat Haroon said, 'How have you been pregnant for two months?' His voice was clear. Runa sat silently on the edge of their bed. She said, 'That is a long story. You want to hear it now or are you very tired?'

'I want to hear it now.'

With a long sigh and without leaving out anything she told Haroon the whole story. He listened in silence. Then he said, 'You and your parents are all dishonest people. In the guise of gentility, you are evil, wicked, abominable deceivers. All of you deserve punishment, serious punishment.'

'Yes, we deserve it. Do come and hit me, hit me hard. I deserve it.' Runa said, crying, and at the same time getting up and advancing a cheek. Haroon slapped her hard. The force of his slap made Runa fall on the floor. Haroon put his foot on her throat and said, 'I could kill you.'

'Yes, kill me. That would be my real deliverance. Don't stop, do kill me. I don't want to live…'.

Haroon took his foot away. He went and sat on the bed and began to pant. Runa covered her face with her hands sobbing.

Haroon suddenly got up, and said loudly, 'Tomorrow, you'll leave my flat. I'll send you the divorce letter later.'

'I'll leave tomorrow night.'

Haroon said nothing. Runa slowly got up from the floor and then went in the sitting room and spent the night there.

Runa packed and tried to rest in the afternoon. Their telephone rang. Reluctantly she picked it up and wrote down the name and details. In the evening, she sent for a rickshaw. As she was leaving the house she saw Haroon in the hallway and stopped to say, 'I'm very, very sorry for putting you through this. But maybe it is better for you.'

Haroon didn't look at Runa.

Runa continued, 'Your female friend, Ayaka, called from Japan this afternoon.'

Haroon slowly turned his head towards Runa. But she had gone.

Waiting for the Moving Van

Steve Jackson
England

THE RINGING PHONE BREAKS into my wasteful thoughts

It's still early, and I'm sitting out on the porch, thinking. I guess I've done too much of that over the past weeks. Still, there's no going back now. Deeds are signed, plans made, and ... and what? Like usual these days, I'm lost in what comes next. There's nothing to keep me here now. The steelworks closed over a year since. Not that my troubles didn't start way before that. That just about finished things off though. All I can do is hope that ...

The ringing phone breaks into my wasteful thoughts.

"I tell you, Judd, I seen them starting to put boxes and stuff in Ben's truck. I guess they'll be loaded and gone before long."

Looks like today's the day. The words from Frank over at Rosemont set me flying out the house.

Frank Caplan and me go way back. We went through school and college together. Both worked at Capital. Then 'Nam, both in the same unit in '70. Saw out the next two years together, till Frank got shot up. I finished out in '73. Frank had pretty much recovered by then. Well, as much as he could, still 'lame but game' as he used to say. One way and another, the war damaged just about everyone. We both went back to work at Capital. I guess just about everyone I knew worked at Capital Mill. They gave Frank a desk job, but his health wasn't up to much, and he soon had to quit to live off welfare. He lived on in his parents' old house at Rosemont after they died. All his confidence gone, though, since 'Nam. He lived alone, never seemed to get going again. Always appeared quiet and content, but deep down I knew he was hurting. We stuck close for a while after the war, and while I was dating Molly. Frank loved his guns, and we'd go out hunting weekends. But I guess, once I met Beth, I kind of abandoned him for a while.

Into my truck, then, and away, a cloud of red dust from under the spinning tyres drifting across the meadow in the light morning breeze. Up to the highway and south, picking up what speed my old Chevy could muster. Five minutes on, and a left turn onto the blacktop, into the morning sun and down to Rosemont, past Frank's place to Molly's house at the end of the track.

I'd met Molly Parkes right when I started back at the Mill. Morgantown wasn't exactly Steel City, but there was plenty of work back then. Paid well, too. I was young, keen, knew how to spend as well as earn. Molly was different too, them days, slim, long dark hair, exciting, someone to be seen with. She lived with her parents in Rosemont, near Frank, just up the highway from my place at Hackberry. Rosemont's nothing but a few houses set back off the highway down a gravel track, built around where an old well used to be. The old windmill water pump's still there, immobile, half its rusted blades missing. The houses down there are much the same as mine: timber-framed, blistered white paint, each set back from the track a piece, surrounded by cornfields. My place is almost on the edge of town now, but it hasn't reached out as far as Rosemont yet, so those houses'll remain intact awhile.

We dated on and off, Molly and me, though I see now she was getting more serious about things. Then Beth came home. Molly's younger sister, she'd been away looking after an old aunt in Indianapolis. Driving Molly home one night, I met her on the porch. She took my breath clean away, just as she was, dressed casual in t-shirt and jeans, blue eyes, long corn-blonde hair. I reckon Molly read, straight off, how things were going to unfold. It got pretty cool between me and Molly after that night, and not long after, we broke up for good. Things got plain ugly between us, though, soon as I started showing up to date Beth.

Beth was so different to Molly, different in so many ways. We'd still go out on the town, me and Beth, but somehow, it was less crazy. We gradually left the wild crowd behind, and grew closer, more in love I guess. Such times as I saw Molly, things were downright bitter. Even those days she was feeding Beth lies about me, trying to do me down every chance she got. But it wasn't going to change how things were. Soon enough, I persuaded Beth to move in with me at Hackberry, get her away from Molly's acid tongue, and pretty soon we were married. Next year Molly married too, a quiet, sober guy called Luther Schwarz, and they lived on with her folks at Rosemont. Didn't seem to stop her bitterness any, though.

Beth and me had two kids in our first three years, Paulie and Kate, and after that I seemed to be pretty bound up with family life, what with fixing the house and working shifts now, to earn more money. They were the happiest years we could possibly've had. But I guess that nothing good in life lasts for ever. The steel industry was starting to die back even them days. Over-production and cheap foreign steel. So no surprise when the work dropped off some. I began working the late shift, four till midnight, on a regular basis - the best paid option, but the worst to do because it took men away from their families. I should'a seen the signs. A lot of the guys on this shift were single, separated, divorced - you can see what's coming.

I hooked up again with Frank those days. He'd drive down to Morrow's Bar to meet the crowd of us after the shift, and, we'd hit that bar till dawn sometimes, most of us young men turned old by the war. I was still bringing the money in fine, but gradually saw less and less of Beth and the kids. They were slipping away from me and I didn't see it. Beth was loyal as she could be, but there was a snake in the grass: Molly. Her bitter mind soon invented enough tales about what I was supposed to be about. She poured her vitriol down the phone into Beth's ear day after day. Women, gambling, drugs. Beth didn't want to believe, but I didn't help make it look any better, me being always out late and home with the dawn, stink of Morrow's still on me, to crash out till the next shift fell due. Stuff I used to do around the house, for Beth, for the kids, it didn't happen no more.

Suddenly, Beth and the kids are gone. They've moved down to Rosemont, with her Mom and Pop - and Molly. I'm pole-axed. I get my act together, fix the place up, fix myself up, drive down to Rosemont, and crawl my apologies. They come home, I start coming home nights straight after the shift, and everything's just fine - for a while. But old habits die hard. There's talk of redundancies. Suddenly, wages take a cut. They pay off the day guys, and the late shift becomes a split shift, twelve midday till five, and seven till midnight. You got to take both shifts to make a living wage. So you don't get home hardly at all. Morrow's Bar's the only business making a profit now.

Then, just like it's happened before, Molly's done her evil work just like she has before, filling Beth's head with how much better off things could be without me. So Beth and the kids have gone to Rosemont again. I get my act together just like before. But this time, it's different. Seems she's not coming back. Molly'n the folks've have convinced her to ship out for good, start over in some new place. I get to talk to her only on the phone. She's unhappy, scared of the future, but doesn't think *we've* got one any more, specially at Hackberry. While she's talking, crying on the phone to me, I can sense Molly standing behind her, prompting, pushing, doing everything she can to prevent us getting back together.

Next thing I learn is the rumour that Capital's gone bust, and I'm out of a job. I turn up at the gates to find all the others there. Angry, but no fight in them. We get a handout from management. No option but to close. There's some payoff, but not much. Then nothing. There's no jobs this side of Pittsburgh, and Pittsburgh's steelworks are more dead than alive as well.

I get to talk to Beth again on the phone. They've heard the news. Now, she's sure *our* life's over. She's talking of moving back to Indianapolis. She's still got a cousin there who 'Molly says' will help her start out. If not, maybe Chicago ...

I still don't give up. I fix the house, get it on the property market. The realtor's pessimistic. With Capital closing, values've taken a dive.

Even so, I pull off a sale. Guy from Columbus wants to knock it down, build a new place. Frank talks to the neighbours down at Rosemont. They say Beth and the kids are going to 'napolis any time now. One more day, and I'm free of *this* place, free to try to win her back one more time. All I can do is hope that ...

The ringing phone breaks into my wasteful thoughts.

I turn up the gravel track and spin past Frank's house. I see him on his porch, left hand shading his eyes as he looks across to Molly's house. He raises his right hand in greeting, and I wave back. I'm outside Molly's now, looking at her rusting, old red Pinto, and next to it Ben's double-cab Toyota truck, half turned around and facing the cornfield. There's stuff already piled in back, and the passenger side doors are both swung open.

As I pull up in a shower of gravel, Ben appears on Molly's porch, carrying two suitcases. Grizzled, bent a little by age, he still carries himself well. I always got on good with Ben. He's been a great pa-in-law to me, but he's been turned by Molly as well, recent times. Seeing my truck, he stops short, and after a moment, puts the cases down, and calls out.

"Judd, you shouldn't be here, you know that."

"Ben ... I had to come." I ease myself out the truck, and stand facing him, maybe ten paces away. As I speak, I can still taste last night's rye whiskey sour in my mouth, reminding me where most of this trouble came from.

"I didn't think ... Beth'd be leaving any time soon."

Ben looks uneasy. I always thought he believed in me, but I guess he has to listen to his older daughter as well: she's kin after all. His voice kinda gives him away though, how much he seems defeated by Molly's constant lies.

"Well, she is. I guess it's out your hands now - if she don't want to come back, it's gotta be none of your business no more. Seems you've used all your chances up."

I try again, hoping to persuade him to believe better of me.

"I've sold the house, Ben. Can't bring the job back. Work's gone from here for good, it seems. But ... but we could all move someplace, me and Beth and the kids, start over. There's a big country out there ..."

Ben lowers his head sheepishly, shakes it slow from side to side like a boxer trying to un-fog his mind after a heavy punch. I try again.

"Ben, you know this is all Molly's doing, all her lies. She's painted me blacker than the ace of spades. I know I could have done better, but ..."

Next thing, Molly bursts out of the house, crashing the screen door back against a nearby chair, and pushes past him. Her hand's already up in the air, finger jabbing in my direction.

"Judd Barron, you got no business here. The show's over. God knows you've had your chances times over, and you've blown'em all. Beth and the kids have had enough, and there's no going back. You hear?"

I square up to Molly, just like I always do. Fat, interfering bitch, she's still getting between me and Beth, feeding her mind with lies about my behaviour and crazy notions of how she deserves better, doing me down in every way she can. She stands there now, solid, assured on her own front porch, hands on hips, staring me down with a look of triumph I ache to slap from her face.

"This is none of your business, Molly."

I try to act calm, but my voice rises as I carry on.

"Like always, you're an interfering shit-stirring cow. Let me talk to Beth, let's get this sorted. She shouldn't be here anyways. You tempted her away with your lying talk of a better life without me. We could still have a better future ..."

"Any life's better than her future with you."

Molly advances a step, while Ben remains mute, hangdog, unsure whether to pick up the cases and carry on. Molly continues, her voice also rising.

"You better get this into your head. She's leaving today. With Pop. With the kids. Where she's going's none of your business. She'll find her future just fine, without you dragging her down ..."

Ede eases out onto the porch, to stand between Ben and Molly. I've always liked Ede. Still slim and elegant, the years hardly telling on her. Her hair silver now. Molly looks nothing like her. Beth's taken after her, same build, same corn-blonde hair she'd had. Ede looks uneasily across at me. The sun shines a little stronger now, over the waving cornfields behind the house. The breeze picks up a little for a moment. For a long minute, nobody moves.

Suddenly, to break the moment, Ben picks up the suitcases again, and clumps down the porch steps. Looking at me all the while, he swings them up onto the back of his truck. Still meeting my gaze, he calls back to the house.

"That's the last of it, I reckon. They's no point hanging around now. Let's be gone. Ede, you'd best fetch 'em out."

Without a word, Ede turns and disappears back inside. Molly, alone on the porch, takes a more solid stance, and folds her arms in a determined manner. Pallid, plain, all her beauty gone now she's run to fat, it was hard to see how she'd come from the same parents as Beth. But, pushy as usual, she can't resist saying more.

"You've finally got your comeuppance, Mister. This time, they're gone for good."

This time, I hate her more than ever, for her persistent jealousy fixing to ruin my family, my life. Her and Luther, always there to interfere. It isn't Luther, though. Never was Luther. He's just under her thumb, goes along with her scheming.

Course, I'd known this day was coming, known Beth and the kids'd be gone from Rosemont before long. But, now with the moment on me, I guess something breaks inside me. I can't let it happen. Not now. Not yet ...

I take a step forward from my truck.

"Ben, I don't want you to take 'em. Not yet. Let me talk to Beth first. I need to ..."

A loud metallic click interrupts me. On the porch, Molly's pulled both hammers back on Luther's twin-barrelled shotgun. She must'a had it ready on the old table. It's now cocked and held across her body, still pointed towards the ground. She snarls out a challenge.

"I thought you'd still be willing to cause trouble, Judd. This here'll make sure this thing's gonna happen, right now."

"Don't be stupid, Moll."

This from Ben, looking alarmed at his daughter's behaviour.

"Judd understands what's happening here. He's not going to do anything stupid ..."

Molly rests the gun a little on her hip, but remains defiant.

"He sure ain't, with my shotgun in his face. Stand back, Judd, or even better, get back in your truck and drive on."

Ede re-appears, pushing Paulie and Kate ahead of her. She and the kids have obviously heard none of this, and she looks with puzzlement at the change in the people around her. She doesn't seem to notice the shotgun at first, and she and the kids start down the porch steps towards Ben's Toyota. The kids both look tearful. My heart cries out for them. It's almost like I call out, because they both suddenly become aware I'm here. Paulie's holding Kate's hand, and they both stop at the side of Ben's truck, just looking at me, uncertain what to do. I long to go over to them, to hold them and tell them everything's OK, just like I should. But I don't move, afraid to break the deadlock around me. Ede catches up with the kids and coaxes them into the back seats. From there they both kneel and look out at me through the cab's back window with its gun rack, their two sets of eyes visible between Ben's rifle and shotgun.

A noise at my side, and I turn slowly to check it out. It's Frank, limping over from his house up the way a little. He gives me a nod of greeting, and comes to stand alongside me. He tries to calm things a little.

"Come on, Molly, you can't go threatening anyone over this. Judd's not going to get violent about things. He just wants to talk. Once more. After all, it's still his wife and kids that this is all about."

"Well, he ain't gonna. This here shotgun'll see to that, if needs be."

At that, Frank moves slightly in front of me. Glancing down, I see his old Colt revolver and his Glock semi-auto both tucked in the back of his jeans waistband. He's brought one for me, for sure. He's seen Molly armed, and thought he'd level things a little for me.

Just then, Luther appears behind Molly. Luther, poor sap, browbeaten into submission by Molly's acid tongue. He whispers to her, moves back a little, looking uncertain as ever. Uncertain or not, he's hanging a Smith & Wesson from his right hand, pointed at the floorboards for now. Molly shouts, triumphant.

"You hear that, Judd? Austin's on his way. That means the law's gonna make sure there's no trouble from you. Just wait until ..."

Suddenly Beth comes out the front door, and my heart stops for a moment. She's beautiful as ever, corn-blonde hair tangled, eyes red with crying. She comes down the steps and stands between us all, halfway between me and the truck with the kids. I can feel tears start in the corners of my own eyes. She looks so vulnerable, so helpless, I long to reach out to her, pull her from the web of scheming lies Molly's spun. I know I've got to speak, got to try again.

"Beth ... Beth, don't do this, don't listen to Molly, she's trying to break us up for good ... Beth, let's talk, we can sort this out ..."

But Molly won't let this ride.

"Beth, get in the truck. You know he's a lying, cheating bastard. Lord knows, you've suffered enough from him. Get in the truck and get gone. Pop, help her."

If Austin *was* coming, it's time to act, now, before ever he gets here. Local sheriff, Luther's cousin, he ain't likely to take my side. I reach out, and take Frank's Glock. Frank takes a step back. Slipping the safety off, I make sure everyone sees the gun. There's a reaction all round. Luther lifts his pistol to point vaguely in my direction. Frank, seeing that, eases his Colt from his waistband, and points it downwards towards the porch steps. There's a moment's silence. Even the wind seems to pause.

Ben is first to react. From where he's standing, he probably can't see either Luther's gun or Frank's Colt. Even so, he's felt the rising tension.

"Come on, Judd, this is starting to go too far. Molly, for God's sake put the shotgun down. Judd, do the same with that handgun. I'm sure we can work this out ..."

But it's already too late to change the course of things. The distant sound of gravel snapping and pinging under tyres breaks the tension, but only for a moment. We all half-turn to look at the Chevy patrol car, easing down the track past Frank's house, and pulling up behind my truck. Austin, in uniform and on duty, eases his bulk out of the driver's door. Halfway to his feet, he sees me holding the Glock. He pauses for a moment, but when he's finally heaved himself upright, his own gun's already in his hand. His gaze swings around the lot, and his jaw tightens when he sees all them other guns.

Ben moves over to put his arm around Beth, still stood motionless and tearful between us all. He looks puzzled, unsure. Ede moves to stand close behind him, looking just as puzzled. Molly shouts again.

"Beth, get in the truck. Austin, ain't you going to disarm Judd and Frank?" Austin's clearly torn between his official role and his family relationships, but tries to sort the situation.

"They's too many guns here. Judd, Frank, Luther, Molly, all of you, put them guns down, and let's sort this out peaceably."

Molly turns towards him, even more flushed now with anger. Her voice cracks as she snarls.

"You should know who you're defending, Austin Parkes. I'm on my own front porch here, and Judd's just a lying, cheating trespasser. Git him out of here!"

Molly raises her shotgun, seeming to point it at Austin. Her hands are shaking. Ben looks alarmed this time. In the car the kids, sensing the rising tension, are both crying freely. Ede, nearest, turns and climbs in to comfort them. Finally, Beth looks up at me through her tears. She looks like she wants to come over, but just now, Ben's hand on her shoulder holds her in check. Molly turns to look at me once more, and gestures with the shotgun.

"Get out of here now. This is your last warning."

Time stands still again, like most of the world's stopped. There's near silence, the only sound, the whisper of the wind across the corn. On the gravel track between us all, little dust devils rise and go spinning across the way.

Ben suddenly seems to come to a decision.

"Judd, this has gone on long enough, too long. We've all listened to too much lies, too much dissent. Beth, this is your choice. No one else's. Your choice. You want to go with Judd, or away to ... someplace else?"

Molly is beside herself with rage.

"Pop, what you saying? Beth needs to go, needs to ..."

Ben turns to look at her, a new light in his eyes. He's made up his mind. His voice is clear and calm.

"It's time for Beth to decide. You've been doing her thinking for her far too long. Beth?"

As he turns away from Molly, Ben takes his arm from Beth's shoulders. He doesn't see Molly raise the shotgun to her shoulder. Sobbing freely now, Beth takes a hesitant step towards me. She's sobbing, her voice cracked.

"Judd ..."

She's coming with me! She wants to come with me! Suddenly, I can only see her and Ben. Everyone else is somewhere in the background, unimportant, gone. I hear Ben's voice again, speaking direct to me.

"Judd, your kids'n all your family's stuff's in my truck. You and Beth take it and drive back to your place for now. I'll come over later in *your* truck, and we'll sort things out some more."

Taking the Toyota keys from his pocket, he hefts them over to me. They sail into the air, catch the morning sunlight. I raise my left hand to catch them, my right hand still holding the Glock ready. As that old silver dollar on Ben's key-ring flashes in the morning sunlight, there's suddenly other flashes in the shadows around me in the places I'm no longer seeing, and something punches me in the chest. There's sounds in the background too, that I can't quite make out, shouts and screams, maybe. The flash of light from that silver dollar stays in my eyes, seems to hang in the air, and spread, then suddenly, the whole of the sky is filled with blinding white light that just goes on and on.

The Trapped Duck

Susan Coons
USA

"I MISS YOU MOM," Evan whispers after his Dad leaves the room.

It's Tuesday night after the first day of school. The kids were left with the daunting task of spending the evening at their father's house. I tried to call to find out how their day was, how they like their teachers, what the cafeteria lunch was like, and if they made any new friends. Evan calls me back at 9:30pm with enthusiasm and excitement in his voice. I'm on speaker phone being monitored by the kids' Dad. Kenzie can't speak to me. It makes her heart hurt to hear my voice and be separated from me and she cries. She's not allowed to tell her Dad she's upset that she can't come home to me. She fears that he may hit her. I envision their rooms in the basement of their father's house. The rest of the family sleeps upstairs. He designed and built that house and put the room of his third child upstairs and left my kids in the basement. Kenzie has a fear of being abducted in the night. When she is at home she makes sure all of the doors in the house are locked each and every night. It is her ritual to check the front then the back then has me double check them. When they are not with me I complete the ritual for her and then speak out loud, "Kenzie, the doors are locked," as if she could hear me.

When sleeping at their father's home they lay in their rooms and listen to the sounds of yelling, fighting, swearing, bumping, crying, pleas for the abuse to stop, and they lay in the dark waiting for it to end. They can hear it all from their basement domiciles. After the fighting is finished someone comes to check on them. They pretend to be asleep. After the adults are back upstairs Kenzie sneaks into Evan's room to make sure he is okay then she falls asleep at some point in her own room. She wouldn't dare let her father catch her out of bed.

He was arrested two Christmas' ago for beating his girlfriend while she was balled up on the floor in the foetal position. He topped off the beating by dumping a bottle of water on her as she lay on the floor. As many victims' do she tried to get the assault and harassment charges against him dropped but the court let him enter ARD for domestic violence instead. Those fines, four hours of Batterers and Abusers Class, and community service sure didn't stop him from laying his hands on her again. Kenzie bravely asked his girlfriend if they would stop fighting at night because it keeps her awake. Now they know the kids can hear it or at least she does.

"Please don't make us go," they plead on the days their father has to pick them up. "Why can't we just stay with you?" I explain that their Dad loves them and that we have a custody agreement that I must follow. Inside I'm hurting for them. I feel helpless with the knowledge that domestic violence offenders get custody too. As long as they are not physically hurting the kids enough to leave bruises or land them in the hospital the kids are forced to endure the suffering.

I am a survivor of his abuse. I was ashamed to speak out. I wish I would have but we can't go back. I speak out now so that others know how staying in these cyclical abusive relationships has an eternal effect on not only our lives but the lives of our children. I endure the abuse still when I see him. He told me the last time I saw him that I "sure did put on a lot of weight." I reminded him his daughter could hear him. Seeing him brings up the wounds of the past. He reminds me of the nightmare of a life I was living while we were together. Not a day went by towards the end when he did not degrade me in some way. It depended on his mood. Some days he threw things at me. Other days he would punch me. He would sometimes smash things. He forced himself on me sexually even after I had waited in the bathtub hoping he would fall asleep before I entered the bedroom. He pushed me off chairs and onto the floor. He gripped my arms so hard that it left bruises the shape of his hands on my arms. He tried to segregate me from my family. I refused to turn my back on my family. They were always loyal and dependable.

After all of this he still walks free. He still terrorises others. He still torments me. He still influences my children. He is a walking time bomb and all I can do is pray that when he has his next explosion that my kids are not involved. In some way, however, they always are. He is their father. When his current girlfriend kicked him out for six months, my kids were moved into a piss-stained town house. The carpets were changed but it still smelled of urine. I would come to pick my kids up and he would answer the door naked. He just didn't care. Other times my kids would answer the door and they would have to go wake him. They are six and their younger brother is two. The young one once had a diaper on that was so full it was dripping down his pant-less legs.

I actually felt sorry for him during this time. At least I am still capable of empathy after it all. Slowly, his girlfriend let him move back into the house he built for her. The kids came too but their things did not. They first slept on the floor and couches. After a few visits they were upgraded to an air mattress that deflated nightly. Finally, after a call was made to Children and Youth regarding unlocked weapons, their beds were brought back. That's right, I said unlocked weapons. After an overnight stay Evan reported that he and his brother were playing with guns that were left on the floor. After their Dad caught them he reprimanded them but left the weapons out.

When we are young these are things we just do not think about. Each choice has an eternal consequence whether it be positive or negative. The defining moment that changed my life forever was winning a car from the local county fair. I wanted to give back to the organisation that I won the car from and the kids' Dad was my sponsor. We spent time together at the club, then began dating, and before I knew it, he moved in with me. We had fun. It felt like it was meant to be. He made me laugh and helped me with things around my house. He once helped a duck escape that was trapped in my chimney. Once the duck got out it ran around my living room, out my sliding glass back doors, and flew off my back deck. I wonder how that duck is making out.

When my grandfather died the twins' Dad left a sympathy card at my door. I spent the rest of the night trying to bury my own grief and drinking at the bar across the street with my future abuser. My grandfather and I were closer than close and his death hit me hard. We had a special bond. When I was a little girl we would go recycle cans together and he would take me to the VFW. He helped teach me how to drive. As I grew older I would skip Sunday mass and go visit Grandpa and Grandma Leonard for an hour. When I turned twenty-one he always kept cold Miller Lite's and veggie burgers waiting for me at his home. When my father threw a tantrum because I didn't want to go to Easter Mass with the family, my Grandpa send me to church with a few airplane bottles of Jack Daniels stuffed into my purse. He would have hated my ex. He wouldn't have minded that I was drinking my sorrows away at a local dive bar and dominating the juke box.

So, the car, the sponsorship, the duck, the death; all were parts of the story that brought us together. I overlooked the red flag that while we were getting to know each other he was healing from a beating given to him by his ex-girlfriend's family. As a young woman the tough guy act seemed sexy and reassuring. I thought I had someone who would fight for me if push came to shove. He made sure to mark his territory in bars and made sure that no other men dare to speak to me unless he liked them.

We were in a whirlwind romance and I lost myself. Isn't that what happens so many times. We meet someone and our realities collide. Some couples start dressing alike, others start talking alike, listening to the same music, growing together or falling apart together. We fell to pieces together yet we stayed together. The first time he laid his hands on me he pushed me up against a wall and strangled me. If only I had walked away. I did not. I decided to start photographing my bruises thinking that would help me later if I ever decided enough was enough. It did not help me.

Listen up world! Every choice matters. Every single one. I hold my son tight and ask him to promise me that he will never, "lose his sweet."

I snuggle my daughter and massage her and let her know that she always deserves to be touched with loving hands. We all have our struggles. We all have the obstacles that are passed down from generation to generation. Think about what the possible lifelong struggles that we are passing on to our children could be. Will my son be an abuser like his father and his grandfather? Will my daughter accept abuse like her mother and her father's girlfriend whom she's known since she was two years old?

Only they can decide the answers to those questions. In my home we have an open honesty agreement. They know that they can tell me anything and I will never get mad at them. They also know that I will never lie to them. This works really well. They trust me because they have experienced that I am a safe person to confide in even when they are the ones who make mistakes. Some days they get in the car and I feel like I am in a confessional. We discuss it all. We discuss things I have never even discussed with my parents. They know they can ask me anything and it's okay. If I feel the answer to their question is not appropriate for their age, I tell them. I do not make up stories to cover the truth. If they ask about Santa, or the tooth fairy, or their Dad, I ask them what they think. I challenge them to be introspective.

I challenge every young person to be introspective, to look at their current situations and to envision what their life with their partner could look like if they stay on the same path. I challenge my readers to think back and think about tell-tale signs and red flags that they could have noticed if they were mindful. I encourage parents of teenagers who are beginning to date to share this story with them. Use it as a jumping off point for discussion. Making blanket statements like, "Never date an abuser," or "having a child changes your life forever," isn't good enough. We need to go deeper so that future generations don't pass on our mistakes. We need to stop turning our heads in the other direction and look right into our children's eyes. Their eyes are watching us. Their ears are listening. Their hearts are feeling and sometimes hardening. We don't want children to have hardened hearts and the inability to put an end to eternal suffering. We need our children to think about their actions and the actions around them.

If you asked me when I was a child and at various different stages in my life what I wanted to be when I grow up, I would never have said that I want to be a survivor of domestic violence. I'm sure the twins' Dad would never have said that he wanted to be a woman beater. Ask a child what he wants to be or do with this chance at life. They want to be dancers and scientists, zookeepers and paediatricians. Let's keep it that way. My kids shouldn't be fearing that their Dad's girlfriend is dead. They should be counting sheep. I shouldn't have to be reading books to my six-year-olds about why adults sometimes lose their temper and how to handle it. I should be reading anything else. I never want my son or daughter to turn into the man that fathered them. I have to focus on the good people that they are every day so that they remember their goodness and know their value. The cycle of abuse does not have to be eternal.

The Anderson Shelter

Ted Stanley
England

MUSCULAR MEN, STRIPPED TO THE WAIST in the August heat, rip the corrugated sheets from the ground and stack them neatly against the garden wall. Refusing the coins offered by Grandpa, the men leave. Grandma watches from the kitchen door.

Outside on the street, the familiar cries of the rag and bone man ripple through the stillness of the muggy morning air: rumpled cloth cap, tatty clothes on a gaunt frame befitting his trade. Cart wheels' rumble over the cobbled street of neat terraced houses: front steps scrubbed clean; front walls bearing stubs of metal railings gone to the war. A black suit and mop of white hair stride purposefully down the pavement: Grandpa going about his community business.

I'm sitting on the edge of the pavement with my best friend, Billy Conner, waiting for the sun to soften the pitch between the cobbles. We swap comics: my *Dandy* for his *Beano*, 'Dennis the Menace' in trouble again. Soon we will be able to dig out the pitch with our penknives, mould it into pear-shaped balls and play 'Bomb the Hun'. Coal black smoke from the towering factory chimneys invades the innocence of a virgin blue sky as the thrump, thrump of the drop hammers sound a monotonous metronome to the working day.

Moments after the plodding grey mare lays her sweet-smelling gift on the warm cobbles, an army of pinafored women armed with brushes and buckets march across their cardinal red doorsteps. Mrs Conner, Billy's mom, hair in metal curlers, laddered nylons drooping around her ankles, is the first to reach the steaming pile. Sweeping it swiftly into her bucket, she carries away her prize with a self-satisfied step. Standing down, the other women return to their chores or peer around net curtains, seeking other opportunities for garden fertilisation or fertile gossip.

The pitch softens as the sun rises higher in the smoke-spoilt sky. Billy is already inserting a lollipop stick and match head into his first 'bomb'. I inhale the rich mineral smell of pitch as I roll it in my palms, thinner and thinner, longer and longer, foreshadowing the beginnings of my working life: red-hot steel, spewing from mill rollers; strong men wielding heavy tongs, sweating bodies shining in the Bessemer glow.

I'm chalking targets on the pavement: Berlin, Dresden, Frankfurt, when Grandma beckons the tinker to the steps of the bay windowed house reserved for the factory foreman. It has a garden, given over to growing vegetables and a front parlour where an upright piano endures my daily practice. A large aspidistra stands on a small table in the bay window; the fragrance of lavender-scented mothballs fills the air. Lavender under my pillow still comforts me on restless nights.

A mutual nod of heads concludes a short conversation. Corrugated sheets find their way onto the tinker's cart; a few coins find their way into grandma's purse, Billy's bombs find their first target: Berlin.

The smell of baking bread and fresh laundry greet me as gentle hands cup my face. "So….what would my little soldier like for lunch today?" I tuck into freshly baked bread, butter melting through it, homemade strawberry jam coating the surface. Grandma warns of indigestion.

A wide moustache flows past the window as Grandpa returns from his social duties: a quarrel settled; a grieving family comforted. Sometimes, on fine days, he walks with me to Brinsworth Fields, or Tinsley Top where the four winds blow: carries me home on his shoulders when I'm tired. At Whitsuntide, I march at his side, behind the Baptist banner, to High Hazels Park.

Leaving the kitchen, Grandma follows him to the edge of the garden. I trail behind at a safe distance, sensing trouble brewing.

"Where's the Anderson gone?" Grandpa demands, in the ominous voice of an approaching storm.

"Gone where it will do some good," defends Grandma, arms folded tightly across her chest, her dainty feet planted wide. "Helping to get this country back on its feet."

"What about my tool shed," he broods, the storm getting closer. "I was going to use it as a tool shed."

"You'd soon complain if there was no food on the table," she retorts. "There's still rationing you know and god knows when it will end, now Atlee's re-elected.

"I need space to store stuff: to work," he persists.

"Work? To fiddle around you mean, when you could be helping me with the chores."

"I do what is mine to do and you do what is yours," he preaches.

"Then I need that land to grow more vegetables," she responds, entrenching her position.

A stern look from Grandpa's towering figure is normally enough to move anything in his path, but grandma is a rock that is refusing to budge. Tears are filling my eyes.

"I could have sold that shelter," he complains, the storm abating.

"I did," she retorted, rattling the coins in her purse, consolidating her position on the high ground.

The impasse continues in silence, then Grandpa's face breaks into a smile, then a grin, then a chuckle and soon he is roaring with laughter. I wipe away the tears. Grandma hesitates, making sure he isn't laughing at her, before allowing herself a slow smile.

"You know it's for the best," she consoles, trying not to sound smug.

As they walk back to the house, he rests a gentle arm around her shoulders.

"One condition, Lilly," he demands.

"What's that?" she asks warily, taking my hand as they pass.

"We plant carrots and sprouts."

"Carrots and sprouts it is, George," she concedes, stroking the packet of onion seeds in her apron pocket.

The Price of Eternity

Vlad Silvas
Romania

PROLOGUE

'SAND ... JUST A GRAIN OF SAND,' he thought, contemplating the small planet that was slowly changing its consistency and colour, from the nacre of a pearl to ruby, only to become cold, metal blue. 'In this endless universe, at the edge of a tiny galaxy, in a microscopic star system ... here, I hid the spark that will light the infinite and bring us immortality! For this, I will sacrifice everything!'

* * *

Sand, she thought for a second, not really knowing if it actually was her thought ... all she could see was the reddish infinity of a desert lighted by the sunset. A gentle breeze stroked her childish face and, like a nature's thrust of pride, tossed a tiny sand swirl toward her celestial blue eyes. She closed them quickly and to defy the desert, she imagined for a second the chaotic waves of the sea. Suddenly, a few splashing drops invaded her senses, with seaweed's stinging smell. When she opened her eyes, an endless ocean was stretching at her feet, across the horizon, sharply bypassing a small patch of sand, the last memory of the desert that Anna stood upon a moment before.

With a slow, familiar push of her heels in the wet sand, Anna slightly rose over the waves, defying the giant ocean. At a stunning speed, she began to fly toward the sun, a burning disk that sank into the sea. She let the waves touch her body and wet her face, then plunged into the clear sky, so high that she seemed only a tiny spot in the vast blue, all alone.

'I'm so bored, I'm tired of listening to your advice ... it's worthless to me ... I just want to stop hearing you!!!' Anna cried aloud to the Voice she has been always hearing in her mind, guiding her steps, her loneliness, and teaching her that her own thoughts were the true force of nature.

'Anna, my dear Anna ... you still have so much to learn about yourself and the world around you.'

'I know everything about this world,' shuddered her eyebrows. 'I can bring the storm and change it into a breeze. I can turn the deepest gorge into the highest mountain ... you have nothing else to teach me!'

'But I'm nothing but a Thought and my sole purpose is to help you discover your strengths, know your limits. In the end, you will choose your destiny ... until then, you will keep hearing me ..." said the Voice in quiet amusement.

'All right ...' Anna responded with defying tone ... 'Then answer these questions ... Why am I alone in this world? ... Why is there nothing that moves out of my own will? ... How about You? ... Do you even exist?!'

'Hmm ... these questions ... I cannot answer them ... you are not ready to hear the answers, not yet anyway ...'

'See ... you're starting again ... you're telling me lies ... you always hide something, you teach me, but never tell me everything there is to know... I'm sick of your riddles' ... and with a firm gesture of her hand, a tall and smooth rock raised from the sea, as dark as her thoughts.

Without realising it, the sky turned into a lead boiler, while the gray clouds were threatening to crush everything under their weight. The silver flashes crossed the eye of the storm and threw demonic reflections into Anna's eyes, while the wind was blowing through her black hair locks, playing the hellish concert like a bandmaster.

She sat with her legs crossed and her eyes closed while repeating without pause: 'I want you to disappear ... disappear ... disappear.'

Suddenly, a thought flashed her mind, illuminating her face and casting away the storm, like a nasty dream. The sea retreated, obedient, out of her way, leaving behind fine and damp sand. Anna fell on her knees and slowly moved her soft palm, pressing gently and leaving the outline of her tender hand, with scattered fingers, as if trying to measure it.

I am ready to find out if I now have the power and the knowledge to succeed, Anna fiercely thought, hoping that the Voice would hear her, as it usually did.

She stood up as if she had been expecting a miracle. After a few breaths, she cast a look at that ephemeral handprint one last time and turned with disappointment. Her idea had not worked. She was astonished though, to see that her hand, so young and fine, was now a little wrinkled ... aged.

She frowned back to her tiny experiment and noticed how that fingerprint started gaining volume, slowly turning into a living palm that moved toward the sky, like the hand of a being trying to break free from the everlasting darkness to the light of life. After a few minutes the creature was finally whole and similar to her in all aspects, only it was all made of sand. It moved blindly, only feeling the place where her creator was sitting. At first, Anna was horrified. Then, with a tremble on her spine, the most tremendous feeling she'd ever had throughout her existence came to her: 'I've made it!'

* * *

'How could you make such an error? ... You have created a monster ... you have violated all the rules of this universe ...' said a baritone voice, accustomed to command and be obeyed.

'Everything is under control ... I know exactly what's going on in Anna's mind ...' he said defensively.

'Hmm ... you are so sure of yourself ... even though you know that you cannot control such an experiment ... you created a being with intelligence ... it is forbidden ...' said another Voice, thinner and smoother, simulating diplomacy.

'A total reckless gesture. I honestly expected that from you ...' the third Voice attacked him aggressively, with a frightening tone.

'But ... SHE is our legacy! Anna will show us a perspective that we have forgotten ... this universe can survive only if we take risks, only if we dare to discover more and more of its mysteries. This is exactly how we, ourselves, evolved ... have you forgotten?! It is the natural course of Existence ...'

'You are the one who forgets that it's been billions of years since our ancestor's experiment gave us, by mere chance, the gift of life and reason ...' said the Leader Voice.

'Maybe what I've achieved ... will surpass the accomplishment of the ancestors, as this was not a mistake, but a well thought-through project ... think about it, Anna is only a few thousand years old ...'

'Again, you are not listening ... it's those billions of years that gave us true power ... we have learned from mistakes, we have evolved slowly, step by step, and we have known true power only when it had not brought us childish satisfaction anymore. The latter, I have no doubt; it is what your Creature feels at this moment ...' the Warrior Voice bluntly spoke.

'I am convinced that Anna is an incredibly beautiful creation ...' said the Wise Voice, trying to brighten him up, 'but her existence endangers the whole balance of the Universe ... you know very well, she has become the God creator of a whole civilisation. Right now, there are millions of beings born only by her sheer will ... and they are not just helpless creatures ... she has endowed them with reason and with an immense adaptability to any living environment ... nothing will stand in their way ... ocean, earth or fire!'

'I understand your objections and I assumed this risk ... but maybe, they will evolve faster than we did ... and they will open for us new doorways ... to worlds that we have never dreamt of before. Have you ever contemplated that for us there is nothing in this universe that would bring the sublime thrill of a new discovery? You must admit that we have lost the magic of the Void ... Anna and her creatures are our only chance ... at REBIRTH!'

'This civilisation will not endure the test of time! They will self-destruct or, worse, destroy entire galaxies on the way … we will not assume this risk in your name … we have already decided … our will shall be fulfilled!'

INTERLUDE

The eons passed quickly over the small experiment planet and Anna learned that everything had a price in this universe and that eternity would require a toll that even the Living God of this world was not ready to pay. Each passing century, and each creature conceived from her own being, added a wrinkle to her formerly younger face. Sometimes, a thread of her dark hair turned snow-white as a reminder of her sacrifice.

'I wonder if you also went through the same pain when you gave me life?'

A tear, is what she allowed herself as a solitary sign of weakness, while her mind tried in vain to find again the Voice that she had, so eagerly, tried to escape long ago.

* * *

Endless rows of grotesque creatures, in different shapes and sizes, some with dozens of eyes, others with several hands or hundreds of feet … some thin and wobbly, others massive, even gigantic, staring at the smaller ones and threatening to crush them. All were advancing as a hypnotised living mass, with only one goal … to see their goddess … the one who gave them life … Anna.

A high temple of dark granite was the place where the goddess chose for her offspring to pay tribute and venerate her. The monolith rose in the middle of a huge field and its smooth surface reflected, sumptuously, the rays of the two suns, located at equal distances, on both sides of the sacred place.

An aged woman with silver-white hair and wax composure watched the sea of worshipers. Those celestial eyes were still unchanged … and glowed with satisfaction.

'My sacrifice was not in vain … maybe I will not live forever … but through all of you, I've gained my immortality…' she said, her face mesmerised in awe. The thought was interrupted by a familiar feeling … a presence she had not felt for a long time … maybe too long …

'Anna, my child …' sighed the Voice, 'the day has come for us to say farewell …'

'We have not spoken for quite some time, Teacher, look at what I have accomplished … you taught me well without realising it … see?! They are my children …' she spoke with a mixture of nostalgia and pride.

'I have to tell you the truth … I owe you this much …'

'You reappear in My world, suddenly interested by my fate … all right … I will listen to you … but know that I am no longer the naive girl you once knew …' arrogantly gestured Anna.

'I do not have much time, so indulge me one last act of selfishness …' whispered the Voice.

Anna waved in acceptance with a lazy gesture.

'We are an old race. Thousands of eons have passed over us. We have never tried to bring life in this motionless cosmos. We remained numb in our immortality, not caring that a tiny spot of motion, imbued with living force, is all we need to bring back the unpredictability into our existence and give us the very REASON to be born anew … You are unique in this Cosmos … so close to perfection, yet so far from it. You only perceive me as a Voice in your mind … but my words do not really exist. The very quiet buzz of the planets, the thunder of the stellar explosions … they are our voices. What you are hearing right now is the music of the universe. Now you understand the long path that you should have walked, until you could have possibly earned the right to create other living beings like yourself?'

'Yeah … and you said I was an egocentric,' she smiled ironically.

'You were my hope in bringing this world to the long awaited rebirth … but now I understand that I have failed … and I, like yourself, will bear the consequences …'

His last words could barely be heard. Dismayed, Anna saw the sky transforming from spotless blue into blood red.

Rivers of fire began to flow from the incandescent sky. The ground itself shuddered, spreading dark bottomless mouths, swallowing the millions of terrified creatures that were running, screaming, crying, and raising desperate prayers for their goddess to save them. Anna only had the time for a last thought: 'Blinded by my selfishness, I never understood until now. You were right, but it's too late ...'

EPILOGUE

Anna's latter regret still lingered, a sinister echo, while he watched the whole planet - his precious experiment, being swallowed within itself, in a chaotic, painfully slow, and almost theatrical implosion.

'It is your fault for the loss of these lives. You have threatened our very existence with your insubordination. For this you shall be punished! We will forget you for Eternity and you will never hear us or ever sense any of us ... you are an Outlaw ... condemned to eternal Loneliness ...' uttered, accusatory, all three Voices.

A tense, impenetrable silence fell over his entire universe. He was now all alone, but a nagging thought still kept him alive: 'I will begin a new experiment ... and I will call it ... Adam.'

The Flight of a Nobody

Wen Xie
USA

HIS NAME IS ZAR AND HE IS NOBODY. He farms land in a forgotten village whose name is spoken on no one's lips. There may be a few in this world who know the frigid terrains of the remote Gansu mountain alcove where this little town sits, surrounded by rocky plains. Its only access to the world beyond is by means of a single road made for foot travel that ran through two mountain passes for a full two days' journey to the next town. Almost everyone who might know or give remembrance to this lonely village have gone east after the Great Famine, most of them leaving with nothing but the clothes on their backs and a few sacks of onion or garlic bulbs scraped from the dry ground as they headed to the coastal cities, all to escape a home that had birthed nothing but war, famine, natural disaster, and grief. Nobody stayed…nobodies like Zar, and those too old and sick to survive a voyage east. They were the ones who resigned to consume just enough to remain alive, waiting for the next life to mercifully claim them.

Sometimes the memories of Xiamen would take Zar's thoughts far away, to a time when he believed he had escaped this fate, and those vicious memories would penetrate his soul most cruelly at moments like this – with his bare hands to the hoe, marred by splinters from rubbing against the ancient wood on one side and cracked to the bitter wind on the other. He pulled his collar up over his nose to block the inhale of the heavy-dusted air, his eyes squinting beneath the rising morning sun.

There must be another here, there must be, he thought as he beat the unforgiving soil for a bulb of garlic that he could make into a stew for her. But the earth has not relented from his hours of toil. Zar dropped his hoe to the ground like a weapon of defeat and he turned to the tiny thatched-roof house, held up by a scaffold of dry wood and walls of pale yellow clay.

His mother lay alone on a thin and dirty mattress with no covering. Her body remained motionless, but her eyes moved to him when he reached the threshold of the home's entrance. Zar walked slowly towards her and sank both knees onto the naked ground to kneel at her side. He leaned in to study her face and for an instant she looked at him in return. But the moment of acknowledgement dissipated as quickly as its onset, and her gaze faded to the lifeless look of blank wonderment that she had worn since his return from Xiamen.

Zar pressed his hands against the mattress to push himself back up onto his feet and walked over to the clay pot sitting over a thin, dying fire. He opened the lid and put in three dry bulbs of garlic from his pant pocket, so small that they all fit into the palm of one hand. He decided to leave the skin on, anything edible is food and he poured in what remained from their water jug, turning it over completely so every drop made it into the pot. *Must go to the well tomorrow*, he thought to himself, all the while hoping it hadn't run dry from the summer drought, which is not unusual for this time of year. Otherwise he would have to make the journey to the lake adjacent to the next town beyond the mountain pass. He did not want to do that, for the lake was claimed by villagers of the other town where decent people had resorted to malevolent acts in the face of starvation and thirst.

He turned to look at his mother's frail body, lying limply to one side with her arm outstretched over the edge of the bed as if she had been in the act of reaching for something that was not there. His thoughts went to his father. Sometimes she saw him and would lift a hopeful arm, touching nothingness, and calling out to space. Her fleeting expression of hope would fade upon the realisation that there was no one before her and she would succumb to her expressionless grief once more.

This was not the life his father wanted for his family. This was not the ending that he had paid so dearly for. Zar reached for the *Yuan* notes wadded in his inside shirt pocket and pressed it against his chest, rising and falling, his breath still going like an ever-moving reminder. He had kept this money in the exact same place since father gave it to him on the day of his passing. Sometimes, when he exerted himself in the fields, he could feel the beat of his heart against the pad, and he would think about that day.

Almost one year ago exact, during the summer of 1976, the Cultural Revolution was at its wane and the newspapers were forbidden to report the foreboding health of Chairman Mao. The politburo would not stand for any comments to suggest the mortality of the man who expunged the foreign invaders. Zar had been in Xiamen for two years and was still surprised to learn that life in civilisation could be in many ways less free than life in the arid mountains of northern China. But he accepted what was done, as it was always done, and the daring would pay with their foolishly courageous lives and the lives of their loved ones. Still, news had to be reported and this was the life he chose - a dream of his pursuit - and he quietly suppressed the faint voice within that reproached him in the dead of night, urging him to be one of the foolish.

It was during lunchtime when the phone call came. Zar was at his desk of the Xiamen newspaper, one hand spooning himself the contents of his boxed lunch, the other hand furiously scribbling notes under the impending 4pm deadline. His eyes occasionally wandered to the photograph of demolished buildings, a corner of which stuck out from beneath a pile of story drafts and handwritten notes on his desk. A publisher's censorship notice accompanied the photograph, distributed earlier that day to the writers on staff. It was written on a flimsy sheet of rice paper with the words "do not report."

An 8.0 magnitude earthquake razed Sichuan province last week, taking near 70,000 souls. 20,000 remain missing. Over 7,000 school buildings fell to the earth that day, covering children beneath a rubble of cardboard and tofu used to construct the buildings. Almost all the buildings had been built in the past five years and received approval from the municipal Building Code Inspector. At the corner of the photograph Zar saw a tiny group of grieving parents standing in a line amidst the wreckage, holding up photographs of their lost children to what appeared to be the one building that remained standing. It was the Minister's building. These parents had marched to the provincial capital of Chengdu to seek official recognition of the wrongful approval of building inspections. The other side of the photograph read "Renegade protestors, do not report."

Zar's fingers tapped on his desk restlessly.

"Phone call for you in the boss's office," a colleague said in passing while heading for his own station. Zar's heart beat a little faster at that moment, and something twisted in his gut. Telephones were not a very accessible commodity, and someone must have staked a great effort to track down the phone number of a workplace where no one knew he worked. After all, he is nobody.

The receiver was heavy in his hand when he picked it up. He pushed the earpiece firmly to his face as if it would somehow ameliorate the heavy static.

"Zar-ah …" he finally heard on the other line. It was a moment before he recognised the voice of Chief Wang, the village leader, speaking in his thick mountain accent. "Your father was in a car accident." Wang's usual gruff voice was consoling. "Xie Ming's boy, you remember … the one that used to call you Uncle Shar … he accidentally sat on a spike when he was playing with his brothers. No one knows how but he somehow sat on a spike that pierced his rear. The child was badly injured. The mother came to me for help … poor woman … she was almost hysterical. Your father was with me; it was our daily chess time. She needed someone to take the boy to a doctor. No one here has a vehicle, you know, and those Zhou bastards refused to lend their mule for travel. So your father took his wheelbarrow, remember that old wooden one, he set the boy in there with his mom holding him. They headed to the clinic in the next town."

Over the muddle of typewriters and busy conversations, Zar could still hear Old Wang's heavy sigh.

"That good-for-nothing doctor there told them the injury was minor and to return home. That boy was *not* alright ... I saw his entrails leaking from his buttocks. Asshole ... he wanted bribe money; that's how these doctors operate now. He's only 4 ... must have been crying in pain, I imagine. He was a good little boy. When he left he insisted it didn't hurt. But his whole little body was shaking as your father settled him into that wooden wheelbarrow ..."

Chief Wang's voice trailed off.

"Your father, stubborn crow, is a kind man and he wouldn't give up," Chief Wang continued indignantly. "He wheeled the boy and his mother to Lanzhou, hoping that a larger hospital would take pity and treat the boy without money. They were turned away again. On their return ... the old buzzard must have been tired by then ... they'd been gone for almost two days now ... on foot the whole way too ... All at his age ... wheeling a boy and a woman across the mountain roads ..."

There was a long pause followed by a deep breath, and Zar felt the pain in his gut as the news hit.

"A black car hit them from behind. Your father was found by a young boy at the side of the road who he was able to call out to for help. The boy and his older brother brought your father home in a cattle wagon ... kind-hearted folks ... rare these days ... Xie Ming's boy and his mother did not survive. Those poor boys without their mother now ... Xie Ming's gone to the city and we have not been able to reach him ... " There was another pause. "We think it was a government car from the description. It did not even stop." The last words were spat with acid bitterness.

Zar continued to listen in silence as Chief Wang told him of his father's condition, his mother's state. Father is home now, but his injuries are grave. It is best if Zar could come back, quite possibly to say his goodbyes.

Most likely Zar did not say anything to Chief Wang during that conversation. He listened with his heart in his throat and a numbed expression on his face. He then hung up the receiver and returned to his apartment without a glance at anyone at his office nor any passers-by on the streets. Only until he asked Yien Yien to come with him did words eventually leave his mouth. He presented her with a thin gold chain that he had used all of his savings to purchase so that her family might not look down at his proposal of marriage. She took one glance at the chain and said no. The following day, Zar made the journey returning home on his own. He found his father on the same mattress that now held his mother, a still fallen figure, bent and broken.

"Here," Old Huang had said as he reached into his shirt pocket and pulled out an envelope to his son. It was one of those small red envelopes used for gifting money, usually decorated with gold inscriptions depicting lucky phrases and figures of auspicious animals. The envelope appeared ancient, its well-wishing messages hardly decipherable. "This is what your mother and I have saved," he said weakly as he put the envelope in Zar's hand. "This was supposed to allow us to purchase a plot of land in Chengdu. But it was not enough."

Zar's father paused as he turned his face away from his son and towards the ceiling as if to study the bits of thatch and dirt that fell gently throughout the room, painting the air into a curtain of gray. He did not turn away from the droplets of rainwater that had seeped through the rivets. Each made a tiny splat as it landed on his face and trickled down the sides of his cheeks like the smallest waterfalls.

"Your mother and I left you for fifteen years and the money is not enough." Old Huang stated all this as if he was reciting facts from a history book, his gaze remained fixed on the thatched roof.

"Was your grandmother good to you while we were gone?" he asked after a while. Father's eyes were watery now. Zar could not tell whether the old man was crying or if the tears were from the dust falling in his eyes that he did not bother to avert.

"She was," was all Zar could manage.

His father had never asked him about how it had been when they left. Zar was only five but he understood why. There was no food, there were no jobs, they had no money. He stood at the entrance of their thatched-roof house, wearing a dark blue coat that his mother made for him from an old comforter to keep him warm in the winter. His grandmother's hands held his firmly as his father wheeled his mother away on a wheelbarrow with their possessions. The wheelbarrow had only one wheel and two handles for pushing. Zar quietly watched his father's back arching up and down with each stride as he pushed the barrow across the rocky terrain. It felt like hours before they were out of sight and the child finally returned to his house. His grandmother had gone in long before.

He was almost twenty when they returned, both hardly recognisable to him and unable to say much. Conversation could not have come easily for parents who left their five-year-old son to be raised by a single grandmother, being forced by famine and poverty to become migrant workers in Guangzhou. Nan Ping and her husband sent all of their savings home for their boy. Zar learned much later in life that his parents did not even see each other during those fifteen years they had been gone. His father worked as a construction worker and his mother lived as a maid with a well-to-do family. *Did they ever beat her?* He sometimes wondered. *Was she ever mistreated?* Nan Ping and Huang Ge left as two youths in their mid-twenties and returned looking as if they had lived a hundred years. His mother's back was forever hunched forward, forcing her to rely on a wooden stick whenever she had to be on her feet. His father bore a deep and everlasting cough from the years of inhaling cement dust.

It was only two weeks after their return that Zar told them that he was leaving their home so that he could pursue a future in Xiamen in the prosperous coast of the Fujian Province. "I am the only person in this place who can read and write," he had said to them. Being a villager with a sad family farm in remote northern China was not his path. Neither of his parents said anything when they received the news. The goodbyes the following day were terse. During his bus journey, Zar opened his fabric bundle to discover several loaves of *mantou* and a package of dried meats. It had been their family's entire ration for that month.

The man closed his eyes firmly to block the oncoming of tears. When he looked down, he realised the water had been boiling. He poured the hot liquid into a wooden bowl and walked towards his mother, gingerly holding the bowl between both hands. He knelt down beside her. Slowly and gently, he spooned a little bit of soup and put the spoon to his mother's parched lips. She did not respond and the thin liquid leaked down the sides of her mouth. Zar set the bowl on the ground and wiped his mother's face softly with the edge of his sleeve. He studied the lines on her face, long and deep and seemed to cover every bit of her aged countenance, leaving not a trace unmarred. Her gaze was far off and distant.

"Mama ..."

The word escaped from his lips unexpectedly. At the sound, Nan Ping finally looked at her son. Slowly and with great effort, she reached towards his face with her outstretched hand that had been dangling off the edge of the mattress. With the back of her hand, she stroked a tear from his cheek that he did not know had fallen. Mother and son looked at each other for some time in that tiny thatched-roof house with no address, built on a road with no name, each holding the other's cheek in one palm. With a final relinquishing sigh, Nan Ping gave her last breath.

The candlelight had died, leaving a thin wisp of smoke that danced in the air when Zar finally went outside. Rising from the western horizon was a roiling storm that slowly covered the sky. He watched the storm approach; it seemed to be moving straight toward him like a target to be consumed. The monolith covered the expanse, a massive blanket that slowly blocked out the sun and cast a black shadow, consuming the land in every direction. Zar watched unmoving as the darkness made its way to the thatched-roof house. Determinedly. Resolute. When the darkness almost came upon Zar and his home, a voice woke him from his numbed stillness. It was the same voice that spoke to him in dead of night, the one that beckoned him to be foolish and courageous.

"*Fly*," it said.

Zar remained still, paralysed by his fear and sadness.

The darkness was close now, the edge of the shadow almost reaching him.

"*FLY!!!!!!!!!!!!*"

And suddenly, this nobody flew.

A social enterprise membership organisation founded by students at the University Centre Grimsby and run by volunteers. We aim to encourage and support creative talent in art and literature providing opportunities for members to showcase their work and develop a successful career

Our current activities include Publishing, Literary Competitions, Film Making, TV Production, Writing Workshop, Festivals and Community Engagement Programmes.

Members benefit from reduced competitions fees, and opportunities to showcase their work or get involved in our range of creative activities.

We are planning to offer a range of publishing options to new writers, and expand our programme of engaging with isolated people in both rural and urban the communities through art and literature

www.hammondhousepublishing.com

University Centre Grimsby

2017 International Literary Prize

The second year of this prestigious literary prize saw a record number of entries spread across five continents.

WINNER	In Memoriam	**Bridget Blankley**
2nd Place	Swallow Chick	Lucy Grace
3rd Place	At a Junction	Rhiannon Lewis

Twenty-five entries were short listed, three were highly commended and five were commended from entries received from countries where the first language isn't English.

JUDGES

Peter True, Anjali Wierny, Hugh Riches, Stuart Spendlow, Ted Stanley and Steve Jackson.

Awarded by the University Centre Grimsby

Sponsored by Kenwick Park Estate: Golf Hotel and Spa

HAMMOND
HOUSE

www.hammondhousepublishing.com

2018
International Literary Prize
1st Prize £500
2nd £100   3rd £50

Worldwide Publication
for the top 25 stories

Theme: PRECIOUS
Short Story of 2000 - 5000 Words
Entries open 1st January 2018
Submission deadline 30th September 2018

OTHER 2018 COMPETITIONS

International Poetry Prize
International Screenwriting Prize

www.hammondhousepublishing.com

The University Centre Grimsby, as part of the Grimsby Institute, is built on high expectations, a focus on learning, commitment to achievement and an engaged, practical education for all students.

A wide range of degree level courses are available including BA (hons) Creative and Professional Writing.

www.grimsby.ac.uk

KENWICK PARK ESTATE
Golf Hotel and Spa

Country house hotel in 320 acres of woodlands, parks, and manicured grounds with woodland lodges, club spa, evergreen spa, tennis courts and championship golf course. The perfect place to relax and recuperate

www.kenwick-park.co.uk

BILLBOARD TV

Theatre, Music, Movies, Art and Literature

BILLBOARD is produced by members of the Hammond House group at the University Centre Grimsby, including students from the creative arts, media and writing faculties, graduates, and members of the local community.

The programme covers Theatre, Music, Arts and Literature across the Humber region, going behind the scenes of your favourite shows, reviewing the latest film releases, books and art exhibitions, interviewing local celebrities and showcasing local musicians.

Billboard provides a great opportunity to showcase member's skills and pursue the Hammond House mission to encourage local talent and engage with the local people.

Broadcast frequently on range of popular TV channels and always available at www.billboardtv.uk

Estuary TV - Channel 7 - Freeview 8 - Virgin Media 159

www.billboardtv.uk

HAMMOND HOUSE

OTHER PUBLICATIONS

ETERNAL – Award-Winning Poetry from around the world from our 2017 International Poetry Prize

CONFICT - Award winning short stories from our 2017 International Literary Prize

WHO'S AFRAID OF THE DARK - Illustrated children's story featuring augmented reality.

SHAKESPEARE IN DEBT - Hilarious Elizabethan farce

FORTHCOMING FILMS
Hammond House Productions

SPIN – An uncover police woman is torn between live and duty. Featuring a replica of one of the most expensive cars in the world, the Ferrari 250 SWB California.

EIGHT BALL – Winner of the 2018 University Centre Grimsby International Screenplay Prize. Candidate for the Asthetica Film Festival

www.hammondhousepublishing.com

www.ingramcontent.com/pod-product-compliance
Lightning Source LLC
Chambersburg PA
CBHW030916120726
47906CB00002B/355